GOTHIC

BLACK
SCI-FI
SHORT STORIES

Anthology of New & Classic Tales
Foreword by Temi Oh
Introduction by Dr. Sandra M. Grayson

FLAME TREE PUBLISHING

FANTASY

This is a FLAME TREE Book

Publisher & Creative Director: Nick Wells
Editorial Director: Catherine Taylor
Associate Editor: Tia Ross
Senior Project Editor: Josie Karani
Editorial Board: Gillian Whitaker, Taylor Bentley, Tia Ross and
the Black Writers Collective

Publisher's Note: Due to the historical nature of the classic text, we're aware
that there may be some language used which has the potential to cause offence
to the modern reader. However, wishing overall to preserve the integrity of the
text, rather than imposing contemporary sensibilities, we have left it unaltered.

FLAME TREE PUBLISHING
6 Melbray Mews, Fulham,
London SW6 3NS, United Kingdom
www.flametreepublishing.com

First published 2021

BLACK SCI-FI

SHORT STORIES

Anthology of New & Classic Tales
Foreword by Temi Oh
Introduction by Dr. Sandra M. Grayson

FLAME TREE PUBLISHING

Contents

CONTENTS

Foreword: Black Sci-Fi Short Stories

A COUPLE OF months ago, I discovered that the American composer, and one of the most important figures in musical theatre, Stephen Sondheim, grew up next to and was mentored by Oscar Hammerstein (one half of the musical theatre duo 'Rogers and Hammerstein'). In a couple of different interviews, I've heard Sondheim say, "If Hammerstein was a geologist, I would have studied rocks." Which makes my head spin. Could Sondheim ever have been a geologist? Or was something in him poised to ring like a tuning fork the first time he encountered musical theatre? Was it only chance? Or did it seek him out?

And what about the rest of us, does our calling seek us all out?

I remember the day that science fiction found me. It began with Ray Bradbury's *Fahrenheit 451*, which my mother had plucked on some maternal intuition from the local bookstore. I still remember how she said those first words to me, at the kitchen table; "It was a pleasure to burn. To see things blackened and changed..." and then handed me the thin tome. I read *Fahrenheit 451*, *Brave New World*, and a dystopian young adult trilogy by Scott Westerfeld called *Uglies*, all in the same spring just before I turned thirteen. When I finished, I promised myself – the way I used to promise other girls that we would be friends forever – that I'd never write anything but science fiction. I always wonder what I'd be writing now if she'd handed me *The Perks of Being a Wallflower* or *A Short History of Nearly Everything*.

Whenever I ask myself what exactly drew me to it then, and sustains me now, my mind always balks. It is as hard to describe what I love about science fiction – and what is worth loving – as it is to describe what I love about a good friend of mine, or my sister. It's a hundred things. Science fiction has given us visions of the kind of worlds we don't want, 'Orwellian' for example, or the women dressed as handmaids protesting outside the supreme court. But also the kind of worlds that we do.

As a science-fiction writer, I feel as if I have a sacred duty. Our human tendency is to turn like Lot's wife back to the past, to lean into nostalgia, or to try to categorise and analyse the present moment and its febrile movements. Our job as science-fiction writers is to keep eyes trained on the future. To shout like prophets, to return with solemn cautions or glad tidings. To fill everyone's hearts with hope. It's not always easy to conceive of the future. Not even for me. I'm writing this in 2020 and all year my mind has lurched towards imagined catastrophe. In times of real uncertainty, simply imagining a future feels like a radical act.

A lot of people say that some aspects of the black experience are comparable to science fiction. There are elements of dystopia, there are alien invasions and abductions. And yet, growing up, in many conceptions I saw of the future, in novels and movies, I didn't see very much of the black experience reflected. That's why discovering, in my twenties, the work of Octavia Butler or Nnedi Okorafor was like a revelation.

You can't build it if you can't imagine it. The first time I saw Wakanda on a screen my heart leapt. It was the kind of wish fulfilment I'd never felt before. It's a wonderfully black utopian vision. Where hovering cars touch down on sand-paved streets or fly through loops above market stalls selling wax-print cloth. Delightfully familiar, yet totally novel.

I watched it with my grandmother and her eyes glittered as well. "Back home," she'd said laughing at the vision. I did too, as I pictured Lagos or Nairobi in a couple of decades.

How would Neil Armstrong have felt, as a boy, watching Georges Méliès' *A Trip to the Moon*, the first science fiction movie? Would he have held his breath in anticipation? Would he have pressed his hands against the prickly surface of the cathode-ray tube television and made a promise to himself? Science fiction shows us the dream, and it's up to all of us to realise it.

Temi Oh
www.theonlytemioh.com

Introduction

SCIENCE FICTION writers of African descent are engaged in a genre that initially was hostile toward and excluded Black people. Charles R. Saunders observed that in early science fiction, outer space was segregated, and the genre was 'as white as a Ku Klux Klan meeting':

> *A black man or woman in a spacesuit was an image beyond the limits of early science fiction writers' imaginations: even the infamous BEM (Bug-eyed Monster) was more palatable to the tastes of the science fiction readership of those formative years, yet at that time the genre was no more or less racist than any other facet of North American life.*

Similarly, LeVar Burton stated, 'What I always found lacking in [science fiction] stories were heroes who looked like me. Rarely did I encounter characters of African descent or other people of color populating those worlds.' In the 1999 interview 'Nalo Hopkinson Subverts Science Fiction,' Hopkinson[1] observed:

> *...in the West, [science fiction] is still predominately written by white people for white people. At some metaphorical level, the message I get is that white people are humans and people of color are aliens ... It doesn't feel like deliberate exclusion of other voices – more like a systematic deafness to them. We're almost invisible.*

Science fiction is changing from the early years. However, Tom Hunter (award administrator for the Arthur C. Clarke Award) pointed out that given that out of 124 submissions from forty-six publishers and imprints only seven per cent were people of color, 'Diversity in science fiction needs action now' (qtd. in Roberts).

The number of Black science-fiction writers is slowly increasing. Their works often reflect sociocultural concerns and consistently represent people of African descent in complex, central roles. In addition, many of the narratives are cautionary tales that focus on the potential for catastrophe in a society when members do not pay attention to the course of events, entities, and/or technology around them. By simultaneously looking back and forward, the narratives reflect a construction of time as a pendulum moving in patterns of recurrence that represent inseparability among the past, present, and future. Often, the works conceptualize societies that recognize all nations and people as connected to a larger global community. The following sections explore Black science fiction in historical and contemporary contexts.

The Formation of Black Science Fiction

The 1859 introductory comments in *The Anglo-African Magazine*, a publication founded and published by Thomas Hamilton, emphasized that Black people 'must speak for themselves; no outside tongue, however gifted with eloquence, can tell their story.' The magazine symbolized an independent voice where people of African descent told their stories though poetry, fiction, and nonfiction. *Blake: or the Huts of America* by Martin R. Delany was among the works featured in the magazine.[2] Most of Part I of *Blake* was published serially in *The Anglo-African Magazine* in 1859. The entire novel was published serially in *The Weekly Anglo-African* newspaper from 1861 to 1862.[3] From a contemporary viewpoint, *Blake* can be categorized as a science-fiction style alternate history novel in that it is set in the historical past (1853), but some details contradict known facts of history. For example, Cuban poet Gabriel de la Concepción Valdés (pseudonym *Placido*) is placed in 1853 and helps plan a rebellion, although the actual person was suspected of plotting an insurrection during the 1840s.

In addition, the United States Supreme Court's 1857 decision in the Dred Scott case is incorporated into the novel, although the setting is before that date. Scott sued for his freedom in 1847. After going through several state courts, the case came before the United States Supreme Court in 1856. In March 1857, the Supreme Court ruled against Dred Scott, denied the citizenship of all Blacks, and opened all federal territory to slavery. The Supreme Court also declared that people of African descent were 'an inferior order, and altogether unfit to associate with the white race, either in social or political relations; and so far inferior, that they had no rights which the white man was bound to respect.' This decision impinged on the rights of free Blacks and slaves and gave legal sanction to the common practice of revoking the rights of Blacks in the United States. According to the Supreme Court, people of African descent were not and could not be citizens of the United States. During a protest meeting held in Philadelphia on 3 April 1857 that was reported in *The Liberator* on 10 April 1857, Robert Purvis, a leading abolitionist, expressed the position held by many Blacks: under the US Constitution and government, people of African descent 'can be nothing but an alien, disfranchised and degraded class.' Purvis resolved, 'The only duty the colored man owes to a Constitution under which he is declared to be an inferior and degraded being … is to denounce and repudiate it.' In a speech given at the fourth anniversary of the New York Anti-Slavery Society on 13 May 1857, Frances Ellen Watkins Harper (writer, orator, activist, and abolitionist) stated, 'I stand at the threshold of the Supreme Court and ask for justice, simple justice. Upon my tortured heart is thrown the mocking words, "You are a negro; you have no rights which white men are bound to respect!"' In *Blake*, repeated allusions to the Supreme Court's decision in the Dred Scott case remind the Black characters of the legal status of Black people in the United States and the continued and urgent necessity to fight for equality, as well as for physical and psychological freedom.

Blake also reflects Delany's belief stated in his 1854 speech, 'Political Destiny of the Colored Race,' on the American Continent to the Colored Inhabitants of the United States,' presented during the National Emigration Convention of Colored People held in Cleveland:

> We must make an issue, create an event, and establish for ourselves a position. This is essentially necessary for our effective elevation as a people, in shaping our national development, directing our destiny, and redeeming ourselves as a race.

In the novel, the Black characters make issues, create events, and establish positions to gain physical and psychological freedom. The novel focuses on Henry Blake (previously known as Carolus Henrico Blacus), a free Black man who is sold into slavery to Colonel Franks. He later marries Maggie, a slave, and they have one child. After Maggie is sold, Henry escapes the Franks plantation and travels through the South, helps several slaves escape, and then goes to Cuba where he finds his wife. After Maggie buys her freedom, she and Henry remain in Cuba. He finds his cousin, the poet Placido. Henry explains, 'I have come to Cuba to help to free my race; and that which I desire here to do, I've done in another place.' Placido has also thought about insurrection. Subsequently, Henry is selected to be 'General-in-Chief of the army of emancipation of the oppressed men and women of Cuba.' Pan-African in vision, the plot of *Blake* (similar to Delany's multifaceted career) spans across multiple nations. Although the novel was published in the United States, Delany's vision and his work in the United States, Africa, England, and Canada, make *Blake* significant to the formation of Black science fiction across nations.

Proto-science Fiction by Writers of African Descent

Similar to Delany's *Blake*, from a contemporary viewpoint, the following works by Black writers from the United States, Lesotho, Cameroon, and Nigeria can be categorized as speculative fiction: Sutton Griggs' *Imperium in Imperio* (1899); Pauline Hopkins' *Of One Blood* (1902–03); Edward Johnson's *Light Ahead for the Negro* (1904); W.E.B. DuBois' 'The Comet' (1920); Thomas Mfolo's *Chaka* (1925); Jean-Louis Njemba Medou's *Nnanga Kon* (1932); Muhammadu Bello Kagara's *Gandoki* (1934); and Daniel Olorunfemi Fagunwa's *Ogboju Ode Ninu Igbo Irunmale (Forest of a Thousand Daemons: A Hunter's Saga* [1938]).[4] In *Imperium in Imperio* (set in the late 1800s), Black people have a secret, underground government called the Imperium in Imperio that developed from a secret society of the revolutionary period. The original objectives of the society were to secure equal rights for free Blacks and to secure freedom and equal rights for all enslaved Africans. Belton Piedmont, a member of the secret government, recommends that the Imperium in Imperio plan to lawfully take over Texas by majority vote and live separately in the United States. Under President Bernard Belgrave's leadership, however, the Imperium in Imperio adopts the plan to seize Texas, take over the United States Navy, and demand the surrender of Texas and Louisiana. They plan to keep Texas as a separate nation (where Black people would have equal rights) and give Louisiana to their foreign allies.

In 1900, the writer and social activist Pauline Elizabeth Hopkins became a founding member of the *Colored American Magazine*. Hazel Carby observed that the *Colored American Magazine* 'tried to create the literary and political climate for a black renaissance in Boston two decades before the emergence of what' is now referred to as the 'Harlem Renaissance.' An editorial statement in the first (May 1900) issue of the *Colored American Magazine* stated, in part,

> *America citizens of color, have long realized that for them there exists no monthly magazine, distinctively devoted to their interests and to the development of Afro-American art and literature … The Colored American Magazine proposes to meet this want, and to offer the colored people of the United States, a medium through which they can demonstrate their ability and tastes, in fiction, poetry, and art, as well as in the arena of historical, social and economic literature.*

Hopkins' novel *Of One Blood* was originally published serially in the *Colored American Magazine* (November–December 1902 and January–November 1903). In *Of One Blood*, Reuel Briggs, the protagonist, is on an expedition in Ethiopia to search for buried cities and treasures. Subsequently, he is taken to the hidden city of Telassar, where the descendants of the people of Meroe (ancient Kush) are protected by mountains from intrusion from the outside world. They are governed by a female monarch (named/titled Candance) and a council of twenty-five sages who plan to restore the nation of Kush. Reuel's mother Mira, an enslaved African who has supernatural powers and could foretell the future, is a descendant of the monarchs of ancient Kush, a rich and powerful ancient African nation. Reuel inherits his mysticism and supernatural powers from Mira.

In Edward Johnson's *Light Ahead for the Negro*, the protagonist Gilbert Twitchell spends 100 years (1906–2006) in suspended animation after an accident in a 'dirigible airship' (air balloon-like machine) leaves him unconscious. He revives in Phoenix, Georgia, in 2006 – a time when the United States is a socialist country and significant progress has been made in race relations.

W.E.B. Du Bois' 'The Comet' explores the temporary erasure of the *color line* as a result of the impact of a comet. The 'color line' refers to racial segregation in the United States after slavery was abolished. The phrase became more well-known after W.E.B. Du Bois used the phrase in his book *The Souls of Black Folk*. Du Bois stated, 'The problem of the twentieth century is the problem of the color-line – the relation of the darker to the lighter races of men in Asia and Africa, in America and the islands of the sea.' In the short story, when the comet hits New York, the Black protagonist Jim Davis is in the lower vaults of the bank where he works as a messenger. He later finds Julia, a white woman. After searching the city, they conclude that the devastation from the comet is global. Julia begins to view Jim as a man and an equal, not as an outcast or inferior. However, her change in perspective is disrupted when her father arrives with a white man named Fred, who explains that only New York had been devastated by the comet. The color line is restored with the return of Julia's father, Fred, and a crowd.

A pioneer in Sesotho literature, Thomas Mfolo was born in Khojane, Lesotho. Like his first two novels, his third novel *Chaka* (1925) was originally published in the Sesotho language. *Chaka* is a fictional account of the heroic Zulu king Sigidi kaSenzangakhona (Shaka). From a contemporary viewpoint, *Chaka* can be categorized as a science-fiction style alternate history novel in that it is set in the historical past (about 1787–1828), but many details contradict known facts of history. Regarding the deviation from historical fact in the novel, Mfolo stated,

> *I am not writing history, I am writing a tale, or I should rather say I am writing what actually happened, but to which a great deal has been added, and from which a great deal has been removed, so that much has been left out, and much has been written that did not actually happen, with the aim solely of fulfilling my purpose in writing this book.* (qtd. in Kunene)

Similarly in the novel, the narrator says, 'But since it is not our purpose to recount all the affairs of his [Chaka's] life, we have chosen only one part which suits our present purpose.'

Daniel P. Kunene concluded that in most of the instances where fact and fiction are at variance in *Chaka,* the effect is to 'build up greater intensity in the plot, and to increase dramatic tensions by creating new juxtapositions of highly volatile events and situations.'

Nnanga Kon (1932) by Cameroonian author Jean-Louis Njemba Medou was originally published in the Bulu language. This first-contact novel is based on the arrival of Adolphus Clemens Good, a white American missionary, in Bulu territory. His appearance earns him the name Nnanga Kon, white ghost or phantom albino. In 'Writing in Cameroon, the First Hundred Years,' Eloise A. Brière stated, 'Despite the French injunction against publishing in local languages [*Nnanga Kon*] was published in Bulu under American auspices at the Presbyterian Mission's Hasley Memorial Press of Elat in Ebolowa.' *Nnanga Kon* won the London African Institute's Margaret Wrong Prize in 1932.

Gandoki (1934) by the Nigerian writer Muhammadu Bello Kagara was originally published in the Hausa language. The novella was one of the winners of a writing competition that was organized by Rupert M. East, a colonial official of the Literature Bureau in northern Nigeria. In the novella, which incorporates the Hausa oral tradition, the protagonist Gandoki fights against the British. Subsequently, jinns bring him to a new, imagined world. In 'Hausa Creative Writing in the 1930s: An Exploration in Postcolonial Theory,' Graham Furniss stated that in the new world the 'specificity of time and space is immediately circumvented by the participation of both friendly and malevolent jinns who can transport themselves and our heroes instantly from place to place, seen or unseen.'

First published in Nigeria in 1938, *Ogboju Ode Ninu Igbo Irunmale (Forest of a Thousand Daemons: A Hunter's Saga)* by Daniel Olorunfemi Fagunwa was originally published in the Yoruba language. The novel focuses on the adventures of Akara-ogun (Compound-of-Spells), a legendary hunter who has magical powers. Akara-ogun recounts his journeys into Irunmale, the Forest of a Thousand Daemons. This forest is the home of ghommids, supernatural beings that are not human or animal. After his second journey into Irunmale, the king asks Akara-ogun to undertake a mission to the city of Mount Langbodo to obtain an object that would bring an abundance of peace and well-being to the nation.

Akara-ogun, along with other hunters who also have magical powers, travel through Irunmale to reach Mount Langbodo. Throughout their journey, they encounter supernatural entities.

Defining Black Science Fiction

The phrase *Black science fiction* generally refers to works by people of African descent who write science fiction or speculative fiction, whether or not the subject of the narratives focuses on Black people or themes. The term *afrofuturism* was coined by Mark Dery in 1993. In 'Black to the Future: Interviews with Samuel R. Delany, Greg Tate, and Tricia Rose,' Dery defined *afrofuturism* as speculative fiction 'that treats African-American themes and addresses African-American concerns in the context of twentieth-century technoculture – and, more generally, African-American signification that appropriates images of technology and a prosthetically enhanced future.'[5] The definition of *afrofuturism* continues to broaden and the term now generally refers to various forms of Black people's artistic endeavors (including literature, music, and film) that use science fiction to explore, create, and/or re-imagine experiences of people of African descent.

Although the formation of Black science fiction is evident prior to the 1960s, Black science fiction writers first emerged post-1960 with Samuel R. Delany,[6] Octavia E. Butler, Charles R. Saunders, and Steven Barnes. Beginning in 1962 with *The Jewels of Aptor*, Samuel R. Delany has specialized in complexly structured science fiction. His awards include the Nebula, Hugo, and Pilgrim. Delany explained that his experience as a Black person runs through all of his works, but the traces are not stereotypes. In *Silent Interviews,* he stated that as a Black person what he writes 'is part of the definition, the reality, the evidence of blackness.' Octavia E. Butler was one of the first writers to introduce the experiences of Black women into science fiction. Her numerous awards include the Nebula, Hugo, and the MacArthur Foundation 'Genius' Grant. Butler said of her characters, 'The black women I write about aren't struggling to make ends meet, but they are the descendants of generations of those who did' (qtd. in Mixon). Charles R. Saunders is best known for his sword and sorcery works such as the *Imaro* series, which is set in a parallel world equivalent of Africa that Saunders called 'Nyumbani.' In a 1984 interview, Saunders described his literary project as 'taking African storytelling traditions and adapting the content of those traditions to Western storytelling technique.' In 'Testimonial: SF Writer Steven Barnes Talks,' Ursula P. Watson observed that Steven Barnes is credited with creating a 'new pantheon of black [science fiction] heroes' in his highly kinetic action/adventure novels.

Exploring Black Science Fiction

While many of the works by Samuel R. Delany, Octavia E. Butler, Charles R. Saunders, and Steven Barnes are set in the future, they often reflect the past. For example, a key issue throughout Samuel R. Delany's *The Einstein Intersection* (1967) is the social standing of the citizens (the elite determine who is human), a point of historical concern to Black people, and one that serves as the primary intersection between the novel and the history of people of African descent. The scene that epitomizes this link is the deliberation over Friza's social standing; she has the appearance of a Black woman. Although race is not the marker that problematizes her position in the community, that she looks like a Black woman is significant. In the novel, the titles 'La,' 'Lo,' and 'Le' indicate a person's social standing as a pure 'norm/fully functional' human. Those without a title are deemed 'nonfunctional' (not human) and caged. Because Friza is mute, some of the elders do not consider her fully functional. The elite do not realize that Friza is telepathic and has telekinetic abilities. The debate is represented through two elders (Lo Hawk and La Dire) with opposing positions over Friza's social status. Lo Hawk argues that the titles 'La' and 'Lo' should be reserved for total norms, and he contends that the old ways must be preserved. La Dire, who believes that customs must change, counters that the titles should be bestowed on any functional person. She moves to give Friza the title 'La.' Friza, however, is not given the title. Although she is not returned to the 'kage' (a restricted area surrounded by an electrified fence where she was confined as a baby), she, like those who remain kaged, is relegated to the margins of the society. The fictional scene in which Friza's status in society is debated then determined (her position as a citizen denied) can be seen as a metaphor for the historical reality of the Supreme Court's 1857 decision in the Dred Scott case. In addition, the situation with Friza can be thematically connected to Imaro, who is also an outsider. He is described as an alien among the people (the Ilayssai) and to the land (the Tamburure). Imaro's isolation, alienation, and enslavement can be seen as a metaphor for the alienation and enslavement of people of African descent during the antebellum period in the United States. Questions about the citizenship of Black people are also explored in Derrick Bell's 'The Space Traders' (1992). In the story, aliens referred to as 'Space Traders' arrive on Earth in 2000 and offer the United States three much-needed items – gold for the nearly bankrupt governments, chemicals to restore the environment, and safe nuclear engines – in exchange for the African Americans living in the United States. The Space Traders want to take the Black people to the aliens' home planet. After much debate (which also explores historical and contemporary issues of racism and discrimination in the United States), the government forces all African Americans to leave with the Space Traders. At the end of the story, the narrator observes that Black people left America as their ancestors had arrived – in chains.

Similar to *The Einstein Intersection*, in Octavia E. Butler's *Dawn* (1987) the future recalls the past. However, in the case of *Dawn* aliens called the Oankali dictate the future for humans. The protagonist, Lilith Iyapo (a Black woman), is taken from Earth and transported to the Oankali ship, where she is held in a confined area against her will, treated like an animal, and scarred by the Oankali – a mark which is a constant reminder to her that the Oankali can do what they want with her body. These details recall the Middle Passage from Africa to the Americas and the scarring and branding of enslaved Africans. Lilith is denied writing materials because the Oankali have forbidden her to read or write, a practice that echoes the laws that deemed it illegal for enslaved Africans to read and write or to be taught such skills. The actions of the Oankali are similar to those of European colonizers of the past – to colonize the minds and the land of their captives. According to Franz Fanon,

> *Colonialism is not satisfied merely with holding a people in its grip and emptying the native's brain of all form and content. By a kind of perverted logic, it turns to the past of the oppressed people, and distorts, disfigures, and destroys it.*

By what seems to be a similar type of 'perverted logic,' the Oankali seek to erase all Earth history and to manipulate human genes. To that end, they destroy all artifacts on Earth (the remains of human culture), forbid humans access to books from Earth, and experiment with human genes. Although the novel reflects parallels to the antebellum period in the United States, *Dawn* is also a metaphor for contemporary American society, where humans often use science to destroy other people and the environment.

Another example of the future and past intersecting is represented in Steven Barnes's *Firedance* (1994). However, in this novel the past is connected to the origin of the protagonist Aubry Knight and is a source of strength. Before Aubry can move forward, he must first travel back. The path that takes him to Africa and to ancient beliefs is represented by the Ibandi (an invented people) and the Ibandi proverbs. Although the Ibandi are not a real African people, they symbolize a return to origin; for Aubry, that means unveiling and recognizing his true self. Among the Ibandi, Aubry is reborn and completes the traditional Ibandi education and initiation. Old Man, an Ibandi elder, reveals to Aubry his heritage:

When Aubry was a baby, Thomas Jai, an Ibandi warrior, brought him to America to protect him. Aubry has returned home. Old Man refers to Aubry as 'a lost child' and 'a child of the Ibandi, raised in America.'

Contemporary Science Fiction by Writers of African Descent

The current landscape of Black science fiction includes established and emerging writers across nations, many of whom have won prestigious awards. For example, Temi Oh, a British-born Nigerian writer, won the 2020 American Library Association's Alex Award for *Do you Dream of Terra-Two?* In 2019 Tade Thompson, a British-born Yoruba writer, won the Arthur C. Clarke Award for *Rosewater*. Colson Whitehead, an African American writer, won the 2017 Pulitzer Prize and the 2017 Arthur C. Clarke Award for *The Underground Railroad*. African-American writer N. K. Jemisin won three consecutive Hugo awards for best science fiction novel – *Fifth Season* in 2016, *The Obelisk Gate* in 2017, and *The Stone Sky* in 2018. Among Nigerian-American writer Nnedi Okorafor's numerous awards are the Hugo, Nebula, and Nommo for her 2015 novella *Benti*. These are just a few examples of the current work of Black science fiction writers.

In the 1827 editorial for *Freedom's Journal*, the first Black owned and operated newspaper in the United States, the editors Samuel Cornish and John B. Russwurm stated, 'We wish to plead our own cause. Too long have others spoken for us. Too long has the public been deceived by misrepresentations, in things which concern us dearly.' Black people's quest to tell their own stories continues in the current landscape. Established and emerging Black science fiction writers accomplish this goal by using science fiction to create worlds where people of African descent are central.

Dr. Sandra M. Grayson

Footnotes for the Introduction

1. Nalo Hopkinson won the 1998 Warner Aspect First Novel Award and the 1999 Locus First Novel Award for her novel *Brown Girl in the Ring*. She grew up in Jamaica, Trinidad, and Guyana; she moved with her family to Canada in 1977 and now lives in the United States.
2. Martin R. Delany was born free in Virginia on May 6, 1812. His mother was free, and his father was a slave. In 1822, his mother took her family to Pennsylvania after 'Virginia authorities threatened to imprison her for teaching her children to read and write' (Levine 1). His father joined them later. Delany had a multifaceted career that included work as 'social activist and reformer, black nationalist, abolitionist, physician, reporter and editor, explorer, jurist, realtor, politician, publisher, educator, army officer, ethnographer, novelist, and political and legal theorist. A sketch of his career can only hint at the range of his interests, activities, and accomplishments' (Levine 1).
3. Note that Martin R. Delany was not a science fiction writer. It is also important to consider *Blake* within the historical and political contexts within which the novel was written. Through fiction, *Blake* explores 'the political and social milieu of the 1850s: slavery as an institution, Cuba as the prime interest of Southern expansionists, the "practicality" of militant slave revolution, and, most importantly, the psychological liberation possible through collective action' (Miller xii).
4. Note that, like Martin R. Delany, these authors were not science fiction writers. It is also important to consider their works within the historical and political contexts within which the texts were written.

5. Mark Dery also observed that African Americans 'inhabit a sci-fi nightmare in which unseen but no less impassable force fields of intolerance frustrate their movements; official histories undo what has been done; and technology is too often brought to bear on black bodies (branding, forced sterilization, the Tuskegee experiment, and tasers come readily to mind).'
6. No relation to Martin R. Delany.

Publisher's Note

This is a special title in our long-running series of Gothic Fantasy short-story collections. Many of the themes in science fiction reveal the world as it is to others, show us how to improve it, and give voice to the many different expressions of a future for humankind. So sci-fi written by, for and about Black people can be a powerful genre. Though not a new phenomenon at all, it has not had enough of the mainstream attention it deserves. More broadly, diversity in general and especially the representation of Black voices in all aspects of publishing still have a long way to go. So, as well as offering a fabulous selection of stories that deserve to be more widely read, this book is for us as a publisher a long-overdue first step towards proactively rectifying the imbalance, by devoting a whole volume to work by Black writers, new and old, as well as involving Black voices at all stages of the creative process: promotion, submissions reading, editing and discussion (including the foreword by Alex Award-winning novelist Temi Oh and the introduction by Sandra M. Grayson, author of *Visions of the Third Millennium: Black Science Fiction Novelists Write the Future*, 2003). As usual, variances in spelling due to differing geographical origins have been retained, to reflect the authors' voices, including in the introduction and foreword.

Space travel, dystopia, cloning, gene therapy, biological manipulation, new diseases, hyper-technological worlds, robotics, gene-splicing and much more are explored here in fantastic stories, to lesser or greater degree informed specifically by the Black experience. To give perspective and foundation, the selected submissions have been combined with writing of an older tradition: early speculative and proto-science fiction by the authors W.E.B. Du Bois (1868–1963), Martin R. Delany (1812–85), Pauline Hopkins (1859–1930), Edward Johnson (1860–1944) and Sutton Griggs (1872–1933), whose first-hand experience of slavery and denial created their living dystopias. From fantastical imaginings to unsettling visions of entirely conceivable near-futures, the stories in this book may deal in invention but they vibrate with real human experience.

GOTHIC

BLACK
SCI-FI
SHORT STORIES

Anthology of New & Classic Tales
Foreword by Temi Oh
Introduction by Dr. Sandra M. Grayson

FLAME TREE PUBLISHING

FANTASY

An Empty, Hollow Interview

James Beamon

MY FIRST interview question with Hope Lange-Nova is incredibly selfish.

"Why me?"

Those of you who follow my work know this isn't one of those "how'd I get to be the go-lucky chosen Negro?" kind of why me's. For those of you who are strictly Hope Lange-Nova fans and you're only here to see what she has to say after her three-year hiatus, understand you're going to get something different than you asked for. I hate Hope Lange-Nova.

Allow me to fine tune my last statement. I am antagonistic toward celebrities in general, Hope Lange-Nova in specific and the decadent excess of Hollywood by and large. I find celebrity gossip to be vapid drivel. This is no big secret, so when the *Times* pulled my assignment to Caracas, where civil war and real news was breaking, because Hope Lange-Nova asked for me by name to interview her, "why me?" is the one question I've been asking to every editor up my chain with no satisfactory answer for the last two days.

Hope Lange-Nova smiles flawlessly, demurely at the question. She wears a sun yellow shift dress, low heels, large sunglasses resting on the top of her flaxen hair. She is out of time with modern fashion – a perfect facsimile of the original Hope Lange as she looked in the 1960's, a regular blonde Jackie Onassis.

"Why not you?" she counters.

We're seated in a secluded corner of a gene clinic's reception area, us and a half dozen others scattered about in fabric cushioned chairs grouped between small coffee tables hosting magazines. TMZ's on the television, which is likely the only news these clients care about. The waiting room is unremarkable save for the fact that the biggest nova celebrity that ever emerged from a gene therapy tank is sitting in it.

"Sherrice Day over in our Celebrity News section's been following you with starry eyes for years now. She'd kill to be able to ask you questions."

"Oh, Mr. Sturgis," she shakes her head at my answer. "I do ever appreciate your tact and diplomacy, but we both know that's not the real truth of why not you."

"Hard truth is like hard water," I tell her, "a bitch to stomach without a filter. But let's see if your perfectly-scienced stomach's strong enough. Celebrity gossip and chatter is fuckall non-news, a waste of everyone's time, not just mine. More to the point, I've been all over the developing world and I've seen first-hand the unintended consequences of the lifestyle you popularized. I'm more than simply not a fan, I'm an anti-fan, which I'm assuming you knew already when you asked for me by name. Hence I ask why."

"Please don't find this churlish," she responds, "but in a world where I can have anything I want, I wanted you. Perhaps I was looking for this raw, standoffish energy, but I'm disinclined to outright tell you. That said, I do assure you there's a reason, Mr. Sturgis. You're a top investigator and I have every confidence you'll divine it."

I can't recall the last time I've heard the word 'churlish' spoken aloud. She even talks a half-step out of time.

"Guess I got myself a mystery," I say.

I cast quick furtive glances around the room, a habit built out of a lifetime of checking for thieves, kidnappers and hostile foreign agents in unwelcoming countries. No, this is still Los Angeles. Around us, beautiful people who have no apparent need for gene therapy sit and wait for it anyway, trying ineptly to not stare at the biggest star in the room, the epitome of all their professional aspirations.

"This a confessional?" I ask. "Apprehensive about your refresh?"

She should be. You should be for her. Most folks tend to think gene therapy is a rather pedestrian, harmless procedure and it is when you're rewriting one or two things, adding freckles or taking away the likelihood of Parkinson's. We forget it's still surgery, a journey people sometimes don't make it back from, whether it's the heart kind or the plastic. And gene therapy, even the annual refresh variety, is a wholly different animal for a nova.

This nova, *the* nova that managed to spawn an entire industry and subculture, bats a dismissive, playful hand at my question.

"If there's anything I must confess, I found your article about the New Leopolders of the Congo quite fascinating."

"Fascinating? Is that what you call a macabre trade you're partly responsible for?"

Writing over your own genetic map with a complete stranger's is dangerous to say the least. Yet people are doing it, whether they're chasing stardom on film or seeking the perfect body to flaunt locally, in large part because of Hope Lange-Nova. Organ failure has become so common for novas and near novas it's created a demand that can only be satisfied through the black market. The New Leopolders are just one of many guerrilla rebel factions who fund themselves off organ sales. I've seen first-hand the mass graves full of innocents opened up and hollowed out, many of them skinned and eyeless. Don't forget those are organs too.

She looks at me with eyes that the camera loves, makes a straight man aspire to be her love interest. "What do you know about me?" she asks.

Hers is not the standard Hollywood tale of being a new face cast in the right part in the right movie which becomes a runaway success, at least not strictly. Hope Lange-Nova's success is directly tied to the industry's failure.

I'm sure you all remember about a decade ago, when the nameless, faceless execs behind the studios got the big idea to acquire the DNA rights to as many dead celebrities as they could. Then they trotted out Marilyn Monroe-Nova, Jimmy Stewart-Nova, Audrey Hepburn-Nova and a parade of other Golden Age clones in a move that was designed to both eliminate the need to develop new talent and secure big names to draw crowds to the theater.

The original stars were iconic, larger than life, which is exactly the problem when they're pared down to living people, acting for audiences with modern sensibilities. The vitriol was worse than when disco died. Backlash and boycotts nearly bankrupted three studios.

But this is the stuff I already knew about the industry and the origins of novas in general. The things I learned about Hope Lange-Nova are two days fresh, courtesy of Sherrice Day at the *Times*.

"The directors and producers were clueless to you being a nova when they cast you for 'Handle with Care.' The film blows up, serious movie buffs uncover your secret six seconds after opening weekend and you become the poster child of success as a nova actress. The one thing I wasn't able to find anywhere in your own words, why'd you pick Hope Lange?"

She looks at me with an appraising eyebrow. "Do you realize how utterly uncouth your question is?"

I nod. "Yep."

"And yet you query regardless?"

I shrug. "I completely respect the fact you're Hope Lange-Nova. I made no moves to discover your prior identity to invoke your birth name. I don't believe in the purist movement and wouldn't dream of calling you a GMO. Still, that respect doesn't dissuade my investigative nature. I wanna remind you that I said Sherrice Day would've asked better questions."

The current wave of novas say their celebrity gene choice wasn't a choice because they always felt they were that celebrity on the inside and they were simply bringing the inside out for the world to see. I find that offensive to trans people everywhere. How would those yesteryear stars feel if they were able to come back and see that a bunch of random people have used their DNA without permission? Flattered? Must be the reason why all the current stars living today have aggressively locked down their DNA rights and are lobbying Congress to make their DNA exempt from public domain… all that flattery.

Hope Lange-Nova nods. "I truthfully don't mind your question, Mr. Sturgis. If I wanted softball I would've requested your Sherrice Day. Tell me, have you seen the original Hope Lange's work, specifically the movie *Peyton Place* or 'The Ghost and Mrs. Muir' television show?"

"'Fraid not. TV's a bit different in Burkina Faso, Iran and along the Amazon to say the least."

She leans toward me conspiratorially. "You should watch them, as therein lies the secret to my success. I'm the ingénue."

"'Scuse me?"

She raised an eyebrow. "Don't tell me after all the stories where I've learned from you, from secret Chinese re-education camps to the Young Sauds, it's my turn to teach the redoubtable Arnour Sturgis?"

"I gotta admit I didn't take you as a fan of my work," I say, "and I guess so."

"How capital! Well, the ingénue is a stock character in literature and film, generally a young woman who has the fawn-eyed, endearing innocence of a child but with a subtle sex appeal," Ms. Lange-Nova holds up fingers and begins to count them off. "She's beautiful, kind, gentle, sweet, virginal, often naïve, in mental or emotional danger or even physical danger, usually a target of the cad; whom she may have mistaken for the hero. I do not care how few movies you may have seen, Mr. Sturgis, I know you've seen the type."

"Gotta admit I have," I tell her.

"Of course you have," she says with a self-satisfied smirk. "But a lot of people still attribute my success to the prior Lange's longevity, indeed laudable with over four decades in the business, the comfort food of her, you see. They don't account for Dennis Hopper-Nova's failed career despite the source being much more storied in Hollywood than Hope Lange. Everyone looks at me and thinks there's some sort of scientific ratio between level of fame and years in film of the gene contributor. They forget I didn't have anything to look at when the first wave of novas failed, except the perfect failure rate of novas, that is. I didn't choose Lange because of some Venn diagram. I choose her because she was the ingénue. Now I am the ingénue."

I lack a response, mostly because I lack an education in literature and film history to either confirm or counter argue. I'm mulling over her theory of her own success while wishing I had Sherrice here to field some questions, when a handsome, dark-haired nurse in blue scrubs comes over.

"The doctor's ready to see you now, Ms. Lange," he says with a winning smile.

Her mouth makes a moue. "Oh, this really won't do, Darion," she says. "I'm afraid I'm not quite done talking to Mr. Sturgis here. Could you be a rare gem and tell Dr. Yuen to wait please?"

"Of course," he says, "just come to the front when you're ready."

It's this kind of decadent display that's given me an aversion to Hollywood and the people that inhabit it. Most folks, me included, don't have a health care plan that allows us the ability to tell the doctor to wait and expect the doctor to actually do so or to be able to afford the dollar per minute charges that rack up while the doctor's idle. Coming from countries where doctors may not have enough potable water to clean their instruments, this is obscene to me.

The nurse leaves us and I field the only question I could think of, which is again incredibly selfish.

"Is this why you asked for me? Because I don't know enough about the history of Hollywood to even see the strawman in your argument?"

"Heavens, no. Even if you had quality counterpoints I imagine all that would do is fuel debate among the scholars." She leans closer. "I'm not wrong, though."

"So how come the original Hope Lange didn't become a super megastar under the power of this trope... the almighty Ingénue Engine?"

"Her problem was timing. Her career started at the edge of the decaying Golden Age when virtually all movies had the ingénue along with noble heroes and bad guys who were bad for badness sake. People were tired of it. Films began pushing the envelope to be racier and edgier. Movies and the world as a whole have been through so much since then. Now that we've seen the distant, bloody edge of racy, edgy, frayed, gristled, gruesome and gory there's an insatiable hunger for nostalgia. In this climate, Hope Lange is right on time."

A twenty-somethings red-haired girl approaches timidly. She asks for an autograph and when Hope nods, the girl hands her the only paper in her possession in this digital age, the DNA ownership certificate for Lana Turner.

I recognize Hope's look as she signs the document. I've seen it the world over in both autocratic presidents and the rebel leaders seeking to overthrow them. A world-weary fatigue, a bone-deep tiredness of the war they're fighting, the onus of being the only one they trust to fight it.

What was it about the fan that caused this reaction? The fan doesn't notice as she retreats with her precious autograph, thanking Ms. Lange-Nova profusely. Meanwhile, I'm like a dog on a scent.

"Hold up, why are we even in this waiting room? Celebrities don't wait. Whether they're buying surgery or shoes, they do it without a crowd."

Hope's stare is a thousand miles away, looking through the television. "It takes me back. I used to be her. And like I said, we have an insatiable hunger for nostalgia."

What she says, the way she says it, it brings to mind a thing unthinkable yet I think it anyway. Somehow, I just know.

"This ain't a refresh. You're giving it all up."

Her smile is a bittersweet.

"As I declared, a top investigator."

"Why?"

"Well, Mr. Sturgis, after one working kidney, a leaky bowel, an absent spleen and a failing liver, I've finally finished what I started out to do." She reaches into her clutch and pulls out a worn picture of a Black girl. The girl sports an enviable smile of unvarnished hope and exuberance that makes all youths beautiful. Hope speaks more to the girl in the photo than me.

"When I first started in this business, the few roles I could land were all stereotypes: slave extra, daughter of the maid, Civil Rights sit-in protester. Then I got a decent part as the girlfriend of one of the leads in a buddy comedy. It was an 'anygirl' wholly uninformed by Black American culture. I realized I was there to cross a diversity checkbox, to bring a touch of color to a part that a white woman could play, and probably more honestly than I."

She turns her eyes up from the photo and looks at me. "Then the novas came. Brand new Anne Bankcrofts, Bette Davises, Liz Taylors. It only reinforced what I already knew but no one spoke aloud... Hollywood was for white people."

I'm sure I was unable to mask the stupefaction on my face. "Wait... so you're telling me America's Sweetheart underneath the gene wash is a sista?"

She gives a small-lipped smile. "When was the last time America's Sweetheart was black?"

"It could've been around the last time folks saw a black war reporter," I reply. "Sometimes you gotta blaze your own trail in this world."

"Perhaps you're right, Mr. Sturgis, in this world." She points to the celebrity news happening on the television. "That world, however, is an illusion, a fabrication. It is a realm of fanciful stories. There are people who control those stories, and say which ones are worthy of being told and who gets to tell them. All I wished for was an honest shot to tell those stories."

Sorry, Hope Lange-Nova fans, but I lose it here with your idol, that is if she's still your idol after you've realized she is black. "That's what you call this, Hope, 'an honest shot?' What's honest about you? You traded in the Struggle for an easier time with a lesser struggle."

Despite my words, her anger never rises. "I was honest about that world and my place in it, Arnour. But you'd prefer I break down barriers. Tell me, who is reporting on the issues concerning our people: the racial-wealth gap, colorism, police brutality, poisoned water, a legion of women who look like me calling the cops on men who look like you while you're on location in Gaza and Jakarta and Caracas reporting on the plight of others?" She shakes her head. "I'm not the only one who swapped out struggles."

"You're wrong, Hope. It's etched in the skin. I carry the fight wherever I go, sista."

"Agreed, Arnour. I'm just of the mind that you shouldn't have to."

"So you didn't."

"I decided," Hope says, "that if they wanted a white girl, I'd give them exactly that. And I've shown them, the whole world really, I had the talent, talent enough to live my life in a perpetual state of method acting and never break character. Now, Arnour, I've decided to no longer give them anything."

I look around the room again. It's still Los Angeles, and it's reflected in the diversity in the waiting room. Besides the redhead who asked for the autograph there's an Arab woman in a hijab, a Latino youth with his black hair slicked back, others of varying shades of skin hue that are considered non-white.

Apparently race still matters in Hollywood in this age of idealized nostalgia. How many of these people were planning to go into the gene tanks and flush out their heritage for a shot of being closer in line with what the industry considered star quality?

"My god," I say, to no one in particular. "How many novas have already erased their culture?"

"An excellent question," Hope Lange-Nova says. "And if anyone could find the answer to such a query, I suspect it would be you. Hopefully, God willing, I'll be able to follow your progress when I'm a different person, the old made new again."

I don't have to tell her of all people the danger of what she intends. The old parts adhere to the old instructions. She will sit for a year or more in a vat of stem cells, sedatives and proprietary goo while nanomachines systematically flay off all her skin, break and remove bones to adjust height and facial features, irradiate her vocal cords and a hundred other macro and micro procedures to get the new parts moving to the new genetic map while trying to cajole the old parts like the heart and lungs from a mutiny that can be truly murderous.

All I ask is a simple, "Are you sure?"

She looks up at the TV. The wistful smile on her face says her mind's a million miles away. "My favorite Hope Lange work was 'The Ghost and Mrs. Muir', a 1960's sitcom about a young widow and the ghost of a roguishly handsome sea captain who had died in his prime a century prior. What drew me to it was the love story, this beautiful couple whose affection for one another was professed, profound, yet completely unobtainable. Sad, don't you think?"

I nod. Her reply is wondrous in how it doesn't answer my question yet answers it. Shirley Temple, Black not the nova, once said, "Any star can be devoured by human adoration, sparkle by sparkle."

Perhaps stars don't only get consumed from the outside, but from the inside out as well. I think about this person beside me, who's both attained the unattainable and yet hasn't, a person, in her own way, is as opened up and hollowed out as those poor bodies filling mass graves around the world. And I sit with her until she is ready to see the doctor.

The Comet

W.E.B. Du Bois

HE STOOD a moment on the steps of the bank, watching the human river that swirled down Broadway. Few noticed him. Few ever noticed him save in a way that stung. He was outside the world – "nothing!" as he said bitterly. Bits of the words of the walkers came to him.

"The comet?"

"The comet—"

Everybody was talking of it. Even the president, as he entered, smiled patronizingly at him, and asked: "Well, Jim, are you scared?"

"No," said the messenger shortly.

"I thought we'd journeyed through the comet's tail once," broke in the junior clerk affably.

"Oh, that was Halley's," said the president; "this is a new comet, quite a stranger, they say – wonderful, wonderful! I saw it last night. Oh, by the way, Jim," turning again to the messenger, "I want you to go down into the lower vaults today."

The messenger followed the president silently. Of course, they wanted *him to* go down to the lower vaults. It was too dangerous for more valuable men. He smiled grimly and listened.

"Everything of value has been moved out since the water began to seep in," said the president; "but we miss two volumes of old records. Suppose you nose around down there, – it isn't very pleasant, I suppose."

"Not very," said the messenger, as he walked out.

"Well, Jim, the tail of the new comet hits us at noon this time," said the vault clerk, as he passed over the keys; but the messenger passed silently down the stairs. Down he went beneath Broadway, where the dim light filtered through the feet of hurrying men; down to the dark basement beneath; down into the blackness and silence beneath that lowest cavern. Here with his dark lantern he groped in the bowels of the earth, under the world.

He drew a long breath as he threw back the last great iron door and stepped into the fetid slime within. Here at last was peace, and he groped moodily forward. A great rat leaped past him and cobwebs crept across his face. He felt carefully around the room, shelf by shelf, on the muddied floor, and in crevice and corner. Nothing. Then he went back to the far end, where somehow the wall felt different. He sounded and pushed and pried. Nothing. He started away. Then something brought him back. He was sounding and working again when suddenly the whole black wall swung as on mighty hinges, and blackness yawned beyond. He peered in; it was evidently a secret vault – some hiding place of the old bank unknown in newer times. He entered hesitatingly. It was a long, narrow room with shelves, and at the far end, an old iron chest. On a high shelf lay the two missing volumes of records, and others. He put them carefully aside and stepped to the chest. It was old, strong, and rusty. He looked at the vast and old-fashioned lock and flashed his light on the hinges. They were deeply incrusted with rust. Looking about, he found a bit of iron and began to pry. The rust had eaten a hundred years, and it had gone deep. Slowly, wearily, the old lid lifted, and with a last, low groan lay bare its treasure – and he saw the dull sheen of gold!

"Boom!"

A low, grinding, reverberating crash struck upon his ear. He started up and looked about. All was black and still. He groped for his light and swung it about him. Then he knew! The great stone door had swung to. He forgot the gold and looked death squarely in the face. Then with a sigh he went methodically to work. The cold sweat stood on his forehead; but he searched, pounded, pushed, and worked until after what seemed endless hours his hand struck a cold bit of metal and the great door swung again harshly on its hinges, and then, striking against something soft and heavy, stopped. He had just room to squeeze through. There lay the body of the vault clerk, cold and stiff. He stared at it, and then felt sick and nauseated. The air seemed unaccountably foul, with a strong, peculiar odor. He stepped forward, clutched at the air, and fell fainting across the corpse.

He awoke with a sense of horror, leaped from the body, and groped up the stairs, calling to the guard. The watchman sat as if asleep, with the gate swinging free. With one glance at him the messenger hurried up to the sub-vault. In vain he called to the guards. His voice echoed and re-echoed weirdly. Up into the great basement he rushed. Here another guard lay prostrate on his face, cold and still. A fear arose in the messenger's heart. He dashed up to the cellar floor, up into the bank. The stillness of death lay everywhere and everywhere bowed, bent, and stretched the silent forms of men. The messenger paused and glanced about. He was not a man easily moved; but the sight was appalling! "Robbery and murder," he whispered slowly to himself as he saw the twisted, oozing mouth of the president where he lay half-buried on his desk. Then a new thought seized him: If they found him here alone – with all this money and all these dead men – what would his life be worth? He glanced about, tiptoed cautiously to a side door, and again looked behind. Quietly he turned the latch and stepped out into Wall Street.

How silent the street was! Not a soul was stirring, and yet it was high-noon – Wall Street? Broadway? He glanced almost wildly up and down, then across the street, and as he looked, a sickening horror froze in his limbs. With a choking cry of utter fright he lunged, leaned giddily against the cold building, and stared helplessly at the sight.

In the great stone doorway a hundred men and women and children lay crushed and twisted and jammed, forced into that great, gaping doorway like refuse in a can – as if in one wild, frantic rush to safety, they had rushed and ground themselves to death. Slowly the messenger crept along the walls, wetting his parched mouth and trying to comprehend, stilling the tremor in his limbs and the rising terror in his heart. He met a business man, silk-hatted and frock-coated, who had crept, too, along that smooth wall and stood now stone dead with wonder written on his lips. The messenger turned his eyes hastily away and sought the curb. A woman leaned wearily against the signpost, her head bowed motionless on her lace and silken bosom. Before her stood a street car, silent, and within – but the messenger but glanced and hurried on. A grimy newsboy sat in the gutter with the "last edition" in his uplifted hand: "Danger!" screamed its black headlines. "Warnings wired around the world. The Comet's tail sweeps past us at noon. Deadly gases expected. Close doors and windows. Seek the cellar." The messenger read and staggered on. Far out from a window above, a girl lay with gasping face and sleevelets on her arms. On a store step sat a little, sweet-faced girl looking upward toward the skies, and in the carriage by her lay – but the messenger looked no longer. The cords gave way – the terror burst in his veins, and with one great, gasping cry he sprang desperately forward and ran, – ran as only the frightened run, shrieking and fighting the air until with one last wail of pain he sank on the grass of Madison Square and lay prone and still.

When he rose, he gave no glance at the still and silent forms on the benches, but, going to a fountain, bathed his face; then hiding himself in a corner away from the drama of death, he quietly gripped himself and thought the thing through: The comet had swept the earth and this was the end. Was everybody dead? He must search and see.

He knew that he must steady himself and keep calm, or he would go insane. First he must go to a restaurant. He walked up Fifth Avenue to a famous hostelry and entered its gorgeous, ghost-haunted halls. He beat back the nausea, and, seizing a tray from dead hands, hurried into the street and ate ravenously, hiding to keep out the sights.

"Yesterday, they would not have served me," he whispered, as he forced the food down.

Then he started up the street, – looking, peering, telephoning, ringing alarms; silent, silent all. Was nobody – nobody – he dared not think the thought and hurried on.

Suddenly he stopped still. He had forgotten. My God! How could he have forgotten? He must rush to the subway – then he almost laughed. No – a car; if he could find a Ford. He saw one. Gently he lifted off its burden, and took his place on the seat. He tested the throttle. There was gas. He glided off, shivering, and drove up the street. Everywhere stood, leaned, lounged, and lay the dead, in grim and awful silence. On he ran past an automobile, wrecked and overturned; past another, filled with a gay party whose smiles yet lingered on their death-struck lips; on past crowds and groups of cars, pausing by dead policemen; at 42nd Street he had to detour to Park Avenue to avoid the dead congestion. He came back on Fifth Avenue at 57th and flew past the Plaza and by the park with its hushed babies and silent throng, until as he was rushing past 72nd Street he heard a sharp cry, and saw a living form leaning wildly out an upper window. He gasped. The human voice sounded in his ears like the voice of God.

"Hello – hello – help, in God's name!" wailed the woman. "There's a dead girl in here and a man and – and see yonder dead men lying in the street and dead horses – for the love of God go and bring the officers—" And the words trailed off into hysterical tears.

He wheeled the car in a sudden circle, running over the still body of a child and leaping on the curb. Then he rushed up the steps and tried the door and rang violently. There was a long pause, but at last the heavy door swung back. They stared a moment in silence. She had not noticed before that he was a Negro. He had not thought of her as white. She was a woman of perhaps twenty-five – rarely beautiful and richly gowned, with darkly-golden hair, and jewels. Yesterday, he thought with bitterness, she would scarcely have looked at him twice. He would have been dirt beneath her silken feet. She stared at him. Of all the sorts of men she had pictured as coming to her rescue she had not dreamed of one like him. Not that he was not human, but he dwelt in a world so far from hers, so infinitely far, that he seldom even entered her thought. Yet as she looked at him curiously he seemed quite commonplace and usual. He was a tall, dark workingman of the better class, with a sensitive face trained to stolidity and a poor man's clothes and hands. His face was soft and slow and his manner at once cold and nervous, like fires long banked, but not out.

So a moment each paused and gauged the other; then the thought of the dead world without rushed in and they started toward each other.

"What has happened?" she cried. "Tell me! Nothing stirs. All is silence! I see the dead strewn before my window as winnowed by the breath of God, – and see—" She dragged him through great, silken hangings to where, beneath the sheen of mahogany and silver, a little French maid lay stretched in quiet, everlasting sleep, and near her a butler lay prone in his livery.

The tears streamed down the woman's cheeks and she clung to his arm until the perfume of her breath swept his face and he felt the tremors racing through her body.

"I had been shut up in my dark room developing pictures of the comet which I took last night; when I came out – I saw the dead!

"What has happened?" she cried again.

He answered slowly:

"Something – comet or devil – swept across the earth this morning and – many are dead!"

"Many? Very many?"

"I have searched and I have seen no other living soul but you."

She gasped and they stared at each other.

"My – father!" she whispered.

"Where is he?"

"He started for the office."

"Where is it?"

"In the Metropolitan Tower."

"Leave a note for him here and come."

Then he stopped.

"No," he said firmly – "first, we must go – to Harlem."

"Harlem!" she cried. Then she understood. She tapped her foot at first impatiently. She looked back and shuddered. Then she came resolutely down the steps.

"There's a swifter car in the garage in the court," she said.

"I don't know how to drive it," he said.

"I do," she answered.

In ten minutes they were flying to Harlem on the wind. The Stutz rose and raced like an airplane. They took the turn at 110th Street on two wheels and slipped with a shriek into 135th.

He was gone but a moment. Then he returned, and his face was gray. She did not look, but said:

"You have lost – somebody?"

"I have lost – everybody," he said, simply – "unless—"

He ran back and was gone several minutes – hours they seemed to her.

"Everybody," he said, and he walked slowly back with something film-like in his hand which he stuffed into his pocket.

"I'm afraid I was selfish," he said. But already the car was moving toward the park among the dark and lined dead of Harlem – the brown, still faces, the knotted hands, the homely garments, and the silence – the wild and haunting silence. Out of the park, and down Fifth Avenue they whirled. In and out among the dead they slipped and quivered, needing no sound of bell or horn, until the great, square Metropolitan Tower hove in sight. Gently he laid the dead elevator boy aside; the car shot upward. The door of the office stood open. On the threshold lay the stenographer, and, staring at her, sat the dead clerk. The inner office was empty, but a note lay on the desk, folded and addressed but unsent:

> *Dear Daughter:*
> *I've gone for a hundred mile spin in Fred's new Mercedes. Shall not be back before dinner. I'll bring Fred with me.*
> *J.B.H.*

"Come," she cried nervously. "We must search the city."

Up and down, over and across, back again – on went that ghostly search. Everywhere was silence and death – death and silence! They hunted from Madison Square to Spuyten Duyvel; they rushed across the Williamsburg Bridge; they swept over Brooklyn; from the Battery and Morningside Heights they scanned the river. Silence, silence everywhere, and no human sign. Haggard and bedraggled they puffed a third time slowly down Broadway, under the broiling sun, and at last stopped. He sniffed the air. An odor – a smell – and with the shifting breeze a sickening stench filled their nostrils and brought its awful warning. The girl settled back helplessly in her seat.

"What can we do?" she cried.

It was his turn now to take the lead, and he did it quickly.

"The long distance telephone – the telegraph and the cable – night rockets and then – flight!"

She looked at him now with strength and confidence. He did not look like men, as she had always pictured men; but he acted like one and she was content. In fifteen minutes they were at the central telephone exchange. As they came to the door he stepped quickly before her and pressed her gently back as he closed it. She heard him moving to and fro, and knew his burdens – the poor, little burdens he bore. When she entered, he was alone in the room. The grim switchboard flashed its metallic face in cryptic, sphinx-like immobility. She seated herself on a stool and donned the bright earpiece. She looked at the mouthpiece. She had never looked at one so closely before. It was wide and black, pimpled with usage; inert; dead; almost sarcastic in its unfeeling curves. It looked – she beat back the thought – but it looked, – it persisted in looking like – she turned her head and found herself alone. One moment she was terrified; then she thanked him silently for his delicacy and turned resolutely, with a quick intaking of breath.

"Hello!" she called in low tones. She was calling to the world. The world *must answer*. Would the world *answer? W*as the world—

Silence!

She had spoken too low.

"Hello!" she cried, full-voiced.

She listened. Silence! Her heart beat quickly. She cried in clear, distinct, loud tones: "Hello – hello – hello!"

What was that whirring? Surely – no – was it the click of a receiver?

She bent close, she moved the pegs in the holes, and called and called, until her voice rose almost to a shriek, and her heart hammered. It was as if she had heard the last flicker of creation, and the evil was silence. Her voice dropped to a sob. She sat stupidly staring into the black and sarcastic mouthpiece, and the thought came again. Hope lay dead within her. Yes, the cable and the rockets remained; but the world – she could not frame the thought or say the word. It was too mighty – too terrible! She turned toward the door with a new fear in her heart. For the first time she seemed to realize that she was alone in the world with a stranger, with something more than a stranger, – with a man alien in blood and culture – unknown, perhaps unknowable. It was awful! She must escape – she must fly; he must not see her again. Who knew what awful thoughts—

She gathered her silken skirts deftly about her young, smooth limbs – listened, and glided into a sidehall. A moment she shrank back: the hall lay filled with dead women; then she leaped to the door and tore at it, with bleeding fingers, until it swung wide. She looked out. He was standing at the top of the alley, – silhouetted, tall and black, motionless. Was he looking at her or away? She did not know – she did not care. She simply leaped and ran – ran until she found herself alone amid the dead and the tall ramparts of towering buildings.

She stopped. She was alone. Alone! Alone on the streets – alone in the city – perhaps alone in the world! There crept in upon her the sense of deception – of creeping hands behind her back – of silent, moving things she could not see, – of voices hushed in fearsome conspiracy. She looked behind and sideways, started at strange sounds and heard still stranger, until every nerve within her stood sharp and quivering, stretched to scream at the barest touch. She whirled and flew back, whimpering like a child, until she found that narrow alley again and the dark, silent figure silhouetted at the top. She stopped and rested; then she walked silently toward him, looked at him timidly; but he said nothing as he handed her into the car. Her voice caught as she whispered:

"Not – that."

And he answered slowly: "No – not that!"

They climbed into the car. She bent forward on the wheel and sobbed, with great, dry, quivering sobs, as they flew toward the cable office on the east side, leaving the world of wealth and prosperity for the world of poverty and work. In the world behind them were death and silence, grave and grim, almost cynical, but always decent; here it was hideous. It clothed itself in every ghastly form of terror, struggle, hate, and suffering. It lay wreathed in crime and squalor, greed and lust. Only in its dread and awful silence was it like to death everywhere.

Yet as the two, flying and alone, looked upon the horror of the world, slowly, gradually, the sense of all-enveloping death deserted them. They seemed to move in a world silent and asleep, – not dead. They moved in quiet reverence, lest somehow they wake these sleeping forms who had, at last, found peace. They moved in some solemn, world-wide *Friedhof, a*bove which some mighty arm had waved its magic wand. All nature slept until – until, and quick with the same startling thought, they looked into each other's eyes – he, ashen, and she, crimson, with unspoken thought. To both, the vision of a mighty beauty – of vast, unspoken things, swelled in their souls; but they put it away.

Great, dark coils of wire came up from the earth and down from the sun and entered this low lair of witchery. The gathered lightnings of the world centered here, binding with beams of light the ends of the earth. The doors gaped on the gloom within. He paused on the threshold.

"Do you know the code?" she asked.

"I know the call for help – we used it formerly at the bank."

She hardly heard. She heard the lapping of the waters far below, – the dark and restless waters – the cold and luring waters, as they called. He stepped within. Slowly she walked to the wall, where the water called below, and stood and waited. Long she waited, and he did not come. Then with a start she saw him, too, standing beside the black waters. Slowly he removed his coat and stood there silently. She walked quickly to him and laid her hand on his arm. He did not start or look. The waters lapped on in luring, deadly rhythm. He pointed down to the waters, and said quietly:

"The world lies beneath the waters now – may I go?"

She looked into his stricken, tired face, and a great pity surged within her heart. She answered in a voice clear and calm, "No."

Upward they turned toward life again, and he seized the wheel. The world was darkening to twilight, and a great, gray pall was falling mercifully and gently on the sleeping dead. The ghastly glare of reality seemed replaced with the dream of some vast romance. The girl lay silently back, as the motor whizzed along, and looked half-consciously for the elf-queen to wave life into this dead world again. She forgot to wonder at the quickness with which he had learned to drive her car. It seemed natural. And then as they whirled and swung into Madison Square and at the door of the Metropolitan Tower she gave a low cry, and her eyes were great! Perhaps she had seen the elf-queen?

The man led her to the elevator of the tower and deftly they ascended. In her father's office they gathered rugs and chairs, and he wrote a note and laid it on the desk; then they ascended to the roof and he made her comfortable. For a while she rested and sank to dreamy somnolence, watching the worlds above and wondering. Below lay the dark shadows of the city and afar was the shining of the sea. She glanced at him timidly as he set food before her and took a shawl and wound her in it, touching her reverently, yet tenderly. She looked up at him with thankfulness in her eyes, eating what he served. He watched the city. She watched him. He seemed very human, – very near now.

"Have you had to work hard?" she asked softly.

"Always," he said.

"I have always been idle," she said. "I was rich."

"I was poor," he almost echoed.

"The rich and the poor are met together," she began, and he finished:

"The Lord is the Maker of them all."

"Yes," she said slowly; "and how foolish our human distinctions seem – now," looking down to the great dead city stretched below, swimming in unlightened shadows.

"Yes – I was not – human, yesterday," he said.

She looked at him. "And your people were not my people," she said; "but today—" She paused. He was a man, – no more; but he was in some larger sense a gentleman, – sensitive, kindly, chivalrous, everything save his hands and – his face. Yet yesterday—

"Death, the leveler!" he muttered.

"And the revealer," she whispered gently, rising to her feet with great eyes. He turned away, and after fumbling a moment sent a rocket into the darkening air. It arose, shrieked, and flew up, a slim path of light, and scattering its stars abroad, dropped on the city below. She scarcely noticed it. A vision of the world had risen before her. Slowly the mighty prophecy of her destiny overwhelmed her. Above the dead past hovered the Angel of Annunciation. She was no mere woman. She was neither high nor low, white nor black, rich nor poor. She was primal woman; mighty mother of all men to come and Bride of Life. She looked upon the man beside her and forgot all else but his manhood, his strong, vigorous manhood – his sorrow and sacrifice. She saw him glorified. He was no longer a thing apart, a creature below, a strange outcast of another clime and blood, but her Brother Humanity incarnate, Son of God and great All-Father of the race to be.

He did not glimpse the glory in her eyes, but stood looking outward toward the sea and sending rocket after rocket into the unanswering darkness. Dark-purple clouds lay banked and billowed in the west. Behind them and all around, the heavens glowed in dim, weird radiance that suffused the darkening world and made almost a minor music. Suddenly, as though gathered back in some vast hand, the great cloud-curtain fell away. Low on the horizon lay a long, white star – mystic, wonderful! And from it fled upward to the pole, like some wan bridal veil, a pale, wide sheet of flame that lighted all the world and dimmed the stars.

In fascinated silence the man gazed at the heavens and dropped his rockets to the floor. Memories of memories stirred to life in the dead recesses of his mind. The shackles seemed to rattle and fall from his soul. Up from the crass and crushing and cringing of his caste leaped the lone majesty of kings long dead. He arose within the shadows, tall, straight, and stern, with power in his eyes and ghostly scepters hovering to his grasp. It was as though some mighty Pharaoh lived again, or curled Assyrian lord. He turned and looked upon the lady, and found her gazing straight at him.

Silently, immovably, they saw each other face to face – eye to eye. Their souls lay naked to the night. It was not lust; it was not love – it was some vaster, mightier thing that needed neither touch of body nor thrill of soul. It was a thought divine, splendid.

Slowly, noiselessly, they moved toward each other – the heavens above, the seas around, the city grim and dead below. He loomed from out the velvet shadows vast and dark. Pearl-white and slender, she shone beneath the stars. She stretched her jeweled hands abroad. He lifted up his mighty arms, and they cried each to the other, almost with one voice, "The world is dead."

"Long live the—"

"Honk! Honk!" Hoarse and sharp the cry of a motor drifted clearly up from the silence below. They started backward with a cry and gazed upon each other with eyes that faltered and fell, with blood that boiled.

"Honk! Honk! Honk! Honk!" came the mad cry again, and almost from their feet a rocket blazed into the air and scattered its stars upon them. She covered her eyes with her hands, and her shoulders heaved. He dropped and bowed, groped blindly on his knees about the floor. A blue flame spluttered lazily after an age, and she heard the scream of an answering rocket as it flew.

Then they stood still as death, looking to opposite ends of the earth.

"Clang – crash – clang!"

The roar and ring of swift elevators shooting upward from below made the great tower tremble. A murmur and babel of voices swept in upon the night. All over the once dead city the lights blinked, flickered, and flamed; and then with a sudden clanging of doors the entrance to the platform was filled with men, and one with white and flying hair rushed to the girl and lifted her to his breast. "My daughter!" he sobbed.

Behind him hurried a younger, comelier man, carefully clad in motor costume, who bent above the girl with passionate solicitude and gazed into her staring eyes until they narrowed and dropped and her face flushed deeper and deeper crimson.

"Julia," he whispered; "my darling, I thought you were gone forever."

She looked up at him with strange, searching eyes.

"Fred," she murmured, almost vaguely, "is the world – gone?"

"Only New York," he answered; "it is terrible – awful! You know, – but you, how did you escape – how have you endured this horror? Are you well? Unharmed?"

"Unharmed!" she said.

"And this man here?" he asked, encircling her drooping form with one arm and turning toward the Negro. Suddenly he stiffened and his hand flew to his hip. "Why!" he snarled. "It's – a – nigger – Julia! Has he – has he dared—"

She lifted her head and looked at her late companion curiously and then dropped her eyes with a sigh.

"He has dared – all, to rescue me," she said quietly, "and I – thank him – much." But she did not look at him again. As the couple turned away, the father drew a roll of bills from his pockets.

"Here, my good fellow," he said, thrusting the money into the man's hands, "take that, – what's your name?"

"Jim Davis," came the answer, hollow-voiced.

"Well, Jim, I thank you. I've always liked your people. If you ever want a job, call on me." And they were gone.

The crowd poured up and out of the elevators, talking and whispering.

"Who was it?"

"Are they alive?"

"How many?"

"Two!"

"Who was saved?"

"A white girl and a nigger – there she goes."

"A nigger? Where is he? Let's lynch the damned—"

"Shut up – he's all right-he saved her."

"Saved hell! He had no business—"

"Here he comes."

Into the glare of the electric lights the colored man moved slowly, with the eyes of those that walk and sleep.

"Well, what do you think of that?" cried a bystander; "of all New York, just a white girl and a nigger!"

The colored man heard nothing. He stood silently beneath the glare of the light, gazing at the money in his hand and shrinking as he gazed; slowly he put his other hand into his pocket and brought out a baby's filmy cap, and gazed again. A woman mounted to the platform and looked about, shading her eyes. She was brown, small, and toil-worn, and in one arm lay the corpse of a dark baby. The crowd parted and her eyes fell on the colored man; with a cry she tottered toward him.

"Jim!"

He whirled and, with a sob of joy, caught her in his arms.

Élan Vital

K. Tempest Bradford

THE FEW MINUTES I had to spend in the Institute's waiting room were my least favorite part of coming up to visit my mother. It felt more like a dialysis room, the visitors sunk into the overly-soft couches and not speaking, just drinking orange juice and recovering. There were no magazines and no television, just cold air blowing from the vents and generic music flowing with it. I'd finished my juice and was beginning to brood on my dislike for overly air-conditioned buildings when my mother arrived attended by a nurse.

I kissed and hugged her, automatically asking how she was, mouthing the answer she always gave as she gave it again.

"I'm fine, same as always."

It wasn't strictly true, but true enough.

"Let's go on out," she said, shrugging off the nurse's continued assistance. "It's too cold in here."

Despite the hint, the nurse tried to help Mom over the threshold. As always, she rebuffed any attempt to treat her like an old person.

"Where to today?" she asked, slipping her arm into mine as we escaped the frigid building.

"Just down to the lake," I said. "Don't want to overexert you."

She squeezed my arm as her feet slid carefully over the cobbled path. I wanted her to use a wheelchair, or a walker, at least. She wouldn't.

"What you mean is that we haven't got so much time today," she said.

I shrugged instead of answering. I didn't want to go into why I couldn't afford much this trip.

"Next time I'll come for a couple of days, at least. I promise."

"No, that's all right," she said. "I don't like it when you spend so much for days and more. A few hours is fine."

I helped her past the immaculately landscaped gardens and small orchards. The scent of flowers, herbs, and fresh-cut grass wafting at us in turn. I glanced at the garden entrances as we passed by, catching quick glances of other people in the middle of visits. A young couple who'd been in the waiting room with me knelt by a small, bald girl as she splashed in the koi pond. Two elderly women stood under a weeping willow, their heads close, lips barely moving. A large group of people speaking Mandarin milled around the waterfall in the rock garden. I could still hear faint traces of their melodic din all the way down by the lake.

I preferred this spot – the flora was less regimented and more natural. And no walls. Just an open space, water gently flicking the shoreline, a beautiful view down the hill, and the occasional cat wandering by.

"This hasn't changed much," my mom said as I helped her down on one of the small benches by the water. "I thought they were going to get ducks or geese or something."

I chose a nearby rock for my own perch. "I think they're having trouble with permits or whatever you need nowadays."

The wind kicked up, sending freckles of reflected light across her face. Her skin was still perfect, beautiful and dark brown, though stretched across her cheekbones a little too tight. I hated that

I never had enough to restore her round cheeks and full figure. I have to look at pictures just to remember her that way.

"You haven't changed much, either," she said while fussing with my hair. I'd bought some dye the week before, knowing she'd notice it. "How long has it been?"

"Three months."

She let out a familiar sigh – part exhaustion, part exasperation, part sadness, I suppose. "That's too soon."

"It's your birthday, though."

"Is it? It's fall already?" She looked out over the small forest that edged the Institute's boundary a few miles away. The trees were still green with no hint of turning. It always felt and looked like summer there; one of the reasons the administrators chose the location. "I miss the seasons. Fall colors, Christmas snow..."

"You never did when you had to shovel it."

That got her to smile.

I reached out and held her hand; still a little cold even in the full sunlight. "Besides, I missed you."

"I know. But..."

"And I won't be able to come back until after the new year, anyway, so I wanted to squeeze in one more visit. Since today is special..."

Years ago I used to bring her cake and presents on her birthday. She couldn't really eat the cake – one of the side effects of whatever they did when they brought her back. The presents had to go back home with me since she didn't have any place to put them and couldn't wear clothing or jewelry once she went back to sleep. I hated having to give that up, too.

"Okay, I'll give you a pass this time." She kissed my cheek, seeming more like her old self. "Where are you off to?"

"Rwanda. For a dig. Dr. Berman promised I'd be more than a glorified volunteer wrangler this trip. And they want me for a year. Still, I'll try to come back and see you sooner than that."

"No, you should concentrate on your work. I'll still be here." My mother never changed.

It was the same when she was sick. I wanted to take a break from college and stay home with her. It was pretty clear that her death was inevitable by that time, the only question being: how long? I wanted to be with her, she wanted me back in class. *If you take a leave of absence you might never go back*, she'd said. So I went back.

"For me it'll seem like you've gone and come back right away." Trying to reassure me again.

"I know," I said. "Must be strange, not being able to perceive the passage of time."

We didn't say anything for a while. This was the part of the visit where one of us either addressed the elephant in the room or steered the conversation around it.

"At least I'm not as bad as Ella," she said. And we both laughed.

My aunt, her older sister, was so notorious for being late that we started her funeral a few hours behind schedule because it just felt right. My cousin Brandon joked that we should have carved an epitaph on her headstone: "I'll be back in five minutes."

"Remember the time she was supposed to pick me up from rehearsal or something?"

"And you waited for her, caught the bus, and was home before she'd even left the house!"

Mom kept me laughing for a long time, recounting trips she'd taken with Ella and their cousins and everything that went wrong because they were never on time anywhere. Stories I'd heard dozens of times before and wouldn't have minded hearing a hundred times again. More and more, her laughs ended with a small coughing fit. I checked the time; we had about forty-five minutes left.

"Do you want to head back?" I asked. "Sit inside a bit before you..."

"Die?"

"You don't die."

"Technically, I do. According to the doctors, anyway."

I didn't argue. I didn't even want to be talking about it. I was never there when my mother went 'back under', as the nurses put it. It was against Institute rules. I suppose for some people it might have been upsetting to see their loved ones in the capsules residents stayed in. Too much like a coffin. For me, it felt wrong not to be by her side when it happened. I was with her when she first died, after all.

Seeing that I wasn't going to go there, mom leaned back and turned her face to the sunlight. "No, let's stay out here a little bit longer. It's a nice day."

"I could come back tomorrow, get a few more hours," I said. It wouldn't matter if I stayed a little longer. There wasn't anyone waiting for me back at home.

"You know how I feel about that." Her look was semi-stern. "You don't want to end up in here yourself. Not for a long time, if ever."

"At least we'd be together," I said, smiling.

"But who would bring us back?"

"I'm sure I could bribe Brandon's kids to do it." I wasn't particularly close to my cousin anymore, though his oldest called me on the holidays. My guess was she'd been coveting my share of our grandmother's house.

"You've given this a lot of thought. I'm surprised."

I knew I had to tread very carefully. "It may come up. Someday. You haven't said you want to stop. And if anything happens to me, it's in my will that I want to come here if I can."

Mom gazed at me steadily for what felt like a long time. "Are you sure that's what you want?"

That alarmed me more than a little. "Why? Is there... I mean, something that isn't right? Is it..." When you avoid talking about something for so long, it's hard to know how to start. "Is it bad?"

"The dying? I don't know, really. They always induce sleep before that moment."

Though I had always been more reluctant to talk about this, I could tell my mother was holding back, not saying some things. That scared me even more. She was always very upfront with me except when it came to what was going on with her. Usually when it was really bad.

"What's it like? Afterwards. While you're... gone."

She shook her head slowly, her look far away. "To be honest, I don't know."

Better than the answer I'd been dreading. Answers, plural, actually. Nothing I could imagine made me feel particularly good. Either I was ripping my mother away from the glories of heaven or giving her only small respites from the tortures of hell. The preachers and protestors all had their own variations on those themes and loved to scream them at me (or anyone else driving past the gates) whenever I came up. 'I don't know' was, at least, not guilt-inducing.

"It's a little like waking up from a dream," she said after a couple of minutes. "I know that I've been dreaming, and I even intend to remember the dream, but I can't recall a single element once I wake up."

"That must be frustrating." I sometimes dreamed of what she did and where she went while I was gone. Many times I was there with her. Those were my favorite.

"It's the way things are," she said and shrugged. "Ironic, though, isn't it? I don't know anymore about the afterlife than anyone else and I've been dead how many years?"

"Seven."

"Hmm." She smiled my favorite smile – the one where the corners of her mouth turned down and yet it was still somehow a smile. "I guess I am having trouble with time. I thought it had been longer."

I still couldn't get over the fact that it had happened at all. It wasn't fair. I was too young to lose my mother and she was too young to be dying. Only fifty-three. Not fair at all. So when the UR Institute approached me in the hospital I was primed to listen and agree. They would handle all of the funeral arrangements and costs and even buy a crypt for her in the cemetery where her mother and father and brother were buried. No one else would know that she wasn't in there. Only I knew that she was actually resting in the Institute waiting to be re-animated. You could have your mother back for a couple of days a few times a year, they'd said. Holidays, birthdays, your wedding day. They had me from hello.

It didn't matter that the only reason they were prepared to foot the bills was that they wanted to study how people who died from cancer reacted to the resurrection process. It didn't matter that I couldn't tell the rest of the family. Only a few people knew then that the Institute wasn't just reanimating rich old ladies' cats anymore. It didn't matter that I would have to provide the élan vital necessary to reanimate her again for those few hours or days. Or that these transfusions shortened my own life span, sometimes caused considerable health problems in other 'donors', and took the ability to have children of my own. It didn't matter. I just wanted my mother back.

"It can't have only been seven years." Mom was frowning now.

"Oh, right. It's been more like ten." My hand went to the nape of my neck, rubbing the tender spot they always used for access. I thought I'd gotten rid of that tic.

"Has it?" She was paging back through her memory. I could tell from her look.

I exuded casualness – my only defense against a mother's ability to catch you in a lie. "Like you said, the process messes with your sense of time."

I had developed this tendency to treat her like a doddering old woman. She was only fifty-three and would always be fifty-three. She never aged, just backed up from death a few steps before going ahead again. The resurrection process didn't work very well on cancer patients, particularly cancers of the blood. She was perpetually sick-seeming, though the pain wasn't as bad. That made it easy to fool myself by thinking she was getting old and forgetful when her memory was as sharp as ever.

"I've been resurrected twenty-six times. I know because someone told me when I hit twenty."

They weren't supposed to tell her stuff like that.

"Six visits should have been three years ago," she continued. "How long has it actually been?"

And of course she was giving me that look. The one mothers have when you've been caught forging a report card signature or sneaking into a movie when you're supposed to be in Algebra. There was no point lying then.

"A little over a year," I admitted. I could see her ramping up. "Mom, it's—"

"When I agreed to do this it was on the condition that you only do two transfusions a year. Three at most. Now you're telling me six!"

"No, listen—"

"Shannon, that's too many. It's dangerous! You're throwing away years—"

"I'm not!"

"*Years* of your life on the past!"

There was more to the speech but a chime interrupted. Each patient had an electronic monitor bracelet to keep track of vital signs, warn of danger, and countdown the time left. It chimed again, informing us that we had twenty minutes.

"We should start back." I said, knowing she didn't need the whole twenty for the walk.

"No. Sit down."

"Mom, please, we need to go."

She pointed at my rock. "Not until we talk about this."

There was nothing to do but give in.

"You can't keep doing this," she said, using The Voice. Like I was a small child and she was explaining why I couldn't have something I'd begged and begged for at the store. "This five or six or however many times a year. You promised me."

"I know. And I'm sorry I lied. But I didn't want you to worry. And I couldn't afford it any other way."

"Afford what? I thought they said this was free."

There had been several times I'd wanted to tell her this. To tell anyone, really. But she wouldn't have just listened. She would have made me stop.

"The 'storage' is free," I said. I hated that word and the way they used it. "But the resurrection isn't. The fees went up once they went public. I couldn't always afford it. And I couldn't wait years between seeing you again. Then they developed a way to transfer vital force between non-family members."

I wanted to turn away, but I forced myself to look her in the eye. "People pay a lot of money for that."

I have only seen my mother cry a few times in my life. Seeing tears in her eyes broke me down to the child I was when I first saw them. When you're three (or thirty) and your mother cries because of something you've done, you want to turn back time or vow to be the perfect daughter for the rest of your life. Anything to make it better.

"Every time I do it for someone else they let me do it for you, too. For the short visits. Then I earn enough money to buy longer ones."

"You have to stop." She squeezed my hand tight and drew me over to the bench.

"Mom, it's okay. I'm fine. The process is much more refined now, much less dangerous."

"No. This isn't right."

"But I'm helping people. Helping them hang on to life a little longer."

Mom made me look her in the eyes. "Why aren't their family members doing it for them? Why are they paying someone else to do it?"

There are probably dozens of legitimate reasons I could have given her. But, in the end, it all came down to the fact that people with that kind of money to throw around didn't need to give of themselves to fulfill their desires, so they didn't. Nor did they have to when there were plenty of people like me around.

The monitor chimed again. She pressed a button to silence it, then took it off altogether.

"Mom!"

"Shannon, I love you. I would do anything for you. I did this for you."

I was the one crying now. "You didn't really want to though, did you?"

"No, baby, I did." She wiped the tears from my cheek. A futile act as they were near torrential. "When I— when I died I had no regrets but one: that I was leaving you. I wouldn't get to see you graduate college or get married or be a mother yourself. I would miss *your* life and I hated that thought."

It was nearly dark. The lights around the lake blinked on and illuminated her hollow face. My mother's body wasted away by cancer. Cancer that would kill her again right in front of my eyes if we stayed any longer. They warned every resident to get back to the Institute before... Before. They said if the proper procedure wasn't followed it could result in damage, or worse.

"How many years has this taken from you? Not just the seven we've been doing this, but the years they leeched?"

I closed my eyes, seeing my face as it looked in the mirror each morning. No wrinkles to speak of – that was down to her genes. But the grey hairs, the stiff joints, and the fatigue made me feel older than thirty. Hell, older than forty, most days. "They don't know. It's hard to tell. They just don't know. And it doesn't matter."

"Of course it matters!"

"No, it doesn't. Because you're my mother. Because I'm supposed to take care of you. Because I wasn't there when you had your operations or when you had chemo or all the other times you needed me. I was off sorting through dead people's things and wondering which pottery sherd came from which dynasty and other bullshit that didn't matter!"

The bracelet beeped again. I took a few minutes to calm down, knowing that minutes was all I had left. But my throat was so tight I could barely breathe and I didn't want to lose it.

"I thought of you every day," she said with effort. "But every day I was glad you weren't there to see me like that. I didn't want that to be how you remembered me. Sending you back to college was an easy excuse."

I wiped my face dry as best I could, then swept away the tears on her cheeks. "So. Atonement for us both, then."

"I let it go on for too long, though," she said. It was obvious that she was in a great deal of pain and did not intend to do anything about it. "I just didn't want to leave you again."

"So don't."

"At some point, I have to. I'm dead, baby. You can bring me back a hundred times and nothing will change that."

"It's not fair."

She wrapped her arms around me. "No one ever promised you fair."

No, no one ever did. Not even her.

* * *

Five minutes before we were supposed to be back at the main building, a nurse found us, my mom's head resting on my shoulder, my arm holding her close.

"Ma'am, do you need help getting back?" he asked.

"She's not going back," I said, my eyes never leaving the water.

"But Miss Tidmore, she needs to get back if we're—"

"I'm exercising my right to allow my mother a full and natural death."

The minutes ticked away. Mom's body started to tremble, the pain kicking in as her time ran out. She'd lost consciousness just after the nurse went to get help. Or reinforcements. It was hard, sitting there, knowing that she was in pain.

In the end, she left the decision up to me. Just like she had seven years before in the hospital. My aunts had been taking care of her, but I had the power of attorney. I could let her go or I could let the Institute bring her back. Now, by the lake, footsteps approaching, it was the same. I could let her go or I could bring her back.

When they came back, I knew, they would try to change my mind. They would argue and reason and sound very convincing. They couldn't force me, though. It was in the contract.

I held her hand. I waited forever. It was over too soon.

But I was there.

The Orb

Tara Campbell

EVERY TIME I stir the biomass, I feel lucky to have been chosen. The stirrer is flat and smooth, made of blonde wood; the biomass is thick and smells of overripe fruit. I look down into the buttery orange swirls in the bucket, and it amazes me that just a few months ago I was helping a friend paint her new nursery walls a similar color. But before her baby arrived, I was selected, and now I'm here making history.

I walk across the dusty field to the wooden shed in our small corner of the 'estate' – which is more like a compound – and press my palm to the scanner, one of the Master's few concessions to modern technology. Electricity and running water seem almost out of place here. Everything else on the compound is rustic: the big farmhouse in which he lives; the bunkhouse where the assistants sleep; a couple of small cabins, one of which is crammed with materials, the other which I claimed for myself by virtue of being the first. This was a fortunate turn of events, given that the assistants are in their twenties and I'm – not.

The air inside the shed is a sweeter, rottener version of the biomass. Although the fumes aren't harmful, the odor would overwhelm at length. I hold my breath against the stink of seaweed, the rot of fertility. The Master doesn't want us wearing masks anymore. He doesn't want the Orb to think it's unwelcome. We created it, after all.

I roll up my sleeves, then dip my hands into the bucket and slather the Orb with biomass. We aren't supposed to use gloves, for purposes of bonding. I enjoy the lushness of the substance – thick, smooth, slightly grainy – and the swell of the Orb under my palms. Its surface is silky and taut, but pliable. There's muscle under there. From time to time I feel it contract.

I start with the Orb's sides and bottom, then climb onto a stepstool to reach the very top of it. By now I can do this without soaking my apron and skirt. After I smooth biomass into the last bit of its skin, I keep my hand in place, waiting for another contraction. Sometimes, if I wait long enough, there's a rumble underneath my fingers. A purr.

* * *

The Orb continues to grow, to the point where even with a stepstool, we can't reach the top of it. One of the assistants suggested using a long-handled brush, but the Master insists that human touch is essential. He's ordered me to build a scaffold around the Orb so we can reach all of it. Luckily one of the assistants is a carpenter – I wouldn't know how to begin.

I've had to ask for the assistants' help so many times. I'm not their leader, per se, but the Master has developed a habit of giving all the orders through me, and through some twisted alchemy of misplaced guilt, the orders become favors the assistants are doing for me, adding to my account on some imaginary ledger.

I don't get that feeling from Michael, the carpenter. He arrived with his girlfriend Sarah a month ago. Julian, however – he's been here twice as long, doing the bare minimum, and yet is jealous of anyone else the Master notices and seems to appreciate. No matter that Julian's work is sloppy, such that I have to check his batches to make sure he's mixed the biomass properly; he's still angry at those of us who are doing well. He's sure to be piqued when Michael invents some ingenious articulated system that expands along with the growth of the Orb. The Master loves this sort of thing, praises intricate inventiveness, admires the time and effort lavished on any sort of niche, analog, temporary measure.

Soon Julian, Lucy, and I will finish the new structure for the Orb. It's something of the Master's design. It looks like a Quonset hut, but we call it a hangar because he finds the former term too militaristic. Even though it will involve destruction, he reminds us, the Great Devouring is ultimately about peace.

* * *

The Orb is now over ten feet in diameter. Still in the old structure, we've expanded Michael's scaffolding as far as it will go, leaving only a small gap for us to slip through with our buckets between it and the wall. Even Julian, the tallest of us, can barely reach the top of the Orb from the scaffolding, and the rest of us must resort to slopping biomass over the last bit we can't get to. We'll have to take down the wall to get it out of the shed.

But the new hangar isn't ready yet. It doesn't sit right. We tried to follow the Master's instructions, but the frame is listing to the side, and we don't dare compound the problem by finishing it. Julian's complaining throughout has not only been demoralizing, but, as it turns out, there may be some truth to it: the blueprints were more sketches than actual plans. The Master is angry, of course, but as he says, he was wrong to expect a team of non-builders to interpret his design correctly.

That's why he's bringing on Hamish, a *real* builder. He's very busy, says the Master, because he's *qualified*, and he will only be here long enough to build the hangar. The Master warns us not so speak with Hamish about the project, or if we must, tell him it's art. That's what the rest of the 'estate' is for, after all, this five-hundred-acre art colony with its ramshackle pavilions and gallery barns; its outdoor sculpture and scrap-metal whirligigs spiraling in the wind; its massive, rusted robot looming vast on the western horizon.

The Master has arranged for us to be in this little fenced-off area, courtesy of the absentee matron who owns the estate. She has a history of funding mysterious projects by mysterious male artists, demanding they surprise and delight her with the first viewing in exchange for absolute secrecy. Perhaps she likes the feeling of power, of creation. Perhaps she thinks it gives her an edge of danger in her dotage.

If she only knew.

* * *

Hamish is here.

The night before he arrived, Sarah complained to me that we shouldn't have extra people coming in and out, 'willy-nilly.' She claimed to be concerned about having an outsider so close to the project, but I suspect she's more annoyed that the Master didn't give Michael an opportunity to redesign the hut. I told her to have faith in the Master's judgment, and she didn't say anything, but I could tell by her expression she wasn't entirely satisfied.

I didn't dare admit to her that *my* main concern was losing my cabin for the new builder's lodging. Fortunately, the Master had us clear out the second cabin for his use. And when Hamish arrived, I grasped the wisdom of this decision, as he appears to be close to my age, and similarly desiring and deserving of some privacy. *Especially* someone like him, who seems the type that would draw other people toward him: strong build, muscular from work; a clever designer's mind; a welcoming smile and kind eyes. I can understand why he might need his own space to get away to.

At any rate, Sarah hardly needs to worry that Hamish will see something he shouldn't, because he and the Master spend all of their time together conferring in the farmhouse, then coming out to stare at our shamefully tilted attempt while holding up drawings as wide as their arms can spread. We watch from a distance, the Master's eyes warning us away. But I've caught a peek at the new drawings, which I assume are Hamish's due to their clean, straight lines. The Master's updated the hangar, adding more scaffolding and thicker walls.

I think about those drawings and marvel at how far we've come from the days of the earthen hut with a padlock and a thousand-gallon tank.

* * *

Before I arrived, the Master says, the Orb was no more than a seashell, the perfection of the infinite designer spiraling outward in the golden ratio. At first the shell was small enough to fit on the palm of his hand, and looked laughably small in its five-foot cube of fluid. Of course I would never laugh at the Orb – it was already up to my knees when I arrived – so I have to take the Master's word for its modest beginnings.

As it grew, he says, the spiraling of the shell disappeared, erased by a layer of pinkish matter accumulating on its surface. But shortly after I arrived, I was witness to a wonder: the gelatinous matter developed a subtle formation of bulges spiraling from the top to the bottom of the sphere. This sense of memory, this intelligence, convinced me that I was part of something truly life-altering, that I had been chosen to help build this new life. That the Master and I would be the architects of a new age.

Back then it was just the two of us. Every day he and I would add nutrients to the tank and take measurements – temperature, salinity, alkalinity, ammonia, nitrate, phosphate, ionic strength, viscosity, and so on. As the Orb grew, its surface morphed from a rosy ooze into something more substantive, condensing itself into something resembling the skin we know now. It hardly looked like something that would subvert the world order, but this was the stage the Master was waiting for, the indication that the Orb was ready to come out of the tank. Now was the time, he said, for a new assistant to join us.

Not 'an assistant' but 'a *new* assistant.'

I told myself the twinge I felt was merely protectiveness of the project. And I was indeed wary of a new person joining our work, but the Master assured me he'd screened Lucy the same way he'd screened me: she'd found his 'art project' online (another necessary concession to modernity), read deeply of his teachings, passed multiple interviews with him, agreed to travel here.

"The path to power," says the Master, "is strewn with the bodies of those who wanted to save the world. It is a golden staircase littered with the remains of those who tried – and failed – to protect vulnerable animals and ecosystems, to rescue the planet itself."

He means the victims of corporate greed: environmentalists, journalists, protestors, activists. But as far as I'm concerned, these corpses include everyone in the world, all of our bodies rotting from poisoned water and filthy air and processed food. The Orb will protect *all* of us by crushing the drills, poaching the poachers, strong-arming the strongmen, and bleeding out greedy CEOs – devouring the devourers until human beings finally have to respect the power of the earth.

This 'art' is very real. When the Master speaks, he doesn't share exactly *how* it will happen, but he has his reasons for keeping that knowledge safe. He has a plan, and it's not for us to question it. Our calling is to care for the Orb. The Master will share the rest of his vision when the time comes.

* * *

The morning Lucy arrived, and the Master winched the Orb out of the water and positioned it over a bedding of damp blankets, she didn't hesitate to reach up and help guide it, dripping, to its nest.

It would need frequent feeding and watering now, said the Master. We were weaning it off the tank. Toughening it.

I volunteered for the first shift, advising Lucy to go and rest. The Master offered to show her the project notes and help her get caught up. I don't like to recall how petty I felt, noticing how he placed a hand on the small of her back as he guided her out of the hut.

But Lucy has turned out to be trustworthy. Unlike me, she moved naturally in the clothing from the start. I've yet to see her fidget with her bonnet, and she's always used the apron for its actual purpose, rather than keeping it clean like part of a costume she'd have to return later.

Knowing now how reliable she is, I don't like to recall how during those first few weeks I listened after she'd bedded down for the evening, alert for any footsteps around her bunkhouse, any stirring inside. How I watched for any deviation in the Master's path from the farmhouse to the hut protecting the Orb.

Lucy was never the problem.

* * *

Hamish has come and built and left, though I can't say I wished for the last of those things. But there would have been no way to fully shield the Orb as we transferred it, and no one uninitiated can see it yet. Michael devised a way to gently lift and transport the Orb to its new hangar. At the same time, the Master has screened and initiated a new batch of assistants, bringing us up to almost a dozen now. I'm grateful for the additional help with the Orb's care, as well as with chores around the compound – the Master has brought in chickens for eggs and cows for milk, and we've begun gardening and baking bread to minimize the necessity for contact with the outside. He says his patroness was very supportive of the investment, finding this all very mysterious and amusing; not realizing, of course, that we are also fortifying our compound to exist in the new world order we are ushering in. But this influx of people leaves me more uneasy than relieved.

I observe the new trainees stirring their buckets of biomass. The buckets are metal now, as are the stirrers, and we're all required to wear elbow-high gloves and full-body aprons, men and women alike. The Master has changed the formula. It's green now, and runnier, and smells of rosemary and vinegar.

When the biomass is ready, I lead everyone up a set of exterior steps to the rooftop, show them how to pour their buckets into the chute, explain how this chute will bathe the Orb in the nutrients it needs to grow. Tell them their contributions are much appreciated.

The new trainees, however, have never seen the Orb, let alone touched it. The Master says this physical closeness is no longer necessary because we are biologically engineered into the Orb (he once admitted to me how surprised he was that HeLa cells were so readily available, even for artistic endeavors, which allows him to describe his work this way). The Orb is already enough like us – *of* us – for the connection he wanted to create. Early touch, he says, was sufficient to activate its sense of empathy, its instinctual bond with those of us who mean it well. Like will protect like.

Now we are supposed to treat it with respect, which doesn't include touch. Anymore. At least, not for the Orb.

After the last trainee empties her bucket, I show them all how to clean the equipment and send them off on their next assignments. This is where the genders separate again, some of the women cooking and cleaning in the farmhouse with Lucy, others gardening with Sarah, the few men fixing things around the compound under Michael's guidance, Julian monitoring the Orb's development (and fuming) under my supervision. It's clear to everyone, even the Master, that he would rather have a team of his own; add to that the sting that Michael and Sarah were given permission to move into the cabin after Hamish's departure.

I walk back out to the hangar and palm the scanner to unlock it. Everyone except the Master, Julian, and I have been programmed out.

Inside, the air is fragrant. The sickly rot of the previous shed has given way to something fresh and green, a field after rain.

The Orb is still slick with a dull gleam of biomass. Still feeding. I climb the newer, bigger scaffold so I won't have to crane my neck to look up into its swelling form. I walk the catwalk around its perimeter, where only those of us who have been here since the beginning are allowed tread.

Up close, I can hear it growing, crinkling with a tiny, wet *snick*.

* * *

Life before the Orb seems so distant now.

It's been a week since anyone has seen Julian.

The last time I saw him, I was on my way out of the hangar. I stopped – it's not that I'd done something wrong, but I didn't have a particular reason for being with the Orb just then. It was night, and I wasn't sure if he'd seen me, so I hurried around the corner out of sight.

My first thought was to just go to my cabin and forget it, but I couldn't. Julian had been stirring things up recently, disgruntled by Michael's increasing prominence, accusing the Master of being attached to certain new trainees – although, I have to admit, it does seem that the Master has taken a special interest in the new recruits.

I only got a few steps before I turned back to see what Julian was up to himself, sneaking around at night. Perhaps I was paranoid, but when I saw that he was heading toward the Master's farmhouse, I was alarmed – what if he'd seen me just then? What if he'd seen me all those other times, visiting the Orb when I wasn't supposed to?

I followed him at a distance, and by the time I reached the farmhouse, the Master had already let him inside. Standing in the shadows outside, I couldn't hear anything in particular, just muffled voices rising and falling. After several minutes, the voices got louder and footsteps pounded the floorboards. I ducked around the corner of the house, and from there I heard the front door creak open. Two sets of shoes clomped across the porch and down the front steps.

"Let me show you, Julian," I heard the Master say. "You deserve to see."

That was a week ago, and no one has seen him since.

* * *

Man is the apex predator. We all knew this before the Master told us; it's why we came. We're here to balance the scales, to create another life form that can mitigate our domination over all other life on the planet. For the good of the Earth, we're here to create something more powerful, more durable than humans and all of our technology – something to keep us in check.

The Orb shares our genetic material. It will have a deep knowledge of us, the way a stem cell 'knows' how to build itself into skin or muscle, blood or bone. It will know what we need. Our weaknesses. How to kill us.

And, I believe, it will share our instinct to save itself above all other forms of life.

But it had to be done. Just like the Master tells us, other systems for mitigating human control – earthquakes, floods, disease, drought, crop infestation – were random and untargeted. Nature doesn't care who it kills, and oligarchs have the means to avoid these plagues: stockpiles of food and supplies in undisclosed locations, private planes to escape, hired guards for protection, and piles of money to keep them loyal. As long as the same corrupt figures remain in charge of manmade systems, he says, they will continue to be destructive.

But I've been thinking: what if it's not just specific people that are to blame? What if human nature is to blame? Amassing of resources leads to the fear of losing them, which leads to the amassing of more resources to prevent losing the original resources. I get that; coming here is what broke me out of that perilous cycle myself. So maybe it isn't certain individuals that need to be eliminated, but our entire flawed species that needs to be put in check. There has to be a counterpoint to our absolute power – doesn't there?

The Master believes we can teach the Orb who to target.

He and I might simply have different ideas of how wide the net needs to be.

Either way, we needed to create something more powerful than us, something we couldn't kill.

It was the only way.

* * *

Last night I saw the Orb give birth.

It was in the hangar. I was concerned for the Orb, because even these few weeks after the move, it's already beginning to outgrow its new environment. The Master says we don't have enough funding to expand the structure, so we're creating space in the other direction, excavating into the ground. Instead of starting right away, as I thought he should, the Master wasted days on additional training and an oath-taking ceremony before allowing the newest recruits to enter the hangar and see her.

The work has been slow, with pickaxes to break through concrete floors, shovels to clear away rocky dirt. I fear we're not moving quickly enough, but the Master doesn't want to upset the Orb with the noise and exhaust of more powerful tools. We've got to dig deep and wide, far enough so she won't roll in by accident, but close enough that we can gently tip her in when her new nest is complete.

I need to stop calling it 'she'. The Master says that's sloppy anthropomorphizing.

Last night I'd come into the hangar to massage the Orb with oil, to soothe its skin during its rapid expansion. Her – its skin is soft and fragrant, as always, but it's begun seeping a milky substance. The Master sees it, of course, but he hasn't told us what, if anything, to do about it. The oils are all I can think of, and at that point it had been three days since I'd been able to apply any.

I don't have the luxury of a special blend; I just have to take what I can sneak out of the kitchen. I've been varying my schedule and keeping the main lights off to avoid attracting attention. Master has changed the Orb's schedule to include times when it must not be disturbed, mimicking our sleep patterns. During these times the lights are kept at a low, golden glow, to provide a comforting environment for rest. I don't think the Master believes that the Orb actually sleeps; this is merely his way of continuing its training in our ways.

I walked around the Orb, running my fingers lightly over its skin to check for lesions. I don't know if the Orb can feel pain, but her skin is so taut, I can only imagine she does – another thing that doesn't seem to concern the Master. Now we are not only discouraged from touching her: it's forbidden. I'm not sure how he imagines this tipping-in will work.

I hadn't even completed a circuit around the Orb when she began to shudder. The milky fluid rose to the surface of her skin, cresting in a cloudy, glistening slick. This time, however, the liquid didn't simply run down the sides and drip to the floor. It coalesced, growing thicker, until I spotted a bulge high up on her side – it must have begun at the very top, too far up for me to see. The bulge spiraled downward along the shuddering Orb, circumnavigating her, gathering up the milky sheen as it traveled. I realized that this bulge was not just covering itself in the viscous liquid, but growing itself out of it. It *was* the milk. When it reached the bottom, it rolled off the Orb onto the floor. It was now a separate, autonomous orb in itself.

The Orb's shuddering slowed, then stopped. The smaller orb, about half my height, leaned against the larger one, suckling a few deposits of milky fluid it had missed, absorbing them into itself. Then it rolled toward me.

I quickly stepped to the side and the new orb headed toward the door. For a moment I panicked, but the door was locked, and the orb couldn't reach the release bar. Somehow, I was convinced that its lack of height was all that stopped it from pressing the bar and freeing itself.

I followed the little orb as it explored the hangar, rolling across the floor until stopped by a wall, then following along that wall until the next barrier – shelving, a desk, a pile of boxes. I followed it the way one might follow a baby or a puppy, lingering at a solicitous distance as it investigated its world.

The small orb completed a circuit of the hangar before returning to its mother. I realize calling her – it – 'mother' is more 'sloppy anthropomorphizing', but then the Master wanted to create something close to human.

And it was very human in this: the smaller orb approached its mother once more, absorbed the last few drops of milk, then rolled itself down into the excavated hole in the floor. I ran to the edge and looked down just as the last of its body slipped into the earth.

I don't know how long I stared into the hole. Eventually I sensed a wetness between my legs and went back to the privacy of my cabin. There I found my underwear damp with a milky discharge that smelled of vinegar and rosemary.

I should tell someone. In all of his planning, the Master has never spoken of anything like this. I can't tell him, though: he'd tighten access, lock me out of the palm scanner, keep me farthest away of all because I broke the rules. I wasn't even supposed to be there.

No, I can't tell him. But it's not because I'm concerned for myself.

I'm not the one who needs protection now.

It's *her*.

* * *

I haven't been able to concentrate for days now, ever since I saw the birth. I need to tell someone – but who? They all feel like part of the Master now.

He chooses a new young man or woman every couple of weeks, lingering near them as they work, calling it mentorship. It's clear which ones are interested, how they straighten their backs and lean their heads a certain way. Smile with a certain warmth. Later, he'll bump into one of them on his stroll, invite them to the farmhouse for dinner. More than a few of the young workers have developed a fondness for solitary walks.

I'm too old to be of interest to him. He wants the young, the beautiful, the bountiful, bound to him. The Master has fierce appetites and a golden tongue, and they are all mesmerized. From the very beginning, they were invested in our project, content to be part of a larger whole – he's merely adjusted the details of the arrangement.

I'm not bitter that he's never come to me. That Hamish never noticed me. I'm past caring. This just means I have more time for my work, for the Orb.

For now, I'll scratch my misgivings into the dirt with a fingernail, whisper them into the grass for safekeeping. I'll continue to rub the Mother with oil and reassure her that – unlike Julian, who is still missing – her child will return.

* * *

I awake from a deep sleep, my underwear damp with milky discharge.

I change and rush to the hangar, expecting a birth. That's when I find the skull.

As though the Orb has been expecting me, the skull lies next to her where I would see it as soon as I entered. I cannot breathe.

One by one, the Orb lays the rest of the bones out for me, spiraling them down the milky ooze of her bulk as she did with her baby orb several days prior; first an arm bone, then a leg bone, a series of ribs, a cascade of tiny wrist and ankle bones. And last, a golden ring, an Irish design of two hands holding a crowned heart. I'd always been fond of the pattern, and had said so to Julian the first time I met him, when I shook his hand and noticed this very same ring.

I don't know what to do, and there's no time – a digging crew is due any minute. As the Orb grows, the Master has grown impatient, and the excavation work now starts before dawn.

I gather the bones in a wheelbarrow and push them out past the fence to a far corner of the estate. Part of me wants the wheel to squeak, wants to be discovered, wants the Master to be exposed, to pay for what he's done.

But then what would then happen to the Orb? We designed her to be a competitor. A murderer. Despite this, no one seems to see her as a danger.

Yet.

The bones knock together with a sticky, dull *thunking* as I dump them onto the ground. As I wash out the wheelbarrow, I tell myself this is for the safety of the Orb, and the benefit of our project. With luck, some animal will carry the remains away to suck the marrow.

With luck, they'll never be seen again.

* * *

This morning we settled the Orb into the hole – her nest, as the Master calls it. The pit is large enough for the moment, but we're all aware it won't last. The Master is nevertheless relieved at the time we've gained, time for him to find the next solution. I know he doesn't want to write to his patroness for more funding – he doesn't want any outside contact at all anymore – but I'm not sure what other options he has. I know we haven't dug enough. Soon enough the Orb will press against the sides of the pit. I wonder if it will hurt her.

Still, for the moment the Master exudes relaxation. He has solved more than one problem – one of the new trainees has been sent away. There's been no announcement, but we hear the Master's judgment in whispers, in second-hand snippets: she wasn't careful enough, and that kind of carelessness wouldn't do around the Orb.

She – the trainee – was beginning to show.

Some of us wonder in whispers who the father is, what will happen to him. But this is all theater, meant to signal innocence.

We all know nothing will happen to the father.

* * *

Another night of discharge. Another dash to the hangar.

Another baby orb is coming.

The process goes more smoothly this time; the Orb a practiced mother. This baby orb is more confident in its perambulations, traveling the room in fluid arcs. This time there is no hole for the baby to sink into – it has been taken over by the bulk of the Orb. I open the door and let the offspring out into the night.

The afterbirth comes more quickly now as well. Another skull, more bones. Another skeleton's birth.

No ring this time.

The trainee who was sent away wore no rings.

But the absence of proof is not proof.

This time I want to leave the bones. I want someone else to find them – but aside from Julian, whose palm no longer exists, the only ones with access are the Master and me.

I think about hauling the bones outside and leaving them there. I want for there to be repercussions, but on the other hand I can't bear the thought that there might not *be* any, that this might be accepted as just punishment for the carelessness the Master accused her of. That he might – would surely – be excused, even vindicated by her death.

But once again, I must consider what might happen to the Orb. I cannot betray her. We created her.

And she's a mother, after all.

As I load the bones into the wheelbarrow, I must also admit that I enjoy the power a secret creates. *I know* are two of the most powerful words on earth.

I roll the bones to the same far corner of the estate. The others have long since disappeared. I tip the new remains out onto the same spot.

Throwing away the proof of one secret is a small price to keep another.

* * *

He thinks we'll never tell. Somehow he thinks we won't even remember any of this because he has taken away all our computers, all paper and pens, all sticks. But I will remember it. It will not be forgotten, because I'm whispering it to the trees and thrumming it at bees as they buzz by. I'm writing it into the air with my fingers. At night I bend down and mumble it into the earth.

Why was he so certain the Orb would know the difference between our enemies and us?

We tried. That was the idea behind touching the Orb, letting it feel our intention. Surely, he thought, it would remember those who wanted it to thrive, and surely it would recognize that we were different from those in power who threatened it, destroyed its environment. We wanted to create a way to fight back.

Was it the Master's sudden directive against touch that was flawed, or was it the original plan? Were we doomed from the start?

All of this is to say that the Orb has disappeared. Not by some magic poof into thin air – there are signs, streaks of gelatinous matter between the seams of the walls, the cracks in the floor, the slats of the roof, as though it exploded outward in all directions, all at once.

The Master is angry at everyone, least of all himself, which is as we've all come to expect, but of course cannot say. Everyone thinks the Orb has failed, that we've lost it, that we'll have to start again. But I don't believe this is true.

Every few nights since the Orb has disappeared, a worker has gone missing. The Master accuses them of cowardice, of running away to escape his wrath. I might agree, except each time it happens, I wake with the sympathetic discharge of another birth. I've taken to lining my underwear with rags, and the spot where I twice took my wheelbarrow is now gathering bones without me. My little pile has become an altar. The Orb is preparing the earth, just as we planned.

We just don't know what for.

* * *

Michael and Sarah are packing their belongings. It's down to four of us now: the two of them, the Master, and me. Up until the moment of their departure, they ask me to come with them, but I merely wish them well as they walk the path to the main road. The chickens cluck and scratch for food in their dusty wake.

The bone altar grows.

* * *

Eggs are a fine and fitting meal, if not a bit monotonous. I've kept up a little vegetable plot of my own, and there are nuts and berries to forage. But it's all right, because there's only myself to feed – I haven't seen the Master in weeks now – and I find I'm not that hungry anyway.

Now I'm the one who goes for solitary walks, not hoping to meet the Master I initially served, but seeking the new one. Seeking *her*.

I walk and I search for her in a fragment of bone, in a viscous slick on a blade of grass, in a whiff of sweetness on a breeze. I want to place my hand on her skin and know if she still recognizes me. I want to know how many children she's delivered, if she will bear my presence in peace, or if she will consume me.

I search for her, but I also want to believe she's not searching for me, that she's looking instead for the destroyers of the earth, her enemies, her destiny.

I want to believe she would sense the cloudy wetness we still share.

But if not, if she did consider me her enemy – would I dissolve away into nothing, extruded into a pile of bones in the wilderness, never to be found or mourned by another soul? Or would I become one of them: an orb, one of *her*? One *with* her?

And still I search for her, and still am left to wonder: Will she someday circle back to find me? Will I ever know what it is to dissolve all the evils of mankind and slip away, down into the dirt, an avenging angel of the earth?

Blake, or The Huts of America

Martin R. Delany

Chapter I
The Project

ON ONE OF THOSE exciting occasions during a contest for the presidency of the United States, a number of gentlemen met in the city of Baltimore. They were few in number, and appeared little concerned about the affairs of the general government. Though men of intelligence, their time and attention appeared to be entirely absorbed in an adventure of self-interest. They met for the purpose of completing arrangements for refitting the old ship "Merchantman," which then lay in the harbor near Fell's Point. Colonel Stephen Franks, Major James Armsted, Captain Richard Paul, and Captain George Royer composed those who represented the American side – Captain Juan Garcia and Captain Jose Castello, those of Cuban interest.

Here a conversation ensued upon what seemed a point of vital importance to the company; it related to the place best suited for the completion of their arrangements. The Americans insisted on Baltimore as affording the greatest facilities, and having done more for the encouragement and protection of the trade than any other known place, whilst the Cubans, on the other side, urged their objections on the ground that the continual increase of liberal principles in the various political parties, which were fast ushering into existence, made the objection beyond a controversy. Havana was contended for as a point best suited for adjusting their arrangements, and that too with many apparent reasons; but for some cause, the preference for Baltimore prevailed.

Subsequently to the adjustment of their affairs by the most complete arrangement for refitting the vessel, Colonel Franks took leave of the party for his home in the distant state of Mississippi.

Chapter II
Colonel Franks at Home

ON THE RETURN of Colonel Stephen Franks to his home at Natchez, he met there Mrs. Arabella, the wife of Judge Ballard, an eminent jurist of one of the Northern States. She had arrived but a day before him, on a visit to some relatives, of whom Mrs. Franks was one. The conversation, as is customary on the meeting of Americans residing in such distant latitudes, readily turned on the general policy of the country.

Mrs. Ballard possessed the highest intelligence, and Mrs. Maria Franks was among the most accomplished of Southern ladies.

"Tell me, Madam Ballard, how will the North go in the present issue?" enquired Franks.

"Give yourself no concern about that, Colonel," replied Mrs. Ballard, "you will find the North true to the country."

"What you consider true, may be false – that is, it might be true to you, and false to us," continued he.

"You do not understand me, Colonel," she rejoined, "we can have no interests separate from yours; you know the time-honored motto, 'united we stand,' and so forth, must apply to the American people under every policy in every section of the Union."

"So it should, but amidst the general clamor in the contest for ascendancy, may you not lose sight of this important point?"

"How can we? You, I'm sure, Colonel, know very well that in our country commercial interests have taken precedence of all others, which is a sufficient guarantee of our fidelity to the South."

"That may be, madam, but we are still apprehensive."

"Well, sir, we certainly do not know what more to do to give you assurance of our sincerity. We have as a plight of faith yielded Boston, New York, and Philadelphia – the intelligence and wealth of the North – in carrying out the Compromise measures for the interests of the South; can we do more?"

"True, Madam Ballard, true! I yield the controversy. You have already done more than we of the South expected. I now remember that the Judge himself tried the first case under the Act, in your city, by which the measures were tested."

"He did, sir, and if you will not consider me unwomanly by telling you, desired me, on coming here, to seek every opportunity to give the fullest assurance that the judiciary are sound on that question. Indeed, so far as an individual might be concerned, his interests in another direction – as you know – place him beyond suspicion," concluded Mrs. Ballard.

"I am satisfied, madam, and by your permission, arrest the conversation. My acknowledgements, madam!" bowed the Colonel, with true Southern courtesy.

"Maria, my dear, you look careworn; are you indisposed?" inquired Franks of his wife, who during conversation sat silent.

"Not physically, Colonel," replied she, "but—"

Just at this moment a servant, throwing open the door, announced dinner.

Besides a sprightly black boy of some ten years of age, there was in attendance a prepossessing, handsome maidservant, who generally kept, as much as the occasion would permit, behind the chair of her mistress. A mutual attachment appeared to exist between them, the maid apparently disinclined to leave the mistress, who seemed to keep her as near her person as possible.

Now and again the fat cook, Mammy Judy, would appear at the door of the dining room bearing a fresh supply for the table, who with a slight nod of the head, accompanied with an affectionate smile and the word "Maggie," indicated a tie much closer than that of mere fellow servants.

Maggie had long been the favorite maidservant of her mistress, having attained the position through merit. She was also nurse and foster mother to the two last children of Mrs. Franks, and loved them, to all appearance, as her own. The children reciprocated this affection, calling her "Mammy."

Mammy Judy, who for years had occupied this position, ceded it to her daughter; she preferring, in consequence of age, the less active life of the culinary department.

The boy Tony would frequently cast a comic look upon Mrs. Ballard, then imploringly gaze in the face of his mistress. So intent was he in this, that twice did his master admonish him by a nod of the head.

"My dear," said the Colonel, "you are dull today; pray tell me what makes you sad?"

"I am not bodily afflicted, Colonel Franks, but my spirit is heavy," she replied.

"How so? What is the matter?"

"That will be best answered at another time and place, Colonel."

Giving his head an unconscious scratch accompanied with a slight twitch of the corner of the mouth, Franks seemed to comprehend the whole of it.

On one of her Northern tours to the watering places – during a summer season some two years previous, having with her Maggie the favorite – Mrs. Franks visited the family of the Judge, at which time Mrs. Ballard first saw the maid. She was a dark mulatto of a rich, yellow, autumnlike complexion, with a matchless, cushionlike head of hair, neither straight nor curly, but handsomer than either.

Mrs. Franks was herself a handsome lady of some thirty-five summers, but ten years less in appearance, a little above medium height, between the majestic and graceful, raven-black hair, and dark, expressive eyes. Yet it often had been whispered that in beauty the maid equalled if not excelled the mistress. Her age was twenty-eight.

The conduct of Mrs. Franks toward her servant was more like that of an elder sister than a mistress, and the mistress and maid sometimes wore dresses cut from the same web of cloth. Mrs. Franks would frequently adjust the dress and see that the hair of her maid was properly arranged. This to Mrs. Ballard was as unusual as it was an objectionable sight, especially as she imagined there was an air of hauteur in her demeanor. It was then she determined to subdue her spirit.

Acting from this impulse, several times in her absence, Mrs. Ballard took occasion to administer to the maid severities she had never experienced at the hands of her mistress, giving her at one time a severe slap on the cheek, calling her an "impudent jade."

At this, Mrs. Franks, on learning, was quite surprised; but on finding that the maid gave no just cause for it, took no further notice of it, designedly evading the matter. But before leaving, Mrs. Ballard gave her no rest until she gave her the most positive assurance that she would part with the maid on her next visit to Natchez. And thus she is found pressing her suit at the residence of the Mississippi planter.

Chapter III
The Fate of Maggie

AFTER DINNER Colonel Franks again pressed the inquiry concerning the disposition of his lady. At this time the maid was in the culinary department taking her dinner. The children having been served, she preferred the company of her old mother whom she loved, the children hanging around, and upon her lap. There was no servant save the boy Tony present in the parlor.

"I can't, I won't let her go! she's a dear good girl!" replied Mrs. Franks. "The children are attached to her, and so am I; let Minny or any other of them go – but do not, for Heaven's sake, tear Maggie from me!"

"Maria, my dear, you've certainly lost your balance of mind! Do try and compose yourself," admonished the Colonel. "There's certainly no disposition to do contrary to your desires; try and be a little reasonable."

"I'm sure, cousin, I see no cause for your importunity. No one that I know of designs to hurt the Negro girl. I'm sure it's not me!" impatiently remarked Mrs. Ballard.

During this, the boy had several times gone into the hall, looking toward the kitchen, then meaningly into the parlor as if something unusual were going on.

Mammy Judy becoming suspicious, went into the hall and stood close beside the parlor door, listening at the conversation.

"Cousin, if you will listen for a moment, I wish to say a word to you," said Mrs. Ballard. "The Judge, as you know, has a countryseat in Cuba near the city of Havana, where we design making every year our winter retreat. As we cannot take with us either free Negroes or white servants, on account of the existing restrictions, I must have a slave, and of course I prefer a well-trained one, as I know all yours to be. The price will be no object; as I know it will be none to you, it shall be none to me."

"I will not consent to part with her, cousin Arabella, and it is useless to press the matter any further!" emphatically replied Mrs. Franks.

"I am sure, cousin Maria, it was well understood between the Colonel and the Judge, that I was to have one of your best-trained maidservants!" continued Mrs. Ballard.

"The Colonel and the Judge! If any such understanding exist, it is without my knowledge and consent, and —"

"It is true, my dear," interposed the Colonel, "but —"

"Then," replied she, "heaven grant that I may go too! from—"

"Pah, pah! cousin Maria Franks, I'm really astonished at you to take on so about a Negro girl! You really appear to have lost your reason. I would not behave so for all the Negroes in Mississippi."

"My dear," said Franks, "I have been watching the conduct of that girl for some time past; she is becoming both disobedient and unruly, and as I have made it a rule of my life never to keep a disobedient servant, the sooner we part with her the better. As I never whip my servants, I do not want to depart from my rule in her case."

Maggie was true to her womanhood, and loyal to her mistress, having more than once communicated to her ears facts the sounds of which reflected no credit in his. For several repulses such as this, it was that she became obnoxious to her master.

"Cousin Maria, you certainly have forgotten; I'm sure, when last at the North, you promised in presence of the girl, that I was to have her, and I'm certain she's expecting it," explained Mrs. Ballard.

"This I admit," replied Mrs. Franks, "but you very well know, cousin Arabella, that that promise was a mere ruse, to reconcile an uneasiness which you informed me you discovered in her, after over-hearing a conversation between her and some free Negroes, at Saratoga Springs."

"Well, cousin, you can do as you please," concluded Mrs. Ballard.

"Colonel, I'm weary of this conversation. What am I to expect?" enquired Mrs. Franks.

"It's a settled point, my dear, she must be sold!" decisively replied Franks.

"Then I must hereafter be disrespected by our own slaves! You know, Colonel, that I gave my word to Henry, her husband, your most worthy servant, that his wife should be here on his return. He had some misgiving that she was to be taken to Cuba before his return, when I assured him that she should be here. How can I bear to meet this poor creature, who places every confidence in what we tell him? He'll surely be frantic."

"Nonsense, cousin, nonsense," sneered Mrs. Ballard. "Frantic, indeed! Why you speak of your Negro slaves as if speaking of equals. Make him know that whatever you order, he must be contented with."

"I'll soon settle the matter with him, should he dare show any feelings about it!" interposed Franks. "When do you look for him, Maria?"

"I'm sure, Colonel, you know more about the matter than I do. Immediately after you left, he took the horses to Baton Rouge, where at the last accounts he was waiting the conclusion of the races. Judge Dilbreath had entered them according to your request – one horse for each day's races. I look for him every day. Then there are more than him to reconcile. There's old Mammy Judy, who will run mad about her. You know, Colonel, she thought so much of her, that she might be treated tenderly the old creature gave up her situation in the house as nurse and foster mother to our children, going into the kitchen to do the harder work."

"Well, my dear, we'll detain your cousin till he comes. I'll telegraph the Judge that, if not yet left, to start him home immediately."

"Colonel, that will be still worse, to let him witness her departure; I would much rather she'd leave before his return. Poor thing!" she sighed.

"Then she may go!" replied he.

"And what of poor old mammy and his boy?"

"I'll soon settle the matter with old Judy."

Mrs. Franks looking him imploringly in the face, let drop her head, burying her face in the palms of her hands. Soon it was found necessary to place her under the care of a physician.

Old Mammy Judy had long since beckoned her daughter, where both stood in breathless silence catching every word that passed.

At the conclusion, Maggie, clasping her hands, exclaimed in suppressed tones,."O mammy, O mammy! what shall I do? O, is there no hope for me? Can't you beg master – can't you save me!"

"Look to de Laud, my chile! Him ony able to bring yeh out mo' nah conkeh!" was the prayerful advice of the woe-stricken old mother. Both, hastening into the kitchen, falling upon their knees, invoked aloud the God of the oppressed.

Hearing in that direction an unusual noise, Franks hastened past the kitchen door, dropping his head, and clearing his throat as he went along. This brought the slaves to an ordinary mood, who trembled at his approach.

Chapter IV
Departure of Maggie

THE COUNTRYSEAT of Franks, or the "great house" of the cotton plantation, was but a short distance from the city. Mrs. Franks, by the advice of her physician, was removed there to avoid the disturbance of the town, when at the same time Mrs. Ballard left with her slave Maggie en route for Baltimore, whither she designed leaving her until ready to sail for Cuba.

"Fahwell, my chile! fahwell; may God A'mighty be wid you!" were the parting words of the poor old slave, who with streaming eyes gazed upon her parting child for the last time.

"O mammy! Can't you save me? O Lord, what shall I do? O my husband! O my poor child! O my! O my!" were the only words, the sounds of which died upon the breeze, as the cab hastily bore her to a steamer then lying at the wharf.

Poor old Mammy Judy sat at the kitchen door with elbows resting upon her knee, side of the face resting in the palm of the hand, tears streaming down, with a rocking motion, noticing nothing about her, but in sorrow moaning just distinctly enough to be understood: "Po' me! Po' me! Po' me!"

The sight was enough to move the heart of anyone, and it so affected Franks that he wished he had "never owned a Negro."

Daddy Joe, the husband of Mammy Judy, was a field hand on the cotton place, visiting his wife at the town residence every Saturday night. Colonel Franks was a fine, grave, senatorial-looking man, of medium height, inclined to corpulency, black hair, slightly grey, and regarded by his slaves as a good master, and religiously as one of the best of men.

On their arrival at the great house, those working nearest gathered around the carriage, among whom was Daddy Joe.

"Wat a mautta wid missus?" was the general inquiry of the gang.

"Your mistress is sick, boys," replied the master.

"Maus, whah's Margot?" enquired the old man, on seeing his mistress carried into the house without the attendance of her favorite maidservant.

"She's in town, Joe," replied Franks.

"How's Judy, seh?"

"Judy is well."

"Tank'e seh!" politely concluded the old man, with a bow, turning away in the direction of his work – with a countenance expressive of anything but satisfaction – from the interview.

The slaves, from their condition, are suspicious; any evasion or seeming design at suppressing the information sought by them frequently arouses their greatest apprehension.

Not unfrequently the mere countenance, a look, a word, or laugh of the master, is an unerring foreboding of misfortune to the slave. Ever on the watch for these things, they learn to read them with astonishing precision.

This day was Friday, and the old slave consoled himself with the thought that on the next evening he would be able to see and know for himself the true state of things about his master's residence in town. The few hours intervening were spent with great anxiety, which was even observed by his fellow slaves.

At last came Saturday evening and with it, immediately after sunset, Daddy Joe made his appearance at the hall door of the great house, tarrying only long enough to inquire "How's missus?" and receive the reply, "she's better," when a few moments found him quite out of sight, striding his way down the lane toward the road to the city.

The sudden and unexpected fate of Maggie had been noised among the slaves throughout the entire neighborhood; many who had the opportunity of doing so, repairing to the house to learn the facts.

In the lower part of the town, bordering on the river there is a depot or receptacle for the slave gangs brought by professional traders. This part of the town is known as "Natchez-under-the-Hill." It is customary among the slaves when any of their number are sold, to say that they are gone "under the hill," and their common salutation through the day was that "Franks' Mag had gone under the hill."

As with quickened steps Daddy Joe approached the town, his most fearful apprehensions became terribly realized when meeting a slave who informed him that "Margot had gone under the hill." Falling upon his knees, in the fence corner, the old man raised his voice in supplication of Divine aid: "O Laud! dow has promis' in dine own wud, to be a fadah to de fadaless, an' husban to de widah! O Laud, let dy wud run an' be glorify! Sof'en de haud haut ob de presseh, an' let my po' chile cum back! an'—"

"Stop that noise there, old nigger!" ordered a patrol approaching him. "Who's boy are you?"

"Sahvant, mausta!" saluted the old slave, "I b'long to cunel Frank, seh!"

"Is this old Joe?"

"Dis is me maus Johnny."

"You had better trudge along home then, as it's likely old Judy wants to see you about this time."

"Tank'e seh," replied the old man, with a bow, feeling grateful that he was permitted to proceed.

"Devilish good, religious old Negro," he remarked to his associates, as the old man left them in the road.

A few minutes more, and Daddy Joe entered the kitchen door at his master's residence. Mammy Judy, on seeing him, gave vent afresh to bitter wailing, when the emotion became painfully mutual.

"O husban'! Husban! Onah po' chile is gone!" exclaimed the old woman, clasping him around the neck.

"Laud! dy will be done!" exclaimed he. "Ole umin, look to de Laud! as he am suffishen fah all tings"; both, falling on their knees, breathed in silence their desires to God.

"How long! How long! O Laud how long!" was the supplicating cry of the old woman being overcome with devotion and sorrow.

Taking the little grandchild in his arms, "Po' chile," said the old man, "I wish yeh had nebeh been baun!" impressing upon it kisses whilst it slept.

After a fervant and earnest prayer to God for protection to themselves, little grandson Joe, the return of his mother their only child, and blessings upon their master and the recovery of their mistress, the poor old slaves retired to rest for the evening, to forget their sorrows in the respite of sleep.

Chapter V
A Vacancy

THIS MORNING the sun rose with that beauty known to a Southern sky in the last month of autumn. The day was Sabbath, and with it was ushered in every reminiscence common to the customs of that day and locality.

That she might spend the day at church for the diversion of her mind, Mrs. Franks was brought in to her city residence; and Natchez, which is usually gay, seemed more so on this day than on former occasions.

When the bells began to signal the hour of worship, the fashionable people seemed en masse to crowd the streets. The carriages ran in every direction, bearing happy hearts and cheerful faces to the various places of worship – there to lay their offerings on the altar of the Most High for the blessings they enjoyed, whilst peering over every gate, out of every alley, or every kitchen door, could be seen the faithful black servants who, staying at home to prepare them food and attend to other domestic duties, were satisfied to look smilingly upon their masters and families as they rode along, without for a moment dreaming that they had a right to worship the same God, with the same promise of life and salvation.

"God bless you, missus! Pray fah me," was the honest request of many a simplehearted slave who dared not aspire to the enjoyment of praying for himself in the Temple of the living God.

But amidst these scenes of gaiety and pleasure, there was one much devoted to her church who could not be happy that day, as there to her was a seeming vacancy which could not be filled – the seat of her favorite maidservant. The Colonel, as a husband and father, was affectionate and indulgent; but his slave had offended, disobeyed his commands, and consequently, had to be properly punished, or he be disrespected by his own servants. The will of the master being absolute, his commands should be enforced, let them be what they may, and the consequences what they would. If slavery be right, the master is justifiable in enforcing obedience to his will; deny him this, and you at once deprive him of the right to hold a slave – the one is a necessary sequence of the other. Upon this principle Colonel Franks acted, and the premise justified the conclusion.

When the carriage drove to the door, Mrs. Franks wept out most bitterly, refusing to enter because her favorite maid could not be an incumbent. Fears being entertained of seriousness in her case, it was thought advisable to let her remain quietly at home.

Daddy Joe and Mammy Judy were anxious spectators of all that transpired at the door of the mansion, and that night, on retiring to their humble bed, earnestly petitioned at the altar of Grace that the Lord would continue upon her his afflictions until their master, convinced of his wrongs, would order the return of their child.

This the Colonel would have most willingly done without the petition of Joe or Judy, but the case had gone too far, the offense was too great, and consequently there could be no reconsideration.

"Poor things," muttered Mrs. Franks in a delirium, "she served him right! And this her only offense! Yes, she was true to me!"

Little Joe, the son of Maggie, in consequence of her position to the white children – from whom her separation had been concealed – had been constantly with his grandmother, and called her "mammy." Accustomed to being without her, he was well satisfied so long as permitted to be with the old woman Judy.

So soon as her condition would permit, Mrs. Franks was returned to her countryseat to avoid the contingencies of the city.

Chapter VI
Henry's Return

EARLY ON MONDAY MORNING, a steamer was heard puffing up the Mississippi. Many who reside near the river, by custom can tell the name of every approaching boat by the peculiar sound of the steampipe, the one in the present instance being the "Sultana."

Daddy Joe had risen and just leaving for the plantation, but stopped a moment to be certian.

"Hush!" admonished Mammy Judy. "Hush! Sho chile, do'n yeh heah how she hollah? Sholy dat's de wat's name! wat dat yeh call eh? 'Suckana,' wat not; sho! I ain' gwine bautha my head long so – sho! See, ole man see! Dah she come! See dat now! I tole yeh so, but yeh uden bleve me!" And the old man and woman stood for some minutes in breathless silence, although the boat must have been some five miles distant, as the escape of steam can be heard on the western waters a great way off.

The approach toward sunrise admonished Daddy Joe of demands for him at the cotton farm, when after bidding "good monin' ole umin," he hurried to the daily task which lay before him.

Mammy Judy had learned – by the boy Tony – that Henry was expected on the "Sultana," and at the approach of every steamer, her head had been thrust out of the door or window to catch a distinct sound. In motionless attitude after the departure of her husband this morning, the old woman stood awaiting the steamer, when presently the boat arrived. But then to be certain that it was the expected vessel – now came the suspense.

The old woman was soon relieved from this most disagreeable of all emotions, by the cry of newsboys returning from the wharf: "'Ere's the 'Picayune,' 'Atlas,' 'Delta'! Lates' news from New Orleans by the swift steamer 'Sultana'!"

"Dah now!" exclaimed Mammy Judy in soliloquy. "Dah now! I tole yeh so! – de wat's name come!" Hurrying into the kitchen, she waited with anxiety the arrival of Henry.

Busying about the breakfast for herself and other servants about the house – the white members of the family all being absent – Mammy Judy for a time lost sight of the expected arrival. Soon however, a hasty footstep arrested her attention, when on looking around it proved to be Henry who came smiling up the yard.

"How'd you do, mammy! How's Mag' and the boy?" inquired he, grasping the old woman by the hand.

She burst into a flood of tears, throwing herself upon him.

"What is the matter!" exclaimed Henry. "Is Maggie dead?"

"No chile," with increased sobs she replied, "much betteh she wah."

"My God! Has she disgraced herself?"

"No chile, may be betteh she dun so, den she bin heah now an' not sole. Maus Stephen sell eh case she! – I dun'o, reckon dat's da reason."

"What! – Do you tell me, mammy, she had better disgraced herself than been sold! By the—!"

"So, Henry! yeh ain't gwine swah! hope yeh ain' gwine lose yeh 'ligion? Do'n do so; put yeh trus' in de Laud, he is suffishen fah all!"

"Don't tell me about religion! What's religion to me? My wife is sold away from me by a man who is one of the leading members of the very church to which both she and I belong! Put my trust in the Lord! I have done so all my life nearly, and of what use is it to me? My wife is sold from me just the same as if I didn't. I'll—"

"Come, come, Henry, yeh mus'n talk so; we is po' weak an' bline cretehs, an' cah see de way uh da Laud. He move' in a mystus way, his wundahs to puhfaum."

"So he may, and what is all that to me? I don't gain anything by it, and—"

"Stop, Henry, stop! Ain' de Laud bless yo' soul? Ain' he take yeh foot out de miah an' clay, an' gib yeh hope da uddah side dis vale ub teahs?"

"I'm tired looking the other side; I want a hope this side of the vale of tears. I want something on this earth as well as a promise of things in another world. I and my wife have been both robbed of our liberty, and you want me to be satisfied with a hope of heaven. I won't do any such thing; I have waited long enough on heavenly promises; I'll wait no longer. I—"

"Henry, wat de mauttah wid yeh? I neveh heah yeh talk so fo' – yeh sin in de sight ub God; yeh gone clean back, I reckon. De good Book tell us, a tousan' yeahs wid man, am but a day wid de Laud. Boy, yeh got wait de Laud own pinted time."

"Well, mammy, it is useless for me to stand here and have the same gospel preached into my ears by you, that I have all my life time heard from my enslavers. My mind is made up, my course is laid out, and if life last, I'll carry it out. I'll go out to the place today, and let them know that I have returned."

"Sho boy! What yeh gwine do, bun house down? Bettah put yeh trus' in de Laud!" concluded the old woman.

"You have too much religion, mammy, for me to tell you what I intend doing," said Henry in conclusion.

After taking up his little son, impressing on his lips and cheeks kisses for himself and tears for his mother, the intelligent slave left the abode of the careworn old woman, for that of his master at the cotton place.

Henry was a black – a pure Negro – handsome, manly and intelligent, in size comparing well with his master, but neither so fleshy nor heavy built in person. A man of good literary attainments – unknown to Colonel Franks, though he was aware he could read and write – having been educated in the West Indies, and decoyed away when young. His affection for wife and child was not excelled by Colonel Franks's for his. He was bold, determined and courageous, but always mild, gentle and courteous, though impulsive when an occasion demanded his opposition.

Going immediately to the place, he presented himself before his master. Much conversation ensued concerning the business which had been entrusted to his charge, all of which was satisfactorily transacted, and full explanations concerning the horses, but not a word was uttered concerning the fate of Maggie, the Colonel barely remarking "your mistress is unwell."

After conversing till a late hour, Henry was assigned a bed in the great house, but sleep was far from his eyes. He turned and changed upon his bed with restlessness and anxiety, impatiently awaiting a return of the morning.

Chapter VII
Master and Slave

EARLY ON TUESDAY morning, in obedience to his master's orders, Henry was on his way to the city to get the house in readiness for the reception of his mistress, Mrs. Franks having improved in three or four days. Mammy Judy had not yet risen when he knocked at the door.

"Hi Henry! yeh heah ready! huccum yeh git up so soon; arter some mischif I reckon? Do'n reckon yeh arter any good!" saluted Mammy Judy.

"No, mammy," replied he, "no mischief, but like a good slave such as you wish me to be, come to obey my master's will, just what you like to see."

"Sho boy! none yeh nonsens'; huccum I want yeh bey maus Stephen? Git dat nonsens' in yeh head las' night long so, I reckon! Wat dat yeh gwine do now?"

"I have come to dust and air the mansion for their reception. They have sold my wife away from me, and who else would do her work?" This reply excited the apprehension of Mammy Judy.

"Wat yeh gwine do, Henry? Yeh arter no good; yeh ain' gwine 'tack maus Stephen, is yeh?"

"What do you mean, mammy, strike him?"

"Yes! Reckon yeh ain' gwine hit 'im?"

"Curse—!"

"Henry, Henry, membeh wat ye 'fess! Fah de Laud sake, yeh ain' gwine take to swahin?" interupted the old woman.

"I make no profession, mammy. I once did believe in religion, but now I have no confidence in it. My faith has been wrecked on the stony hearts of such pretended Christians as Stephen Franks, while passing through the stormy sea of trouble and oppression! And—"

"Hay, boy! yeh is gittin high! Yeh call maussa 'Stephen'?"

"Yes, and I'll never call him 'master' again, except when compelled to do so."

"Bettah g'long ten' t' de house fo' wite folks come, an' nebeh mine talkin' 'bout fightin' 'long wid maus Stephen. Wat yeh gwine do wid white folks? Sho!"

"I don't intend to fight him, Mammy Judy, but I'll attack him concerning my wife, if the words be my last! Yes, I'll—!" and, pressing his lips to suppress the words, the outraged man turned away from the old slave mother with such feelings as only an intelligent slave could realize.

The orders of the morning were barely executed when the carriage came to the door. The bright eyes of the footboy Tony sparkled when he saw Henry approaching the carriage.

"Well, Henry! Ready for us?" enquired his master.

"Yes, sir," was the simple reply. "Mistress!" he saluted, politely bowing as he took her hand to assist her from the carriage.

"Come, Henry my man, get out the riding horses," ordered Franks after a little rest.

"Yes, sir."

A horse for the Colonel and lady each was soon in readiness at the door, but none for himself, it always having been the custom in their morning rides, for the maid and manservant to accompany the mistress and master.

"Ready, did you say?" enquired Franks on seeing but two horses standing at the stile.

"Yes, sir."

"Where's the other horse?"

"What for, sir?"

"What for? Yourself, to be sure!"

"Colonel Franks!" said Henry, looking him sternly in the face. "When I last rode that horse in company with you and lady, my wife was at my side, and I will not now go without her! Pardon me – my life for it, I won't go!"

"Not another word, you black imp!" exclaimed Franks, with an uplifted staff in a rage, "or I'll strike you down in an instant!"

"Strike away if you will, sir, I don't care – I won't go without my wife!"

"You impudent scoundrel! I'll soon put an end to your conduct! I'll put you on the auction block, and sell you to the Negro-traders."

"Just as soon as you please sir, the sooner the better, as I don't want to live with you any longer!"

"Hold your tongue, sir, or I'll cut it out of your head! You ungrateful black dog! Really, things have come to a pretty pass when I must take impudence off my own Negro! By gracious! – God forgive me for the expression – I'll sell every Negro I have first! I'll dispose of him to the hardest Negro-trader I can find!" said Franks in a rage.

"You may do your mightiest, Colonel Franks. I'm not your slave, nor never was and you know it! And but for my wife and her people, I never would have stayed with you till now. I was decoyed away when young, and then became entangled in such domestic relations as to induce me to remain with you; but now the tie is broken! I know that the odds are against me, but never mind!"

"Do you threaten me, sir! Hold your tongue, or I'll take your life instantly, you villain!"

"No, sir, I don' threaten you, Colonel Franks, but I do say that I won't be treated like a dog. You sold my wife away from me, after always promising that she should be free. And more than that, you sold her because—! And now you talk about whipping me. Shoot me, sell me, or do anything else you please, but don't lay your hands on me, as I will not suffer you to whip me!"

Running up to his chamber, Colonel Franks seized a revolver, when Mrs. Franks, grasping hold of his arm, exclaimed, "Colonel! what does all this mean?"

"Mean, my dear? It's rebellion! A plot – this is but the shadow of a could that's fast gathering around us! I see it plainly, I see it!" responded the Colonel, starting for the stairs.

"Stop, Colonel!" admonished his lady. "I hope you'll not be rash. For Heaven's sake, do not stain your hands in blood!"

"I do not mean to, my dear! I take this for protection!" Franks hastening down stairs, when Henry had gone into the back part of the premises.

"Dah now! Dah now!" exclaimed Mammy Judy as Henry entered the kitchen. "See wat dis gwine back done foh yeh! Bettah put yo' trus' in de Laud! Henry, yeh gone clean back t' de wuhl ghin, yeh knows it!"

"You're mistaken, Mammy; I do trust the Lord as much as ever, but I now understand him better than I use to, that's all. I dont intend to be made a fool of any longer by false preaching."

"Henry!" interrogated Daddy Joe – who, apprehending difficulties in the case, had managed to get back to the house. "Yeh gwine lose all yo' 'ligion? Wat yeh mean, boy!"

"Religion!" replied Henry rebukingly. "That's always the cry with black people. Tell me nothing about religion when the very man who hands you the bread at communion has sold your daughter away from you!"

"Den yeh 'fen' God case man 'fen' yeh! Take cah, Henry, take cah! mine wat yeh 'bout; God is lookin' at yeh, an' if yeh no' willin' trus' 'im, yeh need'n call on 'im in time o' trouble."

"I dont intend, unless He does more for me then than He has done before. 'Time of need!' If ever man needed His assistance, I'm sure I need it now."

"Yeh do'n know wat yeh need; de Laud knows bes'. On'y trus' in 'im, an' 'e bring yeh out mo' nah conkah. By de help o' God I's heah dis day, to gib yeh cumfut!"

"I have trusted in Him, Daddy Joe, all my life, as I told Mammy Judy this morning, but—"

"Ah boy, yeh's gwine back! Dat on't do Henry, dat on't do!"

"Going back from what? My oppressor's religion! If I could only get rid of his inflictions as easily as I can his religion, I would be this day a free man, when you might then talk to me about 'trusting.'"

"Dis, Henry, am one uh de ways ob de Laud; 'e fus 'flicks us an' den he bless us."

"Then it's a way I don't like."

"Mine how yeh talk, boy! 'God moves in a myst'us way His wundahs to pehfaum,' an—"

"He moves too slow for me, Daddy Joe; I'm tired waiting so—"

"Come Henry, I hab no sich talk like dat! yeh is gittin' rale weaked; yeh gwine let de debil take full 'session on yeh! Take cah boy, mine how yeh talk!"

"It is not wickedness, Daddy Joe; you don't understand these things at all. If a thousand years with us is but a day with God, do you think that I am required to wait all that time?"

"Don't, Henry, don't! De wud say 'stan' still an' see de salbation.'"

"That's no talk for me, Daddy Joe; I've been 'standing still' long enough – I'll 'stand still' no longer."

"Den yeh no call t' bey God wud? Take cah boy, take cah!"

"Yes I have, and I intend to obey it, but that part was intended for the Jews, a people long since dead. I'll obey that intended for me."

"How yeh gwine bey it?"

"'Now is the accepted time, today is the day of salvation.' So you see, Daddy Joe, this is very different to standing still."

"Ah boy, I's feahd yeh's losen yeh 'ligion!"

"I tell you once for all, Daddy Joe, that I'm not only 'losing' but I have altogether lost my faith in the religion of my oppressors. As they are our religious teachers, my estimate of the thing they give is no greater than it is for those who give it."

With elbows upon his knees, and face resting in the palms of his hands, Daddy Joe for some time sat with his eyes steadily fixed on the floor, whilst Ailcey who for a part of the time had been an auditor to the conversation, went into the house about her domestic duties.

"Never mind, Henry! I hope it will not always be so with you. You have been kind and faithful to me and the Colonel, and I'll do anything I can for you!" sympathetically said Mrs. Franks, who, having been a concealed spectator of the interview between Henry and the old people, had just appeared before them.

Wiping away the emblems of grief which stole down his face, with a deep-toned voice upgushing from the recesses of a more than iron-pierced soul, he enquired, "Madam, what can you do! Where is my wife?" To this, Mrs. Franks gave a deep sigh. "Never mind, never mind!" continued he, "yes, I will mind, and by—!"

"O! Henry, I hope you've not taken to swearing! I do hope you will not give over to wickedness! Our afflictions should only make our faith the stronger."

"'Wickedness.' Let the righteous correct the wicked, and the Christian condemn the sinner!"

"That is uncharitable in you, Henry! As you know I have always treated you kindly, and God forbid that I should consider myself any less than a Christian! And I claim as much at least for the Colonel, though like frail mortals he is liable to err at times."

"Madam!" said he with suppressed emotion – starting back a pace or two – "Do you think there is anything either in or out of hell so wicked, as that which Colonel Franks has done to my wife, and now about to do to me? For myself I care not – my wife!"

"Henry!" said Mrs. Franks, gently placing her hand upon his shoulder. "There is yet a hope left for you, and you will be faithful enough, I know, not to implicate any person. It is this: Mrs. Van Winter, a true friend of your race, is shortly going to Cuba on a visit, and I will arrange with her to purchase you through an agent on the day of your sale, and by that means you can get to Cuba, where probably you may be fortunate enough to get the master of your wife to become your purchaser."

"Then I have two chances!" replied Henry.

Just then Ailcey, thrusting her head in the door, requested the presence of her mistress in the parlor.

Chapter VIII
The Sale

"DAH NOW, dah now!" exclaimed Mammy Judy. "Jis wat ole man been tellin' on yeh! Yeh go out yandah, yeh kick up yeh heel, git yeh head clean full proclamation an' sich like dat, an' let debil fool yeh, den go fool long wid wite folks long so, sho! Bettah go 'bout yeh bisness; been sahvin' God right, yeh no call t'do so eh reckon!"

"I don't care what comes! my course is laid out and my determination fixed, and nothing they can do can alter it. So you and Daddy Joe, mammy, had just as well quit your preaching to me the religion you have got from your oppressors."

"Soul-driveh git yeh, yeh cah git way fom dem eh doh recken! Sho chile, yeh ain' dat mighty!" admonished Mammy Judy.

"Henry, my chile, look to de Laud! Look to de Laud! Case 'e 'lone am able t' bah us up in ouah trouble! An—"

"Go directly sir, to Captain John Harris' office and ask him to call immediately to see me at my house!" ordered Franks.

Politely bowing, Henry immediately left the premises on his errand.

"Laud a' messy maus Stephen!" exclaimed Mammy Judy, on hearing the name of John Harris the Negro-trader. "Hope yeh arteh no haum! Gwine sell all on us to de tradehs?"

"Hoot-toot, hoot-toot! Judy, give yourself no uneasiness about that till you have some cause for it. So you and Joe may rest contented, Judy," admonished Franks.

"Tank'e maus Stephen! Case ah heahn yeh tell Henry dat yeh sell de las' nig—"

"Hush, ole umin, hush! Yeh tongue too long! Put yeh trus' in de Laud!" interrupted Daddy Joe.

"I treat my black folks well," replied Franks, "and all they have to—"

Here the doorbell having been rung, he was interrupted with a message from Ailcey, that a gentleman awaited his presence in the parlor.

At the moment which the Colonel left the kitchen, Henry stepped over the stile into the yard, which at once disclosed who the gentleman was to whom the master had been summoned. Henry passed directly around and behind the house.

"See, ole man, see! Reckon 'e gwine dah now!" whispered Mammy Judy, on seeing Henry pass through the yard without going into the kitchen.

"Whah?" enquired Daddy Joe.

"Dun'o out yandah, whah 'e gwine way from wite folks!" she replied.

The interview between Franks and the trader Harris was not over half an hour duration, the trader retiring, Franks being prompt and decisive in all of his transactions, making little ceremony.

So soon as the front door was closed, Ailcey smiling bore into the kitchen a half-pint glass of brandy, saying that her master had sent it to the old people.

The old man received it with compliments to his master, pouring it into a black jug in which there was both tansy and garlic, highly recommending it as a "bitters" and certain antidote for worms, for which purpose he and the old woman took of it as long as it lasted, though neither had been troubled with that particular disease since the days of their childhood.

"Wat de gwine do wid yeh meh son?" enquired Mammy Judy as Henry entered the kitchen.

"Sell me to the soul-drivers! what else would they do?"

"Yeh gwin 'tay 'bout till de git yeh?"

"I shant move a step! and let them do their—"

"Maus wants to see yeh in da front house, Henry," interrupted Ailcey, he immediately obeying the summons.

"Heah dat now!" said mammy Judy, as Henry followed the maid out of the kitchen.

"Carry this note, sir, directly to Captain Jack Harris!" ordered Franks, handing to Henry a sealed note. Receiving it, he bowed politely, going out of the front door, directly to the slave prison of Harris.

"Eh heh! I see," said Harris on opening the note, "Colonel Frank's boy; walk in here," passing through the office into a room which proved to be the first department of the slave prison. "No common Negro, I see! You're a shade higher. A pretty deep shade too! Can read, write, cipher; a good religious fellow, and has a Christian and sir name. The devil you say! Who's your father? Can you preach?"

"I have never tried," was the only reply.

"Have you ever been a member of Congress?" continued Harris with ridicule.

To this Henry made no reply.

"Wont answer, hey! Beneath your dignity. I understand that you're of that class of gentry who dont speak to common folks! You're not quite well enough dressed for a gentleman of your cloth. Here! Mr. Henry, I'll present you with a set of ruffles: give yourself no trouble sir, as I'll dress you! I'm here for that purpose," said Harris, fastening upon the wrists of the manly bondman a heavy pair of handcuffs.

"You hurt my wrist!" admonished Henry.

"New clothing will be a little tight when first put on. Now sir!" continued the trader, taking him to the back door and pointing into the yard at the slave gang there confined. "As you have been respectably dressed, walk out and enjoy yourself among the ladies and gentlemen there; you'll find them quite a select company."

Shortly after this the sound of the bellringer's voice was heard – a sound which usually spread terror among the slaves: "Will be sold this afternoon at three o'clock by public outcry, at the slave prison of Captain John Harris, a likely choice Negro fellow, the best trained body servant in the state, trained to the business by the most accomplished lady and gentleman Negro-trainers in the Mississippi Valley. Sale positive without a proviso."

"Dah, dah! Did'n eh tell yeh so? Ole man, ole man! heah dat now! Come heah. Dat jis what I been tellin on im, but 'e uden bleve me!" ejaculated old Mammy Judy on hearing the bell ring and the handbill read.

Falling upon their knees, the two old slaves prayed fervently to God, thanking him that it was as "well with them" as it was.

"Bless de Laud! My soul is happy!" cried out Mammy Judy being overcome with devotion, clapping her hands.

"Tang God, fah wat I feels in my soul!" responded Daddy Joe.

Rising from their knees with tears trickling down their cheeks, the old slaves endeavored to ease their troubled souls by singing,

> *Oh, when shall my sorrows subside,*
> *And when shall my troubles be ended;*
> *And when to the bosom of Christ be conveyed,*
> *To the mansions of joy and bliss;*
> *To the mansions of joy and bliss!*

"Wuhthy to be praise! Blessed be de name uh de Laud! Po' black folks, de Laud o'ny knows sats t' come ob us!" exclaimed Mammy Judy.

"Look to de Laud ole umin, 'e's able t' bah us out mo' neh conkeh. Keep de monin' stah in sight!" advised Daddy Joe.

"Yes, ole man, yes, dat I done dis many long day, an' ah ain' gwine lose sight uh it now! No, God bein' my helpeh, I is gwine keep my eyes right on it, dat I is!"

As the hour of three drew near, many there were going in the direction of the slave prison, a large number of persons having assembled at the sale.

"Draw near, gentlemen, draw near!" cried Harris. "The hour of sale is arrived: a positive sale with no proviso, cash down, or no sale at all!" A general laugh succeeded the introduction of the auctioneer.

"Come up here my lad!" continued the auctioneer, wielding a long red rawhide. "Mount this block, stand beside me, an' let's see which is the best looking man! We have met before, but I never had the pleasure of introducing you. Gentlemen one and all, I take pleasure in introducing to you Henry – pardon me, sir – Mr. Henry Holland, I believe – am I right, sir? – Mr. Henry Holland, a good looking fellow you will admit.

"I am offered one thousand dollars; one thousand dollars for the best looking Negro in all Mississippi! If all the negro boys in the state was as good looking as him, I'd give two thousand dollars for 'em all myself!" This caused another laugh. "Who'll give me one thousand five—"

Just then a shower of rain came on.

"Gentlemen!" exclaimed the auctioneer. "Without a place can be obtained large enough to shelter the people here assembled, the sale will have to be postponed. This is a proviso we couldn't foresee, an' therefore is not responsible for it." There was another hearty laugh.

A whisper went through the crowd, when presently a gentleman came forward, saying that those concerned had kindly tendered the use of the church which stood nearby, in which to continue the sale.

"Here we are again, gentlemen! Who bids five hundred more for the likely Negro fellow? I am offered fifteen hundred dollars for the finest Negro servant in the state! Come, my boy, bestir yourself an' don't stan' there like a statute; can't you give us a jig? whistle us a song! I forgot, the Negro fellow is religious; by the by, an excellent recommendation, gentlemen. Perhaps he'll give us a sermon. Say, git up there old fellow, an' hold forth. Can't you give us a sermon on Abolition? I'm only offered fifteen hundred dollars for the likely Negro boy! Fifteen, sixteen, sixteen hundred, just agoing at – eighteen, eighteen, nineteen hundred, nineteen hundred! Just agoing at nineteen hundred dollars for the best body servant in the state; just agoing at nineteen and without a better bid I'll – Going! Going! Go—!"

Just at this point a note was passed up the aisle to the auctioneer, who after reading it said, "Gentlemen! Circumstances beyond my control make it necessary that the sale be postponed until one day next week; the time of continuance will be duly announced," when, bowing, he left the stand.

"That's another proviso not in the original bill!" exclaimed a voice as the auctioneer left the stand, at which there were peals of laughter.

To secure himself against contingency, Harris immediately delivered Henry over to Franks.

There were present at the sale, Crow, Slider, Walker, Borbridge, Simpson, Hurst, Spangler and Williams, all noted slave traders, eager to purchase, some on their return home, and some with their gangs en route for the Southern markets.

The note handed the auctioneer read thus:

> CAPT. HARRIS: – Having learned that there are private individuals at the sale, who design purchasing my Negro man, Harry, for his own personal advantage, you will peremptorily postpone the sale – making such apology as the occasion demands – and effect a private sale with Richard Crow, Esq., who offers me two thousand dollars for him. Let the boy return to me. Believe me to be,
> Very Respectfully,
> STEPHEN FRANKS
> Capt. John Harris. Natchez, Nov. 29th, 1852.

"Now, sir," said Franks to Henry, who had barely reached the house from the auction block, "take this pass and go to Jackson and Woodville, or anywhere else you wish to see your friends, so that you be back against Monday afternoon. I ordered a postponement of the sale, thinking that I would try you awhile longer, as I never had cause before to part with you. Now see if you can't be a better boy!"

Eagerly taking the note, thanking him with a low bow, turning away, Henry opened the paper, which read:

> *Permit the bearer my boy Henry, sometimes calling himself Henry Holland – a kind of*
> *negro pride he has – to pass and repass wherever he wants to go, he behaving himself properly.*
> *STEPHEN FRANKS*
> *To all whom it may concern. Natchez, Nov. 29th, 1852.*

Carefully depositing the charte volante in his pocket wallet, Henry quietly entered the hut of Mammy Judy and Daddy Joe.

Chapter IX
The Runaway

"DE LAUD'S GOOD – bless his name!" exclaimed Mammy Judy wringing her hands as Henry entered their hut. "'e heahs de prahs ob 'is chilen. Yeh hab reason t' tang God yeh is heah dis day!"

"Yes Henry, see wat de Laud's done fah yeh. Tis true's I's heah dis day! Tang God fah dat!" added Daddy Joe.

"I think," replied he, after listening with patience to the old people, "I have reason to thank our Ailcey and Van Winter's Biddy; they, it seems to me, should have some credit in the matter."

"Sho boy, g'long whah yeh gwine! Yo' backslidin' gwine git yeh in trouble ghin eh reckon?" replied Mammy Judy.

Having heard the conversation between her mistress and Henry, Ailcey, as a secret, informed Van Winter's Derba, who informed her fellow servant Biddy, who imparted it to her acquaintance Nelly, the slave of esquire Potter, Nelly informing her mistress, who told the 'Squire, who led Franks into the secret of the whole matter.

"Mus'n blame me, Henry!" said Ailcey in an undertone. "I di'n mean de wite folks to know wat I tole Derba, nor she di'n mean it nuther, but dat devil, Pottah's Nell! us gals mean da fus time we ketch uh out, to duck uh in da rivah! She's rale wite folk's nigga, dat's jus' wat she is. Nevah mine, we'll ketch her yit!"

"I don't blame you Ailcey, nor either of Mrs. Van Winter's girls, as I know that you are my friends, neither of whom would do anything knowingly to injure me. I know Ailcey that you are a good girl, and believe you would tell me—"

"Yes Henry, I is yo' fren' an' come to tell yeh now wat da wite folks goin' to do."

"What is it Ailcey; what do you know?"

"Wy dat ugly ole devil Dick Crow – God fah gim me! But I hate 'im so, case he nothin' but po' wite man, no how – I know 'im he come from Fagina on—"

"Never mind his origin, Ailcey, tell me what you know concerning his visit in the house."

"I is goin' to, but da ugly ole devil, I hates 'im so! Maus Stephen had 'im in da pahla, an' 'e sole yeh to 'im, dat ugly ole po' wite devil, fah – God knows how much – a hole heap a money; 'two' somethin."

"I know what it was, two thousand dollars, for that was his selling price to Jack Harris."

"Yes, dat was da sum, Henry."

"I am satisfied as to how much he can be relied on. Even was I to take the advice of the old people here, and become reconciled to drag out a miserable life of degradation and bondage under them, I would not be permitted to do so by this man, who seeks every opportunity to crush out my lingering manhood, and reduce my free spirit to the submission of a slave. He cannot do it, I will not submit to it, and I defy his power to make me submit."

"Laus a messy, Henry, yeh free man! huccum yeh not tell me long'o? Sho boy, bettah go long whah yeh gwine, out yandah, an' not fool long wid wite folks!" said Mammy Judy with surprise, "wat bring yeh heah anyhow?"

"That's best known to myself, mammy."

"Wat make yeh keep heah so long den, dat yeh ain' gone fo' dis?"

"Your questions become rather pressing, mammy; I can't tell you that either."

"Laud, Laud, Laud! So yeh free man? Well, well, well!"

"Once for all, I now tell you old people what I never told you before, nor never expected to tell you under such circumstances; that I never intend to serve any white man again. I'll die first!"

"De Laud a' messy on my po' soul! An' huccum yeh not gone befo'?"

"Carrying out the principles and advice of you old people 'standing still, to see the salvation.' But with me, 'now is the accepted time, today is the day of salvation.'"

"Well, well, well!" sighed Mammy Judy.

"I am satisfied that I am sold, and the wretch who did it seeks to conceal his perfidy by deception. Now if ever you old people did anything in your lives, you must do it now."

"Wat dat yeh want wid us?"

"Why, if you'll go, I'll take you on Saturday night, and make our escape to a free country."

"Wat place yeh call dat?"

"Canada!" replied Henry, with emotion.

"How fah yeh gwine take me?" earnestly enquired the old woman.

"I can't just now tell the distance, probably some two or three thousand miles from here, the way we'd have to go."

"De Laus a messy on me! An' wat yeh gwine do wid little Joe; ain gwine leave 'im behine?"

"No, Mammy Judy, I'd bury him in the bottom of the river first! I intend carrying him in a bundle on my back, as the Indians carry their babies."

"Wat yeh gwine do fah money; yeh ain' gwine rob folks on de road?"

"No mammy, I'll starve first. Have you and Daddy Joe saved nothing from your black-eye peas and poultry selling for many years?"

"Ole man, how much in dat pot undeh de flo' dah; how long since yeh count it?"

"Don'o," replied Daddy Joe, "las' time ah count it, da wah faughty guinea* uh sich a mauttah, an' ah put in some six-seven guinea mo' since dat."

"Then you have some two hundred and fifty dollars in money."

"Dat do yeh?" enquired Mammy Judy.

"Yes, that of itself is enough, but—"

"Den take it an' go long whah yeh gwine; we ole folks too ole fah gwine headlong out yandah an' don'o whah we gwine. Sho boy! take de money an' g'long!" decisively replied the old woman after all her inquisitiveness.

"If you don't know, I do, mammy, and that will answer for all."

"Dat ain' gwine do us. We ole folks ain' politishon an' undestan' de graumma uh dese places, an' w'en we git dah den maybe do'n like it an cahn' git back. Sho chile, so long whah yeh gwine!"

"What do you say, Daddy Joe? Whatever you have to say, must be said quick, as time with me is precious."

"We is too ole dis time a day, chile, t'go way out yauah de Laud knows whah; bettah whah we is."

"You'll not be too old to go if these whites once take a notion to sell you. What will you do then?"

"Trus' to de Laud!"

"Yes, the same old slave song – 'Trust to the Lord.' Then I must go, and—"

"Ain' yeh gwine take de money, Henry?" interrupted the old woman.

"No, mammy, since you will not go, I leave it for you and Daddy Joe, as you may yet have use for it, or those may desire to use it who better understand what use to make of it than you and Daddy Joe seem willing to be instructed in."

"Den yeh 'ont have de money?"

"I thank you and Daddy most kindly, Mammy Judy, for your offer, and only refuse because I have two hundred guineas about me."

"Sho boy, yeh got all dat, no call t'want dat little we got. Whah yeh git all dat money? Do'n reckon yeh gwine tell me! Did'n steal from maus Stephen, do'n reckon?"

"No, mammy, I'm incapable of stealing from any one, but I have, from time to time, taken by littles, some of the earnings due me for more than eighteen years' service to this man Franks, which at the low rate of two hundred dollars a year, would amount to sixteen hundred dollars more than I secured, exclusive of the interest, which would have more than supplied my clothing, to say nothing of the injury done me by degrading me as a slave. 'Steal' indeed! I would that when I had an opportunity, I had taken fifty thousand instead of two. I am to understand you old people as positively declining to go, am I?"

"No, no, chile, we cahn go! We put ouh trus' in de Laud, he bring us out mo' nah conkah."

"Then from this time hence, I become a runaway. Take care of my poor boy while he's with you. When I leave the swamps, or where I'll go, will never be known to you. Should my boy be suddenly missed, and you find three notches cut in the bark of the big willow tree, on the side away from your hut, then give yourself no uneasiness; but if you don't find these notches in the tree, then I know nothing about him. Goodbye!" And Henry strode directly for the road to Woodville.

"Fahwell me son, fahwell, an' may God a'mighty go wid you! May de Laud guide an' 'tect yeh on de way!"

The child, contrary to his custom, commenced crying, desiring to see Mamma Maggie and Dadda Henry. Every effort to quiet him was unavailing. This brought sorrow to the old people's hearts and tears to their eyes, which they endeavored to soothe in a touching lamentation:

> *See wives and husbands torn apart,*
> *Their children's screams, they grieve my heart.*
> *They are torn away to Georgia!*
> *Come and go along with me—*
> *They are torn away to Georgia!*
> *Go sound the Jubilee!*

Chapter X
Merry Making

THE DAY IS SATURDAY, a part of which is given by many liberal masters to their slaves, the afternoon being spent as a holiday, or in vending such little marketable commodities as they might by chance possess.

As a token of gratitude, it is customary in many parts of the South for the slaves to invite their masters to their entertainments. This evening presented such an occasion on the premises of Colonel Stephen Franks.

This day Mammy Judy was extremely busy, for in addition to the responsibility of the culinary department, there was her calico habit to be done up – she would not let Potter's Milly look any better than herself – and an old suit of the young master George's clothes had to be patched and darned a little before little Joe could favorably compare with Craig's Sooky's little Dick. And the cast-off linen given to her husband for the occasion might require a "little doing up."

"Wat missus sen' dis shut heah wid de bres all full dis debilment an' nonsense fah?" said Mammy Judy, holding up the garment, looking at the ruffles. "Sho! Missus mus' be crack, sen' dis heah! Ole man ain' gwine sen' he soul to de ole boy puttin' on dis debilment!" And she hastened away with the shirt, stating to her mistress her religious objections. Mrs. Franks smiled as she took the garment, telling her that the objections could be easily removed by taking off the ruffles.

"Dat look sumphen like!" remarked the old woman, when Ailcey handed her the shirt with the ruffles removed.

"Sen' dat debilment an' nonsense heah! Sho!" And carrying it away smiling, she laid it upon the bed.

The feast of the evening was such as Mammy Judy was capable of preparing when in her best humor, consisting of all the delicacies usually served up on the occasion of corn huskings in the graingrowing region.

Conscious that he was not entitled to their gratitude, Colonel Franks declined to honor the entertainment, though the invitation was a ruse to deceive him, as he had attempted to deceive them.

The evening brought with it much of life's variety, as may be seen among the slave population of the South. There were Potter's slaves, and the people of Mrs. Van Winter, also those of Major Craig, and Dr. Denny, all dressed neatly, and seemingly very happy.

Ailcey was quite the pride of the evening, in an old gauze orange dress of her mistress, and felt that she deserved to be well thought of, as proving herself the friend of Henry, the son-in-law of Daddy Joe and Mammy Judy, the heads of the entertainment. Mammy Judy and Potter's Milly were both looking matronly in their calico gowns and towlinen aprons, and Daddy Joe was the honored and observed of the party, in an old black suit with an abundance of surplus.

"He'p yeh se'f, chilen!" said Mammy Judy, after the table had been blessed by Daddy Joe. "Henry ain' gwine be heah, 'e gone to Woodville uh some whah dah, kick'n up 'e heel. Come, chilen, eat haughty, mo' whah dis come f'om. He'p yeh se'f now do'n—"

"I is, Aun' Judy; I likes dis heah kine a witals!" drawled out Potter's Nelse, reaching over for the fifth or sixth time. "Dis am good shaut cake!"

"O mammy, look at Jilson!" exclaimed Ailcey, as a huge, rough field hand – who refused to go to the table with the company, but sat sulkily by himself in one corner – was just walking away, with two whole "cakes" of bread under his arm.

"Wat yeh gwine do wid dat bread, Jilson?" enquired the old woman.

"I gwine eat it, dat wat I gwine do wid it! I ain' had no w'eat bread dis two hauvest!" he having come from Virginia, where such articles of food on harvest occasion were generally allowed the slave.

"Big hog, so 'e is!" rebukingly said Ailcey, when she saw that Jilson was determined in his purpose.

"Nebeh mine dat childen, plenty mo'!" responded Mammy Judy.

"Ole umin, dat chile in de way dah; de gals haudly tu'n roun," suggested Daddy Joe, on seeing the pallet of little Joe crowded upon as the girls were leaving the table, seating themselves around the room.

"Ailcey, my chile, jes' run up to de hut wid 'im, 'an lay 'im in de bed; ef yeh fuhd, Van Wintah' Ben go wid yeh; ah knows 'e likes to go wid de gals," said Mammy Judy.

Taking up his hat with a bland smile, Ben obeyed orders without a demur.

The entertainment was held at the extreme end of a two-acre lot in the old slave quarters, while the hut of Mammy Judy was near the great house. Ailcey thought she espied a person retreat into the shrubbery and, startled, she went to the back door of the hut, but Ben hooted at the idea of any person out and about on such an occasion, except indeed it was Jilson with his bread. The child being carefully placed in bed, Ailcey and her protector were soon mingled with the merry slaves.

There were three persons generally quite prominent among the slaves of the neighborhood, missed on this occasion; Franks' Charles, Denny's Sam, and Potter's Andy; Sam being confined to bed by sickness.

"Ailcey, whah's Chaules – huccum 'e not heah?" enquired Mammy Judy.

"Endeed, I dun'o mammy."

"Huccum Pottah's Andy ain' heah muddah?"

"Andy a' home tonight, Aun' Judy, an' uh dun'o whah 'e is," replied Winny.

"Gone headlong out yandah, arteh no good, uh doh reckon, an' Chaules 'e gone dah too," replied the old woman.

"Da ain' nothin' mattah wid dis crowd, Aun' Judy," complimented Nelse as he sat beside Derba. At this expression Mammy Judy gave a deep sigh, on the thought of her absent daughter.

"Come, chilen," suggested Mammy Judy, "yeh all eat mighty hauty, an' been mighty merry, an' 'joy yehse'f much; we now sing praise to de Laud fah wat 'e done fah us," raising a hymn in which all earnestly joined:

> *Oh! Jesus, Jesus is my friend,*
> *He'll be my helper to the end,...*

"Young folk, yeh all bettah git ready now an' go, fo' de patrollas come out. Yeh all 'joy yeh se'f much, now time yeh gone. Hope yeh all sauv God Sunday. Ole man fo' de all gone, hab wud uh prah," advised the old woman; the following being sung in conclusion:

> *The Lord is here, and the Lord is all around us;*
> *Canaan, Canaan's a very happy home—*
> *O, glory! O, glory! O, glory! God is here,*

when the gathering dispersed, the slaves going cheerfully to their homes.

"Come ole man, yeh got mautch? light sum dem shavens dah, quick. Ah cah fine de chile heah on dis bed!" said Mammy Judy, on entering the hut and feeling about in the dark for little Joe. "Ailcey, wat yeh done wid de chile?"

"E's dah, Mammy Judy, I lain 'im on de bed, ah spose 'e roll off." The shavings being lit, here was no child to be found.

"My Laud, ole man! whah's de chile? Wat dis mean! O, whah's my po' chile gone; my po' baby!" exclaimed Mammy Judy, wringing her hands in distress.

"Stay, ole 'umin! De tree! De tree!" When, going out in the dark, feeling the trunk of the willow, three notches in the bark were distinct to the touch.

"Ole 'umin!" exclaimed Daddy Joe in a suppressed voice, hastening into the hut. "It am he, it am Henry got 'im!"

"Tang God, den my po' baby safe!" responded Mammy Judy, when they raised their voices in praise of thankfulness:

> *'O, who's like Jesus!*
> *Hallelujah! praise ye the Lord;*
> *O, who's like Jesus!*
> *Hallelujah! love and serve the Lord!'*

Falling upon their knees, the old man offered an earnest, heartful prayer to God, asking his guardianship through the night, and protection through the day, especially upon their heartbroken daughter, their runaway son-in-law, and the little grandson, when the two old people retired to rest with spirits mingled with joy, sorrow, hope, and fear; Ailcey going into the great house.

Chapter XI
A Shadow

"AH, BOYS! Here you are, true to your promise," said Henry, as he entered a covert in the thicket adjacent the cotton place, late on Sunday evening, "have you been waiting long?"

"Not very," replied Andy, "not mo' dan two-three ouahs."

"I was fearful you would not come, or if you did before me, that you would grow weary, and leave."

"Yeh no call to doubt us Henry, case yeh fine us true as ole steel!"

"I know it," answered he, "but you know, Andy, that when a slave is once sold at auction, all respect for him—"

"O pshaw! we ain' goin' to heah nothin' like dat a tall! case—"

"No!" interrupted Charles, "all you got to do Henry, is to tell we boys what you want, an' we're your men."

"That's the talk for me!"

"Well, what you doin' here?" enquired Charles.

"W'at brought yeh back from Jackson so soon?" further enquired Andy.

"How did you get word to meet me here?"

"By Ailcey; she give me the stone, an' I give it to Andy, an' we both sent one apiece back. Didn't you git 'em?"

"Yes, that's the way I knew you intended to meet me," replied Henry.

"So we thought," said Charles, "but tell us, Henry, what you want us to do."

"I suppose you know all about the sale, that they had me on the auction block, but ordered a postponement, and—"

"That's the very pint we can't understand, although I'm in the same family with you," interrupted Charles.

"But tell us Henry, what yeh doin' here?" impatiently enquired Andy.

"Yes," added Charles, "we want to know."

"Well, I'm a runaway, and from this time forth, I swear – I do it religiously – that I'll never again serve any white man living!"

"That's the pint I wanted to git at before," explained Charles, "as I can't understan' why you run away, after your release from Jack Harris, an'—"

"Nah, I nuthah!" interrupted Andy.

"It seems to me," continued Charles, "that I'd 'ave went before they 'tempted to sell me, an' that you're safer now than before they had you on the block."

"Dat's da way I look at it," responded Andy.

"The stopping of the sale was to deceive his wife, mammy, and Daddy Joe, as he had privately disposed of me to a regular soul-driver by the name of Crow."

"I knows Dick Crow," said Andy, "'e come f'om Faginy, whah I did, da same town."

"So Ailcey said of him. Then you know him without any description from me," replied Henry.

"Yes 'n deed! an' I knows 'im to be a inhuman, mean, dead-po' white man, dat's wat I does."

"Well, I was privately sold to him for two thousand dollars, then ordered back to Franks, as though I was still his slave, and by him given a pass, and requested to go to Woodville where there were arrangements to seize me and hold me, till Crow ordered me, which was to have been on Tuesday evening. Crow is not aware of me having been given a pass; Franks gave it to deceive his wife, in case of my not returning, to make the impression that I had run away, when in reality I was sold to the trader."

"Then our people had their merrymaking all for nothin'," said Charles, "an' Franks got what 'e didn't deserve – their praise."

"No, the merrymaking was only to deceive Franks, that I might have time to get away. Daddy Joe, Mammy Judy, and Ailcey knew all about it, and proposed the feast to deceive him."

"Dat's good! Sarve 'im right, da 'sarned ole scamp!" rejoined Andy.

"It couldn't be better!" responded Charles.

"Henry uh wish we was in yo' place an' you none da wus by it," said Andy.

"Never mind, boys, give yourselves no uneasiness, as it wont be long before we'll all be together."

"You think so, Henry?" asked Charles.

"Well uh hope so, but den body can haudly 'spect it," responded Andy.

"Boys," said Henry, with great caution and much emotion, "I am now about to approach an important subject and as I have always found you true to me – and you can only be true to me by being true to yourselves – I shall not hesitate to impart it! But for Heaven's sake! – perhaps I had better not!"

"Keep nothin' back, Henry," said Charles, "as you know that we boys 'll die by our principles, that's settled!"

"Yes, I wants to die right now by mine; right heah, now!" sanctioned Andy.

"Well it is this – close, boys! close!" when they gathered in a huddle, beneath an underbush, upon their knees, "you both go with me, but not now. I—"

"Why not now?" anxiously enquired Charles.

"Dat's wat I like to know!" responded Andy.

"Stop, boys, till I explain. The plans are mine and you must allow me to know more about them than you. Just here, for once, the slave-holding preacher's advice to the black man is appropriate, 'Stand still and see the salvation.'"

"Then let us hear it, Henry," asked Charles.

"Fah God sake!" said Andy, "let us heah w'at it is, anyhow, Henry; yeh keep a body in 'spence so long, till I's mose crazy to heah it. Dat's no way!"

"You shall have it, but I approach it with caution! Nay, with fear and trembling, at the thought of what has been the fate of all previous matters of this kind. I approach it with religious fear, and hardly think us fit for the task; at least, I know I am not. But as no one has ever originated, or given us anything of the kind, I suppose I may venture."

"Tell it! tell it!" urged both in a whisper.

"Andy," said Henry, "let us have a word of prayer first!" when they bowed low, with their heads to the ground, Andy, who was a preacher of the Baptist pursuasion among his slave brethren, offering a solemn and affecting prayer, in whispers to the Most High, to give them knowledge and courage in the undertaking, and success in the effort.

Rising from their knees, Andy commenced an anthem, by which he appeared to be much affected, in the following words:

> *About our future destiny,*
> *There need be none debate—*
> *Whilst we ride on the tide,*
> *With our Captain and his mate.*

Clasping each other by the hand, standing in a band together, as a plight of their union and fidelity to each other, Henry said, "I now impart to you the secret, it is this: I have laid a scheme, and matured a plan for a general insurrection of the slaves in every state, and the successful overthrow of slavery!"

"Amen!" exclaimed Charles.

"God grant it!" responded Andy.

"Tell us, Henry, how's dis to be carried out?" enquired Andy.

"That's the thing which most concerns me, as it seems that it would be hard to do in the present ignorant state of our people in the slave States," replied Charles.

"Dat's jis wat I feah!" said Andy.

"This difficulty is obviated. It is so simple that the most stupid among the slaves will understand it as well as if he had been instructed for a year."

"What!" exclaimed Charles.

"Let's heah dat again!" asked Andy.

"It is so just as I told you! So simple is it that the trees of the forest or an orchard illustrate it; flocks of birds or domestic cattle, fields of corn, hemp, or sugar cane; tobacco, rice, or cotton, the whistling of the wind, rustling of the leaves, flashing of lightning, roaring of thunder, and running of streams all keep it constantly before their eyes and in their memory, so that they can't forget it if they would."

"Are we to know it now?" enquired Charles.

"I'm boun' to know it dis night befo' I goes home, 'case I been longin' fah ole Pottah dis many day, an' uh mos' think uh got 'im now!"

"Yes boys, you've to know it before we part, but—"

"That's the talk!" said Charles.

"Good nuff talk fah me!" responded Andy.

"As I was about to say, such is the character of this organization, that punishment and misery are made the instruments for its propagation, so—"

"I can't understan' that part—"

"You know nothing at all about it Charles, and you must—"

"Stan' still an' see da salvation!" interrupted Andy.

"Amen!" responded Charles.

"God help you so to do, brethren!" admonished Henry.

"Go on Henry tell us! give it to us!" they urged.

"Every blow you receive from the oppressor impresses the organization upon your mind, making it so clear that even Whitehead's Jack could understand it as well as his master."

"We are satisfied! The secret, the secret!" they importuned.

"Well then, first to prayer, and then to the organization. Andy!" said Henry, nodding to him, when they again bowed low with their heads to the ground, whilst each breathed a silent prayer, which was ended with "Amen" by Andy.

Whilst yet upon their knees, Henry imparted to them the secrets of his organization.

"O, dat's da thing!" exclaimed Andy.

"Capital, capital!" responded Charles. "What fools we was that we didn't know it long ago!"

"I is mad wid myse'f now!" said Andy.

"Well, well, well! Surely God must be in the work," continued Charles.

"'E's heah; Heaven's nigh! Ah feels it! It's right heah!" responded Andy, placing his hand upon his chest, the tears trickling down his cheeks.

"Brethren," asked Henry, "do you understand it?"

"Understand it? Why, a child could understand, it's so easy!" replied Charles.

"Yes," added Andy, "ah not only undestan' myse'f, but wid da knowledge I has uv it, ah could make Whitehead's Jack a Moses!"

"Stand still, then, and see!" said he.

"Dat's good Bible talk!" responded Andy.

"Well, what is we to do?" enquired Charles.

"You must now go on and organize continually. It makes no difference when, nor where you are, so that the slaves are true and trustworthy, as the scheme is adapted to all times and places."

"How we gwine do Henry, 'bout gittin' da things 'mong da boys?" enquired Andy.

"All you have to do, is to find one good man or woman – I don't care which, so that they prove to be the right person – on a single plantation, and hold a seclusion and impart the secret to them, and make them the organizers for their own plantation, and they in like manner impart it to some other next to them, and so on. In this way it will spread like smallpox among them."

"Henry, you is fit fah leadah ah see," complimentingly said Andy.

"I greatly mistrust myself, brethren, but if I can't command, I can at least plan."

"Is they anything else for us to do Henry?" enquired Charles.

"Yes, a very important part of your duties has yet to be stated. I now go as a runaway, and will be suspected of lurking about in the thickets, swamps and caves; then to make the ruse complete, just as often as you think it necessary, to make a good impression, you must kill a shoat, take a lamb, pig, turkey, goose, chickens, ham of bacon from the smoke house, a loaf of bread or crock of butter from the spring house, and throw them down into the old waste well at the back of the old quarters, always leaving the heads of the fowls lying about and the blood of the larger animals. Everything that is missed dont hesitate to lay it upon me, as a runaway, it will only cause them to have the less suspicion of your having such a design."

"That's it – the very thing!" said Charles. "An it so happens that they's an ole waste well on both Franks' and Potter's places, one for both of us."

"I hope Andy, you have no religious objections to this?"

"It's a paut ah my 'ligion Henry, to do whateveh I bleve right, an' shall sholy do dis, God being my helpah!"

"Now he's talkin!" said Charles.

"You must make your religion subserve your interests, as your oppressors do theirs!" advised Henry. "They use the Scriptures to make you submit, by preaching to you the texts of 'obedience to your masters' and 'standing still to see the salavation,' and we must now begin to understand the Bible so as to make it of interest to us."

"Dat's gospel talk," sanctioned Andy. "Is da anything else yeh want tell us boss – I calls 'im boss, 'case 'e aint nothing else but 'boss' – so we can make 'ase an' git to wuck? 'case I feels like goin' at 'em now, me!"

"Having accomplished our object, I think I have done, and must leave you tomorrow."

"When shall we hear from you, Henry?" enquired Charles.

"Not until you shall see me again; when that will be, I don't know. You may see me in six months, and might not not in eighteen. I am determined, now that I am driven to it, to complete an organization in every slave state before I return, and have fixed two years as my utmost limit."

"Henry, tell me before we part, do you know anything about little Joe?" enquired Charles.

"I do!"

"Wha's da chile?" enquired Andy.

"He's safe enough, on his way to Canada!" at which Charles and Andy laughed.

"Little Joe is on 'is way to Canada?" said Andy. "Mighty young travelah!"

"Yes," replied Henry with a smile.

"You're a-joking Henry?" said Charles, enquiringly.

"I am serious, brethren," replied he. "I do not joke in matters of this kind. I smiled because of Andy's surprise."

"How did 'e go?" further enquired Andy.

"In company with his 'mother' who was waiting on her 'mistress!'" replied he quaintly.

"Eh heh!" exclaimed Andy. "I knows all 'bout it now; but whah'd da 'mammy' come from?"

"I found one!"

"Aint 'e high!" said Andy.

"Well, brethren, my time is drawing to a close," said Henry, rising to his feet.

"O!" exclaimed Andy. "Ah like to forgot, has yeh any money Henry?"

"Have either of you any?"

"We has."

"How much?"

"I got two-three hundred dollahs!" replied Andy.

"An' so has I, Henry!" added Charles.

"Then keep it, as I have two thousand dollars now around my waist, and you'll find use for all you've got, and more, as you will before long have an opportunity of testing. Keep this studiously in mind and impress it as an important part of the scheme of organization, that they must have money, if they want to get free. Money will obtain them everything necessary by which to obtain their liberty. The money is within all of their reach if they only knew it was right to take it. God told the Egyptian slaves to 'borrow from their neighbors' – meaning their oppressors – 'all their jewels;' meaning to take their money and wealth wherever they could lay hands upon it, and depart from Egypt. So you must teach them to take all the money they can get from their masters, to enable them to make the strike without a failure. I'll show you when we leave for the North, what money will do for you, right here in Mississippi. Bear this in mind; it is your certain passport through the white gap, as I term it."

"I means to take all ah can git; I bin doin' dat dis some time. Ev'ry time ole Pottah leave 'is money pus, I borrys some, an' e' all'as lays it on Miss Mary, but 'e think so much uh huh, dat anything she do is right wid 'im. Ef 'e 'spected me, an' Miss Mary say 'twant me, dat would be 'nough fah 'im."

"That's right!" said Henry. "I see you have been putting your own interpretation on the Scriptures, Andy, and as Charles will now have to take my place, he'll have still a much better opportunity than you, to "borrow from his master.' "

"You needn't fear, I'll make good use of my time!" replied Charles.

The slaves now fell upon their knees in silent communion, all being affected to the shedding of tears, a period being put to their devotion by a sorrowful trembling of Henry's voice singing to the following touching words:

Farewell, farewell, farewell!
My loving friends farewell!
Farewell old comrades in the cause,
I leave you here, and journey on;
And if I never more return,
Farewell, I'm bound to meet you there!

"One word before we part," said Charles. "If we never should see you again, I suppose you intend to push on this scheme?"

"Yes!"

"Insurrection shall be my theme!

My watchword 'Freedom or the grave!'
Until from Rappahannock's stream,
To where the Cuato waters lave,
One simultaneous war cry
Shall burst upon the midnight air!
And rouse the tyrant but to sigh –
Mid sadness, wailing, and despair!"

Grasping each eagerly by the hand, the tears gushing from his eyes, with an humble bow, he bid them finally "farewell!" and the runaway was off through the forest.

Chapter XII
The Discovery

"IT CAN'T BE; I won't believe it!" said Franks at the breakfast table on Sunday morning, after hearing that little Joe was missed. "He certainly must be lost in the shrubbery."

After breakfast a thorough search was made, none being more industrious than Ailcey in hunting the little fugitive, but without success.

"When was he last seen?" enquired Franks.

"He wah put to bed las' night while we wuh at de suppeh seh!" replied Ailcey.

"There's something wrong about this thing, Mrs. Franks, and I'll be hanged if I don't ferret out the whole before I'm done with it!" said the Colonel.

"I hope you don't suspect me as—"

"Nonsense! my dear, not at all – nothing of the sort, but I do suspect respectable parties in another direction."

"Gracious, Colonel! Whom have you reference to? I'm sure I can't imagine."

"Well, well, we shall see! Ailcey, call Judy."

"Maus Stephen, yeh sen' fah me?" enquired the old woman, puffing and blowing.

"Yes, Judy. Do you know anything about little Joe? I want you to tell me the truth!" sternly enquired Franks.

"Maus Stephen! I cah lie! so long as yeh had me, yu nah missus neveh knows me tell lie. No, bless de Laud! Ah sen' my soul to de ole boy dat way? No maus Stephen, ah uhdn give wat I feels in my soul—"

"Well never mind, Judy, about your soul, but tell us about—"

"Ah! maus Stephen, ah 'spects to shout wen de wul's on fiah! an—"

"Tell us about the boy, Judy, and we'll hear about your religion another time."

"If you give her a little time, Colonel, I think she'll be able to tell about him!" suggested Mrs. Franks on seeing the old woman weeping.

"Sho, mammy!" said Ailcey in a whisper with a nudge, standing behind her, "wat yeh stan' heah cryin' befo' dese ole wite folks fah!"

"Come, come, Judy! what are you crying about! let us hear quickly what you've got to say. Don't be frightened!"

"No maus Stephen, I's not feahed; ah could run tru troop a hosses an' face de debil! My soul's happy, my soul's on fiah! Whoo! Blessed Jesus! Ride on, King!" when the old woman tossed and tumbled about so dexterously, that the master and mistress considered themselves lucky in getting out of the way.

"The old thing's crazy! We'll not be able to get anything out of her, Mrs. Franks."

"No maus Stephen, blessed be God a'mighty! I's not crazy, but sobeh as a judge! An—"

"Then let us hear about little Joe, as you can understand so well what is said around you, and let us have no more of your whooping and nonsense, distracting the neighborhood!"

"Blessed God! Blessed God! Laud sen' a nudah gale! O, fah a nudah showeh!"

"I really believe she's crazy! We've now been here over an hour, and no nearer the information than before."

"I think she's better now!" said Mrs. Franks.

"Judy, can you compose yourself long enough to answer my questions?" enquired Franks.

"O yes, mausta! ah knows wat I's 'bout, but w'en mausta Jesus calls, ebry body mus' stan' back, case 'e's 'bove all!"

"That's all right, Judy, all right; but let us hear about little Joe – do you know anything about him, where he is, or how he was taken away?"

"'E wah dah Sattiday night, maus Stephen."

"What time, Judy, on Saturday evening was he there?"

"W'en da wah eatin suppeh, seh."

"How do you know, when you were at the lower quarters, and he in your hut?"

"'E wah put to bed den."

"Who put him to bed – you?"

"No, seh, Ailcey."

"Ailcey – who went with her, any one?"

"Yes seh, Van Wintah Ben went wid uh."

"Van Winter's Ben! I thought we'd get at the thieves presently; I knew I'd ferret it out! Well now, Judy, I ask you as a Christian, and expect you to act with me as one Christian with another – has not Mrs. Van Winter been talking to you about this boy?"

"No seh, nebeh!"

"Nor to Henry?"

"No seh!"

"Did not she, to your knowledge, send Ben there that night to steal away little Joe?"

"No, seh!"

"Did you not hear Ailcey tell some one, or talking in her sleep, say that Mrs. Van Winter had something to do with the abduction of that boy?"

"Maus Stephen, ah do'n undehstan' dat duckin uh duckshun, dat w'at yeh call it – dat big wud!"

"O! 'abduction' means stealing away a person, Judy."

"Case ah waun gwine tell nothin 'bout it."

"Well, what do you know, Judy?"

"As dah's wud a troof in me, ah knows nothin' 'bout it."

"Well, Judy, you can go now. She's an honest old creature, I believe!" said Franks, as the old fat cook turned away.

"Yes, poor old black fat thing! She's religious to a fault," replied Mrs. Franks.

"Well, Ailcey, what do you know about it?" enquired the master.

"Nothin' seh, o'ny Mammy Judy ask me toat 'im up to da hut an' put 'im in bed."

"Well, did you do it?"

"Yes, seh!"

"Did Ben go with you?"

"Yes, seh!"

"Did he return with you to the lower quarters?"

"Yes, seh!"

"Did he not go back again, or did he remain in the house?"

"'E stay in."

"Did you not see some one lurking about the house when you took the boy up to the hut?"

"Ah tot ah heahn some un in da bushes, but Ben say 'twan no one."

"Now Ailcey, don't you know who that was?"

"No, seh!"

"Was'nt it old Joe?"

"No, seh, lef' 'im in de low quahteh."

"Was it Henry?"

"Dun no, seh!"

"Wasn't it Mrs. Van Winter's—"

"Why Colonel!" exclaimed Mrs. Franks with surprise.

"Negroes, I mean! You didn't let me finish the sentence, my dear!" explained he, correcting his error.

"Ah dun'o, seh!"

"Now tell me candidly, my girl, who and what you thought it was at the time?"

"Ah do'n like to tell!" replied the girl, looking down.

"Tell, Ailcey! Who do you think it was, and what they were after?" enquired Mrs. Franks.

"Ah do'n waun tell, missus!"

"Tell, you goose you! did you see any one?" continued Franks.

"Ah jis glance 'em."

"Was the person close to you?" further enquired Mrs. Franks.

"Yes, um, da toched me on da shouldeh an' run."

"Well, why don't you tell then, Ailcey, who you thought it was, and what they were after, you stubborn jade you, speak!" stormed Franks, stamping his foot.

"Don't get out of temper, Colonel! make some allowance for her under the circumstances. Now tell, Ailcey, what you thought at the time?" mildly asked Mrs. Franks.

"Ah tho't t'wah maus Stephen afteh me."

"Well, if you know nothing about it, you may go now!" gruffly replied her master. "These Negroes are not to be trusted. They will endeavor to screen each other if they have the least chance to do so. I'll sell that girl!"

"Colonel, don't be hasty in this matter, I beg of you!" said Mrs. Franks earnestly.

"I mean to let her go to the man she most hates, that's Crow."

"Why do you think she hates Crow so badly?"

"By the side looks she gives him when he comes into the house."

"I pray you then, Colonel, to attempt no more auction sales, and you may avoid unpleasant association in that direction."

"Yes, by the by, speaking of the auction, I really believe Mrs. Van Winter had something to do with the abduction of that little Negro."

"I think you do her wrong, Colonel Franks; she's our friend, and aside from this, I don't think her capable of such a thing."

"Such friendship is worse than open enmity, my dear, and should be studiously shunned."

"I must acquit her, Colonel, of all agency in this matter."

"Well, mark what I tell you, Mrs. Franks, you'll yet hear more of it, and that too at no distant day."

"Well it may be, but I can't think so."

"'May be'! I'm sure so. And more: I believe that boy has been induced to take advantage of my clemency, and run away. I'll make an example of him, because what one Negro succeeds in doing, another will attempt. I'll have him at any cost. Let him go on this way and there won't be a Negro in the neighborhood presently."

"Whom do you mean, Colonel?"

"I mean that ingrate Henry, that's who."

"Henry gone!"

"I have no doubt of it at all, as he had a pass to Woodville and Jackson; and now that the boy is stolen by someone, I've no doubt himself. I might have had some leniency towards him had he not committed a theft, a crime of all others the most detestable in my estimation."

"And Henry is really gone?" with surprise again enquired Mrs. Franks.

"He is, my dear, and you appear to be quite inquisitive about it!" remarked Franks as he thought he observed a concealed smile upon her lips.

"I am inquisitive, Colonel, because whatever interests you should interest me."

"By Monday evening, hanged if I don't know all about this thing. Ailcey, call Charles to get my saddle horse!"

"Charles ain' heah, maus Stephen."

"Where's old Joe?"

"At de hut, seh."

"Tell him to saddle Oscar immediately, and bring him to the door."

"Yes, seh!" replied the girl, lightly tripping away.

The horse was soon at the door, and with his rider cantering away.

"Tony, what is Mammy Judy about?" enquired Mrs. Franks as evening approached.

"She's sif'en meal, missus, to make mush fah ouah suppah."

"You must tell mammy not to forget me, Tony, in the distribution of her mush and milk."

"Yes, missus, ah tell uh right now!" when away ran Tony bearing the message, eager as are all children to be the agents of an act of kindness.

Mammy Judy, smiling, received the message with the assurance of "Yes, dat she shall hab much as she want!" when, turning about, she gave strict orders that Ailcey neglect not to have a china bowl in readiness to receive the first installment of the hasty pudding.

The hut of Mammy Judy served as a sort of headquarters on Saturday and Sunday evenings for the slaves from the plantation, and those in town belonging to the "estate," who this evening enjoyed a hearty laugh at the expense of Daddy Joe.

Slaves are not generally supplied with light in their huts; consequently, except from the fat of their meat and that gathered about the kitchen with which they make a "lamp," and the use of pinewood tapers, they eat and do everything about their dwellings in the dark.

Hasty pudding for the evening being the bill of fare, all sat patiently awaiting the summon of Mammy Judy, some on blocks, some on logs of wood, some on slab benches, some on inverted buckets and half-barrel wash tubs, and whatever was convenient, while many of the girls and other young people were seated on the floor around against the wall.

"Hush, chilen!" admonished Mammy Judy, after carefully seeing that each one down to Tony had been served with a quota from the kettle.

"Laud, make us truly tankful fah wat we 'bout to 'ceive!" petitioned Daddy Joe with uplifted hands. "Top dah wid yo' nause an' nonsense ole people cah heah deh yeahs to eat!" admonished the old man as he took the pewter dish between his knees and commenced an earnest discussion of its contents. "Do'n yeh heah me say hush dah? Do'n yeh heah!"

"Joe!" was the authoritative voice from without.

"Sah!"

"Take my horse to the stable!"

"Yes, sah!" responded the old man, sitting down his bowl of mush and milk on the hearth in the corner of the jam. "Do'n any on yeh toch dat, yeh heah?"

"We ain gwine to, Daddy Joe," replied the young people.

"Huccum de young folks, gwine eat yo' mush and milk? Sho, ole man, g'long whah yeh gwine, ad' let young folk 'lone!" retorted Mammy Judy.

On returning from the stable, in his hurry the old man took up the bowl of a young man who sat it on his stool for the moment.

"Yoheh, Daddy Joe, dat my mush!" said the young man.

"Huccum dis yone?" replied the old man.

"Wy, ah put it dah; yeh put yone in de chimbly connoh."

"Ah! Dat eh did!" exclaimed he, taking up the bowl eating heartily. "Wat dat yeh all been doin' heah? Some on yeh young folks been prankin' long wid dis mush an' milk!" continued the old man, champing and chewing in a manner which indicated something more solid than mush and milk.

"Deed we did'n, Daddy Joe; did'n do nothin' to yo' mush an' milk, so we did'n!" replied Ailcey, whose word was always sufficient with the old people.

"Hi, what dis in heah! Sumpen mighty crisp!" said Daddy Joe, still eating heartily and now and again blowing something from his mouth like coarse meal husks. "Sumpen heah mighty crisp, ah tells yeh! Ole umin, light dat pine knot dah; so dahk yeh cah'n see to talk. Git light dah quick ole umin! Sumpen heah mighty crisp in dis mush an' milk! – Mighty crisp!"

"Good Laud! see dah now! Ah tole yeh so!" exclaimed Mammy Judy when, on producing a light, the bowl was found to be partially filled with large black house roaches.

"Reckon Daddy Joe do'n tank'im fah dat!" said little Tony, referring to the blessing of the old man; amidst an outburst of tittering and snickering among the young people.

Daddy Joe lost his supper, when the slaves retired for the evening.

Chapter XIII
Perplexity

EARLY ON MONDAY morning Colonel Franks arose to start for Woodville and Jackson in search of the fugitive.

"My dear, is Ailcey up? Please call Tony," said Mrs. Franks, the boy soon appearing before his mistress. "Tony, call Ailcey," continued she, "your master is up and going to the country."

"Missus Ailcey ain' dah!" replied the boy, returning in haste from the nursery.

"Certainly she is; did you go into the nursery?"

"Yes, um!"

"Are the children there?"

"Yes, um, boph on 'em."

"Then she can't be far – she'll be in presently."

"Missus, she ain' come yit," repeated the boy after a short absence.

"Did you look in the nursery again?"

"Yes, um!"

"Are the children still in bed?"

"Yes, um, boph sleep, only maus George awake."

"You mean one asleep and the other awake!" said Mrs. Franks, smiling.

"Yes um boph wake!" replied the boy.

"Didn't you tell me, Tony, that your master George only was awake?" asked the mistress.

"Miss Matha sleep fus, den she wake up and talk to maus George," explained the boy, his master laughing, declared that a Negro's skull was too thick to comprehend anything.

"Don't mistake yourself, Colonel!" replied Mrs. Franks. "That boy is anything but a blockhead, mind that!"

"My dear, can't you see something about that girl?" said the Colonel.

"Run quickly, Tony, and see if Ailcey is in the hut," bade Mrs. Franks.

"Dear me," continued she, "since the missing of little Joe, she's all gossip, and we needn't expect much of her until the thing has died away."

"She'll not gossip after today, my dear!" replied the Colonel decisively, "as I'm determined to put her in my pocket in time, before she is decoyed away by that ungrateful wretch, who is doubtless ready for anything, however vile, for revenge."

Ailcey was a handsome black girl, graceful and intelligent, but having been raised on the place, had not the opportunity of a house maid for refinement. The Colonel, having had a favorable opinion of her as a servant, frequently requested that she be taken from the field, long before it had been done. This had not the most favorable impression upon the mind of his lady, who since the morning of the interview, the day before, had completely turned against the girl.

Mrs. Franks was an amiable lady and lenient mistress, but did a slave offend, she might be expected to act as a mistress; and still more, she was a woman; but concerning Ailcey she was mistaken, as a better and more pure-hearted female slave there was not to be found; and as true to her mistress and her honor, as was Maggie herself.

"Missus, she ain't dare nudder! aun' Judy ain seed 'er from las' night!" said the boy who came running up the stairs.

"Then call Charles immediately!" ordered she; when away went he and shortly came Charles.

"Servant, mist'ess!" saluted Charles, as he entered her presence.

"Charles, do you know anything of Ailcey?" enquired she.

"No mist'ess I don't."

"When did you see her last?"

"Last night, ma'm."

"Was she in company with anyone?"

"Yes ma'm, Potter's Rachel."

"What time in the evening was it, Charles?"

"After seven o'clock, ma'm."

"O, she was home after that and went to bed in the nursery, where she has been sleeping for several nights."

"My dear, this thing must be probed to the bottom at once! things are taking such a strange course, that we don't know whom to trust. I'll be hanged if I understand it!" The carriage being ordered, they went directly down to 'squire Potter's.

"Good morning Mrs. Potter! – you will pardon us for the intrusion at so early an hour, but as the errand may concern us all, I'll not stop to be ceremonious – do I find the 'squire in?"

The answer being in the affirmative, a servant being in attendance, the old gentleman soon made his appearance.

"Good morning, Colonel and Madam Franks!" saluted he.

"Good morning, 'squire! I shan't be ceremonious, and to give you a history of my errand, and to make a short story of a long one, we'll 'make a lump job of it,' to use a homely phrase."

"I know the 'squire will be interested!" added Mrs. Franks.

"No doubt of it at all, ma'm!" replied Mrs. Potter, who seemed to anticipate them.

"It is this," resumed the Colonel. "On Friday I gave my boy Henry verbal permission to go to the country, when he pretended to leave. On Saturday evening during the Negro-gathering at the old quarters, my little Negro boy Joe was stolen away, and on last evening, our Negro girl Ailcey the nurse, cleared out, and it seems was last seen in company with your Negro girl Rachel."

"Titus, call Rachel there! No doubt but white men are at the bottom of it," said Potter.

"Missus, heah I is!" drawled the girl awkwardly, with a curtsy.

"Speak to your master there; he wants you," ordered Mrs. Potter.

"Mausta!" saluted the girl.

"Rachel, my girl, I want you to tell me, were you with Colonel Franks' black girl Ailcey on last evening?"

"Yes seh, I wah."

"Where, Rachel?" continued the master.

"Heah seh, at ouah house."

"Where did you go to?"

"We go down to docteh Denny."

"What for – what took you down to Dr. Denny's, Rachel?"

"Went 'long wid Ailcey."

"What did Ailcey go there for – do you know?"

"Went dah to see Craig' Polly."

"Craig's Polly, which of Mr. Craig's Negro girls is that?"

"Dat un w'ot mos' white."

"Well, was Polly there?"

"She waun dah w'en we go, but she soon come."

"Why did you go to Dr. Denny's to meet Polly?"

"Ailcey say Polly go'n to meet uh dah."

"Well, did they leave there when you did?"

"Yes, seh."

"Where did you go to then?"

"I come home, seh."

"Where did they go?"

"Da say da go'n down undah da Hill."

"Who else was with them besides you?"

"No un, seh."

"Was there no man with them, when they left for under the Hill?"

"No, seh."

"Did you see no man about at all, Rachel?"

"No, seh."

"Now don't be afraid to tell: was there no white person at all spoke to you when together last night?"

"None but some white gent'men come up an' want walk wid us, same like da al'as do we black girls w'en we go out."

"Did the girls seem to be acquainted and glad to see them?"

"No seh, the girls run, and da gent'men cus—"

"Never mind that, Rachel, you can go now," concluded her master.

"Well, 'squire, hanged if this thing mus'nt be stopped! Four slaves in less than that many days gone from under our very eyes, and we unable to detect them! It's insufferable, and I believe whites to be at the head of it! I have my suspicions on a party who stands high in the community, and—"

"Now Colonel, if you please!" interrupted Mrs. Franks.

"Well, I suppose we'll have for the present to pass that by," replied he.

"Indeed, something really should be done!" said the 'squire.

"Yes, and that quickly, if we would keep our Negroes to prevent us from starving."

"I think the thing should at once be seen into; what say you, Colonel?"

"As I have several miles to ride this morning," said Franks, looking at his watch, it now being past nine o'clock, "I must leave so as to be back in the evening. Any steps that may be taken before my return, you have the free use of my name. Good morning!"

A few minutes and the Colonel was at his own door, astride of a horse, and on his way to Woodville.

Chapter XIV
Gad and Gossip

THIS DAY the hut of Mammy Judy seemed to be the licensed resort for all the slaves of the town; and even many whites were seen occasionally to drop in and out, as they passed along. Everyone knew the residence of Colonel Franks, and many of the dusky inhabitants of the place were solely indebted to the purse-proud occupants of the "great house" for their introduction to that part of Mississippi.

For years he and Major Armsted were the only reliable traders upon whom could be depended for a choice gang of field Negroes and other marketable people. And not only this section, but the whole Mississippi Valley to some extent was to them indebted. First as young men the agents of Woolford, in maturer age their names became as household words and known as the great proprietary Mississippi or Georgia Negro-traders.

Domestic service seemed for the time suspended, and little required at home to do, as the day was spent as a kind of gala-day, in going about from place to place talking of everything.

Among the foremost of these was Mammy Judy, for although she partially did, and was expected to stay and be at home today, and act as an oracle, yet she merely stole a little time to run over to Mrs. Van Winter's, step in at 'squire Potter's to speak a word to Milly, drop by Dr. Denny's, and just poke in her head at Craig's a moment.

"Ah been tellin' on 'em so! All along ah been tellin' on 'em, but da uden bleve me!" soliloquized Mammy Judy, when the first dash of news through the boy Tony reached her, that Ailcey had gone and taken with her some of 'squire Potter's people, several of Dr. Denny's, a gang of Craig's, and half of Van Winter's. "Dat jis wat ah been tellin' on 'em all along, but da uden bleve me!" concluded she.

"Yeah heah de news!" exclaimed Potter's Minney to Van Winter's Biddy.

"I heah dat Ailcey gone!" replied Biddy.

"Dat all; no mo?" enquired the girl with a high turban of Madras on her head.

"I heahn little Joe go too!"

"Didn yeh heah dot Denny' Sookey, an' Craig' Polly, took a whole heap uh Potteh' people an' clah'd out wid two po' white mens, an' dat da all seen comin' out Van Winteh de old ablish'neh, soon in de monin' fo' day?"

"No!" replied the good-natured, simple-hearted Biddy, "I did'n!"

"Yes, sho's yeh baun dat true, case uhly dis monin' cunel Frank' an' lady come see mausta – and yeh know 'e squiah an' make de law – an' mauster ghin 'em papehs, an' da go arter de Judge to put heh in jail!"

"Take who to jail?"

"Wy, dat ole ablish'neh, Miss Van Winteh! Ah wish da all dead, dese ole ablish'nehs, case da steal us an' sell us down souph to haud maustas, w'en we got good places. Any how she go'n to jail, an' I's glad!"

Looking seriously at her, Biddy gave a long sigh, saying nothing to commit herself, but going home, communicated directly to her mistress that which she heard, as Mrs. Van Winter was by all regarded as a friend to the Negro race, and at that time the subject of strong suspicion among the slaveholders of the neighborhood.

Eager to gad and gossip, from place to place the girl Minney passed about relating the same to each and all with whom she chanced to converse, they imparting to others the same strange story, until reaching the ears of intelligent whites who had heard no other version, it spread through the city as a statement of fact.

Learning as many did by sending to the house, that the Colonel that day had gone in search of his slaves, the statement was confirmed as having come from Mrs. Franks, who was known to be a firm friend of Mrs. Van Winter.

"Upon my word!" said Captain Grason on meeting Sheriff Hughes. "Sheriff, things are coming to a pretty pass!"

"What's that, Captain?" enquired the Sheriff.

"Have you not heard the news yet, concerning the Negroes?"

"Why, no! I've been away to Vicksburg the last ten days, and just getting back."

"O, Heavens! we're no longer safe in our own houses. Why, sir, we're about being overwhelmed by an infamous class of persons who live in our midst, and eat at our tables!"

"You surprise me, Captain! what's the matter?"

"Sir, it would take a week to relate the particulars, but our slaves are running off by wholesale. On Sunday night a parcel of Colonel Franks' Negroes left, a lot of Dr. Denny's, some of 'squire Potter's, and a gang of Craig's, aided by white men, whom together with the Negroes were seen before day in the morning coming out of the widow Van Winters, who was afterwards arrested, and since taken before the judge on a writ of habeas corpus, but the circumstances against her being so strong she was remanded for trial, which so far strengthens the accusation. I know not where this thing will end!"

"Surprising indeed, sir!" replied Hughes. "I had not heard of it before, but shall immediately repair to her house, and learn all the facts in the case. I am well acquainted with Mrs. Van Winter – in fact she is a relation of my wife – and must hasten. Good day, sir!"

On ringing the bell, a quick step brought a person to the door, when on being opened, the Sheriff found himself in the warm embraces of the kind-hearted and affectionate Mrs. Van Winter herself.

After the usual civilities, she was the first to introduce the subject, informing him of their loss by their mutual friends Colonel Franks and lady, with others, and no surprise was greater than that on hearing the story current concerning herself.

Mammy Judy was as busy as she well could be, in hearing and telling news among the slaves who continually came and went through the day. So overwhelmed with excitement was she, that she had little else to say in making a period, then "All a long ah been tellin' on yeh so, but yeh uden bleve me!"

Among the many who thronged the hut was Potter's Milly. She in person is black, stout and fat, bearing a striking resemblance to the matronly old occupant Mammy Judy. For two hours or more letting a number come in, gossip, and pass out, only to be immediately succeeded by another; who like the old country woman who for the first time in visiting London all day stood upon the sidewalk of the principal thoroughfare waiting till the crowd of people and cavalcade of vehicles passed, before she made the attempt to cross the street; she sat waiting till a moment would occur by which in private to impart a secret to her friend alone. That moment did at last arrive.

"Judy!" said the old woman in a whisper. "Ah been waitin' all day long to see yeh fah sumpen' ticlar!"

"W'at dat, Milly?" whispered Mammy Judy scarcely above her breath.

"I's gwine too!" and she hurried away to prepare supper for the white folks, before they missed her, though she had been absent full two hours and a half, another thirty minutes being required for the fat old woman to reach the house.

"Heah dat now!" whispered Mammy Judy. "Ah tole yeh so!"

"Well, my dear, not a word of that graceless dog, the little Negro, nor that girl," said Franks who had just returned from the country, "but I am fully compensated for the disappointment, on learning of the arrest and imprisonment of that—!"

"Who, Colonel?" interrupted his wife.

"I hope after this you'll be willing to set some estimation on my judgment – I mean your friend Mrs. Van Winter the abolitionist!"

"I beg your pardon, Colonel, as nothing is farther from the truth! From whom did you receive that intelligence?"

"I met Captain Grason on his way to Woodville, who informed me that it was current in town, and you had corroborated the statement. Did you see him?"

"Nothing of the kind, sir, and it has not been more than half an hour since Mrs. Van Winter left here, who heartily sympathizes with us, though she has her strange notions that black people have as much right to freedom as white."

"Well, my dear, we'll drop the subject!" concluded the Colonel with much apparent disappointment.

The leading gentlemen of the town and neighborhood assembled inaugurating the strictest vigilant police regulations, when after free and frequent potations of brandy and water, of which there was no scarcity about the Colonel's mansion, the company separated, being much higher spirited, if not better satisfied, than when they met in council.

This evening Charles and Andy met each other in the street, but in consequence of the strict injunction on the slaves by the patrol law recently instituted, they only made signs as they passed, intending to meet at a designated point. But the patrol reconnoitred so closely in their track, they were driven entirely from their purpose, retiring to their homes for the night.

Chapter XV
Interchange of Opinion

THE LANDING of a steamer on her downward trip brought Judge Ballard and Major Armsted to Natchez. The Judge had come to examine the country, purchase a cotton farm, and complete the arrangements of an interest in the "Merchantman." Already the proprietor of a large estate in Cuba, he was desirous of possessing a Mississippi cotton place. Disappointed by the absence of his wife abroad, he was satisfied to know that her object was accomplished.

Major Armsted was a man of ripe intelligence, acquired by years of rigid experience and close observation, rather than literary culture, though his educational attainments as a business man were quite respectable. He for years had been the partner in business with Colonel Stephen Franks. In Baltimore, Washington City, Annapolis, Richmond, Norfolk, Charlestown, and Winchester, Virginia, a prison or receptacle for coffle-gangs of slaves purchased and sold in the market, comprised their principal places of business in the slaveowning states of the Union.

The Major was a great jester, full of humor, and fond of a good joke, ever ready to give and take such even from a slave. A great common sense man, by strict attention to men and things, and general observation, had become a philosopher among his fellows.

"Quite happy to meet you, Judge, in these parts!" greeted Franks. "Wonder you could find your way so far south, especially at such a period, these being election times!"

"Don't matter a bit, as he's not up for anything I believe just now, except for Negro-trading! And in that he is quite a proselyte, and heretic to the teachings of his Northern faith!" jocosely remarked Armsted.

"Don't mistake me, gentlemen, because it was the incident of my life to be born in a nonslaveholding state. I'm certain that I am not at all understood as I should be on this question!" earnestly replied the Judge.

"The North has given you a bad name, Judge, and it's difficult to separate yourself now from it, holding the position that you do, as one of her ablest jurists," said Armsted.

"Well, gentlemen!" seriously replied the Judge. "As regards my opinion of Negro slavery, the circumstances which brought me here, my large interest and responsibility in the slave-labor products of Cuba, should be, I think, sufficient evidence of my fidelity to Southern principles, to say nothing of my official records, which modesty should forbid my reference to."

"Certainly, certainly, Judge! The Colonel is at fault. He has lost sight of the fact that you it was who seized the first runaway Negro by the throat and held him by the compromise grasp until we Southern gentlemen sent for him and had him brought back!"

"Good, good, by hookie!" replied the Colonel, rubbing his hands together.

"I hope I'm understood, gentlemen!" seriously remarked the Judge.

"I think so, Judge, I think so!" replied Armsted, evidently designing a full commitment on the part of the Judge. "And if not, a little explanation will set us right."

"It is true that I have not before been engaged in the slave trade, because until recently I had conscientious scruples about the thing – and I suppose I'm allowed the right of conscience as well as other folks," smilingly said the Judge, "never having purchased but for peopling my own plantation. But a little sober reflection set me right on that point. It is plain that the right to buy implies the right to hold, also to sell; and if there be right in the one, there is in the other; the premise being right, the conclusion follows as a matter of course. I have therefore determined, not only to buy and hold, but buy and sell also. As I have heretofore been interested for the trade I will become interested in it."

"Capital, capital, by George! That's conclusive. Charles! A pitcher of cool water here; Judge, take another glass of brandy."

"Good, very good!" said Armsted. "So far, but there is such a thing as feeding out of two cribs – present company, you know, and so – ahem! – therefore we should like to hear the Judge's opinion of equality, what it means anyhow. I'm anxious to learn some of the doctrines of human rights, not knowing how soon I may be called upon to practice them, as I may yet marry some little Yankee girl, full of her Puritan notions. And I'm told an old bachelor 'can't come it' up that way, except he has a 'pocket full of rocks,' and can talk philanthropy like old Wilberforce."

"Here, gentlemen, I beg to make an episode, before replying to Major Armsted," suggested the Judge. "His jest concerning the Yankee girl reminds me – and I hope it may not be amiss in saying so – that my lady is the daughter of a clergyman, brought up amidst the sand of New England, and I think I'll not have to go from the present company to prove her a good slaveholder. So the Major may see that we northerners are not all alike."

"How about the Compromise measures, Judge? Stand up to the thing all through, and no flinching."

"My opinion, sir, is a matter of record, being the first judge before whom a case was tested, which resulted in favor of the South. And I go further than this; I hold as a just construction of the law, that not only has the slaveholder a right to reclaim his slave when and wherever found, but by its provision every free black in the country, North and South, are liable to enslavement by any white person. They are freemen by sufferance or slaves-at-large, whom any white person may claim at discretion. It was a just decision of the Supreme Court – though I was in advance of it by action – that persons of African descent have no rights that white men are bound to respect!"

"Judge Ballard, with this explanation, I am satisfied; indeed as a Southern man I would say, that you've conceded all that I could ask, and more than we expected. But this is a legal disquisition; what is your private opinion respecting the justice of the measures?"

"I think them right, sir, according to our system of government."

"But how will you get away from your representative system, Judge? In this your blacks are either voters, or reckoned among the inhabitants."

"Very well, sir, they stand in the same relation as your Negroes. In some of the states they are permitted to vote, but can't be voted for, and this leaves them without any political rights at all. Suffrage, sir, is one thing, franchisement another; the one a mere privilege – a thing permitted – the other a right inherent, that which is inviolable – cannot be interfered with. And my good sir, enumeration is a national measure, for which we are not sectionally responsible."

"Well, Judge, I'm compelled to admit that you are a very good Southerner; upon the whole, you are severe upon the Negroes; you seem to allow them no chance."

"I like Negroes well enough in their place!"

"How can you reconcile yourself to the state of things in Cuba, where the blacks enter largely into the social system?"

"I don't like it at all, and never could become reconciled to the state of things there. I consider that colony as it now stands, a moral pestilence, a blighting curse, and it is useless to endeavor to disguise the fact; Cuba must cease to be a Spanish colony, and become American territory. Those mongrel Creoles are incapable of self-government, and should be compelled to submit to the United States."

"Well, Judge, admit the latter part of that, as I rather guess we are all of the same way of thinking – how do you manage to get on with society when you are there?"

"I cannot for a moment tolerate it! One of the hateful customs of the place is that you must exchange civilities with whomsoever solicits it, consequently, the most stupid and ugly Negro you meet in the street may ask for a 'light' from your cigar."

"I know it, and I invariably comply with the request. How do you act in such cases?"

"I invariably comply, but as invariably throw away my cigar! If this were all, it would not be so bad, then the idea of meeting Negroes and mulattoes at the levees of the Captain General is intolerable! It will never do to permit this state of things so near our own shores."

"Why throw away the cigar, Judge? What objection could there be to it because a negro took a light from it?"

"Because they are certain to take hold of it with their black fingers!"

"Just as I've always heard, Judge Ballard. You Northerners are a great deal more fastidious about Negroes than we of the South, and you'll pardon me if I add, 'more nice than wise,' to use a homily. Did ever it occur to you that black fingers made that cigar, before it entered your white lips! – all tobacco preparations being worked by Negro hands in Cuba – and very frequently in closing up the wrapper, they draw it through their lips to give it tenacity."

"The deuce! Is that a fact, Major!"

"Does that surprise you, Judge? I'm sure the victuals you eat is cooked by black hands, the bread kneaded and made by black hands, and the sugar and molasses you use, all pass through black hands, or rather the hands of Negroes pass through them; at least you could not refrain from thinking so, had you seen them as I have frequently, with arms full length immersed in molasses."

"Well, Major, truly there are some things we are obliged to swallow, and I suppose these are among them."

"Though a Judge, Your Honor, you perceive that there are some things you have not learned."

"True, Major, true; and I like the Negro well enough in his place, but there is a disposition peculiar to the race, to shove themselves into the notice of the whites."

"Not peculiar to them, Judge, but common to mankind. The black man desires association with the white, because the latter is regarded his superior. In the South it is the poor white man with the wealthy, and in Europe the common with the gentlefolks. In the North you have not made these distinctions among the whites, which prevents you from noticing this trait among yourselves."

"Tell me, Major, as you seem so well to understand them, why a Negro swells so soon into importance?"

"Simply because he's just like you, Judge, and I! It is simply a manifestation of human nature in an humble position, the same as that developed in the breast of a conqueror. Our strictures are not just on this unfortunate race, as we condemn in them that which we approve in ourselves. Southerner as I am, I can joke with a slave just because he is a man; some of them indeed, fine warmhearted fellows, and intelligent, as was the Colonel's Henry."

"I can't swallow that, Major! Joking with a Negro is rather too large a dose for me!"

"Let me give you an idea of my feeling about these things: I have on my place two good-natured black fellows, full of pranks and jokes – Bob and Jef. Passing along one morning Jef was approaching me, when just as we met and I was about to give him the time of day, he made a sudden halt, placing himself in the attitude of a pugilist, grasping the muscle of his left arm, looking me full in the eyes exclaimed, 'Maus Army, my arm aches for you!' when stepping aside he gave the path for me to pass by."

"Did you not rebuke him for the impudence?"

"I laid my hand upon his shoulders as we passed, and gave him a laugh instead. At another time, passing along in company, Bob was righting up a section of fence, when Jef came along. 'How is yeh, Jef?' saluted Bob, without a response. Supposing he had not seen me, I hallooed out: 'How are you Jef!' but to this, he made no reply. A gentleman in company with me who enjoyed the joke, said: 'Why Jef, you appear to be above speaking to your old friends!' Throwing his head slightly down with a rocking motion in his walk, elongating his mouth after the manner of a sausage – which by the way needed no improvement in that direction – in a tone of importance still looking down he exclaimed, 'I totes a meat!' He had indeed, a fine gammon on his shoulder from which that evening, he doubtless intended a good supper with his wife, which made him feel important, just as Judge Ballard feels, when he receives the news that 'sugar is up,' and contemplates large profits from his crop of that season."

"I'll be plagued, Major, if your love of the ludicrous don't induce you to give the freest possible license to your Negroes! I wonder they respect you!"

"One thing, Judge, I have learned by my intercourse with men, that pleasantry is the life and soul of the social system; and good treatment begets more labor from the slave than bad. A smile from the master is better than cross looks, and one crack of a joke with him is worth a hundred cracks of the whip. Only confide in him, and let him be satisfied that you respect him as a man, he'll work himself to death to prove his worthiness."

"After all, Major, you still hold them as slaves, though you claim for them the common rights of other people!"

"Certainly! And I would just as readily hold a white as a black in slavery, were it the custom and policy of the country to do so. It is all a matter of self-interest with me; and though I am morally opposed to slavery, yet while the thing exists, I may as well profit by it, as others."

"Well, Major," concluded the Judge, "let us drop the subject, and I hope that the free interchange of opinion will prove no detriment to our future prospects and continued friendship."

"Not at all, sir, not at all!" concluded the Major with a smile.

Chapter XVI
Solicitude and Amusement

MRS. FRANKS SOUGHT the earliest opportunity for an interview with the Major concerning her favorite, Maggie. The children now missed her, little George continued fretful, and her own troubled soul was pressed with anxiety.

On conversing with the Major, to her great surprise she learned that the maid had been sold to a stranger, which intelligence he received from Mrs. Ballard herself, whom he met on the quay as he left Havana. The purchaser was a planter formerly of Louisiana, a bachelor by the name of Peter Labonier. This person resided twelve miles from Havana, the proprietor of a sugar estate.

The apprehension of Mrs. Franks, on learning these facts, were aroused to a point of fearful anxiety. These fears were mitigated by the probable chance, in her favor by a change of owners, as his first day's possession of her, turned him entirely against her. He would thus most probably part with her, which favored the desires of Mrs. Franks.

She urged upon the Major as a favor to herself, to procure the release of Maggie, by his purchase and enfranchisement with free papers of unconditional emancipation.

To this Major Armsted gave the fullest assurance, at the earliest possible opportunity. The company were to meet at no distant day, when he hoped to execute the orders.

"How did you leave cousin Arabella, Judge?" enquired Mrs. Franks, as he and the Colonel entered the parlor directly from the back porch, where they had been engaged for the last two hours in close conversation.

"Very well, Maria, when last heard from; a letter reaching me just before I left by the kindness of our mutual friend the Major. By the way, your girl and she did not get on so well, I be—!"

An admonitory look from Franks arrested the subject before the sentence was completed.

Every reference to the subject was carefully avoided, though the Colonel ventured to declare that henceforth towards his servants, instead of leniency, he intended severity. They were becoming every day more and more troublesome, and less reliable. He intended, in the language of his friend the Judge, to "lay upon them a heavy hand" in future.

"I know your sentiments on this point," he said in reply to an admonition from Armsted, "and I used to entertain the same views, but experience has taught me better."

"I shall not argue the point Colonel, but let you have your own way!" replied Armsted.

"Well, Judge, as you wish to become a Southerner; you must first 'see the sights,' as children say, and learn to get used to them. I wish you to ride out with me to Captain Grason's, and you'll see some rare sport; the most amusing thing I ever witnessed," suggested Franks.

"What is it?" enquired the Major.

"The effect is lost by previous knowledge of the thing," replied he. "This will suit you, Armsted, as you're fond of Negro jokes."

"Then, Colonel, let's be off," urged the Major.

"Off it is!" replied Franks, as he invited the gentlemen to take a seat in the carriage already at the door.

"Halloo, halloo, here you are, Colonel! Why Major Armsted, old fellow, 'pon my word!" saluted Grason, grasping Armsted by the hand as they entered the porch.

"Judge Ballard, sir," said Armsted.

"Just in time for dinner, gentlemen! Be seated," invited he, holding the Judge by the hand. "Welcome to Mississippi, Sir! What's up, gentlemen?"

"We've come out to witness some rare sport the Colonel has been telling us about," replied the Major.

"Blamed if I don't think the Colonel will have me advertised as a showman presently! I've got a queer animal here; I'll show him to you after dinner," rejoined Grason. "Gentlemen, help yourself to brandy and water."

Dinner over, the gentlemen walked into the pleasure grounds, in the rear of the mansion.

"Nelse, where is Rube? Call him!" said Grason to a slave lad, brother to the boy he sent for.

Shortly there came forward, a small black boy about eleven years of age, thin visage, projecting upper teeth, rather ghastly consumptive look, and emaciated condition. The child trembled with fear as he approached the group.

"Now gentlemen," said Grason, "I'm going to show you a sight!" having in his hand a long whip, the cracking of which he commenced, as a ringmaster in the circus.

The child gave him a look never to be forgotten; a look beseeching mercy and compassion. But the decree was made, and though humanity quailed in dejected supplication before him, the command was imperative, with no living hand to stay the pending consequences. He must submit to his fate, and pass through the ordeal of training.

"Wat maus gwine do wid me now? I know wat maus gwine do," said this miserable child, "he gwine make me see sights!" when going down on his hands and feet, he commenced trotting around like an animal.

"Now gentlemen, look!" said Grason. "He'll whistle, sing songs, hymns, pray, swear like a trooper, laugh, and cry, all under the same state of feelings."

With a peculiar swing of the whip, bringing the lash down upon a certain spot on the exposed skin, the whole person being prepared for the purpose, the boy commenced to whistle almost like a thrush; another cut changed it to a song, another to a hymn, then a pitiful prayer, when he gave utterance to oaths which would make a Christian shudder, after which he laughed outright; then from the fullness of his soul he cried:

"O maussa, I's sick! Please stop little!" casting up gobs of hemorrhage.

Franks stood looking on with unmoved muscles. Armsted stood aside whittling a stick; but when Ballard saw, at every cut the flesh turn open in gashes streaming down with gore, till at last in agony he appealed for mercy, he involuntarily found his hand with a grasp on the whip, arresting its further application.

"Not quite a Southerner yet Judge, if you can't stand that!" said Franks on seeing him wiping away the tears.

"Gentlemen, help yourself to brandy and water. The little Negro don't stand it nigh so well as formerly. He used to be a trump!"

"Well, Colonel," said the Judge, "as I have to leave for Jackson this evening, I suggest that we return to the city."

The company now left Grason's, Franks for the enjoyment of home, Ballard and Armsted for Jackson, and the poor boy Reuben, from hemorrhage of the lungs, that evening left time for eternity.

Chapter XVII
Henry at Large

ON LEAVING the plantation carrying them hanging upon his arm, thrown across his shoulders, and in his hands Henry had a bridle, halter, blanket, girt, and horsewhip, the emblems of a faithful servant in discharge of his master's business.

By shrewdness and discretion – such was his management as he passed along – that he could tell the name of each place and proprietor long before he reached them. Being a scholar, he carefully kept a record of the plantations he had passed, that when accosted by a white, as an overseer or patrol, he invariably pretended to belong to a back estate, in search of his master's racehorse. If crossing a field, he was taking a near cut; but if met in a wood, the animal was in the forest, as being a great leaper no fence could debar him, though the forest was fenced and posted. The blanket, a substitute for a saddle, was in reality carried for a bed.

With speed unfaltering and spirits unflinching, his first great strive was to reach the Red River, to escape from his own state as quickly as possible. Proceeding on in the direction of the Red River country, he met with no obstruction except in one instance, when he left his assailant quietly upon the earth. A few days after an inquest was held upon the body of a deceased overseer – verdict of the Jury, "By hands unknown."

On approaching the river, after crossing a number of streams, as the Yazoo, Ouchita, and such, he was brought to sad reflections. A dread came over him, difficulties lay before him, dangers stood staring him in the face at every step he took. Here for the first time since his maturity of manhood responsibilities rose up in a shape of which he had no conception. A mighty undertaking, such as had never before been ventured upon, and the duty devolving upon him, was too much for a slave with no other aid than the aspirations of his soul panting for liberty. Reflecting upon the peaceful hours he once enjoyed as a professing Christian, and the distance which slavery had driven him from its peaceful portals, here in the wilderness, determining to renew his faith and dependence upon Divine aid, when falling upon his knees he opened his heart to God, as a tenement of the Holy Spirit.

"Arm of the Lord, awake! Renew my faith, confirm my hope, perfect me in love. Give strength, give courage, guide and protect my pathway, and direct me in my course!" Springing to his feet as if a weight had fallen from him, he stood up a new man.

The river is narrow, the water red as if colored by iron rust, the channel winding. Beyond this river lie his hopes, the broad plains of Louisiana with a hundred thousand bondsmen seeming anxiously to await him.

Standing upon a high bank of the stream, contemplating his mission, a feeling of humbleness and a sensibility of unworthiness impressed him, and that religious sentiment which once gave comfort to his soul now inspiring anew his breast, Henry raised in solemn tones amidst the lonely wilderness:

> *Could I but climb where Moses stood,*
> *And view the landscape o'er;*
> *Not Jordan's streams, nor death's cold flood,*
> *Could drive me from the shore!*

To the right of where he stood was a cove, formed by the washing of the stream at high water, which ran quite into the thicket, into which the sun shone through a space among the high trees.

While thus standing and contemplating his position, the water being too deep to wade, and on account of numerous sharks and alligators, too dangerous to swim, his attention was attracted by the sound of a steamer coming up the channel. Running into the cove to shield himself, a singular noise disturbed him, when to his terror he found himself amidst a squad of huge alligators, which sought the advantages of the sunshine.

His first impulse was to surrender himself to his fate and be devoured, as in the rear and either side the bank was perpendicular, escape being impossible except by the way he entered, to do which would have exposed him to the view of the boat, which could not have been avoided. Meantime the frightful animals were crawling over and among each other, at a fearful rate.

Seizing the fragment of a limb which lay in the cove, beating upon the ground and yelling like a madman, giving them all possible space, the beasts were frightened at such a rate, that they reached the water in less time than Henry reached the bank. Receding into the forest, he thus escaped the observation of the passing steamer, his escape serving to strengthen his fate in a renewed determination of spiritual dependence.

While gazing upon the stream in solemn reflection for Divine aid to direct him, logs came floating down, which suggested a proximity to the raft with which sections of that stream is filled, when going but a short distance up, he crossed in safety to the Louisiana side. His faith was now fully established, and thenceforth, Henry was full of hope and confident of success.

Reaching Alexandria with no obstruction, his first secret meeting was held in the hut of aunt Dilly. Here he found them all ready for an issue.

"An dis you, chile?" said the old woman, stooping with age, sitting on a low stool in the chimney corner. "Dis many day, I heahn on yeh!" though Henry had just entered on his mission. From Alexandria he passed rapidly on to Latuer's, making no immediate stops, prefering to organize at the more prominent places.

This is a mulatto planter, said to have come from the isle of Guadaloupe. Riding down the road upon a pony at a quick gallop was a mulatto youth, a son of the planter, an old black man on foot keeping close to the horse's heels.

"Whose boy are you?" enquired the young mulatto, who had just dismounted, the old servant holding his pony.

"I'm in search of master's race horse."

"What is your name?" further enquired the young mulatto.

"Gilbert, sir."

"What do you want?"

"I am hungry, sir."

"Dolly," said he to an old black woman at the woodpile, "show this man into the Negro quarter, and give him something to eat; give him a cup of milk. Do you like milk, my man?"

"Yes, sir, I have no choice when hungry; anything will do."

"Da is none heah but claubah, maus Eugene," replied the old cook.

"Give him that," said the young master. "You people like that kind of stuff I believe; our Negroes like it."

"Yes, sir," replied Henry when the lad left.

"God knows 'e needn' talk 'bout wat we po' black folks eat, case da don' ghin us nothin' else but dat an' caun bread," muttered the old woman.

"Don't they treat you well, aunty?" enquired Henry.

"God on'y knows, my chile, wat we suffeh."

"Who was that old man who ran behind your master's horse?"

"Dat Nathan, my husban'."

"Do they treat him well, aunty?"

"No, chile, wus an' any dog, da beat 'im foh little an nothin'."

"Is uncle Nathan religious?"

"Yes, chile, ole man an' I's been sahvin' God dis many day, fo yeh baun! Wen any one on 'em in de house git sick, den da sen foh 'uncle Nathan' come pray foh dem; 'uncle Nathan' mighty good den!"

"Do you know that the Latuers are colored people?"

"Yes, chile; God bless yeh soul yes! Case huh mammy ony dead two-three yehs, an' she black as me."

"How did they treat her?"

"Not berry well; she nus da childen; an eat in a house arter all done."

"What did Latuer's children call her?"

"Da call huh 'mammy' same like wite folks childen call de nus."

"Can you tell me, aunty, why they treat you people so badly, knowing themselves to be colored, and some of the slaves related to them?"

"God bless yeh, hunny, de wite folks, dese plantehs make 'em so; da run heah, an' tell 'em da mus'n treat deh niggers well, case da spile 'em."

"Do the white planters frequently visit here?"

"Yes, hunny, yes, da heah some on 'em all de time eatin' an' drinkin' long wid de old man; da on'y tryin' git wat little 'e got, dat all! Da 'tend to be great frien' de ole man; but laws a massy, hunny, I doh mine dese wite folks no how!"

"Does your master ever go to their houses and eat with them?"

"Yes, chile, some time 'e go, but den half on 'em got nothin' fit to eat; da hab fat poke an' bean, caun cake an' sich like, dat all da got, some on 'em."

"Does Mr. Latuer give them better at his table?"

"Laws, hunny, yes; yes'n deed, chile! 'E got mutton – some time whole sheep mos' – fowl, pig, an' ebery tum ting a nuddeh, 'e got so much ting dah, I haudly know wat cook fus."

"Do the white planters associate with the family of Latuer?"

"One on 'em, ten 'e coatin de dahta; I don't recon 'e gwine hab heh. Da cah fool long wid 'Toyeh's gals dat way."

"Whose girls, Metoyers?"

"Yes, chile."

"Do you mean the wealthy planters of that name?"

"Dat same, chile.'

"Well, I want to understand you; you don't mean to say that they are colored people?"

"Yes, hunny, yes; da good culed folks anybody. Some five-six boys' an five-six gals on 'em; da all rich."

"How do they treat their slaves?"

"Da boys all mighty haud maustas, de gals all mighty good; sahvants all like 'em."

"You seem to understand these people very well, aunty. Now please tell me what kind of masters there are generally in the Red River country."

"Haud 'nough, chile, haud 'nough, God on'y knows!"

"Do the colored masters treat theirs generally worse than the whites?"

"No, hunny, 'bout da same."

"That's just what I want to know. What are the usual allowances for slaves?"

"Da 'low de fiel' han' two suit a yeah; foh umin one long linen coat,* make suit; an' foh man, pantaloon an' jacket."

"How about eating?"

"Half-peck meal ah day foh family uh fo!"

"What about weekly privileges? Do you have Saturday to yourselves?"

"Laud, honny, no! No, chile, no! Da do'n 'low us no time, 'tall. Da 'low us ebery uddeh Sunday wash ouh close; dat all de time we git."

"Then you don't get to sell anything for yourselves?"

"No, hunny, no. Da don' 'low pig, chicken, tucky, goose, bean, pea, tateh, nothin' else."

"Well, aunty. I'm glad to meet you, and as evening's drawing nigh, I must see your husband a little, then go."

"God bless yeh, chile, whah ebeh yeh go! Yeh ain' arteh no racehos, dat yeh ain't."

"You got something to eat, my man, did you?" enquired the lad Eugene, at the conclusion of his interview with uncle Nathan.

"I did, sir, and feasted well!" replied Henry in conclusion. "Good bye!" and he left for the next plantation suited to his objects.

"God bless de baby!" said old aunt Dolly as uncle Nathan entered the hut, referring to Henry.

"Ah, chile!" replied the old man with tears in his eyes; "my yeahs has heahn dis day!"

Chapter XVIII
Fleeting Shadows

IN HIGH SPIRITS Henry left the plantation of Latuer, after sowing seeds from which in due season, he anticipated an abundant harvest. He found the old man Nathan all that could be desired, and equal to the task of propagating the scheme. His soul swelled with exultation on receiving the tidings, declaring that though nearly eighty years of age, he never felt before an implied meaning, in the promise of the Lord.

"Now Laud!" with uplifted hand exclaimed he at the conclusion of the interview. "My eyes has seen, and meh yeahs heahn, an' now Laud! I's willin' to stan' still an' see dy salvation!"

On went Henry to Metoyers, visiting the places of four brothers, having taken those of the white planters intervening, all without detection or suspicion of being a stranger.

Stopping among the people of Colonel Hopkins at Grantico summit, here as at Latuer's and all intermediate places, he found the people patiently looking for a promised redemption. Here a pet female slave, Silva, espied him and gave the alarm that a strange black was lurking among the Negro quarters, which compelled him to retirement sooner than intended.

Among the people of Dickson at Pine Bluff, he found the best of spirits. There was Newman, a young slave man born without arms, who was ready any moment for a strike.

"How could you fight?" said Henry. "You have no arms!"

"I am compelled to pick with my toes, a hundred pound of cotton a day,* and I can sit on a stool and touch off a cannon!" said this promising young man whose heart panted with an unsuppressed throb for liberty.

Heeley's, Harrison's, and Hickman's slaves were fearfully and pitiably dejected. Much effort was required to effect a seclusion, and more to stimulate them to action. The continual dread "that maus wont let us!" seemed as immovably fixed as the words were constantly repeated; and it was not until an occasion for another subject of inquest, in the person of a pest of an old black slave man, that an organization was effected.

Approaching Crane's on Little River, the slaves were returning from the field to the gin. Many – being females, some of whom were very handsome – had just emptied their baskets. So little clothing had they, and so loosely hung the tattered fragments about them, that they covered themselves behind the large empty baskets tilted over on the side, to shield their person from exposure.

The overseer engaged in another direction, the master absent, and the family at the great house, a good opportunity presented for an inspection of affairs.

"How do you do, young woman?" saluted Henry.

"How de do, sir!" replied a sprightly, comely young mulatto girl, who stood behind her basket with not three yards of cloth in the tattered relic of the only garment she had on.

"Who owns this place?"

"Mr. Crane, sir," she politely replied with a smile.

"How many slaves has he?"

"I don'o, some say five 'a six hunded."

"Do they all work on this place?"

"No, sir, he got two-three places."

"How many on this place?"

"Oveh a hundred an' fifty."

"What allowances have you?"

"None, sir."

"What! no Saturday to yourselves?"

"No, sir."

"They allow you Sundays, I suppose."

"No, sir, we work all day ev'ry Sunday."

"How late do you work?"

"Till we can' see to pick no mo' cotton; but w'en its moon light we pick till ten o'clock at night."

"What time do you get to wash your clothes?"

"None, sir; da on'y 'low us one suit ev'ry New Yehs day,* an' us gals take it off every Satady night aftah de men all gone to bed and wash it fah Sunday."

"Why do you want clean clothes on Sunday, if you have to work on that day?"

"It's de Laud's day, an' we wa to be clean, and we feel betteh."

"How do the men do for clean clothes?"

"We wash de men's clothes afteh da go to bed."

"And you say you are only allowed one suit a year? Now, young woman, I don't know your name but—"

"Nancy, sir."

"Well, Nancy, speak plainly, and dont be backward; what does your one suit consist of?"

"A frock, sir, made out er coarse tow linen."

"Only one piece, and no underclothes at all?"

"Dat's all, sir!" replied she modestly looking down and drawing the basket, which sufficiently screened her, still closer to her person.

"Is that which you have on a sample of the goods your clothes are made of?"

"Yes, sir, dis is da kine."

"I would like to see some other of your girls."

"Stop, sir, I go call Susan!" when, gathering up and drawing around and before her a surplus of the back section, the only remaining sound remnant of the narrow tattered garment that she wore, off she ran behind the gin, where lay in the sun, a number of girls to rest themselves during their hour of "spell."

"Susan!" she exclaimed rather loudly. "I do'n want you gals!" she pleasantly admonished, as the whole twelve or fifteen rose from their resting place, and came hurriedly around the building, Nancy and Susan in the lead. They instinctively as did Nancy, drew their garments around and about them, on coming in sight of the stranger. Standing on the outside of the fence, Henry politely bowed as they approached.

"Dis is Susan, sir!" said Nancy, introducing her friend with bland simplicity.

"How de do, sir!" saluted she, a modest and intelligent, very pretty young black girl, of good address.

"Well, Susan!" replied Henry. "I don't want anything but to see you girls; but I will ask you this question: how many suits of clothes do they give you a year?"

"One, sir."

"How many pieces make a suit?"

"Jus' one frock," and they simultaneously commenced drawing still closer before, the remnant of coarse garment, which hung in tatters about them.

"Don't you have shoes and stockings in winter?"

"We no call foh shoes, case 'taint cole much; on'y some time little fros'."

"How late in the evening do you work?"

"Da fiel' han's dah," pointing to those returning to the field, "da work till bedtime, but we gals heah, we work in de gin, and spell each other ev'ey twelve ouahs."

"You're at leisure now; who fills your places?"

"Nutha set a' han's go to work, fo' you come."

"How much cotton do they pick for a task?"

"Each one mus' pick big basket full, an' fetch it in f'om da fiel' to de gin, else da git thirty lashes."

"How much must the women pick as a task?"

"De same as de men."

"That can't be possible!" said Henry, looking over the fence down upon their baskets. "How much do they hold?"

"I dis membeh sir, but good 'eal."

"I see on each basket marked 225 pounds; is that the quantity they hold?"

"Yes, sir, dat's it."

"All mus' be in gin certain ouah else da git whipped; sometime de men help 'em."

"How can they do this when they have their own to carry?"

"Da put derse on de head, an' ketch holt one side de women basket. Sometimes they leave part in de fiel', an' go back afteh it."

"Do you get plenty to eat?"

"No, sir, da feeds us po'ly; sometime, we do'n have mo'n half nough!"

"Did you girls ever work in the field?"

"O yes, sir! all uv us, on'y we wan't strong nough to fetch in ouh cotton, den da put us in de gin."

"Where would you rather; in the gin or in the field?"

"If 'twant foh carryin' cotton, we'a rather work in de fiel'."

"Why so, girls?"

"Case den da would'n be so many ole wite plantehs come an' look at us, like we was show!"

"Who sees that the tasks are all done in the field?"

"Da Driveh."

"Is he a white man?"

"No sir, black."

"Is he a free man?"

"No, sir, slave."

"Have you no white overseer?"

"Yes, sir, Mr. Dorman."

"Where is Dorman when you are at work."

"He out at de fiel too."

"What is he doing there?"

"He watch Jesse, da drivah."

"Is Jesse a pretty good fellow?"

"No, sir, he treat black folks like dog, he all de time beat 'em, when da no call to do it."

"How did he treat you girls when you worked in the field?"

"He beat us if we jist git little behind de rest in pickin'! Da wite folks make 'im bad."

"Point him out to me and after tonight, he'll never whip another."

"Now, girls, I see that you are smart intelligent young women, and I want you to tell me why it is, that your master keeps you all here at work in the gin, when he could get high prices for you, and supply your places with common cheap hands at half the money?"

"Case we gals won' go! Da been mo'n a dozen plantehs heah lookin' at us, an' want to buy us foh house keepehs, an' we wont go; we die fus!" said Susan with a shudder.

"Yes," repeated Nancy, with equal emotion, "we die fus!"

"How can you prevent it, girls; won't your master sell you against your will?"

"Yes, sir, he would, but da plantehs da don't want us widout we willin' to go."

"I see! Well girls, I believe I'm done with you; but before leaving let me ask you, is there among your men, a real clever good trusty man? I don't care either old or young, though I prefer an old or middle-aged man."

"O yes, sir," replied Nancy, "da is some mong 'em."

"Give me the name of one," said Henry, at which request Nancy and Susan looked hesitatingly at each other.

"Don't be backward," admonished he, "as I shan't make a bad use of it." But still they hesitated, when after another admonition Nancy said, "Dare's uncle Joe—"

"No, uncle Moses, uncle Moses!" in a suppressed tone interrupted the other girls.

"Who is uncle Moses?" enquired Henry.

"He' my fatha," replied Susan, "an—"

"My uncle!" interrupted Nancy.

"Then you two are cousins?"

"Yes, sir, huh fatha an my motha is brotha an sisteh," replied Nancy.

"Is he a religious man, girls?"

"Yes, sir, he used to preach but'e do'n preach now," explained Susan.

"Why?"

"Case da 'ligions people wo'n heah im now."

"Who, colored people?"

"Yes, sir."

"When did they stop hearing him preach?"

"Good while ago."

"Where at?"

"Down in da bush meetin', at da Baptism."

"He's a Baptist then – what did he do?"

Again became Susan and Nancy more perplexed than before, the other girls in this instance failing to come to their relief.

"What did he do girls? Let me know it quick, as I must be off!"

"Da say – da say – I do'n want tell you!" replied Susan hesitating, with much feeling.

"What is it girls, can't some of you tell me?" earnestly enquired Henry.

"Da say befo' 'e come heah way down in Fagina, he kill a man, ole po' wite ovehseeah!"

"Is that it, girls?" enquired he.

"Yes, sir!" they simultaneously replied.

"Then he's the very man I want to see!" said Henry. "Now don't forget what I say to you; tell him that a man will meet him tonight below here on the river side, just where the carcass of an ox lies in the verge of the thicket. Tell him to listen and when I'm ready, I'll give the signal of a runaway – the screech of the panther* – when he must immediately obey the summons. One word more, and I'll leave you. Every one of you as you have so praiseworthily concluded, die before surrendering to such base purposes as that for which this man who holds you wishes to dispose of you. Girls, you will see me no more. Fare—"

"Yo' name sir, yo' name!" they all exclaimed.

"My name is – Farewell, girls, farewell!" – when Henry darted in the thickest of the forest, leaving the squad of young maiden slaves in a state of bewildering inquiry concerning the singular black man.

The next day Jesse the driver was missed, and never after heard of. On inquiry being made of the old man Moses concerning the stranger, all that could be elicited was, "Stan' still child'en, and see da salvation uv da Laud!"

Chapter XIX
Come What Will

LEAVING THE PLANTATION of Crane with high hopes and great confidence in the integrity of uncle Moses and the maiden gang of cotton girls, Henry turned his course in a retrograde direction so as again to take the stream of Red River, Little River, where he then was, being but a branch of that water.

Just below its confluence with the larger stream, at the moment when he reached the junction, a steam cotton trader hove in view. There was no alternative but to stand like a freeman, or suddenly escape into the forest, thus creating suspicions and fears, as but a few days previous a French planter of the neighborhood lost a desperate slave, who became a terror to the country around. The master was compelled to go continually armed, as also other white neighbors, and all were afraid after nightfall to pass out the threshold of their own doors. Permission was given to every white man to shoot him if ever seen within rifle shot, which facts having learned the evening before, Henry was armed with this precaution.

His dress being that of a racegroom – small leather cap with long front piece, neat fitting roundabout, high boots drawn over the pantaloon legs, with blanket, girth, halter, whip and bridle – Henry stood upon the shore awaiting the vessel.

"Well boy!" hailed the captain as the line was thrown out, which he caught, making fast at the root of a tree. "Do you wish to come aboard?"

"Good man!" approvingly cried the mate, at the expert manner which he caught the line and tied the sailor knot.

"Have you ever steamboated, my man?" continued the captain.

"Yes, sir," replied Henry.

"Where?"

"On the Upper and Lower Mississippi, sir."

"Whom do you know as masters of steamers on the Upper Mississippi?"

"Captains Thogmorton, Price, Swan, and—"

"Stop, stop! That'll do," interrupted the captain, "you know the master of every steamer in the trade, I believe. Now who in the Lower trade?"

"Captains Scott, Hart, and—"

"What's Captain Hart's Christian name?" interrupted the captain.

"Jesse, sir."

"That'll do, by George you know everybody! Do you want to ship?"

"No, sir."

"What are you doing here?"

"I'm hunting master's stray racehorse."

"Your master's race horse! Are you a slave boy?"

"Yes, sir."

"How did you come to be on the Mississippi River?"

"I hired my time, sir."

"Yes, yes, boy, I see!"

"Who is your master?"

"Colonel Sheldon; I used to belong to Major Gilmore."

"Are you the boy Nepp, the great horse trainer the Major used to own?"

"No, sir, I'm his son."

"Are you as good at training horses as the old chap?"

"They call me better, sir."

"Then you're worth your weight in gold. Will your master sell you?"

"I don't know, sir."

"How did your horse come to get away?"

"He was bought from the Major by Colonel Sheldon to run at the great Green Wood Races, Texas, and while training he managed to get away, leaping the fences, and taking to the forest."

"Then you're Major Tom's race rider Gilbert! You're a valuable boy; I wonder the Major parted with you."

The bell having rung for dinner, the captain left, Henry going to the deck.

Among those on deck was a bright mulatto young man, who immediately recognized Henry as having seen him on the Upper Mississippi, he being a free man. On going up to him, Henry observed that he was laden with heavy manacles.

"Have I not seen you somewhere before?" enquired he.

"Yes; my name is Lewis Grimes, you saw me on the Upper Mississippi," replied the young man. "Your name is Henry Holland!"

"What have you been doing?" enquired Henry, on seeing the handcuffs.

"Nothing at all!" replied he with eyes flashing resentment and suffused with tears.

"What does this mean?" continued he, pointing at the handcuffs.

"I am stolen and now being taken to Texas, where I am to be enslaved for life!" replied Lewis sobbing aloud.

"Who did this vile deed?" continued Henry in a low tone of voice, pressing his lips to suppress his feelings.

"One Dr. Johns of Texas, now a passenger on this boat!"

"Was that the person who placed a glass to your lips which you refused, just as I came aboard?"

"Yes, that's the man."

"Why don't you leave him instantly?" said Henry, his breast heaving with emotion.

"Because he always handcuffs me before the boat lands, keeping me so during the time she lies ashore."

"Why don't you jump overboard when the boat is under way?"

"Because he guards me with a heavy loaded rifle, and I can't get a chance."

"He 'guards' you! 'You can't get a chance!' Are there no nights, and does he never sleep?"

"Yes, but he makes me sleep in the stateroom with him, keeping his rifle at his bedside."

"Are you never awake when he's asleep?"

"Often, but I'm afraid to stir lest he wakens."

"Well don't you submit, die first if thereby you must take another into eternity with you! Were it my case and he ever went to sleep where I was, he'd never waken in this world!"

"I never thought of that before, I shall take your advice the first opportunity. Good-bye sir!" hastily said the young man, as the bell tapped a signal to start, and Henry stepped on shore.

"Let go that line!" sternly commanded the captain, Henry obeying orders on the shore, when the boat glided steadily up the stream, seemingly in unison with the lively though rude and sorrowful song of the black firemen—

I'm a-goin' to Texas – O! O-O-O!
I'm a-goin' to Texas – O! O-O-O!

Having in consequence of the scarcity of spring houses and larders along his way in so level and thinly settled country, Henry took in his pouch from the cook of the boat an ample supply of provisions for the suceeding four or five days. Thus provided for, standing upon the bank for a few minutes, with steady gaze listening to the sad song of his oppressed brethren as they left the spot, and reflecting still more on the miserable fate of the young mulatto freeman Lewis Grimes held by the slave-holder Dr. Johns of Texas, he, with renewed energy, determined that nothing short of an interference by Divine Providence should stop his plans and progress. In soliloquy said Henry, "Yes!

If every foe stood martialed in the van,
I'd fight them single combat, man to man!"

and again he started with a manly will, as fixed and determined in his purpose as though no obstructions lay in his pathway.

From plantation to plantation did he go, sowing the seeds of future devastation and ruin to the master and redemption to the slave, an antecedent more terrible in its anticipation than the warning voice of the destroying Angel in commanding the slaughter of the firstborn of Egypt. Himself careworn, distressed and hungry, who just being supplied with nourishment for the system, Henry went forth a welcome messenger, casting his bread upon the turbid waters of oppression, in hopes of finding it after many days.

Holding but one seclusion on each plantation, his progress was consequently very rapid, in whatever direction he went.

With a bold stride from Louisiana, he went into Texas. Here he soon met with the man of his wishes. This presented in the person of Sampson, on the cotton place of proprietor Richardson. The master here, though represented wealthy, with an accomplished and handsome young daughter, was a silly, stupid old dolt, an inordinate blabber and wine bibber. The number of his slaves was said to be great and he the owner of three plantations, one in Alabama, and the others in Texas.

Sampson was a black, tall, stoutly built, and manly, possessing much general intelligence, and a good-looking person. His wife a neat, intelligent, handsome little woman, the complexion of himself, was the mother of a most interesting family of five pretty children, three boys and two girls. This family entered at once into the soul of his mission, seeming to have anticipated it.

With an amply supply of means, buried in a convenient well-marked spot, he only awaited a favorable opportunity to effect his escape from slavery. With what anxiety did that wife gaze smilingly in his face, and a boy and girl cling tightly each to a knee, as this husband and father in whispers recounted his plans and determination of carrying them out. The scheme of Henry was at once committed to his confidence, and he requested to impart them wherever he went.

Richardson was a sportsman and Sampson his body servant, they traveled through every part of the country, thus affording the greatest opportunity for propagating the measures of the secret organization. From Portland in Maine to Galveston in Texas, Sampson was as familiar as a civil engineer.

"Sampson, Sampson, stand by me! Stand by me, my man; stand at your master's back!" was the language of this sottish old imbecile he kept continually reveling at a gambling table, and who from excessive fatigue would sometimes squat or sit down upon the floor behind him. "Sampson, Sampson! are you there? Stand by your master, Sampson!" again would he exclaim, so soon as the tall commanding form of his black protector was missed from his sight.

Sampson and his wife were both pious people, believing much in the Providence of God, he, as he said, having recently had it "shown to" him – meaning a presentiment – that a messenger would come to him and reveal the plan of deliverance.

"I am glad to see that you have money," said Henry, "you are thereby well qualified for your mission. With money you may effect your escape almost at any time. Your most difficult point is an elevated obstruction, a mighty hill, a mountain; but through that hill there is a gap, and money is your passport through that White Gap to freedom. Mark that! It is the great range of White mountains and White river which are before you, and the White Gap that you must pass through to reach the haven of safety. Money alone will carry you through the White mountains or across the White river to liberty."

"Brother, my eyes is open, and my way clear!" responded Sampson to this advice.

"Then," said Henry, "you are ready to 'rise and shine' for—"

"My light has come!—" interrupted Sampson. "But—"

"The glory of God is not yet shed abroad!" concluded Henry, who fell upon Sampson's neck with tears of joy in meeting unexpectedly one of his race so intelligent in that region of country.

Sampson and wife Dursie, taking Henry by the hand wept aloud, looking upon him as the messenger of deliverance foreshown to them.

Kneeling down a fervent prayer was offered by Sampson for Henry's protection by the way, and final success in his "mighty plans," with many Amens and "God grants," by Dursie.

Partaking of a sumptuous fare on 'ash cake and sweet milk – a dainty diet with many slaves – and bidding with a trembling voice and tearful eye a final "Farewell!" in six hours he had left the state of Texas to the consequences of a deep-laid scheme for a terrible insurrection.

Chapter XX
Advent Among the Indians

FROM TEXAS Henry went into the Indian Nation near Fort Towson, Arkansas.

"Make yourself at home, sir," invited Mr. Culver, the intelligent old Chief of the United Nation, "and Josephus will attend to you," referring to his nephew Josephus Braser, an educated young chief and counselor among his people.

"You are slaveholders, I see, Mr. Culver!" said Henry.

"We are, sir, but not like the white men," he replied.

"How many do you hold?"

"About two hundred on my two plantations."

"I can't well understand how a man like you can reconcile your principles with the holding of slaves and—"

"We have had enough of that!" exclaimed Dr. Donald, with a tone of threatening authority.

"Hold your breath, sir, else I'll stop it!" in a rage replied the young chief.

"Sir," responded the Doctor, "I was not speaking to you, but only speaking to that Negro!"

"You're a fool!" roared Braser, springing to his feet.

"Come, come, gentlemen!" admonished the old Chief. "I think you are both going mad! I hope you'll behave something better."

"Well, uncle, I can't endure him! he assumes so much authority!" replied he. "He'll make the Indians slaves just now, then Negroes will have no friends."

Donald was a white man, married among the Indians a sister of the old Chief and aunt to the young, for the sake of her wealth and a home. A physician without talents, he was unable to make a business and unwilling to work.

"Mr. Bras—"

"I want nothing more of you," interrupted Braser, "and don't—"

"Josephus, Josephus!" interrupted the old chief. "You will surely let the Doctor speak!"

Donald stood pale and trembling before the young Choctaw born to command, when receiving no favor he left the company muttering "nigger!"

"Now you see," said Mr. Culver as the Doctor left the room, "the difference between a white man and Indian holding slaves. Indian work side by side with black man, eat with him, drink with him, rest with him and both lay down in shade together; white man even won't let you talk! In our Nation Indian and black all marry together. Indian like black man very much, ony he don't fight 'nough. Black man in Florida fight much, and Indian like 'im heap!"

"You make, sir, a slight mistake about my people. They would fight if in their own country they were united as the Indians here, and not scattered thousands of miles apart as they are. You should also remember that the Africans have never permitted a subjugation of their country by foreigners as the Indians have theirs, and Africa today is still peopled by Africans, whilst America, the home of the Indian – who is fast passing away – is now possessed and ruled by foreigners."

"True, true!" said the old Chief, looking down reflectingly. "Too true! I had not thought that way before. Do you think the white man couldn't take Africa if he wanted?"

"He might by a combination, and I still am doubtful whether then he could if the Africans were determined as formerly to keep him out. You will also remember, that the whites came in small numbers to America, and then drove the Indians from their own soil, whilst the blacks got in Africa as slaves, are taken by their own native conquerors, and sold to white men as prisoners of war."

"That is true, sir, true!" sighed the old Chief. "The Indian, like game before the bow, is passing away before the gun of the white man!"

"What I now most wish to learn is, whether in case that the blacks should rise, they may have hope or fear from the Indian?" asked Henry.

"I'm an old mouthpiece, been puffing out smoke and talk many seasons for the entertainment of the young and benefit of all who come among us. The squaws of the great men among the Indians in Florida were black women, and the squaws of the black men were Indian women. You see the vine that winds around and holds us together. Don't cut it, but let it grow till bimeby, it git so stout and strong, with many, very many little branches attached, that you can't separate them. I now reach to you the pipe of peace and hold out the olive-branch of hope! Go on young man, go on. If you want white man to love you, you must fight im!" concluded the intelligent old Choctaw.

"Then, sir, I shall rest contented, and impart to you the object of my mission," replied Henry.

"Ah hah!" exclaimed the old chief after an hour's seclusion with him. "Ah hah! Indian have something like that long-go. I wonder your people ain't got it before! That what make Indian strong; that what make Indian and black man in Florida hold together. Go on young man, go on! may the Great Spirit make you brave!" exhorted Mr. Culver, when the parties retired for the evening, Henry rooming with the young warrior Braser.

By the aid of the young Chief and kindness of his uncle the venerable old brave, Henry was conducted quite through the nation on a pony placed at his service, affording to him an ample opportunity of examining into the condition of things. He left the settlement with the regrets of the people, being the only instance in which his seclusions were held with the master instead of the slave.

Chapter XXI
What Not

LEAVING THE UNITED NATION of Chickasaw and Choctaw Indians, Henry continued his travel in this the roughest, apparently, of all the states. Armed with bowie knives and revolvers openly carried belted around the person, he who displays the greatest number of deadly weapons seems to be considered the greatest man. The most fearful incivility and absence of refinement was apparent throughout this region. Neither the robes of state nor gown of authority is sufficient to check the vengeance of awakened wrath in Arkansas. Law is but a fable, its ministration a farce, and the pillars of justice but as stubble before the approach of these legal invaders.

Hurriedly passing on in the darkness of the night, Henry suddenly came upon a procession in the wilderness, slowly and silently marching on, the cortege consisting principally of horsemen, there being but one vehicle, advanced by four men on horseback. Their conversation seemed at intervals of low, muttering, awestricken voices. The vehicle was closely covered, and of a sad, heavy sound by the rattling of the wheels upon the unfinished path of the great Arkansas road. Here he sat in silence listening, waiting for the passage of the solemn procession, but a short distance from whence in the thicket stood the hut of the slave to whom he was sent.

"Ole umin! done yeh heah some 'un trampin' round de house? Hush! evedroppehs 'bout!" admonished Uncle Jerry.

"Who dat?" enquired Aunt Rachel, as Henry softly rapped at the back window.

"A friend!" was the reply.

"What saut frien' dat go sneak roun' people back windah stid comin' to de doh!"

"Hush, ole umin, yeh too fas'! how yeh know who 'tis? Frien', come roun' to de doh," said the old man.

Passing quickly around, the door was opened, a blazing hot fire shining full in his face, the old man holding in his hand a heavy iron poker in the attitude of defence.

"Is dis you, my frien'?" enquired Uncle Jerry, to whom Henry was an entire stranger.

"Yes, uncle, this is me," replied he.

"God bless yeh, honey! come in; we didn know 'twos you, chile! God bless de baby!" added Aunt Rachel. "Ole man, heah yeh comin' an' we been lookin' all day long. Dis evenin' I git some suppeh, an' I don'o if yeh come uh no."

"How did you know I was coming, aunty?"

"O! honey, da tell us," replied she.

"Who told you?"

"De folks up dah."

"Up where?"

"Up dah, 'mong de Injins, chile."

"Indians told you?"

"No, honey; some de black folks, da all'as gwine back and for'ard, and da lahn heap from dem up dah; an' da make 'ase an' tell us."

"Can you get word from each other so far apart, that easy?"

"Yes 'ndeed, honey! some on 'em all de time gwine; wite folks know nothin' 'bout it. Some time some on 'em gone two-three day, an' ain miss; white folks tink da in the woods choppin'."

"Why, that's the very thing! you're ahead of all the other states. You folks in Arkansas must be pretty well organized already."

"Wat dat yeh mean, chile, dat 'organ' so?"

"I mean by that, aunty, a good general secret understanding among yourselves."

"Ah, chile! dat da is. Da comin' all de time, ole man hardly time to eat mou'full wen 'e come in de hut night."

"Tell me, aunty, why people like you and uncle here, who seem to be at the head of these secrets, are not more cautious with me, a stranger?"

"Ole umin, I lisenin at yeh!" said Uncle Jerry, after enough had been told to betray them; but the old people well understood each other, Aunt Rachel by mutual consent being the mouthpiece.

"How we knows you!" rejoined the old woman. "Wy, chile, yeh got mahk dat so soon as we put eye on yeh, we knows yeh. Huccum yeh tink we gwine tell yeh so much wen we don'o who yeh is? Sho, chile, we ain't dat big fool!"

"Then you know my errand among you, aunty?"

"Yes, meh son, dat we does, an' we long been waitin' foh some sich like you to come 'mong us. We thang God dis night in ouh soul! We long been lookin' foh ye, chile!" replied Uncle Jerry.

"You are closely watched in this state, I should think, uncle."

"Yes, chile, de patrolas da all de time out an' gwine in de quahtehs an' huntin' up black folks wid der 'nigga-dogs' as da call 'em."

"I suppose you people scarcely ever get a chance to go anywhere, then?"

"God bless yeh, honey, da blacks do'n mine dem noh der 'niggadogs' nutha. Patrolas feahd uh de black folks, an' da black folks charm de dogs, so da cahn heht 'em," said Aunt Rachel.

"I see you understand yourselves! Now, what is my best way to get along through the state?"

"Keep in de thicket, chile, as da patrolas feahd to go in de woods, da feahd runaway ketch 'em! Keep in da woods, chile, an' da ain' goin' dah bit! Da talk big, and sen' der dog, but da ain' goin' honey!" continued the old woman.

"Ah spose, meh son, yeh know how to chaum dogs?" enquired Uncle Jerry.

"I understand the mixed bull, but not the full-bred Cuba dog," replied Henry.

"Well, chile, da keep boph kine heah, de bull dog an' bloodhoun' an' fo' yeh go, I lahn yeh how to fix 'em all! Da come sneakin' up to yeh! da cahn bite yeh!"

"Thank you, Uncle Jerry! I'll try and do as much for you in some way."

"Yeh no call foh dat, meh son; it ain' nothin' mo' nah onh—"

"Hush! ole man; ain' dat dem?" admonished Aunt Rachel, in a whisper, as she went to the door, thrusting out her head in the dark.

"Who? Patrols?" with anxiety enquired Henry.

"No, chile, de man da kill down yondah; all day long da been lookin' foh 'em to come."

"A procession passed just before I came to your door, which I took for a funeral."

"Yes, chile, dat's it, da kill im down dah."

On enquiry, it appeared that in the senate a misunderstanding on the rules of order and parliamentary usage occurred, when the Speaker, conceiving himself insulted by the senator who had the floor, deliberately arose from his chair, when approaching the senator, drove a bowie knife through his body from the chest, which laid him a corpse upon the senate floor.

"There he is! There he is!" stormed the assassin, pointing with defiance at the lifeless body, his hand still reeking with blood. "I did it!" slapping his hand upon his own breast in triumph of his victory.

They had just returned with the body of the assassinated statesman to the wretched home of his distracted family, some ten miles beyond the hut of Uncle Jerry.

"Is this the way they treat each other, aunty?"

"Yes, chile, wus den dat! da kill one-notha in cole blood, sometime at de table eatin'. Da all'as choppin' up some on 'em."

"Then you black people must have a poor chance among them, if this is the way they do each other!"

"Mighty po', honey; mighty po' indeed!" replied Uncle Jerry.

"Well, uncle, it's now time I was doing something; I've been here some time resting. Aunty, see to your windows and door; are there any cracks in the walls!"

"No, honey, da dob good!" whispered the old woman as a wellpatched, covering quilt to shield the door was hung, covering nearly one side of the hut, and a thickly-patched linsey gown fully shielded the only window of four eight-by-ten lights.

These precautions taken, they drew together in a corner between the head of the bed and well-daubed wall to hold their seclusion.

"Laud!" exclaimed Uncle Jerry, after the secrets were fully imparted to them. "Make beah dine all-conquering ahm! strike off de chains dat dy people may go free! Come, Laud, a little nigh, eh!"

"Honah to 'is name!" concorded Aunt Rachel. "Wuthy all praise! Tang God fah wat I seen an' heahn dis night! dis night long to be membed! Meh soul feels it! It is heah!" pressing her hand upon her breast, exclaimed she.

"Amen! Laud heah de cry uh dy children! Anseh prah!" responded the old man, in tears; when Aunt Rachel in a grain of sorrowful pathos, sung to the expressive words in the slaves' lament:

> *"In eighteen hundred and twenty-three*
> *They said their people should be free!*
> *It is wrote in Jeremiah,*
> *Come and go along with me!*
> *It is wrote in Jeremiah,*
> *Go sound the Jubilee!"*

At the conclusion of the last line, a sudden sharp rap at the door startled them, when the old woman, hastening, took down the quilt, enquiring, "Who dat?"

"Open the door, Rachel!" was the reply, in an authoritative tone from a posse of patrols, who on going their evening rounds were attracted to the place by the old people's devotion, and stood sometime listening around the hut.

"You seem to be happy here, Jerry," said Ralph Jordon, the head of the party. "What boy is this you have here?"

"Major Morgan's sir," replied Henry, referring to the proprietor of the next plantation above.

"I don't remember seeing you before, boy," continued Jordon.

"No, sir; lately got me," explained Henry.

"Aye, aye, boy; a preacher, I suppose."

"No, sir."

"No, Maus Rafe, dis brotheh no preacheh; but 'e is 'logious, and come to gib us little comfit, an' bless God I feels it now; dat I does, blessed be God!" said the old woman.

"Well, Rachel, that's all right enough; but, my boy, its high time that you were getting towards home. You've not yet learned our rules here; where are you from?"

"Louisiana, sir."

"Yes, yes, that explains it. Louisiana Negroes are permitted to go out at a much later hour than our Negroes."

"Maus Rafe, ah hope yah let de brotheh eat a mouph'l wid us fo' go?"

"O yes, Rachel! give the boy something to eat before he goes; I suppose the 'laborer is worthy of his hire,' " looking with a smile at his comrades.

"Yes 'ndeed, seh, dat he is!" replied the old woman with emphasis.

"Rachel, I smell something good! What have you here, spare rib?" enquired Ralph Jordon, walking to the table and lifting up a clean check apron which the old woman had hurriedly thrown over it to screen her homely food from the view of the gentlemen patrols. "Good! spare rib and ash cake, gentlemen! What's better? Rachel, give us some seats here!" continued Ralph.

Hurrying about, the old woman made out to seat the uninvited guests with a half barrel tub, an old split bottom chair, and a short slab bench, which accommodated two.

"By gum! This is fine," said Ralph Jordon, smacking his mouth, and tearing at a rib. "Gentlemen, help yourselves to some spirits," setting on the table a large flask of Jamaica rum, just taken from his lips.

"Nothing better," replied Tom Hammond; "give me at any time the cooking in the Negro quarters before your great-house dainties."

"So say I," sanctioned Zack Hite, champing like a hungry man. "The Negroes live a great deal better than we do."

"Much better, sir, much better," replied Ralph. "Rachel, don't you nor Jerry ever take any spirits?"

"No, Maus Rafe, not any," replied the old woman.

"May be your friend there will take a little."

"I don't drink, sir," said Henry.

Rising from the homely meal at the humble board of Aunt Rachel and Uncle Jerry, they emptied their pockets of crackers, cold biscuits and cheese, giving the old man a plug of honey-cured tobacco, to be divided between himself and wife, in lieu of what they had, without invitation, taken the liberty of eating. The patrol this evening were composed of the better class of persons, principally business men, two of whom, being lawyers who went out that evening for a mere "frolic among the Negroes."

Receiving the parting hand, accompanied with a "good bye, honey!" and "God bless yeh, meh son!" from the old people, Henry left the hut to continue his course through the forest. Hearing persons approaching, he stepped aside from the road to conceal himself, when two parties at the junction of two roads met each other, coming to a stand.

"What's up tonight, Colonel?" enquired one.

"Nothing but the raffle."

"Are you going?"

"Yes, the whole party here; won't you go?"

"I dun'o; what's the chances?"

"Five dollars only."

"Five dollars a chance! What the deuce is the prize!"

"Oh, there's several for the same money."

"What are they?"

"That fine horse and buggy of Colonel Sprout, a mare and colt, a little Negro girl ten years of age, and a trail of four of the finest Negro-dogs in the state."

"Hallo! all them; why, how many chances, in the name of gracious, are there?"

"Only a hundred and fifty."

"Seven hundred and fifty dollars for the whole; that's cheap. But, then, all can't win, and it must be a loss to somebody."

"Will you go, Cap'n?"

"Well, I don't care – go it is!" when the parties started in the direction of the sport, Henry following to reconnoiter them.

On approaching the tavern, the rafflers, who waited the rest of the company to gather, could be seen and heard through the uncurtained windows and the door, which was frequently opened, standing around a blazing hot fire, and in groups over the barroom floor, amusing themselves with jests and laughter. Henry stood in the verge of the forest in a position to view the whole of their proceedings.

Presently there was a rush out of doors with glee and merriment. Old Colonel Sprout was bringing out his dogs, to test their quality previous to the raffle.

"Now, gentlemen!" exclaimed he, "them is the best trained dogs in this part of the state. Be dad, they's the bes' dogs in the country. When you say 'nigger,' you needn't fear they'll ever go after anything but a nigger."

"Come, Colonel, give them a trial; we must have something going on to kill time," suggested one of the party.

"But what will he try 'em on?" said another; "there's no niggers to hunt."

"Send them out, and let them find one, be George; what else would you have them do?" replied a third.

"Where the deuce will they get one?" rejoined a fourth.

"Just as a hunting dog finds any other game," answered a fifth; "where else?"

"O, by golly, gentlemen, you need's give yourselves no uneasiness about the game. They'll find a nigger, once started if they have to break into some Negro quarter and drag 'm out o' bed. No mistake 'bout them, I tell you, gentlemen," boasted Sprout.

"But won't a nigger hurt 'em when he knows he's not a runaway?" enquired Richard Rester Rutherford.

"What, a nigger hurt a bloodhound! By, gracious, they're fearder of a bloodhound than they is of the devil himself! Them dogs is dogs, gentlemen, an' no mistake; they is by gracious!" declared Sprout.

"Well, let them loose, Colonel, and let's have a little sport, at any rate!" said Ralph Jordon, the patrol, who had just arrived; "we're in for a spree tonight, anyhow."

"Here, Caesar, Major, Jowler, here Pup! Niggers about! Seek out!" hissed the Colonel, with a snap of the finger, pointing toward the thicket, in the direction of which was Henry. With a yelp which sent a shudder through the crowd, the dogs started in full chase for the forest.

"By George, Colonel, that's too bad! Call them back!" said Ralph Jordon, as the savage brutes bounded in search of a victim.

"By thunder, gentlemen, it's too late! they'll have a nigger before they stop. They'll taste the blood of some poor black devil before they git back!" declared Sprout.

Having heard every word that passed between them, in breathless silence Henry waited the approach of the animals. The yelping now became more anxious and eager, until at last it was heard as a short, impatient, fretful whining, indicating a near approach to their prey, when growing less and less, they ceased entirely to be heard.

"What the Harry does it mean! the dogs has ceased to bay!" remarked Colonel Sprout.

"Maybe they caught a nigger," replied John Spangler.

"It might be a Tartar!" rejoined Ralph Jordon.

"Maybe a nigger caught them!" said the Sheriff of the county, who was present to superintend the raffle, and receive the proceeds of the hazard.

"What!" exclaimed the old gentleman, to enhance the value of the prizes. "What! My Caesar, Major, Jowler, and Pup, the best dogs in all Arkansas! – A nigger kill them! No, gentlemen, once let loose an' on their trail, an' they's not a gang o' niggers to be found out at night they couldn't devour! Them dogs! Hanged if they didn't eat a nigger quicker as they'd swaller a piece o' meat!"

"Then they're the dogs for me!" replied the Sheriff.

"And me," added Spangle, a noted agent for catching runaway slaves.

"The raffle, the raffle!" exclaimed several voices eager for a chance, estimating at once the value of the dogs above the aggregate amount of the stakes.

"But the dogs, the dogs, gentlemen! They're not here! Give us the dogs first," suggested an eager candidate for competition in the prizes.

"No matter, gentlemen; be sartin," said the Colonel, "when they's done they'll come back agin."

"But how will they be managed in attacking strange Negroes?" enquired Ralph Jordon.

"O, the command of any white man is sufficient to call 'em off, an' they's plenty o' them all'as wherever you find niggers."

"Then, Colonel, we're to understand you to mean, that white men can't live without niggers."

"I'll be hanged, gentlemen, if it don't seem so, for wherever you find one you'll all'as find tother, they's so fully mixed up with us in all our relations!" peals of laughter following the explanation.

"Come, Colonel, I'll be hanged if we stand that, except you stand treat!" said Ralph.

"Stand what? Let us understand you; what'd I say?"

"What did you say? why, by George, you tell us flatly that we are related to niggers!"

"Then, gentlemen, I'll stand treat; for on that question I'll be consarned if some of us don't have to knock under!" at which there were deafening roars of laughter, the crowd rushing into the barroom, crying, "Treat! Treat!! That's too good to be lost!"

Next day after the raffle, the winners having presented the prizes back to their former owner, it was whispered about that the dogs had been found dead in the woods, the mare and colt were astray, the little slave girl was in a pulmonary decline, the buggy had been upset and badly worsted the day before the raffle, and the horse had the distemper; upon which information the whole party met at a convenient place on a fixed day, going out to his house in a body, who ate, drank, and caroused at his expense during the day and evening.

"Sprout," said Ralph Jordon, "with your uniform benevolence, generosity and candor, how did you ever manage to depart so far from your old principles and rule of doing things? I can't understand it."

"How so? Explain yourself," replied Sprout.

"Why you always give rather than take advantage, your house and means always being open to the needy, even those with whom you are unacquainted."

"I'm sure I ain't departed one whit from my old rule," said Sprout; "I saw you was all strangers to the thing, an' I took you in; I'm blamed if I didn't!" the crowd shouting with laughter.

"One word, Sprout," said Jordon. "When the dogs ceased baying, didn't you suspect something wrong?"

"I know'd at once when they stopped that they was defeated; but I thought they'd pitched headlong into a old wellhole some sixty foot deep, where the walls has tumbled in, an' made it some twenty foot wide at the top. I lis'ened every minute 'spectin' to hear a devil of a whinin' 'mong 'em' but I was disapinted."

"Well, its a blamed pity, anyhow, that such fine animals were killed; and no clue as yet, I believe, to the perpetration of the deed," said the Sheriff.

"They was, indeed," replied Sprout, "as good a breed o' dogs as ever was, an' if they'd a been trained right, nothin' could a come up with them; but consarn their picters, it serves 'em right, as they wos the cussedest cowards I ever seed! 'Sarn them, if a nigger ony done so – jis' made a pass at 'em, an' I'll be hanged if they didn't yelp like wild cats, an almost kill 'emselves runin' away!" at which explanation the peals of laughter were deafening.

"Let's stay a week, stay a week, gentlemen!" exclaimed Ralph Jordon, in a convulsion of laughter.

"Be gracious, gentlemen!" concluded Sprout. "If you stay till eternity it won't alter the case one whit; case, the mare an' colt's lost, the black gal's no use to anybody, the buggy's all smashed up, the hos' is got the distemper, and the dogs is dead as thunder!"

With a boisterous roar, the party, already nearly exhausted with laughter, commenced gathering their hats and cloaks, and left the premises declaring never again to be caught at a raffling wherein was interested Colonel Joel Sprout.

The dogs were the best animals of the kind, and quickly trailed out their game; but Henry, with a well-aimed weapon, slew each ferocious beast as it approached him, leaving them weltering in their own blood instead of feasting on his, as would have been the case had he not overpowered them. The rest of the prizes were also valuable and in good order, and the story which found currency depreciating them, had its origin in the brain and interest of Colonel Sprout, which resulted, as designed, entirely in his favor.

Hastening on to the Fulton landing Henry reached it at half-past two o'clock in the morning, just in time to board a steamer on the downward trip, which barely touched the shore to pick up a package. Knowing him by reputation as a great horse master, the captain received him cheerfully, believing him to have been, from what he had learned, to the Texas races with horses for his master.

Being now at ease, and faring upon the best the vessel could afford, after a little delay along the cotton trading coast, Henry was safely landed in the portentous city of New Orleans.

Chapter XXII
New Orleans

THE SEASON is the holidays, it is evening, and the night is beautiful. The moon, which in Louisiana is always an object of impressive interest, even to the slave as well as those of enlightened and scientific intelligence, the influence of whose soft and mellow light seems ever like the enchanting effect of some invisible being, to impart inspiration – now being shed from the crescent of the first day of the last quarter, appeared more interesting and charming than ever.

Though the cannon at the old fort in the Lower Faubourg had fired the significant warning, admonishing the slaves as well as free blacks to limit their movement, still there were passing to and fro with seeming indifference Negroes, both free and slaves, as well as the whites and Creole quadroons, fearlessly along the public highways, in seeming defiance of the established usage of Negro limitation.

This was the evening of the day of Mardi Gras, and from long-established and time-honored custom, the celebration which commenced in the morning was now being consummated by games, shows, exhibitions, theatrical performances, festivals, masquerade balls, and numerous entertainments and gatherings in the evening. It was on this account that the Negroes had been allowed such unlimited privileges this evening.

Nor were they remiss to the utmost extent of its advantages.

The city which always at this season of the year is lively, and Chartier street gay and fashionable, at this time appeared more lively, gay and fashionable than usual. This fashionable thoroughfare, the pride of the city, was thronged with people, presenting complexions of every shade and color. Now could be seen and realized the expressive description in the popular song of the vocalist Cargill:

> *I suppose you've heard how New Orleans*
> *Is famed for wealth and beauty;*
> *There's girls of every hue, it seems,*
> *From snowy white to sooty.*

The extensive shops and fancy stores presented the presence behind their counters as saleswomen in attendance of numerous females, black, white, mulatto and quadroon, politely bowing, curtsying, and rubbing their hands, in accents of broken English inviting to purchase all who enter the threshold, or even look in at the door:

"Wat fa you want something? Walk in, sire, I vill sell you one nice present fa one young lady."

And so with many who stood or sat along the streets and at the store doors, curtsying and smiling they give the civil banter:

"Come, sire, I sell you one pretty ting."

The fancy stores and toy shops on this occasion were crowded seemingly to their greatest capacity. Here might be seen the fashionable young white lady of French or American extraction, and there the handsome, and frequently beautiful maiden of African origin, mulatto, quadroon, or sterling black, all fondly interchanging civilities, and receiving some memento or keepsake from the hand of an acquaintance. Many lively jests and impressive flings of delicate civility noted the greetings of the passersby. Freedom seemed as though for once enshielded by her sacred robes and crowned with cap and wand in hand, to go forth untrammeled through the highways of the town. Along the private streets, sitting under the verandas, in the doors with half-closed jalousies, or promenading unconcernedly the public ways, mournfully humming in solace or chanting in lively glee, could be seen and heard many a Creole, male or female, black, white or mixed race, sometimes in reverential praise of

> *Father, Son and Holy Ghost—*
> *Madonna, and the Heavenly Host!*

in sentimental reflection on some pleasant social relations, or the sad reminiscence of ill-treatment or loss by death of some loved one, or worse than death, the relentless and insatiable demands of slavery.

In the distance, on the levee or in the harbor among the steamers, the songs of the boatmen were incessant. Every few hours landing, loading and unloading, the glee of these men of sorrow was touchingly appropriate and impressive. Men of sorrow they are in reality; for if there be a class of men anywhere to be found, whose sentiments of song and words of lament are made to reach the sympathies of others, the black slave-boatmen of the Mississippi river is that class. Placed in positions the most favorable to witness the pleasures enjoyed by others, the tendency is only to augment their own wretchedness.

Fastened by the unyielding links of the iron cable of despotism, reconciling themselves to a lifelong misery, they are seemingly contented by soothing their sorrows with songs and sentiments of apparently cheerful but in reality wailing lamentations. The most attracting lament of the evening was sung to words, a stanza of which is presented in pathos of delicate tenderness, which is but a spray from the stream which gushed out in insuppressible jets from the agitated fountains of their souls, as if in unison with the restless current of the great river upon which they were compelled to toil, their troubled waters could not be quieted. In the capacity of leader, as is their custom, one poor fellow in pitiful tones led off the song of the evening:

> *Way down upon the Mobile river,*
> *Close to Mobile bay;*
> *There's where my thoughts is running ever,*
> *All through the livelong day:*
> *There I've a good and fond old mother,*
> *Though she is a slave;*
> *There I've a sister and a brother,*

> *Lying in their peaceful graves.*
> *Then in chorus joined the whole company—*
> *O, could I somehow a'nother,*
> *Drive these tears way;*
> *When I think about my poor old mother,*
> *Down upon the Mobile bay.*

Standing in the midst of and contemplating such scenes as these, it was that Henry determined to finish his mission in the city and leave it by the earliest conveyance over Pontchartrain for Alabama – Mobile being the point at which he aimed. Swiftly as the current of the fleeting Mississippi was time passing by, and many states lay in expanse before him, all of which, by the admonishing impulses of the dearest relations, he was compelled to pass over as a messenger of light and destruction.

Light, of necessity, had to be imparted to the darkened region of the obscure intellects of the slaves, to arouse them from their benighted condition to one of moral responsibility, to make them sensible that liberty was legitimately and essentially theirs, without which there was no distinction between them and the brute. Following as a necessary consequence would be the destruction of oppression and ignorance.

Alone and friendless, without a home, a fugitive from slavery, a child of misfortune and outcast upon the world, floating on the cold surface of chance, now in the midst of a great city of opulence, surrounded by the most despotic restrictions upon his race, with renewed determination Henry declared that nothing short of an unforeseen Providence should impede his progress in the spread of secret organization among the slaves. So aroused, he immediately started for a house in the Lower Faubourg.

"My frien', who yeh lookin' foh?" kindly enquired a cautious black man, standing concealed in the shrubbery near the door of a low, tile-covered house standing back in the yard.

"A friend," replied Henry.

"Wat's 'is name?" continued the man.

"I do not rightly know."

"Would yeh know it ef yeh heahed it, my fren'?"

"I think I would."

"Is it Seth?"

"That's the very name!" said Henry.

"Wat yeh want wid 'im, my fren'?"

"I want to see him."

"I spose yeh do, fren'; but dat ain' answer my questin' yet. Wat yeh want wid 'em?"

"I would rather see him, then I'll be better able to answer."

"My fren'," replied the man, meaningly, "ah see da is somethin' in yeh; come in!" giving a significant cough before placing his finger on the latchstring.

On entering, from the number and arrangement of the seats, there was evidence of an anticipated gathering; but the evening being that of the Mardi Gras, there was nothing remarkable in this. Out from another room came a sharp, observing, shrewd little dark brown-skin woman, called in that community a griffe. Bowing, sidling and curtsying, she smilingly came forward.

"Wat brotha dis, Seth?" enquired she.

"Ah don'o," carelessly replied he with a signal of caution, which was not required in her case.

"Ah!" exclaimed Henry. "This is Mr. Seth! I'm glad to see you."

After a little conversation, in which freely participated Mrs. Seth, who evidently was deservingly the leading spirit of the evening, they soon became reconciled to the character and mission of their unexpected and self-invited guest.

"Phebe, go tell 'em," said Seth; when lightly tripping away she entered the door of the other room, which after a few moments' delay was partially opened, and by a singular and peculiar signal, Seth and the stranger were invited in. Here sat in one of the most secret and romantic-looking rooms, a party of fifteen, the representatives of the heads of that many plantations, who that night had gathered for the portentous purpose of a final decision on the hour to strike the first blow. On entering, Henry stood a little in check.

"Trus' 'em!" said Seth. "Yeh fine 'em da right saut uh boys – true to deh own color! Da come fom fifteen diffent plantation."

"They're the men for me!" replied Henry, looking around the room. "Is the house all safe?"

"Yes brotha, all safe an' soun', an' a big dog in da yahd, so dat no one can come neah widout ouah knowin' it."

"First, then, to prayer, and next to seclusion," said Henry, looking at Seth to lead in prayer.

"Brotha, gib us wud a' prah," said Seth to Henry, as the party on their knees bowed low their heads to the floor.

"I am not fit, brother, for a spiritual leader; my warfare is not Heavenly, but earthly; I have not to do with angels, but with men; not with righteousness, but wickedness. Call upon some brother who has more of the grace of God than I. If I ever were a Christian, slavery has made me a sinner; if I had been an angel, it would have made me a devil! I feel more like cursing than praying – may God forgive me! Pray for me, brethren!"

"Brotha Kits, gib us wud a prah, my brotha!" said Seth to an athletic, powerful black man.

"Its not fah ouah many wuds, noah long prah – ouah 'pinion uh ouah self, nah sich like, dat Dou anseh us; but de 'cerity ob ouah hahts an ouah 'tentions. Bless de young man dat come 'mong us; make 'im fit fah 'is day, time, an' genration! Dou knows, Laud, dat fah wat we 'semble; anseh dis ouah 'tition, an' gib us token ob Dine 'probation!" petitioned Kits, slapping his hand at the conclusion down upon and splitting open a pine table before him.

"Amen," responded the gathering.

"Let da wud run an' be glorify!" exclaimed Nathan Seth.

The splitting of the table was regarded as ominous, but of doubtful signification, the major part considering it as rather unfavorable. Making no delay, lest a despondency ensue through fear and superstition, Henry at once entered into seclusion, completing an organization.

"God sen' yeh had come along dis way befo'!" exclaimed Phebe Seth.

"God grant 'e had!" responded Nathan.

"My Laud! I feels like a Sampson! ah feels like gwine up to take de city mehself!" cried out Kits, standing erect in the floor with fists clenched, muscles braced, eyes shut, and head thrown back.

"Yes, yes!" exclaimed Phebe. "Blessed be God, brotha Kits, da King is in da camp!"

"Powah, powah!" responded Seth. "Da King is heah!"

"Praise 'is name!" shouted Phebe clapping and rubbing her hands. "Fah wat I feels an' da knowledge I has receive dis night! I been all my days in darkness till now! I feels we shall be a people yit! Thang' God, thang God!" when she skidded over the floor from side to side, keeping time with a tune sung to the words—

> *"We'll honor our Lord and Master;*
> *We'll honor our Lord and King;*
> *We'll honor our Lord and Master,*

> *And bow at His command!*
> *O! brothers, did you hear the news?*
> *Lovely Jesus is coming!*
> *If ever I get to the house of the Lord,*
> *I'll never come back any more."*

"It's good to be heah!" shouted Seth.

"Ah! dat it is, brotha Seth!" responded Kits. "Da Laud is nigh, dat 'e is! 'e promise whahsomeveh two-three 'semble, to be in da mids' and dat to bless 'em, an' 'is promise not in vain, case 'e heah tonight!"

At the moment which Phebe took her seat, nearly exhausted with exercise, a loud rap at the door, preceded by the signal for the evening, alarmed the party.

"Come in, brotha Tib – come quick, if yeh comin!" bade Seth, in a low voice hastily, as he partially opened the door, peeping out into the other room.

"O, pshaw!" exclaimed Phebe, as she and her husband yet whispered; "I wish he stay away. I sho nobody want 'em! he all'as half drunk anyhow. Good ev'nin', brotha Tib. How yeh been sense we see yeh early paut da night?"

"Reasable, sistah – reasable, thang God. Well, what yeh all 'cided on? I say dis night now au neveh!" said Tib, evidently bent on mischief.

"Foolishness, foolishness!" replied Phebe. "It make me mad see people make fool uh demself! I wish 'e stay home an' not bothen heah!"

"Ah, 'spose I got right to speak as well as da rest on yeh! Yeh all ain' dat high yit to keep body fom talkin', ah 'spose. Betta wait tell yeh git free fo' ye 'temp' scrow oveh people dat way! I kin go out yeh house!" retorted the mischievous man, determined on distracting their plans.

"Nobody odeh yeh out, but I like see people have sense, specially befo' strangehs! an' know how behave demself!"

"I is gwine out yeh house," gruffly replied the man.

"My friend," said Henry, "listen a moment to me. You are not yet ready for a strike; you are not yet ready to do anything effective. You have barely taken the first step in the matter, and—"

"Strangeh!" interrupted the distracter. "Ah don'o yeh name, yeh strangeh to me—I see yeh talk 'bout 'step'; how many step man got take fo' 'e kin walk? I likes to know dat! Tell me that fus, den yeh may ax me what yeh choose!"

"You must have all the necessary means, my brother," persuasively resumed Henry, "for the accomplishment of your ends. Intelligence among yourself on everything pertaining to your designs and project. You must know what, how, and when to do. Have all the instrumentalities necessary for an effective effort, before making the attempt. Without this, you will fail, utterly fail!"

"Den ef we got wait all dat time, we neveh be free!" gruffly replied he. "I goes in foh dis night! I say dis night! Who goes—"

"Shet yo' big mouth! Sit down! Now make a fool o' yo'self!" exclaimed several voices with impatience, which evidently only tended to increase the mischief.

"Dis night, dis night au neveh!" boisterously yelled the now infuriated man at the top of his voice. "Now's da time!" when he commenced shuffling about over the floor, stamping and singing at the top of his voice—

> *Come all my brethren, let us take a rest,*
> *While the moon shines bright and clear;*
> *Old master died and left us all at last,*

> *And has gone at the bar to appear!*
> *Old master's dead and lying in his grave;*
> *And our blood will now cease to flow;*
> *He will no more tramp on the neck of the slave,*
> *For he's gone where slaveholders go!*
> *Hang up the shovel and the hoe – o – o – o!*
> *I don't care whether I work or no!*
> *Old master's gone to the slaveholders rest—*
> *He's gone where they all ought to go!*

pointing down and concluding with an expression which indicated anything but a religious feeling.

"Shame so it is dat he's 'lowed to do so! I wish I was man foh 'im, I'd make 'im fly!" said Phebe much alarmed, as she heard the great dog in the yard, which had been so trained as to know the family visitors, whining and manifesting an uneasiness unusual with him. On going to the back door, a person suddenly retreated into the shrubbery, jumping the fence, and disappearing.

Soon, however, there was an angry low heavy growling of the dog, with suppressed efforts to bark, apparently prevented by fear on the part of the animal. This was succeeded by cracking in the bushes, dull heavy footsteps, cautious whispering, and stillness.

"Hush! Listen!" admonished Phebe. "What is dat? Wy don't Tyger bark? I don't understan' it! Seth, go out and see, will you? Wy don't some you men make dat fool stop? I wish I was man, I'd break 'is neck, so I would!" during which the betrayer was shuffling, dancing, and singing at such a pitch as to attract attention from without.

Seth seizing him from behind by a firm grasp of the collar with both hands, Tib sprang forward, slipping easily out of it, leaving the overcoat suspended in his assailant's hands, displaying studded around his waist a formidable array of deathly weapons, when rushing out of the front door, he in terrible accents exclaimed—

"Insurrection! Insurrection! Death to every white!"

With a sudden spring of their rattles, the gendarmes, who in cloisters had surrounded the house, and by constant menacing gestures with their maces kept the great dog, which stood back in a corner, in a snarling position in fear, arrested the miscreant, taking him directly to the old fort calaboose. In the midst of the confusion which necessarily ensued, Henry, Seth, and Phebe, Kits and fellow-leaders from the fifteen plantations, immediately fled, all having passes for the day and evening, which fully protected them in any part of the city away from the scene of disturbance.

Intelligence soon reached all parts of the city, that an extensive plot for rebellion of the slaves had been timely detected. The place was at once thrown into a state of intense excitement, the military called into requisition, dragoons flying in every direction, cannon from the old fort sending forth hourly through the night, thundering peals to give assurance of their sufficiency, and the infantry on duty traversing the streets, stimulating with martial air with voluntary vocalists, who readily joined in chorus to the memorable citing words in the Southern States of—

> *Go tell Jack Coleman,*
> *The Negroes are arising!*

Alarm and consternation succeeded pleasure and repose, sleep for the time seemed to have departed from the eyes of the inhabitants, men, women and children ran every direction through the streets, seeming determined if they were to be massacred, that it should be done in the open highways rather than secretly in their own houses. The commotion thus continued till the morning;

meanwhile editors, journalists, reporters, and correspondents, all were busily on the alert, digesting such information as would form an item of news for the press, or a standing reminiscence for historical reference in the future.

Chapter XXIII
The Rebel Blacks

FOR THE REMAINDER of the night secreting themselves in Conti and Burgundi streets, the rebel proprietors of the house in which was laid the plot for the destruction of the city were safe until the morning, their insurrectionary companions having effected a safe retreat to the respective plantations to which they belonged that evening.

Jason and Phebe Seth were the hired slaves of their own time from a widower master, a wealthy retired attorney at Baton Rouge, whose only concern about them was to call every ninety days at the counter of the Canal Bank of New Orleans, and receive the price of their hire, which was there safely deposited to his credit by the industrious and faithful servants. The house in which the rebels met had been hired for the occasion, being furnished rooms kept for transient accommodation.

On the earliest conveyance destined for the City of Mobile, Henry left, who, before he fled, admonished as his parting counsel, to "stand still and see the salvation"; the next day being noted by General Ransom, as an incident in his history, to receive a formal visit of a fortnight's sojourn, in the person of his slaves Jason and Phebe Seth.

The inquisition held in the case of the betrayer Tib developed fearful antecedents of extensive arrangements for the destruction of the city by fire and water, thereby compelling the white inhabitants to take refuge in the swamps, whilst the blacks marched up the coast, sweeping the plantations as they went.

Suspicions were fixed upon many, among whom was an unfortunate English schoolteacher, who was arrested and imprisoned, when he died, to the last protesting his innocence. Mr. Farland was a good and bravehearted man, disdaining to appeal for redress to his country, lest it might be regarded as the result of cowardice.

Taking fresh alarm at this incident, the municipal regulations have been most rigid in a system of restriction and espionage toward Negroes and mulattoes, almost destroying their self-respect and manhood, and certainly impairing their usefulness.

Chapter XXIV
A Flying Cloud

SAFELY IN Mobile Henry landed without a question, having on the way purchased of a passenger who was deficient of means to bear expenses, a horse by which he made a daring entry into the place. Mounting the animal which was fully caparisoned, he boldly rode to the principal livery establishment, ordering for it the greatest care until his master's arrival.

Hastening into the country he readily found a friend and seclusion in the hut of Uncle Cesar, on the plantation of Gen. Audly. Making no delay, early next morning he returned to the city to effect a special object. Passing by the stable where the horse had been left, a voice loudly cried out:

"There's that Negro boy, now! Hallo, there, boy! didn't you leave a horse here?"

Heeding not the interrogation, but speedily turning the first corner, Henry hastened away and was soon lost among the inhabitants.

"How yeh do, me frien'?" saluted a black man whom he met in a by-street. "Ar' yeh strangeh?"

"Why?" enquired Henry.

"O, nothin'! On'y I hearn some wite men talkin'j's now, an' da say some strange nigga lef' a hoss dar, an' da blev 'e stole 'em, an' da gwine ketch an' put 'em in de jail."

"If that's all, I live here. Good morning!" rejoined he who soon was making rapid strides in the direction of Georgia.

Every evening found him among the quarters of some plantations, safely secreted in the hut of some faithful, trustworthy slave, with attentive, anxious listeners, ready for an issue. So, on he went with flying haste, from plantation to plantation, till Alabama was left behind him.

In Georgia, though the laws were strict, the Negroes were equally hopeful. Like the old stock of Maryland and Virginia blacks from whom they were descended, they manifested a high degree of intelligence for slaves. Receiving their messenger with open arms, the aim of his advent among them spread like fire in a stubble. Everywhere seclusions were held and organizations completed, till Georgia stands like a city at the base of a burning mountain, threatened with destruction by an overflow of the first outburst of lava from above. Clearing the state without an obstruction, he entered that which of all he most dreaded, the haughty South Carolina.

Here the most relentless hatred appears to exist against the Negro, who seems to be regarded but as an animated thing of convenience or a domesticated animal, reared for the service of his master. The studied policy of the whites evidently is to keep the blacks in subjection and their spirits below a sentiment of self-respect. To impress the Negro with a sense of his own inferiority is a leading precept of their social system; to be white is the only evidence necessary to establish a claim to superiority. To be a "master" in South Carolina is to hold a position of rank and title, and he who approaches this the nearest is heightened at least in his own estimation.

These feelings engendered by the whites have been extensively incorporated with the elements of society among the colored people, giving rise to the "Brown Society" an organized association of mulattos, created by the influence of the whites, for the purpose of preventing pure-blooded Negroes from entering the social circle, or holding intercourse with them.

Here intelligence and virtue are discarded and ignored, when not in conformity with these regulations. A man with the prowess of Memnon, or a woman with the purity of the "black doves" of Ethiopia and charms of the "black virgin" of Solomon, avails them nothing, if the blood of the oppressor, engendered by wrong, predominates not in their veins.

Oppression is the author of all this, and upon the heads of the white masters let the terrible responsibility of this miserable stupidity and ignorance of their mulatto children rest; since to them was left the plan of their social salvation, let upon their consciences rest the penalties of their social damnation.

The transit of the runaway through this state was exceedingly difficult, as no fabrication of which he was capable could save him from the penalties of arrest. To assume freedom would be at once to consign himself to endless bondage, and to acknowledge himself a slave was at once to advertise for a master. His only course of safety was to sleep through the day and travel by night, always keeping to the woods.

At a time just at the peep of day when making rapid strides the baying of hounds and soundings of horns were heard at a distance.

Understanding it to be the sport of the chase, Henry made a hasty retreat to the nearest hiding place which presented, in the hollow of a log. On attempting to creep in a snarl startled him, when out leaped the fox, having counterrun his track several times, and sheltered in a fallen sycamore. Using his remedy for distracting dogs, he succeeded the fox in the sycamore, resting in safety during the day without molestation, though the dogs bayed within thirty yards of him, taking a contrary course by the distraction of their scent.

For every night of sojourn in the state he had a gathering, not one of which was within a hut, so closely were the slaves watched by patrol, and sometimes by mulatto and black overseers. These gatherings were always held in the forest. Many of the confidants of the seclusions were the much-dreaded runaways of the woods, a class of outlawed slaves, who continually seek the lives of their masters.

One day having again sought retreat in a hollow log where he lay sound asleep, the day being chilly, he was awakened by a cold application to his face and neck, which proved to have been made by a rattlesnake of the largest size, having sought the warmth of his bosom.

Henry made a hasty retreat, ever after declining the hollow of a tree. With rapid movements and hasty action, he like a wind cloud flew through the State of South Carolina, who like "a thief in the night" came when least expected.

Henry now entered Charleston, the metropolis, and head of the "Brown Society," the bane and dread of the blacks in the state, an organization formed through the instrumentality of the whites to keep the blacks and mulattos at variance. To such an extent is the error carried, that the members of the association, rather than their freedom would prefer to see the blacks remain in bondage. But many most excellent mulattos and quadroons condemn with execration this auxiliary of oppression. The eye of the intelligent world is on this "Brown Society"; and its members when and wherever seen are scanned with suspicion and distrust. May they not be forgiven for their ignorance when proving by repentance their conviction of wrong?

Lying by till late next morning, he entered the city in daylight, having determined boldly to pass through the street, as he might not be known from any common Negro. Coming to an extensive wood-yard he learned by an old black man who sat at the gate that the proprietors were two colored men, one of whom he pointed out, saying:

"Dat is my mausta."

Approaching a respectable-looking mulatto gentleman standing in conversation with a white, his foot resting on a log:

"Do you wish to hire help, sir?" enquired Henry respectfully touching his cap.

"Take off your hat, boy!" ordered the mulatto gentleman. Obeying the order, he repeated the question.

"Who do you belong to?" enquired the gentleman.

"I am free, sir!" replied he.

"You are a free boy? Are you not a stranger here?"

"Yes, sir."

"Then you lie, sir," replied the mulatto gentleman, "as you know that no free Negro is permitted to enter this state. You are a runaway, and I'll have you taken up!" at the same time walking through his office looking out at the front door as if for an officer.

Making a hasty retreat, in less than an hour he had left the city, having but a few minutes tarried in the hut of an old black family on the suburb, one of the remaining confidentials and adherents of the memorable South Carolina insurrection, when and to whom he imparted his fearful scheme.

"Ah!" said the old man, throwing his head in the lap of his old wife, with his hands around her neck, both of whom sat near the chimney with the tears coursing down their furrowed cheeks. "Dis many a day I been prayin' dat de Laud sen' a nudder Denmark 'mong us! De Laud now anseh my prar in dis young man! Go on, my son – go on – an' may God A'mighty bress yeh!"

North Carolina was traversed mainly in the night. When approaching the region of the Dismal Swamp, a number of the old confederates of the noted Nat Turner were met with, who hailed the daring young runaway as the harbinger of better days. Many of these are still long-suffering, hard-laboring slaves on the plantations; and some bold, courageous, and fearless adventurers, denizens of the mystical, antiquated, and almost fabulous Dismal Swamp, where for many years they have defied the approach of their pursuers.

Here Henry found himself surrounded by a different atmosphere, an entirely new element. Finding ample scope for undisturbed action through the entire region of the Swamp, he continued to go scattering to the winds and sowing the seeds of a future crop, only to take root in the thick black waters which cover it, to be grown in devastation and reaped in a whirlwind of ruin.

"I been lookin' fah yeh dis many years," said old Gamby Gholar, a noted high conjurer and compeer of Nat Turner, who for more than thirty years has been secluded in the Swamp, "an' been tellin' on 'em dat yeh 'ood come long, but da 'ooden' heah dat I tole 'em! Now da see! Dis many years I been seein' on yeh! Yes, 'ndeed, chile, dat I has!" and he took from a gourd of antiquated appearance which hung against the wall in his hut, many articles of a mysterious character, some resembling bits of woollen yarn, onionskins, oystershells, finger and toenails, eggshells, and scales which he declared to be from very dangerous serpents, but which closely resembled, and were believed to be those of innocent and harmless fish, with broken iron nails.

These he turned over and over again in his hands, closely inspecting them through a fragment of green bottle glass, which he claimed to be a mysterious and precious "blue stone" got at a peculiar and unknown spot in the Swamp, whither by a special faith he was led – and ever after unable to find the same spot – putting them again into the gourd, the end of the neck being cut off so as to form a bottle, he rattled the "goombah," as he termed it, as if endeavoring to frighten his guest. This process ended, he whispered, then sighted into the neck, first with one eye, then with the other, then shook, and so alternately whispering, sighting and shaking, until apparently getting tired, again pouring them out, fumbling among them until finding a forked breast-bone of a small bird, which, muttering to himself, he called the "charm bone of a treefrog."

"Ah," exclaimed Gamby as he selected out the mystic symbol handing it to Henry, "got yeh at las'. Take dis, meh son, an' so long as yeh keep it, da can' haum yeh, dat da can't. Dis woth money, meh son; da ain't many sich like dat in de Swamp! Yeh never want for nothin' so long as yeh keep dat!"

In this fearful abode for years of some of Virginia and North Carolina's boldest black rebels, the names of Nat Turner, Denmark Veezie, and General Gabriel were held by them in sacred reverence; that of Gabriel as a talisman. With delight they recounted the many exploits of whom they conceived to be the greatest men who ever lived, the pretended deeds of whom were fabulous, some of the narrators claiming to have been patriots in the American Revolution.

"Yeh offen hearn on Maudy Ghamus," said an old man stooped with age, having the appearance of a centenarian. "Dat am me – me heah!" continued he, touching himself on the breast. "I's de frien' on Gamby Gholar; an' I an' Gennel Gabel fit in de Malution wah, an' da want no sich fightin' dare as dat in Gabel wah!"

"You were then a soldier in the Revolutionary War for American independence, father?" enquired Henry.

"Gau bress yeh, hunny. Yes, 'ndeed, chile, long 'for yeh baun; dat I did many long day go! Yes, chile, yes!"

"And General Gabriel, too, a soldier of the American Revolution?" replied Henry.

"Ah, chile, dat 'e did fit in de Molution wah, Gabel so, an' 'e fit like mad dog! Wen 'e sturt, chile, da can't stop 'im; da may as well let 'im go long, da can't do nuffin' wid 'im."

Henry subscribed to his eminent qualifications as a warrior, assuring him that those were the kind of fighting men they then needed among the blacks. Maudy Ghamus to this assented, stating that the Swamp contained them in sufficient number to take the whole United States; the only difficulty in the way being that the slaves in the different states could not be convinced of their strength. He had himself for years been an emissary; also, Gamby Gholar, who had gone out among them with sufficient charms to accomplish all they desired, but could not induce the slaves to a general rising.

"Take plenty goomba an' fongosa 'long wid us, an' plant mocasa all along, an' da got nuffin' fah do but come, an' da 'ooden come!" despairingly declared Maudy Ghamus.

Gamby Gholar, Maudy Ghamus, and others were High Conjurors, who as ambassadors from the Swamp, were regularly sent out to create new conjurers, lay charms, take off "spells" that could not be reached by Low Conjurors, and renew the art of all conjurors of seven years existence, at the expiration of which period the virtue was supposed to run out; holding their official position by fourteen years appointments. Through this means the revenue is obtained for keeping up an organized existence in this much-dreaded morass – the Dismal Swamp.

Before Henry left they insisted upon, and anointed him a priest of the order of High Conjurors, and amusing enough it was to him who consented to satisfy the aged devotees of a time-honored superstition among them. Their supreme executive body called the "Head" consists in number of seven aged men, noted for their superior experience and wisdom. Their place of official meeting must be entirely secluded, either in the forest, a gully, secluded hut, an underground room, or a cave.

The seven old men who, with heightened spirits, hailed his advent among them, led Henry to the door of an ample cave – their hollow – at the door of which they were met by a large sluggish, lazily-moving serpent, but so entirely tame and petted that it wagged its tail with fondness toward Maudy as he led the party. The old men, suddenly stopping at the approach of the reptile, stepping back a pace, looked at each other mysteriously shaking their heads:

"Go back!" exclaimed Maudy waving his hand. "Go back, my chile! 'e in terrible rage! 'e got seben long toof, any on 'em kill yeh like flash!" tapping it slightly on the head with a twig of grapevine which he carried in his hand.

Looking at the ugly beast, Henry had determined did it approach to harm, to slay it; but instead, it quietly coiled up and lay at the door as if asleep, which reminded him of queer and unmeaning sounds as they approached, uttered by Gholar, which explained that the animal had been trained to approach when called as any other pet. The "Head" once in session, they created him conjuror of the highest degree known to their art.* With this qualification he was licensed with unlimited power – a power before given no one – to go forth and do wonders. The "Head" seemed, by the unlimited power given him, to place greater reliance in the efforts of Henry for their deliverance than in their own seven heads together.

"Go, my son," said they, "an' may God A'mighty hole up yo' han's an' grant us speedy 'liverence!"

Being now well refreshed – having rested without the fear of detection – and in the estimation of Gholar, Ghamus and the rest of the "Heads," well qualified to prosecute his project amidst the prayers, blessings, wishes, hopes, fears, pow-wows and promises of a never failing conjuration, and tears of the cloudy inhabitants of this great seclusion, among whom were the frosty-headed, bowed-down old men of the Cave, Henry left that region by his usual stealthy process, reaching Richmond, Virginia, in safety.

Chapter XXV
Like Father, Like Son

WITH HIS USUAL ADROITNESS, early in the morning, Henry entered Richmond boldly walking through the streets. This place in its municipal regulations, the customs and usages of society, the tastes and assumptious pride of the inhabitants, much resembles Charleston, South Carolina, the latter being a modified model of the former.

The restrictions here concerning Negroes and mulattos are less rigid, as they may be permitted to continue in social or religious gatherings after nine o'clock at night provided a white person be present to inspect their conduct; and may ride in a carriage, smoke a cigar in daylight, or walk with a staff at night.

According to an old-existing custom said to have originated by law, a mulatto or quadroon who proved a white mother were themselves regarded as white: and many availing themselves of the fact, took advantage of it by leaving their connections with the blacks and turning entirely over to the whites. Their children take further advantage of this by intermarrying with the whites, by which their identity becomes extinct, and they enter every position in society both social and political. Some of the proudest American statesmen in either House of the Capital, receive their poetic vigor of imagination from the current of Negro blood flowing in their veins.

Like those of Charleston, some of the light mixed bloods of Richmond hold against the blacks and pure-blooded Negroes the strongest prejudice and hatred, all engendered by the teachings of their Negro-fearing master-fathers. All of the terms and epithets of disparagement commonly used by the whites toward the blacks are as readily applied to them by this class of the mixed bloods. Shy of the blacks and fearful of the whites, they go sneaking about with the countenance of a criminal, of one conscious of having done wrong to his fellows. Spurned by the one and despised by the other, they are the least happy of all the classes. Of this class was Mrs. Pierce, whose daughter stood in the hall door, quite early enjoying the cool air this morning.

"Miss," enquired Henry of the young quadroon lady, "can you inform me where I'll find the house of Mr. Norton, a colored family in this city?" politely raising his cap as he approached her.

With a screech she retreated into the house, exclaiming, that a black Negro at the door had given her impudence. Startled at this alarm so unexpected to him – though somewhat prepared for such from his recent experience in Charleston – Henry made good a most hasty retreat before the father, with a long red "hide" in his hand, could reach the door. The man grimaced, declaring, could he have his way, every black in the country would be sold away to labor.

Finding the house of his friend, he was safely secluded until evening, when developing his scheme, the old material extinguished and left to mould and rot after the demonstration at Southampton, was immediately rekindled, never again to be suppressed until the slaves stood up the equal of the masters. Southampton – the name of Southampton to them was like an electric shock.

"Ah, Laud!" replied Uncle Medly, an old man of ninety-four years, when asked whether or not he would help his brethren in a critical time of need. "Dat I would. Ef I do noffin' else, I pick up dirt an' tro' in der eye!" meaning in that of their masters.

"Glory to God!" exclaimed his wife, an old woman of ninety years.

"Hallelujah!" responded her daughter, the wife of Norton, the man of the house.

"Blessed be God's eternal name!" concluded the man himself. "I've long been praying and looking, but God has answered me at last."

"None could answer it, but a prayer-hearing God!" replied the wife.

"None would answer it, but a prayer-hearing God!" responded the husband.

"None did answer it, but a prayer-hearing God!" exclaimed the woman. "Glory to God! Glory to God! 'Tis none but He can deliver!"

They fell on their knees to pray, when fervent was their devotion; after which Henry left, but on account of a strict existing patrol regulation, was obliged for three days to be in the wood, so closely watched was he. The fourth evening he effected most adroitly an escape from his hiding place, passing through a strong guard of patrol all around him, entering the District of Columbia at early dawn, soon entering the City of Washington.

The slave prison of Williams and Brien conspicuously stood among the edifices; high in the breeze from the flagstaff floated defiantly the National Colors, stars as the pride of the white man, and stripes as the emblem of power over the blacks. At this the fugitive gave a passing glance, but with hurried steps continued his course, not knowing whither he would tarry. He could only breathe in soliloquy, "How long, O Lord of the oppressed, how long shall this thing continue?"

Passing quietly along, gazing in at every door, he came to a stop on the corner of Pennsylvania avenue and Sixth Street. On entering, looking into the establishment, his eye unexpectedly caught that of a person who proved to be a mulatto gentleman, slowly advancing toward the door.

His first impulse was to make a retreat, but fearing the effort would be fatal, bracing his nerves, he stood looking the person full in the face.

"Do you want anything, young man?" enquired the mulatto gentleman, who proved to be the proprietor.

"I am hungry, sir!" Henry quickly replied.

"You're a stranger, then, in the city?"

"I am, sir."

"Never here before?"

"Never before, sir."

"Have you no acquaintance in the place?"

"None at all, sir."

"Then, sir, if you'll come in, I'll see if I can find as much as you can eat." replied the goodhearted man.

Setting him down to a comfortable breakfast, the wife and niece of the proprietor kindly attended upon him, filling his pouch afterwards with sufficient for the day's travel.

Giving him a parting hand, Henry left with, "God Almighty bless the family!" clearing the city in a short time.

"I understand it all," replied the gentleman in response, "and may the same God guide and protect you by the way!" justly regarding him as a fugitive.

The kindness received at the hands of this family* brought tears of gratitude to the eyes of the recipient, especially when remembering his treatment from the same class in Charleston and Richmond. About the same time that Henry left the city, the slave of a distinguished Southern statesman also left Washington and the comforts of home and kindness of his master forever.

From Washington taking a retrograde course purposely to avoid Maryland, where he learned they were already well advised and holding gatherings, the margin of Virginia was cut in this hasty passage, so as to reach more important points for communication. Stealing through the neighborhood and swimming the river, a place was reached called Mud Fort, some four miles distant from Harper's Ferry, situated on the Potomac.

Seeing a white man in a field near by, he passed on as if unconscious of his presence, when the person hailing him in broken English questioned his right to pass.

"I am going to Charleston, sir." replied Henry.

"Vat fahr?" inquired the Dutchman.

"On business," replied he.

"You nagher, you! dat ish not anzer mine question! I does ax you vat fahr you go to Charleston, and you anzer me dat!"

"I told you, sir, that I am going on business."

"You ish von zaucy nagher, andt I bleve you one runaway! Py ching, I vill take you pack!" said the man instantly climbing the fence to get into the road where the runaway stood.

"That will do," exclaimed Henry, "you are near enough – I can bring you down there," at the same time presenting a well-charged six-barrel weapon of death; when the affrighted Dutchman fell on the opposite side of the fence unharmed, and Henry put down his weapon without a fire.

Having lurked till evening in a thicket near by, Charleston was entered near the depot, just at the time when the last train was leaving for Washington. Though small, this place was one of the most difficult in which to promote his object, as the slaves were but comparatively few, difficult to be seen, and those about the depot and house servants, trained to be suspicious and mistrustful of strange blacks, and true and faithful to their masters. Still, he was not remiss in finding a friend and a place for the seclusion.

This place was most admirably adapted for the gathering, being held up a run or little stream, in a bramble thicket on a marshy meadow of the old Brackenridge estate, but a few minutes walk from the town. This evening was that of a strict patrol watch, their headquarters for the night being in Worthington's old mills, from which ran the race, passing near which was the most convenient way to reach the place of gathering for the evening.

While stealthily moving along in the dark, hearing a cracking in the weeds and a soft tramping of feet, Henry secreted himself in a thick high growth of Jamestown weeds along the fence, when he slightly discerned a small body of men as if reconnoitering the neighborhood. Sensible of the precariousness of his condition, the fugitive lie as still as death, lest by dint he might be discovered, as much fear and apprehension then prevaded the community.

Charleston, at best, was a hard place for a Negro, and under the circumstances, had he been discovered, no plea would have saved him. Breathlessly crouched beneath the foliage and thorns of the fetid weed, he was startled by a voice suddenly exclaiming—

"Hallo there! who's that?" which provided to be that of one of the patrol, the posse having just come down the bank of the race from the mill.

"Sahvant, mausta!" was the humble reply.

"Who are you?" further enquired the voice.

"Zack Parker, sir."

"Is that you, old Zack?"

"Yes, mausta – honner bright."

"Come, Zack, you must go with us! Don't you know that Negroes are not allowed to be out at night alone, these times? Come along!" said Davy Hunter.

"Honner bright, maus Davy – honner bright!" continued the old black slave of Colonel Davenport, quietly walking beside them along the mill race, the water of which being both swift and deep. "Maus Davy, I got some mighty good rum here in dis flas' – you gentmen hab some? Mighty good! Mine I tells you, maus Davy – mighty good!"

"Well, Zack, we don't care to take a little," replied Bob Flagg. "Have you had your black mouth to this flask?"

"Honner bright, maus Bobby – honner bright!" replied the old man.

Hunter raised the flask to his mouth, the others gathering around, each to take a draught in turn, when instantly a plunge in the water was heard, and the next moment old Zack Parker was swinging his hat in triumph on the opposite bank of the channel, exclaiming, "Honner bright, gentmen! Honner bright! Happy Jack an' no trouble!" – the last part of the sentence being a cant phrase commonly in use in that part of the country, to indicate a feeling free from all cares.

In a rage the flask was thrown in the dark, and alighted near his feet upright in the tufts of grass, when the old man in turn seizing the vessel, exclaiming aloud, "Yo' heath, gentmen! Yo' good heath!" Then turning it up to his mouth, the sound heard across the stream gave evidence of his enjoyment of the remainder of the contents. "Thank'e, gentmen – good night!" when away went Zack to the disappointment and even amusement of the party.

Taking advantage of this incident, Henry, under a guide, found a place of seclusion, and a small number of good willing spirits ready for the counsel.

"Mine, my chile!" admonished old Aunt Lucy. "Mine hunny, how yeh go long case da all'as lookin' arter black folks."

Taking the nearest course through Worthington's woods, he reached in good time that night the slave quarters of Captain Jack Briscoe and Major Brack Rutherford. The blacks here were united by the confidential leaders of Moore's people, and altogether they were rather a superior gathering of slaves to any yet met with in Virginia. His mission here soon being accomplished, he moved rapidly on to Slaughter's, Crane's and Washington's old plantations, where he caused a glimmer of light, which until then had never been thought of, much less seen, by them.

The night rounds of the patrol of the immediate neighborhood, caused a hurried retreat from Washington's – the last place at which he stopped – and daybreak the next morning found him in near proximity to Winchester, when he sought and obtained a hiding place in the woods of General Bell.

The people here he found ripe and ready for anything that favored their redemption. Taylor's, Logan's, Whiting's and Tidball's plantations all had crops ready for the harvest.

"An' is dis de young man," asked Uncle Talton, stooped with the age of eighty-nine years, "dat we hearn so much ob, dat's gwine all tru de country 'mong de black folks? Tang God a'mighty for wat I lib to see!" and the old man straightened himself up to his greatest height, resting on his staff, and swinging himself around as if whirling on the heel as children sometimes do, exclaimed in the gladness of his heart and the bouyancy of his spirits at the prospect of freedom before him: "I dont disagard none on 'em," referring to the whites.

"We have only 'regarded' them too long, father," replied Henry with a sigh of sorrow, when he looked upon the poor old time and care-worn slave, whose only hope for freedom rested in his efforts.

"I neber 'spected to see dis! God bless yeh, my son! May God 'long yeh life!" continued the old man, the tears streaming down his cheeks.

"Amen!" sanctioned Uncle Ek.

"God grant it!" replied Uncle Duk.

"May God go wid yeh, my son, wheresomeber yeh go!" exclaimed the old slaves present; when Henry, rising from the block of wood upon which he sat, being moved to tears, reaching out his hand, said, "Well, brethren, mothers, and fathers! My time with you is up, and I must leave you – farewell!" when this faithful messenger of his oppressed brethren, was soon in the woods, making rapid strides towards Western Virginia.

Wheeling, in the extreme Western part of Virginia, was reached by the fugitive, where the slaves, already restless and but few in number in consequence of their close proximity to a free state – Ohio being on the opposite side of the river, on the bank of which the town is situated – could never thereafter become contented.

The "Buckeye State" steamer here passed along on a downward trip, when boarding her as a black passenger, Cincinnati in due season was reached, when the passengers were transferred to the "Telegraph No. 2," destined for Louisville, Kentucky. Here crowding in with the passengers, he went directly to Shippenport, a small place but two miles below – the rapids or falls preventing the large class of steamers from going thence except at the time of high water – the "Crystal Palace," a beautiful packet, was boarded, which swiftly took him to Smithland, at the confluence of the Cumberland and Ohio rivers.

From this point access up the Cumberland was a comparatively easy task, and his advent into Nashville, Tennessee, was as unexpected at this time to the slaves, as it was portentous and ominous to the masters.

There was no difficulty here in finding a seclusion, and the introduction of his subject was like the application of fire to a drought-seasoned stubble field. The harvest was ripe and ready for the scythe, long before the reaper and time for gathering came. In both town and country the disappointment was sad, when told by Henry that the time to strike had not yet come; that they for the present must "Stand still and see the salvation!"

"How long, me son, how long we got wait dis way?" asked Daddy Luu, a good old man and member of a Christian church for upwards of forty years.

"I can't tell exactly, father, but I suppose in this, as in all other good works, the Lord's own annointed time!" replied he.

"An' how long dat gwine be, honey? case I's mighty ti'ed waitin' dis way!" earnestly responded the old man.

"I can't tell you how long, father; God knows best."

"An' how we gwine know w'en 'E is ready?"

"When we are ready, He is ready, and not till then is His time."

"God sen we was ready, now den!" concluded the old man, blinded with tears, and who, from the reverence they had for his age and former good counsel among them, this night was placed at the head of the Gathering.

Carrying with him the prayers and blessings of his people here, Henry made rapid strides throughout this state, sowing in every direction seeds of the crop of a future harvest.

From Tennessee Henry boldly strode into Kentucky, and though there seemed to be a universal desire for freedom, there were few who were willing to strike. To run away, with them, seemed to be the highest conceived idea of their right to liberty. This they were doing, and would continue to do on every favorable opportunity, but their right to freedom by self-resistance, to them was forbidden by the Word of God. Their hopes were based on the long-talked-of promised emancipation in the state.

"What was your dependence," inquired he of an old man verging on the icy surface of ninety winters' slippery pathways, "before you had this promise of emancipation?"

"Wy, dar war Guvneh Metcalf, I sho 'e good to black folks," replied Uncle Winson.

"Well, uncle, tell me, supposing he had not been so, what would you have then done?"

"Wy, chile, I sho 'e raise up dat time 'sides dem maus Henry and maus John."

"But what good have they ever done you? I don't see that you are any better off than had they never lived."

"Ah, chile! Da good to we black folks," continued the old man, with a fixed belief that they were emancipationists and the day of freedom, to the slaves drew near.

Satisfied that self-reliance was the furthest from their thoughts, but impressing them with new ideas concerning their rights, the great-hearted runaway bid them "Good bye, and may God open your eyes to see your own condition!" when in a few minutes Lexington was relieved of an enemy, more potent than the hostile bands of red men who once defied the military powers of Kentucky.

In a few days this astonishing slave was again on the smooth waters of the beautiful Ohio, making speed as fast as the steamer "Queen of the West" could carry him down stream towards Grand Gulf on the great river of the Southwest.

Chapter XXVI
Return to Mississippi

THE EVENING, for the season, was very fine; the sky beautiful; the stars shining unusually bright; while Henry, alone on the hurricane deck of the "Queen of the West," stood in silence abaft the wheel-house, gazing intently at the golden orbs of Heaven. Now shoots a meteor, then seemingly shot a comet, again glistened a brilliant planet which almost startled the gazer; and while he yet stood motionless in wonder looking into the heavens, a blazing star whose scintillations dazzled the sight, and for the moment bewildered the mind, was seen apparently to vibrate in a manner never before observed by him.

At these things Henry was filled with amazement, and disposed to attach more than ordinary importance to them, as having an especial bearing in his case; but the mystery finds interpretation in the fact that the emotions were located in his own brain, and not exhibited by the orbs of Heaven.

Through the water plowed the steamer, the passengers lively and mirthful, sometimes amusingly noisy, whilst the adventurous and heart-stricken fugitive, without a companion or friend with whom to share his grief and sorrows, and aid in untangling his then deranged mind, threw himself in tribulation upon the humble pallet assigned him, there to pour out his spirit in communion with the Comforter of souls on high.

The early rising of the passengers aroused him from apparently an abridged night of intermitting sleep, when creeping away into a by-place, he spent the remainder of the day. Thus by sleeping through the day, and watching in the night – induced by the proximity to his old home – did the runaway spend the time during the first two days of his homeward journey.

Falling into a deep sleep early on the evening of the third day, he was suddenly aroused about eleven o'clock by the harsh singing of the black firemen on the steamer:

Natchez under the Hill!
Natchez under the Hill!

sung to an air with which they ever on the approach of a steamer, greet the place, as seemingly a sorrowful reminiscence of their ill-fated brethren continually sold there; when springing to his feet and hurrying upon deck, he found the vessel full upon the wharf boat stationed at the Natchez landing.

Taking advantage of the moment – passing from the wheelhouse down the ladder to the lower deck – thought by many to have gone forever from the place, Henry effected without detection an easy transit to the wharf, and from thence up the Hill, where again he found himself amid the scenes of his saddest experience, and the origination and organization of the measures upon which were based his brightest hopes and expectations for the redemption of his race in the South.

Chapter XXVII
A Night of Anxiety

ON SATURDAY EVENING, about half past seven, was it that Henry dared again to approach the residence of Colonel Franks. The family had not yet retired, as the lights still burned brilliantly in the great house, when, secreted in the shrubbery contiguous to the hut of Mammy Judy and Daddy Joe, he lay patiently awaiting the withdrawal in the mansion.

"There's no use in talkin,' Andy, he's gittin' suspicious of us all," said Charles, "as he threatens us all with the traders; an' if Henry don't come soon, I'll have to leave anyhow! But the old people, Andy, I can't think of leavin' them!"

"Do you think da would go if da had a chance, Charles?"

"Go? yes 'ndeed, Andy, they'd go this night if they could git off. Since the sellin' of Maggie, and Henry's talkin' to 'em, and his goin' an' takin' little Joe, and Ailcey, an' Cloe, an' Polly an' all clearin' out, they altered their notion about stayin' with ole Franks."

"Wish we could know when Henry's comin' back. Wonder what 'e is," said Andy.

"Here!" was the reply in a voice so cautiously suppressed, and so familiarly distinct that they at once recognized it to be that of their long-absent and most anxiously looked-for friend. Rushing upon him, they mutually embraced, with tears of joy and anxiety.

"How have you been anyhow, Henry?" exclaimed Charles in a suppressed tone. "I's so glad to see yeh, dat I ain't agwine to speak to yeh, so I ain't!" added Andy.

"Come, brethren, to the woods!" said Henry; when the three went directly to the forest, two and half miles from the city.

"Well now, Henry, tell us all about yourself. What you been doin'?" inquired Charles.

"I know of nothing about myself worth telling," replied he.

"Oh, pshaw! wot saut a way is dat, Henry; yeh wont tell a body nothin'. Pshaw, dats no way," grumbled Andy.

"Yes, Andy, I've much to tell you; but not of myself; 'tis about our poor oppressed people everywhere I've been! But we have not now time for that."

"Why, can't you tell us nothin'?"

"Well, Andy, since you must have something, I'll tell you this much: I've been in the Dismal Swamp among the High Conjurors, and saw the heads, old Maudy Ghamus and Gamby Gholar."

"Hoop! now 'e's a talkin'! Ef 'e wasn't I wouldn't tell yeh so! An' wat da sa to yeh, Henry?"

"They welcomed me as the messenger of their deliverance; and as a test of their gratitude, made me a High Conjuror after their own order."

"O pshaw, Henry! Da done what? Wy, ole feller, yeh is high sho 'nough!"

"What good does it do, Henry, to be a conjuror?" inquired Charles.

"It makes the more ignorant slaves have greater confidence in, and more respect for, their headmen and leaders."

"Oh yes, I see now! Because I couldn't see why you would submit to become a conjuror if it done no good."

"That's it, Charles! As you know, I'll do anything not morally wrong, to gain our freedom; and to effect this, we must take the slaves, not as we wish them to be, but as we really find them to be."

"You say it gives power, Henry; is there any reality in the art of conjunction?"

"It only makes the slaves afraid of you if you are called a conjuror, that's all!"

"Oh, I understand it well enough now!" concluded Charles.

"I undehstood well 'nough fuss, but I want to know all I could, dat's all!" added Andy. "Ole Maudy's a high feller, aint 'e, Henry?"

"Oh yes! he's the Head," replied Charles.

"No," explained Henry, "he's not now Head, but Gamby Gholar, who has for several years held that important position among them. Their Council consists of Seven, called the 'Heads,' and their Chief is called 'the Head.' Everything among them, in religion, medicine, laws, or politics, of a public character, is carried before the Head in Council to be settled and disposed of."

"Now we understan'," said Andy, "but tell us, Henry, how yeh get 'long 'mong de folks whar yeh bin all dis time?"

"Very well; everywhere except Kentucky, and there you can't move them toward a strike!"

"Kentucky!" rejoined Andy. "I all'as thought dat de slaves in dat state was de bes' treated uv any, an' dat da bin all 'long spectin' to be free."

"That's the very mischief of it, Andy! 'Tis this confounded 'good treatment' and expectation of getting freed by their oppressors, that has been the curse of the slave. All shrewd masters, to keep their slaves in check, promise them their freedom at their, the master's death, as though they were certain to die first. This contents the slave, and makes him obedient and willing to serve and toil on, looking forward to the promised redemption. This is just the case precisely now in Kentucky. It was my case. While Franks treated me well, and made promises of freedom to my wife" – and he gave a deep sigh – "I would doubtless have been with him yet; but his bad treatment – his inhuman treatment of my wife – my poor, poor wife! – poor Maggie! was that which gave me courage, and made me determined to throw off the yoke, let it cost me what it would. Talk to me of a good master! A 'good master' is the very worst of masters. Were they all cruel and inhuman, or could the slaves be made to see their treatment aright, they would not endure their oppression for a single hour!"

"I sees it, I sees it!" replied Andy.

"An' so do I," added Charles, "who couldn't see that?"

"I tells yeh, Henry, it was mighty haud for me to make up my mine to leave ole Potteh; but even sence you an' Chaules an' me made de vow togedder, I got mo' an' mo' to hate 'im. I could chop 'is head off sometime, I get so mad. I bleve I could chop off Miss Mary' head; an' I likes hur; she mighty good to we black folks."

"Pshaw! yes 'ndeed' ole Frank's head would be nothin' for me to chop off; I could chop off mistess head, an' you know she's a good woman; but I mus' be mighty mad fus'!" said Charles.

"That's it, you see. There is no danger that a 'good' master or mistress will ever be harmed by the slaves. There's neither of you, Andy, could muster up courage enough to injure a 'good master' or mistress. And even I now could not have the heart to injure Mrs. Franks," said Henry.

"Now me," replied Charles.

"Yes, 'ndeed, dats a fac', case I knows I couldn' hurt Miss Mary Potteh. I bleve I'd almos' chop off anybody's head if I see 'em 'tempt to hurt 'e!" added Andy; when they heartily laughed at each other.

"Just so!" said Henry. "A slave has no just conception of his own wrongs. Had I dealt with Franks as he deserved, for doing that for which he would have taken the life of any man had it been his case – tearing my wife from my bosom! – the most I could take courage directly to do, was to leave him, and take as many from him as I could induce to go. But maturer reflection drove me to the expedient of avenging the general wrongs of our people, by inducing the slave, in his might, to scatter red ruin throughout the region of the South. But still, I cannot find it in my heart to injure an individual, except in personal conflict."

"An has yeh done it, Henry?" earnestly inquired Andy.

"Yes, Andy; yes, I have done it! and I thank God for it! I have taught the slave that mighty lesson: to strike for Liberty. 'Rather to die as freemen, than live as slaves!'"

"Thang God!" exclaimed Charles.

"Amen!" responded Andy.

"Now, boys, to the most important event of your lives!" said Henry.

"Wat's dat?" asked Andy.

"Why, get ready immediately to leave your oppressors tonight!" replied he.

"Glory to God!" cried Andy.

"Hallelujah!" responded Charles.

"Quietly! Softly! Easy, boys, easy!" admonished Henry, when the party in breathless silence, on tiptoe moved off from the thicket in which they were then seated, toward the city.

It was now one o'clock in the night, and Natchez shrouded in darkness and quiet, when the daring and fearless runaway with his companions, entered the enclosure of the great house grounds, and approached the door of the hut of Daddy Joe and Mammy Judy.

"Who dat! Who dat, I say? Ole man, don' yeh hear some un knockin' at de doh?" with fright said Mammy Judy in a smothered tone, hustling and nudging the old man, who was in a deep sleep, when Henry rapped softly at the door.

"Wat a mautta, ole umin?" after a while inquired the old man, rubbing his eyes.

"Some un at de doh!" she replied.

"Who dar?" inquired Daddy Joe.

"A friend!" replied Henry with suppressed voice.

"Ole man, open de doh quick! I bleve in me soul dat Henry! Open de doh!" said mammy.

On the door being opened, the surprise and joy of the old woman was only equalled by the emotion of her utterance.

"Dar! dar now, ole man! I tole 'em so, but da 'uden bleve me! I tole 'em 'e comin', but da 'uden lis'en to me! Did yeh git 'er, me son? Little Joe cum too? O Laud! whar's my po' chile! What's Margot?"

To evade further inquiry, Henry replied that they were all safe, and hoping to see her and the old man.

"How yeh bin, my chile? I'se glad to see yeh, but mighty sorry eh cum back; case de wite folks say, da once git der hands on yeh da neber let yeh go 'g'in! Potteh, Craig, Denny, and all on 'em, da tryin' to fine whar yeh is, hunny!"

"I am well, mammy, and come now to see what is to be done with you old people," said Henry.

"We 'ont to be hear long, chile; de gwine sell us all to de traders!" replied mammy with a deep sigh.

"Yes chile," added Daddy Joe, "we all gwine to de soul-driveh!"

"You'll go to no soul-drivers!" replied Henry, the flash of whose eyes startled Mammy Judy.

"How yeh gwine help it, chile?" kindly asked Daddy Joe.

"I'll show you. Come, come, mammy! You and daddy get ready, as I've come to take you away, and must be at the river before two o'clock," said Henry, who with a single jerk of a board in the floor of the hut, had reached the hidden treasure of the old people.

"Who gwine wid us, chile?" inquired Mammy Judy.

"Charles, Andy, and his female friend, besides some we shall pick up by the way!" replied Henry.

"Now he's a-talkin'!" jocosely said Charles, looking at Andy with a smile, at the mention of his female friend.

"'E ain' doin' nothin' else!" replied Andy.

"Wat become o' po' little Tony! 'E sleep here tonight case he not berry well. Po' chile!" sighed the old woman.

"We'll take him too, of course; and I would that I could take every slave in Natchez!" replied Henry. "It is now half-past one," said he, looking at his watch, "and against two we must be at the river. Go Andy, and get your friend, and meet us at the old burnt sycamore stump above the ferry. Come mammy and daddy, not a word for your lives!" admonished Henry, when taking their package on his back, and little Tony by the hand, they left forever the great house premises of Colonel Stephen Franks in Natchez.

On approaching the river a group was seen, which proved to consist of Andy, Clara (to whom his integrity was plighted), and the faithful old stump, their guidepost for the evening. Greeting each other with tears of joy and fearful hearts, they passed down to the water's edge, but a few hundred feet below.

The ferry boat in this instance was a lightly built yawl, commanded by a white man; the ferry one of many such selected along the shore, expressly for such occasions.

"Have you a pass?" demanded the boatman as a ruse, lest he might be watched by a concealed party. "Let me see it!"

"Here, sir," said Henry, presenting to him by the light of a match which he held in his hand for the purpose, the face of a half eagle.

"Here is seven of you, an' I can't do it for that!" in an humble undertone supplicating manner, said the man. "I axes that for one!"

The weight of seven half eagles dropped into his hand, caused him eagerly to seize the oars, making the quickest possible time to the opposite side of the river.

Chapter XXVIII
Studying Head Work

"NOW HENRY," said Andy, after finding themselves in a safe place some distance from the landing, "you promise' w'en we stauted to show us de Noth Star – which is it?" On looking up the sky was too much obscured with clouds.

"I can't show it to you now, but when we stop to refresh, I'll then explain it to you," replied he.

"It high time now, chil'en, we had a mou'full to eat ef we got travel dis way!" suggested Mammy Judy, breaking silence for the first time since they left the great house.

"Yes," replied Andy, "Clara and little Tony mus' wan' to eat, an' I knows wat dis chile wants!" touching himself on the breast.

The runaways stopped in the midst of an almost impenetrable thicket, kindled a fire to give them light, where to take their fare of cold meat, bread and butter, and cheese, of which the cellar and pantry of Franks, to which Mammy Judy and Charles had access, afforded an ample supply.

Whilst the others were engaged in refreshing, Henry, aside of a stump, was busily engaged with pencil and paper.

"Whar's Henry, dat 'e ain't hear eatin?" inquired Mammy Judy, looking about among the group.

"I sho, ole umin, 'e's oveh dar by de stump," replied Daddy Joe.

"Wat dat boy doin' dar? Henry, wat yeh doin'? Mus' be studyin' headwuck, I reckon! Sho boy! betteh come 'long an' git a mou'full to eat. Yeh ain' hungry I reckon," said the old woman.

"Henry, we dun eatin' now. You mos' ready to tell us 'bout de Noth Star?" said Andy.

"Yes, I will show you," said Henry, walking forward and setting himself in the center of the group. "You see these seven stars which I've drawn on this piece of paper – numbered 1, 2, 3, 4, 5, 6, 7? From the peculiarity of the shape of their relative position to each other, the group is called the 'Dipper,' because to look at them they look like a dipper or a vessel with a long handle.

"I see it; don't you see dat, Chaules?" said Andy.

"Certainly, anybody could see that," replied Charles.

"Ole umin," said Daddy Joe, "don' yeh see it?"

"Sho', ole man! Ain't I lookin!" replied the old woman.

"You all see it then, do you?" inquired Henry.

"Yes, yes!" was the response.

"Now then," continued Henry; "for an explanation by which you can tell the North Star, when or from whatever place you may see it. The two stars of the Dipper, numbered 6 and 7, are called the pointers, because they point directly to the North Star, a very small, bright star, far off from the pointers, generally seeming by itself, especially when the other stars are not very bright.

"The star numbered 8, above the pointer, a little to the left, is a dim, small star, which at first sight would seem to be in a direct line with it; but by drawing a line through 7 to 8, leaves a space as you see between the star 6 and lower part of the line; or forms an angle (as the 'book men' call it, Andy) of ten degrees. The star number 9 in the distance, and a little to the right, would also seem to be directly opposite the pointers; but by drawing a line through 7 to 9, there is still a space left between the lower end of the line and 6. Now trace the dotted line from 6 through the center of 7, and it leads directly to 10. This is the North Star, the slave's great Guide to Freedom! Do you all now understand it?"

"See it!" replied Andy. "Anybody can't see dat, ain' got sense' 'nuff to run away, an' no call to be free, dat's all! I knows all about it. I reckon I a'mos' know it betteh dan you, Henry!"

"Dar, dar, I tole yeh so! I tole yeh dat boy studyin' head wuck, an yeh 'uden bleve me! 'E run about yendeh so much an' kick up 'e heel dat'e talk so much gramma an' wot not, dat body haudly undehstan'! I knows dat 'e bin 'splainin do. Ole man, yeh understan' im?" said Mammy Judy.

"Ah, ole umin, dat I does! An' I' been gone forty years 'ago, I' know'd dis much 'bout it!" replied Daddy Joe.

"Above number 2 the second star of the handle of the Dipper, close to it, you will see by steadily looking, a very small star, which I call the knob or thumb-holt of the handle. You may always tell the Dipper by the knob of the handle; and the North star by the Dipper. The Dipper, during the night you will remember, continues to change its position in relation to the earth, so that it sometimes seems quite upside down."

"See here, Henry, does you know all—"

"Stop, Andy, I've not done yet!" interrupted he.

"Uh, heh!" said Andy.

"When the North star cannot be seen," continued Henry, "you must depend alone upon nature for your guide. Feel, in the dark, around the trunks or bodies of trees, especially oak, and whenever you feel moss on the bark, that side on which the moss grows is always to the north. One more explanation and then we'll go. Do you see this little round metallic box? This is called a—"

"Wat dat you call 'talic, Henry? Sho, boy! yeh head so full ob gramma an' sich like dat yeh don' know how to talk!" interrupted Mammy Judy.

"That only means iron or brass, or some hard thing like that, mammy," explained he. "The little box of which I was speaking has in it what is called a compass. It has a face almost like a clock or watch, with one straight hand which reaches entirely across the face, and turns or shakes whenever you move the box. This hand or finger is a piece of metal called 'loadstone' or 'magnet,' and termed the needle of the compass; and this end with the little cross on it, always points in one direction, and that is to the north. See; it makes no difference which way it is moved, this point of the needle turns back and points that way."

"An mus' ye al'as go de way it pints, Henry?" inquired Andy.

"No; not except you are running away from the South to Canada, or the free States; because both of these places are in the north. But when you know which way the north is, you can easily find any other direction you wish. Notice this, all of you."

"When your face is to the north, your back is to the south; your right hand to the east, and your left to the west. Can you remember this?"

"O yes, easy!" replied Andy.

"Then you will always know which way to go, by the compass showing you which is north," explained Henry.

"What does dese letters roun' hear mean, Henry?" further inquired Andy.

"Only what I have already explained; meaning north, east, west, and south, with their intermediate—"

"Dar!" interrupted Mammy Judy. "'E gone into big talk g'in! Sho!"

"Intermediate means between, mammy," explained Henry.

"Den ef dat's it, I lis'en at yeh; case I want gwine bautheh my head wid you' jography an' big talk like dat!" replied the old woman.

"What does a compass cost?" inquired Charles, who had been listening with intense interest and breathless silence at the information given by their much-loved fellow bondman.

"One-half a dollar, or four bits, as we call it, so that every slave who will, may get one. Now, I've told you all that's necessary to guide you from a land of slavery and long suffering, to a land of liberty and future happiness. Are you now all satisfied with what you have learned?"

"Chauls, aint 'e high! See here, Henry, does yeh know all dat yeh tell us? Wy, ole feller, you is way up in de hoobanahs! Wy, you is conjure sho'nuff. Ef I only know'd dis befo', ole Potteh neven keep me a day. O, pshaw! I bin gone long 'go!"

"He'll do!" replied Charles.

"Well, well, well!" apostrophized Mammy Judy. "Dat beats all! Sence I was baun, I nebber hear de like. All along I been tellen on yeh, dat 'e got 'is head chuck cleanfull ob cumbustable, an' all dat, but yeh 'ud'n bleve me! Now yeh see!"

"Ole umin, I 'fess dat's all head wuck! Dat beats Punton! dat boy's nigh up to Maudy Ghamus! Dat boy's gwine to be mighty!" with a deep sigh replied Daddy Joe.

"Come, now, let's go!" said Henry.

On rising from where they had all been sitting with fixed attention upon their leader and his instruction, the sky was observed through the only break in the thicket above their heads, when suddenly they simultaneously exclaimed:

"There's the Dipper! there's the North Star!" all pointing directly to the Godlike beacon of liberty to the American slave.

Leaving Mammy Judy and Daddy Joe, Clara and little Tony, who had quite recovered from his indisposition the early part of the night, in charge of a friend who designedly met them on the Louisiana side of the river, with heightened spirits and a new impulse, Henry, Charles and Andy, started on their journey in the direction of their newly described guide, the North Star.

> *Star of the North thou art not bigger,*
> *Than the diamond in my ring;*
> *Yet every black star-gazing nigger,*
> *Looks up to thee as some great thing!*

was the apostrophe of an American writer to the sacred orb of Heaven, which in this case was fully verified.

During the remainder of the night and next day, being Sabbath, they continued their travel, only resting when overcome wth fatigue. Continuing in Louisiana by night, and resting by day, Wednesday morning, before daybreak, brought them to the Arkansas river. At first they intended to ford, but like the rivers generally of the South, its depth and other contingencies made it necessary to seek some other means. After consultation in a canebreak, day beginning to dawn, walking boldly up to a man just loosening a skiff from its fastenings, they demanded a passage across the river. This the skiffman refused peremptorily on any pretext, rejecting the sight of a written pass.

"I want none of yer nigger passes!" angrily said he. "They ain't none uv 'em good 'or nothin', no how! It's no use to show it to me, ye's can't git over!"

First looking meaningly and determinedly at Charles and Andy – biting his lips – then addressing himself to the man, Henry said:

"Then I have one that will pass us!" presenting the unmistaking evidence of a shining gold eagle, at the sight of which emblem of his country's liberty, the skiffman's patriotism was at once awakened, and their right to pass as American freemen indisputable.

A few energetic muscular exertions with the oars, and the sturdy boatman promptly landed his passengers on the other side of the river.

"Now, gentlm'n, I done the clean thing, didn't I, by jingo! Show me but half a chance an' I'll ack the man clean out. I dont go in for this slaveholding o' people in these Newnited States uv the South, nohow, so I don't. Dog gone it, let every feller have a fair shake!"

Dropping into his hand the ten-dollar gold piece, the man bowed earnestly, uttering—

"I hope ye's good luck, gent'men! Ye'll al'as fine me ready when ye's come 'long this way!"

Chapter XXIX
The Fugitives

WITH MUCH APPREHENSION, Henry and comrades passed hastily through the State of Arkansas, he having previously traversed it partly, had learned sufficient to put him on his guard.

Traveling in the night, to avoid the day, the progress was not equal to the emergency. Though Henry carried a pocket compass, they kept in sight of the Mississippi river, to take their chance of the first steamer passing by.

The third night out, being Monday, at daybreak in the morning, their rest for the day was made at a convenient point within the verge of a forest. Suddenly Charles gave vent to hearty laughter, at a time when all were supposed to be serious, having the evening past, been beset by a train of three Negro-dogs, which, having first been charmed, they slew at the instant; the dogs probably not having been sent on trail of them, but, after the custom of the state, baying on a general round to intimidate the slaves from clandestinely venturing out, and to attack such runaways as might by chance be found in their track.

"Wat's da mauttah, Chauls?" enquired Andy.

"I was just thinking," replied he, "of the sight of three High Conjurers, who if Ghamus and Gholar be true, can do anything they please, having to escape by night, and travel in the wild woods, to evade the pursuit of white men, who do not pretend to know anything about such things."

"Dat's a fack," added Andy, "an' little, scronny triflin' weak, white men at dat – any one uv us heah, ought to whip two or three uv 'em at once. Dares Hugh's a little bit a feller, I could take 'im in one han' an' throw 'im oveh my head, an' ole Pottah, for his pant, he so ole an' good foh nothin, I could whip wid one hand half a dozen like 'im."

"Now you see, boys," said Henry, "how much conjuration and such foolishness and stupidity is worth to the slaves in the South. All that it does, is to put money into the pockets of the pretended conjurer, give him power over others by making them afraid of him; and even old Gamby Gholar and Maudy Ghamus and the rest of the Seven Heads, with all of the High Conjurors in the Dismal Swamp, are depending more upon me to deliver them from their confinement as prisoners in the Swamp and runaway slaves, than all their combined efforts together. I made it a special part of my mission, wherever I went, to enlighten them on this subject."

"I wandah you didn't fend 'em," replied Andy.

"No danger of that, since having so long, to no purpose, depended upon such persons and nonsense, they are sick at heart of them, and waiting willing and ready, for anything which may present for their aid, even to the destruction of their long cherished, silly nonsense of conjuration."

"Thang God foh dat!" concluded Andy.

Charles having fallen asleep, Andy became the sentinel of the party, as it was the arrangement for each one alternately, every two hours during rest, to watch while the other two slept. Henry having next fallen into a doze, Andy heard a cracking among the bushes, when on looking around, two men approached them. Being fatigued, drowsy, and giddy, he became much alarmed, arousing his comrades, all springing to their feet. The men advanced, who, to their gratification proved to be Eli and Ambrose, two Arkansas slaves, who having promised to meet Henry on his return, had effected their escape immediately after first meeting him, lurking in the forest in the direction which he had laid out to take.

Eli was so fair as to be taken, when first seen, to be a white man. Throwing their arms about Henry, they bestowed upon him their blessing and thanks, for his advent into the state as the means of their escape.

While thus exchanging congratulations, the approach upstream of a steamer was heard, and at once Henry devised the expedient, and determined boldly to hail her and demand a passage. Putting Eli forward as the master, Ambrose carrying the portmanteaus which belonged to the two, and the others with bundles in their hands, all rushed to the bank of the river on the verge of the thicket; Eli held up a handkerchief as a signal. The bell tolled, and the yawl immediately lowered, made for the shore. It was agreed that Eli should be known as Major Ely, of Arkansas.

Seeing that blacks were of the company, when the yawl approached, the mate stood upon her forecastle.

"What's the faction here?" cried out the sturdy mate.

"Where are you bound?" enquired Eli.

"For St. Louis."

"Can I get a passage for myself and four Negroes?"

"What's the name, sir?"

"Major Ely, of Arkansas," was the reply.

"Aye, aye, sir, come aboard," said the mate; when, pulling away, the steamer was soon reached, the slaves going to the deck, and the master to the cabin.

On application for a stateroom, the clerk, on learning the name, desired to know his destination.

"The State of Missouri, sir," said Eli, "between the points of the mouth of the Ohio and St. Genevieve."

"Ely," repeated the clerk, "I've heard that name before – it's a Missouri name – any relation to Dr. Ely, Major?"

"Yes, a brother's son," was the prompt reply.

"Yes, yes, I thought I knew the name," replied the clerk. "But the old fellow wasn't quite of your way of thinking concerning Negroes, I believe?"

"No, he is one man, and I'm another, and he may go his way, and I'll go mine," replied Eli.

"That's the right feeling, Major," replied the clerk, "and we would have a much healthier state of politics in the country, if men generally would only agree to act on that principle."

"It has ever been my course," said Eli.

"Peopling a new farm I reckon, Major?"

"Yes, sir."

The master, keeping a close watch upon the slaves, was frequently upon deck among them, and requested that they might be supplied with more than common fare for slaves, he sparing no expense to make them comfortable. The slaves, on their part, appeared to be particularly attached to him, always smiling when he approached, apparently regretting when he left for the cabin.

Meanwhile, the steamer gracefully plowing up the current, making great headway, reached the point desired, when the master and slaves were safely transferred from the steamer to the shore of Missouri.

Chapter XXX
The Pursuit

THE ABSENCE of Mammy Judy, Daddy Joe, Charles, and little Tony, on the return early Monday morning of Colonel Franks and lady from the country, unmistakably proved the escape of their slaves, and the further proof of the exit of 'squire Potter's Andy and Beckwith's Clara, with the remembrance of the stampede a few months previously, required no further confirmation of the fact, when the neighborhood again was excited to ferment. The advisory committee was called into immediate council, and ways and means devised for the arrest of the recreant slaves recently left, and to prevent among them the recurrence of such things; a pursuit was at once commenced, which for the three succeeding days was carried in the wrong direction – towards Jackson, whither, it was supposed in the neighborhood, Henry had been lurking previous to the last sally upon their premises, as he had certainly been seen on Saturday evening, coming from the landing.

No traces being found in that direction, the course was changed, the swiftest steamer boarded in pursuit for the Ohio river. This point being reached but a few hours subsequent to that of the fugitives, when learning of their course, the pursuers proceeded toward the place of their destination, on the Mississippi river.

This point being the southern part of Missouri but a short distance above the confluence of the Ohio and Mississippi, the last named river had, of necessity, to be passed, being to the fugitives only practicable by means of a ferry. The ferryman in this instance commanded a horse-boat, he residing on the opposite side of the river. Stepping up to him – a tall, raw-boned athletic, rough looking, bearded fellow – Eli saluted:

"We want to cross the river, sir!"

"Am yers free?" enquired the ferryman.

"Am I free! Are you free?" rejoined Eli.

"Yes, I be's a white man!" replied the boatman.

"And so am I!" retorted Eli. "And you dare not tell me I'm not."

"I'll swong, stranger, yer mus' 'scuse me, as I did n' take notice on yez! But I like to know if them air black folks ye got wey yer am free, cause if they arn't, I be 'sponsible for 'em 'cording to the new law, called, I 'bleve the Nebrasky Complimize Fugintive Slave Act, made down at Californy, last year," apologized and explained the somewhat confused ferryman.

"Yes," replied Henry, "we are free, and if we were not, I do'nt think it any part of your business to know. I thought you were here to carry people across the river."

"But frien'," rejoined the man, "yer don't understan' it. This are a law made by the Newnited States of Ameriky, an' I be 'bliged to fulfill it by ketchin' every fugintive that goes to cross this way, or I mus' pay a thousand dollars, and go to jail till the black folks is got, if that be's never. Yer see yez can't blame me, as I mus' 'bey the laws of Congress I'll swong it be's hardly a fair shake nuther, but I be 'bliged to 'bey the laws, yer know."

"Well sir," replied Henry, "we want to cross the river."

"Let me see yez papers frien'?" asked the ferryman.

"My friend," said Henry, "are you willing to make yourself a watch dog for slaveholders, and do for them that which they would not do for themselves, catch runaway slaves? Don't you know that this is the work which they boast on having the poor white men at the North do for them? Have you not yet learned to attend to your own interests instead of theirs? Here are our free papers," holding out his open hand, in which lay five half eagle pieces.

"Jump aboard!" cried the ferryman. "Quick, quick!" shouted he, as the swift feet of four hourses were heard dashing up the road.

Scarcely had the boat moved from her fastenings, till they had arrived; the riders dismounted, who presenting revolvers, declared upon the boatman's life, instantly, if he did not change the direction of his boat and come back to the Missouri shore. Henry seized a well-charged rifle belonging to the boatman, his comrades each with a well-aimed six-barreled weapon.

"Shoot if you dare!" exclaimed Henry, the slaveholders declining their arms – when, turning to the awestricken ferryman, handing him the twenty-five dollars, said, "your cause is a just one, and your reward is sure; take this money, proceed and you are safe – refuse, and you instantly die!"

"Then I be to do right," declared the boatman, "if I die by it," when applying the whip to the horses, in a few moments landed them on the Illinois shore.

This being the only ferry in the neighborhood, and fearing a bribe or coercion by the people on the Illinois side, or the temptation of a high reward from the slave-catchers, Henry determined on eluding, if possible, every means of pursuit.

"What are your horses worth?" enquired he.

"They can't be no use to your frien' case they is both on 'em bline, an' couldn't travel twenty miles a day, on a stretch!"

"Have you any other horses?"

"They be all the horses I got; I gineraly feed a spell this side. I lives over here – this are my feedin' trip," drawled the boatman.

"What will you take for them?"

"Well, frien', they arn't wuth much to buy, no how, but wuth good lock to me for drawin' the boat over, yer see."

"What did they cost you in buying them?"

"Well, I o'ny giv six-seven dollars apiece, or sich a maiter for 'em' when I got 'em, an' they cos me some two-three dollars, or sich a matter, more to get 'em in pullin' order, yer see."

"Will you sell them to me?"

"I hadn't ort to part wey 'em frien', as I do good lock o' bisness hereabouts wey them air nags, bline as they be."

"Here are thirty dollars for your horses," said Henry, putting into his hand the money in gold pieces, when, unhitching them from their station, leading them out to the side of the boat, he shot them, pushing them over into the river.

"Farewell, my friend," saluted Henry, he and comrades leaving the astonished ferryman gazing after them, whilst the slaveholders on the other shore stood grinding their teeth, grimacing their faces, shaking their fists, with various gesticulations of threat, none of which were either heard, heeded or cared for by the fleeting party, or determined ferryman.

Taking a northeasterly course of Indiana, Andy being an accustomed singer, commenced, in lively glee and cheerful strains, singing to the expressive words:

We are like a band of pilgrims,
In a strange and foreign land,
With our knapsacks on our shoulders,
And our cudgels in our hands,
We have many miles before us.
But it lessens not our joys,

> *We will sing a merry chorus,*
> *For we are the tramping boys.*
> *Then joined in chorus the whole party—*
> *We are all jogging,*
> *Jog, jog, jogging,*
> *And we're all jogging,*
> *We are going to the North!*

The Wabash river becoming the next point of obstruction, a ferry, as in the last case, had also to be crossed, the boatman residing on the Indiana side.

"Are you free?" enquired the boatman, as the party of blacks approached.

"We are," was the reply of Henry.

"Where are you from?" continued he.

"We are from home, sir," replied Charles, "and the sooner you take us across the river, just so much sooner will we reach it."

Still doubting their right to pass he asked for their papers, but having by this time become so conversant with the patriotism and fidelity of these men to their country, Charles handing the Indianan a five dollar piece, who on seeing the outstretched wings of the eagle, desired no further evidence of their right to pass, conveying them into the state, contrary to the statutes of the Commonwealth.

On went the happy travelers without hinderance, or molestation, until the middle of the week next ensuing.

Chapter XXXI
The Attack, Resistance, Arrest

THE TRAVEL for the last ten days had been pleasant, save the necessity in the more southern part of the state, of lying-by through the day and traveling at night – the fugitives cheerful and full of hope, nothing transpiring to mar their happiness, until approaching a village in the center of northern Indiana.

Supposing their proximity to the British Provinces made them safe, with an imprudence not before committed by the discreet runaways, when nearing a blacksmith's shop a mile and a half from the village, Andy in his usual manner, with stentorian voice, commenced the following song:

> *I'm on my way to Canada,*
> *That cold and dreary land:*
> *The dire effects of slavery,*
> *I can no longer stand.*
> *My soul is vexed within me so,*
> *To think that I'm a slave,*
> *I've now resolved to strike the blow,*
> *For Freedom or the grave.*
> *All uniting in the chorus,*
> *O, righteous Father*
> *Wilt thou not pity me;*
> *And aid me on to Canada,*
> *Where fugitives are free?*

I heard old England plainly say,
If we would all forsake,
Our native land of Slavery,
And come across the lake.

"There, Ad'line! I golly, don't you hear that?" said Dave Starkweather, the blacksmith, to his wife, both of whom on hearing the unusual noise of singing, thrust their heads out of the door of a little log hut, stood patiently listening to the song, every word of which they distinctly caught. "Them's fugertive slaves, an' I'll have 'em tuck up; they might have passed, but for their singin' praise to that darned Queen! I can't stan' that no how!"

"No," replied Adaline, "I'm sure I don't see what they sing to her for; she's no 'Merican. We ain't under her now, as we Dave?"

"No we ain't, Ad'line, not sence the battle o' Waterloo, an' I golly, we wouldn't be if we was. The 'Mericans could whip her a darned sight easier now than what they done when they fit her at Waterloo."

"Lah me, Dave, you could whip 'er yourself, she ai'nt bigger nor tother wimin is she?" said Mrs. Starkweather.

"No she ain't, not a darn' bit!" replied he.

"Dave, ask em in the shop to rest," suggested the wife in a hurried whisper, elbowing her husband as the party advanced, having ceased singing so soon as they saw the faces of white persons.

"Travlin', I reckon?" interrogated the blacksmith. "Little tired, I spose?"

"Yes sir, a little so," replied Henry.

"Didn't come far, I 'spect?" continued he.

"Not very," carelessly replied Henry.

"Take seat there, and rest ye little," pointing to a smoothly-worn log, used by the visitors of the shop.

"Thank you," said Henry, "we will," all seating themselves in a row.

"Take little somethin?" asked he; stepping back to a corner, taking out a caddy in the wall, a rather corpulent green bottle, turning it up to his mouth, drenching himself almost to strangulation.

"We don't drink, sir," replied the fugitives.

"Temperance, I reckon?" enquired the smith.

"Rather so," replied Henry.

"Kind o' think we'll have a spell o' weather?"

"Yes," said Andy, "dat's certain; we'll have a spell a weatheh!"

On entering the shop, the person at the bellows, a tall, able-bodied young man, was observed to pass out at the back door, a number of persons of both sexes to come frequently look in, and depart, succeeded by others; no import being attached to this, supposing themselves to be an attraction, partly from their singing, and mainly from their color being a novelty in the neighborhood.

During conversation with the blacksmith, he after eyeing very closely the five strangers, was observed to walk behind the door, stand for some minutes looking as if reading, when resuming his place at the anvil, after which he went out the back door. Curiosity now, with some anxiety induced Henry to look for the cause of it, when with no little alarm, he discovered a handbill fully descriptive of himself and comrades, having been issued in the town of St. Genevieve, offering a heavy reward, particularizing the scene at the Mississippi ferry, the killing of the horses as an aggravated offense, because depriving a poor man of his only means of livelihood, being designed to strengthen inducements to apprehend them, the bill being signed "John Harris."

Evening now ensuing, Henry and comrades, the more easily to pass through the village without attraction, had remained until this hour, resting in the blacksmith shop. Enquiring for some black family in the neighborhood, they were cited to one consisting of an old man and woman, Devan by name, residing on the other side, a short distance from the village.

"Ye'll fine ole Bill of the right stripe," said the blacksmith knowingly. "Ye needn' be feard o' him. Ye'll fine him and ole Sally just what they say they is; I'll go bail for that. The first log hut ye come to after ye leave the village is thern; jist knock at the door, an' ye'll fine ole Bill an' Sally all right blame if ye don't. Jis name me; tell 'em Dave Starkweather sent ye there, an' blamed if ye don't fine things at high water mark; I'm tellin' ye so, blamed if I ain't!" was the recommendation of the blacksmith.

"Thank you for your kindness," replied Henry, politely bowing as they rose from the log. "Goodbye, sir!"

"Devilish decent lookin' black fellers," said the man of the anvil, complimenting designedly for them to hear. "Blamed if they ain't as free as we is – I golly they is!"

Without, as they thought, attracting attention, passing through the village a half mile or more, they came to a log hut on the right side of the way.

"How yeh do fren? How yeh come on?" saluted a short, rather corpulent, wheezing old black man. "Come in. Hi! Dahs good many on yeh; ole 'omin come, heah's some frens!" calling his wife Sally, an old woman, shorter in stature, but not less corpulent than he, sitting by a comfortable dry-stump fire.

"How is yeh, frens? How yeh do? come to da fiah, mighty cole!" said the old woman.

"Quite cool," replied Andy, rubbing his hands, spreading them out, protecting his face from the heat.

"Yeh is travelin, I reckon, there is good many go' long heah; we no call t'ask 'em whah da gwine, we knows who da is, case we come from dah. I an, ole man once slave in Faginny; mighty good country fah black folks."

Sally set immediately about preparing something to give her guests a good meal. Henry admonished them against extra trouble, but they insisted on giving them a good supper.

Deeming it more prudent, the hut being on the highway, Henry requested to retire until summoned to supper, being shown to the loft attained by a ladder and simple hatchway, the door of which was shut down, and fastened on the lower side.

The floor consisting of rough, unjointed board, containing great cracks through which the light and heat from below passed up, all could be both seen and heard, which transpired below.

Seeing the old man so frequently open and look out at the door, and being suspicious from the movements of the blacksmith and others, Henry affecting to be sleepy, requested Billy and his wife when ready, to awaken them, when after a few minutes, all were snoring as if fast asleep, Henry lying in such a position as through a knothole in the floor, to see every movement in all parts of the room. Directly above him in the rafter within his reach, hung a mowing scythe.

"Now's yeh time, ole man; da all fas' asleep, da snorin' good!" said old Sally, urging Billy to hasten, who immediately left the hut.

The hearts of the fugitives were at once "in their mouths," and with difficulty it was by silently reaching over and heavily pressing upon each of them, Henry succeeded in admonishing each to entire quietness and submission.

Presently entered a white man, who whispering with Sally left the room. Immediately in came old Bill, at the instant of which, Henry found his right hand above him, involuntarily grasped firmly on the snath of the scythe.

"Whah's da?" enquired old Bill, on entering the hut.

"Sho da whah yeh lef' em!" replied the old woman.

"Spose I kin bring 'em in now?" continued old Bill.

"Bring in who?"

"Da white folks: who else I gwine fetch in yeh 'spose?"

"Bettah let em 'tay whah da is, an' let de po' men lone, git sumpen t' eat, an' go 'long whah da gwine!" replied Sally, deceptively.

"Huccum yeh talk dat way? Sho yeh tole me go!" replied Billy.

"Didn' reckon yeh gwine bring 'em on da po' cretahs dis way, fo' da git moufful t' eat an' git way so."

"How I gwine let 'em go now de white folks all out dah? Say Sally? Dat jis what make I tell yeh so!"

"Bettah let white folks 'lone, Willum! dat jis what I been tellin' on yeh. Keep foolin' 'long wid white folks, bym'by da show yeh! I no trus' white man, no how. Sho! da no fren' o' black folks. Bus spose body 'blige keep da right side on 'em long so."

"Ole 'omin," said Bill, "yeh knows we make our livin' by da white folks, an' mus' do what da tell us, so whah's da use talkin' long so. 'Spose da come in now?"

"Sho, I tole yeh de man sleep? gwine bring white folks on 'em so? give po' cretahs no chance? Go long, do what yeh gwine do; yeh fine out one dese days!" concluded Sally.

Having stealthily risen to their feet standing in a favorable position, Henry in whispers declared to his comrades that with that scythe he intended mowing his way into Canada.

Impatient for their entrance, throwing wide open the door of the hut, which being the signal, in rushed eleven white men, headed by Jud Shirly, constable, Dave Starkweather the blacksmith, and Tom Overton as deputies; George Grove, a respectable well-dressed villager, stood giving general orders.

With light and pistol in hand, Franey, mounting the stairway commanded a surrender. Eli, standing behind the hatchway, struck the candle from his hand, when with a swing of the scythe there was a screech, fall, and groan heard, then with a shout and leap, Henry in the lead, they cleared the stairs to the lower floor, the white men flying in consternation before them, making their way to the village, alarming the inhabitants.

The fugitives fled in great haste continuing their flight for several miles, when becoming worn down and fatigued, retired under cover of a thicket a mile from a stage tavern kept by old Isaac Slusher of German descent.

The villagers following in quick pursuit, every horse which could be readily obtained being put on the chase, the slaves were overtaken, fired upon – a ball lodging in Charles' thigh – overpowered, and arrested. Deeming it, from the number of idlers about the place, and the condition of the stables, much the safest imprisonment, the captives were taken to the tavern of Slusher, to quarter for the night.

On arriving at this place, a shout of triumph rent the air, and a general cry "take them into the barroom for inspection! Hang them! Burn them!" and much more.

Here the captives were derided, scoffed at and ridiculed, turned around, limbs examined, shoved about from side to side, then ordered to sit down on the floor, a noncompliance with which, having arranged themselves for the purpose, at a given signal, a single trip by an equal number of whites, brought the four poor prisoners suddenly to the floor on the broad of their back, their heads striking with great force. At this abuse of helpless men, the shouts of laughter became deafening. It caused them to shun the risk of standing, and keep seated on the floor.

Charles having been wounded, affected inability to stand, but the injury being a flesh wound, was not serious.

"We'll show ye yer places, ye black devils!" said Ned Bradly, a rowdy, drawing back his foot to kick Henry in the face, as he sat upon the floor against the wall, giving him a slight kick in the side as he passed by him.

"Don't do that again, sir!" sternly said Henry, with an expression full of meaning, looking him in the face.

Several feet in an instant were drawn back to kick, when Slusher interfering, said, "Shendlemans! tem black mans ish prishners! You tuz pring tem into mine housh, ant you shandt puse tem dare!" when the rowdies ceased abusing them.

"Well, gentlemen," said Tom Overton, a burly, bullying barroom person, "we'd best git these blacks out of the way, if they's any fun up tonight."

"I cot plendy peds, shendlemans, I ondly vants to know who ish to bay me," replied Slusher.

"I golly," retorted Starkweather, "you needn't give yourself no uneasiness about that Slusher. I think me, and Shirly, and Grove is good for a night's lodging for five niggers, anyhow!"

"I'm in that snap, too!" hallooed out Overton.

"Golly! Yes, Tom, there's you we like to forgot, blamed if we didn't!" responded Starkweather.

"Dat ish all right nough zo far as te plack man's ish gonzern, put ten dare ish to housh vull o' peoples, vot vare must I gheep tem?"

"We four," replied Grove, "will see you paid, who else? Slusher, we want it understood, that we four stand responsible for all expenses incurred this night, in the taking of these Negroes," evidently expecting to receive as they claimed, the reward offered in the advertisement.

"Dat vill too, ten," replied Slusher. "Vell, I ish ready to lite tese black mans to ped."

"No Slusher," interrupted Grove, "that's not the understanding, we don't pay for beds for niggers to sleep in!"

"No, by Molly!" replied Overton. "Dogged if that ain't going a leetle too far! Slusher, you can't choke that down, no how you can fix in. If you do as you please with your own house, these niggers is in our custody, and we'll do as we please with them. We want you to know that we are white men, as well as you are, and can't pay for niggers to sleep in the same house with ourselves."

"Gents," said Ned Bradly, "do you hear that?"

"What?" enquired several voices.

"Why, old Slusher wants to give the niggers a room upstairs with us!"

"With who?" shouted they.

"With us white men."

"No, blamed if he does!" replied Starkweather.

"We won't stand that!" exclaimed several voices.

"Where's Slusher?" enquired Ben West, a discharged stage driver, who hung about the premises, and now figured prominently.

"Here ish me, shendlemans!" answered Slusher, coming from the back part of the house. "Andt you may do you please midt tem black mans, pud iv you dempt puse me, I vill pudt you all out mine housh!"

"The stable, the stable!" they all cried out. "Put the niggers in the stable, and we'll be satisfied!"

"Tare ish mine staple – you may pud tem vare you blease," replied the old man, "budt you shandt puse me!"

Securely binding them with cords, they were placed in a strongly built log stable closely weather-boarded, having but a door and window below, the latter being closely secured, and the door locked on the outside with a staple and padlock. The upper windows being well secured, the blacks thus locked in, were left to their fate, whilst their captors comfortably housed, were rioting in triumph through the night over the misfortune, and blasted prospects for liberty.

Chapter XXXII
The Escape

THIS NIGHT THE INMATES of the tavern revelled with intoxication; all within the building, save the exemplary family of the stern old German, Slusher, who peremptorily refused from first to last, to take any part whatever with them, doubtless, being for the evening the victims of excessive indulgence in the beverage of ardent spirits. Now and again one and another of the numerous crowd gathered from the surrounding neighborhood, increasing as the intelligence spread, went alone to the stable to examine the door, reconnoiter the premises, and ascertain that the prisoners were secure. The company getting in such high glee that, fearing a neglect of duty, it became advisable to appoint for the evening a corps of sentinels whose special duty, according to their own arrangements, should be to watch and guard the captives. This special commission being one of pecuniary consideration, Jim Franey, the township constable, the rowdy Ned Bradly, and Ben West the discharged stage driver, who being about the premises, readily accepted the office, entering immediately on the line of duty.

The guard each alternately every fifteen minutes went out to examine the premises, when one and a half of the clock again brought around the period of Ben West's duty. Familiar with the premises and the arrangement of the stables, taking a lantern, West designed closely to inspect their pinions, that no lack of duty on his part might forfeit his claim to the promised compensation.

When placing them in the stable, lights then being in requisition, Henry discovered in a crevice between the wall an the end of the feed-trough a common butcher knife used for the purpose of repairing harness. So soon as the parties left the stable, the captives lying with their heads resting on their bundles, Henry arising, took the knife, cutting loose himself and companions, but leaving the pinions still about their limbs as though fastened, resumed his position upon the bundle of straw. The scythe had been carelessly hung on a section of the worm fence adjoining the barn, near the door of the prison department, their weapons having been taken from them.

"Well, boys," enquired West, holding up the lantern, "you're all here, I see: do you want anything? Take some whiskey!" holding in his hand a quart bottle.

"The rope's too tight around my ankle!" complained Charles. "Its took all the feeling out of my leg."

Dropping upon his knees to loosen the cord, at this moment, Henry standing erect brandishing the keen glistening blade of the knife before him – his companions having sprung to their feet – "Don't you breathe," exclaimed the intrepid unfettered slave, "or I'll bury the blade deep in your bosom! One hour I'll give you for silence, a breach of which will cost your life." Taking a tin cup which West brought into the stable, pouring it full to the brim, "Drink this!" said Henry, compelling the man who was already partially intoxicated, to drink as much as possible, which soon rendered him entirely insensible.

"Come, boys!" exclaimed he, locking the stable, putting the key into his pocket, leaving the intoxicated sentinel prostrated upon the bed of straw intended for them, and leaving the tavern house of the old German Slusher forever behind them.

The next period of watch, West being missed, Ned Bradly, on going to the stable, finding the door locked, reported favorably, supposing it to be still secure. Overton in turn did the same. When drawing near daylight – West still being missed – Franey advised that a search be made for him. The bedrooms, and such places into which he might most probably have retired, were repeatedly searched in vain, as calling at the stable elicited no answer, either from him nor the captives.

The sun was now more than two hours high, and word was received from the village to hasten the criminals in for examination before the magistrate. Determining to break open the door, which being done, Ben West was found outstretched upon the bed of straw, who, with difficulty, was aroused from his stupor. The surprise of the searchers on discovering his condition, was heightened on finding the escape of the fugitives. Disappointment and chagrin now succeeded high hopes and merriment, when a general reaction ran throughout the neighborhood; for the sensation at the escape even became greater than on the instance of the deed of resistance and success of the capture.

Of all the disappointments connected with this affair, there was none to be regretted save that of the old German tavern keeper, Isaac Slusher, who, being the only pecuniary sufferer, the entire crowd revelling at his expense.

"Gonvound dish bishnesh!" exclaimed Slusher with vexation. "Id alwaysh cosht more dan de ding ish wordt. Mine Got! afder dish I'll mindt mine own bishnesh. Iv tem Soudt Amerigans vill gheep niggersh de musht gedch dem demzelve. Mine ligger ish ghon, I losht mine resht, te niggersh rhun avay, an' I nod magk von zent!"

Immediate pursuit was sent out in search of the runaways but without success; for, dashing on, scythe in hand, with daring though peaceable strides through the remainder of the state and that of Michigan, the fugitives reached Detroit without further molestation or question from any source on the right of transit, the inhabitants mistaking them for resident blacks out from their homes in search of employment.

Chapter XXXIII
Happy Greeting

AFTER THEIR FORTUNATE escape from the stables of Isaac Slusher in Indiana, Henry and comrades safely landed across the river in Windsor, Essex County, Canada West, being accompanied by a mulatto gentleman resident of Detroit, who from the abundance of his generous heart, with others there, ever stands ready and has proven himself an uncompromising, true and tried friend of his race, and every weary traveler-on a fugitive slave pilgrimage, passing that way.

"Is dis Canada? Is dis de good ole British soil we hear so much 'bout way down in Missierppi?" exclaimed Andy. "Is dis free groun'? De lan' whar black folks is free! Thang God a'mighty for dis privilege!" When he fell upon his hands and knees and kissed the earth.

Poor fellow! he little knew the unnatural feelings and course pursued toward his race by many Canadians, those too pretending to be Englishmen by birth, with some of whom the blacks had fought side by side in the memorable crusade made upon that fairest portion of Her Majesty's Colonial Possessions, by Americans in disguise, calling themselves "Patriots." He little knew that while according to fundamental British Law and constitutional rights, all persons are equal in the realm, yet by a systematic course of policy and artifice, his race with few exceptions in some parts, excepting the Eastern Province, is excluded from the enjoyment and practical exercise of every right, except mere suffrage-voting – even to those of sitting on a jury as its own peer, and the exercise of military duty. He little knew the facts, and as little expected to find such a state of things in the long-talked of and much-loved Canada by the slaves. He knew not that some of high intelligence and educational attainments of his race residing in many parts of the Provinces, were really excluded from and practically denied their rights, and that there was no authority known to the colony to give redress and make restitution on the petition or application of these representative men of his race, which had frequently been done with the reply from the Canadian functionaries that they had no power to reach their case. It had never entered the mind of poor Andy, that in going to Canada in search of freedom, he was then in a country where privileges were denied him which are common to the slave in every Southern state – the right of going into the gallery of a public building – that a few of the most respectable colored ladies of a town in Kent County, desirous through reverence and respect, to see a British Lord Chief Justice on the Bench of Queen's Court, taking seats in the gallery of the court house assigned to females and other visitors, were ruthlessly taken hold of and shown down the stairway by a man and "officer" of the Court of Queen's Bench for that place. Sad would be to him the fact when he heard that the construction given by authority to these grievances, when requested to remedy or remove them, was, that they were "local contingencies to be reached alone by those who inflicted the injuries." An emotion of unutterable indignation would swell the heart of the determined slave, and almost compel him to curse the country of his adoption. But Andy was free – being on British soil – from the bribes of slaveholding influences; where the unhallowed foot of the slavecatcher dare not tread; where no decrees of an American Congress sanctioned by a president born and bred in a free state and himself once a poor apprentice boy in a village, could reach.

Thus far, Andy was happy; happy in the success of their escape, the enlarged hopes of future prospects in the industrial pursuits of life; and happy in the contemplation of meeting and seeing Clara.

There were other joys than those of Andy, and other hopes and anticipations to be realised. Charles, Ambrose, and Eli, who, though with hearts overflowing with gratitude, were silent in holy praise to heaven, claiming to have emotions equal to his, and conjugal expectations quite as sacred if not yet as binding.

"The first thing now to be done is to find our people!" said Henry with emotion, after the excess of Andy had ceased.

"Where are they?" inquired the mulatto gentleman. "And what are their names?"

"Their names at home were Frank's Ailcey, Craig's Polly, and Little Joe, who left several months ago; and an old man and woman called Daddy Joe and Mammy Judy; a young woman called Clara Beckwith, and a little boy named Tony, who came on but a few days before us."

"Come with me, and I'll lead you directly to him!" replied the mulatto gentlemen; when taking a vehicle, he drove them to the country a few miles from Windsor, where the parties under feelings such as never had been experienced by them before, fell into the embrace of each other.

"Dar now, dar! wat I tell you? Bless de laud, ef dar ain' Chaules an' Henry!" exclaimed Mammy Judy, clapping her hands, giving vent to tears which stole in drops from the eyes of all. "My po' chile! My po' Margot!" continued she in piteous tones as the bold and manly leader pressed closely to his bosom his boy, who now was the image of his mother. "My son, did'n yeh hear nothing bout er? did'n yeh not bring my po' Margot?"

"No, mammy, no! I have not seen and did not bring her! No, mammy, no! But—!" When Henry became choked with grief which found an audible response from the heart of every child of sorrow present.

Clara commenced, seconded by Andy and followed by all except him the pierce to whose manly heart had caused it, in tones the most affecting:

> *O, when shall my sorrow subside!*
> *And when shall my troubles be ended;*
> *And when to the bosom of Christ be conveyed,*
> *To the mansions of joy and bliss!*
> *To the mansions of joy and bliss!*

Falling upon their knees, Andy uttered a most fervent prayer, invoking Heaven's blessing and aid.
"Amen!" responded Charles.
"Hallelujah!" cried Clara, clapping her hands.
"Glory, glory, glory!" shouted Ailcey.
"O laud! W'en shall I get home!" mourned Mammy Judy.

"Tis good to be here, chilen! 'Tis good to be here!" said Daddy Joe, rubbing his hands quite wet with tears – when all rising to their feet met each other in the mutual embraces of Christian affection, with heaving hearts of sadness.

"We have reason, sir," said Henry addressing himself to the mulatto gentleman who stood a tearful eye witness to the scenes, "we have reason to thank God from the recesses of our hearts for the providential escape we've made from slavery!" which expression was answered only by trickles down the gentleman's cheeks.

The first care of Henry was to invest a portion of the old people's money by the purchase of fifty acres of land with improvements suitable, and provide for the schooling of the children until he should otherwise order. Charles by appointment in which Henry took part, was chosen leader of the runaway party, Andy being the second, Ambrose and Eli respectively the keepers of their money and accounts, Eli being a good penman.

"Now," said Henry, after two days rest, "the time has come and I must leave you! Polly, as you came as the mistress, you must now become the mother and nurse of my poor boy! Take good care of him – mammy will attend to you. Charles, as you have all secured land close to, I want you to stand by the old people; Andy, you, Ambrose, and Eli, stand by Charles and the girls, and you must succeed, as nothing can separate you; your strength depending upon your remaining together."

"Henry, is yeh guine sho' nuff?" earnestly enquired Andy.

"Yes, I must go!"

"Wait little!" replied Andy, when after speaking aside with Eli and Ambrose, calling the girls they all whispered for sometime together; occasional evidence of seriousness, anxiety, and joy marking their expressions of countenance.

The Provincial regulations requiring a license, or three weeks report to a public congregation, and that many sabbaths from the altar of a place of worship to legalise a marriage, and there being now no time for either of these, the mulatto gentleman who was still with them being a clergyman, declared, that in this case no such restrictions were binding; being originally intended for the whites and the free, and not for the panting runaway slave.

"Thank God for that! That's good talk!" said Charles.

"Ef it aint dat, 'taint nothin! Dat's wat I calls good black talk!" replied Andy, causing the clergyman and all to look at each other with a smile.

The party gathered standing in a semicircle, the clergyman in the center, a hymn being sung and prayer offered – rising to their feet, and an exhortation of comfort and encouragement being given, with the fatherly advice and instructions of their domestic guidance in after life by the aged man of God; the sacred and impressively novel words: "I join you together in the bonds of matrimony!" gave Henry the pleasure before leaving of seeing upon the floor together, Charles and Polly, Andy and Clara, Eli and Ailcey, "as man and wife forever."

"Praise God!" exclaimed poor old mammy, whose heart was most tenderly touched by the scene before her, contrasting it by reflection with the sad reminiscence of her own sorrowful and hopeless union with Daddy Joe, with whom she had lived fifty years as happily as was possible for slaves to do.

"Bless de laud!" responded the old man.

The young wives all gave vent to sobs of sympathy and joy, when the parson as a solace sung in touching sentiments:

Daughters of Zion! awake from thy sadness!
Awake for they foes shall oppress thee no more.
Bright o'er the hills shines the day star of gladness
Arise! for the night of they sorrow is o'er;
Daughters of Zion, awake from thy sadness!

Awake for they foes shall oppress thee no more!

"O glory!" exclaimed Mammy Judy, when the scene becoming most affecting; hugging his boy closely to his bosom, upon whose little cheek and lips he impressed kisses long and affectionate, when laying him in the old woman's lap and kissing little Tony, turning to his friends with a voice the tone of which sent through them a thrill, he said:

"By the instincts of a husband, I'll have her if living! If dead, by impulses of a Heaven-inspired soul, I'll avenge her loss unto death! Farewell, farewell!" the tears streaming as he turned from his child and its grandparents; when but a few minutes found the runaway leader seated in a car at the Windsor depot, from whence he reached the Suspension Bridge at Niagara en route for the Atlantic.

Chapter XXXIV
A Novel Adventure

FROM THE SUSPENSION BRIDGE through the great New York Central Railway to Albany, and thence by the Hudson River, Henry reached the city on the steamer "Hendrick Hudson," in the middle of an afternoon. First securing a boarding house – a new thing to him – he proceeded by direction to an intelligence office, which he found kept by a mulatto gentleman. Here inquiring for a situation as page or valet on a voyage to Cuba, he deposited the required sum, leaving his address as "Gilbert Hopewell, 168 Church St." – changing the name to prevent all traces of himself out of Canada, whither he was known to have gone, to the free states of America, and especially to Cuba whence he was going, the theater of his future actions.

In the evening Henry took a stroll through the great thoroughfare, everything being to him so very novel, that eleven o'clock brought him directly in front of doubtless the handsomest saloon of the kind in the world, situated on the corner of Broadway and Franklin street. Gazing in at the luxurious and fashionable throng and gaieties displayed among the many in groups at the tables, there was one which more than all others attracted his attention, though unconscious at the time of its doing so.

The party consisted of four; a handsome and attractive young lady, accompanied by three gentlemen, all fine looking, attractive persons, wearing the undress uniforms of United States naval officers. The elder of these was a robust, commanding person in appearance, black hair, well mixed with white, seemingly some sixty years of age. One of the young gentlemen was tall, handsome, with raven-black hair, moustache, and eyes; the other, medium height, fair complexion, hair, moustache and whiskers, with blue eyes; while the young lady ranked of medium proportions in height and size, drab hair, fair complexion, plump cheeks and hazel eyes, and neatly dressed in a maroon silk habit, broadly faced in front and cuffed with orange satin, the collar being the same, neatly bound with crimson.

While thus musing over the throng continually passing in and out, unconsciously Henry had his attention so fixed on this group, who were passing out and up Broadway, involuntarily leaving the window through which he had been gazing, he found himself following them in the crowd which throng the street closely, foot to foot.

Detecting himself and about to turn aside, he overheard the elderly gentleman in reply to a question by the lady concerning the great metropolis, say, that in Cuba where in a few days they would be, recreation and pleasure were quite equal to that of New York. Now drawing more closely he learned that the company were destined for Havana, to sail in a few days. His heart beat with joy, when turning and making his way back, he found his boarding house without difficulty.

Henry once more spent a sleepless night, noted by restless anxiety; and the approach of morning seemed to be regulated by the extent of the city. If thoughts could have done it, the great Metropolis would have been reduced to a single block of houses, reducing in like manner the night to a few fleeting moments.

Early in the morning he had risen, and impatiently pacing the floor, imagined that the people of that city were behind the age in rising. Presently the summons came for breakfast, and ere he was seated a note was handed him reading thus:

> *Intelligence Office – Leonard St., New York, March 5th, 1853*
> *Gilbert Hopewell:*
> *There is now an opportunity offered to go to Cuba, to attend on a party of four – a lady and three gentlemen – who sail for Havana direct (see Tribune of this morning). Be at my office at half past ten o'clock, and you will learn particulars, which, by that time I will have obtained.*
> *Respectfully, B.A.P.*

Though the delay was but an hour, Henry was restless, and when the time came was punctually in his place. The gentleman who called to meet him at the Intelligence office Henry recognized as one of the party seen the previous evening at the great saloon in Broadway. Arrangements having been completed concerning his attendance and going with them, "Meet me in an hour at the St. Nicholas, and commence your duties immediately," said the gentleman, when politely bowing, Henry turned away with a heart of joy, and full of hope.

Promptly to the time he was at the hotel, arranging for a start; when he found that his duties consisted in attendance particularly on the young lady and one of the young gentlemen, and the other two as occasion might require. The company was composed of Captain Richard Paul, the elderly gentleman; Lieutenant Augustus Seeley, the black-haired; passed Midshipman Lawrence Spencer, the light-haired gentleman, and Miss Cornelia Woodward.

Miss Woodward was modest and retiring, though affable, conversant and easy in manner. In her countenance were pictured an expression of definite anxiety and decisive purpose, which commanded for her the regard and esteem of all whom she approached. Proud without vanity, and graceful without affectation, she gained the esteem of everyone; a lady making the remark that she was one of the most perfect of American young ladies.

After breakfast the next morning they embarked on the steam packet "Isabella," to sail that day at eleven o'clock.

Of the gentlemen, Augustus Seeley gave to Miss Woodward the most attention, though nothing in her manner betrayed attachment except an occasional sigh.

Henry, for the time, appeared to be her main dependence; as shortly after sailing she manifested a disposition to keep in retirement as much as possible. Though a girl of tender affections, delicate sentiments, and elevated Christian graces, Cornelia was evidently inexperienced and unprepared for the deceptious impositions practiced in society. Hence, with the highest hopes and expectations, innocently unaware of the contingencies in life's dangerous pathway, hazarding her destiny on the simple promise of an irresponsible young man, but little more than passed midshipman, she reached the quay at Moro Castle in less than six days from the Port of New York.

The Floating City of Pengimbang

Michelle F. Goddard

KADE TURNED her head and breathed through her nose. The smell of the champaca flower tucked behind her ear and the salt air briefly replaced that of tar and scorched metal. She stood lightly on the jukung as the boat bobbed on the sea, hands folded, face a mirror of a still pond. In the distance, the ground crew shuffled into action. Galoshes splashed through pools of water, making droplets skitter across the oily surface of the runway. Waves prowled at the edge of the landing plateau, a man-made butte that barely stood above the water, commandeered from the last significant landmass in the South Pacific closest to an island once known as Bali.

The wind changed, a slight caress that played across Kade's skin, causing the fine black hairs on her arm to flutter. Her lips parted. She drank in a hint of tart ozone. The cumulous clouds widened, bullying their way across the sky. The signs were subtle, easy to miss, but Kade noted the slight change of pressure registering in the bone below her ear and was certain.

"The storm will be earlier than you indicated," she said.

Beside her, her grandfather, Darma, appeared not to hear. He sat on the bench at the front of the skiff, his gaze fixed skyward.

Kade raised her face as the clouds parted. "Perhaps this was not the best time for Adi's visit."

The belly of the transport ship descended from the sky. Jets of flame shot from rotating thrusters on either side of the craft toward the landing pad below. Waves of heat blossomed out, shimmering the air into a veil that warped the image of the ship. The transport settled, belching out fuel and flames. Where plants had encroached on the tarmac, the fire scolded their temerity. Some burned until they were ash. Others were extinguished by a merciful wave of sea water.

"Fire does not forgive," Darma said. "But water may, given enough time and a truly contrite heart."

Kade nodded, acknowledging his words but unsure of his meaning. If Darma was seeking contrition from Adi, he had not waited long enough. Likewise, there was nothing in her grandfather's stiff-backed, jutting-jaw posture that indicated anything as pliable as forgiveness.

"Kade, your assistance with Water-Web has been immeasurable."

"Thank you, grandfather."

"It will continue to be so."

"Yes?"

"But Adi was always meant to succeed me."

"What? But—"

Darma put up his hand to silence her. Kade gripped her hands tighter and pressed her lips together. She breathed in slowly, calming the storm within as it pressed against her chest, making it hard to breathe as if she were drowning. Her mind floundered, casting about for any reason for his decision, but there was nothing to hold to. Or else it was no shore she was capable of reaching.

Darma smiled and Kade squinted into the distance. The ship was now resting on the tarmac, and the passenger shuttle had reached the docking moors. A lone figure disembarked and walked towards the wharf where Darma and Kade waited in their boat. Darma rose smoothly, considering his age and the waves that kicked up their small watercraft as if it too was excited to see Adi.

"Grandfather." Adi stepped onto the boat and the men embraced, an arm locking maneuver that drew even more attention to Darma's frailness and Adi's, robust energy. "Cousin." Adi nodded toward Kade.

"You look well," Kade said.

"You look pale," Darma said. "But soon you'll have a nice glow about you."

Adi stiffened and frowned. "I think that will take longer to achieve than my schedule will allow."

With a glance from Darma, Kade moved aside making room for the two men. She engaged the solar sails and set the return destination toward home through the navcom, her fingers numb on the dials. The wind slipped through the wisps of her hair, tossing it aside as easily as Darma's words had her dreams.

The jukung, though shaped in the traditional mold of a Balinese skiff was none-the-less powered by modern means. Soon Pengimbang came into view. A ring of bamboo supports spread out like the loose ends of a woven basket from the tiny island in its centre. Between the longest two spokes, jetties that poked like accusing fingers toward the sea, stood the harbour and floating market.

Kade guided the boat into dock, throwing the line to the dock-hands. "Secure all the boats and exterior docks. A storm surge is on its way."

A burly dock-hand shouldered his way through the crowd.

"What of the Water-Web, Darma? The last surge damaged many fishing boats, ruined several sea farms and the outlying buildings are still under repair."

Adi strode forward, eyes ablaze. "There is nothing keeping you here."

"You're more off-worlder than native now aren't you, Adi." The man folded his thick arms across his chest. "What do you have to say about it?"

"You can't hold back the tide."

A laugh erupted from Darma. He clapped both hands on Adi's shoulder as he pushed him through the crowd. "We shall see."

"Kade," the dock-hand said, his gaze tight under a furrowed brow.

Kade addressed the group of villagers loosely scattered around the dock. "We all have work to do, yes."

They nodded. Some even bowed. Kade bowed deeply, awed by the unexpected respect. But she knew she was only the avatar of their hope, of their fear. She hurried after her grandfather and cousin, using the spring of the bamboo under her feet to hasten her way.

A canter-levered bamboo bridge linked the harbor to the neighboring village, a collection of floating bamboo huts. Vertical gardens hung on south facing walls emitting a heady concoction from the delicate flowers and savoury herbs. A few dwellings jumped and jerked as damaged float barrels were repaired by the divers below. Kneeling on the dock, the homes' occupants looked on, eyes narrowed, as if by sheer will they could speed matters on.

A ping came through her synaptic relay. Kade accepted the message.

"Grandfather, the storm is confirmed." She refrained from mentioning early, as I said. Would Adi have been so sure?

Having received the message, villagers around Kade, began preparing. Homes were lashed together to offer more stable structures. Roofs made up of operable louvers were closed to create rounded tops to minimize wind exposure. Small boats and skiffs were pulled inside and homes secured. Soon, evacuations to the three largest bespoke structures on Pengimbang would begin, if they hadn't already.

"Bowing to nature," Adi said. "Is that your solution? A storm comes and you scurry like rats, your lives at the whim of the weather and the water."

"Perhaps that is our penance," Kade said.

"Why? We have Mars and Europa."

"*Some* have Mars and Europa," Kade said, nodding at the men from the repair team as they rushed by, tools in hand. "The rest of us must adapt."

It was a relief to see the drills had been paying off; urgency with focus, procedure, not panic. If only the Water-Web would work as well. But was Adi the missing component? Adi's strength? His fierceness? He was certainly as unrelenting as Darma, the two men being so alike. Is that why Darma had chosen him instead of Kade?

They passed a hut that had been winched off the water with the help of its neighbors and a complex pulley system. Repairmen were now lowering the hut as their eyes raked the darkening sky.

"We've taken steps backwards, not forwards." Adi shook his head at the hoisted hut. "We would have been shamed to live in bamboo."

"There is no shame in this," Kade said, gesturing toward the bowered entrance to the three-story bespoke structure that stood on the edge of the island.

She led them through the fifteen metre long curved tunnel. At intervals, arched openings like wide mouthed grins lolled their tongues of rattan toward the sea. Boats that were moored there rocked and pitched with increasing agitation. Walkways branched off to other parts of the village that ultimately connected the three largest bespoke structures and the island that lay in the centre; a web sheltering a plump green bristled spider.

At the end of the passage the foyer rose to a ten meter arch. The floors above ran the circumference, supported with bamboo trusses bent and woven so that the inside of the structure stood like a gigantic fish trap. The funnel spiraled up to the peaked roof. Cool sea air swirled in eddies, carrying the smell of flowering shrubs that sat in fat pots near the pane-less windows.

Kade stiffened as a message came through.

"Barometric pressure is dropping," she said. "It is time." She led them toward large double doors at the other end of the hall as the wind grew brisk and urgent. The three passed through an office housing a single desk in a smooth curling wave design, a sleek chair, and a large bay window that looked out on the harbor. A seamless door on the far wall slid open to reveal a room beyond.

Except for the entrance that closed so completely it was as if it had never been there, the walls of this new space were bare, smooth and dark. In the centre stood an s-shaped chair, anchored to the floor and affixed with armrests that ended in shallow basins. The structure was made of the same material and glowed blue, the only light in the room. Streams of neon flowed within, an apparition of living water.

Darma pulled back his shoulders and approached it. He sat and leaned back. As he did, a tendril sprung from the chair and probed the back of his head. Darma grunted and his gaze became distant, his face pinched and hard. He was plugged into the Water-Web. The chair softened, molding to Darma's body, the spirit of liquidity becoming irrefutable as it cradled him. He pressed his hands into the basins which were now of a jelly-like consistency.

Kade gripped her hands tighter. She could already feel them submerged in the gel, the nano-mites crawling across her skin like the spiders she imagined them to be. Then the sensation of expansion. It was not unpleasant, only strange to feel herself in one place and in many at the same time. Darma insisted that was impossible. This anthropomorphizing was not scientific; she was not the water.

"Is this it?" Adi asked, scanning the chair with an intensity hard enough to be a touch. "The Water-Web?" He reached out to the chair, and Kade's hand darted out to stop him.

"Not while the Controller is engaged."

Adi retreated a step.

"And this is merely the interface," Kade said, her voice strained as she wavered between pride and resentment. She swallowed her frustration. "During a storm, Darma directs the technology, interfacing with the web and directing the nano-mites. Normally they are in a passive state, filaments sent out into the atmosphere, through the water, collecting data and calculating all variables in regard to the weather."

"The advanced warning system," Adi said. "Much like the old SLOSH surge forecasts."

"Yes, but this is better adapted to deal with the volatile human interference on the weather systems. With so many island states and their competing technologies, the weather has become even more unpredictable."

Darma moaned and his face pulled back into a rictus grin. Kade leaned over him but did not touch him. The system would alert her to any problem, but she wanted her grandfather to feel her presence, her support. He would scold her if he saw this frivolous action.

Adi joined her at Darma's side, but he seemed too busy focusing on the techno-port on the back of Darma's head to take note of the pain written on the old man's face. Kade tensed at his brazen scrutiny, but she knew the message beneath Darma's words on the skiff; she would be expected to do her duty.

"The system is not only predictive," Kade continued to explain. "Using this interface, the nano-mites are activated. They spin a microscopic spider silk derivative that creates a network around the city. Under the controller's directive, the system stabilizes the city during the storms and acts as a living force-field."

Kade envisioned lines of spider-silk thrown out, the web spreading to hold Pengimbang safe. The wind would blow, and the people would feel the shadow of its ferocity, but nothing more. The tide would surge. If the system worked to specifications, inside the Water-Web Pengimbang would reach up to kiss the dark cheek of the sky. The image hung in her mind and Kade smiled, buoyed by the thought.

"But that would take considerable power," Adi said. "Pengimbang doesn't have access to that kind of power."

"We use the tidal surge itself," Kade said. "The stronger the storm, the more power we have to use."

Kade felt the stabilization begin to root before the report came in and exhaled in relief. It spread, but then stopped. A shudder fluttered inside, fear, caught like a bird in her rib cage. She gasped as a turbulent force overwhelmed her mind. A thought erupted in her as if someone had shouted it. The storm would be worse than they anticipated.

Kade looked to her grandfather. Darma scowled, then winced. His hands closed into fists and his body became rigid. The chair stiffened beneath him. He cried out and jerked to his feet. Adi caught the old man as he began to fall.

Kade darted toward the machine. She thrust her hands into the jelly and felt the floor beneath her disappear. She gasped breathless, drowning, pulled apart until she was the smallest part of herself. Her spirit spread out thinner and thinner. Too thin. Then, as if an elastic snapped back into place, she was once more herself in the room. The sense of the space around her tilted for a moment and then slid back into place, like a boat listing and then suddenly righting itself on a wave.

"Darma," Adi said, wrapping his arms tighter around his grandfather's frail shoulders. "Darma, what happened?"

"I am fine. Fine." Darma struggled out of Adi's arms to stand on his own, though he leaned heavily on the young man. "Just weakened. It will pass."

Kade withdrew her hands. The liquid, viscous yet silken, receded like a reluctant lover. The chair once more adopted its sinuous shape.

"Report," Darma said.

Kade blinked and shook her head. She reached out through her synaptics. All the messages came at once. Without pause, she sorted and analyzed the data.

"All citizens have been accounted for. Evacuation successful. Minor injuries, but no casualties. The Water Web is holding."

Darma motioned them toward the door leading back into the office. He was always eager to leave, always needing to look out the large window in the office, as if he couldn't sense the embrace of the web and needed confirmation it was there. Or perhaps it was still a wonder he needed to see with his own eye. Understandable. The Water-Web was always a stunning sight, and this time even more so.

Inside the office, Kade pushed free the slats of the window to open them wider. Darma had reached farther than he had before, though debris floated on the outer rim where the web met the sea. The docks she could see from the window looked shorn off at the end; the metal tie-off pilings hung precariously from shattered bamboo planks. Kade noted several huts bobbing like drunken men without hats, their louvered shutters torn from them. Inside the web, Pengimbang was far safer than outside.

Beyond the web's reach, the seas roiled, white foam spray atop grey waves, rising up in protest to slash ribbons into crinkled black velvet skies. The web, a scintillating wall erected around the city, flashed with each angry blow. The floating city undulated, grinding and moaning as it rode the surge. Fat raindrops pelted the roofs, drumming the storms disdain against the huts, until it became a grumbling hum.

Kade moved aside as Adi crept forward. Resting his hands on the windowsill he stared out, eyes wide and mouth agape. He wet his lips slowly, eyes narrowing. As if a decision were made, Adi nodded. "I have to show you something. I need a secure link."

Kade closed the shutters. She stepped to the desk, pulling the chair out and offering it to Darma before she leaned over the table. Her fingers flew upon its surface. The desk pulsed once before throwing its light upward to form a screen that curved one hundred and eighty degrees around them. Kade stepped aside before Adi could shoulder past. He touched his middle finger to his palm. A virtual keyboard spread out before him at waist height. He entered a code and data ran across the virtual screen. Adi hit enter. A globe materialized in the air above them.

"What is this?" Darma asked, peering up at the planet.

"A new home," Adi said, his eyes alight with the glow from the sphere. "You want to keep your way of life. Imagine it without the storms and the flooding. Without constantly living in a state of emergency, just barely surviving."

"That is not how we live," Kade said.

"We can start fresh."

The orb's surface gleamed brilliant turquoise, deepening to midnight in ribbons that wound along the equator. The poles shimmered icy aqua capping the jewel of a planet. Land masses dotted the sphere, a planet of archipelagos, with only a half dozen once-upon-a-time Australia-size continents. Kade reached toward the image and spread her fingers wide, magnifying it. Rotation ceased, showing one continent with a long string of islands sweeping across the southern ocean, each island like an emerald on a cerulean velvet mat.

"Beautiful," Kade said. "And there must be many island states vying for re-settlement."

"Not yet," Adi said. "This is classified information."

"Then how did you get this?"

Adi glared at Kade. "I have *some* skill." He stared at the planet. "But, imagine it; Pengimbang on one of these islands."

"And they'll take everyone?" Kade asked.

"There's a screening process."

"Of course, there is," Kade said, her voice flat.

"Kade," Darma said. "What has gotten into you?"

"Seeding is a considerable investment," Adi said. "But, Grandfather, with this," Adi glanced toward the window, "now *that* is technology they could find useful on a planet like this."

Kade stared at the spinning globe. Beneath her feet she felt the bamboo shift. Did they have bamboo on this planet? Did the water there feel warm and smooth? Would it welcome her people after they abandoned this planet? Should it?

"But we have to move quickly," Adi said, shutting down the program. "Make a proposal—"

"The Water-Web is not a bargaining chip," Darma said. He rose and rested his hands on Adi's shoulder. "It is for you. To use for Pengimbang."

Adi stared at Darma for a moment but then gave a stiff nod. "I have much to consider."

"We shall leave you to it."

Kade glided to Darma's side. She walked him toward the door, though the old man made every effort to appear as if her help was unnecessary. She led him back to the fish-trap foyer and toward one of the windows that offered a wide view over the city. A favorite spot of Darma's to rest after a session with the Water-Web, a chaise was already waiting and the area held only the distant echoes of voices that floated down from the other floors.

"Grandfather," Kade said, helping him into the seat. "I think you are wrong about Adi."

Darma breathed heavily as he leaned back in the chair. He stared up at Kade.

"I do not like this person I am seeing, Kade. I do not like this hardness, this recalcitrance. Where is my sweet girl?"

Kade bowed her head, turning her face away as if to block the heat of his words from burning her. She bit her lip, the pain enough to goad her past shame.

"I only mean to say that he has his own destiny. Away from here. That planet. It is quite beautiful. I can understand the potential—"

"You wish to go?"

Her head jerked up, her face unable to hide the shock and pain. Was this what he thought of her? So weak-willed? So easily swayed? She shook her head, one stiff twitch of denial. Her chin rose as she looked at Darma.

"But Adi clearly does."

Darma turned away and pursed his lips and gazed out over the city. The matter was closed. He would not listen to her but perhaps he would listen to Adi.

Kade returned to the room but did not find Adi in it. The entrance to the Water-Web room stood ajar. Kade wondered how he had bypassed the security. She imagined Darma would be pleased by his initiative.

"Adi, I would speak with you," Kade said.

"What is it, cousin?" Adi said, his gaze fixed on the chair.

Now that she faced him, Kade's resolve wavered. She closed her eyes. In her mind's eye, she watched the storm beat against the force-field, a pulse that mirrored her own anxious heart. Yet the Water-Web held, withstood the assault. She took a breath and faced her cousin.

"It is obvious to me that your heart is in resettlement."

"And?"

Adi moved around the chair scanning every curve. He knelt down and peered closely at the streams, following the flow until he stood staring into the basin. He pressed his finger against the pliant surface. Kade winced with the intrusion.

"Darma is getting old," Kade said.

"Are you here to beg me to stay?"

"I am here to ask you to speak to Darma on my behalf. I may not be his first choice but—"

"He is set on me. And what Darma wants—"

"I know you do not want to stay. I have already been trained on the Water-Web. I believe I have an affinity. If only Darma would give me a chance. If you would talk to him…"

Adi slid into the chair and leaned back. His eyes narrowed. His brow furrowed.

"What are you doing?" Kade said.

"I am exploring my legacy," Adi said as he touched his middle finger to his palm.

A thin tendril leaked from the headrest. Adi grabbed it and pressed it to the back of his head. Kade felt a flash of heat as if a burning lance had run through her.

"Stop," Kade said. "You don't know what you are doing."

"I am accessing the system," Adi said as he pushed his hands down into the basin. "If Darma won't see reason, I still might be able to convince—"

The chair solidified. It bucked and Adi flew across the room. He landed on all fours, shaking his head and groaning. His arms trembled and his legs kicked and slipped against the floor as he struggled to find his feet.

Uncertainty permeated Kade's limbs. Distress calls flashed through her synaptics. The Water-Web was dissolving.

Kade gritted her teeth and staggered toward the chair.

"No, Kade. You must not."

Darma stood on the threshold, hunched and gasping as if each breath were being torn from him. He took a step toward the chair, but only the one. Darma braced himself against the wall with his left hand, fingers clutching for purchase, his right pressed to his side, his chest a bellows.

"You are too weak, grandfather," Kade said.

"I would not risk you."

Kade gazed at her grandfather. "You are afraid. You are afraid. For me." Her hands rose toward the interface "But I am not."

The chair liquefied. A delicate tendril sprung forth and crept toward Kade. It rose to meet her hand, spiraling as it slid up her arm. With a sigh, Kade embraced the sensation. The interface flowed until Kade was completely cocooned in a brilliant blue aura. Only a finger-thick band of the interface remained attached to the floor. Cool electricity ran the length of Kade's body. It sent her reaching for the floor, her head thrown back, her vision bathed in neon.

Kade could sense the nano-mites, as if holding their breath, waiting for her direction. With a wave of her fingers, they responded, lacing together the rent that Adi had torn. She was the spider and wove the Water-Web higher and wider and stronger, the city now encased within a sparkling azure sphere.

She did not need to see to know it was so. She did not need confirmation when her awareness lived everywhere. But she would not be contained, confined, constrained. Kade moved toward the door.

Somewhere close by, there was movement. Kade turned a part of her mind there.

"Kade," Darma said, shuffling toward her Adi beside him, the two men leaning on each other. "You cannot leave this room. Not like this. It is too dangerous."

Kade looked back. The Water-Web interface billowed out behind her; a veil blown by her passage. One thin blue thread of it remained affixed to the floor. Kade beckoned. It sprung free and wrapped around her finger.

Darma stared, eyes growing wide, glowing with the neon of the interface, or perhaps in awe, as tears streamed down his face and he reached but did not touch her.

"Kade," Darma said.

Kade smiled. At least she believed she did and hoped her grandfather knew he was forgiven as she walked out of the room.

The New Colossuses

Harambee K. Grey-Sun

IT TOOK HALF A MOMENT for Ollie to realize he'd been buried alive. He spent the second half – and several moments after – trying not to panic as he squirmed his horizontal body, attempting to discover his boundaries.

He dared not open his eyes or mouth. He could feel the dirt – or whatever – firmly encasing his body. The only air he had was that trapped inside his lungs; he had to be wise about conserving it.

The soil was looser above him – that resting on his face, chest, stomach, and knees. He was mostly clothed, but his feet were bare. His arms, at his sides. His palms, downward. He couldn't use his hands as shovels; his toes were of limited use. He was left to wriggling his entire self while making frequent, desperate attempts at leg-lifts and sit-ups.

It wasn't a totally unique experience. He'd been involuntarily buried under soaked blankets, trash, and other objects while trying to sleep peacefully in parks or on sidewalks. He'd always gotten out to see another day.

Presently, it took some doing, but eventually he managed to sit up to a point where his face felt more air than dirt. With the aid of replenished lungs, he managed to sit up properly and crawl free. Twitchy eyelids eventually allowed his eyes to find daylight…saturated with periwinkle.

He'd emerged into a day as blue as he was in the face. Yet, he'd came out of the grave into good air, despite its traces of decay. He gulped it down as quickly as he could get it while jerkily swiveling his head to his left and right, checking for the presence of others. No other figures nearby, not that he could make out anyway in the haze brooding over this land of soil and refuse bleached of distinct markings by time and the weather.

Cans, here; plastic stuff, there. And him – another discard. Whoever had buried him had done a poor job. For such a shallow grave, the diggers could've at least checked if he was actually dead first.

Involuntarily – and stiffly – he shook his head at the waste then attempted to heave himself to his feet. Through grunts and winces, he made his best efforts to stretch his weary limbs as he checked himself over.

Best he could readily tell, he wore a tight yet roomy enough jumpsuit, much of it caked in moist dirt. He did his best to brush himself off, giving up after a minute or so. Though it felt like burlap against his moist skin, the suit had a foil-like sheen. A few tears, here and there – more than a few of them claiming thin yet tenacious worms, attempting to wriggle their way in or out. He picked off the ones he saw.

His limited round of stretching hadn't done much good. His joints still ached. His head throbbed. Every so often, his ears popped, as if bubbles were bursting on the surface of his eardrums. Breathing was laborious. But he was *alive*.…. Standing unsteadily on spongy ground, under a pale lavender sky that lent its hue to the ubiquitous haze of moist air – yet, *alive*.

If he wanted to remain so, he figured he'd better get moving. He'd need food, water – preferably soon.

He started off in a direction to which he gave no thought. He couldn't see much more than fifteen feet in either direction; so there was no point to *where*. He was simply focused on *why*.

Who could've done it?

He guessed someone had gotten tired of seeing him camped out in front of their favorite fast food joint; or nursing a cup of coffee in the corner of the chain café, parked too close to the rest rooms; or haunting the rows between library shelves, envying the pages held close by covers, despite their dust and mold.

Youngish and able-bodied, Ollie didn't look like he should be homeless – maybe that's precisely why he attracted disgust instead of sympathy. Derisive words instead of a helping hand. But he'd gotten by. Gotten by as well as the voices had allowed him to.

He was a survivor, even if – as he now considered – some deranged worker at one of the shelters he'd frequented had made up their own mind to dispose of him.

But just where had they tried to bury him? And how long ago?

A steadier crackling had joined the sporadic popping in his ears. The traces of decay were now intermixed with more aromatic scents, just as faint, yet reminiscent of women's perfumes, those his nostrils had often sampled from passersby on the sidewalks. Ollie may've closed his eyes to take a deeper breath, dredging up pleasant memories, just long enough for his foot to glance against something hard and cold, sending him to stumble. Regaining his footing, he turned and cast his eyes downward to focus on a large, rusted metal rectangle, lying flat, half buried. The words he could make out read 'Reclaimed Land. Wildlife Refuge. Owned by Automotive—'

That had to be the joke of the day. He'd heard no birds. No barking or baying or any other animal calls. Far as he could tell, only he was here. He and the worms, in this dying day.

It was late afternoon, of that he was now certain as the haze seemed to thin, permitting him a greater range of vision. He began to make out trees. Leafless and sparse – easy to avoid. There was no sun. Yet close to the ground, on the horizon, he glimpsed spires – golden, gleaming, curving like horns – amassed like a tuft of giant, unyielding weeds. Fixated, he slogged on toward them.

The ground was uneven, all around, with pits and trenches, steady inclines and declines. The trees grew less scattered yet remained like skeletal arms reaching from the ground, long having given up any struggle for life, yet still imbued with a spirit strong enough to prevent falling.

Ollie paid little attention to avoiding obstacles; his swaying body seemed to do just fine on its own as he moved along, the haze continuing to thin into wisps. More and more the terrain felt to his feet like cold oatmeal, infused with menthol. Firm, yet pliable; emitting a cooling sensation with each step, that made its way upward from the soles, easing any physical pain one would normally feel on such a trek, while serenading the nostrils with the faint scent of mint.

He'd gone on for he hadn't known how long – bringing the distant gargantuan spires into greater view, counting four thus far, and trying to guess how many hundreds of feet they stood above the ground – before he noticed, to his left and his right, other upright bodies beyond himself and the dead trees. Men and women, trudging in the same direction as he. Others – *alive*.

He didn't stare. He gave them only glances. Those around him were big and small, all shapes and sizes, yet similarly garbed. The light wasn't fair to any – but many that he saw seemed weathered, on the north side of middle-aged. Their expressions, dour. Their pallors, those of winter warriors who'd lost to the season. And yet all of them seemed possessed of the same determined spirit – to reach the spires.

None spoke. None even made the effort. Not even a pretense. Only hurried looks passed between fellow travelers – those nearer and farther away – before each and every woman and man returned their gaze toward those golden horns.

Ollie didn't need to converse with the others. The voices in his head carried on their usual conversations, their usual discussions of regrets and whatevers and what-ifs, digressing every now and then to gas empty words about the here and now.

The inner voices were familiar – mostly. But as he and his fellow travelers grew thicker in mass and drew nearer the spires. The tones in his mind began to vary – become lighter and darker – more and more foreign – intruding…

Why shouldn't I spend my energies on ephemeral partners fifteen plus or minus instead of more age appropriate? The younger are all about play…the older – after a few harsh breaks – have come back around that way…

Another thought, wafting in…

Life and love seem incompatible…Is there a choice? There must a choice. One is an exercise in the moderation of pain…The other is an inconstant schedule of intense pain and release…. Where is the love as I've seen it advertised?

Were these the thoughts of his fellow travelers? Ollie glanced around – as did the multitude of others – only to find attention ineluctably reverting toward the gleaming spires while another thought found its way into his consciousness.

If only I'd gotten into the right school…the preschool my parents just knew would be right for me…but, no…And how do I end up? A fast-food franchisee….They're right to hate me…. Everyone's right to hate me….

Another:

Lousy dad trying to buy me with pricey gifts…. The time to do that was when I was a kid…the most expensive one of all – the gift of attention…. The present of his presence…. But, no – he didn't have the time at the time…. Now I don't want his damned gifts, or his calls, or his attention…. Who has the time?

Yet another:

I wanted to go out with her – so badly – and she expressed interest…. Smiled at me, even spoke a few nice words…. But if I go down that road, I lose myself…. I need to finish my sketches, my paintings, those two sculptures…. All the ideas in my head…. Only then can I safely pursue a healthy relationship….

And yet another:

How dare she take credit for my success…. I grew up to be a success in spite of her…. What, did she think her parenting method of negligence seasoned with sporadic yelling and threats had a hand in molding me to become the perfect white-collar cog in the wheel? I can't wait until some news organization tries to interview Dear Mother again….

And another…. And another…. Many, many others… They trudged along as one mass, one body. Were they all sharing one another's thoughts? Regrets and resentments and whatever else weaving in on different wavelengths?

Ollie only knew his head was full of others' preoccupations; his own were almost lost to him – though not entirely. Most importantly, he wasn't lost. None among this great mass of travelers were.

The structure toward which they all lumbered came into greater view: A geodesic dome, a mile or more wide, dimpled like a big silvery blue golf ball and encircled by gleaming golden spires, jutting from the soil, slanting away from the dome, stretching for hundreds of feet. From Ollie's perspective – it almost seemed like a bizarre sculpture of the sun, half submerged, struggling to rise from the earth.

A steady white noise in his ears, he felt a rapid thumping in his chest – his heart. Pumping all this time, he was sure, but he only now became cognizant of its working, perhaps due to the exertion of walking for so long. Looking over his shoulders, taking in the sheer number of fellow travelers, he realized that they all had traveled up a hill – not a steep one, but one that had placed them at a substantial height.

Hundreds of dirty, jumpsuited men and women had ascended or were ascending from all sides. Many slowed their pace as they neared – perhaps out of awe, perhaps due to weariness hammering at their bodies – but none among the dreary, bedraggled caravan stopped completely. They converged upon the structure. Ollie was no exception. The journey hadn't ended.

Many brushed a hand across a spire as they passed, if they happened to near one; but most went straight toward the dome – and seemed to pass right through. It wasn't exactly transparent; the surface seemed more iridescent, fading from one hue to another as he neared. Yet, no matter his position, others still seemed to disappear upon reaching and touching the surface. In the environment's fading light, Ollie figured his eyes were playing tricks on him. Only when he drew close enough to the dome's panels to reach and out to touch did he begin to understand, while keeping his hands to himself.

Without touching, he'd no hope of guessing their composition – metal, plastic, glass, or something completely unknown – but the surface provided a faint reflection, one clear and detailed enough for him to see he was not the young man he remembered. Wrinkles, thin gray hair – like his fellow travelers, he wasn't a day under sixty. The panels also acted as a slightly tinted window, giving view to all manners of tubes, configured in a variety of ways, each filled with a multihued mist or a radiant, undulating glob of something.

One dollop – fluctuating between golden brown and dull orange – caught his eye, seemed to call to him. Without thinking, he pressed his hands and face to the glass for a better look, only to be sucked in.

He'd instinctively shut his eyes when he'd felt his body being jerked forward; opening them, he saw only the hues that had fascinated him – golden brown fading to dull orange and gradually going back to brown. He still had a body – but it was immobile, upright, experiencing odd sensations. The glob had him.

"Welcome" – a disembodied, slightly feminine voice invaded his sense of sound – "you who are forlorn, you who yearn, you who are lost, you refuse of tempests…"

The voice had a long list of the types it welcomed, all of whom seemed like miserable sorts, wretched beings for whom no one had any use – save for this structure, this grand structure in which he was now entrapped.

As the voice droned on, Ollie's body shivered. His jumpsuit seemed to shred itself, falling away from his trembling body in slivers. He tried to shut his eyes, his ears, blacking out the colors and tuning out the voice – but the glob had his body and senses, deranging them.

While what felt like tendrils swooped in from every which way – darting, piercing, plucking, jerking – sweeping Ollie's naked body, his senses were being acquisitioned, repurposed, moving on from sight, hearing, smell, taste, and touch – far beyond.

He struggled – God, he struggled – but he ultimately gave in, having little else to give other than his spirit. His senses no longer belonged to him. His body was converting to another state of being.

The colors faded to white as the voice faded away. Gradually, he became aware of a new voice speaking. It sounded like an old flame. It sounded like his mother. His father. It sounded like everyone who had ever cared for him, even momentarily. It explained that the Earth, much of its resources having been spent, had entered a new age. Humankind had failed in its half-hearted mission to colonize any other planets; thus, the greatest minds left among the greatly reduced population had banded together to build structures such as these.

The whiteness gave way to an aerial view of the structure and the surrounding land. From the sky, the structure indeed looked like a sun or a blooming flower. The land itself was a grand island, receiving large boats on its various shores. Men and women in contamination suits drove carts filled with unconscious bodies from the ships to various points on the island, where they proceeded to bury the men and women in shallow graves, allowing the contaminated soil to further prepare the bodies – and regress the minds – for the inevitable lurching toward…

"…this dome of imprisoned static, this factory of new age music, this – the mother of exiles from other worlds who shall come and replenish ours. Thank you, retirees, for your selfless contributions, to giving your whole selves to the dying Earth's beacon, this dome of imprisoned static, this…"

A sudden shift in perspective showed a mostly black sky filled with stars, and some planets. And possibly other objects.

Ollie no longer heard voices or static or anything else as his final conversion neared its completion. Like the others for whom the Earth had one final use, he was a part – one small part – of providing the raw material, the memories of lives and loves wasted, for the music being broadcast outward, beyond the solar system, out toward beings who might exist, who might feel the groove enough to launch their ships, leaving their own planets to dance toward the Earth – hopefully with their own songs of rejuvenation, their own instruments of renewal.

Planted among the temporary graves for the undead – the retired – this or one of the other Final Music factories dotting the earth, sending pleasing pleas across the universe, might reach saviors or conquerors. At this point, no one cared which, so long as they came.

Imperium in Imperio

Sutton E. Griggs

Chapter I
A Small Beginning

"**CUM ER** long hunny an' let yer mammy fix yer 'spectabul, so yer ken go to skule. Yer mammy is 'tarmined ter gib yer all de book larning dar is ter be had eben ef she has ter lib on bred an' herrin's, an' die en de a'ms house."

These words came from the lips of a poor, ignorant negro woman, and yet the determined course of action which they reveal vitally affected the destiny of a nation and saved the sun of the Nineteenth Century, proud and glorious, from passing through, near its setting, the blackest and thickest and ugliest clouds of all its journey; saved it from ending the most brilliant of brilliant careers by setting, with a shudder of horror, in a sea of human blood.

Those who doubt that such power could emanate from such weakness; or, to change the figure, that such a tiny star could have dimensions greater than those of earth, may have every vestige of doubt removed by a perusal of this simple narrative.

Let us now acquaint ourselves with the circumstances under which the opening words of our story were spoken. To do this, we must need lead our readers into humble and commonplace surroundings, a fact that will not come in the nature of a surprise to those who have traced the proud, rushing, swelling river to the mountain whence it comes trickling forth, meekly and humbly enough.

The place was Winchester, an antiquated town, located near the northwestern corner of the State of Virginia.

In October of the year 1867, the year in which our story begins, a white man by the name of Tiberius Gracchus Leonard had arrived in Winchester, and was employed as teacher of the school for colored children.

Mrs. Hannah Piedmont, the colored woman whom we have presented to our readers as addressing her little boy, was the mother of five children, – three girls and two boys. In the order of their ages, the names of her children were: James Henry, aged fifteen, Amanda Ann, aged thirteen, Eliza Jane, aged eleven, Belton, aged eight, and Celestine, aged five. Several years previous to the opening of our history, Mr. Piedmont had abandoned his wife and left her to rear the children alone.

School opened in October, and as fast as she could get books and clothing Mrs. Piedmont sent her children to school. James Henry, Amanda Ann, and Eliza Jane were sent at about a week's interval. Belton and Celestine were then left – Celestine being regarded as too young to go. This morning we find Belton's mother preparing him for school, and we shall stand by and watch the preparations.

The house was low and squatty and was built of rock. It consisted of one room only, and over this there was a loft, the hole to climb into which was in plain view of any one in the room. There was only one window to the house and that one was only four feet square. Two panes of this were broken out and the holes were stuffed with rags. In one corner of the room there stood a bed in which Mrs. Piedmont and Amanda Ann slept. Under this was a trundle bed in which Eliza Jane and Celestine slept at the head, while Belton slept at the foot. James Henry climbed into the loft and slept there on a pallet of straw. The cooking was done in a fireplace which was on the side of the house opposite the window. Three chairs, two of which had no backs to them, completed the articles in the room.

In one of these chairs Mrs. Piedmont was sitting, while Belton stood before her all dressed and ready to go to school, excepting that his face was not washed.

It might be interesting to note his costume. The white lady for whom Mrs. Piedmont washed each week had given her two much-torn pairs of trousers, discarded by her young son. One pair was of linen and the other of navy blue. A leg from each pair was missing; so Mrs. Piedmont simply transferred the good leg of the linen pair to the suit of the navy blue, and dressed the happy Belton in that suit thus amended. His coat was literally a conglomeration of patches of varying sizes and colors. If you attempted to describe the coat by calling it by the name of the color that you thought predominated, at least a half dozen aspirants could present equal claims to the honor. One of Belton's feet was encased in a wornout slipper from the dainty foot of some young woman, while the other wore a turned over boot left in town by some farmer lad who had gotten himself a new pair. His hat was in good condition, being the summer straw last worn by a little white playfellow (when fall came on, this little fellow kindly willed his hat to Belton, who, in return for this favor, was to black the boy's shoes each morning during the winter).

Belton's mother now held in her hand a wet cloth with which she wished to cleanse his face, the bacon skin which he gnawed at the conclusion of his meal having left a circle of grease around his lips. Belton did not relish the face washing part of the programme (of course hair combing was not even considered). Belton had one characteristic similar to that of oil. He did not like to mix with water, especially cold water, such as was on that wet cloth in his mother's hand. However, a hint in reference to a certain well-known leather strap, combined with the offer of a lump of sugar, brought him to terms.

His face being washed, he and his mother marched forth to school, where he laid the foundation of the education that served him so well in after life.

A man of tact, intelligence, and superior education moving in the midst of a mass of ignorant people, ofttimes has a sway more absolute than that of monarchs.

Belton now entered the school-room, which in his case proves to be the royal court, whence he emerges an uncrowned king.

Chapter II
The School

THE HOUSE in which the colored school was held was, in former times, a house of worship for the white Baptists of Winchester. It was a long, plain, frame structure, painted white. Many years prior to the opening of the colored school it had been condemned as unsafe by the town authorities, whereupon the white Baptists had abandoned it for a more beautiful modern structure.

The church tendered the use of the building to the town for a public school for the colored children. The roof was patched and iron rods were used to hold together the twisting walls. These improvements being made, school was in due time opened. The building was located on the outskirts of the town, and a large open field surrounded it on all sides.

As Mrs. Piedmont and her son drew near to this building the teacher was standing on the door-steps ringing his little hand bell, calling the children in from their recess. They came running at full speed, helter skelter. By the time they were all in Mrs. Piedmont and Belton had arrived at the step. When Mr. Leonard saw them about to enter the building an angry scowl passed over his face, and he muttered half aloud: "Another black nigger brat for me to teach."

The steps were about four feet high and he was standing on the top step. To emphasize his disgust, he drew back so that Mrs. Piedmont would pass him with no danger of brushing him. He drew back rather too far and began falling off the end of the steps. He clutched at the door and made such a scrambling noise that the children turned in their seats just in time to see his body rapidly disappearing in a manner to leave his feet where his head ought to be.

Such a yell of laughter as went up from the throats of the children! It had in it a universal, spontaneous ring of savage delight which plainly told that the teacher was not beloved by his pupils.

The back of the teacher's head struck the edge of a stone, and when he clambered up from his rather undignified position his back was covered with blood. Deep silence reigned in the school-room as he walked down the aisle, glaring fiercely right and left. Getting his hat he left the school-room and went to a near-by drug store to have his wounds dressed.

While he was gone, the children took charge of the school-room and played pranks of every description. Abe Lincoln took the teacher's chair and played "'fessor."

"Sallie Ann ain't yer got wax in yer mouf?"

"Yes sar."

"Den take dis stick and prop yer mouf opun fur half hour. Dat'll teach yer a lesson."

"Billy Smith, yer didn't know yer lessun," says teacher Abe. "Yer may stan' on one leg de ballunce ob de ebenning."

"Henry Jones, yer sassed a white boy ter day. Pull off yer jacket. I'll gib yer a lessun dat yer'll not furgit soon. Neber buck up to yer s'periors."

"John Jones, yer black, nappy head rascal, I'll crack yer skull if yer doan keep quiut."

"Cum year, yer black, cross-eyed little wench, yer. I'll teach yer to go to sleep in here." Annie Moore was the little girl thus addressed.

After each sally from Abe there was a hearty roar of laughter, he imitated the absent teacher so perfectly in look, voice, manner, sentiment, and method of punishment.

Taking down the cowhide used for flogging purposes Abe left his seat and was passing to and fro, pretending to flog those who most frequently fell heir to the teacher's wrath. While he was doing this Billy Smith stealthily crept to the teacher's chair and placed a crooked pin in it in order to catch Abe when he returned to sit down.

Before Abe had gone much further the teacher's face appeared at the door, and all scrambled to get into their right places and to assume studious attitudes. Billy Smith thought of his crooked pin and had the "cold sweats." Those who had seen Billy put the pin in the chair were torn between two conflicting emotions. They wanted the pin to do its work, and therefore hoped. They feared Billy's detection and therefore despaired.

However, the teacher did not proceed at once to take his seat. He approached Mrs. Piedmont and Belton, who had taken seats midway the room and were interested spectators of all that had been going on. Speaking to Mrs. Piedmont, he said: "What is your name?"

She replied: "Hannah Lizabeth Piedmont."

"Well, Hannah, what is your brat's name?"

"His name am Belton Piedmont, arter his grandaddy."

"Well, Hannah, I am very pleased to receive your brat. He shall not want for attention," he added, in a tone accompanied by a lurking look of hate that made Mrs. Piedmont shudder and long to have her boy at home again. Her desire for his training was so great that she surmounted her misgivings and carried out her purposes to have him enrolled.

As the teacher was turning to go to his desk, hearing a rustling noise toward the door, he turned to look. He was, so to speak, petrified with astonishment. There stood on the threshold of the door a woman whose beauty was such as he had never seen surpassed. She held a boy by the hand. She was a mulatto woman, tall and graceful. Her hair was raven black and was combed away from as beautiful a forehead as nature could chisel. Her eyes were a brown hazel, large and intelligent, tinged with a slight look of melancholy. Her complexion was a rich olive, and seemed especially adapted to her face, that revealed not a flaw.

The teacher quickly pulled off his hat, which he had not up to that time removed since his return from the drug store. As the lady moved up the aisle toward him, he was taken with stage fright. He recovered self-possession enough to escort her and the boy to the front and give them seats. The whole school divided its attention between the beautiful woman and the discomfitted teacher. They had not known that he was so full of smiles and smirks.

"What is your name?" he enquired in his most suave manner.

"Fairfax Belgrave," replied the visitor.

"May I be of any service to you, madam?"

At the mention of the word madam, she colored slightly. "I desire to have my son enter your school and I trust that you may see your way clear to admit him."

"Most assuredly madam, most assuredly." Saying this, he hastened to his desk, opened it and took out his register. He then sat down, but the next instant leapt several feet into the air, knocking over his desk. He danced around the floor, reaching toward the rear of his pants, yelling: "Pull it out! pull it out! pull it out!"

The children hid their faces behind their books and chuckled most gleefully. Billy Smith was struck dumb with terror. Abe was rolling on the floor, bellowing with uncontrollable laughter.

The teacher finally succeeded in extricating the offending steel and stood scratching his head in chagrin at the spectacle he had made of himself before his charming visitor. He took an internal oath to get his revenge out of Mrs. Piedmont and her son, who had been the innocent means of his double downfall that day.

His desk was arranged in a proper manner and the teacher took his pen and wrote two names, now famous the world over.

"Bernard Belgrave, age 9 years."

"Belton Piedmont, age 8 years."

Under such circumstances Belton began his school career.

Chapter III
The Parson's Advice

WITH HEAVY HEART and with eyes cast upon the ground, Mrs. Piedmont walked back home after leaving Belton with his teacher. She had intended to make a special plea for her boy, who had all along displayed such precociousness as to fill her bosom with the liveliest hopes. But the teacher was so repulsive in manner that she did not have the heart to speak to him as she had intended.

She saw that the happenings of the morning had had the effect of deepening a contemptuous prejudice into hatred, and she felt that her child's school life was to be embittered by the harshest of maltreatment.

No restraint was put upon the flogging of colored children by their white teachers, and in Belton's case his mother expected the worst. During the whole week she revolved the matter in her mind. There was a conflict in her bosom between her love and her ambition. Love prompted her to return and take her son away from school. Ambition bade her to let him stay. She finally decided to submit the whole matter to her parson, whom she would invite to dinner on the coming Sunday.

The Sabbath came and Mrs. Piedmont aroused her family bright and early, for the coming of the parson to take dinner was a great event in any negro household. The house was swept as clean as a broom of weeds tied together could make it. Along with the family breakfast, a skillet of biscuits was cooked and a young chicken nicely baked.

Belton was very active in helping his mother that morning, and she promised to give him a biscuit and a piece of chicken as a reward after the preacher was through eating his dinner. The thought of this coming happiness buoyed Belton up, and often he fancied himself munching that biscuit and biting that piece of chicken. These were items of food rarely found in that household.

Breakfast over, the whole family made preparations for going to Sunday school. Preparations always went on peacefully until it came to combing hair. The older members of the family endured the ordeal very well; but little "Lessie" always screamed as if she was being tortured, and James Henry received many kicks and scratches from Belton before he was through combing Belton's hair.

The Sunday school and church were always held in the day-school building. The Sunday school scholars were all in one class and recited out of the "blue back spelling book." When that was over, members of the school were allowed to ask general questions on the Bible, which were answered by anyone volunteering to do so. Everyone who had in any way caught a new light on a passage of scripture endeavored, by questioning, to find out as to whether others were as wise as he, and if such was not the case, he gladly enlightened the rest.

The Sunday school being over, the people stood in groups on the ground surrounding the church waiting for the arrival of the parson from his home, Berryville, a town twelve miles distant. He was pastor of three other churches besides the one at Winchester, and he preached at each one Sunday in the month. After awhile he put in his appearance. He was rather small in stature, and held his head somewhat to one side and looked at you with that knowing look of the parrot. He wore a pair of trousers that had been black, but were now sleet from much wear. They lacked two inches of reaching down to the feet of his high-heeled boots. He had on a long linen cluster that reached below his knees. Beneath this was a faded Prince Albert coat and a vest much too small. On his head there sat, slightly tipped, a high-topped beaver that seemed to have been hidden between two mattresses all the week and taken out and straightened for Sunday wear. In his hand he held a walking cane.

Thus clad he came toward the church, his body thrown slightly back, walking leisurely with the air of quiet dignity possessed by the man sure of his standing, and not under the necessity of asserting it overmuch in his carriage.

The brothers pulled off their hats and the sisters put on their best smiles as the parson approached. After a cordial handshake all around, the preacher entered the church to begin the services. After singing a hymn and praying, he took for his text the following "passige of scripter:"

"It air harder fur a camel to git through de eye of a cambric needle den fur a rich man to enter de kingdom of heben."

This was one of the parson's favorite texts, and the members all settled themselves back to have a good "speritual" time.

The preacher began his sermon in a somewhat quiet way, but the members knew that he would "warm up bye and bye." He pictured all rich men as trying to get into heaven, but, he asserted, they invariably found themselves with Dives. He exhorted his hearers to stick to Jesus. Here he pulled off his collar, and the sisters stirred and looked about them. A little later on, the preacher getting "warmer," pulled off his cuffs. The brethren laughed with a sort of joyous jumping up and down all the while – one crying "Gib me Jesus," another "Oh I am gwine home," and so on.

One sister who had a white lady's baby in her arms got happy and flung it entirely across the room, it falling into Mrs. Piedmont's lap, while the frenzied woman who threw the child climbed over benches, rushed into the pulpit, and swung to the preacher's neck, crying – "Glory! Glory!

Glory!" In the meanwhile Belton had dropped down under one of the benches and was watching the proceedings with an eye of terror.

The sermon over and quiet restored, a collection was taken and given to the pastor. Mrs. Piedmont went forward to put some money on the table and took occasion to step to the pulpit and invite the pastor to dinner. Knowing that this meant chicken, the pastor unhesitatingly accepted the invitation, and when church was over accompanied Mrs. Piedmont and her family home.

The preacher caught hold of Belton's hand as they walked along. This mark of attention, esteemed by Belton as a signal honor, filled his little soul with joy. As he thought of the manner in which the preacher stirred up the people, the amount of the collection that had been given him, and the biscuits and chicken that now awaited him, Belton decided that he, too, would like to become a preacher.

Just before reaching home, according to a preconcerted plan, Belton and James Henry broke from the group and ran into the house. When the others appeared a little later on, these two were not to be seen. However, no question was asked and no search made. All things were ready and the parson sat down to eat, while the three girls stood about, glancing now and then at the table. The preacher was very voracious and began his meal as though he "meant business."

We can now reveal the whereabouts of Belton and James Henry. They had clambered into the loft for the purpose of watching the progress of the preacher's meal, calculating at each step how much he would probably leave. James Henry found a little hole in the loft directly over the table, and through this hole he did his spying. Belton took his position at the larger entrance hole, lying flat on his stomach. He poked his head down far enough to see the preacher, but held it in readiness to be snatched back, if the preacher's eyes seemed to be about to wander his way.

He was kept in a state of feverish excitement, on the one hand, by fear of detection, and on the other, by a desire to watch the meal. When about half of the biscuits were gone, and the preacher seemed as fresh as ever, Belton began to be afraid for his promised biscuit and piece of chicken. He crawled to James Henry and said hastily – "James, dees haf gone," and hurriedly resumed his watch. A moment later he called out in a whisper, "He's tuck anudder." Down goes Belton's head to resume his watch. Every time the preacher took another biscuit Belton called out the fact to James.

All of the chicken was at last destroyed and only one biscuit remained; and Belton's whole soul was now centered on that biscuit. In his eagerness to watch he leaned a good distance out, and when the preacher reached forth his hand to take the last one Belton was so overcome that he lost his balance and tumbled out of his hole on the floor, kicking, and crying over and over again: "I knowed I wuzunt goin' to git naren dem biscuits."

The startled preacher hastily arose from the table and gazed on the little fellow in bewilderment. As soon as it dawned upon him what the trouble was, he hastily got the remaining biscuit and gave it to Belton. He also discovered that his voracity had made enemies of the rest of the children, and very adroitly passed a five cent piece around to each.

James Henry, forgetting his altitude and anxious not to lose his recompense, cried out loudly from the loft: "Amanda Ann you git mine fur me."

The preacher looked up but saw no one. Seeing that his request did not have the desired effect, James Henry soon tumbled down full of dust, straw and cobwebs, and came into possession of his appeasing money. The preacher laughed heartily and seemed to enjoy his experience highly.

The table was cleared, and the preacher and Mrs. Piedmont dismissed the children in order to discuss unmolested the subject which had prompted her to extend an invitation to the parson. In view of the intense dislike the teacher had conceived for Belton, she desired to know if it were not best to withdraw him from school altogether, rather than to subject him to the harsh treatment sure to come.

"Let me gib yer my advis, sistah Hannah. De greatest t'ing in de wul is edification. Ef our race ken git dat we ken git ebery t'ing else. Dat is de key. Git de key an' yer ken go in de house to go whare you please. As fur his beatin' de brat, yer musn't kick agin dat. He'll beat de brat to make him larn, and won't dat be a blessed t'ing? See dis scar on side my head? Old marse Sampson knocked me down wid a single-tree tryin' to make me stop larning, and God is so fixed it dat white folks is knocking es down ef we don't larn. Ef yer take Belton out of school yer'll be fighting 'genst de providence of God."

Being thus advised by her shepherd, Mrs. Piedmont decided to keep Belton in school. So on Monday Belton went back to his brutal teacher, and thither we follow him.

Chapter IV
The Turning of a Worm

AS TO WHO Mr. Tiberius Gracchus Leonard was, or as to where he came from, nobody in Winchester, save himself, knew.

Immediately following the close of the Civil War, Rev. Samuel Christian, a poor but honorable retired minister of the M.E. Church, South, was the first teacher employed to instruct the colored children of the town.

He was one of those Southerners who had never believed in the morality of slavery, but regarded it as a deep rooted evil beyond human power to uproot. When the manacles fell from the hands of the Negroes he gladly accepted the task of removing the scales of ignorance from the blinded eyes of the race.

Tenderly he labored, valiantly he toiled in the midst of the mass of ignorance that came surging around him. But only one brief year was given to this saintly soul to endeavor to blast the mountains of stupidity which centuries of oppression had reared. He fell asleep.

The white men who were trustees of the colored school, were sorely puzzled as to what to do for a successor. A Negro, capable of teaching a school, was nowhere near. White young men of the South, generally, looked upon the work of teaching "niggers" with the utmost contempt; and any man who suggested the name of a white young lady of Southern birth as a teacher for the colored children was actually in danger of being shot by any member of the insulted family who could handle a pistol.

An advertisement was inserted in the Washington Post to the effect that a teacher was wanted. In answer to this advertisement Mr. Leonard came. He was a man above the medium height, and possessed a frame not large but compactly built. His forehead was low and narrow; while the back of his head looked exceedingly intellectual. Looking at him from the front you would involuntarily exclaim: "What an infamous scoundrel." Looking at him from the rear you would say: "There certainly is brain power in that head."

The glance of Mr. Leonard's eye was furtive, and his face was sour looking indeed. At times when he felt that no one was watching him, his whole countenance and attitude betokened the rage of despair.

Most people who looked at him felt that he carried in his bosom a dark secret. As to scholarship, he was unquestionably proficient. No white man in all the neighboring section, ranked with him intellectually. Despite the lack of all knowledge of his moral character and previous life, he was pronounced as much too good a man to fritter away his time on "niggers."

Such was the character of the man into whose hands was committed the destiny of the colored children of Winchester.

As his mother foresaw would be the case, Belton was singled out by the teacher as a special object on which he might expend his spleen. For a man to be as spiteful as he was, there must have been something gnawing at his heart. But toward Bernard none of this evil spirit was manifested. He seemed to have chosen Bernard for his pet, and Belton for his "pet aversion." To the one he was all kindness; while to the other he was cruel in the extreme.

Often he would purchase flowers from the florist and give to Bernard to bear home to his mother. On these days he would seemingly take pains to give Belton fresh bruises to take home to *his* mother. When he had a particularly good dinner he would invite Bernard to dine with him, and would be sure to find some pretext for forbidding Belton to partake of his own common meal.

Belton was by no means insensible to all these acts of discrimination. Nor did Bernard fail to perceive that he, himself, was the teacher's pet. He clambered on to the teacher's knees, played with his mustache, and often took his watch and wore it. The teacher seemed to be truly fond of him.

The children all ascribed this partiality to the color of Bernard's skin, and they all, except Belton, began to envy and despise Bernard. Of course they told their parents of the teacher's partiality and their parents thus became embittered against the teacher. But however much they might object to him and desire his removal, their united protests would not have had the weight of a feather. So the teacher remained at Winchester for twelve years. During all these years he instructed our young friends Belton and Bernard.

Strangely enough, his ardent love for Bernard and his bitter hatred of Belton accomplished the very same result in respect to their acquirements. The teacher soon discovered that both boys were talented far beyond the ordinary, and that both were ambitious. He saw that the way to wound and humiliate Belton was to make Bernard excel him. Thus he bent all of his energies to improve Bernard's mind. Whenever he heard Belton recite he brought all of his talents to bear to point out his failures, hoping thus to exalt Bernard, out of whose work he strove to keep all blemishes. Thus Belton became accustomed to the closest scrutiny, and prepared himself accordingly. The result was that Bernard did not gain an inch on him.

The teacher introduced the two boys into every needed field of knowledge, as they grew older, hoping always to find some branch in which Bernard might display unquestioned superiority. There were two studies in which the two rivals dug deep to see which could bring forth the richest treasures; and these gave coloring to the whole of their afterlives. One, was the History of the United States, and the other, Rhetoric.

In history, that portion that charmed them most was the story of the rebellion against the yoke of England. Far and wide they went in search of everything that would throw light on this epoch. They became immersed in the spirit of that heroic age.

As a part of their rhetorical training they were taught to declaim. Thanks to their absorption in the history of the Revolution, their minds ran to the sublime in literature; and they strove to secure pieces to declaim that recited the most heroic deeds of man, of whatever nationality.

Leonidas, Marco Bozarris, Arnold Winklereid, Louis Kossuth, Robert Emmett, Martin Luther, Patrick Henry and such characters furnished the pieces almost invariably declaimed. They threw their whole souls into these, and the only natural thing resulted. No human soul can breathe the atmosphere of heroes and read with bated breath their deeds of daring without craving for the opportunity to do the like. Thus the education of these two young men went on.

At the expiration of twelve years they had acquired an academic education that could not be surpassed anywhere in the land. Their reputation as brilliant students and eloquent speakers had spread over the whole surrounding country.

The teacher decided to graduate the young men; and he thought to utilize the occasion as a lasting humiliation of Belton and exaltation of his favorite, Bernard Belgrave. Belton felt this.

In the first part of this last school year of the boys, he had told them to prepare for a grand commencement exercise, and they acted accordingly. Each one chose his subject and began the preparation of his oration early in the session, each keeping his subject and treatment secret from the other.

The teacher had announced that numerous white citizens would be present; among them the congressman from the district and the mayor of the town. Belton determined upon two things, away down in his soul. He determined to win in the oratorical contest, and to get his revenge on his teacher on the day that the teacher had planned for his – (Belton's) humiliation. Bernard did not have the incentive that Belton did; but defeat was ever galling to him, and he, too, had determined to win.

The teacher often reviewed the progress made by Bernard on his oration, but did not notice Belton's at all. He strove to make Bernard's oration as nearly perfect as labor and skill could make it. But Belton was not asleep as to either of the resolutions he had formed. Some nights he could be seen stealing away from the congressman's residence. On others he could be seen leaving the neighborhood of the school, with a spade in one hand and a few carpenter's tools in the other.

He went to the congressman, who was a polished orator with a national reputation, in order that he might purge his oration from its impurities of speech. As the congressman read the oration and perceived the depth of thought, the logical arrangement, the beauty and rhythm of language, and the wide research displayed, he opened his eyes wide with astonishment. He was amazed that a young man of such uncommon talents could have grown up in his town and he not know it. Belton's marvelous talents won his respect and admiration, and he gave him access to his library and criticized his oration whenever needed.

Secretly and silently preparations went on for the grand conflict. At last the day came. The colored men and women of the place laid aside all work to attend the exercises. The forward section of seats was reserved for the white people. The congressman, the mayor, the school trustees and various other men of standing came, accompanied by their wives and daughters.

Scholars of various grades had parts to perform on the programme, but the eyes of all sought the bottom of the page where were printed the names of the two oratorical gladiators:

BELTON PIEDMONT. BERNARD BELGRAVE.

The teacher had given Bernard the last place, deeming that the more advantageous. He appointed the congressman, the mayor, and one of the school trustees to act as judges, to decide to whom he should award a beautiful gold medal for the more excellent oration. The congressman politely declined and named another trustee in his stead. Then the contest began. As Belton walked up on the platform the children greeted him with applause. He announced as his subject: "The Contribution of the Anglo-Saxon to the Cause of Human Liberty." In his strong, earnest voice, he began to roll off his well turned periods. The whole audience seemed as if in a trance. His words made their hearts burn, and time and again he made them burst forth in applause.

The white people who sat and listened to his speech looked upon it as a very revelation to them, they themselves not having had as clear a conception of the glory of their race as this Negro now revealed. When he had finished, white men and women crowded to the front to congratulate him upon his effort, and it was many minutes before quiet was restored sufficiently to allow the programme to proceed.

Bernard took his position on the platform, announcing as his subject: "Robert Emmett." His voice was sweet and well modulated and never failed to charm. Admiration was plainly depicted on every face as he proceeded. He brought to bear all the graces of a polished orator, and more than once tears came into the eyes of his listeners. Particularly affecting was his description of Emmett's death. At the conclusion it was evident that his audience felt that it would have been difficult to have handled that subject better.

The judges now retired to deliberate as to whom to give the prize. While they are out, let us examine Belton's plans for carrying out the second thing, upon the accomplishment of which he was determined; viz., revenge.

In the rear of the schoolhouse, there stood an old wood-shed. For some slight offence the teacher had, two or three years back, made Belton the fire-maker for the balance of his school life instead of passing the task around according to custom. Thus the care of the wood-house had fallen permanently to Belton's lot.

During the last year Belton had dug a large hole running from the floor of the wood-shed to a point under the platform of the school room. The dirt from this underground channel he cast into a deep old unused well, not far distant. Once under the platform, he kept on digging, making the hole larger by far. Numerous rocks abounded in the neighborhood, and these he used to wall up his underground room, so that it would hold water. Just in the middle of the school-room platform he cut, from beneath, a square hole, taking in the spot where the teacher invariably stood when addressing the school. He cut the boards until they lacked but a very little, indeed, of being cut through. All looked well above, but a baby would not be safe standing thereon. Belton contrived a kind of prop with a weight attached. This prop would serve to keep the cut section from breaking through. The attached weight was at rest in a hole left in the wall of the cavity near its top. If you dislocated the weight, the momentum that it would gather in the fall would pull down the prop to which it was attached.

Finally, Belton fastened a strong rope to the weight, and ran the rope under the schoolhouse floor until it was immediately beneath his seat. With an auger he made a hole in the floor and brought the end through. He managed to keep this bit of rope concealed, while at the same time he had perfect command of his trap door.

For two or three nights previous to commencement day Belton had worked until nearly morning filling this cistern with water. Now when through delivering his oration, he had returned to his seat to await the proper moment for the payment of his teacher. The judges were out debating the question as to who had won. They seemed to be unable to decide who was victorious and beckoned for the teacher to step outside.

They said: "That black nigger has beat the yellow one all to pieces this time, but we don't like to see nigger blood triumph over any Anglo-Saxon blood. Ain't there any loop-hole where we can give it to Bernard, anyhow?"

"Well, yes," said the teacher eagerly, "on the ground of good behavior."

"There you hit it," said the Mayor. "So we all decide."

The judges filed in, and the Mayor arose to announce their decision. "We award," said he to the breathless audience, "the prize to Bernard Belgrave."

"No! no! no!" burst forth from persons all over the house. The congressman arose and went up to Belton and congratulated him upon his triumph over oratory, and lamented his defeat by prejudice. This action caused a perceptible stir in the entire audience.

The teacher went to his desk and produced a large gold medal. He took his accustomed place on the platform and began thus:

"Ladies and Gentlemen, this is the proudest moment of my life." He got no further. Belton had pulled the rope, the rope had caused the weight to fall, and the weight had pulled the prop and down had gone the teacher into a well of water.

"Murder! Murder! Murder!" he cried "Help! Help! Help! I am drowning. Take me out, it is cold."

The audience rushed forward expecting to find the teacher in a dangerous situation; but they found him standing, apparently unharmed, in a cistern, the water being a little more than waist deep. Their fright gave way to humor and a merry shout went up from the throats of the scholars.

The colored men and women laughed to one side, while the white people smiled as though they had admired the feat as a fine specimen of falling from the sublime to the ridiculous. Bending down over the well, the larger students caught hold of the teacher's arms and lifted him out.

He stood before the audience wet and shivering, his clothes sticking to him, and water dripping from his hair. The medal was gone. The teacher dismissed the audience, drew his last month's pay and left that night for parts unknown.

Sometimes, even a worm will turn when trodden upon.

Chapter V
Belton Finds a Friend

LONG BEFORE the rifle ball, the cannon shot, and the exploding shell were through their fiendish task of covering the earth with mortals slain; while the startled air was yet busy in hurrying to Heaven the groans of the dying soldier, accompanied as they were by the despairing shrieks of his loved ones behind; while horrid War, in frenzied joy, yet waved his bloody sword over the nation's head, and sought with eager eagle eyes every drop of clotted gore over which he might exult; in the midst of such direful days as these, there were those at the North whom the love of God and the eye of faith taught to leap over the scene of strife to prepare the trembling negro for the day of freedom, which, refusing to have a dawn, had burst in meridian splendor upon his dazzled gaze.

Into the southland there came rushing consecrated Christians, men and women, eager to provide for the negro a Christian education. Those who stayed behind gathered up hoarded treasures and gladly poured them into the lap of the South for the same laudable purpose. As a result of the coming of this army of workers, bearing in their arms millions of money, ere many years had sped, well nigh every southern state could proudly boast of one or more colleges where the aspiring negro might quench has thirst for knowledge.

So when Bernard and Belton had finished their careers at the Winchester public school, colleges abounded in the South beckoning them to enter. Bernard preferred to go to a northern institution, and his mother sent him to enter Harvard University.

Belton was poor and had no means of his own with which to pursue his education; but by the hand of providence a most unexpected door was opened to him. The Winchester correspondent of the *Richmond Daily Temps* reported the commencement exercises of the Winchester public school of the day that Belton graduated. The congressman present at the exercises spoke so highly of Belton's speech that the correspondent secured a copy from Belton and sent it to the editor of *The Temps*.

This was printed in *The Temps* and created a great sensation in political and literary circles in every section of the country. Every newspaper of any consequence reproduced the oration in full. It was published and commented upon by the leading journals of England. The President of the United States wrote a letter of congratulation to Belton. Everywhere the piece was hailed as a classic.

After reading the oration, Mr. V.M. King, editor of *The Temps*, decided to take it home with him and read it to his wife. She met him at the door and as he kissed her she noticed that there was a sober look in his eye. Tenderly he brushed back a few stray locks of his wife's hair, saying as he did so, in a somewhat troubled tone: "Wife, it has come at last. May the good Lord cease not to watch over our beloved but erring land." She inquired as to what he meant. He led her to his study and read to her Belton's oration.

In order to understand the words which we have just quoted as being spoken by him to his wife, let us, while he reads, become a little better acquainted with Mr. King and his paper, *The Temps*.

Mr. King was born and reared in Virginia, was educated at a Northern University, and had sojourned for several years in England. He was a man of the broadest culture. For several years he had given the negro problem most profound study. His views on the subject were regarded by the white people of the South as ultra-liberal. These views he exploited through his paper, *The Temps*, with a boldness and vigor, gaining thereby great notoriety.

Though a democrat in politics, he was most bitterly opposed to the practice, almost universal in the South, of cheating the negro out of his right to vote. He preached that it was unjust to the negro and fatal to the morals of the whites.

On every possible occasion he viciously assaulted the practice of lynching, denouncing it in most scathing terms. In short, he was an outspoken advocate of giving the negro every right accorded him by the Constitution of the United States.

He saw the South leading the young negro boy and girl to school, where, at the expense of the state, they were taught to read history and learn what real liberty was, and the glorious struggles through which the human race had come in order to possess it. He foresaw that the rising, educated negro would allow his eye to linger long on this bloody but glorious page until that most contagious of diseases, devotion to liberty, infected his soul.

He reasoned that the negro who had endured the hardships of slavery might spend his time looking back and thanking God for that from which he had made his escape; but the young negro, knowing nothing of physical slavery, would be peering into the future, measuring the distance that he had yet to go before he was truly free, and would be asking God and his own right arm for the power to secure whatever rights were still withheld.

He argued that, living as the negro did beneath the American flag, known as the flag of freedom, studying American history, and listening on the outer edge of great Fourth of July crowds to eloquent orators discourse on freedom, it was only a matter of a few years before the negro would deify liberty as the Anglo-Saxon race had done, and count it a joy to perish on her altar.

In order that the Republic might ever stand, he knew that the principles of liberty would have to be continually taught with all the eloquence and astuteness at command; and if this teaching had the desired effect upon the white man it would also be powerful enough to awaken the negro standing by his side.

So, his ear was to the ground, expecting every moment to hear the far off sounds of awakened negroes coming to ask for liberty, and if refused, to slay or be slain.

When he read Belton's oration he saw that the flame of liberty was in his heart, her sword in his hand, and the disdain of death stamped on his brow. He felt that Belton was the morning star which told by its presence that dawn was near at hand.

Thus it was that he said to his wife: "Wife, it has come at last. May the good Lord cease not to watch over our beloved land."

This expression was not the offspring of fear as to the outcome of a possible conflict, for, Anglo-Saxon like, that was with him a foregone conclusion in favor of his own race. But he shuddered at the awful carnage that would of necessity ensue if two races, living house to house, street to street, should be equally determined upon a question at issue, equally disdainful of life, fighting with the rancor always attendant upon a struggle between two races that mutually despise and detest each other.

He knew that it was more humane, more in accordance with right, more acceptable with God, to admit to the negro that Anglo-Saxon doctrine of the equality of man was true, rather than to murder the negro for accepting him at his word, though spoken to others.

Feeling thus, he pleaded with his people to grant to the negro his rights, though he never hinted at a possible rebellion, for fear that the mention of it might hasten the birth of the idea in the brain of the negro.

That evening, after he had read the oration to his wife and told her of his forebodings, he sat with his face buried in his hands, brooding over the situation. Late in the night he retired to rest, and the next morning, when he awoke, his wife was standing by his bed, calling him. She saw that his sleep was restless and thought that he was having troubled dreams. And so he was.

He dreamed that a large drove of fatted swine were munching acorns in a very dense forest of oaks, both tall and large. The oaks were sending the acorns down in showers, and the hogs were greedily consuming them. The hogs ate so many that they burst open, and from their rotting carcasses fresh oaks sprang and grew with surprising rapidity. A dark cloud arose and a terrible hurricane swept over the forest; and the old and new oaks fought furiously in the storm, until a loud voice, like unto that of a God, cried out above all the din of the hurricane, saying in tones of thunder: "Know ye not that ye are parents and children? Parents, recognize your children. Children, be proud of the parents from whom you spring."

The hurricane ceased, the clouds sped away as if in terror, and the oaks grew up together under a clear sky of the purest blue, and beautiful birds of all kinds built their nests in the trees, and carolled forth the sweetest songs.

He placed upon the dream the following interpretation:

The swine were the negroes. The oak trees were the white people. The acorns were the doctrine of human liberty, everywhere preached by Anglo-Saxons. The negroes, feasting off of the same thought, had become the same kind of being as the white man, and grew up to a point of equality. The hurricane was the contest between the two races over the question of equality. The voice was intended to inform the whites that they had brought about these aspirations in the bosom of the negro, and that the liberty-loving negro was their legitimate offspring, and not a bastard. The whites should recognize their own doings. On the other hand, the negro should not be over boastful, and should recognize that the lofty conception of the dignity of man and value and true character of liberty were taught him by the Anglo-Saxon. The birds betokened a happy adjustment of all differences; and the dream that began in the gloom of night ended in the dawn of day.

Mr. King was very cheerful, therefore, and decided to send to Winchester for Belton, thinking that it might be a wise thing to keep an eye and a friendly hand on a young negro of such promise. In the course of a couple of days, Belton, in response to his request, arrived in Richmond. He called at the office of *The Temps* and was ushered into Mr. King's office.

Mr. King had him take a seat. He enquired of Belton his history, training, etc. He also asked as to his plans for the future. Finding that Belton was desirous of securing a college education, but was destitute of funds, Mr. King gladly embraced the opportunity of displaying his kind interest. He offered to pay Belton's way through college, and the offer was gladly accepted.

He told Belton to call at his home that evening at seven o'clock to receive a check for his entire college course. At the appointed hour Belton appeared at Mr. King's residence.

Mr. King was sitting on his front porch, between his wife and aged mother, while his two children, a girl and boy, were playing on the lawn. Belton was invited to take a seat, much to his surprise.

Seeing a stranger, the children left their play and came to their father, one on each side. They looked with questioning eyes from father to Belton, as if seeking to know the purpose of the visit.

Mr. King took the check from his pocket and extended it toward Belton, and said: "Mr. Piedmont, this will carry you through college. I have only one favor to ask of you. In all your dealings with my people recognize the fact that there are two widely separated classes of us, and that there is a good side to the character of the worst class. Always seek for and appeal to that side of their nature."

Belton very feelingly thanked Mr. King, and assured him that he would treasure his words. He was true to his promise, and decided from that moment to never class all white men together, whatever might be the provocation, and to never regard any class as totally depraved.

This is one of the keys to his future life. Remember it.

Chapter VI
A Young Rebel

IN THE CITY of Nashville, Tennessee, there is a far famed institution of learning called Stowe University, in honor of Mrs. Harriet Beecher Stowe, author of "Uncle Tom's Cabin."

This institution was one of the many scores of its kind, established in the South by Northern philanthropy, for the higher education of the Negro. Though called a university, it was scarcely more than a normal school with a college department attached.

It was situated just on the outskirts of the city, on a beautiful ten-acre plot of ground. The buildings were five in number, consisting of a dormitory for young men, two for young ladies, a building for recitations, and another, called the teachers' mansion; for the teachers resided there. These buildings were very handsome, and were so arranged upon the level campus as to present a very attractive sight.

With the money which had been so generously given him by Mr. King, Belton entered this school. That was a proud day in his life when he stepped out of the carriage and opened the University gate, feeling that he, a Negro, was privileged to enter college. Julius Cæsar, on entering Rome in triumph, with the world securely chained to his chariot wheels; Napoleon, bowing to receive the diadem of the Cæsars' won by the most notable victories ever known to earth; General Grant, on his triumphal tour around the globe, when kings and queens were eager rivals to secure from this man of humble birth the sweeter smile; none of these were more full of pleasurable emotion than this poor Negro lad, who now with elastic step and beating heart marched with head erect beneath the arch of the doorway leading into Stowe University.

Belton arrived on the Saturday preceding the Monday on which school would open for that session. He found about three hundred and sixty students there from all parts of the South, the young women outnumbering the young men in about the proportion of two to one.

On the Sunday night following his arrival the students all assembled in the general assembly room of the recitation building, which room, in the absence of a chapel, was used as the place for religious worship. The president of the school, a venerable white minister from the North, had charge of the service that evening. He did not on this occasion preach a sermon, but devoted the hour to discoursing upon the philanthropic work done by the white people of the North for the freedmen of the South.

A map of the United States was hanging on the wall, facing the assembled school. On this map there were black dots indicating all places where a school of learning had been planted for the colored people by their white friends of the North. Belton sat closely scrutinizing the map. His eyes swept from one end to the other. Persons were allowed to ask any questions desired, and Belton was very inquisitive.

When the hour of the lecture was over he was deeply impressed with three thoughts: First, his heart went out in love to those who had given so freely of their means and to those who had dedicated their lives to the work of uplifting his people.

Secondly, he saw an immense army of young men and women being trained in the very best manner in every section of the South, to go forth to grapple with the great problems before them.

He felt proud of being a member of so promising an army, and felt that they were to determine the future of the race. In fact, this thought was reiterated time and again by the president.

Thirdly, Belton was impressed that it was the duty of those receiving such great blessings to accomplish achievements worthy of the care bestowed. He felt that the eyes of the North and of the civilized world were upon them to see the fruits of the great labor and money spent upon them.

Before he retired to rest that night, he besought God to enable him and his people, as a mark of appreciation of what had been done for the race, to rise to the full measure of just expectation and prove worthy of all the care bestowed. He went through school, therefore, as though the eyes of the world were looking at the race enquiringly; the eyes of the North expectantly; and the eyes of God lovingly, – three grand incentives to his soul.

When these schools were first projected, the White South that then was, fought them with every weapon at its command. Ridicule, villification, ostracism, violence, arson, murder were all employed to hinder the progress of the work. Outsiders looked on and thought it strange that they should do this. But, just as a snake, though a venomous animal, by instinct knows its enemy and fights for its life with desperation, just so the Old South instinctively foresaw danger to its social fabric as then constituted, and therefore despised and fought the agencies that were training and inspiring the future leaders of the Negro race in such a manner as to render a conflict inevitable and of doubtful termination.

The errors in the South, anxious for eternal life, rightfully feared these schools more than they would have feared factories making powder, moulding balls and fashioning cannons. But the New South, the South that, in the providence of God, is yet to be, could not have been formed in the womb of time had it not been for these schools. And so the receding murmurs of the scowling South that was, are lost in the gladsome shouts of the South which, please God, is yet to be.

But lest we linger too long, let us enter school here with Belton. On the Monday following the Sunday night previously indicated, Belton walked into the general assembly room to take his seat with the other three hundred and sixty pupils. It was the custom for the school to thus assemble for devotional exercises. The teachers sat in a row across the platform, facing the pupils. The president sat immediately in front of the desk, in the center of the platform, and the teachers sat on either side of him.

To Belton's surprise, he saw a colored man sitting on the right side of and next to the president. He was sitting there calmly, self-possessed, exactly like the rest. He crossed his legs and stroked his beard in a most matter of fact way. Belton stared at this colored man, with his lips apart and his body bent forward. He let his eyes scan the faces of all the white teachers, male and female, but would end up with a stare at the colored man sitting there. Finally, he hunched his seat-mate with his elbow and asked what man that was. He was told that it was the colored teacher of the faculty.

Belton knew that there was a colored teacher in the school but he had no idea that he would be thus honored with a seat with the rest of the teachers. A broad, happy smile spread over his face, and his eyes danced with delight. He had, in his boyish heart, dreamed of the equality of the races and sighed and hoped for it; but here, he beheld it in reality. Though he, as a rule, shut his eyes when prayer was being offered, he kept them open that morning, and peeped through his fingers at that thrilling sight, – a colored man on equal terms with the white college professors.

Just before the classes were dismissed to their respective class rooms, the teachers came together in a group to discuss some matter, in an informal way. The colored teacher was in the center of the group and discussed the matter as freely as any; and he was listened to with every mark of respect. Belton kept a keen watch on the conference and began rubbing his hands and chuckling to himself with delight at seeing the colored teacher participating on equal terms with the other teachers.

The colored teacher's views seemed about to prevail, and as one after another the teachers seemed to fall in line with him Belton could not contain himself longer, but clapped his hands and gave a loud, joyful, "Ha! ha!"

The eyes of the whole school were on him in an instant, and the faculty turned around to discover the source and cause of the disorder. But Belton had come to himself as soon as he made the noise, and in a twinkling was as quiet and solemn looking as a mouse.

The faculty resumed its conference and the students passed the query around as to what was the matter with the "newcomer." A number tapped their heads significantly, saying: "Wrong here." How far wrong were they! They should have put their hands over their hearts and said: "The fire of patriotism here;" for Belton had here on a small scale, the gratification of the deepest passion of his soul, viz., Equality of the races. And what pleased him as much as anything else was the dignified, matter of fact way in which the teacher bore his honors. Belton afterwards discovered that this colored man was vice-president of the faculty.

On a morning, later in the session, the president announced that the faculty would hold its regular weekly meeting that evening, but that he would have to be in the city to attend to other masters. Belton's heart bounded at the announcement. Knowing that the colored teacher was vice-president of the faculty, he saw that he would preside. Belton determined to see that meeting of the faculty if it cost him no end of trouble. He could not afford, under any circumstances, to fail to see that colored man preside over those white men and women.

That night, about 8:30 o'clock, when the faculty meeting had progressed about half way, Belton made a rope of his bed clothes and let himself down to the ground from the window of his room on the second floor of the building. About twenty yards distant was the "mansion," in one room of which the teachers held their faculty meetings. The room in which the meeting was held was on the side of the "mansion" furthest from the dormitory from which Belton had just come. The "mansion" dog was Belton's friend, and a soft whistle quieted his bark. Belton stole around to the side of the house, where the meeting was being held. The weather was mild and the window was hoisted. Belton fell on his knees and crawled to the window, and pulling it up cautiously peeped in. He saw the colored teacher in the chair in the center of the room and others sitting about here and there. He gazed with rapture on the sight. He watched, unmolested, for a long while.

One of the lady teachers was tearing up a piece of paper and arose to come to the window to throw it out. Belton was listening, just at that time, to what the colored teacher was saying, and did not see the lady coming in his direction. Nor did the lady see the form of a man until she was near at hand. At the sight she threw up her hands and screamed loudly from fright. Belton turned and fled precipitately. The chicken-coop door had been accidentally left open and Belton, unthinkingly, jumped into the chicken house. The chickens set up a lively cackle, much to his chagrin. He grasped an old rooster to stop him, but missing the rooster's throat, the rooster gave the alarm all the more vociferously. Teachers had now crowded to the window and were peering out. Some of the men started to the door to come out. Belton saw this movement and decided that the best way for him to do was to play chicken thief and run. Grasping a hen with his other hand, he darted out of the chicken house and fled from the college ground, the chickens squalling all the while. He leapt the college fence at a bound and wrung off the heads of the chickens to stop the noise.

The teachers decided that they had been visited by a Negro, hunting for chickens; laughed heartily at their fright and resumed deliberations. Thus again a patriot was mistaken for a chicken thief; and in the South to-day a race that dreams of freedom, equality, and empire, far more than is imagined, is put down as a race of chicken thieves. As in Belton's case, this conception diverts attention from places where startling things would otherwise be discovered.

In due time Belton crept back to the dormitory, and by a signal agreed upon, roused his room-mate, who let down the rope, by means of which he ascended; and when seated gave his room-mate an account of his adventure.

Sometime later on, Belton in company with another student was sent over to a sister University in Nashville to carry a note for the president. This University also had a colored teacher who was one point in advance of Belton's. This teacher ate at the same table with the white teachers, while Belton's teacher ate with the students. Belton passed by the dining room of the teachers of this sister University and saw the colored teacher enjoying a meal with the white teachers. He could not enjoy the sight as much as he would have liked, from thinking about the treatment his teacher was receiving. He had not, prior to this, thought of that discrimination, but now it burned him.

He returned to his school and before many days had passed he had called together all the male students. He informed them that they ought to perfect a secret organization and have a password. They all agreed to secrecy and Belton gave this as the pass word: "Equality or Death."

He then told them that it was his ambition and purpose to coerce the white teachers into allowing the colored teacher to eat with them. They all very readily agreed; for the matter of his eating had been thoroughly canvassed for a number of sessions, but it seemed as though no one dared to suggest a combination. During slavery all combinations of slaves were sedulously guarded against, and a fear of combinations seems to have been injected into the Negro's very blood.

The very boldness of Belton's idea swept the students away from the lethargic harbor in which they had been anchored, and they were eager for action. Belton was instructed to prepare the complaint, which they all agreed to sign. They decided that it was to be presented to the president just before devotional exercises and an answer was to be demanded forthwith. One of the young men had a sister among the young lady students, and, through her Belton's rebellion was organized among the girls and their signatures secured.

The eventful morning came. The teachers glanced over the assembled students, and were surprised to see them dressed in their best clothes as though it was the Sabbath. There was a quiet satisfied look on their faces that the teachers did not understand.

The president arrived a little late and found an official envelope on his desk. He hurriedly broke the seal and began to read. His color came and went. The teachers looked at him wonderingly. The president laid the document aside and began the devotional exercises. He was nervous throughout, and made several blunders. He held his hymn book upside down while they were singing, much to the amusement of the school. It took him some time to find the passage of scripture which he desired to read, and after reading forgot for some seconds to call on some one to pray.

When the exercises were through he arose and took the document nervously in hand. He said; "I have in my hands a paper from the students of this institution concerning a matter with which they have nothing to do. This is my answer. The classes will please retire." Here he gave three strokes to the gong, the signal for dispersion. But not a student moved. The president was amazed. He could not believe his own eyes. He rang the gong a second time and yet no one moved. He then in nervous tones repeated his former assertions and then pulled the gong nervously many times in succession. All remained still. At a signal from Belton, all the students lifted their right hands, each bearing a small white board on which was printed in clear type: "Equality or Death."

The president fell back, aghast, and the white teachers were all struck dumb with fear. They had not dreamed that a combination of their pupils was possible, and they knew not what it foreboded. A number grasped the paper that was giving so much trouble and read it. They all then held a hurried consultation and assured the students that the matter should receive due attention.

The president then rang the gong again but the students yet remained. Belton then arose and stated that it was the determination of the students to not move an inch unless the matter was adjusted then and there. And that faculty of white teachers beat a hasty retreat and held up the white flag! They agreed that the colored teacher should eat with them.

The students broke forth into cheering, and flaunted a black flag on which was painted in white letters; "Victory." They rose and marched out of doors two by two, singing "John Brown's Body lies mouldering in the grave, and we go marching on."

The confused and bewildered teachers remained behind, busy with their thoughts. They felt like hens who had lost their broods. The cringing, fawning, sniffling, cowardly Negro which slavery left, had disappeared, and a new Negro, self-respecting, fearless, and determined in the assertion of his rights was at hand.

Ye who chronicle history and mark epochs in the career of races and nations must put here a towering, gigantic, century stone, as marking the passing of one and the ushering in of another great era in the history of the colored people of the United States. Rebellions, for one cause or another, broke out in almost every one of these schools presided over by white faculties, and as a rule, the Negro students triumphed.

These men who engineered and participated in these rebellions were the future leaders of their race. In these rebellions, they learned the power of combinations, and that white men could be made to capitulate to colored men under certain circumstances. In these schools, probably one hundred thousand students had these thoughts instilled in them. These one hundred thousand went to their respective homes and told of their prowess to their playmates who could not follow them to the college walls. In the light of these facts the great events yet to be recorded are fully accounted for.

Remember that this was Belton's first taste of rebellion against the whites for the securing of rights denied simply because of color. In after life he is the moving, controlling, guiding spirit in one on a far larger scale; it need not come as a surprise. His teachers and school-mates predicted this of him.

Chapter VII
A Sermon, A Sock and a Fight

BELTON REMAINED at Stowe University, acquiring fame as an orator and scholar. His intellect was pronounced by all to be marvelously bright.

We now pass over all his school career until we come to the closing days of the session in which he graduated. School was to close on Thursday, and the Sunday night previous had been designated as the time for the Baccalaureate sermon. On this occasion the entire school assembled in the general assembly room, – the graduating class occupying the row of front seats stretching across the room. The class, this year, numbered twenty-five; and they presented an appearance that caused the hearts of the people to swell with pride.

Dr. Lovejoy, president of the University, was to preach the sermon. He chose for his text, "The Kingdom of God is within us." We shall choose from his discourse just such thoughts as may throw light upon some events yet to be recorded, which might not otherwise be accounted for:

"Young men, we shall soon push you forth into the midst of a turbulent world, to play such a part as the voice of God may assign you. You go forth, amid the shouts and huzzahs of cheering friends, and the anxious prayers of the faithful of God. The part that you play, the character of your return journey, triumphant or inglorious, will depend largely upon how well you have learned the lesson of this text. Remember that the kingdom of God is within you. Do not go forth into the world to demand favors of the world, but go forth to give unto the world. Be strong in your own hearts.

"The world is like unto a wounded animal that has run a long way and now lies stretched upon the ground, the blood oozing forth from gaping wounds and pains darting through its entire frame.

The huntsman, who comes along to secure and drink the feverish milk of this animal that is all but a rotting carcass, seriously endangers his own well being. So, young men, do not look upon this dying, decaying world to feed and support you. You must feed and support it. Carry fresh, warm, invigorating blood in your veins to inject into the veins of the world. This is far safer and nobler than sticking the lance into the swollen veins of the world, to draw forth its putrid blood for your own use. I not only exhort you but I warn you. You may go to this dying animal as a surgeon, and proceed to cut off the sound portions for your own use. You may deceive the world for awhile, but it will, ere long, discover whether you are a vandal or a surgeon; and if it finds you to be the former, when you are closest to its bosom, it will squeeze you tightly and tear your face to shreds.

"I wish now to apply these thoughts to your immediate circumstances.

"You shall be called upon to play a part in the adjusting of positions between the negro and Anglo-Saxon races of the South. The present status of affairs cannot possibly remain. The Anglo-Saxon race must surrender some of its outposts, and the negro will occupy these. To bring about this evacuation on the part of the Anglo-Saxon, and the forward march of the negro, will be your task. This is a grave and delicate task, fraught with much good or evil, weal or woe. Let us urge you to undertake it in the spirit to benefit the world, and not merely to advance your own glory.

"The passions of men will soon be running high, and by feeding these passions with the food for which they clamor you may attain the designation of a hero. But, with all the energy of my soul, I exhort you to not play with fire, merely for the sake of the glare that it may cast upon you. Use no crisis for self-aggrandizement. Be so full of your own soul's wealth that these temptations may not appeal to you. When your vessel is ploughing the roughest seas and encountering the fiercest gales, consult as your chart the welfare of the ship and crew, though you may temporarily lose fame as a captain.

"Young men, you are highly favored of God. A glorious destiny awaits your people. The gates of the beautiful land of the future are flung wide. Your people stand before these gates peering eagerly within. They are ready to march. They are waiting for their commanders and the command to move forward. You are the commanders who must give the command. I urge, I exhort, I beseech you, my dear boys, to think not of yourselves. Let your kingdom be within. Lead them as they ought to be led, taking no thought to your own glory.

"If you heed my voice you shall become true patriots. If you disregard it, you will become time-serving demagogues, playing upon the passions of the people for the sake of short-lived notoriety. Such men would corral all the tigers in the forest and organize them into marauding regiments simply for the honor of being in the lead. Be ye none of these, my boys. May your Alma Mater never feel called upon to cry to God in anguish to paralyze the hand that she herself has trained.

"Be not a burrowing parasite, feasting off of the world's raw blood. Let the world draw life from you. Use not the misfortunes of your people as stones of a monument erected to your name. If you do, the iron fist of time will knock it over on your grave to crumble your decaying bones to further dust.

"Always serve the world as the voice of good conscience, instructed by a righteous God, may direct. Do this and thou shalt live; live in the sweetened memory of your countrymen; live in the heart of your Alma Mater; live when the earth is floating dust, when the stars are dead, when the sun is a charred and blackened ruin; live on the bosom of your Savior, by the throne of his God, in the eternal Heavens."

The teacher's soul was truly in his discourse and his thoughts sank deep into the hearts of his hearers. None listened more attentively than Belton. None were more deeply impressed than he. None more readily incorporated the principles enumerated as a part of their living lives.

When the preacher sat down he bowed his head in his hands. His frame shook. His white locks fluttered in the gentle spring breeze. In silence he prayed. He earnestly implored God to not allow his work and words to be in vain. The same fervent prayer was on Belton's lips, rising from the center of his soul. Somewhere, these prayers met, locked arms and went before God together. In due time the answer came.

This sermon had much to do with Belton's subsequent career. But an incident apparently trivial in itself was the occasion of a private discourse that had even greater influence over him. It occurred on Thursday following the night of the delivery of the sermon just reported. It was on this wise:

Belton had, in everything, excelled his entire class, and was, according to the custom, made valedictorian. His room-mate was insanely jealous of him, and sought every way possible to humiliate him. He had racked his brain for a scheme to play on Belton on commencement day, and he at last found one that gave him satisfaction.

There was a student in Stowe University who was noted for his immense height and for the size and scent of his feet. His feet perspired freely, summer and winter, and the smell was exceedingly offensive. On this account he roomed to himself. Whenever other students called to see him he had a very effective way of getting rid of them, when he judged that they had stayed long enough. He would complain of a corn and forthwith pull off a shoe. If his room was crowded, this act invariably caused it to be empty. The fame of these feet spread to the teachers and young ladies, and, in fact, to the city. And the huge Mississippian seemed to relish the distinction.

Whenever Belton was to deliver an oration he always arranged his clothes the night beforehand. So, on the Wednesday night of the week in question, he carefully brushed and arranged his clothes for the next day. In the valedictory there were many really touching things, and in rehearsing it before his room-mate Belton had often shed tears. Fearing that he might he so touched that tears would come to his eyes in the final delivery, he had bought a most beautiful and costly silk handkerchief. He carefully stowed this away in the tail pocket of his handsome Prince Albert suit of lovely black. He hung his coat in the wardrobe, very carefully, so that he would merely have to take it down and put it on the next day.

His room-mate watched his movements closely, but slyly. He arose when he saw Belton hang his coat up. He went down the corridor until he arrived at the room occupied by the Mississippian. He knocked, and after some little delay, was allowed to enter.

The Mississippian was busy rehearsing his oration and did not care to be bothered. But he sat down to entertain Belton's room-mate for a while. He did not care to rehearse his oration before him and he felt able to rout him at any time. They conversed on various things for a while, when Belton's room-mate took up a book and soon appeared absorbed in reading. He was sitting on one side of a study table in the center of the room while the Mississippian was on the other. Thinking that his visitor had now stayed about long enough, the Mississippian stooped down quietly and removed one shoe. He slyly watched Belton's room-mate, chuckling inwardly. But his fun died away into a feeling of surprise when he saw that his shoeless foot was not even attracting attention.

He stooped down and pulled off the other shoe, and his surprise developed into amazement when he saw that the combined attack produced no result. Belton's room-mate seemed absorbed in reading.

The Mississippian next pulled off his coat and pretending to yawn and stretch, lifted his arms just so that the junction of his arm with his shoulder was on a direct line with his visitor's nose. Belton's room-mate made a slight grimace, but kept on reading. The Mississippian was dumbfounded.

He then signified his intention of retiring to bed and undressed, eyeing his visitor all the while, hoping that the scent of his whole body would succeed.

He got into bed and was soon snoring loudly enough to be heard two or three rooms away; but Belton's room-mate seemed to pay no attention to the snoring.

The Mississippian gave up the battle in disgust, saying to himself: "That fellow regards scents and noises just as though he was a buzzard, hatched in a cleft of the roaring Niagara Falls." So saying, he fell asleep in reality and the snoring increased in volume and speed.

Belton's room-mate now took a pair of large new socks out of his pocket and put them into the Mississippian's shoes, from which he took the dirty socks already there. Having these dirty socks, he quietly tips out of the room and returns to his and Belton's room.

Belton desired to make the speech of his life the next day, and had retired to rest early so as to be in prime nervous condition for the effort. His room-mate stole to the wardrobe and stealthily extracted the silk handkerchief and put these dirty socks in its stead. Belton was then asleep, perhaps dreaming of the glories of the morrow.

Thursday dawned and Belton arose, fresh and vigorous. He was cheerful and buoyant that day; he was to graduate bedecked with all the honors of his class. Mr. King, his benefactor, was to be present. His mother had saved up her scant earnings and had come to see her son wind up the career on which she had sent him forth, years ago.

The assembly room was decorated with choice flowers and presented the appearance of the Garden of Eden. On one side of the room sat the young lady pupils, while on the other the young men sat. Visitors from the city came in droves and men of distinction sat on the platform. The programme was a good one, but all eyes dropped to the bottom in quest of Belton's name; for his fame as an orator was great, indeed. The programme passed off as arranged, giving satisfaction and whetting the appetite for Belton's oration. The president announced Belton's name amid a thundering of applause. He stepped forth and cast a tender look in the direction of the fair maiden who had contrived to send him that tiny white bud that showed up so well on his black coat. He moved to the center of the platform and was lustily cheered, he walked with such superb grace and dignity.

He began his oration, capturing his audience with his first sentence and bearing them along on the powerful pinions of his masterly oratory; and when his peroration was over the audience drew its breath and cheered wildly for many, many minutes. He then proceeded to deliver the valedictory to the class. After he had been speaking for some time, his voice began to break with emotion. As he drew near to the most affecting portion he reached to his coat tail pocket to secure his silk handkerchief to brush away the gathering tears. As his hand left his pocket a smile was on well-nigh every face in the audience, but Belton did not see this, but with bowed head, proceeded with his pathetic utterances.

The audience of course was struggling between the pathos of his remarks and the humor of those dirty socks.

Belton's sweetheart began to cry from chagrin and his mother grew restless, anxious to tell him or let him know in some way. Belton's head continued bowed in sadness, as he spoke parting words to his beloved classmates, and lifted his supposed handkerchief to his eyes to wipe away the tears that were now coming freely. The socks had thus come close to Belton's nose and he stopped of a sudden and held them at arm's length to gaze at that terrible, terrible scent producer. When he saw what he held in his hand he flung them in front of him, they falling on some students, who hastily brushed them off.

The house, by this time, was in an uproar of laughter; and the astonished Belton gazed blankly at the socks lying before him. His mind was a mass of confusion. He hardly knew where he was or what he was doing. Self-possession, in a measure, returned to him, and he said: "Ladies and gentlemen, these socks are from Mississippi. I am from Virginia."

This reference to the Mississippian was greeted by an even louder outburst of laughter. Belton bowed and left the platform, murmuring that he would find and kill the rascal who had played that trick on him. The people saw the terrible frown on his face, and the president heard the revengeful words, and all feared that the incident was not closed.

Belton hurried out of the speakers' room and hastily ran to the city to purchase a pistol. Having secured it, he came walking back at a furious pace. By this time the exercises were over and friends were returning to town. They desired to approach Belton and compliment him, and urge him to look lightly on his humorous finale; but he looked so desperate that none dared to approach him.

The president was on the lookout for Belton and met him at the door of the boys' dormitory. He accosted Belton tenderly and placed his hand on his shoulder. Belton roughly pushed him aside and strode into the building and roamed through it, in search of his room-mate, whom he now felt assured did him the trick.

But his room-mate, foreseeing the consequences of detection, had made beforehand every preparation for leaving and was now gone. No one could quiet Belton during that whole day, and he spent the night meditating plans for wreaking vengeance.

The next morning the president came over early, and entering Belton's room, was more kindly received. He took Belton's hand in his and sat down near his side. He talked to Belton long and earnestly, showing him what an unholy passion revenge was. He showed that such a passion would mar any life that yielded to it.

Belton, he urged, was about to allow a pair of dirty socks to wreck his whole life. He drew a picture of the suffering Savior, crying out between darting pains the words of the sentence, the most sublime ever uttered: "Lord forgive them for they know not what they do." Belton was melted to tears of repentance for his unholy passion.

Before the president left Belton's side he felt sure that henceforth a cardinal principle of his life would be to allow God to avenge all his wrongs. It was a narrow escape for Belton; but he thanked God for the lesson, severe as it was, to the day of his death. The world will also see how much it owes to God for planting that lesson in Belton's heart.

Let us relate just one more incident that happened at the winding up of Belton's school life. As we have intimated, one young lady, a student of the school, was very near to Belton. Though he did not love her, his regard for her was very deep and his respect very great.

School closed on Thursday, and the students were allowed to remain in the buildings until the following Monday, when, ordinarily, they left. The young men were allowed to provide conveyances for the young ladies to get to the various depots. They esteemed that a very great privilege.

Belton, as you know, was a very poor lad and had but little money. After paying his expenses incident to his graduation, and purchasing a ticket home, he now had just one dollar and a quarter left. Out of this one dollar and a quarter he was to pay for a carriage ride of this young lady friend to the railway station. This, ordinarily, cost one dollar, and Belton calculated on having a margin of twenty-five cents. But you would have judged him the happy possessor of a large fortune, merely to look at him.

The carriage rolled up to the girls' dormitory and Belton's friend stood on the steps, with her trunks, three in number. When Belton saw that his friend had three trunks, his heart sank. In order to be sure against exorbitant charges the drivers were always made to announce their prices before the journey was commenced. A crowd of girls was standing around to bid the young lady adieu. In an off-hand way Belton said: "Driver what is your fee?" He replied: "For you and the young lady and the trunks, two dollars, sir."

Belton almost froze in his tracks, but, by the most heroic struggling, showed no signs of discomfiture on his face. Endeavoring to affect an air of indifference, he said: "What is the price for the young lady and the trunks?"

"One dollar and fifty cents."

Belton's eyes were apparently fixed on some spot in the immensity of space. The driver, thinking that he was meditating getting another hackman to do the work, added: "You can call any hackman you choose and you won't find one who will do it for a cent less."

Belton's last prop went with this statement. He turned to his friend smilingly and told her to enter, with apparently as much indifference as a millionaire. He got in and sat by her side; but knew not how on earth he was to get out of his predicament.

The young lady chatted gayly and wondered at Belton's dullness. Belton, poor fellow, was having a tough wrestle with poverty and was trying to coin something out of nothing. Now and then, at some humorous remark, he would smile a faint, sickly smile. Thus it went on until they arrived at the station. Belton by this time decided upon a plan of campaign.

They alighted from the carriage and Belton escorted his friend into the coach. He then came back to speak to the driver. He got around the corner of the station house, out of sight of the train and beckoned for the driver to come to him. The driver came and Belton said: "Friend, here is one dollar and a quarter. It is all I have. Trust me for the balance until tomorrow."

"Oh! no," replied the driver. "I must have my money to-day. I have to report to-night and my money must go in. Just fork over the balance, please."

"Well," said Belton rather independently – for he felt that he now had the upper hand, "I have given you all the money that I have. And you have got to trust me for the balance. You can't take us back," and Belton started to walk away.

The driver said: "May be that girl has some money. I'll see her."

Terror immediately seized Belton, and he clutched at the man eagerly, saying: "Ah, no, now, don't resort to any such foolishness. Can't you trust a fellow?" Belton was now talking very persuasively.

The driver replied: "I don't do business that way. If I had known that you did not have the money I would not have brought you. I am going to the young lady."

Belton was now thoroughly frightened and very angry; and he planted himself squarely in front of the driver and said: "You shall do no such thing!"

The driver heard the train blow and endeavored to pass. Belton grasped him by the collar and putting a leg quickly behind him, tripped him to the ground, falling on top of him. The driver struggled, but Belton succeeded in getting astride of him and holding him down. The train shortly pulled out, and Belton jumped up and ran to wave a good-bye to his girl friend.

Later in the day, the driver had him arrested and the police justice fined him ten dollars. A crowd of white men who heard Belton's story, admired his respect for the girl, and paid the fine for him and made up a purse.

At Stowe University, Belton had learned to respect women. It was in these schools that the work of slavery in robbing the colored women of respect, was undone. Woman now occupied the same position in Belton's eye as she did in the eye of the Anglo-Saxon.

There is hope for that race or nation that respects its women. It was for the smile of a woman that the armored knight of old rode forth to deeds of daring. It is for the smile of women that the soldier of to-day endures the hardships of the camp and braves the dangers of the field of battle.

The heart of man will joyfully consent to be torn to pieces if the lovely hand of woman will only agree to bind the parts together again and heal the painful wounds.

The Negro race had left the last relic of barbarism behind, and this young negro, fighting to keep that cab driver from approaching the girl for a fee, was but a forerunner of the negro, who, at the voice of a woman, will fight for freedom until he dies, fully satisfied if the hand that he worships will only drop a flower on his grave.

Belton's education was now complete, as far as the school-room goes.

What will he do with it?

Chapter VIII
Many Mysteries Cleared Up

ON THE DAY prior to the one on which Bernard first entered the public school of Winchester, Fairfax Belgrave had just arrived in the town.

A costly residence, beautifully located and furnished in the most luxurious manner, was on the eve of being sold. Mrs. Belgrave purchased this house and installed herself as mistress thereof. Here she lived in isolation with her boy, receiving no callers and paying no visits. Being a devoted Catholic, she attended all the services of her church and reared Bernard in that faith.

For a time white and colored people speculated much as to who Mrs. Belgrave was, and as to what was the source of her revenue; for she was evidently a woman of wealth. She employed many servants and these were plied with thousands of questions by people of both races. But the life of Mrs. Belgrave was so circumspect, so far removed from anything suspicious, and her bearing was so evidently that of a woman of pure character and high ideals that speculation died out after a year or two, and the people gave up the finding out of her history as a thing impossible of achievement. With seemingly unlimited money at her command, all of Bernard's needs were supplied and his lightest wishes gratified. Mrs. Belgrave was a woman with very superior education. The range of her reading was truly remarkable. She possessed the finest library ever seen in the northern section of Virginia, and all the best of the latest books were constantly arriving at her home. Magazines and newspapers arrived by every mail. Thus she was thoroughly abreast with the times.

As Bernard grew up, he learned to value associating with his mother above every other pleasure. She superintended his literary training and cultivated in him a yearning for literature of the highest and purest type. Politics, science, art, religion, sociology, and, in fact, the whole realm of human knowledge was invaded and explored. Such home training was an invaluable supplement to what Bernard received in school. When, therefore, he entered Harvard, he at once moved to the front rank in every particular. Many white young men of wealth and high social standing, attracted by his brilliancy, drew near him and became his fast friends. In his graduating year, he was so popular as to be elected president of his class, and so scholarly as to be made valedictorian.

These achievements on his part were so remarkable that the Associated Press telegraphed the news over the country, and many were the laudatory notices that he received. The night of his graduation, when he had finished delivering his oration that swept all before it as does the whirlwind and the hurricane, as he stepped out of the door to take his carriage for home, a tall man with a broad face and long flowing beard stepped up behind him and tapped him on the shoulder.

Bernard turned and the man handed him a note. Tearing the envelope open he saw in his mother's well known handwriting the following:

> "*Dear Bernie:*
> "*Follow this man and trust him as you would your loving mother.*
> "*Fairfax Belgrave.*"

Bernard dismissed his carriage, ordered to take him to his lodging, and spoke to the man who had accosted him, saying that he was at his service. They walked a distance and soon were at the railroad station. They boarded the train and in due time arrived in Washington, D.C., Bernard asking no questions, knowing that a woman as habitually careful as his mother did not send that message without due care and grave purpose.

In Washington they took a carriage and were driven to one of the most fashionable portions of the city, and stopped before a mansion of splendid appearance. Bernard's escort led the way into the house, having a key to which all of the doors responded. Bernard was left in the parlor and told to remain until some one called for him. The tall man with long flowing beard went to his room and removed his disguise.

In a few minutes a negro servant, sent by this man, appeared and led Bernard to a room in the rear of the house on the second floor. It was a large room having two windows, one facing the east and the other the north.

As he stepped into the room he saw sitting directly facing him a white man, tall and of a commanding appearance. His hair, and for that matter his whole noble looking head and handsome face bore a striking resemblance to Bernard's own. The latter perceived the likeness and halted in astonishment. The man arose and handed Bernard a note. Bernard opened it and found it exactly resembling the one handed him just prior to his journey to Washington.

The man eyed Bernard from head to foot with a look that betrayed the keenest interest. Opening one of the drawers of his desk he drew forth a paper. It was a marriage certificate, certifying to a marriage between Fairfax Belgrave and —.

"I am your mother's lawful husband, and you are my legitimate child."

Bernard knew not what to say, think, or feel. His mother had so carefully avoided any mention of her family affairs that he regarded them as among things sacred, and he never allowed even his thoughts to wander in that direction.

"I am Senator — from the state of —, chairman of — committee."

The information contained in that sentence made Bernard rise from his seat with a bound. The man's name was a household word throughout the nation, and his reputation was international.

"Be seated, Bernard, I have much to say to you. I have a long story to tell. I have been married twice. My first wife's brother was Governor of — and lived and died a bachelor. He was, however, the father of a child, whose mother was a servant connected with his father's household. The child was given to my wife to rear, and she accepted the charge. The child bloomed into a perfect beauty, possessed a charming voice, could perform with extraordinary skill on the piano, and seemed to have inherited the mind of her father, whose praises have been sung in all the land.

"When this child was seventeen years of age my wife died. This girl remained in our house. I was yet a young man. Now that my wife was gone, attending to this girl fell entirely into my hands. I undertook her education. As her mind unfolded, so many beauteous qualities appeared that she excited my warm admiration.

"By chance, I discovered that the girl loved me; not as a father, but as she would a lover. She does not know to this day that I made the discovery when I did. As for myself, I had for some time been madly in love with her. When I discovered, that my affections were returned, I made proposals, at that time regarded as honorable enough by the majority of white men of the South.

"It seemed as though my proposition did not take her by surprise. She gently, but most firmly rejected my proposal. She told me that the proposal was of a nature to occasion deep and lasting repugnance, but that in my case she blamed circumstances and conditions more than she did me. The quiet, loving manner in which she resented insult and left no tinge of doubt as to her virtue, if possible, intensified my love. A few days later she came to me and said: 'Let us go to Canada and get married secretly. I will return South with you. No one shall ever know what we have done, and for the sake of your political and social future I will let the people apply whatever name they wish to our relationship.'

"I gladly embraced the proposal, knowing that she would keep faith even unto death; although I realized how keenly her pure soul felt at being regarded as living with me dishonorably. Yet, love and interest bade her bow her head and receive the public mark of shame.

"Heroic soul! That is the marriage certificate which I showed you. You were born. When you were four years old your mother told me that she must leave, as she could not bear to see her child grow up esteeming her an adulteress.

"The war broke out, and I entered the army, and your mother took you to Europe, where she lived until the war was over, when she returned to Winchester, Virginia. Her father was a man of wealth, and you own two millions of dollars through your mother. At my death you shall have eight millions more.

"So much for the past. Let me tell you of my plans and hopes for your future. This infernal race prejudice has been the curse of my life. Think of my pure-hearted, noble-minded wife, branded as a harlot, and you, my own son, stigmatized as a bastard, because it would be suicide for me to let the world know that you both are mine, though you both are the direct descendants of a governor, and a long line of heroes whose names are ornaments to our nation's history.

"I want you to break down this prejudice. It is the wish of your mother and your father. You must move in the front, but all that money and quiet influence can do shall be done by me for your advancement. I paid Mr. Tiberius Gracchus Leonard two thousand dollars a year to teach you at Winchester. His is a master mind. One rash deed robbed the world of seeing a colossal intellect in high station. I shall tell you his history presently.

"I desire you to go to Norfolk County, Virginia, and hang up your sign as an attorney at law. I wish you to run for congress from that district. Leonard is down there. As you will find out, he will be of inestimable service to you.

"Now let me give you his history. Leonard was the most brilliant student that ever entered — University in the state of —. Just prior to the time when he would have finished his education at school, the war broke out and he enlisted in the Confederate Army, and was made a colonel of a regiment. I was also a colonel, and when our ranks became depleted the two regiments were thrown into one. Though he was the ranking officer, our commander, as gallant and intrepid an officer as ever trod a battle field, was put in command. This deeply humilitated Leonard and he swore to be avenged.

"One evening, when night had just lowered her black wings over the earth, we were engaging the enemy. Our commander was in advance of his men. Suddenly the commander fell, wounded. At first it was thought that the enemy bad shot him, but investigation showed that the ball had entered his back. It was presumed, then, that some of his own men had mistook him for an enemy and had shot him through mistake. Leonard had performed the nefarious deed knowingly. By some skillful detective work, I secured incontestible evidence of his guilt. I went to him with my proof and informed him of my intentions to lay it before a superior officer. His answer was: 'If you do, I will let the whole world know about your nigger wife.' I fell back as if stunned. Terror seized me. If he knew of my marriage might not others know it? Might not it be already generally known? These were the thoughts that coursed through my brain. However, with an effort I suppressed my alarm. Seeing that each possessed a secret that meant death and disgrace to the other (for I shall certainly kill myself if I am ever exposed) I entered into an agreement with him.

"On the condition that he would prepare a statement confessing his guilt and detailing the circumstances of the crime and put this paper in my hand, I would show him my marriage certificate; and after that, each was to regard the other's secret as inviolate.

"We thus held each other securely tied. His conscience, however, disturbed him beyond measure; and every evening, just after dusk, he fancied that he saw the form of his departed commander. It made him cowardly in battle and he at last deserted.

"He informed me as to how my secret came into his possession. Soon after he committed his crime he felt sure that I was in possession of his secret, and he thought to steal into my tent and murder me. He stole in there one night to perpetrate the crime. I was talking in my sleep. In my slumber I told the story of my secret marriage in such circumstantial detail that it impressed him as being true. Feeling that he could hold me with that, he spared my life, determined to wound me deeper than death if I struck at him.

"You see that he is a cowardly villain; but we sometimes have to use such.

"Now, my son, go forth; labor hard and climb high. Scale the high wall of prejudice. Make it possible, dear boy, for me to own you ere I pass out of life. Let your mother have the veil of slander torn from her pure form ere she closes her eyes on earth forever."

Bernard, handsome, brilliant, eloquent, the grandson of a governor, the son of a senator, a man of wealth, to whom defeat was a word unknown, steps out to battle for the freedom of his race; urged to put his whole soul into the fight because of his own burning desire for glory, and because out of the gloom of night he heard his grief stricken parents bidding him to climb where the cruel world would be compelled to give its sanction to the union that produced such a man as he.

Bernard's training was over. He now had a tremendous incentive. Into life he plunges.

Chapter IX
Love and Politics

ACTING ON HIS FATHER'S advice Bernard arrived in Norfolk in the course of a few days. He realized that he was now a politician and decided to make a diligent study of the art of pleasing the populace and to sacrifice everything to the goddess of fame. Knowing that whom the people loved they honored, he decided to win their love at all hazards. He decided to become the obedient servant of the people that he might thus make all the people his servants.

He took up his abode at Hotel Douglass, a colored hotel at which the colored leaders would often congregate. Bernard mingled with these men freely and soon had the name among them of being a jovial good fellow.

While at Harvard, Bernard had studied law simultaneously with his other studies and graduated from both the law and classical departments the same year.

Near the city court house, in a row of somewhat dilapidated old buildings, he rented a law office. The rowdy and criminal element infested this neighborhood. Whenever any of these got into difficulties, Bernard was always ready to defend them. If they were destitute of funds he would serve them free of charge and would often pay their fines for them. He was ever ready to go on bonds of any who got into trouble. He gave money freely to those who begged of him. In this manner he became the very ideal of the vicious element, though not accounted by them as one of their number.

Bernard was also equally successful in winning favor with the better element of citizens. Though a good Catholic at heart, he divided his time among all denominations, thus solving the most difficult problem for a Negro leader to solve; for the religious feeling was so intense that it was carried into almost every branch of human activity.

Having won the criminal and religious circles, he thought to go forth and conquer the social world and secure its support. He decided to enter society and pay marked attention to that young lady that would most increase his popularity. We shall soon see how this would-be conqueror stood the very first fire.

His life had been one of such isolation that he had not at all moved in social circles before this, and no young woman had ever made more than a passing impression on him.

There was in Norfolk a reading circle composed of the brightest, most talented young men and women of the city. Upon taking a short vacation, this circle always gave a reception which was attended by persons of the highest culture in the city. Bernard received an invitation to this reception, and, in company with a fellow lawyer attended. The reception was held at the residence of a Miss Evangeline Leslie, a member of the circle.

The house was full of guests when Bernard and his friend arrived. They rang the door bell and a young lady came to the door to receive them.

She was a small, beautifully formed girl with a luxuriant growth of coal black hair that was arranged in such a way as to impart a queenly look to her shapely head. Her skin was dark brown, tender and smooth in appearance. A pair of laughing hazel eyes, a nose of the prettiest possible size and shape, and a chin that tapered with the most exquisite beauty made her face the Mecca of all eyes.

Bernard was so struck with the girl's beauty that he did not greet her when she opened the door. He stared at her with a blank look. They were invited in.

Bernard pulled off his hat and walked in, not saying a word but eyeing that pretty girl all the while. Even when his back was turned toward her, as he walked, his head was turned over his shoulders and his eye surveyed all the graceful curves of her perfect form and scanned those features that could but charm those who admire nature's work.

When he had taken a seat in the corner of a room by the side of his friend he said: "Pray, who is that girl that met you at the door? I really did not know that a dark woman could look so beautiful."

"You are not the only one that thinks that she is surpassingly beautiful," said his friend. "Her picture is the only Negro's picture that is allowed to hang in the show glasses of the white photographers down town. White and colored pay homage to her beauty."

"Well," said Bernard, "that man who denies that girl's beauty should be sent to the asylum for the cure of a perverted and abnormal taste."

"I see you are rather enthusiastic. Is it wise to admire mortgaged property?" remarked his friend.

"What's that?" asked Bernard, quickly. "Is any body in my way?"

"In your way?" laughed his friend. "Pray what do you mean? I don't understand you."

"Come," said Bernard, "I am on pins. Is she married or about to be?"

"Well, not exactly that, but she has told me that she cares a good bit for me."

Bernard saw that his friend was in a mood to tease him and he arose and left his side.

His friend chuckled gleefully to himself and said: "The would-be catcher is caught. I thought Viola Martin would duck him if anybody could. Tell me about these smile-proof bachelors. When once they are struck, they fall all to pieces at once."

Bernard sought his landlady, who was present as a guest, and through her secured an introduction to Miss Viola Martin. He found her even more beautiful, if possible, in mind than in form and he sat conversing with her all the evening as if enchanted.

The people present were not at all surprised; for as soon as Bernard's brilliancy and worth were known in the town and people began to love him, it was generally hoped and believed that Miss Martin would take him captive at first sight.

Miss Viola Martin was a universal favorite. She was highly educated and an elocutionist of no mean ability. She sang sweetly and was the most accomplished pianist in town. She was bubbling over with good humor and her wit and funny stories were the very life of any circle where she happened to be. She was most remarkably well-informed on all leading questions of the day, and men of brain always enjoyed a chat with her. And the children and older people fairly worshipped her; for she paid especial attention to these. In all religious movements among the women she was the leading spirit.

With all these points in her favor she was unassuming and bowed her head so low that the darts of jealousy, so universally hurled at the brilliant and popular, never came her way. No one in Norfolk was considered worthy of her heart and hand and the community was tenderly solicitous as to who should wed her.

Bernard had made such rapid strides in their affections and esteem that they had already assigned him to their pet, Viola, or Vie as she was popularly called.

When the time for the departure of the guests arrived, Bernard with great regret bade Miss Martin adieu.

She ran upstairs to get her cloak, and a half dozen girls went tripping up stairs behind her; when once in the room set apart for the ladies' cloaks they began to gleefully pound Viola with pillows and smother her with kisses.

"You have made a catch, Vie. Hold him," said one.

"He'll hold himself," said another. To all of which Viola answered with a sigh.

A mulatto girl stepped up to Viola and with a merry twinkle in her eye said: "Theory is theory and practice is practice, eh, Vie? Well, we would hardly blame you in this case."

Viola earnestly replied: "I shall ask for no mercy. Theory and practice are one with me in this case."

"Bah, bah, girl, two weeks will change that tune. And I, for one, won't blame you," replied the mulatto still in a whisper.

The girls seeing that Viola did not care to be teased about Bernard soon ceased, and she came down stairs to be escorted home by the young man who had accompanied her there.

This young man was, thus early, jealous of Bernard and angry at Viola for receiving his attentions, and as a consequence he was silent all the way home.

This gave Viola time to think of that handsome, talented lawyer whom she had just met. She had to confess to herself that he had aroused considerable interest in her bosom and she looked forward to a promised visit with pleasure. But every now and then a sigh would escape her, such as she made when the girls were teasing her.

Her escort bade her good-night at her father's gate in a most sullen manner, but Viola was so lost in thought that she did not notice it. She entered the house feeling lively and cheerful, but when she entered her room she burst into crying. She would laugh a while and cry a while as though she had a foretaste of coming bliss mixed with bitterness.

Bernard at once took the place left vacant by the dropping away of the jealous young man and became Viola's faithful attendant, accompanying her wherever he could. The more he met Viola, the more beautiful she appeared to him and the more admirable he found her mind.

Bernard almost forgot his political aspirations, and began to ponder that passage of scripture that said man should not be alone. But he did not make such progress with Viola as was satisfactory to him. Sometimes she would appear delighted to see him and was all life and gayety. Again she was scarcely more than polite and seemed perfectly indifferent to him.

After a long while Bernard decided that Viola, who seemed to be very ambitious, treated him thus because he had not done anything worthy of special note. He somewhat slacked up in his attentions and began to devote himself to acquiring wide spread popularity with a view to entering Congress and reaching Viola in this way.

The more he drew off from Viola the more friendly she would seem to him, and he began to feel that seeming indifference was perhaps the way to win her. Thus the matter moved along for a couple of years.

In the mean time, Mr. Tiberius Gracchus Leonard, Bernard's old teacher, was busy in Norfolk looking after Bernard's political interests, acting under instructions from Bernard's father, Senator —.

About this stage of Bernard's courtship Mr. Leonard called on him and told him that the time was ripe for Bernard to announce himself for Congress. Bernard threw his whole soul into the project. He had another great incentive to cause him to wish to succeed, Viola Martin's hand and heart.

In order to understand what followed we must now give a bit of Virginia political history.

In the year — there was a split in the democratic party of Virginia on the question of paying Virginia's debt to England. The bolting section of the party joined hands with the republicans and whipped the regular democrats at the polls. This coalition thus formed was eventually made the Republican party of Virginia.

The democrats, however, rallied and swept this coalition from power and determined to forever hold the state government if they had to resort to fraud. They resorted to ballot box stuffing and various other means to maintain control. At last, they passed a law creating a state electoral commission.

This commission was composed of three democrats. These three democrats were given the power to appoint three persons in each county as an Electoral Board. These county electoral boards would appoint judges for each precinct or voting place in the county. They would also appoint a special constable at each voting booth to assist the illiterate voters.

With rare exceptions, the officials were democrats, and with the entire state's election machinery in their hands the democrats could manage elections according to their "own sweet will." It goes without saying that the democrats always carried any and every precinct that they decided, and elections were mere farces.

Such was the condition of affairs when Bernard came forward as a candidate from the Second Congressional District. The district was overwhelmingly republican, but the democrats always secured the office.

It was regarded as downright foolhardy to attempt to get elected to Congress from the District as a republican; so the nomination was merely passed around as an honor, empty enough.

It was such a feeling that inspired the republicans to nominate Bernard; but Bernard entered the canvass in dead earnest and conducted a brilliant campaign.

The masses of colored people rallied around his flag. Ministers of colored churches came to his support. Seeing that the colored people were so determined to elect Bernard, the white republicans, leaders and followers, fell into line. Viola Martin organized patriotic clubs among the women and aroused whatever voters seemed lethargic.

The day of election came and Bernard was elected by a majority of 11,823 votes; but the electoral boards gave the certificate of election to his opponent, alleging his opponent's majority to be 4,162.

Bernard decided to contest the election in Congress, and here is where Leonard's fine work was shown. He had, for sometime, made it appear in Norfolk that he was a democrat of the most radical school. The leading democrats made his acquaintance and Leonard very often composed speeches for them. He thus became a favorite with certain prominent democrats and they let him into the secret workings of the electoral machinery. Thus informed, Leonard went to headquarters of the Democratic party at Richmond with a view to bribing the clerks to give him inside facts. He found the following to be the character of the work done at headquarters.

A poll of all the voters in the state was made. The number of white and the number of colored voters in each voting precinct was secured. The number of illiterate voters of both races was ascertained. With these facts in their possession, they had conducted all the campaign necessary for them to carry on an election. Of course speakers were sent out as a sham, but they were not needed for anything more than appearances.

Having the figures indicated above before them, they proceeded to assign to each district, each county, each city, each precinct just such majorities as they desired, taking pains to make the figures appear reasonable and differ somewhat from figures of previous years. Whenever it would do no harm, a precinct was granted to the republicans for the sake of appearances.

Ballot boxes of varied patterns were secured and filled with ballots marked just as they desired. Some ballots were for republicans, some for democrats, and some marked wrong so as to indicate the votes of illiterates. The majorities, of course, were invariably such as suited the democrats. The ballots were all carefully counted and arranged; and tabulated statements of the votes cast put in. A sheet for the returns was put in, only awaiting the signatures of the officials at the various precincts in order to be complete. These boxes were carried by trusted messengers to their destinations.

On election day, not these boxes, but boxes similar to them were used to receive the ballots. On the night of the election, the ballot boxes that actually received the votes were burned with all their contents and the boxes and ballots from Richmond were substituted. The judges of election took out the return sheet, already prepared, signed it and returned it to Richmond forthwith. Thus it could always be known thirty days ahead just what the exact vote in detail was to be throughout the entire state. In fact a tabulated statement was prepared and printed long before election day.

Leonard paid a clerk at headquarters five thousand dollars for one of these tabulated statements. With this he hurried on to Washington and secretly placed it before the Republican Congressional Campaign Committee, with the understanding that it was to be used after election day as a basis for possible contest. Fifteen of the most distinguished clergymen in the nation were summoned to Washington and made affidavits, stating that they had seen this tabulated statement twenty days before the election took place.

When Virginia's returns came in they were found to correspond in every detail to this tabulated report.

As nothing but a prophet, direct from God, could have foreseen the results exactly as they did occur, this tabulated statement was proof positive of fraud on a gigantic scale.

With this and a mass of other indisputable evidence at his back, secured by the shrewd Leonard, Bernard entered the contest for his seat. The House of Representatives was democratic by a small majority. The contest was a long and bitter one. The republicans were solidly for Bernard. The struggle was eagerly watched from day to day. It was commonly believed that the democrats would vote against Bernard, despite the clear case in his favor.

The day to vote on the contest at last arrived and the news was flashed over the country that Bernard had triumphed. A handful of democrats had deserted their party and voted with the republicans. Bernard's father had redeemed his promise of secret support. Bernard's triumph in a democratic house caused the nation to rub its eyes and look again in wonder.

The colored people hailed Bernard as the coming Moses. "Belgrave, Belgrave, Belgrave," was on every Negro tongue. Poems were addressed to him. Babies were named after him. Honorary titles were showered upon him. He was in much demand at fairs and gatherings of notable people. He accepted every invitation of consequence, whenever possible, and traveled far and wide winning friends by his bewitching eloquence and his pleasing personality.

The democrats, after that defeat, always passed the second district by and Bernard held his seat in Congress from year to year unmolested. He made application and was admitted to plead law before the Supreme Court of the United States. And when we shall see him again it will be there, pleading in one of the most remarkable cases known to jurisprudence.

Chapter X
Cupid Again at Work

BELTON, AFTER GRADUATING from Stowe University, returned with his mother to their humble home at Winchester. He had been away at school for four years and now desired to see his home again before going forth into the world.

He remained at Winchester several days visiting all the spots where he had toiled or played, mourned or sung, wept or laughed as a child. He entered the old school house and gazed with eyes of love on its twisting walls, decaying floor and benches sadly in need of repair. A somewhat mournful smile played upon his lips as he thought of the revengeful act that he had perpetrated upon his first teacher, Mr. Leonard, and this smile died away into a more sober expression as he remembered how his act of revenge had, like chickens, come home to roost, when those dirty socks had made him an object of laughter at Stowe University on commencement day.

Revenge was dead in his bosom. And it was well for the world that this young negro had been trained in a school where there was a friendly lance to open his veins and let out this most virulent of poisons.

Belton lingered about home, thinking of the great problem of human life. He would walk out of town near sunset and, taking his seat on some grassy knoll would gaze on the Blue Ridge mountains. The light would fade out of the sky and the gloom of evening gather, but the mountains would maintain their same bold appearance. Whenever he cast his eyes in their direction, there they stood firm and immovable.

His pure and lofty soul had an affinity for all things grand and he was always happy, even from childhood, when he could sit undisturbed and gaze at the mountains, huge and lofty, rising in such unconquerable grandeur, upward toward the sky. Belton chose the mountain as the emblem of his life and he besought God to make him such in the moral world.

At length he tore himself loose from the scenes of his childhood, and embracing his fond mother, left Winchester to begin life in the city of Richmond, the capital of the old Confederacy. Through the influence of Mr. King, his benefactor, he secured a position as a teacher in one of the colored schools of that city.

The principal of the school to which Belton was assigned was white, but all the rest of the teachers were young colored women. On the morning of his arrival at the school building Belton was taken in charge by the principal, and by him was carried around to be introduced to the various teachers. Before he reaches a certain room, let us give you a slight introduction to the occupant thereof.

Antoinette Nermal was famed throughout the city for her beauty, intelligence and virtue. Her color was what is termed a light brown skin. We assure you that it was charming enough. She was of medium height, and for grace and symmetry her form was fit for a sculptor's model. Her pretty face bore the stamp of intellectuality, but the intellectuality of a beautiful woman, who was still every inch a woman despite her intellectuality. Her thin well-formed lips seemed arranged by nature in such a manner as to be incomplete without a kiss, and that lovely face seemed to reinforce the invitation. Her eyes were black, and when you gazed in them the tenderness therein seemed to be about to draw you out of yourself. They concealed and yet revealed a heart capable of passionate love.

Those who could read her and wished her well were much concerned that she should love wisely; for it could be seen that she was to love with her whole heart, and to wreck her love was to wreck her life. She had passed through all her life thus far without seriously noticing any young man, thus giving some the impression that she was incapable of love, being so intellectual. Others who read her better knew that she despised the butterfly, flitting from flower to flower, and was preserving her heart to give it whole into the keeping of some worthy man.

She neither sang nor played, but her soul was intensely musical and she had the most refined and cultivated taste in the musical circles in which she moved. She was amiable in disposition, but her amiability was not of the kind to lead her in quest of you; but if you came across her, she would treat you so pleasantly that you would desire to pass that way again.

Belton and the principal are now on the way to her room. As they entered the door her back was to them, as she was gazing out of the window. Belton's eyes surveyed her graceful form and he was so impressed with its loveliness that he was sorry when she began to turn around. But when she was turned full around Belton forgot all about her form, and his eyes did not know which to contemplate longest, that rich complexion, those charming eyes, or those seductive lips. On the other hand, Miss Nermal was struck with Belton's personal appearance and as she contemplated the noble, dignified yet genial appearance which he presented, her lips came slightly apart, rendering her all the more beautiful.

The principal said: "Miss Nermal, allow me to present to you our newly arrived associate in the work, Mr. Belton Piedmont."

Miss Nermal smiled to Belton and said: "Mr. Piedmont, we are glad to have a man of your acknowledged talents in our midst and we anticipate much of you."

Belton felt much flattered, surprised, overjoyed. He wished that he could find the person who had been so very kind as to give that marvelously beautiful girl such a good opinion of himself. But when he opened his mouth to reply he was afraid of saying something that would shatter this good opinion; so he bowed politely and merely said, "Thank you."

"I trust that you will find our association agreeable," said Miss Nermal, smiling and walking toward him.

This remark turned Belton's mind to thoughts that stimulated him to a brisk reply. "Oh assuredly, Miss Nermal. I am already more than satisfied that I shall expect much joy and pleasure from my association with you – I— I— I mean the teachers."

Belton felt that he had made a bad break and looked around a little uneasily at the principal, violently condemning in his heart that rule which led principals to escort young men around; especially when there was a likelihood of meeting with such a lovely girl. If you had consulted Belton's wishes at that moment, school would have been adjourned immediately, the principal excused, and himself allowed to look at and talk to Miss Nermal as much as he desired.

However, this was not to be. The principal moved to the door to continue his tour. Belton reluctantly followed. He didn't see the need of getting acquainted with all the teachers in one day. He thought that there were too many teachers in that building, anyhow. These were Belton's rebellious thoughts as he left Miss Nermal's room.

Nevertheless, he finished his journey around to the various rooms and afterwards assumed charge of his own room. Some might ascribe his awkwardness in his room that day to the fact that the work was new to him. But we prefer to think that certain new and pleasing sensations in his bosom were responsible.

When the young lady teachers got together at noon that day, the question was passed around as to what was thought of Mr. Piedmont. Those teachers whom Belton met before he entered Miss Nermal's room thought him "very nice." Those whom he met after he left her room thought him rather dull. Miss Nermal herself pronounced him "just grand."

All of the girls looked at Miss Nermal rather inquiringly when she said this, for she was understood to usually pass young men by unnoticed. Each of the other girls, previous to seeing Belton, had secretly determined to capture the rising young orator in case his personal appearance kept pace with his acknowledged talents. In debating the matter they had calculated their chances of success and had thought of all possible rivals. Miss Nermal was habitually so indifferent to young men that they had not considered her as a possibility. They were quite surprised, to say the least, to hear her speak more enthusiastically of Belton than any of the rest had done. If Miss Nermal was to be their rival they were ready to abandon the field at once, for the charms of her face, form, and mind were irresistible when in repose; and what would they be if she became interested in winning the heart of a young man?

When school was dismissed that afternoon Belton saw a group of teachers walking homeward and Miss Nermal was in the group. Belton joined them and somehow contrived to get by Miss Nermal's side. How much she aided him by unobserved shifting of positions is not known.

All of the rest of the group lived nearer the school than did Miss Nermal and so, when they had all dropped off at respective gates, Miss Nermal yet had some distance to go. When Belton saw this, he was a happy fellow. He felt that the parents of the teachers had shown such excellent judgment in choosing places to reside. He would not have them change for the world. He figured that he would have five evenings of undisturbed bliss in each week walking home with Miss Nermal after the other teachers had left.

Belton contrived to walk home with the same group each evening. The teachers soon noticed that Miss Nermal and Belton invariably walked together, and they managed by means of various excuses to break up the group; and Belton had the unalloyed pleasure of escorting Miss Nermal from the school-house door to her own front yard. Belton secured the privilege of calling to see Miss Nermal at her residence and he confined his social visits to her house solely.

They did not talk of love to one another, but any one who saw the couple together could tell at a glance what was in each heart. Belton, however, did not have the courage to approach the subject. His passion was so intense and absorbing and filled him with so much delight that he feared to talk on the subject so dear to his heart, for fear of a repulse and the shattering of all the beautiful castles which his glowing imagination, with love as the supervising architect, had constructed. Thus matters moved along for some time; Miss Nermal thoroughly in love with Belton, but Belton prizing that love too highly to deem it possible for him to be the happy possessor thereof.

Belton was anxious for some indirect test. He would often contrive little devices to test Miss Nermal's feelings towards him and in each case the result was all that he could wish, yet he doubted. Miss Nermal thoroughly understood Belton and was anxious for him to find some way out of his dilemma. Of course it was out of the question for her to volunteer to tell him that she loved him – loved him madly, passionately; loved him in every fibre of her soul.

At last the opportunity that Belton was hoping for came. Miss Nermal and Belton were invited out to a social gathering of young people one night. He was Miss Nermal's escort.

At this gathering the young men and women played games such as pinning on the donkey's tail, going to Jerusalem, menagerie, and various other parlor games. In former days, these social gatherings played some games that called for kissing by the young ladies and gentlemen, but Miss Nermal had opposed such games so vigorously that they had long since been dismissed from the best circles.

Belton had posted two or three young men to suggest a play involving kissing, that play being called, "In the well." The suggestion was made and just for the fun of having an old time game played, they accepted the suggestion. The game was played as follows.

Young men and young women would move their chairs as close back to the walls as possible. This would leave the center of the room clear. A young man would take his place in the middle of the floor and say, "I am in the well." A questioner would then ask, "How many feet?" The party in the well would then say, for instance, "Three feet." The questioner would then ask, "Whom will you have to take you out?"

Whosoever was named by the party in the well was required by the rules of the game to go to him and kiss him the number of times equivalent to the number of feet he was in the well.

The party thus called would then be in the well. The young men would kiss the ladies out and vice versa.

Miss Nermal's views on kissing games were well known and the young men all passed her by. Finally, a young lady called Belton to the well to kiss her out. Belton now felt that his chance had came. He was so excited that when he went to the well he forgot to kiss her. Belton was not conscious of the omission but it pleased Antoinette immensely.

Belton said, "I am in the well." The questioner asked, "How many feet?" Belton replied, "ONLY one." "Whom will you have to take you out?" queried the questioner. Belton was in a dazed condition. He was astounded at his own temerity in having deliberately planned to call Miss Nermal to kiss him before that crowd or for that matter to kiss him at all. However he decided to make a bold dash. He averted his head and said, "Miss Antoinette Nermal."

All eyes were directed to Miss Nermal to see her refuse. But she cast a look of defiance around the room and calmly walked to where Belton stood. Their eyes met. They understood each other. Belton pressed those sweet lips that had been taunting him all those many days and sat down, the happiest of mortals.

Miss Nermal was now left in the well to call for some one to take her out. For the first time, it dawned upon Belton that in working to secure a kiss for himself, he was about to secure one for some one else also. He glared around the room furiously and wondered who would be base enough to dare to go and kiss that angel.

Miss Nermal was proceeding with her part of the game and Belton began to feel that she did not mind it even if she did have to kiss some one else. After all, he thought, his test would not hold good as she was, he felt sure, about to kiss another.

While Belton was in agony over such thoughts Miss Nermal came to the point where she had to name her deliverer. She said, "The person who put me in here will have to take me out." Belton bounded from his seat and, if the fervor of a kiss could keep the young lady in the well from drowning, Miss Nermal was certainly henceforth in no more danger.

Miss Nermal's act broke up that game.

On the way home that night, neither Antoinette nor Belton spoke a word. Their hearts were too full for utterance. When they reached Miss Nermal's gate, she opened it and entering stood on the other side, facing Belton.

Belton looked down into her beautiful face and she looked up at Belton. He felt her eyes pulling at the cords of his heart. He stooped down and in silence pressed a lingering kiss on Miss Nermal's lips. She did not move.

Belton said, "I am in the well." Miss Nermal whispered, "I am too." Belton said, "I shall always be in the well." Miss Nermal said, "So shall I." Belton hastily plucked open the gate and clasped Antoinette to his bosom. He led her to a double seat in the middle of the lawn, and there with the pure-eyed stars gazing down upon them they poured out their love to each other.

Two hours later Belton left her and at that late hour roused every intimate friend that he had in the city to tell them of his good fortune.

Miss Nermal was no less reserved in her joy. She told the good news everywhere to all her associates. Love had transformed this modest, reserved young woman into a being that would not have hesitated to declare her love upon a house-top.

Chapter XI
No Befitting Name

HAPPY BELTON now began to give serious thought to the question of getting married. He desired to lead Antoinette to the altar as soon as possible and then he would be sure of possessing the richest treasure known to earth. And when he would speak of an early marriage she would look happy and say nothing in discouragement of the idea. She was Belton's, and she did not care how soon he claimed her as his own.

His poverty was his only barrier. His salary was small, being only fifty dollars a month. He had not held his position long enough to save up very much money. He decided to start up an enterprise that would enable him to make money a great deal faster.

The colored people of Richmond at that time had no newspaper or printing office. Belton organized a joint stock company and started a weekly journal and conducted a job printing establishment. This paper took well and was fast forging to the front as a decided success.

It began to lift up its voice against frauds at the polls and to champion the cause of honest elections. It contended that practicing frauds was debauching the young men, the flower of the Anglo-Saxon race. One particularly meritorious article was copied in *The Temps* and commented upon editorially. This article created a great stir in political circles.

A search was instituted as to the authorship. It was traced to Belton, and the politicians gave the school board orders to dump Belton forthwith, on the ground that they could not afford to feed and clothe a man who would so vigorously "attack Southern Institutions," meaning by this phrase the universal practice of thievery and fraud at the ballot box. Belton was summarily dismissed.

His marriage was of necessity indefinitely postponed. The other teachers were warned to give no further support to Belton's paper on pain of losing their positions. They withdrew their influence from Belton and he was, by this means, forced to give up the enterprise.

He was now completely without an occupation, and began to look around for employment. He decided to make a trial of politics. A campaign came on and he vigorously espoused the cause of the Republicans. A congressional and presidential campaign was being conducted at the same time, and Belton did yeoman service.

Owing to frauds in the elections the Democrats carried the district in which Belton labored, but the vote was closer than was ever known before. The Republicans, however, carried the nation and the President appointed a white republican as post-master of Richmond. In recognition of his great service to his party, Belton was appointed stamping clerk in the Post Office at a salary of sixty dollars per month.

As a rule, the most prominent and lucrative places went to those who were most influential with the voters. Measured by this standard and by the standard of real ability, Belton was entitled to the best place in the district in the gift of the government; but the color of his skin was against him, and he had to content himself with a clerkship.

At the expiration of one year, Belton proudly led the charming Antoinette Nermal to the marriage altar, where they became man and wife. Their marriage was the most notable social event that had ever been known among the colored people of Richmond. All of the colored people and many of the white people of prominence were at the wedding reception, and costly presents poured in upon them. This brilliant couple were predicted to have a glorious future before them. So all hearts hoped and felt.

About two years from Belton's appointment as stamping clerk and one year from the date of his marriage, a congressional convention was held for the purpose of nominating a candidate for Congress. Belton's chief, the postmaster, desired a personal friend to have the honor. This personal friend was known to be prejudiced against colored people and Belton could not, therefore, see his way clear to support him for the nomination. He supported another candidate and won for him the nomination; but the postmaster dismissed him from his position as clerk. Crushed in spirit, Belton came home to tell his wife of their misfortune.

Although he was entitled to the postmastership, according to the ethics of the existing political condition, he had been given a commonplace clerkship. And now, because he would not play the puppet, he was summarily dismissed from that humble position. His wife cheered him up and bade him to not be despondent, telling him that a man of his talents would beyond all question be sure to succeed in life.

Belton began to cast around for another occupation, but, in whatever direction he looked, he saw no hope. He possessed a first class college education, but that was all. He knew no trade nor was he equipped to enter any of the professions. It is true that there were positions around by the thousands which he could fill, but his color debarred him. He would have made an excellent drummer, salesman, clerk, cashier, government official (county, city, state, or national) telegraph operator, conductor, or any thing of such a nature. But the color of his skin shut the doors so tight that he could not even peep in.

The white people would not employ him in these positions, and the colored people did not have any enterprises in which they could employ him. It is true that such positions as street laborer, hod-carrier, cart driver, factory hand, railroad hand, were open to him; but such menial tasks were uncongenial to a man of his education and polish. And, again, society positively forbade him doing such labor. If a man of education among the colored people did such manual labor, he was looked upon as an eternal disgrace to the race. He was looked upon as throwing his education away and lowering its value in the eyes of the children who were to come after him.

So, here was proud, brilliant Belton, the husband of a woman whom he fairly worshipped, surrounded in a manner that precluded his earning a livelihood for her. This set Belton to studying the labor situation and the race question from this point of view. He found scores of young men just in his predicament. The schools were all supplied with teachers. All other doors were effectually barred. Society's stern edict forbade these young men resorting to lower forms of labor. And instead of the matter growing better, it was growing worse, year by year. Colleges were rushing class after class forth with just his kind of education, and there was no employment for them.

These young men, having no employment, would get together in groups and discuss their respective conditions. Some were in love and desired to marry. Others were married and desired to support their wives in a creditable way. Others desired to acquire a competence. Some had aged parents who had toiled hard to educate them and were looking to them for support. They were willing to work but the opportunity was denied them. And the sole charge against them was the color of their skins. They grew to hate a flag that would float in an undisturbed manner over such a condition of affairs. They began to abuse and execrate a national government that would not protect them against color prejudice, but on the contrary actually practiced it itself.

Beginning with passively hating the flag, they began to think of rebelling against it and would wish for some foreign power to come in and bury it in the dirt. They signified their willingness to participate in such a proceeding.

It is true that it was only a class that had thought and spoke of this, but it was an educated class, turned loose with an idle brain and plenty of time to devise mischief. The toiling, unthinking masses went quietly to their labors, day by day, but the educated malcontents moved in and out among them, convincing them that they could not afford to see their men of brains ignored because of color.

Belton viewed this state of affairs with alarm and asked himself, whither was the nation drifting. He might have joined this army of malcontents and insurrection breeders, but that a very remarkable and novel idea occurred to him. He decided to endeavor to find out just what view the white people were taking of the Negro and of the existing conditions. He saw that the nation was drifting toward a terrible cataract and he wished to find out what precautionary steps the white people were going to take.

So he left Richmond, giving the people to understand that he was gone to get a place to labor to support his wife. The people thought it strange that he did not tell where he was going and what he was to do. Speculation was rife. Many thought that it was an attempt at deserting his wife, whom he seemed unable to support. He arranged to visit his wife twice a month.

He went to New York and completely disguised himself. He bought a wig representing the hair on the head of a colored woman. He had this wig made especially to his order. He bought an outfit of well fitting dresses and other garments worn by women. He clad himself and reappeared in Richmond. His wife and most intimate friends failed to recognize him. He of course revealed his identity to his wife but to no one else.

He now had the appearance of a healthy, handsome, robust colored girl, with features rather large for a woman but attractive just the same. In this guise Belton applied for a position as nurse and was successful in securing a place in the family of a leading white man. He loitered near the family circle as much as he could. His ear was constantly at the key holes, listening. Sometimes he would engage in conversation for the purpose of drawing them out on the question of the Negro.

He found out that the white man was utterly ignorant of the nature of the Negro of to-day with whom he has to deal. And more than that, he was not bothering his brain thinking about the Negro. He felt that the Negro was easily ruled and was not an object for serious thought. The barbers, the nurses, cooks and washerwomen, the police column of the newspapers, comic stories and minstrels were the sources through which the white people gained their conception of the Negro. But the real controling power of the race that was shaping its life and thought and preparing the race for action, was unnoticed and in fact unseen by them.

The element most bitterly antagonistic to the whites avoided them, through intense hatred; and the whites never dreamed of this powerful inner circle that was gradually but persistently working its way in every direction, solidifying the race for the momentous conflict of securing all the rights due them according to the will of their heavenly Father.

Belton also stumbled upon another misconception, which caused him eventually to lose his job as nurse. The young men in the families in which Belton worked seemed to have a poor opinion of the virtue of colored women. Time and again they tried to kiss Belton, and he would sometimes have to exert his full strength to keep them at a distance. He thought that while he was a nurse, he would do what he could to exalt the character of the colored women. So, at every chance he got, he talked to the men who approached him, of virtue and integrity. He soon got the name of being a "virtuous prude" and the white men decided to corrupt him at all hazards.

Midnight carriage rides were offered and refused. Trips to distant cities were proposed but declined. Money was offered freely and lavishly but to no avail. Belton did not yield to them. He became the cynosure of all eyes. He seemed so hard to reach, that they began to doubt his sex. A number of them decided to satisfy themselves at all hazards. They resorted to the bold and daring plan of kidnapping and overpowering Belton.

After that eventful night Belton did no more nursing. But fortunately they did not recognize who he was. He secretly left, had it announced that Belton Piedmont would in a short time return to Richmond, and throwing off his disguise, he appeared in Richmond as Belton Piedmont of old. The town was agog with excitement over the male nurse, but none suspected him. He was now again without employment, and another most grievous burden was about to be put on his shoulders. May God enable him to bear it.

During all the period of their poverty stricken condition, Antoinette bore her deprivations like a heroine. Though accustomed from her childhood to plenty, she bore her poverty smilingly and cheerfully. Not one sigh of regret, not one word of complaint escaped her lips. She taught Belton to hope and have faith in himself. But everything seemed to grow darker and darker for him. In the whole of his school life, he had never encountered a student who could surpass him in intellectual ability; and yet, here he was with all his conceded worth, unable to find a fit place to earn his daily bread, all because of the color of his skin. And now the Lord was about to bless him with an offspring. He hardly knew whether to be thankful or sorrowful over this prospective gift from heaven.

On the one hand, an infant in the home would be a source of unbounded joy; but over against this pleasing picture there stood cruel want pointing its wicked, mocking finger at him, anxious for another victim. As the time for the expected gift drew near, Belton grew more moody and despondent. Day by day he grew more and more nervous. One evening the nurse called him into his wife's room, bidding him come and look at his son. The nurse stood in the door and looked hard at Belton as he drew near to the side of his wife's bed. He lifted the lamp from the dresser and approached. Antoinette turned toward the wall and hid her head under the cover. Eagerly, tremblingly, Belton pulled the cover from the little child's face, the nurse all the while watching him as though her eyes would pop out of her head.

Belton bent forward to look at his infant son. A terrible shriek broke from his lips. He dropped the lamp upon the floor and fled out of the house and rushed madly through the city. The color of Antoinette was brown. The color of Belton was dark. But the child was white!

What pen can describe the tumult that raged in Belton's bosom for months and months! Sadly, disconsolately, broken in spirit, thoroughly dejected, Belton dragged himself to his mother's cottage at Winchester. Like a ship that had started on a voyage, on a bright day, with fair winds, but had been overtaken and overwhelmed in an ocean storm, and had been put back to shore, so Belton now brought his battered bark into harbor again.

His brothers and sisters had all married and had left the maternal roof. Belton would sleep in the loft from which in his childhood he tumbled down, when disturbed about the disappearing biscuits. How he longed and sighed for childhood's happy days to come again. He felt that life was too awful for him to bear.

His feelings toward his wife were more of pity than reproach. Like the multitude, he supposed that his failure to properly support her had tempted her to ruin. He loved her still if anything, more passionately than ever. But ah! what were his feelings in those days toward the flag which he had loved so dearly, which had floated proudly and undisturbed, while color prejudice, upheld by it, sent, as he thought, cruel want with drawn sword to stab his family honor to death. Belton had now lost all hope of personal happiness in this life, and as he grew more and more composed he found himself better prepared than ever to give his life wholly to the righting of the wrongs of his people.

Tenderly he laid the image of Antoinette to rest in a grave in the very center of his heart. He covered her grave with fragrant flowers; and though he acknowledged the presence of a corpse in his heart, 'twas the corpse of one he loved.

We must leave our beautiful heroine under a cloud just here, but God is with her and will bring her forth conqueror in the sight of men and angels.

Chapter XII
On the Dissecting Board

ABOUT THIS TIME the Legislature of Louisiana passed a law designed to prevent white people from teaching in schools conducted in the interest of Negroes.

A college for Negroes had been located at Cadeville for many years, presided over by a white minister from the North. Under the operations of the law mentioned, he was forced to resign his position.

The colored people were, therefore, under the necessity of casting about for a successor. They wrote to the president of Stowe University requesting him to recommend a man competent to take charge of the college. The president decided that Belton was an ideal man for the place and recommended him to the proper authorities. Belton was duly elected.

He again bade home adieu and boarded the train for Cadeville, Louisiana. Belton's journey was devoid of special interest until he arrived within the borders of the state. At that time the law providing separate coaches for colored and white people had not been enacted by any of the Southern States. But in some of them the whites had an unwritten but inexorable law, to the effect that no Negro should be allowed to ride in a first-class coach. Louisiana was one of these states, but Belton did not know this. So, being in a first-class coach when he entered Louisiana, he did not get up and go into a second-class coach. The train was speeding along and Belton was quietly reading a newspaper. Now and then he would look out of a window at the pine tree forest near the track. The bed of the railway had been elevated some two or three feet above the ground, and to get the dirt necessary to elevate it a sort of trench had been dug, and ran along beside the track. The rain had been falling very copiously for the two or three days previous, and the ditch was full of muddy water. Belton's eyes would now and then fall on this water as they sped along.

In the meanwhile the train began to get full, passengers getting on at each station. At length the coach was nearly filled. A white lady entered, and not at once seeing a vacant seat, paused a few seconds to look about for one. She soon espied an unoccupied seat. She proceeded to it, but her slight difficulty had been noted by the white passengers.

Belton happened to glance around and saw a group of white men in an eager, animated conversation, and looking in his direction now and then as they talked. He paid no especial attention to this, however, and kept on reading. Before he was aware of what was going on, he was surrounded by a group of angry men. He stood up in surprise to discover its meaning. "Get out of this coach. We don't allow niggers in first-class coaches. Get out at once," said their spokesman.

"Show me your authority to order me out, sir," said Belton firmly.

"We are our own authority, as you will soon find out if you don't get out of here."

"I propose," said Belton, "to stay right in this coach as long—" He did not finish the sentence, for rough fingers were clutching his throat. The whole group was upon him in an instant and he was soon overpowered. They dragged him into the aisle, and, some at his head and others at his feet, lifted him and bore him to the door. The train was speeding along at a rapid rate. Belton grew somewhat quiet in his struggling, thinking to renew it in the second-class coach, whither he supposed they were carrying him. But when they got to the platform, instead of carrying him across they tossed him off the train into that muddy ditch at which Belton had been looking. His body and feet fell into the water while his head buried itself in the soft clay bed.

The train was speeding on and Belton eventually succeeded in extricating himself from his bed of mud and water. Covered from head to foot with red clay, the president-elect of Cadeville College walked down to the next station, two miles away. There he found his satchel, left by the conductor of the train. He remained at this station until the afternoon, when another train passed. This time he entered the second-class coach and rode unmolested to Monroe, Louisiana. There he was to have changed cars for Cadeville. The morning train, the one from which he was thrown, made connection with the Cadeville train, but the afternoon train did not. So he was under the necessity of remaining over night in the city of Monroe, a place of some twenty thousand inhabitants.

Being hungry, he went forth in quest of a meal. He entered a restaurant and asked the white man whom he saw behind the counter for a meal. The white man stepped into a small adjoining room to fill the order, and Belton eat down on a high stool at the eating counter. The white man soon returned with some articles of food in a paper bag. Seeing Belton sitting down, he cried out: "Get up from there, you nigger. It would cost me a hundred dollars for you to be seen sitting there."

Belton looked up in astonishment, "Do you mean to say that I must stand up here and eat?" he asked.

"No, I don't mean any such thing. You must go out of here to eat."

"Then," replied Belton, "I shall politely leave your food on your hands if I cannot be allowed to eat in here."

"I guess you won't," the man replied. "I have cut this ham off for you and you have got to take it."

Belton, remembering his experience earlier in the day, began to move toward the door to leave. The man seized a whistle and in an instant two or three policemen came running, followed by a crowd. Belton stood still to await developments. The clerk said to the policeman: "This high-toned nigger bought a meal of me and because I would not let him sit down and eat like white people he refused to pay me."

The officers turned to Belton and said: "Pay that man what you owe him."

Belton replied: "I owe him nothing. He refuses to accommodate me, and I therefore owe him nothing."

"Come along with me, sir. Consider yourself under arrest."

Wondering what kind of a country he had entered, Belton followed the officer and incredible as it may seem, was locked up in jail for the night. The next morning he was arraigned before the mayor, whom the officer had evidently posted before the opening of court. Belton was fined five dollars for vagrancy and was ordered to leave town within five hours. He paid his fine and boarded the train for Cadeville.

As the train pulled in for Cadeville, a group of white men were seen standing on the platform. One of them was a thin, scrawny looking man with a long beard, very, very white. His body was slightly stooping forward, and whenever he looked at you he had the appearance of bending as if to see you better. When Belton stepped on to the platform this man, who was the village doctor, looked at him keenly.

Belton was a fine specimen of physical manhood. His limbs were well formed, well proportioned and seemed as strong as oak. His manly appearance always excited interest wherever he was seen. The doctor's eyes followed him cadaverously. He went up to the postmaster, a short man with a large head. The postmaster was president of the band of "Nigger Rulers" of that section.

The doctor said to the postmaster: "I'll be durned if that ain't the finest lookin' darkey I ever put my eye on. If I could get his body to dissect, I'd give one of the finest kegs of whiskey in my cellar."

The postmaster looked at Belton and said: "Zakeland," for such was the doctor's name, "you are right. He is a fine looking chap, and he looks a little tony. If we 'nigger rulers' are ever called in to attend to him we will not burn him nor shoot him to pieces. We will kill him kinder decent and let you have him to dissect. I shall not fail to call for that whiskey to treat the boys." So saying they parted.

Belton did not hear this murderous conversation respecting himself. He was joyfully received by the colored people of Cadeville, to whom he related his experiences. They looked at him as though he was a superior being bearing a charmed life, having escaped being killed. It did not come to their minds to be surprised at the treatment accorded him for what he had done. Their wonder was as to how he got off so easily.

Belton took charge of the school and began the faithful performance of his duties. He decided to add an industrial department to his school and traveled over the state and secured the funds for the work. He sent to New Orleans for a colored architect and contractor who drew the plans and accepted the contract for erecting the building.

They decided to have colored men erect the building and gathered a force for that purpose. The white brick-masons of Monroe heard of this. They organized a mob, came to Cadeville and ordered the men to quit work. They took charge of the work themselves, letting the colored brick-masons act as hod carriers for them. They employed a white man to supervise the work. The colored people knew that it meant death to resist and they paid the men as though nothing unusual had happened.

Belton had learned to observe and wait. These outrages sank like molten lead into his heart, but he bore them all. The time for the presidential election was drawing near and he arose in the chapel one morning to lecture to the young men on their duty to vote.

One of the village girls told her father of Belton's speech. The old man was shaving his face and had just shaved off one side of his beard when his daughter told him. He did not stop to pull the towel from around his neck nor to put down his razor. He rushed over to the house where Belton boarded and burst into his room. Belton threw up his hands in alarm at seeing this man come, razor in hand, towel around his neck and beard half off and half on. The man sat down to catch his breath. He began: "Mr. Piedmont, I learn that you are advising our young men to vote. I am sure you don't know in what danger you stand. I have come to give you the political history of this section of Louisiana. The colored people of this region far outnumber the white people, and years ago had absolute control of everything. The whites of course did not tamely submit, but armed themselves to overthrow us. We armed ourselves, and every night patrolled this road all night long looking for the whites to come and attack us. My oldest brother is a very cowardly and sycophantic man. The white people made a spy and traitor out of him. When the people found out that there was treachery in our ranks it demoralized them, and our organization went to pieces.

"We had not the authority nor disposition to kill a traitor, and consequently we had no effective remedy against a betrayal. When the news of our demoralized condition reached the whites it gave them fresh courage, and they have dominated us ever since. They carry on the elections. We stay in our fields all day long on election day and scarcely know what is going on. Not long since a white man came through here and distributed republican ballots. The white people captured him and cut his body into four pieces and threw it in the Ouachita River. Since then you can't get any man to venture here to distribute ballots.

"Just before the last presidential campaign, two brothers, Samuel and John Bowser, colored, happened to go down to New Orleans. Things are not so bad down there as they are up here in Northern Louisiana. These two brothers each secured a republican party ballot, and on election day somewhat boastfully cast them into the ballot box. There is, as you have perhaps heard, a society here known as 'Nigger Rulers.' The postmaster of this place is president of the society, and the teacher of the white public school is the captain of the army thereof.

"They sent word to the Bowser brothers that they would soon be there to whip them. The brothers prepared to meet them. They cut a hole in the front side of the house, through which they could poke a gun. Night came on, and true to their word the 'Nigger Rulers' came. Samuel Bowser fired when they were near the house and one man fell dead. All of the rest fled to the cover of the neighboring woods. Soon they cautiously returned and bore away their dead comrade. They made no further attack that night.

"The brothers hid out in the woods. Hearing of this and fearing that the men would make their escape the whites gathered in force and hemmed in the entire settlement on all sides. For three days the men hid in the woods, unable to escape because of the guard kept by the whites. The third night a great rain came up and the whites sought the shelter of their homes.

"The brothers thus had a chance to escape. John escaped into Arkansas, but Samuel, poor fool, went only forty miles, remaining in Louisiana. The mob forced one of our number, who escorted him on horseback, to inform them of the road that Samuel took. In this way they traced and found him. They tied him on a horse and brought him back here with them. They kept him in the woods three days, torturing him. On the third day we heard the loud report of a gun which we supposed ended his life. None of us know where he lies buried. You can judge from this why we neglect voting."

This speech wound up Belton's political career in Cadeville. He thanked the man for the information, assuring him that it would be of great value to him in knowing how to shape his course.

After Belton had been at Cadeville a few years, he had a number of young men and women to graduate from the various departments of his school. He invited the pastor of a leading white church of Monroe to deliver an oration on the day of commencement exercises. The preacher came and was most favorably impressed with Belton's work, as exhibited in the students then graduating. He esteemed Belton as a man of great intellectual power and invited him to call at his church and house if he ever came to Monroe.

Belton was naturally greatly elated over this invitation from a Southerner and felt highly complimented. One Sabbath morning, shortly thereafter, Belton happened to be in Monroe, and thinking of the preacher's kind invitation, went to his church to attend the morning service. He entered and took a seat near the middle of the church.

During the opening exercises a young white lady who sat by his side experienced some trouble in finding the hymn. Belton had remembered the number given out and kindly took the book to find it. In an instant the whole church was in an uproar. A crowd of men gathered around Belton and led him out of doors. A few leaders went off to one side and held a short consultation. They decided that as it was Sunday, they would not lynch him. They returned to the body of men yet holding Belton and ordered him released. This evidently did not please the majority, but he was allowed to go.

That afternoon Belton called at the residence of the minister in order to offer an explanation. The minister opened the door, and seeing who it was, slammed it in his face. Belton turned away with many misgivings as to what was yet to come. Dr. Zackland always spent his Sundays at Monroe and was a witness of the entire scene in which Belton had figured so prominently. He hastened out of church, and as soon as he saw Belton turned loose, hurried to the station and boarded the train for Cadeville, leaving his hymn book and Bible on his seat in the church. His face seemed lighted up with joy. "I've got him at last. Careful as he has been I've got him," he kept repeating over and over to himself.

He left the train at Cadeville and ran to the postmaster's house, president of the "Nigger Rulers," and he was out of breath when he arrived there. He sat down, fanned himself with his hat, and when sufficiently recovered, said: "Well, we will have to fix that nigger, Piedmont. He is getting too high."

"What's that he has been doing now? I have looked upon him as being an uncommonly good nigger. I have kept a good eye on him but haven't even had to hint at him," said the postmaster."

"Well, he has shown his true nature at last. He had the gall to enter a white church in Monroe this morning and actually took a seat down stairs with the white folks; he did not even look at the gallery where he belonged."

"Is that so?" burst out the postmaster incredulously.

"I should say he did, and that's not all. A white girl who sat by him and could not read very well, failed to find the hymn at once. That nigger actually had the impudence to take her book and find the place for her."

"The infernal scoundrel. By golly, he shall hang," broke in the postmaster.

Dr. Zackland continued: "Naturally the congregation was infuriated and soon hustled the impudent scoundrel out. If services had not been going on, and if it had not been Sunday, there is no telling what would have happened. As it was they turned him loose. I came here to tell you, as he is our 'Nigger' living here at Cadeville, and the 'Nigger Rulers' of Cadeville will be disrespected if they let such presumptuous niggers go about to disturb religious services."

"You are right about that, and we must soon put him out of the way. To-night will be his last night on earth," replied the postmaster.

"Do you remember our bargain that we made about that nigger when he came about here?" asked Dr. Zackland.

"No," answered the postmaster.

"Well, I do. I have been all along itching for a chance to carry it out. You were to give me the nigger's body for dissecting purposes, in return for which I was to give you a keg of my best whiskey," said Dr. Zackland.

"Ha, ha, ha," laughed the postmaster, "I do remember it now."

"Well, I'll certainly stick up to my part of the program if you will stick to yours."

"You can bet on me," returned Dr. Zackland. "I have a suggestion to make about the taking off of the nigger. Don't have any burning or riddling with bullets. Just hang him and fire one shot in the back of his head. I want him whole in the interest of society. That whiskey will be the finest that you will ever have and I want a good bargain for it."

"I'll follow your instructions to the letter," answered the postmaster. "I'll just tell the boys that he, being a kind of decent nigger, we will give him a decent hanging. Meantime, Doctor, I must get out. To-day is Sunday and we must do our work to-morrow night. I must get a meeting of the boys to-night." So saying, the two arose, left the house and parted, one going to gather up his gang and the other to search up and examine his dissecting appliances.

Monday night about 9 o'clock a mob came and took Belton out into the neighboring woods. He was given five minutes to pray, at the expiration of which time he was to be hanged. Belton seemed to have foreseen the coming of the mob, but felt somehow that God was at work to deliver him. Therefore he made no resistance, having unshaken faith in God.

The rope was adjusted around his neck and thrown over the limb of a tree and Belton was swinging up. The postmaster then slipped forward and fired his pistol at the base of his skull and the blood came oozing forth. He then ordered the men to retire, as he did not care for them to remain to shoot holes in the body, as was their custom.

As soon as they retired, three men sent by Dr. Zackland stole out of hiding and cut Belton's body down. Belton was not then dead, for he had only been hanging for seven minutes, and the bullet had not entered the skull but had simply ploughed its way under the skin. He was, however, unconscious, and to all appearances dead.

The three men bore him to Dr. Zackland's residence, and entered a rear door. They laid him on a dissecting table in the rear room, the room in which the doctor performed all surgical operations.

Dr. Zackland came to the table and looked down on Belton with a happy smile. To have such a robust, well-formed, handsome nigger to dissect and examine he regarded as one of the greatest boons of his medical career.

The three men started to retire. "Wait," said Dr. Zackland, "let us see if he is dead."

Belton had now returned to consciousness but kept his eyes closed, thinking it best to feign death. Dr. Zackland cut off the hair in the neighborhood of the wound in the rear of Belton's head and began cutting the skin, trying to trace the bullet. Belton did not wince.

"The nigger is dead or else he would show some sign of life. But I will try pricking his palm." This was done, but while the pain was exceedingly excruciating, Belton showed no sign of feeling. "You may go now," said the doctor to his three attendants, "he is certainly dead."

The men left. Dr. Zackland pulled out his watch and said: "It is now 10 o'clock. Those doctors from Monroe will be here by twelve. I can have everything exactly ready by that time."

A bright ray of hope passed into Belton's bosom. He had two hours more of life, two hours more in which to plan an escape. Dr. Zackland was busy stirring about over the room. He took a long, sharp knife and gazed at its keen edge. He placed this on the dissecting table near Belton's feet. He then passed out of doors to get a pail of water, and left the door ajar.

He went to his cabinet to get out more surgical instruments, and his back was now turned to Belton and he was absorbed in what he was doing. Belton's eyes had followed every movement, but in order to escape attention his eyelids were only slightly open. He now raised himself up, seized the knife that was near his feet and at a bound was at the doctor's side.

The doctor turned around and was in dread alarm at the sight of the dead man returned to life. At that instant he was too terrified to act or scream, and before he could recover his self-possession Belton plunged the knife through his throat. Seizing the dying man he laid him on the dissecting board and covered him over with a sheet.

He went to the writing desk and quickly scrawled the following note.

> "DOCTORS:
> "I have stepped out for a short while.
> Don't touch the nigger until I come.
> "Zackland."

He pinned this note on that portion of the sheet where it would attract attention at once if one should begin to uncover the corpse. He did this to delay discovery and thus get a good start on those who might pursue him.

Having done this he crept cautiously out of the room, leapt the back fence and made his way to his boarding place. He here changed his clothes and disappeared in the woods. He made his way to Baton Rouge and sought a conference with the Governor. The Governor ordered him under arrest and told him that the best and only thing he could do was to send him back to Cadeville under military escort to be tried for murder.

This was accordingly done. The community was aroused over the death of Dr. Zackland at the hands of a negro. The sending of the military further incensed them. At the trial which followed, all evidence respecting the mob was excluded as irrelevant. Robbery was the motive assigned for the deed. The whole family with which Belton lived were arraigned as accomplices, because his bloody clothes were found in his room in their house.

During the trial, the jury were allowed to walk about and mingle freely with the people and be thus influenced by the bitter public sentiment against Belton. Men who were in the mob that attempted Belton's murder were on the jury. In fact, the postmaster was the foreman. Without leaving their seats the jury returned a verdict of guilty in each case and all were sentenced to be hanged.

The prisoners were taken to the New Orleans jail for safe keeping. While incarcerated here awaiting the day of execution, a newspaper reporter of a liberal New Orleans paper called on the prisoners. He was impressed with Belton's personality and promised to publish any statement that Belton would write. Belton then gave a thorough detailed account of every happening. The story was telegraphed broadcast and aroused sympathetic interest everywhere.

Bernard read an account of it and hastened to his friend's side in New Orleans. In response to a telegram from Bernard a certain influential democratic senator came to New Orleans. Influence was brought to bear, and though all precedent was violated, the case was manoeuvred to the Supreme Court of the United States. Before this tribunal Bernard made the speech of his life and added to his fame as an orator. Competent judges said that the like of it had not been heard since the days of Daniel Webster.

As he pleaded for his friend and the others accused the judges of the Supreme Court wept scalding tears. Bernard told of Belton's noble life, his unassuming ways, his pure Christianity. The decision of the lower court was reversed, a change of venue granted, a new trial held and an acquittal secured.

Thus ended the tragic experience that burned all the remaining dross out of Belton's nature and prepared him for the even more terrible ordeal to follow in after years.

Chapter XIII
Married and Yet Not Married

BERNARD WAS NOW at the very acme of fame. He had succeeded in becoming the most noted negro of his day. He felt that the time was not ripe for him to gather up his wealth and honors and lay them, with his heart, at Viola's feet. One afternoon he invited Viola to go out buggy riding with him, and decided to lay bare his heart to her before their return home. They drove out of Norfolk over Campostella bridge and went far into the country, chatting pleasantly, oblivious of the farm hands preparing the soil for seed sowing; for it was in balmy spring. About eight o'clock they were returning to the city and Bernard felt his veins throbbing; for he had determined to know his fate before he reached Viola's home. When midway the bridge he pulled his reins and the horse stood still. The dark waters of the small river swept on beneath them. Night had just begun to spread out her sombre wings, bedecked with silent stars. Just in front of them, as they looked out upon the center of the river, the river took a bend which brought a shore directly facing them. A green lawn began from the shore and ran back to be lost in the shadows of the evening. Amid a group of trees, there stood a little hut that looked to be the hut of an old widower, for it appeared neglected, forsaken, sad.

Bernard gazed at this lonesome cottage and said: "Viola, I feel to-night that all my honors are empty. They feel to me like a load crushing me down rather than a pedestal raising me up. I am not happy. I long for the solitude of those trees. That decaying old house calls eloquently unto something within me. How I would like to enter there and lay me down to sleep, free from the cares and divested of the gewgaws of the world."

Viola was startled by these sombre reflections coming from Bernard. She decided that something must be wrong. She was, by nature, exceedingly tender of heart, and she turned her pretty eyes in astonished grief at Bernard, handsome, melancholy, musing.

"Ah, Mr. Belgrave, something terrible is gnawing at your heart for one so young, so brilliant, so prosperous as you are to talk thus. Make a confidante of me and let me help to remove the load, if I can."

Bernard was silent and eat gazing out on the quiet flowing waters. Viola's eyes eagerly scanned his face as if to divine his secret.

Bernard resumed speaking: "I have gone forth into life to win certain honors and snatch from fame a wreath, and now that I have succeeded, I behold this evening, as never before, that it is not worthy of the purpose for which I designed it. My work is all in vain."

"Mr. Belgrave, you must not talk so sadly," said Viola, almost ready to cry.

Bernard turned and suddenly grasped Viola's hands and said in passionate tones: "Viola, I love you. I have nothing to offer you worthy of you. I can find nothing worthy, attain nothing worthy. I love you to desperation. Will you give yourself to a wretch like me? Say no! don't throw away your beauty, your love on so common a piece of clay."

Viola uttered a loud, piercing scream that dispersed all Bernard's thoughts and frightened the horse. He went dashing across the bridge, Bernard endeavoring to grasp the reins. When he at last succeeded, Viola had fainted. Bernard drove hurriedly towards Viola's home, puzzled beyond measure. He had never heard of a marriage proposal frightening a girl into a faint and he thought that there was surely something in the matter of which he knew nothing. Then, too, he was racking his brain for an excuse to give Viola's parents. But happily the cool air revived Viola and she awoke trembling violently and begged Bernard to take her home at once. This he did and drove away, much puzzled in mind.

He revived the whole matter in his mind, and thoughts and opinions came and went. Perhaps she deemed him utterly unworthy of her. There was one good reason for this last opinion and one good one against it. He felt himself to be unworthy of such a girl, but on the other hand Viola had frequently sung his praises in his own ears and in the ears of others. He decided to go early in the morning and know definitely his doom.

That night he did not sleep. He paced up and down the room glancing at the clock every five minutes or so. He would now and then hoist the window and strain his eyes to see if there were any sign of approaching dawn. After what seemed to him at least a century, the sun at last arose and ushered in the day. As soon as he thought Miss Martin was astir and unengaged, he was standing at the door. They each looked sad and forlorn. Viola knew and Bernard felt that some dark shadow was to come between them.

Viola caught hold of Bernard's hand and led him silently into the parlor. Bernard sat down on the divan and Viola took a seat thereon close by his side. She turned her charming face, sweet in its sadness, up to Bernard's and whispered "kiss me, Bernard."

Bernard seized her and kissed her rapturously. She then arose and sat in a chair facing him, at a distance.

She then said calmly, determinedly, almost icily, looking Bernard squarely in the face: "Bernard, you know that I love you. It was I that asked you to kiss me. Always remember that. But as much as I love you I shall never be your wife. Never, never."

Bernard arose and started toward Viola. He paused and gazed down upon that beautiful image that sat before him and said in anguish: "Oh God! Is all my labor in vain, my honors common dirt, my future one dreary waste? Shall I lose that which has been an ever shining, never setting sun to me? Viola! If you love me you shall be my wife."

Viola bowed her head and shook it sadly, saying: "A power higher than either you or I has decreed it otherwise."

"Who is he? Tell me who he is that dare separate us and I swear I will kill him," cried Bernard in a frenzy of rage.

Viola looked up, her eyes swimming in tears, and said: "Would you kill God?"

This question brought Bernard to his senses and he returned to his seat and sat down suddenly. He then said: "Viola Martin, you are making a fool of me. Tell me plainly why we cannot be man and wife, if you love me as you say you do?"

"Bernard, call here to-morrow at 10 o'clock and I will tell you all. If you can then remove my objections all will be well."

Bernard leaped up eager to get away, feeling that that would somewhat hasten the time for him to return. Viola did not seem to share his feelings of elation. But he did not mind that. He felt himself fully able to demolish any and all objections that Viola could bring. He went home and spent the day perusing his text-book on logic. He would conjure up imaginary objections and would proceed to demolish them in short order. He slept somewhat that night, anticipating a decisive victory on the morrow.

When Bernard left Viola that morning, she threw herself prostrate on the floor, moaning and sobbing. After a while she arose and went to the dining room door. She looked in upon her mother, quietly sewing, and tried to say in a cheerful manner: "Mamma, I shall be busy writing all day in my room. Let no one disturb me." Her mother looked at her gently and lovingly and assured her that no one should disturb her. Her mother surmised that all had not gone well with her and Bernard, and that Viola was wrestling with her grief. Knowing that spats were common to young people in love she supposed it would soon be over.

Viola went upstairs and entered her room. This room, thanks to Viola's industry and exquisite taste, was the beauty spot of the whole house. Pictures of her own painting adorned the walls, and scattered here and there in proper places were articles of fancy work put together in most lovely manner by her delicate fingers. Viola was fond of flowers and her room was alive with the scent of pretty flowers and beautiful roses. This room was a fitting scene for what was to follow. She opened her tiny writing desk. She wrote a letter to her father, one to her mother and one to Bernard. Her letter to Bernard had to be torn up and re-written time and again, for fast falling tears spoiled it almost as fast as she wrote. At last she succeeded in finishing his letter to her satisfaction.

At eventide she came down stairs and with her mother, sat on the rear porch and saw the sun glide gently out of sight, without a struggle, without a murmur. Her eye lingered long on the spot where the sun had set and watched the hidden sun gradually steal all of his rays from the skies to use them in another world. Drawing a heavy sigh, she lovingly caught her mother around the waist and led her into the parlor. Viola now became all gayety, but her mother could see that it was forced. She took a seat at the piano and played and sang. Her rich soprano voice rang out clear and sweet and passers by paused to listen to the glorious strains. Those who paused to hear her sing passed on feeling sad at heart. Beginning in somewhat low tones, her voice gradually swelled and the full, round tones full of melody and pathos seemed to lift up and bear one irresistibly away.

Viola's mother sat by and looked with tender solicitude on her daughter singing and playing as she had never before in her life. "What did it mean?" she asked herself. When Viola's father came from the postoffice, where he was a clerk, Viola ran to him joyously. She pulled him into the parlor and sat on his knee stroking his chin and nestling her head on his bosom. She made him tell her tales as he did when she was a child and she would laugh, but her laugh did not have its accustomed clear, golden ring.

Kissing them good night, she started up to her bed room. When at the head of the stairway she returned and without saying a word kissed her parents again.

When she was gone, the parents looked at each other and shook their heads. They knew that Viola was feeling keenly on account of something but felt that her cheerful nature would soon throw it off. But the blade was in her heart deeper than they knew. Viola entered her room, fastening the door behind her. She went to her desk, secured the three letters that she had written and placed them on the floor a few inches apart in a position where they would attract immediate attention upon entering the room. She then lay down upon her bed and put one arm across her bosom. With her other hand she turned on the gas jet by the head of her bed. She then placed this other hand across her bosom and ere long fell asleep to wake no more.

The moon arose and shed its sad, quiet light through the half turned shutters, through the window pane. It seemed to force its way in in order to linger and weep over such queenly beauty, such worth, meeting with such an accursed end.

Thus in this forbidden path Viola Martin had gone to him who said: "Come unto Me all ye that labor and are heavy laden, and I will give you rest."

Chapter XIV
Married and Yet Not Married (Continued)

AT TEN O'CLOCK on the next day, Bernard called at Viola's residence. Viola's mother invited him in and informed him that Viola had not arisen. Thinking that her daughter had spent much of the night in meditating on whatever was troubling her, She had thought not to awaken her so early. Bernard informed her that Viola had made an engagement with him for that morning at ten o'clock. Mrs. Martin looked alarmed. She knew that Viola was invariably punctual to an appointment and something unusual must be the matter. She left the room hurriedly and her knees smote together as she fancied she discovered the scent of escaping gas. She clung to the banisters for support and dragged her way to Viola's door. As she drew near, the smell of gas became unmistakable, and she fell forward, uttering a loud scream. Bernard had noticed the anxious look on Viola's mother's face and was listening eagerly. He beard her scream and dashed out of the parlor and up the stairs. He rushed past Mrs. Martin and burst open the door to Viola's door. He drew back aghast at the sight that met his gaze. The next instant he had seized her lifeless form, beautiful in death, and smothered those silent lips with kisses.

Mrs. Martin regained sufficient strength to rush into the room, and when she saw her child was dead uttered a succession of piercing shrieks and fell to the floor in a swoon.

This somewhat called Bernard's mind from his own grief. He lay Viola down upon her own bed most tenderly and set about to restore Mrs. Martin to consciousness. By this time the room was full of anxious neighbors.

While they are making inquiry let us peruse the letters which the poor girl left behind.

"MY DEAR, DEAR, HEART-BROKEN MAMA:

"I am in the hands of God. Whatever He does is just, is right, is the only thing to be done. Knowing this, do not grieve after me. Take poor Bernard for your son and love him as you did me. I make that as my sole dying request of you. One long sweet clinging kiss ere I drop into the ocean of death to be lost in its tossing waves.
"Viola."

"BELOVED PAPA:

"Your little daughter is gone. Her heart, though torn, bleeding, dead, gave, as it were, an after throb of pain as it thought of you. In life you never denied me a request. I have one to make from my grave, knowing that you will not deny me. Love Bernard as your son; draw him to you, so that, when in your old age you go tottering to your tomb in quest of me, you may have a son to bear you up. Take my lifeless body on your knee and kiss me as you did of old. It will help me to rest sweetly in my grave.
"Your little Vie."

"DEAR BERNARD:

"Viola has loved and left you. Unto you, above all others, I owe a full explanation of the deed which I have committed; and I shall therefore lay bare my heart to you. My father was a colonel in the Civil War and when I was very young he would make my little heart thrill with patriotic fervor as he told me of the deeds of daring of the gallant Negro soldiers. As a result, when nothing but a tiny girl, I determined to be a heroine and find some outlet for my patriotic feeling. This became a consuming passion. In 18— just two years prior to my meeting you, a book entitled, 'White Supremacy and Negro Subordination,' by the

merest accident came into my possession. That book made a revelation to me of a most startling nature.

"While I lived I could not tell you what I am about to tell you. Death has brought me the privilege. That book proved to me that the intermingling of the races in sexual relationship was sapping the vitality of the Negro race and, in fact, was slowly but surely exterminating the race. It demonstrated that the fourth generation of the children born of intermarrying mulattoes were invariably sterile or woefully lacking in vital force. It asserted that only in the most rare instances were children born of this fourth generation and in no case did such children reach maturity. This is a startling revelation. While this intermingling was impairing the vital force of our race and exterminating it, it was having no such effect on the white race for the following reason. Every half-breed, or for that, every person having a tinge of Negro blood, the white people cast off. We receive the cast off with open arms and he comes to us with his devitalizing power. Thus, the white man was slowly exterminating us and our total extinction was but a short period of time distant. I looked out upon our strong, tender hearted, manly race being swept from the face of the earth by immorality, and the very marrow in my bones seemed chilled at the thought thereof. I determined to spend my life fighting the evil. My first step was to solemnly pledge God to never marry a mulatto man. My next resolve was to part in every honorable way all courting couples of mulatto people that I could. My other and greatest task was to persuade the evil women of my race to cease their criminal conduct with white men and I went about pleading with them upon my knees to desist. I pointed out that such a course was wrong before God and was rapidly destroying the Negro race. I told them of my resolve to never marry a mulatto man. Many had faith in me and I was the means of redeeming numbers of these erring ones. When you came, I loved you. I struggled hard against that love. God, alone, knows how I battled against it. I prayed Him to take it from me, as it was eating my heart away. Sometimes I would appear indifferent to you with the hope of driving you away, but then my love would come surging with all the more violence and sweep me from my feet. At last, you seemed to draw away from me and I was happy. I felt free to you. But you at last proposed to me when I thought all such notions were dead. At once I foresaw my tragic end. My heart shed bloody tears, weeping over my own sad end, weeping for my beloved parents, weeping for my noble Bernard who was so true, so noble, so great in all things.

"Bernard, how happy would I have been, how deliriously happy, could I but have stood beside you at the altar and sworn fidelity to you. Ours would have been an ideal home. But it was not to be. I had to choose between you and my race. Your noble heart, in its sober moments will sanction my choice, I would not have died if I could have lived without proving false to my race. Had I lived, my love and your agony, which I cannot bear, would have made me prove false to every vow.

"Dear Bernard, I have a favor to ask of you. Secure the book of which I spoke to you. Study the question of the intermingling of the races. If miscegenation is in reality destroying us, dedicate your soul to the work of separating the white and colored races. Do not let them intermingle. Erect moral barriers to separate them. If you fail in this, make the separation physical; lead our people forth from this accursed land. Do this and I shall not have died in vain. Visit my grave now and then to drop thereon a flower and a flag, but no tears. If in the shadowy beyond, whose mists I feel gathering about me, there is a place where kindred spirits meet, you and I shall surely meet again. Though I could not in life, I will in death sign myself,

"Your loving wife,

"Viola Belgrave."

Let us not enter this saddened home when the seals of those letters were broken. Let us not break the solemn silence of those who bowed their heads and bore the grief, too poignant for words. Dropping a tear of regret on the little darling who failed to remember that we have one atonement for all mankind and that further sacrifice was therefore needless, we pass out and leave the loving ones alone with their dead.

But, we may gaze on Bernard Belgrave as he emerges from the room where his sun has set to rise no more. His eyes flash, his nostrils dilate, his bosom heaves, he lifts his proud head and turns his face so that the light of the sky may fall full upon it.

And lifting up his hands, trembling with emotion as though supplicating for the strength of a god, he cries out; "By the eternal heavens these abominable horrors shall cease. The races, whose union has been fraught with every curse known to earth and hell, must separate. Viola demands it and Bernard obeys." It was this that sent him forth to where kings were eager to court his favor.

Chapter XV
Weighty Matters

WITH HIS HANDS thrust into his pockets, and his hat pulled over his grief stricken eyes, Bernard slowly wended his way to his boarding place.

He locked himself in his room and denied himself to all callers. He paced to and fro, his heart a cataract of violent, tossing, whirling emotions. He sat down and leaned his head upon the bed, pressing his hand to his forehead as if to restore order there. While thus employed his landlady knocked at the door and called through the key hole, informing him that there was a telegram for him. Bernard arose, came out, signed for and received the telegram, tore it open and read as follows:

Waco, Texas, — 18—
"HON. BERNARD BELGRAVE, M.C.,
"Come to Waco at once. If you fail to come you will make the mistake of your life. Come.
"BELTON PIEDMONT."

"Yes, I'll go," shouted Bernard, "anywhere, for anything." He seemed to feel grateful for something to divert his thoughts and call him away from the scene where his hopes had died. He sent Viola's family a note truthfully stating that he was unequal to the task of attending Viola's funeral, and that for his part she was not dead and never should be. The parents had read Bernard's letter left by Viola and knew the whole story. They, too, felt that it was best for Bernard to go. Bernard took the train that afternoon and after a journey of four days arrived at Waco.

Belton being apprised by telegram of the hour of his arrival, was at the station to meet him. Belton was actually shocked at the haggard appearance of his old play-fellow. It was such a contrast from the brilliant, glowing, handsome Bernard of former days.

After the exchange of greetings, they entered a carriage and drove through the city. They passed out, leaving the city behind. After going about five miles, they came in sight of a high stone wall enclosure. In the middle of the enclosed place, upon a slight elevation, stood a building four stories high and about two hundred feet long and one hundred and eighty feet wide. In the center of the front side arose a round tower, half of it bulging out. This extended from the ground to a point about twenty feet above the roof of the building. The entrance to the building was through a wide door in this tower. Off a few paces was a small white cottage. Here and there trees abounded in patches in the enclosure, which seemed to comprise about twenty acres.

The carriage drove over a wide, gravel driveway which curved so as to pass the tower door, and on out to another gate. Belton and Bernard alighted and proceeded to enter. Carved in large letters on the top of the stone steps were these words: "Thomas Jefferson College." They entered the tower and found themselves on the floor of an elevator, and on this they ascended to the fourth story. The whole of this story was one huge room, devoid of all kinds of furniture save a table and two chairs in a corner. In the center was an elevated platform about ten feet square, and on this stood what might have passed for either a gallows or an acting pole.

Belton led Bernard to the spot where the two chairs and table stood and they sat down. Belton informed Bernard that he had brought him there so that there would be no possibility of anyone hearing what, he had to say. Bernard instantly became all attention. Belton began his recital: "I have been so fortunate as to unearth a foul conspiracy that is being hatched by our people. I have decided to expose them and see every one of them hung,"

"Pray tell me, Belton, what is the motive that prompts you to be so zealous in the work of ferreting out conspirators among your people to be hanged by the whites?"

"It is this," said Belton: "you know as it is, the Negro has a hard time in this country. If we begin to develop traitors and conspirators we shall fare even worse. It is necessary, therefore, that we kill these vipers that come, lest we all be slain as vipers."

"That may be true, but I don't like to see you in that kind of business," said Bernard.

"Don't talk that way," said Belton, "for I counted upon your aid. I desire to secure you as prosecuting attorney in the case. When we thus expose the traitors, we shall earn the gratitude of the government and our race will be treated with more consideration in the future. We will add another page to the glorious record of our people's devotion by thus spurning these traitors."

"Belton, I tell you frankly that my share in that kind of business will be infinitessimally small. But go on. Let me know the whole story, that I may know better what to think and do," replied Bernard.

"Well, it is this," began Belton; "you know that there is one serious flaw in the Constitution of the United States, which has already caused a world of trouble, and there is evidently a great deal more to come. You know that a ship's boilers, engines, rigging, and so forth may be in perfect condition, but a serious leak in her bottom will sink the proudest vessel afloat. This flaw or defect in the Constitution of the United States is the relation of the General Government to the individual state. The vague, unsettled state of the relationship furnished the pretext for the Civil War. The General Government says to the citizen: 'I am your sovereign. You are my citizen and not the citizen of only one state. If I call on you to defend my sovereignty, you must do so even if you have to fight against your own state. But while I am your supreme earthly sovereign I am powerless to protect you against crimes, injustices, outrages against you. Your state may disfranchise you with or without law, may mob you; but my hands are so tied that I can't help you at all, although I shall force you to defend my sovereignty with your lives. If you are beset by Klu Klux, White Cappers, Bulldozers, Lynchers, do not turn your dying eyes on me for I am unable to help you.' Such is what the Federal Government has to say to the Negro. The Negro must therefore fight to keep afloat a flag that can afford him no more protection than could a helpless baby. The weakness of the General Government in this particular was revealed with startling clearness in connection with the murder of those Italians in New Orleans, a few years ago. This government had promised Italy to afford protection to the property and lives of her citizens sojourning in our midst. But when these men were murdered the General Government could not even bring the murderers to trial for their crime. Its treaty had been broken by a handful of its own citizens and it was powerless to punish them. It had to confess its impotence to the world, and paid Italy a specified sum of money. The Negro finds himself an unprotected foreigner in his own home. Whatever outrages may be perpetrated upon him by the people of the state in which he lives, he cannot expect any character of redress from the General Government. So in order to supply this needed protection, this conspiracy of which I have spoken has been formed to attempt to unite all Negroes in a body to do that which the whimpering government childishly but truthfully says it cannot do.

"These men are determined to secure protection for their lives and the full enjoyment of all rights and privileges due American citizens. They take a solemn oath, offering their very blood for the cause. I see that this will lead, eventually, to a clash of arms, and I wish to expose the conspiracy before it is too late. Cooperate with me and glory and honor shall attend us all of our days. Now, Bernard, tell me candidly what you think of the whole matter. May I not rely on you?"

"Well, let me tell you just exactly what I think and just what I shall do," thundered Bernard, rising as he spoke. Pointing his finger at Belton, he said: "I think, sir, that you are the most infernal scoundrel that I ever saw, and those whom you call conspirators are a set of sublime patriots; and further," hissed Bernard in rage through his teeth, "if you betray those men, I will kill you."

To Bernard's surprise Belton did not seem enraged as Bernard thought he would be. Knowing Belton's spirit he had expected an encounter after such words as he had just spoken.

Belton looked indifferent and unconcerned, and arose, as if to yawn, when suddenly he threw himself on Bernard with the agility of a tiger and knocked him to the floor. From secret closets in the room sprang six able bodied men. They soon had Bernard securely bound. Belton then told Bernard that he must retract what he had said and agree to keep his revealed purpose a secret or he would never leave that room alive.

"Then I shall die, and my only regret will be that I shall die at the hands of such an abominable wretch as you are," was Bernard's answer.

Bernard was stood against the wall. The six men retired to their closets and returned with rifles. Bernard gazed at the men unflinchingly. They formed a line, ten paces in front of him. Belton gave Bernard one last chance, as he said, to save his life, by silence as to his plans.

Bernard said: "If I live I shall surely proclaim your infamy to our people and slay you besides. The curse of our doomed race is just such white folks' niggers as you are. Shoot, shoot, shoot, you whelps."

They took aim and, at a command from Belton, fired. When the smoke had lifted, Belton said: "Bernard, those were blank cartridges. I desired to give you another chance. If you consent to leave me unmolested to ferret out those conspirators I will take your word as your bond and spare your life. Will you accept your life at such a low price?"

"Come here and let me give you my answer," said Bernard. "Let me whisper something in your ear."

Belton drew near and Bernard spat in his face and said, "Take that, you knave."

Belton ordered Bernard seized and carried to the center of the room where stood what appeared to be an acting pole, but what was in reality a complete gallows. A black cap was adjusted over Bernard's head and a rope tied to his hands. He was told that a horrible death awaited him. He was informed that the platform on which he stood was a trap door that concealed an opening in the center of the building, that extended to the first floor. He was told that he would be dropped far enough to have his arms torn from his body and would be left to die.

Bernard perceptibly shuddered at the fate before him but he had determined long since to be true to every higher aspiration of his people, and he would die a death however horrible rather than stand by and see aspiring souls slaughtered for organizing to secure their rights at all hazards. He muttered a prayer to God, closed his eyes, gritted his teeth and nerved himself for the ordeal, refusing to answer Belton's last appeal.

Belton gave command to spring the trap door after he had counted three. In order to give Bernard a chance to weaken he put one minute between each count. "One— Two— Three—" he called out.

Bernard felt the floor give way beneath his feet and he shot down with terrific speed. He nerved himself for the shock that was to tear his limbs from his body, but, strange to say, he felt the speed lessening as he fell and his feet eventually struck a floor with not sufficient force to even jar him severely. "Was this death? Was he dead or alive?" he was thinking within himself, when suddenly the mask was snatched from his face and he found himself in a large room containing desks arranged in a semi-circular form. There were one hundred and forty-five desks, and at each a person was seated.

"Where was he? What did that assemblage mean? What did his strange experiences mean?" he asked himself. He stood there, his hands tied, his eye wandering from face to face.

Within a few minutes Belton entered and the assemblage broke forth into cheers. Bernard had alighted on a platform directly facing the assemblage. Belton walked to his side and spread out his hands and said: "Behold the Chiefs of the conspirators whom you would not betray. Behold me, whom they have called the arch conspirator. You have nobly stood the test. Come, your reward awaits you. You are worthy of it and I assure you it is worthy of you."

Bernard had not been killed in his fall because of a parachute which had been so arranged, unknown to him, to save him in the descent.

Chapter XVI
Unwritten History

BELTON, SMILING, locked his arm in Bernard's and said: "Come with me. I will explain it all to you." They walked down the aisle together.

At the sight of these two most conspicuous representatives of all that was good and great in the race, moving down the aisle side by side, the audience began to cheer wildly and a band of musicians began playing "Hail to the Chief."

All of this was inexplicable to Bernard; but he was soon to learn what and how much it meant. Belton escorted him across the campus to the small but remarkably pretty white cottage with green vines clinging to trellis work all around it. Here they entered. The rooms were furnished with rare and antique furniture and were so tastefully arranged as to astonish and please even Bernard, who had been accustomed from childhood to choice, luxuriant magnificence.

They entered a side room, overlooking a beautiful lawn which could boast of lovely flowers and rose bushes scattered here and there. They sat down, facing each other. Bernard was a bundle of expectancy. He had passed through enough to make him so.

Belton said: "Bernard, I am now about to put the keeping of the property, the liberty, and the very lives of over seven million five hundred thousand people into your hands."

Bernard opened his eyes wide in astonishment and waited for Belton to further explain himself.

"Realize," said Belton, "that I am carefully weighing each remark I make and am fully conscious of how much my statement involves." Bernard bowed his head in solemn thought. Viola's recent death, the blood-curdling experiences of the day, and now Belton's impressive words all united to make that a sober moment with him; as sober as any that he had ever had in his life. He looked Belton in the face and said: "May revengeful lightning transfix me with her fiercest bolts; may hell's most fiery pillars roll in fury around me; may I be despised of man and forgotten of my God, if I ever knowingly, in the slightest way, do aught to betray this solemn, this most sacred trust."

Belton gazed fondly on the handsome features of his noble friend and sighed to think that only the coloring of his skin prevented him from being enrolled upon the scroll containing the names of the very noblest sons of earth. Arousing himself as from a reverie he drew near to Bernard and said: "I must begin. Another government, complete in every detail, exercising the sovereign right of life and death over its subjects, has been organized and maintained within the United States for many years. This government has a population of seven million two hundred and fifty thousand."

"Do you mean all that you say, Belton?" asked Bernard eagerly.

"I shall in a short time submit to you positive proofs of my assertion. You shall find that I have not overstated anything."

"But, Belton, how in the world can such a thing be when I, who am thoroughly conversant with every movement of any consequence, have not even dreamed of such a thing."

"All of that shall be made perfectly clear to you in the course of the narrative which I shall now relate."

Bernard leaned forward, anxious to hear what purported to be one of the most remarkable and at the same time one of the most important things connected with modern civilization.

Belton began: "You will remember, Bernard, that there lived, in the early days of the American Republic, a negro scientist who won an international reputation by his skill and erudition. In our school days, we spoke of him often. Because of his learning and consequent usefulness, this negro enjoyed the association of the moving spirits of the revolutionary period. By the publication of a book of science which outranked any other book of the day that treated of the same subject, this negro became a very wealthy man. Of course the book is now obsolete, science having made such great strides since his day. This wealthy negro secretly gathered other free negroes together and organized a society that had a two-fold object. The first object was to endeavor to secure for the free negroes all the rights and privileges of men, according to the teachings of Thomas Jefferson. Its other object was to secure the freedom of the enslaved negroes the world over. All work was done by this organization with the sole stipulation that it should be used for the furtherance of the two above named objects of the society, and for those objects alone.

"During slavery this organization confined its membership principally to free negroes, as those who were yet in physical bondage were supposed to have aspirations for nothing higher than being released from chains, and were, therefore, not prepared to eagerly aspire to the enjoyment of the highest privileges of freedom. When the War of Secession was over and all negroes were free, the society began to cautiously spread its membership among the emancipated. They conducted a campaign of education, which in every case preceded an attempt at securing members. This campaign of education had for its object the instruction of the negro as to what real freedom was. He was taught that being released from chains was but the lowest form of liberty, and that he was no more than a common cur if he was satisfied with simply that. That much was all, they taught, that a dog howled for. They made use of Jefferson's writings, educating the negro to feel that he was not in the full enjoyment of his rights until he was on terms of equality with any other human being that was alive or had ever lived. This society used its influence secretly to have appointed over Southern schools of all kinds for negroes such teachers as would take especial pains to teach the negro to aspire for equality with all other races of men.

"They were instructed to pay especial attention to the history of the United States during the revolutionary period. Thus, the campaign of education moved forward. The negroes gained political ascendancy in many Southern states, but were soon hurled from power, by force in some quarters, and by fraud in others. The negroes turned their eyes to the federal government for redress and a guarantee of their rights. The federal government said: 'Take care of yourselves, we are powerless to help you.' The 'Civil Rights Bill,' was declared null and void, by the Supreme Court. An 'honest election bill' was defeated in Congress by James G. Blaine and others. Separate coach laws were declared by the Supreme Court to be constitutional. State Constitutions were revised and so amended as to nullify the amendment of the Federal Constitution, giving the negro the right to vote. More than sixty thousand defenseless negroes were unlawfully slain. Governors would announce publicly that they favored lynching. The Federal Government would get elected to power by condemning these outrages, and when there, would confess its utter helplessness. One President plainly declared, what was already well known, 'that the only thing that they could do, would be to create a healthy sentiment.' This secret organization of which we have been speaking decided that some means must be found to do what the General Government could not do, because of a defect in the Constitution. They decided to organize a General Government that would protect the negro in his rights. This course of action decided upon, the question was as to how this could be done the most quickly and successfully. You well know that the negro has been a marvelous success since the war, as a builder of secret societies.

"One member of this patriotic secret society, of which we have been speaking, conceived the idea of making use of all of these secret orders already formed by negroes. The idea met with instant approval. A house was found already to hand. These secret orders were all approached and asked to add one more degree and let this added degree be the same in every negro society. This proposition was accepted, and the Government formed at once. Each order remained, save in this last degree where all were one. This last degree was nothing more nor less than a compact government exercising all the functions of a nation. The grand purpose of the government was so apparent, and so needful of attention, that men rushed into this last degree pledging their lives to the New Government.

"All differences between the race were to be settled by this Government, as it had a well organized judiciary. Negroes, members of this Government, were to be no longer seen fighting negroes before prejudiced white courts. An army was organized and every able-bodied citizen enlisted. After the adjournment of the lodge sessions, army drills were always executed. A Congress was duly elected, one member for every fifty thousand citizens. Branch legislatures were formed in each state. Except in a few, but important particulars, the constitution was modeled after that of the United States.

"There is only one branch to our Congress, the members of which are elected by a majority vote, for an indefinite length of time, and may be recalled at any time by a majority vote.

"This Congress passes laws relating to the general welfare of our people, and whenever a bill is introduced in the Congress of the United States affecting our race it is also introduced and debated here.

"Every race question submitted to the United States judiciary, is also submitted to our own. A record of our decisions is kept side by side with the decisions of the United States.

"The money which the scientist left was wisely invested, and at the conclusion of the civil war amounted to many millions. Good land at the South was offered after the war for twenty-five cents an acre. These millions were expended in the purchase of such lands, and our treasury is now good for $500,000,000. Our citizens own about $350,000,000. And all of this is pledged to our government in case it is needed.

"We have at our disposal, therefore, $850,000,000. This money can he used by the Government in any way that it sees fit, so long as it is used to secure the recognition of the rights of our people. They are determined to be free and will give their lives, as freely as they have given their property.

"This place is known as Jefferson College, but it is in reality the Capitol of our Government, and those whom you have just left are the Congressmen."

"But, Belton," broke in Bernard, "how does it happen that I have been excluded from all this?"

"That is explained in this way. The relation of your mother to the Anglo-Saxon race has not been clearly understood, and you and she have been under surveillance for many years.

"It was not until recently deemed advisable to let you in, your loyalty to the race never having fully been tested. I have been a member for years. While I was at Stowe University, though a young man, I was chairman of the bureau of education and had charge of the work of educating the race upon the doctrine of human liberty.

"While I was at Cadeville, La., that was my work. Though not attracting public attention, I was sowing seed broadcast. After my famous case I was elected to Congress here and soon thereafter chosen speaker, which position I now hold.

"I shall now come to matters that concern you. Our constitution expressly stipulates that the first President of our Government should be a man whom the people unanimously desired. Each Congressman had to be instructed to vote for the same man, else there would be no election. This was done because it was felt that the responsibility of the first President would be so great, and have such a formative influence that he should be the selection of the best judgment of the entire nation.

"In the second place, this would ensure his having a united nation at his back. Again, this forcing the people to be unanimous would have a tendency to heal dissensions within their ranks. In other words, we needed a George Washington.

"Various men have been put forward for this honor and vigorous campaigns have been waged in their behalf. But these all failed of the necessary unanimous vote. At last, one young man arose, who was brilliant and sound, genial and true, great and good. On every tongue was his name and in every heart his image. Unsolicited by him, unknown to him, the nation by its unanimous voice has chosen him the President of our beloved Government. This day he has unflinchingly met the test that our Congress decreed and has come out of the furnace, purer than gold. He feared death no more than the caress of his mother, when he felt that that death was to be suffered in behalf of his oppressed people. I have the great honor, on this the proudest occasion of my life, to announce that I am commissioned to inform you that the name of our President is Bernard Belgrave. You, sir, are President of the Imperium In Imperio, the name of our Government, and to you we devote our property, our lives, our all, promising to follow your banner into every post of danger until it is planted on freedom's hill. You are given three months in which to verify all of my claims, and give us answer as to whether you will serve us."

* * *

Bernard took three months to examine into the reality and stability of the Imperium. He found it well nigh perfect in every part and presented a form of government unexcelled by that of any other nation.

Chapter XVII
Crossing the Rubicon

BERNARD ASSUMED the Presidency of the Imperium and was duly inaugurated in a manner in keeping with the importance of his high office. He began the direction of its affairs with such energy and tactful discretion as betokened great achievements.

He familiarized himself with every detail of his great work and was thoroughly posted as to all the resources at his command. He devoted much time to assuaging jealousies and healing breaches wherever such existed in the ranks of the Imperium. He was so gentle, so loving, yet so firm and impartial, that all factional differences disappeared at his approach.

Added to his great popularity because of his talents, there sprang up for him personal attachments, marvelous in depth. He rose to the full measure of the responsibilities of his commanding position, and more than justified the fondest anticipations of his friends and admirers. In the meanwhile he kept an observant eye upon the trend of events in the United States, and his fingers were ever on the pulse of the Imperium. All of the evils complained of by the Imperium continued unabated; in fact, they seemed to multiply and grow instead of diminishing.

Bernard started a secret newspaper whose business it was to chronicle every fresh discrimination, every new act of oppression, every additional unlawful assault upon the property, the liberty or the lives of any of the members of the Imperium. This was an illustrated journal, and pictures of horrors, commented upon in burning words, spread fire-brands everywhere in the ranks of the Imperium. Only members of the Imperium had access to this fiery journal.

At length an insurrection broke out in Cuba, and the whole Imperium watched this struggle with keenest interest, as the Cubans were in a large measure negroes. In proportion as the Cubans drew near to their freedom, the fever of hope correspondingly rose in the veins of the Imperium. The United States of America sent a war ship to Cuba. One night while the sailors slept in fancied security, some powerful engine of destruction demolished the vessel and ended the lives of some 266 American seamen.

A board of inquiry was sent by the United States Government to the scene of the disaster, and, after a careful investigation of a most thorough character, decided that the explosion was not internal and accidental but external and by design. This finding made war between the United States and Spain practically inevitable.

While the whole nation was in the throes of war excitement, a terrible tragedy occurred. President McKinley had appointed Mr. Felix A. Cook, a colored man of ability, culture and refinement as postmaster of Lake City, South Carolina. The white citizens of this place made no protest against the appointment and all was deemed satisfactory.

One morning the country awoke to be horrified with the news that Mr. Cook's home had been assaulted at night by a mob of white demons in human form. The mob set fire to the house while the occupants slept, and when Mr. Cook with his family endeavored to escape from the flames he was riddled with bullets and killed, and his wife and children were wounded. And the sole offense for which this dastardly crime was perpetrated, was that he decided to accept the honor which the government conferred upon him in appointing him postmaster of a village of 300 inhabitants. It was the color of his skin that made this acceptance odious in the eyes of his Anglo-Saxon neighbors!

This incident naturally aroused as much indignation among the members of the Imperium as did the destruction of the war ship in the bosoms of the Anglo-Saxons of the United States. All things considered, Bernard regarded this as the most opportune moment for the Imperium to meet and act upon the whole question of the relationship of the negro race to the Anglo-Saxons.

The Congress of the Imperium was called and assembled in special session at the Capitol building just outside of Waco. The session began on the morning of April – the same day on which the Congress of the United States had under consideration the resolutions, the adoption of which meant war with Spain. These two congresses on this same day had under consideration questions of vital import to civilization.

The proceedings of the Anglo-Saxons have been told to the world in minute detail, but the secret deliberations of the Imperium are herein disclosed for the first time. The exterior of the Capitol at Waco was decorated with American flags, and red, white and blue bunting. Passers-by commented on the patriotism of Jefferson College. But, enveloped in this decoration there was cloth of the color of mourning. The huge weeping willows stood, one on each side of the speaker's desk. To the right of the desk, there was a group of women in widow's weeds, sitting on an elevated platform. There were fifty of these, their husbands having been made the victims of mobs since the first day of January just gone.

To the left of the speaker's desk, there were huddled one hundred children whose garments were in tatters and whose looks bespoke lives of hardship. These were the offsprings robbed of their parents by the brutish cruelty of unthinking mobs.

Postmaster Cook, while alive, was a member of the Imperium and his seat was now empty and draped in mourning. In the seat was a golden casket containing his heart, which had been raked from the burning embers on the morning following the night of the murderous assault. It was amid such surrounding as these that the already aroused and determined members of the Congress assembled.

Promptly at 11 o'clock, Speaker Belton Piedmont took the chair. He rapped for order, and the chaplain offered a prayer, in which he invoked the blessings of God upon the negro race at the most important crisis in its history. Word was sent, by proper committee, across the campus informing the president that Congress was in session awaiting his further pleasure. According to custom, the president came in person to orally deliver his message.

He entered in the rear of the building and marched forward. The Congress arose and stood with bowed heads as he passed through. The speaker's desk was moved back as a sign of the president's superior position, and directly in the center of the platform the president stood to speak. He was dressed in a Prince Albert suit of finest black. He wore a standing collar and a necktie snowy white. The hair was combed away from that noble brow of his, and his handsome face showed that he was nerved for what he regarded as the effort of his life.

In his fierce, determined glance you could discover that latent fires, hitherto unsuspected even in his warm bosom, had been aroused. The whole man was to speak that day. And he spoke. We can give you his words but not his speech. Man can photograph the body, but in the photograph you can only glimpse the soul. Words can portray the form of a speech, but the spirit, the life, are missing and we turn away disappointed. That sweet, well modulated voice, full of tender pathos, of biting sarcasm, of withering irony, of swelling rage, of glowing fervor, according as the occasion demanded, was a most faithful vehicle to Bernard; conveying fully every delicate shade of thought.

The following gives you but a faint idea of his masterly effort. In proportion as you can throw yourself into his surroundings, and feel, as he had felt, the iron in his soul, to that extent will you be able to realize how much power there was in what is now to follow:

The President's Message

"Two terrible and discordant sounds have burst forth upon the erstwhile quiet air and now fill your bosom with turbulent emotions. One is the blast of the bugle, fierce and loud, calling us to arms against a foreign nation to avenge the death of American seamen and to carry the cup of liberty to a people perishing for its healing draught. The other is the crackling of a burning house in the night's dead hours, the piteous cries of pain and terror from the lips of wounded babes; the despairing, heart-rending, maddening shrieks of the wife and mother; the harrowing groans of the dying husband and father, and the gladsome shout of the fiendish mob of white American citizens, who have wrought the havoc just described, a deed sufficiently horrible to make Satan blush and hell hastily hide her face in shame.

"I deem this, my fellow countrymen, as an appropriate time for us to consider what shall be our attitude, immediate and future, to this Anglo-Saxon race, which calls upon us to defend the fatherland and at the same moment treats us in a manner to make us execrate it. Let us, then, this day decide what shall be the relations that shall henceforth exist between us and the Anglo-Saxon race of the United States of America.

"Seven million eyes are riveted upon you, hoping that you will be brave and wise enough to take such action as will fully atone for all the horrors of the past and secure for us every right due to all honorable, loyal, law-abiding citizens of the United States. Pleadingly they look to you to extract the arrow of shame which hangs quivering in every bosom, shame at continued humiliation, unavenged.

"In order to arrive at a proper conclusion as to what the duty of the hour is, it would be well to review our treatment received at the hands of the Anglo-Saxon race and note the position that we are now sternly commanded by them to accept.

"When this is done, to my mind, the path of duty will be as plain before our eyes as the path of the sun across the heavens. I shall, therefore, proceed to review our treatment and analyze our present condition, in so far as it is traceable to the treatment which we now receive from the Anglo-Saxon.

"When in 1619 our forefathers landed on the American shore, the music of welcome with which they were greeted, was the clanking of iron chains ready to fetter them; the crack of the whip to be used to plow furrows in their backs; and the yelp of the blood-hound who was to bury his fangs deep into their flesh, in case they sought for liberty. Such was the music with which the Anglo-Saxon came down to the shore to extend a hearty welcome to the forlorn children of night, brought from a benighted heathen land to a community of Christians!

"The negro was seized and forced to labor hard that the Anglo-Saxon might enjoy rest and ease. While he sat in his cushioned chair, in his luxurious home, and dreamed of the blessedness of freedom, the enforced labor of slaves felled the forest trees, cleared away the rubbish, planted the seed and garnered the ripened grain, receiving therefor no manner of pay, no token of gratitude, no word of coldest thanks.

"That same hammer and anvil that forged the steel sword of the Anglo-Saxon, with which he fought for freedom from England's yoke, also forged the chain that the Anglo-Saxon used to bind the negro more securely in the thralldom of slavery. For two hundred and forty-four years the Anglo-Saxon imposed upon the hapless, helpless negro, the bondage of abject slavery, robbed him of the just recompense of his unceasing toil, treated him with the utmost cruelty, kept his mind shrouded in the dense fog of ignorance, denied his poor sinful soul access to the healing word of God, and, while the world rolled on to joy and light, the negro was driven cowering and trembling, back, back into the darkest corners of night's deepest gloom. And when, at last, the negro was allowed to come forth and gaze with the eyes of a freeman on the glories of the sky, even this holy act, the freeing of the negro, was a matter of compulsion and has but little, if anything, in it demanding gratitude, except such gratitude as is due to be given unto God. For the Emancipation Proclamation, as we all know, came not so much as a message of love for the slave as a message of love for the Union; its primary object was to save the Union, its incident, to liberate the slave. Such was the act which brought to a close two hundred and forty-four years of barbarous maltreatment and inhuman oppression! After all these years of unremitting toil, the negro was pushed out into the world without one morsel of food, one cent of money, one foot of land. Naked and unarmed he was pushed forward into a dark cavern and told to beard the lion in his den. In childlike simplicity he undertook the task. Soon the air was filled with his agonizing cries; for the claws and teeth of the lion were ripping open every vein and crushing every bone. In this hour of dire distress the negro lifted up his voice in loud, long piteous wails calling upon those for help at whose instance and partially for whose sake he had dared to encounter the deadly foe. These whilom friends rushed with a loud shout to the cavern's mouth. But when they saw the fierce eyes of the lion gleaming in the dark and heard his fearful growl, this loud shout suddenly died away into a feeble, cowardly whimper, and these boastful creatures at the crackling of a dry twig turned and scampered away like so many jack-rabbits.

"Having thus briefly reviewed our past treatment at the hand of the Anglo-Saxon, we now proceed to consider the treatment which we receive at his hands to-day.

The Industrial Situation

"During the long period of slavery the Negro race was not allowed to use the mind as a weapon in the great 'battle for bread.'

"The Anglo-Saxon said to the negro, in most haughty tones: 'In this great "battle for bread," you must supply the brute force while I will supply the brain. If you attempt to use your brain I will kill you; and before I will stoop so low as to use my own physical power to earn my daily bread I will kill myself.'

"This edict of the Anglo-Saxon race, issued in the days of slavery, is yet in force in a slightly modified form.

"He yet flees from physical exertion as though it were the leprosy itself, and yet, violently pushes the negro into that from which he has so precipitately fled, crying in a loud voice, 'unclean, unclean.'

"If forced by circumstances to resort to manual labor, he chooses the higher forms of this, where skill is the main factor. But he will not labor even here with the negro, but drives him out and bars the door.

"He will contribute the public funds to educate the negro and then exert every possible influence to keep the negro from earning a livelihood by means of that education.

"It is true, that in the goodness of his heart he will allow the negro community to have a negro preacher, teacher, doctor, pharmacist and jackleg lawyer, but further than this he will not go. Practically all of the other higher forms of labor are hermetically sealed so far as the negro is concerned.

"Thus, like Tantalus of old, we are placed in streams of water up to our necks, but when we stoop down to drink thereof the waters recede; luscious fruit, tempting to the eye and pleasing to the taste, is placed above our heads, only to be wafted away by the winds of prejudice, when, like Tantalus we reach up to grasp and eat.

Our Civil Rights

"An Italian, a Frenchman, a German, a Russian, a Chinaman and a Swede come, let us suppose, on a visit to our country.

"As they draw near our public parks they look up and see placards forbidding somebody to enter these places. They pause to read the signs to see who it is that is forbidden to enter.

"Unable to understand our language, they see a negro child returning from school and they call the child to read and interpret the placard. It reads thus: 'Negroes and dogs not allowed in here.'

"The little negro child, whose father's sweaty, unrequited toil cleared the spot whereon the park now stands, loiters outside of the wicker gate in company with the dogs of the foreigners and gazes wistfully through the cracks at the children of these strangers sporting on the lawn.

"This is but a fair sample of the treatment which our race receives everywhere in the South.

"If we enter a place where a sign tells us that the public is served, we do not know whether we are to be waited upon or driven out like dogs.

"And the most shameful and hopeless feature connected with the question of our civil rights is that the Supreme Court has lent its official sanction to all such acts of discrimination. The highest court in the land is the chief bulwark of caste prejudice in democratic America.

Education

"The race that thinks of us and treats us as we have just indicated has absolute charge of the education of our children.

"They pay our teachers poorer salaries than they do their own; they give us fewer and inferior school buildings and they make us crawl in the dust before the very eyes of our children in order to secure the slightest concessions.

"They attempt to muzzle the mouths of negro teachers, and he who proclaims too loudly the doctrine of equality as taught by Thomas Jefferson, will soon be in search of other employment.

"Thus, they attempt to cripple our guides so that we may go forward at a feeble pace.

"Our children, early in life, learn of our maltreatment, and having confidence in the unused strength of their parents, urge us to right our wrongs.

"We listen to their fiery words and gaze in fondness on their little clinched fists. We then bow our heads in shame and lay bare to them the chains that yet hold our ankles, though the world has pronounced us free.

"In school, they are taught to bow down and worship at the shrine of the men who died for the sake of liberty, and day by day they grow to disrespect us, their parents who have made no blow for freedom. But it will not always be thus!

Courts of Justice

"Colored men are excluded from the jury box; colored lawyers are discriminated against at the bar; and negroes, with the highest legal attainments, are not allowed to even dream of mounting the seat of a judge.

"Before a court that has been lifted into power by the very hands of prejudice, justice need not be expected. The creature will, presumably, serve its creator; this much the creator demands.

"We shall mention just one fact that plainly illustrates the character of the justice to be found in our courts.

"If a negro murders an Anglo-Saxon, however justifiably, let him tremble for his life if he is to be tried in our courts. On the other hand, if an Anglo-Saxon murders a negro in cold blood, without the slightest provocation, he will, if left to the pleasure of our courts, die of old age and go down to his grave in perfect peace.

"A court that will thus carelessly dabble and play in puddles of human blood needs no further comment at my hands.

Mob Law

"The courts of the land are the facile instruments of the Anglo-Saxon race. They register its will as faithfully as the thermometer does the slightest caprice of the weather. And yet, the poor boon of a trial in even such courts as these is denied the negro, even when his character is being painted with hell's black ink and charges that threaten his life are being laid at his door. He is allowed no chance to clear his name; no opportunity to bid a friend good bye; no time to formulate a prayer to God.

"About this way of dealing with criminals there are three horrible features: First, innocent men are often slain and forced to sleep eternally in dishonored graves. Secondly, when men who are innocent are thus slain the real culprits are left behind to repeat their deeds and thus continue to bring reproach upon the race to which they belong. Thirdly, illegal execution always begets sympathy in the hearts of our people for a criminal, however dastardly may be his crime. Thus the execution loses all of its moral force as a deterrent. That wrath, that eloquence, which would all be used in abuse of the criminal is divided between him and his lynchers. Thus the crime for which the man suffers, is not dwelt upon with that unanimity to make it sufficiently odious, and, as a consequence, lynching increases crime. And, too, under the operation of the lynch-law the criminal knows that any old tramp is just as liable as himself to be seized and hanged.

"This accursed practice, instead of decreasing, grows in extent year by year. Since the close of the civil war no less than sixty thousand of our comrades, innocent of all crime, have been hurried to their graves by angry mobs, and to-day their widows and orphans and their own departed spirits cry out to you to avenge their wrongs.

"Woe unto that race, whom the tears of the widows, the cries of starving orphans, the groans of the innocent dying, and the gaping wounds of those unjustly slain, accuse before a righteous God!

Politics

"'Governments are instituted among men, deriving their just powers from the consent of the governed!'

"These words were penned by the man whom the South has taught us to revere as the greatest and noblest American statesman, whether those who are now alive or those who are dead. We speak of Thomas Jefferson. They have taught us that he was too wise to err and that his sayings are truth incarnate. They are ready to anathematize any man in their own ranks who will decry the self-evident truths which he uttered.

"The Bible which the white people gave us, teaches us that we are men. The Declaration of Independence, which we behold them wearing over their hearts, tells us that all men are created equal. If, as the Bible says, we are men; if, as Jefferson says, all men are equal; if, as he further states, governments derive all just powers from the consent of the governed, then it follows that the American government is in duty bound to seek to know our will as respects the laws and the men who are to govern us.

"But instead of seeking to know our will, they employ every device that human ingenuity can contrive to prevent us from expressing our opinion. The monarchial trait seems not to have left their blood. They have apparently chosen our race as an empire, and each Anglo-Saxon regards himself as a petty king, and some gang or community of negroes as his subjects.

"Thus our voice is not heard in the General Government. Our kings, the Anglo-Saxons, speak for us, their slaves. In some states we are deprived of our right to vote by frauds, in others by violence, and in yet others by statutory enactment. But in all cases it is most effectually done.

"Burdens may be put upon our shoulders that are weighing us down, but we have no means of protesting. Men who administer the laws may discriminate against us to an outrageous degree, but we have no power to remove or to punish them.

"Like lean, hungry dogs, we must crouch beneath our master's table and snap eagerly at the crumbs that fall. If in our scramble for these crumbs we make too much noise, we are violently kicked and driven out of doors, where, in the sleet and snow, we must whimper and whine until late the next morning when the cook opens the door and we can then crouch down in the corner of the kitchen.

"Oh! my Comrades, we cannot longer endure our shame and misery!

"We can no longer lay supinely down upon our backs and let oppression dig his iron heel in our upturned pleading face until, perchance, the pity of a bystander may meekly request him to desist.

"Fellow Countrymen, we must be free. The sun that bathes our land in light yet rises and sets upon a race of slaves.

"The question remaining before us, then, is, How we are to obtain this freedom? In olden times, revolutions were effected by the sword and spear. In modern times the ballot has been used for that purpose. But the ballot has been snatched from our hands. The modern implement of revolutions has been denied us. I need not say more. Your minds will lead you to the only gate left open.

"But this much I will say: let not so light, so common, so universal a thing as that which we call death be allowed to frighten you from the path that leads to true liberty and absolute equality. Let that which under any circumstances must come to one and all be no terror to you.

"To the martyr, who perishes in freedom's cause, death comes with a beauteous smile and with most tender touch. But to the man whose blood is nothing but sour swill; who prefers to stay like fattening swine until pronounced fit for the butcher's knife; to such, death comes with a most horrifying visage, and seizing the victim with cold and clammy hands hurries with his disgusting load to some far away dumping ground.

"How glad am I that I can glance over this audience and see written upon your faces utter disdain of death.

"In concluding let me say, I congratulate you that after years of suffering and disunion our faces are now *all* turned toward the golden shores of liberty's lovely land.

"Some tell us that a sea is in our way, so deep that we cannot cross. Let us answer back in joyful tones as our vessels push out from the shore, that our clotted blood, shed in the middle of the sea, will float to the other side, even if we do not reach there ourselves.

"Others tell us that towering, snow-capped mountains enclose the land. To this we answer, if we die on the mountain-side, we shall be shrouded in sheets of whitest snow, and all generations of men yet to come upon the earth will have to gaze upward in order to see our whitened forms.

"Let us then, at all hazards, strike a blow for freedom. If it calls for a Thermopylæ, be free. If it calls for a Valley Forge, be free. If contending for our rights, given unto us by God, causes us to be slain, let us perish on the field of battle, singing as we pass out of the world, 'Sweet Freedom's song,' though every word of this soul-inspiring hymn must come forth wrapped in our hearts' warm blood.

"Gentlemen of the Imperium in Imperio, I await your pleasure."

Chapter XVIII
The Storm's Master

WHEN BERNARD ceased speaking and took his seat the house was as silent as a graveyard. All felt that the time for words had passed and the next and only thing in order was a deed.

Each man seemed determined to keep his seat and remain silent until he had some definite plan to suggest. At length one man, somewhat aged, arose and spoke as follows:

"Fellow citizens, our condition is indeed past enduring and we must find a remedy. I have spent the major portion of my life in close study of this subject, searching for a solution. My impression is that the negro will never leave this country. The day for the wholesale exodus of nations is past. We must, then, remain here. As long as we remain here as a separate and distinct race we shall continue to be oppressed. We must lose our identity. I, therefore, urge that we abandon the idea of becoming anything noteworthy as a separate and distinct race and send the word forth that we amalgamate."

When the word "amalgamate" escaped his lips a storm of hisses and jeers drowned further speech and he quickly crouched down in his seat. Another arose and advocated emigration to the African Congo Free State. He pointed out that this State, great in area and rich in resources, was in the hands of the weak kingdom of Belgium and could be wrested from Belgium with the greatest ease. In fact, it might be possible to purchase it, as it was the personal property of King Leopold.

He further stated that one of his chief reasons for suggesting emigration was that it would be a terrible blow to the South. The proud Southerner would then have his own forests to fell and fields to tend. He pictured the haughty Southern lady at last the queen of her own kitchen. He then called attention to the loss of influence and prestige which the South would sustain in the nation. By losing nearly one half of its population the South's representation in Congress would be reduced to such a point that the South would have no appreciable influence on legislation for one half a century to come. He called attention to the business depression that would ensue when the southern supply merchant lost such an extensive consumer as the negro.

He wound up by urging the Imperium to go where they would enjoy all the rights of free men, and by picturing the demoralization and ruin of the South when they thus went forth. His suggestion met with much favor but he did not make clear the practicability of his scheme.

At length a bold speaker arose who was courageous enough to stick a match to the powder magazine which Bernard had left uncovered in all their bosoms. His first declaration was: "I am for war!" and it was cheered to the echo. It was many minutes before the applause died away. He then began an impassioned invective against the South and recited in detail horror after horror, for which the South was answerable. He described hangings, revolting in their brutality; he drew vivid word pictures of various burnings, mentioning one where a white woman struck the match and ignited the pile of wood that was to consume the trembling negro. He told of the Texas horror, when a colored man named Smith was tortured with a red hot poker, and his eyes gouged out; after which he was slowly roasted to death. He then had Mrs. Cook arise and gather her children about her, and tell her sorrowful story. As she proceeded the entire assembly broke down in tears, and men fell on each other's necks and wept like babes. And oh! Their hearts swelled, their bosoms heaved, their breath came quick with choking passion, and there burst from all their throats the one hoarse cry: "War! war! war!"

Bernard turned his head away from this affecting sight and in his soul swore a terrible oath to avenge the wrongs of his people.

When quiet was sufficiently restored, the man with the match arose and offered the following resolutions:

"WHEREAS, the history of our treatment by the Anglo-Saxon race is but the history of oppression, and whereas, our patient endurance of evil has not served to decrease this cruelty, but seems rather to increase it; and whereas, the ballot box, the means of peaceful revolution is denied us, therefore;

"*Be it Resolved*: That the hour for wreaking vengeance for our multiplied wrongs has come.

"*Resolved* secondly: That we at once proceed to war for the purpose of accomplishing the end just named, and for the further purpose of obtaining all our rights due us as men.

"*Resolved* thirdly: That no soldier of the Imperium leave the field of battle until the ends for which this war was inaugurated are fully achieved."

A dozen men were on their feet at once to move the adoption of these resolutions. The motion was duly seconded and put before the house. The Chairman asked: "Are you ready to vote?" "Ready!" was the unanimous, vociferous response.

The chairman, Belton Piedmont, quietly said: "Not ready." All eyes were then pointed eagerly and inquiringly to him. He called the senior member of the house to the chair and came down upon the floor to speak.

We are now about to record one of the most remarkable feats of oratory known to history. Belton stood with his massive, intellectual head thrown back and a look of determined defiance shot forth from his eyes. His power in debate was well known and the members settled themselves back for a powerful onslaught of some kind; but exactly what to expect they did not know.

Fortunately for Belton's purpose, surprise, wonder, expectancy, had, for the time being, pushed into the background the more violent emotions surging a moment before.

Belton turned his head slowly, letting his eye sweep the entire circle of faces before him, and there seemed to be a force and an influence emanating from the look. He began: "I call upon you all to bear me witness that I have ever in word and deed been zealous in the work of building up this Imperium, whose holy mission it is to grapple with our enemy and wrest from him our stolen rights, given to us by nature and nature's God. If there be one of you that knowest aught against my patriotism, I challenge him to declare it now; and if there be anything to even cast a suspicion upon me, I shall gladly court a traitor's ignoble doom."

He paused here. No one accepted the challenge, for Belton was the acknowledged guiding star that had led the Imperium to the high point of efficiency where Bernard found it.

"By your silence," Belton continued, "I judge that my patriotism is above suspicion; and this question being settled, I shall feel free to speak all that is within me on the subject now before me. I have a word to say in defence of the south—"

"No! No! No! No!" burst from a score of throats. Friends crowded around Belton and begged him to desist. They told him that the current was so strong that it was death to all future usefulness to try to breast it.

Belton waved them away and cried out in impassioned tones: "On her soil I was born; on her bosom I was reared; into her arms I hope to fall in death; and I shall not from fear of losing popular favor desist from pointing out the natural sources from which her sins arise, so that when judgment is pronounced justice will not hesitate to stamp it with her righteous seal."

"Remember your scars!" shouted one.

"Yes, I am scarred," returned Belton. "I have been in the hands of an angry mob; I have dangled from a tree at the end of a rope; I have felt the murderous pistol drive cold lead into my flesh; I have been accounted dead and placed upon the dissecting table; I have felt the sharp surgical knife ripping my flesh apart when I was supposed to be dead; all of these hardships and more besides I have received at the hands of the South; but she has not and cannot drive truth from my bosom, and the truth shall I declare this day."

Seeing that it was useless to attempt to deter him, Belton continued his speech without interruption: "There are many things in the message of our most worthy President that demand attention. It was indeed an awful sin for the Anglo-Saxon to enslave the negro. But in judging a people we must judge them according to the age in which they lived, and the influence that surrounded them.

"If David were on earth alive to-day and the ruler of an enlightened kingdom, he would be impeached forthwith, fined for adultery, imprisoned for bigamy, and hanged for murder. Yet while not measuring up to the standard of morality of to-day, he was the man after God's own heart in his day and generation.

"If Abraham were here to-day he would be expelled from any church that had any regard for decency; and yet, he was the father of the faithful, for he walked according to the little light that struggled through the clouds and reached him.

"When slavery was introduced into America, it was the universal practice of mankind to enslave. Knowing how quick we all are to heed the universal voice of mankind, we should be lenient toward others who are thus tempted and fall.

"It has appeared strange to some that the Americans could fight for their own freedom from England and yet not think of those whom they then held in slavery. It should be remembered that the two kinds of slavery were by no means identical. The Americans fought for a theory and abstract principle. The negro did not even discern the points at issue; and the Anglo-Saxon naturally did not concern himself at that time with any one so gross as not to know anything of a principle for which he, (the Anglo-Saxon) was ready to offer up his life.

"Our President alluded to the fact that the negro was unpaid for all his years of toil. It is true that he was not paid in coin, but he received that from the Anglo-Saxons which far outweighs in value all the gold coin on earth. He received instruction in the arts of civilization, a knowledge of the English language, and a conception of the one true God and his Christ.

"While all of the other races of men were behind the ball of progress rolling it up the steep hill of time, the negro was asleep in the jungles of Africa. Newton dug for the law of gravitation; Herschel swept the starry sky in search of other worlds; Columbus stood upon the prow of the ship and braved the waves of the ocean and the fiercer ridicule of men; Martin Luther, single handed and alone, fought the Pope, the religious guide of the world; and all of this was done while the negro slept. After others had toiled so hard to give the bright light of civilization to the world, it was hardly to be expected that a race that slept while others worked could step up and at once enjoy all the fruits of others' toil.

"Allow me to note this great fact; that by enslavement in America the negro has come into possession of the great English language. He is thus made heir to all the richest thoughts of earth. Had he retained his mother tongue, it would perhaps have been centuries untold before the masterpieces of earth were given him. As it is we can now enjoy the companionship of Shakespeare, Bacon, Milton, Bunyan, together with the favorite sons of other nations adopted into the English language, such as Dante, Hugo, Goethe, Dumas and hosts of others. Nor must we ever forget that it was the Anglo-Saxon who snatched from our idolatrous grasp the deaf images to which we prayed, and the Anglo-Saxon who pointed us to the Lamb of God that takes away the sins of the world.

"So, beloved fellow citizens, when we calmly survey the evil and the good that came to us through American slavery, it is my opinion that we find more good for which to thank God than we find evil for which to curse man.

"Our President truly says that Abraham Lincoln was in such a position that he was forced to set the negro free. But let us remember that it was Abraham Lincoln and those who labored with him that created this position, from which he could turn neither to the right nor to the left.

"If, in his patriotic soul, we see love for the flag of his country overshadowing every other love, let us not ignorantly deny that other loves were there, deep, strong, and incapable of eradication; and let us be grateful for that.

The Labour Question

"Prejudice, pride, self-interest, prompt the whites to oppose our leaving in too large numbers the lower forms of labor for the higher; and they resort to any extreme to carry out their purpose. But this opposition is not an unmixed evil. The prejudice and pride that prompt them to exclude the Negro from the higher forms of labor, also exclude themselves from the lower forms, thus leaving the Negro in undisputed possession of a whole kingdom of labor.

"Furthermore, by denying us clerical positions, and other higher types of labor we shall be forced into enterprises of our own to furnish labor for our own talent. Let us accept the lesson so plainly taught and provide enterprises to supply our own needs and employ our own talents.

"If there is any one thing, more than another, that will push the Negro forth to build enterprises of his own, it will be this refusal of the whites to employ the higher order of labor that the race from time to time produces. This refusal will prove a blessing if we accept the lesson that it teaches. And, too, in considering this subject let us not feel that we are the only people who have a labor problem on hand to be solved. The Anglo-Saxon race is divided into two hostile camps – labor and capital. These two forces are gradually drawing together for a tremendous conflict, a momentous battle. The riots at Homestead, at Chicago, at Lattimer are but skirmishes between the picket lines, informing us that a general conflict is imminent. Let us thank God that we are not in the struggle. Let us thank Him that our labor problem is no worse than it is.

Our Civil Rights

"For our civil rights we are struggling and we must secure them. But if they had all come to us when they first belonged to us, we must frankly admit that we would have been unprepared for them.

"Our grotesque dress, our broken language, our ignorant curiosity, and, on the part of many our boorish manners, would have been nauseating in the extreme to men and women accustomed to refined association. Of course these failings are passing away: but the polished among you have often been made ashamed at the uncouth antics of some ignorant Negroes, courting the attention of the whites in their presence. Let us see to it, then, that we as a people, not a small minority of us, are prepared to use and not abuse the privileges that must come to us.

"Let us reduce the question of our rejection to a question pure and simple of the color of our skins, and by the help of that God who gave us that color we shall win.

"On the question of education much might be said in blame of the South, but far more may be said in her praise.

"The evils of which our president spoke are grave and must be righted, but let us not fail to see the bright side.

"The Anglo-Saxon child virtually pays for the education of the Negro child. You might hold that he might do more. It is equally true that he might do less. When we contrast the Anglo-Saxon, opening his purse and pouring out his money for the education of the Negro, with the Anglo-Saxon plaiting a scourge to flog the Negro aspiring to learn, the progress is marvelous indeed.

"And, let us not complain too bitterly of the school maintained by the Southerner, for it was there that we learned what true freedom was. It was in school that our hearts grew warm as we read of Washington, of Jefferson, of Henry, apostles of human liberty. It was the school of the Southerner that has builded the Imperium which now lifts its hand in power and might to strike a last grand blow for liberty.

Courts of Justice

"As for the courts of justice, I have not one word to say in palliation of the way in which they pander to the prejudices of the people. If the courts be corrupt; if the arbitrator between man and man be unjust; if the wretched victim of persecution is to be stabbed to death in the house of refuge; then, indeed, has mortal man sunk to the lowest level. Though every other branch of organized society may reek with filth and slime, let the ermine on the shoulders of the goddess of justice ever be clean and spotless.

"But remember this, that the Court of last resort has set the example which the lower courts have followed. The Supreme Court of the United States, it seems, may be relied upon to sustain any law born of prejudice against the Negro, and to demolish any law constructed in his interest. Witness the Dred Scott decision, and, in keeping with this, the decision on the Civil Rights Bill and Separate Coach Law.

"If this court, commonly accepted as being constituted with our friends, sets such a terrible example of injustice, it is not surprising that its filthy waters corrupt the various streams of justice in all their ramifications.

Mob Law

"Of all the curses that have befallen the South, this is the greatest. It cannot be too vehemently declaimed against. But let us look well and see if we, as a people, do not bear some share of the responsibility for the prevalence of this curse.

"Our race has furnished some brutes lower than the beasts of the field, who have stirred the passions of the Anglo-Saxon as nothing in all of human history has before stirred them. The shibboleth of the Anglo-Saxon race is the courage of man and the virtue of woman: and when, by violence, a member of a despised race assails a defenseless woman; robs her of her virtue, her crown of glory; and sends her back to society broken and crushed in spirit, longing, sighing, praying for the oblivion of the grave, it is not to be wondered at that hell is scoured by the Southern white man in search of plans to vent his rage. The lesson for him to learn is that passion is ever a blind guide and the more violent the more blind. Let him not cease to resent with all the intensity of his proud soul the accursed crime; but let this resentment pursue such a channel as will ensure the execution of the guilty and the escape of the innocent. As for us, let us cease to furnish the inhuman brutes whose deeds suggest inhuman punishments.

"But, I am aware that in a large majority of cases where lynchings occur, outrages upon women are not even mentioned. This fact but serves as an argument against all lynchings; for when lawlessness breaks forth, no man can set a limit where it will stop. It also warns us as a race to furnish no crime that provokes lynching; for when lynching once gets started, guilty and innocent alike will suffer, and crimes both great and small will be punished alike.

"In regard to the lynching of our Comrade Cook, I have this to say. Every feature connected with that crime but emphasizes its heinousness. Cook was a quiet, unassuming, gentlemanly being, enjoying the respect of all in a remarkable degree. Having wronged no one he was unconscious of having enemies. His wife and loving little ones had retired to rest and were enjoying the deep sleep of the innocent. A band of whites crept to his house under the cover of darkness, and thought to roast all alive. In endeavoring to make their escape the family was pursued by a shower of bullets and Cook fell to the ground, a corpse, leaving his loved ones behind, pursued by a fiendish mob. And the color of Cook's skin was the only crime laid at his door.

"If ye who speculate and doubt as to the existence of a hell but peer into the hearts of those vile creatures who slew poor Cook, you will draw back in terror; for hell, black hell is there. To give birth to a deed of such infamy, their hearts must be hells in miniature. But there is one redeeming feature about this crime. Unlike others, it found no defense anywhere. The condemnation of the crime was universal. And the entire South cried out in bitter tones against the demons who had at last succeeded in putting the crown of infamy of all the ages upon her brow.

Politics

"The South has defrauded us out of the ballot and she must restore it. But in judging her crime let us take an impartial view of its occasion. The ballot is supposed to be an expression of opinion. It is a means employed to record men's ideas. It is not designed as a vehicle of prejudice or gratitude, but of thought, opinion. When the Negro was first given the ballot he used it to convey expression of love and gratitude to the North, while it bore to the South a message of hate and revenge. No Negro, on pain of being ostracised or probably murdered, was allowed to exercise the ballot in any other way than that just mentioned. They voted in a mass, according to the dictates of love and hate.

"The ballot was never designed for such a purpose. The white man snatched the ballot from the Negro. His only crime was, in not snatching it from him also, for he was voting on the same principle. Neither race was thinking. They were both simply feeling, and ballots are not meant to convey feelings.

"But happily that day has passed and both races are thinking and are better prepared to vote. But the white man is still holding on to the stolen ballot box and he must surrender it. If we can secure possession of that right again, we shall use it to correct the many grievous wrongs under which we suffer. That is the one point on which all of our efforts are focused. Here is the storm center. Let us carry this point and our flag will soon have all of our rights inscribed thereon. The struggle is on, and my beloved Congress, let me urge one thing upon you. Leave out revenge as one of the things at which to aim.

"In His Holy Word our most high God has said: 'Vengeance is mine.' Great as is this Imperium, let it not mount God's throne and attempt by violence to rob Him of his prerogatives. In this battle, we want Him on our side and let us war as becometh men who fear and reverence Him. Hitherto, we have seen vengeance terrible in his hands.

"While we, the oppressed, stayed upon the plantation in peace, our oppressors were upon the field of battle engaged in mortal combat; and it was the blood of our oppressor, not our own, that was paid as the price of our freedom. And that same God is alive to-day; and let us trust Him for vengeance, and if we pray let our prayer be for mercy on those who have wronged us, for direful shall be their woes.

"And now, I have a substitute proposition. Fellow Comrades, I am not for internecine war. O! Eternal God, lend unto these, my Comrades, the departed spirit of Dante, faithful artist of the horrors of hell, for we feel that he alone can paint the shudder-making, soul-sickening scenes that follow in the wake of fast moving internecine war.

"Now, hear my solution of the race problem. The Anglo-Saxon does not yet know that we have caught the fire of liberty. He does not yet know that we have learned what a glorious thing it is to die for a principle, and especially when that principle is liberty. He does not yet know how the genius of his institutions has taken hold of our very souls. In the days of our enslavement we did not seem to him to be much disturbed about physical freedom. During the whole period of our enslavement we made only two slight insurrections.

"When at last the war came to set us free we stayed in the field and fed the men who were reddening the soil with their blood in a deadly struggle to keep us in bondage forever. We remained at home and defended the helpless wives and children of men, who if they had been at home would have counted it no crime to have ignored all our family ties and scattered husbands and wives, mothers and children as ruthlessly as the autumn winds do the falling leaves.

"The Anglo-Saxon has seen the eyes of the Negro following the American eagle in its glorious flight. The eagle has alighted on some mountain top and the poor Negro has been seen climbing up the rugged mountain side, eager to caress the eagle. When he has attempted to do this, the eagle has clawed at his eyes and dug his beak into his heart and has flown away in disdain; and yet, so majestic was its flight that the Negro, with tears in his eyes, and blood dripping from his heart has smiled and shouted: 'God save the eagle.'

"These things have caused us to be misunderstood. We know that our patient submission in slavery was due to our consciousness of weakness; we know that our silence and inaction during the civil war was due to a belief that God was speaking for us and fighting our battle; we know that our devotion to the flag will not survive one moment after our hope is dead; but we must not be content with knowing these things ourselves. We must change the conception which the Anglo-Saxon has formed of our character. We should let him know that patience has a limit; that strength brings confidence; that faith in God will demand the exercise of our own right arm; that hope and despair are each equipped with swords, the latter more dreadful than the former. Before we make a forward move, let us pull the veil from before the eyes of the Anglo-Saxon that he may see the New Negro standing before him humbly, but firmly demanding every right granted him by his maker and wrested from him by man.

"If, however, the revelation of our character and the full knowledge of our determined attitude does not procure our rights, my proposition, which I am about to submit, will still offer a solution.

Resolutions

"1. Be it *Resolved*: That we no longer conceal from the Anglo-Saxon the fact that the Imperium exists, so that he may see that the love of liberty in our bosoms is strong enough to draw us together into this compact government. He will also see that each individual Negro does not stand by himself, but is a link in a great chain that must not be broken with impunity.

"2. *Resolved*: That we earnestly strive to convince the Anglo-Saxon that we are now thoroughly wedded to the doctrine of Patrick Henry: 'Give me liberty or give me death,' Let us teach the Anglo-Saxon that we have arrived at the stage of development as a people, where we prefer to die in honor rather than live in disgrace.

"3. *Resolved*: That we spend four years in endeavors to impress the Anglo-Saxon that he has a New Negro on his hands and must surrender what belongs to him. In case we fail by these means to secure our rights and privileges we shall all, at once, abandon our several homes in the various other states and emigrate in a body to the State of Texas, broad in domain, rich in soil and salubrious in climate. Having an unquestioned majority of votes we shall secure possession of the State government.

"4. *Resolved*: That when once lawfully in control of that great state we shall, every man, die in his shoes before we shall allow vicious frauds or unlawful force to pursue us there and rob us of our acknowledged right.

"5. *Resolved*: That we sojourn in the state of Texas, working out our destiny as a separate and distinct race in the United States of America.

"Such is the proposition which I present. It is primarily pacific: yet it is firm and unyielding. It courts a peaceable adjustment, yet it does not shirk war, if war is forced.

"But in concluding, let me emphasize that my aim, my hope, my labors, my fervent prayer to God is for a peaceable adjustment of all our differences upon the high plane of the equality of man. Our beloved President, in his message to this Congress, made a serious mistake when he stated that there were only two weapons to be used in accomplishing revolutions. He named the sword (and spear) and ballot. There is a weapon mightier than either of these. I speak of the pen. If denied the use of the ballot let us devote our attention to that mightier weapon, the pen.

"Other races which have obtained their freedom erect monuments over bloody spots where they slew their fellow men. May God favor us to obtain our freedom without having to dot our land with these relics of barbaric ages.

"The Negro is the latest comer upon the scene of modern civilization. It would be the crowning glory of even this marvelous age; it would be the grandest contribution ever made to the cause of human civilization; it would be a worthy theme for the songs of the Holy Angels, if every Negro, away from the land of his nativity, can by means of the pen, force an acknowledgment of equality from the proud lips of the fierce, all conquering Anglo-Saxon, thus eclipsing the record of all other races of men, who without exception have had to wade through blood to achieve their freedom.

"Amid all the dense gloom that surrounds us, this transcendent thought now and then finds its way to my heart and warms it like a glorious Sun. Center your minds, beloved Congress, on this sublime hope, and God may grant it to you. But be prepared, if he deems us unfit for so great a boon, to buckle on our swords and go forth to win our freedom with the sword just as has been done by all other nations of men.

"My speech is made, my proposition is before you. I have done my duty. Your destiny is in your own hands."

Belton's speech had, like dynamite, blasted away all opposition. He was in thorough mastery of the situation. The waves of the sea were now calm, the fierce winds had abated, there was a great rift in the dark clouds. The ship of state was sailing placidly on the bosom of the erstwhile troubled sea, and Belton was at the helm.

His propositions were adopted in their entirety without one dissenting voice.

When the members left the Congress hall that evening they breathed freely, feeling that the great race problem was, at last, about to be definitely settled.

But, alas! how far wrong they were!

As Belton was leaving the chamber Bernard approached him and put his hands fondly on his shoulders.

Bernard's curly hair was disordered and a strange fire gleamed in his eye. He said: "Come over to the mansion to-night. I wish much to see you. Come about nine P.M."

Belton agreed to go.

Chapter XIX
The Parting of Ways

AT THE HOUR appointed Belton was at the door of the president's mansion and Bernard was there to meet him. They walked in and entered the same room where years before Belton had, in the name of the Congress, offered Bernard the Presidency of the Imperium.

The evening was mild, and the window, which ran down to the floor, was hoisted. The moon was shedding her full light and Bernard had not lighted his lamp. Each of them took seats near the window, one on one side and the other on the other, their faces toward the lawn.

"Belton," said Bernard, "that was a masterly speech you made to-day. If orations are measured according to difficulties surmounted and results achieved, yours ought to rank as a masterpiece. Aside from that, it was a daring deed. Few men would have attempted to rush in and quell that storm as you did. They would have been afraid of being torn to shreds, so to speak, and all to no purpose. Let me congratulate you." So saying he extended his hand and grasped Belton's feelingly.

Belton replied in a somewhat melancholy strain: "Bernard, that speech and its result ended my life's work. I have known long since that a crisis between the two races would come some day and I lived with the hope of being used by God to turn the current the right way. This I have done, and my work is over."

"Ah, no, Belton; greater achievements, by far, you shall accomplish. The fact is, I have called you over here to-night to acquaint you with a scheme that means eternal glory and honor to us both."

Belton smiled and shook his head.

"When I fully reveal my plan to you, you will change your mind."

"Well, Bernard, let us hear it."

"When you closed your speech to-day, a bright light shot athwart my brain and revealed to me something glorious. I came home determined to work it out in detail. This I have done, and now I hand this plan to you to ascertain your views and secure your cooperation." So saying he handed Belton a foolscap sheet of paper on which the following was written:

A Plan of Action for the Imperium in Imperio

1. Reconsider our determination to make known the existence of our Imperium, and avoid all mention of an emigration to Texas.

2. Quietly purchase all Texas land contiguous to states and territories of the Union. Build small commonplace huts on these lands and place rapid fire disappearing guns in fortifications dug beneath them. All of this is to be done secretly, the money to be raised by the issuance of bonds by the Imperium.

3. Encourage all Negroes who can possibly do so to enter the United States Navy.

4. Enter into secret negotiations with all of the foreign enemies of the United States, acquainting them of our military strength and men aboard the United States war ships.

5. Secure an appropriation from Congress to hold a fair at Galveston, inviting the Governor of Texas to be present. It will afford an excuse for all Negro families to pour into Texas. It will also be an excuse for having the war ships of nations friendly to us, in the harbor for a rendezvous.

6. While the Governor is away, let the troops proceed quietly to Austin, seize the capitol and hoist the flag of the Imperium.

7. We can then, if need be, wreck the entire navy of the United States in a night; the United States will then be prostrate before us and our allies.

8. We will demand the surrender of Texas and Louisiana to the Imperium. Texas, we will retain. Louisiana, we will cede to our foreign allies in return for their aid. Thus will the Negro have an empire of his own, fertile in soil, capable of sustaining a population of fifty million people.

Belton ceased reading the paper and returned it to Bernard.

"What is your opinion of the matter, Belton?"

"It is treason," was Belton's terse reply.

"Are you in favor of it?" asked Bernard.

"No. I am not and never shall be. I am no traitor and never shall be one. Our Imperium was organized to secure our rights within the United States and we will make any sacrifice that can be named to attain that end. Our efforts have been to wash the flag free of all blots, not to rend it; to burnish every star in the cluster, but to pluck none out.

"Candidly, Bernard, I love the Union and I love the South. Soaked as Old Glory is with my people's tears and stained as it is with their warm blood, I could die as my forefathers did, fighting for its honor and asking no greater boon than Old Glory for my shroud and native soil for my grave. This may appear strange, but love of country is one of the deepest passions in the human bosom, and men in all ages have been known to give their lives for the land in which they had known nothing save cruelty and oppression. I shall never give up my fight for freedom, but I shall never prove false to the flag. I may fight to keep her from floating over cesspools of corruption by removing the cesspool; but I shall never fight to restrict the territory in which she is to float. These are my unalterable opinions."

Bernard said: "Well, Belton, we have at last arrived at a point of separation in our lives. I know the Anglo-Saxon race. He will never admit you to equality with him. I am fully determined on my course of action and will persevere."

Each knew that further argument was unnecessary, and they arose to part. They stood up, looking each other squarely in the face, and shook hands in silence. Tears were in the eyes of both men. But each felt that he was heeding the call of duty, and neither had ever been known to falter. Belton returned to his room and retired to rest. Bernard called his messenger and sent him for every man of prominence in the Congress of the Imperium.

They all slept in the building. The leaders got out of bed and hurried to the president. He laid before them the plan he had shown Belton. They all accepted it and pronounced it good. He then told them that he had submitted it to Belton but that Belton was opposed. This took them somewhat by surprise, and finding that Belton was opposed to it they were sorry that they had spoken so hastily.

Bernard knew that such would be their feelings. He produced a written agreement and asked all who favored that plan to sign that paper, as that would be of service in bringing over other members. Ashamed to appear vacillating, they signed. They then left.

The Congress assembled next day, and President Belgrave submitted his plan. Belton swept the assembly with his eyes and told at a glance that there was a secret, formidable combination, and he decided that it would be useless to oppose the plan.

The President's plan was adopted. Belton alone voted no.

Belton then arose and said: "Being no longer able to follow where the Imperium leads, I hereby tender my resignation as a member."

The members stood aghast at these words, for death alone removed a member from the ranks of the Imperium, and asking to resign, according to their law was asking to be shot. Bernard and every member of the Congress crowded around Belton and begged him to reconsider, and not be so cruel to his comrades as to make them fire bullets into his noble heart.

Belton was obdurate. According to the law of the Imperium, he was allowed thirty days in which to reconsider his request. Ordinarily those under sentence of death were kept in close confinement, but not so with Belton. He was allowed all liberty. In fact, it was the secret wish of every one that he might take advantage of his freedom and escape. But Belton was resolved to die.

As he now felt that his days on earth were few, his mind began to turn toward Antoinette. He longed to see her once more and just let her know that he loved her still. He at length decided to steal away to Richmond and have a last interview with her. All the pent up passion of years now burst forth in his soul, and as the train sped toward Virginia, he felt that love would run him mad ere he saw Antoinette once more.

While his train goes speeding on, let us learn a little of the woman whom he left years ago.

Antoinette Nermal Piedmont had been tried and excluded from her church on the charge of adultery. She did not appear at the trial nor speak a word in her own defense. Society dropped her as you would a poisonous viper, and she was completely ostracised. But, conscious of her innocence and having an abiding faith in the justice of God, she moved along undisturbed by the ostracism. The only person about whom she was concerned was Belton.

She yearned, oh! so much, to be able to present to him proofs of her chastity; but there was that white child. But God had the matter in hand.

As the child grew, its mother noticed that its hair began to change. She also thought she discovered his skin growing darker by degrees. As his features developed he was seen to be the very image of Belton. Antoinette frequently went out with him and the people began to shake their heads in doubt. At length the child became Antoinette's color, retaining Belton's features.

Public sentiment was fast veering around. Her former friends began to speak to her more kindly, and the people began to feel that she was a martyr instead of a criminal. But the child continued to steadily grow darker and darker until he was a shade darker than his father.

The church met and rescinded its action of years ago. Every social organization of standing elected Antoinette Nermal Piedmont an honorary member. Society came rushing to her. She gently smiled, but did not seek their company. She was only concerned about Belton. She prayed hourly for God to bring him back to her. And now, unknown to her, he was coming.

One morning as she was sitting on her front porch enjoying the morning breeze, she looked toward the gate and saw her husband entering. She screamed loudly, and rushed into her son's room and dragged him out of bed. She did not allow him time to dress, but was dragging him to the door.

Belton rushed into the house. Antoinette did not greet him, but cried in anxious, frenzied tones: "Belton! there is your white child! Look at him! Look at him!"

The boy looked up at Belton, and if ever one person favored another, this child favored him. Belton was dazed. He looked from child to mother and from mother to child. By and by it began to dawn on him that that child was somehow his child.

His wife eyed him eagerly. She rushed to her album and showed him pictures of the child taken at various stages of its growth. Belton discerned the same features in each photograph, but a different shade of color of the skin. His knees began to tremble. He had come, as the most wronged of men, to grant pardon. He now found himself the vilest of men, unfit for pardon.

A picture of all that his innocent wife had suffered came before him, and he gasped: "O, God, what crime is this with which my soul is stained?" He put his hands before his face.

Antoinette divined his thoughts and sprang toward him. She tore his hands from his face and kissed him passionately, and begged him to kiss and embrace her once more.

Belton shook his head sadly and cried: "Unworthy, unworthy."

Antoinette now burst forth into weeping.

The boy said: "Papa, why don't you kiss Mama?"

Hearing the boy's voice, Belton raised his eyes, and seeing his image, which Antoinette had brought into the world, he grasped her in his arms and covered her face with kisses; and there was joy enough in those two souls to almost excite envy in the bosom of angels.

Belton was now recalled to life. He again loved the world. The cup of his joy was full. He was proud of his beautiful, noble wife, proud of his promising son. For days he was lost in contemplation of his new found happiness. But at last, a frightful picture arose before him. He remembered that he was doomed to die, and the day of his death came galloping on at a rapid pace. Thus a deep river of sadness went flowing on through his happy Elysian fields.

But he remained unshaken in his resolve. He had now learned to put duty to country above everything else. Then, too, he looked upon his boy and he felt that his son would fill his place in the world. But Antoinette was so happy that he could not have the heart to tell her of his fate. She was a girl again. She chatted and laughed and played as though her heart was full of love. In her happiness she freely forgave the world for all the wrongs that it had perpetrated upon her.

At length the day drew near for Belton to go to Waco. He took a tender leave of his loved ones. It was so tender that Antoinette was troubled, and pressed him hard for an answer as to when he was to return or send for them. He begged her to be assured of his love and know that he would not stay away one second longer than was necessary. Thus assured, she let him go, after kissing him more than a hundred times.

Belton turned his back on this home of happiness and love, to walk into the embrace of death. He arrived in Waco in due time, and the morning of his execution came.

In one part of the campus there was a high knoll surrounded on all sides by trees. This knoll had been selected as the spot for the execution.

In the early morn while the grass yet glittered with pearls of water, and as the birds began to chirp, Belton was led forth to die. Little did those birds know that they were chirping the funeral march of the world's noblest hero. Little did they dream that they were chanting his requiem.

The sun had not yet risen but had reddened the east with his signal of approach. Belton was stationed upon the knoll, his face toward the coming dawn. With his hands folded calmly across his bosom, he stood gazing over the heads of the executioners, at the rosy east.

His executioners, five in number, stood facing him, twenty paces away. They were commanded by Bernard, the President of the Imperium. Bernard gazed on Belton with eyes of love and admiration. He loved his friend but he loved his people more. He could not sacrifice his race for his dearest friend. Viola had taught him that lesson. Bernard's eyes swam with tears as he said to Belton in a hoarse whisper: "Belton Piedmont, your last hour has come. Have you anything to say?"

"Tell posterity," said Belton, in firm ringing tones that startled the birds into silence, "that I loved the race to which I belonged and the flag that floated over me; and, being unable to see these objects of my love engage in mortal combat, I went to my God, and now look down upon both from my home in the skies to bless them with my spirit."

Bernard gave the word of command to fire, and Belton fell forward, a corpse. On the knoll where he fell he was buried, shrouded in an American flag.

Chapter XX
Personal – (Berl Trout)

I WAS A MEMBER of the Imperium that ordered Belton to be slain. It fell to my lot to be one of the five who fired the fatal shots and I saw him fall. Oh! that I could have died in his stead!

When he fell, the spirit of conservatism in the Negro race, fell with him. He was the last of that peculiar type of Negro heroes that could so fondly kiss the smiting hand.

His influence, which alone had just snatched us from the edge of the precipice of internecine war, from whose steep heights we had, in our rage, decided to leap into the dark gulf beneath, was now gone; his restraining hand was to be felt no more.

Henceforth Bernard Belgrave's influence would be supreme. Born of distinguished parents, reared in luxury, gratified as to every whim, successful in every undertaking, idolized by the people, proud, brilliant, aspiring, deeming nothing impossible of achievement, with Viola's tiny hand protruding from the grave pointing him to move forward, Bernard Belgrave, President of the Imperium In Imperio, was a man to be feared.

As Bernard stood by the side of Belton's grave and saw the stiffened form of his dearest friend lowered to its last resting place, his grief was of a kind too galling for tears. He laughed a fearful, wicked laugh like unto that of a maniac, and said: "Float on proud flag, while yet you may. Rejoice, oh! ye Anglo-Saxons, yet a little while. Make my father ashamed to own me, his lawful son; call me a bastard child; look upon my pure mother as a harlot; laugh at Viola in the grave of a self-murderer; exhume Belton's body if you like and tear your flag from around him to keep him from polluting it! Yes, stuff your vile stomachs full of all these horrors. You shall be richer food for the buzzards to whom I have solemnly vowed to give your flesh."

These words struck terror to my soul. With Belton gone and this man at our head, our well-organized, thoroughly equipped Imperium was a serious menace to the peace of the world. A chance spark might at any time cause a conflagration, which, unchecked, would spread destruction, devastation and death all around.

I felt that beneath the South a mine had been dug and filled with dynamite, and that lighted fuses were lying around in careless profusion, where any irresponsible hand might reach them and ignite the dynamite. I fancied that I saw a man do this very thing in a sudden fit of uncontrollable rage. There was a dull roar as of distant rumbling thunder. Suddenly there was a terrific explosion and houses, fences, trees, pavement stones, and all things on earth were hurled high into the air to come back a mass of ruins such as man never before had seen. The only sound to be heard was a universal groan; those who had not been killed were too badly wounded to cry out.

Such were the thoughts that passed through my mind. I was determined to remove the possibility of such a catastrophe. I decided to prove traitor and reveal the existence of the Imperium that it might be broken up or watched. My deed may appear to be the act of a vile wretch, but it is done in the name of humanity. Long ere you shall have come to this line, I shall have met the fate of a traitor. I die for mankind, for humanity, for civilization. If the voice of a poor Negro, who thus gives his life, will be heard, I only ask as a return that all mankind will join hands and help my poor down-trodden people to secure those rights for which they organized the Imperium, which my betrayal has now destroyed. I urge this because love of liberty is such an inventive genius, that if you destroy one device it at once constructs another more powerful.

When will all races and classes of men learn that men made in the image of God will not be the slaves of another image?

Seven Thieves

Emmalia Harrington

SWEAT ESCAPED the turban Widow Edith Derosiers stuffed under her straw hat, dripping into her eyes. Any attempt to shake off the salty liquid sent droplets flying onto leaves and soil alike. Though a few dashes of perspiration probably wouldn't harm her garden, she grabbed a corner of her neckerchief to swab her russet skin. Eyeing the pump bottle leaning against her kneeling form, she considered applying some mist to her face.

The bottle was filled with the best insect repellent in the Virginia colony, a mixture of witch hazel, lavender and mint extracts suspended in water. She was only a third of the way through with this current batch; a quick spray on herself shouldn't be too wasteful.

Once she shook her hands loose of cramps, Edith pressed her palm against her face. The action flattened her homemade mask, crushing the dried roses and lavender stuffed inside. Edith breathed deep, pulling floral scents both rich and delicate into her lungs, cleansing her innards. Even in her backyard kingdom, to travel unprotected was to court a painful death.

Rising to her feet, she beat dust off of her apron before picking up her tools and heading to her storage shed. Her knees and back complained only a little. Once everything was stowed away, she lingered at the shack door, taking in her treasures.

Herbs and flowers took up most of her land, planted as close together as she dared. Even with the air as still as it was right now, fragrance rose from every leaf and stem. Not one plant bore traces of browning, wilting or insects.

Nestled against her kitchen wall was a black canister large enough for an adult to stand inside with her arms outstretched. Edith didn't miss her childhood days of pumping water and hauling buckets to the kitchen until her arms and hands were one large burn.

Near the back of the property was a brick outbuilding outfitted with a shingled roof and a few tiny windows. Edith kept her still house cleaner than anything, discouraging rogue wisps of perfume.

If crouching for hours in direct sunlight in the height of summer was odious, entering her little laboratory made her want to scream. The only light peeked from around the locked shutters and oozed from mirror slabs. A place so dusky should have condensation on its walls and air that steamed with every breath. Her reality was a reek so stale her floral mask was the only thing keeping her from gagging. Opening the shutters and leaving the door ajar risked contaminating her nascent work with outside miasma.

Giving the mirror slab by the doorway a double tap, captured sunlight filled the room, illuminating slabs which supported large copper pears with drooping stems feeding fragrant liquid into a receiving flask. In one corner stood a device as tall as her, its round glass sides boasting layers of gravel, sand and charcoal. The bottom of the tube held a tap where she could help herself to all the purified water she could carry. Against a far wall were casks of Seven Thieves' Vinegar in the making.

A better world would have all her vinegar mature in six months, allowing her ingredients to penetrate every drop of liquid. The current market demanded so much of the tonic, a single week had to do. Edith's culmination of breeding, composting, weeding and cultivating was hastened into a product any housewife could spit out.

Stretching her arms over her head, working gardening induced knots, Edith headed to a corner filled with vats of spoiled wine and her shelves of distilled essences. All of her stocks were running low, though camphor, peppermint and the other five thieves were nearly gone. Her customers would die or move on to a whiter, less experienced perfumer before her ingredients regrew.

Near the middle of the room sat a table filled with scales, vials and other instruments, scrubbed yesterday until her fingers bloomed angry red. Pulling down the necessary ingredients, Edith measured what she needed to make another vat of vinegar. Part of her wondered if she could pour the exact amounts with her eyes closed. The rest of her liked not being arrested or worse for selling faulty goods to whites.

The ground trembled beneath her in spurts. Straightening, a hand on the small of her back, she turned to find a familiar broad tawny body standing in the doorway. The newcomer was leaning against the frame, with heavy shadows under her eyes. Her gown and apron were rumpled, and her cap went askew as Edith barreled into Widow Marja Anker, delivering a rib creaking hug. Marja returned the hug, the rumbling in her chest indicating a groan.

Edith stepped away, her eyes hardening as she took in her Marja's bare face and dried blood framing her nails.

Marja caught the glare. She mimed coughing into her free hand before turning the palm to Edith, revealing a lack of lung-generated pus.

Removing her mask, Edith rammed it into Marja's open hand before pointing to their house. Marja's lips moved, giving Edith a series of sounds tumbling into one another. Edith spun on her heel, returning to the table. Closing her eyes, she gave a small prayer that her Marja had enough sense to cover her nose at least until she returned indoors.

* * *

A small eternity later, with a flask of skin-cooling rosemary water in hand, Edith crossed her garden to the back door of the main house. The sun was finishing its peak in the sky, and the cramping in her stomach reminded Edith that she hadn't eaten anything since the morning light made its first forays into the day. Before food, she had to deal with more pressing concerns.

Inside her house by the back door rested a custom made paddle fan.

Picking up her fan, Edith followed her nose to the kitchen, where Marja stood with her back to the room, scouring her medical gear with sand and water. Stomping the ground to alert the woman, Edith said "What were you thinking, being out all night?" Marja wilted at the sound of Edith's voice, loud enough for the deaf to hear. "Do you want to give the City Watch a reason to lock you away? You of all people should remember the blacks' plague curfew."

Turning around, Marja waited for Edith to bite her fan before enunciating, "Mrs. Abrams was having a difficult birth." As her words hit the paddle, its cloth and metal hummed, passing the woman's message through teeth and bone. "I spent all night and a good part of yesterday making sure she and her babies would remain on this earth." Her muscles turned to rags, and she slumped against Edith. Marja said something Edith couldn't catch, prompting the woman to tap her Marja's shoulder and point to the fan.

Picking her head off from Edith's chest, Marja told the fan, "She had triplets."

Edith blinked, then softly shoved her Marja towards the nearest chair. Marja resisted the push, her mouth twisted into a thin smile. "Mr. Abrams closed his shop early. He refused to leave the hall outside his bedroom until the last of the afterbirth was delivered. With three new sons, he has no reason to have me jailed."

Opening her mouth wide and using her free hand, Edith mimicked Marja's favorite praying style.

Stepping back to reveal her akimbo stance, Marja said, "Do you think me a fool? I'm not going to witness if a woman and her babies look ready to die in front of me." Relaxing her arms, she added "Mr. Abrams is giving us a favor for this."

Edith raised her eyebrows.

Returning to the basin steaming on the counter, Marja motioned for Edith to follow. Plunging her hands into the gritty water, Marja said, "Mr. Abrams wants to pay me handsomely to spend the next fortnight looking after his wife and heirs. When I explained my other duties, he offered to pay me well and not report me to the Watch."

Filling her lungs with humid kitchen air, Edith yelled "It's not enough to go out into the plague air without protection? You want to be tossed into a cell again with only fleas for food and company?" Her shoulders sagging, she added "They won't let me give you perfume in jail."

As Edith turned away, Marja caught the edge of her sleeve. A strong tug was all she needed to come free. When Marja stomped the kitchen floor, trying to grab her attention, Edith kept walking.

Several minutes later she returned to the kitchen, a box in her hands. Moving with as heavy a step she could manage, she placed the box on the counter, pulled out a spray bottle and headed to the woman now at the table, busy drying a pewter enema syringe. It only took a few pumps to drench it and her Marja's hands with proper Seven Thieves vinegar.

Marja leapt back, dropping the syringe. Her face was contorted into a "What's wrong with you?" look.

"I'm not taking chances," Edith said. Stopping for breath, she started to say more, but noticed Marja's still perplexed visage.

Making a sigh large enough to move her arms and back, her picked up the syringe and walked up to her companion, showing her where droplets still shone on the metal. Marja spoke into Edith's ear. It took a few repeats until she made out, "Won't the water weaken its strength?"

Her face burning, Edith hurried to her box, taking out a brass ball on a cord. The musty floral notes of chamomile seeped from holes punched into the metal. Edith turned to Marja, eyebrows raised, holding up the pomander. Marja lowered her head to give her companion an easier time fastening the chain and its pendant around her neck.

Edith made a point to leave the vinegar bottle by the still-wet midwifery tools.

* * *

When Edith wasn't working on Seven Thieves Vinegar, or sending her goods to wholesalers, she was mixing, distilling, steeping and bottling to keep up with the wealthy's demand for protective fragrances. Some were liquids meant to be dabbed, sprinkled or sprayed onto the skin or clothes, while solid perfumes needed to be rubbed into place or carried around in pomanders, keeping their owners in a fragrant cloud that wouldn't fade within hours.

Vinegar wasn't as elegant as the scents she wore around her neck or peddled to the nicer shops in town, but her recipe was the nicest smelling available, and enough people could afford it. To keep her purse happy, she spent a better part of a week in her garden replenishing her supplies.

In her still room, where none were around to look, Edith removed her shoes and stockings to give her feet room to swell. Her nose turned numb from the steam that escaped when she transferred distillations from one flask to another.

Preparing the vinegar itself required no heat, just a matter of clipping what she needed from her garden, drying the necessary herbs, layering them prepared containers, pouring over vinegar and leaving the mixture to sit.

As long as her hands kept busy, she wouldn't grind her feet into the earth, waiting for stomping that never came. She wouldn't keep scanning her surroundings, looking over her shoulder for traces of that kind tawny face. Edith would do everything in her power to make fragrances that were second to none in keeping disease away. Her pockets would grow so full she'd reinforce them with canvas. Marja would never have to work for others ever again, but drink all the tea and wine she pleased while staying out of prison. There would be no Marja praying for a single water flask to last four days.

If the Abramses caught her Marja witnessing to their slaves, they probably wouldn't call the City Watch, but a judge to send her to the auction block.

It was every bit as likely that Marja would remember to wear a mask or pomander locket, only to give it to a slave or beggar with no protection to speak of. Her Marja's lungs would fill with muck, forcing her to cough until her ribs cracked. No amount of Edith's perfume would bring her back.

These thoughts made Edith's hands shake so badly she dared not handle her perfumes and vinegar. She'd grab a spray bottle and stalk her garden, hunting for insects to blast into submission. By the time her bottle was empty her arms were usually steady enough to resume her work.

Whenever Marja didn't come home one night, Edith had to constantly remind herself that this wasn't the first time. Marja was full of tales of missing curfew in her effort to save souls. She'd only been caught a handful of times.

The next day Edith worked her hands into blisters. From the afternoon onwards, her knees creaked with every movement. By that night, her feet were so swollen she feared having to take scissors to her shoes.

With the way her heart was pounding, and her feet kept twisting against the floor, searching for the tale tell tremble of footsteps, sleep wasn't going to come. No matter, there was plenty to do. Taking the household supply of Seven Thieves vinegar, she swabbed it along every window, door, chamber pot and other areas prone to contamination. By the time she was finished, she couldn't stand, let alone walk without pain shooting up her soles through to her head.

Soaking her afflicted body in a bath of rose petals and lemon balm did wonders for her flesh. The fragrant water served as a reminder of how Marja refused all protection for herself. For a while, Edith couldn't tell if her blood was boiling or if it was the bath.

It took three cups of wine to cool her enough to consider lying down. Sleep remained a stranger, forcing Edith to stare into the dark, captive to her thoughts. If the late Reverend Anker's followers could manage to sneak bread and small beer into the Ankers' cells, perhaps Edith could do the same for her Marja. She tried not to think of how easily guards could sneak up on her. Eventually she succeeded. Thoughts of Marja shoved before an audience, her mouth forced open to prove good health, crowded everything else from Edith's mind.

Her Marja's reputation as a troublemaker would likely get her sold to a sugarcane island. Burns and hunger were rampant, though most slaves took years to die. Edith should probably pray for a Carolina rice farmer to buy her Marja, where malaria would finish her off faster.

Edith might have stayed in her haze forever if a pair of strong hands hadn't shaken her out of it. She jerked upright and overshot, nearly falling onto her bedding. The hands steadied her for a long moment before withdrawing.

Blinking the grogginess from her eyes, Edith felt for the mirror block on her bedside table. The other person beat her to it, awakening a flare that made Edith wince. When her eyes stopped hurting, she made out a familiar shape gesturing with a free hand.

"I can't see you well," Edith said. Hauling her creaky body out of bed, she found her fan and bit it, turning to her Marja.

"I didn't want to wake you," Marja said, leaning to touch foreheads with Edith.

Edith stepped back, pointing out the window to the sliver of moon. Her Marja mimed slow, careful steps, stopping to look over her shoulder. Edith raised her arms and squinted as though aiming a pistol.

Marja shrugged, motioning for Edith to bite her fan. "You shouldn't act as though it's my first time out after curfew," the midwife said, "I've been practicing since before I married."

Edith held out her hand, pretending to give a speech before flipping through pages of an imaginary book. Then she hunched over, faking a coughing fit.

Marja exaggerated a sigh, flopping her arms, before speaking into the fan. "That's not what happened. The triplets kept me busy until well after sunset, and Mrs. Abrams kept a close eye on me. I wasn't able to witness to her slaves." Her hands gathered bunches of her apron, twisting the fabric.

Edith pointed her head to the moon. Marja looked away, mumbling. At Edith's prodding, she walked around the room in an exaggerated march, stopping every so often. When Marja paused, she'd mimic opening a door and preaching the Good Word. A few times she paused by their bed, stroking the imaginary heads of the ailing.

Edith's vision turned grey before she remembered to breathe. Her arms trembling, she forced herself to back away before she did something regrettable. "Even if it's not at the Abramses, witnessing after curfew is still illegal. Why do you want to throw away this life you have?" she shouted, her throat rasping at the force of her words. "Is staying with me so awful, you'd you prefer rotted lungs?"

Marja had winced at Edith's initial outburst, but now stood at her full height, feet braced for whatever may come her way. She pointed to her heart and raised her hands heavenward.

Shoving past Marja, Edith headed for the parlor. The cushions on the chairs were threadbare and starting to lose their stuffing, but a night sleeping on three seats pushed together wouldn't kill her.

Edith changed her mind the next morning. Her shoulders were full of knots, and her neck refused to straighten. Hobbling to the kitchen, she prayed that the solar water heater hadn't cooled too much overnight. A long steam over a basin of flowers followed by a massage with rose hip oil should turn her into a new woman.

Biting her lip and hunching, she stomped her foot. Nothing happened. Glancing about the kitchen and checking the pantry revealed the same amount of bread and clean dishes as last night.

It was impossible to run in her cramped state, forcing Edith to speed-limp to the front door, where Marja kept a bundle of midwifery supplies. The bag was gone. Edith tried not to melt to the floor in relief.

After an endless stretch of time, where her heart refused to slow and she had to remember to breathe, Edith struggled upright. In the kitchen, she brewed some tea and sank into a chair, her mind whirring. She had every reason to be hard on her Marja, and yet... She tried to shake her head, but still couldn't move.

What made Marja Edith's sweet Marja was her devotion to Jesus. "'Under Christ, there is no man or woman, black or white,'" Edith quoted, "'There's only love.'" Edith traced her fingers along her cheek and lips, remembering Marja's gesture as she first told Edith those words.

To block her Marja from offering freedom through Christ made Edith little better than a colony official, and every bit as stupid. If being locked up and left to starve couldn't stop Marja, neither would harsh words. Edith cringed as she remembered last night's words. Was she trying to drive her Marja away? The idea of never sharing a home or bed again with Marja should be destroyed before it could take root.

Rising from the table, Edith checked the water's temperature before dragging out the bathtub. If she was going to act, it would be with a halfway working body.

* * *

Scouring every secondhand shop open to free blacks during the morning hours left Edith in her still shed well into the evening, working by the light of mirror slabs. When her neck cramped, she rubbed rose hip oil into the afflicted spot. If sweat dripped into her eyes, she shook it off. When exhaustion blurred her vision, she used her nose and fingers to find the right herbs and stuff them where they needed to be.

Years of handling trowels, shovels and uncooperative flasks had given Edith leather-hard hands. She gave thanks every night when her labor addled head caused the needle to slip, jabbing her flesh. A more genteel woman would have had more hole than finger by the end of the first night. Then again, a proper lady likely had more time to devote to needle work and make fewer mistakes that caused herbs to dribble out of half pinned hems.

It was two days before Edith found the time to voice her plan to Marja.

When Edith entered the house that evening, her hands were cracked, her muscles were on fire and her joints were made of creaks. Turning into the kitchen, her eyes flicked to the spout that connected to the water heater, before settling on the cupboard where the tub lay, scoured clean and ready for another reviving soak.

Heading to the counter, she reached for the shelves that held her homemade blend of marigold, cornflowers and tea, along with the teapot painted with blue garlands her Marja loved. The hot water spigot helped to make a quick brew. In the pantry were rosewater Shrewsbury cakes that weren't too stale. Adding pitchers of milk and honey to the table, Edith screwed up her courage to seek her Marja.

Rather than stomp on the ground, Edith approached Marja in the parlor, walking into her companion's line of sight and waiting, twisting her fingers. The midwife's eyes remained fixed on her Bible. A thousand flurried heartbeats passed, but Marja didn't turn a page. Clasping her hands together, Edith clutched them against her breast, drooping her head and shoulders.

The air hummed, reminding Edith of a string stretching to its breaking point. Looking up at Marja would spell disaster, revealing a face Edith didn't want to show. No, she would stand here all night and for the next week if she had to, moving only when her Marja signaled her thoughts.

Edith's knees screamed, wanting to know what on earth she was thinking. They'd swell and lock if she kept straining herself.

Marja touched Edith's chin, guiding her face upwards. With trembling teeth, glittering eyes, reddening noses, it was like looking into a mirror. Placing her lips against Edith's ear, Marja whispered her favorite verses before the two of them retreated into the kitchen.

Over tepid tea and Shrewsbury cakes, Edith outlined her plan, pausing and repeating herself with words and hands to make sure Marja understood. Her Marja nodded, tracing notes to herself with her finger on the kitchen table. When asked if she could distribute scented fabric to more than just the Abrams' slaves, Marja's smile threatened to crack her face in two. "Good news is to be shared with all," she said.

* * *

Marja woke her up that midnight, full of fire and inspiration. Even biting the fan, Edith couldn't glean an ounce of sense from her companion. Daybreak and the brief night's sleep cleared Edith's mind enough to understand her Marja.

According to her companion, though Edith was heading down the right path, setting aside time and resources to those who needed the most help, she could take greater steps. Why was she using her cast offs from making Seven Thieves' Vinegar, and dipping into her bumper crop of sage? Surely a slave's health would be better protected with flowers Edith reserved for her wealthiest customers. An elegant bouquet stuffed inside a kerchief would do wonders to protect someone's lungs.

No amount of Edith explaining that she liked to eat would convince her companion otherwise. Staving off a growing headache, Edith left for her garden before she could tell Marja to grow her own herbs.

That night Marja brought home bonus gifts from the Abrams, a basket of worn-out cloth. Making a rude internal gesture at her joints, Edith settled by her Marja's side. Threading a spare needle, she followed her dearest's lead.

Of One Blood

Or, The Hidden Self

Pauline Hopkins

Chapter I

THE RECITATIONS were over for the day. It was the first week in November and it had rained about every day the entire week; now freezing temperature added to the discomforture of the dismal season. The lingering equinoctial whirled the last clinging yellow leaves from the trees on the campus and strewed them over the deserted paths, while from the leaden sky fluttering snow-white flakes gave an unexpected touch of winter to the scene.

The east wind for which Boston and vicinity is celebrated, drove the sleet against the window panes of the room in which Reuel Briggs sat among his books and the apparatus for experiments. The room served for both living and sleeping. Briggs could have told you that the bareness and desolateness of the apartment were like his life, but he was a reticent man who knew how to suffer in silence. The dreary wet afternoon, the cheerless walk over West Boston bridge through the soaking streets had but served to emphasize the loneliness of his position, and morbid thoughts had haunted him all day: To what use all this persistent hard work for a place in the world – clothes, food, a roof? Is suicide wrong? he asked himself with tormenting persistency. From out the storm, voices and hands seemed beckoning him all day to cut the Gordian knot and solve the riddle of whence and whither for all time.

His place in the world would soon be filled; no vacuum remained empty; the eternal movement of all things onward closed up the gaps, and the wail of the newly-born augmented the great army of mortals pressing the vitals of mother Earth with hurrying tread. So he had tormented himself for months, but the courage was yet wanting for strength to rend the veil. It had grown dark early. Reuel had not stirred from his room since coming from the hospital – had not eaten nor drank, and was in full possession of the solitude he craved. It was now five o'clock. He sat sideways by the bare table, one leg crossed over the other. His fingers kept the book open at the page where he was reading, but his attention wandered beyond the leaden sky, the dripping panes, and the sounds of the driving storm outside.

He was thinking deeply of the words he had just read, and which the darkness had shut from his gaze. The book was called *The Unclassified Residuum*, just published and eagerly sought by students of mysticism, and dealing with the great field of new discoveries in psychology. Briggs was a close student of what might be termed 'absurdities' of supernatural phenomena or *mysticism*, best known to the every-day world as 'effects of the imagination', a phrase of mere dismissal, and which it is impossible to make precise; the book suited the man's mood. These were the words of haunting significance:

"All the while, however, the phenomena are there, lying broadcast over the surface of history. No matter where you open its pages, you find things recorded under the name of divinations, inspirations, demoniacal possessions, apparitions, trances, ecstasies, miraculous healing and productions of disease, and occult powers possessed by peculiar individuals over persons and things in their neighborhood.

"The mind-curers and Christian scientists, who are beginning to lift up their heads in our communities, unquestionably get remarkable results in certain cases. The ordinary medical man dismisses them from his attention with the cut-and-dried remark that they are 'only the effects of the imagination.' But there is a meaning in this vaguest of phrases.

"We know a non-hysterical woman who in her trances knows facts which altogether transcend her *possible* normal consciousness, facts about the lives of people whom she never saw or heard of before. I am well aware of all the liabilities to which this statement exposes me, and I make it deliberately, having practically no doubt whatever of its truth."

Presently Briggs threw the book down, and, rising from his chair, began pacing up and down the bare room.

"That is it," at length he said aloud. "I have the power, I know the truth of every word – of all M. Binet asserts, and could I but complete the necessary experiments, I would astonish the world. O Poverty, Ostracism! have I not drained the bitter cup to the dregs!" he apostrophized, with a harsh, ironical laugh.

Mother Nature had blessed Reuel Briggs with superior physical endowments, but as yet he had never had reason to count them blessings. No one could fail to notice the vast breadth of shoulder, the strong throat that upheld a plain face, the long limbs, the sinewy hands. His head was that of an athlete, with close-set ears, and covered with an abundance of black hair, straight and closely cut, thick and smooth; the nose was the aristocratic feature, although nearly spoiled by broad nostrils, of this remarkable young man; his skin was white, but of a tint suggesting olive, an almost sallow color which is a mark of strong, melancholic temperaments. His large mouth concealed powerful long white teeth which gleamed through lips even and narrow, parting generally in a smile at once grave, genial and singularly sweet; indeed Briggs' smile changed the plain face at once into one that interested and fascinated men and women. True there were lines about the mouth which betrayed a passionate, nervous temperament, but they accorded well with the rest of his strong personality. His eyes were a very bright and piercing gray, courageous, keen and shrewd. Briggs was not a man to be despised – physically or mentally.

None of the students associated together in the hive of men under the fostering care of the 'benign mother' knew aught of Reuel Briggs's origin. It was rumored at first that he was of Italian birth, then they 'guessed' he was a Japanese, but whatever land claimed him as a son, all voted him a genius in his scientific studies, and much was expected of him at graduation. He had no money, for he was unsocial and shabby to the point of seediness, and apparently no relatives, for his correspondence was limited to the letters of editors of well known local papers and magazines. Somehow he lived and paid his way in a third-rate lodging-house near Harvard square, at the expense of the dull intellects or the idle rich, with which a great university always teems, to whom Briggs acted as 'coach', and by contributing scientific articles to magazines on the absorbing subject of spiritualistic phenomena. A few of his articles had produced a profound impression. The monotonous pacing continued for a time, finally ending at the mantel, from whence he abstracted a disreputable looking pipe and filled it.

"Well," he soliloquized, as he reseated himself in his chair, "Fate has done her worst, but she mockingly beckons me on and I accept her challenge. I shall not yet attempt the bourne. If I conquer, it will be by strength of brain and willpower. I shall conquer; I must and will."

The storm had increased in violence; the early dusk came swiftly down, and at this point in his revery the rattling window panes, as well as the whistle and shriek of gusts of moaning wind, caught his attention. "Phew! a beastly night." With a shiver, he drew his chair closer to the cylinder stove, whose glowing body was the only cheerful object in the bare room.

As he sat with his back half-turned to catch the grateful warmth, he looked out into the dim twilight across the square and into the broad paths of the campus, watching the skeleton arms of giant trees tossing in the wind, and the dancing snow-flakes that fluttered to earth in their fairy gowns to be quickly transformed into running streams that fairly overflowed the gutters. He fell into a dreamy state as he gazed, for which he could not account. As he sent his earnest, penetrating gaze into the night, gradually the darkness and storm faded into tints of cream and rose and soft moist lips. Silhouetted against the background of lowering sky and waving branches, he saw distinctly outlined a fair face framed in golden hair, with soft brown eyes, deep and earnest – terribly earnest they seemed just then – rose-tinged baby lips, and an expression of wistful entreaty. O how real, how very real did the passing shadow appear to the gazer!

He tried to move, uneasily conscious that this strange experience was but 'the effect of the imagination', but he was powerless. The unknown countenance grew dimmer and farther off, floating gradually out of sight, while a sense of sadness and foreboding wrapped him about as with a pall.

A wilder gust of wind shook the window sashes. Reuel stared about him in a bewildered way like a man awakening from a heavy sleep. He listened to the wail of the blast and glanced at the fire and rubbed his eyes. The vision was gone; he was alone in the room; all was silence and darkness. The ticking of the cheap clock on the mantel kept time with his heart-beats. The light of his own life seemed suddenly eclipsed with the passing of the lovely vision of Venus. Conscious of an odd murmur in his head, which seemed to control his movements, he rose and went toward the window to open it; there came a loud knock at the door.

Briggs did not answer at once. He wanted no company. Perhaps the knocker would go away. But he was persistent. Again came the knock ending in a double rat-tat accompanied by the words:

"I know you are there; open, open, you son of Erebus! You inhospitable Turk!"

Thus admonished Briggs turned the key and threw wide open the door.

"It's you, is it? Confound you, you're always here when you're not wanted," he growled.

The visitor entered and closed the door behind him. With a laugh he stood his dripping umbrella back of the stove against the chimney-piece, and immediately a small stream began trickling over the uncarpeted floor; he then relieved himself of his damo outer garments.

"Son of Erebus, indeed, you ungrateful man. It's as black as Hades in this room; a light, a light! Why did you keep me waiting out there like a drowned rat?"

The voice was soft and musical. Briggs lighted the student lamp. The light revealed a tall man with the beautiful face of a Greek God; but the sculptured features did not inspire confidence. There was that in the countenance of Aubrey Livingston that engendered doubt. But he had been kind to Briggs, was, in fact, his only friend in the college, or, indeed, in the world for that matter.

By an act of generosity he had helped the forlorn youth, then in his freshman year, over obstacles which bade fair to end his college days. Although the pecuniary obligation was long since paid, the affection and worship Reuel had conceived for his deliverer was dog-like in its devotion.

"Beastly night," he continued, as he stretched his full length luxuriously in the only easy chair the room afforded. "What are you mooning about all alone in the darkness?"

"Same old thing," replied Briggs briefly.

"No wonder the men say that you have a twist, Reuel."

"Ah, man! But the problem of whence and whither! To solve it is my life; I live for that alone; let'm talk."

"You ought to be re-named the 'Science of Trance-States,' Reuel. How a man can grind day and night beats me." Livingston handed him a cigar and for a time they smoked in silence.

At length Reuel said:

"Shake hands with Poverty once, Aubrey, and you will solve the secret of many a student's success in life."

"Doubtless it would do me good," replied Livingston with a laugh, "but just at present, it's the ladies, bless their sweet faces who disturb me, ana not delving in books nor weeping over ways and means. Shades of my fathers, forbid that I should ever have to work!

"Lucky dog!" growled Reuel, enviously, as he gazed admiringly at the handsome face turned up to the ceiling and gazing with soft caressing eyes at the ugly whitewashed wall through rings of curling smoke. "Yet you have a greater gift of duality than I," he added dreamily. "Say what you will; ridicule me, torment me, but you know as well as I that the wonders of a material world cannot approach those of the undiscovered country within ourselves – the hidden self lying quiescent in every human soul."

"True, Reuel, and I often wonder what becomes of the mind and morals, distinctive entities grouped in the republic known as man, when death comes. Good and evil in me contend; which will gain the mastery? Which will accompany me into the silent land?"

"Good and evil, God and the devil," suggested Reuel. "Yes, sinner or saint, body or soul, which wins in the life struggle? I am not sure that it matters which," he concluded with a shrug of his handsome shoulders. "I should know if I never saw you again until the struggle was over. Your face will tell its own tale in another five years. Now listen to this:" He caught up the book he had been reading and rapidly turning the leaves read over the various passages that had impressed him.

"A curious accumulation of data; the writer evidently takes himself seriously," Livingston commented.

"And why not?" demanded Reuel.

"You and I know enough to credit the author with honest intentions."

"Yes; but are we prepared to go so far?"

"This man is himself a mystic. He gives his evidence clearly enough."

"And do you credit it?"

"Every word! Could I but get the necessary subject, I would convince you; I would go farther than M. Binet in unveiling the vast scheme of compensation and retribution carried about in the vast recesses of the human soul."

"Find the subject and I will find the money," laughed Aubrey.

"Do you mean it, Aubrey? Will you join me in carrying forward a search for more light on the mysteries of existence?"

"I mean it. And now, Reuel, come down from the clouds, and come with me to a concert."

"Tonight?"

"Yes, 'tonight'" mimicked the other. "The blacker the night, the greater the need of amusement. You go out too little."

"Who gives the concert?"

"Well, it's a new departure in the musical world; something Northerners know nothing of; but I who am a Southerner, born and bred, or as the vulgar have it, 'dyed in the wool,' know and understand Negro music. It is a jubilee concert given by a party of Southern colored people at Tremont Temple. I have the tickets. Redpath has them in charge."

"Well, if you say so, I suppose I must." Briggs did not seem greatly impressed.

"Coming down to the practical, Reuel, what do you think of the Negro problem? Come to think of it, I have never heard you express an opinion about it. I believe it is the only burning question in the whole category of live issues and ologies about which you are silent."

"I have a horror of discussing the woes of unfortunates, tramps, stray dogs and cats and Negroes – probably because I am an unfortunate myself."

They smoked in silence.

Chapter II

THE PASSING of slavery from the land marked a new era in the life of the nation. The war, too, had passed like a dream of horrors, and over the resumption of normal conditions in business and living, the whole country, as one man, rejoiced and heaved a deep sigh of absolute content.

Under the spur of the excitement occasioned by the Proclamation of Freedom, and the great need of schools for the blacks, thousands of dollars were contributed at the North, and agents were sent to Great Britain, where generosity towards the Negroes was boundless. Money came from all directions, pouring into the hands of philanthropists, who were anxious to prove that the country was able, not only to free the slave, but to pay the great debt it owed him – protection as he embraced freedom, and a share in the great Government he had aided to found by sweat and toil and blood. It was soon discovered that the Negro possessed a phenomenal gift of music, and it was determined to utilize this gift in helping to support educational institutions of color in the Southland.

A band of students from Fisk University were touring the country, and those who had been fortunate enough to listen once to their matchless untrained voices singing their heartbreaking minor music with its grand and impossible intervals and sound combinations, were eager to listen again and yet again.

Wealthy and exclusive society women everywhere vied in showering benefits and patronage upon the new prodigies who had suddenly become the pets of the musical world. The Temple was a blaze of light, and crowded from pit to dome. It was the first appearance of the troupe in New England, therefore it was a gala night, and Boston culture was out in force.

The two friends easily found their seats in the first balcony, and from that position idly scanned the vast audience to beguile the tedious waiting. Reuel's thoughts were disturbed; he read over the program, but it carried no meaning to his preoccupied mind; he was uneasy; the face he had seen outlined in the twilight haunted him. A great nervous dread of he knew not what possessed him, and he actually suffered as he sat there answering at random the running fire of comments made by Livingston on the audience, and replying none too cordially to the greetings of fellow-students, drawn to the affair, like himself, by curiosity.

"Great crowd for such a night," observed one. "The weather matches your face, Briggs; why didn't you leave it outside? Why do you look so down?"

Reuel shrugged his shoulders.

"They say there are some pretty girls in the troupe; one or two as white as we," continued the speaker unabashed by Reuel's surliness.

"They range at home from alabaster to ebony," replied Livingston. "The results of amalgamation are worthy the careful attention of all medical experts."

"Don't talk shop, Livingston," said Briggs peevishly.

"You are really more disagreeable than usual," replied Livingston, pleasantly. "Do try to be like the other fellows, for once, Reuel."

Silence ensued for a time, and then the irrepressible one of the party remarked: "The soprano soloist is great; heard her in New York." At this there was a general laugh among the men. Good natured Charlie Vance was generally "stuck" once a month with the "loveliest girl, by jove, you know."

"That explains your presence here, Vance; what's her name?"

"Dianthe Lusk."

"Great name. I hope she comes up to it – the flower of Jove."

"Flower of Jove, indeed! You'll say so when you see her," cried Charlie with his usual enthusiasm.

"What! Again, my son? 'Like Dian's kiss, unmasked, unsought, Love gives itself'" quoted Livingston, with a smile on his handsome face.

"Oh, stow it! Aubrey, even your cold blood will be stirred at sight of her exquisite face; of her voice I will not speak; I cannot do it justice."

"If this is to be the result of emancipation, I for one vote that we ask Congress to annul the Proclamation," said Reuel, drily.

Now conversation ceased; a famous local organist began a concert on the organ to occupy the moments of waiting. The music soothed Reuel's restlessness. He noticed that the platform usually occupied by the speaker's desk, now held a number of chairs and a piano. Certainly, the assiduous advertising had brought large patronage for the new venture, he thought as he idly calculated the financial result from the number in the audience.

Soon the hot air, the glare of lights, the mingling of choice perfumes emanating from the dainty forms of elegantly attired women, acted upon him as an intoxicant. He began to feel the pervading excitement – the flutter of expectation, and presently the haunting face left him.

The prelude drew to a close; the last chord fell from the fingers of the artist; a line of figures – men and women – dark in hue. and neatly dressed in quiet evening clothes, filed noiselessly from the anterooms and filled the chairs upon the platform. The silence in the house was painful. These were representatives of the people for whom God had sent the terrible scourge of blood upon the land to free from bondage. The old abolitionists in the vast audience felt the blood leave their faces beneath the stress of emotion.

The opening number was 'The Lord's Prayer'. Stealing, rising, swelling, gathering, as it thrilled the ear, all the delights of harmony in a grand minor cadence that told of deliverance from bondage and homage to God for his wonderful aid, sweeping the awed heart with an ecstasy that was almost pain; breathing, hovering, soaring, they held the vast multitude in speechless wonder.

Thunders of applause greeted the close of the hymn. Scarcely waiting for a silence, a female figure rose and came slowly to the edge of the platform and stood in the blaze of lights with hands modestly clasped before her. She was not in any way the preconceived idea of a Negro. Fair as the fairest woman in the hall, with wavy bands of chestnut hair, and great, melting eyes of brown, soft as those of childhood; a willowy figure of exquisite mould, clad in a sombre gown of black. There fell a voice upon the listening ear, in celestial showers of silver that passed all conceptions, all comparisons, all dreams; a voice beyond belief – a great soprano of unimaginable beauty, soaring heavenward in mighty intervals.

> "Go down, Moses, way down in Egypt's land,
> Tell ol' Pharaoh, let my people go."

sang the woman in tones that awakened ringing harmonies in the heart of every listener.

"By Jove!" Reuel heard Livingston exclaim. For himself he was dazed, thrilled; never save among the great artists of the earth, was such a voice heard alive with the divine fire.

Some of the women in the audience wept; there was the distinct echo of a sob in the deathly quiet which gave tribute to the power of genius. Spellbound they sat beneath the outpoured anguish of a suffering soul. All the horror, the degradation from which a race had been delivered were in the pleading strains of the singer's voice. It strained the senses almost beyond endurance. It pictured to that self-possessed, highly-cultured New England assemblage as nothing else ever had, the awfulness of the hell from which a people had been happily plucked.

Reuel was carried out of himself; he leaned forward in eager contemplation of the artist; he grew cold with terror and fear. Surely it could not be – he must be dreaming! It was incredible! Even as he whispered the words to himself the hall seemed to grow dim and shadowy; the sea of faces melted away; there before him in the blaze of light – like a lovely phantom – stood a woman wearing the face of his vision of the afternoon!

Chapter III

IT WAS Hallow-eve.

The north wind blew a cutting blast over the stately Charles, and broke the waves into a miniature flood; it swept the streets of the University city, and danced on into the outlying suburbs tossing the last leaves about in gay disorder, not even sparing the quiet precincts of Mount Auburn cemetery. A deep, clear, moonless sky stretched overhead, from which hung myriads of sparkling stars.

In Mount Auburn, where the residences of the rich lay far apart, darkness and quietness had early settled down. The main street seemed given over to die duskiness of the evening, and with one exception, there seemed no light on earth or in heaven save the cold gleam of the stars.

The one exception was in the home of Charlie Vance, or 'Adonis', as he was called by his familiars. The Vance estate was a spacious house with rambling ells, tortuous chimney-stacks, and corners, eaves and ledges; the grounds were extensive and well kept telling silently of the opulence of its owner. Its windows sent forth a cheering light. Dinner was just over.

Within, on an old-fashioned hearth, blazed a glorious wood fire, which gave a rich coloring to the oak-pane!led walls, and fell warmly on a group of young people seated and standing, chatting about the fire. At one side of it, in a chair of the Elizabethan period, sat the hostess, Molly Vance, only daughter of James Vance, Esq., and sister of 'Adonis', a beautiful girl of eighteen.

At the opposite side, leaning with folded arms against the high carved mantel, stood Aubrey Livingston; the beauty of his fair hair and blue eyes was never more marked as he stood there in the gleam of the fire and the soft candlelight. He was talking vivaciously, his eyes turning from speaker to speaker, as he ran on, but resting chiefly with pride on his beautiful betrothed, Molly Vance.

The group was completed by two or three other men, among them Reuel Briggs, and three pretty girls. Suddenly a clock struck the hour.

"Only nine," exclaimed Molly. "Good people, what shall we do to wile the tedium of waiting for the witching hour? Have any one of you enough wisdom to make a suggestion?"

"Music," said Livingston.

"We don't want anything so commonplace."

"Blind Man's Buff," suggested 'Adonis'.

"Oh! Please not that, the men are so rough!"

"Let us," broke in Cora Scott, "tell ghost stories."

"Good, Cora! Yes, yes, yes." "No, no!" exclaimed a chorus of voices.

"Yes, yes," laughed Molly, gaily, clapping her hands. "It is the very thing. Cora, you are the wise woman of the party. It is the very time, tonight is the new moon, and we can try our projects in the Hyde house."

"The moon should be full to account for such madness," said Livingston.

"Don't be disagreeable, Aubrey," replied Molly. "The 'ayes' have it. You're with me, Mr. Briggs?"

"Of course, Miss Vance," answered Reuel, "to go to the North Pole or Hades – only please tell us where is 'Hyde house.'"

"Have you never heard? Why it's the adjoining estate. It is reputed to be haunted, and a lady in white haunts the avenue in the most approved ghostly style."

"Bosh!" said Livingston.

"Possibly," remarked the laughing Molly, "but it is the 'bosh' of a century."

"Go on, Miss Vance; don't mind Aubrey. Who has seen the lady?"

"She is not easily seen," proceeded Molly, "she only appears on Hallow-eve, when the moon is new, as it will be tonight. I had forgotten that fact when I invited you here. If anyone stands, tonight, in the avenue leading to the house, he will surely see the tall veiled figure gliding among the old hemlock trees."

One or two shivered.

"If, however, the watcher remain, the lady will pause, and utter some sentence of prophecy of his future."

"Has anyone done this?" queried Reuel.

"My old nurse says she remembers that the lady was seen once."

"Then, we'll test it again tonight!" exclaimed Reuel, greatly excited over the chance to prove his pet theories.

"Well, Molly, you've started Reuel off on his greatest hobby; I wash my hands of both of you."

"Let us go any way!" chorused the venturesome party.

"But there are conditions," exclaimed Molly. "Only one person must go at a time."

Aubrey laughed as he noticed the consternation in one or two faces.

"So," continued Molly, "as we cannot go together, I propose that each shall stay a quarter of an hour, then whether successful or not, return and let another take his or her place. I will go first."

"No—", it was Charlie who spoke, "I put my veto on that, Molly. If you are mad enough to risk colds in this mad freak, it shall be done fairly. We will draw lots."

"And I add to that, not a girl leave the house; we men will try the charm for the sake of your curiosity, but not a girl goes. You can try the ordinary Hallow-eve projects while we are away."

With many protests, but concealed relief, this plan was reluctantly adopted by the female element. The lots were prepared and placed in a hat, and amid much merriment, drawn.

"You are third, Mr. Briggs," exclaimed Molly who held the hat and watched the checks.

"I'm first," said Livingston, "and Charlie second."

"While we wait for twelve, tell us the story of the house, Molly," cried Cora.

Thus adjured, Molly settled herself comfortably in her chair and began: "Hyde House is nearly opposite the cemetery, and its land joins that of this house; it is indebted for its ill-repute to one of its owners, John Hyde. It has been known for years as a haunted house, and avoided as such by the superstitious. It is low-roofed, rambling, and almost entirely concealed by hemlocks, having an air of desolation and decay in keeping with its ill-repute. In its dozen rooms were enacted the dark deeds which gave the place the name of the 'haunted house.'

"The story is told of an unfaithful husband, a wronged wife and a beautiful governess forming a combination which led to the murder of a guest for his money. The master of the house died from remorse, under peculiar circumstances. These materials give us the plot for a thrilling ghost story."

"Well, where does the lady come in?" interrupted 'Adonis'.

There was a general laugh.

"This world is all a blank without the ladies for Charlie," remarked Aubrey. "Molly, go on with your story, my child."

"You may all laugh as much as you please, but what I am telling you is believed in this section by everyone. A local magazine speaks of it as follows, as near as I can remember:

"'A most interesting story is told by a woman who occupied the house for a short time. She relates that she had no sooner crossed the threshold than she was met by a beautiful woman in flowing robes of black, who begged permission to speak through her to her friends. The friends were thereupon bidden to be present at a certain time. When all were assembled they were directed by invisible powers to kneel. Then the spirit told the tale of the tragedy through the woman. The spirit was the niece of the murderer, and she was in the house when the crime was committed. She discovered blood stains on the door of the woodshed, and told her uncle that she suspected him of murdering the guest, who had mysteriously disappeared. He secured her promise not to betray him. She had always kept the secret. Although both had been dead for many years, they were chained to the scene of the crime, as was the governess, who was the man's partner in guilt. The final release of the niece from the place was conditional on her making a public confession. This done she would never be heard from again. And she never was, except on Hallow-eve, when the moon is new."

"Bring your science and philosophy to bear on this, Reuel. Come, come, man, give us your opinion," exclaimed Aubrey.

"Reuel doesn't believe such stuff; he's too sensible," added Charlie.

"If these are facts, they are only for those who have a mental affinity with them. I believe that if we could but strengthen our mental sight, we could discover the broad highway between this and the other world on which both good and evil travel to earth," replied Reuel.

"And that first highway was beaten out of chaos by Satan, as Milton has it, eh, Briggs?"

"Have it as you like, Smith. No matter. For my own part, I have never believed that the whole mental world is governed by the faculties we understand, and can reduce to reason or definite feeling. But I will keep my ideas to myself; one does not care to be laughed at."

The conversation was kept up for another hour about indifferent subjects, but all felt the excitement underlying the frivolous chatter. At quarter before twelve, Aubrey put on his ulster with the words: "Well, here goes for my lady." The great doors were thrown open, and the company grouped about him to see him depart.

"Mind, honor bright, you go," laughed Charlie.

"Honor bright," he called back.

Then he went on beyond the flood of light into the gloom of the night. Muffled in wraps and ulsters they lingered on the piazzas waiting his return.

"Would he see anything?"

"Of course not!" laughed Charlie and Bert Smith. "Still, we bet he'll be sharp to his time."

They were right. Aubrey returned at five minutes past twelve, a failure.

Charlie ran down the steps briskly, but in ten minutes came hastening back.

"Well," was the chorus, "did you see it?"

"I saw something – a figure in the trees!"

"And you did not wait?" said Molly, scornfully.

"No, I dared not; I own it."

"It's my turn; I'm third," said Reuel.

"Luck to you, old man," they called as he disappeared in the darkness.

Reuel Briggs was a brave man. He knew his own great physical strength and felt no fear as he traversed the patch of woods lying between the two estates. As he reached the avenue of hemlocks he was not thinking of his mission, but of the bright home scene he had just left – of love and home and rest – such a life as was unfolding before Aubrey Livingston and sweet Molly Vance.

"I suppose there are plenty of men in the world as lonely as I am," he mused; "but I suppose it is my own fault. A man though plain and poor can generally manage to marry; and I am both. But I don't regard a wife as one regards bread – better sour bread than starvation; better an uncongenial life-companion than none! What a frightful mistake! No! The woman I marry must be to me a necessity, because I love her; because so loving her, 'all the current of my being flows to her' and I feel she is my supreme need."

Just now he felt strangely happy as he moved in the gloom of the hemlocks, and he wondered many times after that whether the spirit is sometimes mysteriously conscious of the nearness of its kindred spirit; and feels, in anticipation, the "sweet unrest" of the master-passion that rules the world.

The mental restlessness of three weeks before seemed to have possession of him again. Suddenly the "restless, unsatisfied longing," rose again in his heart. He turned his head and saw a female figure just ahead of him in the path, coming toward him. He could not see her features distinctly, only the eyes – large, bright and dark. But their expression! Sorrowful, wistful – almost imploring – gazing straightforward, as if they saw nothing – like the eyes of a person entirely absorbed and not distinguishing one object from another.

She was close to him now, and there was a perceptible pause in her step. Suddenly she covered her face with her clasped hands, as if in uncontrollable grief. Moved by a mighty emotion, Briggs addressed the lonely figure:

"You are in trouble, madam; may I help you?"

Briggs never knew how he survived the next shock. Slowly the hands were removed from the face and the moon gave a distinct view of the lovely features of the jubilee singer – Dianthe Lusk.

She did not seem to look at Briggs, but straight before her, as she said in a low, clear, passionless voice:

"You can help me, but not now; tomorrow."

Reuel's most prominent feeling was one of delight. The way was open to become fully acquainted with the woman who had haunted him sleeping and waking, for weeks past.

"Not now! Yet you are suffering. Shall I see you soon? Forgive me – but, oh! Tell me—"

He was interrupted. The lady moved or floated away from him, with her face toward him and gazing steadily at him.

He felt that his whole heart was in his eyes, yet hers did not drop, nor did her cheek color.

"The time is not yet," she said in the same, clear, calm, measured tones, in which she had spoken before. Reuel made a quick movement toward her, but she raised her hand, and the gesture forbade him to follow her. He paused involuntarily, and she turned away, and disappeared among the gloomy hemlock trees.

He parried the questions of the merry crowd when he returned to the house, with indifferent replies. How they would have laughed at him – slave of a passion as sudden and romantic as that of Romeo for Juliet; with no more foundation than the 'presentments' in books which treat of the 'occult'. He dropped asleep at last, in the early morning hours, and lived over his experience in his dreams.

Chapter IV

ALTHOUGH NOT YET a practitioner, Reuel Briggs was a recognized power in the medical profession. In brain diseases he was an authority.

Early the next morning he was aroused from sleep by imperative knocking at his door. It was a messenger from the hospital. There had been a train accident on the Old Colony road, would he come immediately?

Scarcely giving himself time for a cup of coffee, he arrived at the hospital almost as soon as the messenger.

The usual silence of the hospital was broken; all was bustle and movement, without confusion. It was a great call upon the resources of the officials, but they were equal to it. The doctors passed from sufferer to sufferer, dressing their injuries; then they were borne to beds from which some would never rise again.

"Come with me to the women's ward, Doctor Briggs," said a nurse. "There is a woman there who was taken from the wreck. She shows no sign of injury, but the doctors cannot restore her to consciousness. Doctor Livingston pronounces her dead, but it doesn't seem possible. So young, so beautiful. Do something for her, Doctor."

The men about a cot made way for Reuel, as he entered the ward. "It's no use Briggs," said Livingston to him in reply to his question. "Your science won't save her. The poor girl is already cold and stiff."

He moved aside disclosing to Reuel's gaze the lovely face of Dianthe Lusk!

The most marvellous thing to watch is the death of a person. At that moment the opposite takes place to that which took place when life entered the first unit, after nature had prepared it for the inception of life. How the vigorous life watches the passage of the liberated life out of its earthly environment! What a change is this! How important the knowledge of whither life tends! Here is shown the setting free of a disciplined spirit giving up its mortality for immortality – the condition necessary to know God. Death! There is no death. Life is everlasting, and from its reality can have no end. Life is real and never changes, but preserves its identity eternally as the angels, and the immortal spirit of man, which are the only realities and continuities in the universe, God being over all, Supreme Ruler and Divine Essence from whom comes all life. Somewhat in this train ran Reuel's thoughts as he stood beside the seeming dead girl, the cynosure of all the medical faculty there assembled.

To the majority of those men, the case was an ordinary death, and that was all there was to it. What did this young upstart expect to make of it? Of his skill and wonderful theories they had heard strange tales, but they viewed him coldly as we are apt to view those who dare to leave the beaten track of conventionality.

Outwardly cool and stolid, showing no sign of recognition, he stood for some seconds gazing down on Dianthe: every nerve quivered, every pulse of his body throbbed. Her face held for him a wonderful charm, an extraordinary fascination. As he gazed he knew that once more he beheld what he had vaguely sought and yearned for all his forlorn life. His whole heart went out to her; destiny, not chance, had brought him to her. He saw, too, that no one knew her, none had a clue to her identity; he determined to remain silent for the present, and immediately he sought to impress Livingston to do likewise.

His keen glance swept the faces of the surrounding physicians. "No, not one" he told himself, "holds the key to unlock this seeming sleep of death." He alone could do it. Advancing far afield in the mysterious regions of science, he had stumbled upon the solution of one of life's problems: *the reanimation of the body after seeming death.*

He had hesitated to tell of his discovery to anyone; not even to Livingston had he hinted of the daring possibility, fearing ridicule in case of a miscarriage in his calculations. But for the sake of this girl he would make what he felt to be a premature disclosure of the results of his experiments. Meantime, Livingston, from his place at the foot of the cot, watched his friend with fascinated eyes. He, too, had resolved, contrary to his first intention, not to speak of his knowledge of the beautiful patient's identity. Curiosity was on tiptoe; expectancy was in the air. All felt that something unusual was about to happen.

Now Reuel, with gentle fingers, touched rapidly the clammy brow, the icy, livid hands, the region of the pulseless heart. No breath came from between the parted lips; the life-giving organ was motionless. As he concluded his examination, he turned to the assembled doctors:

"As I diagnose this case, it is one of suspended animation. This woman has been long and persistently subjected to mesmeric influences, and the nervous shock induced by the excitement of the accident has thrown her into a cataleptic sleep."

"But, man!" broke from the head physician in tones of exasperation, "rigor mortis in unmistakable form is here. The woman is dead!"

At these words there was a perceptible smile on the faces of some of the students – associates who resented his genius as a personal affront, and who considered these words as good as a reprimand for the daring student, and a settler of his pretensions. Malice and envy, from Adam's time until today, have loved a shining mark.

But the reproof was unheeded. Reuel was not listening. Absorbed in thoughts of the combat before him, he was oblivious to all else as he bent over the lifeless figure on the cot. He was full of an earnest purpose. He was strung up to a high tension of force and energy. As he looked down upon the unconscious girl whom none but he could save from the awful fate of a death by post-mortem, and who by some mysterious mesmeric affinity existing between them, had drawn him to her rescue, he felt no fear that he should fail.

Suddenly he bent down and took both cold hands into his left and passed his right hand firmly over her arms from shoulder to wrist. He repeated the movements several times; there was no response to the passes. He straightened up, and again stood silently gazing upon the patient. Then, like a man just aroused from sleep, he looked across the bed at Livingston and said abruptly:

"Dr. Livingston, will you go over to my room and bring me the case of vials in my medicine cabinet? I cannot leave the patient at this point."

Livingston started in surprise as he replied: "Certainly, Briggs, if it will help you any."

"The patient does not respond to any of the ordinary methods of awakening. She would probably lie in this sleep for months, and death ensue from exhaustion, if stronger remedies are not used to restore the vital force to a normal condition."

Livingston left the hospital; he could not return under an hour; Reuel took up his station by the bed whereon was stretched an apparently lifeless body, and the other doctors went the rounds of the wards attending to their regular routine of duty. The nurses gazed at him curiously; the head doctor, upon whom the young student's earnestness and sincerity had evidently made an impression, came a number of times to the bare little room to gaze upon its silent occupants, but there was nothing new. When Livingston returned, the group again gathered about the iron cot where lay the patient.

"Gentlemen," said Reuel, with quiet dignity, when they were once more assembled, "will you individually examine the patient once more and give your verdicts?"

Once more doctors and students carefully examined the inanimate figure in which the characteristics of death were still more pronounced. On the outskirts of the group hovered the house-surgeon's assistants ready to transport the body to the operating room for the post-mortem. Again the head physician spoke, this time impatiently.

"We are wasting our time, Dr. Briggs; I pronounce the woman dead. She was past medical aid when brought here."

"There is no physical damage, apparent or hidden, that you can see, Doctor?" questioned Reuel, respectfully.

"No; it is a perfectly healthful organism, though delicate. I agree entirely with your assertion that death was induced by the shock."

"Not *death*, Doctor," protested Briggs.

"Well, well, call it what you like – call it what you like, it amounts to the same in the end," replied the doctor testily.

"Do you all concur in Doctor Hamilton's diagnosis?" Briggs included all the physicians in his sweeping glance. There was a general assent.

"I am prepared to show you that in some cases of seeming death – or even death in reality – consciousness may be restored or the dead brought back to life. I have numberless times in the past six months restored consciousness to dogs and cats after rigor mortis had set in," he declared calmly.

"Bosh!" broke from a leading surgeon. In this manner the astounding statement, made in all seriousness, was received by the group of scientists mingled with an astonishment that resembled stupidity. But in spite of their scoffs, the young student's confident manner made a decided impression upon his listeners, unwilling as they were to be convinced.

Reuel went on rapidly; his eyes kindled; his whole person took on the majesty of conscious power, and pride in the knowledge he possessed. "I have found by research that life is not dependent upon organic function as a principle. It may be infused into organized bodies even after the organs have ceased to perform their legitimate offices. Where death has been due to causes which have not impaired or injured or destroyed tissue formation or torn down the structure of vital organs, life may be recalled when it has become entirely extinct, which is not so in the present case. This I have discovered by my experiments in animal magnetism."

The medical staff was fairly bewildered. Again Dr. Hamilton spoke:

"You make the assertion that the dead can be brought to life, if I understand your drift, Dr. Briggs, and you expect us to believe such utter nonsense." He added significantly, "My colleagues and I are here to be convinced."

"If you will be patient for a short time longer, Doctor, I will support my assertion by action. The secret of life lies in what we call volatile magnetism – it exists in the free atmosphere. You, Dr. Livingston, understand my meaning; do you see the possibility in my words?" he questioned, appealing to Aubrey for the first time.

"I have a faint conception of your meaning, certainly," replied his friend.

"This subtle magnetic agent is constantly drawn into the body through the lungs, absorbed and held in bounds until chemical combination has occurred through the medium of mineral agents always present in normal animal tissue When respiration ceases this magnetism cannot be drawn into the lungs. It must be artificially supplied. This, gentlemen, is my discovery. I supply this magnetism. I have it here in the case Dr. Livingston has kindly brought me." He held up to their gaze a small phial wherein reposed a powder. Physicians and students, now eager listeners, gazed spell-bound upon him, straining their ears to catch every tone of the low voice and every change of the luminous eyes; they pressed forward to examine the contents of the bottle. It passed from eager hand to eager hand, then back to the owner.

"This compound, gentlemen, is an exact reproduction of the conditions existing in the human body. It has common salt for its basis. This salt is saturated with oleo resin and then exposed for several hours in an atmosphere of free ammonia. The product becomes a powder, and *that* brings back the seeming dead to life."

"Establish your theory by practical demonstration, Dr. Briggs, and the dreams of many eminent practitioners will be realized," said Dr. Hamilton, greatly agitated by his words.

"Your theory smacks of the supernatural, Dr. Briggs, charlatanism, or dreams of lunacy," said the surgeon. "We leave such assertions to quacks, generally, for the time of miracles is past."

"The supernatural presides over man's formation always," returned Reuel, quietly. "Life is that evidence of supernatural endowment which originally entered nature during the formation of the units for the evolution of man. Perhaps the superstitious masses came nearer to solving the mysteries of creation than the favored elect will ever come. Be that as it may, I will not contend. I will proceed with the demonstration."

There radiated from the speaker the potent pressence of a truthful mind, a pure, unselfish nature, and that inborn dignity which repels the shafts of lower minds as ocean's waves absorb the drops of rain. Something like respect mingled with awe hushed the sneers, changing them into admiration as he calmly proceeded to administer the so-called lifegiving powder. Each man's watch was in his hand; one minute passed – another – and still another. The body remained inanimate.

A cold smile of triumph began to dawn on the faces of the older members of the profession, but it vanished in its incipiency, for a tremor plainly passed over the rigid form before them. Another second – another convulsive movement of the chest!

"She moves!" cried Aubrey at last, carried out of himself by the strain on his nerves. "Look, gentlemen, she breathes! *She is alive*; Briggs is right! Wonderful! Wonderful!"

"We said there could not be another miracle, and here it is!" exclaimed Dr. Hamilton with strong emotion.

Five minutes more and the startled doctors fell back from the bedside at a motion of Reuel's hand. A wondering nurse, with dilated eyes, unfolded a screen, placed it in position and came and stood beside the bed opposite Reuel. Holding Dianthe's hands, he said in a low voice: "Are you awake?" Her eyes unclosed in a cold, indifferent stare which gradually changed to one of recognition. She looked at him – she smiled, and said in a weak voice, "Oh, it is you; I dreamed of you while I slept."

She was like a child – so trusting that it went straight to the young man's heart, and for an instant a great lump seemed to rise in his throat and choke him. He held her hands and chafed them, but spoke with his eyes only. The nurse said in a low voice: "Dr. Briggs, a few spoonfuls of broth will help her?"

"Yes, thank you, nurse; that will be just right" He drew a chair close beside the bed, bathed her face with water and pushed back the tangle of bright hair. He felt a great relief and quiet joy that his experiment had been successful.

"Have I been ill? Where am I?" she asked after a pause, as her face grew troubled and puzzled.

"No, but you have been asleep a long time; we grew anxious about you. You must not talk until you are stronger."

The muse returned with the broth; Dianthe drank it eagerly and called for water, then with her hand still clasped in Reuel's she sank into a deep sleep, breathing softly like a tired child.

It was plain to the man of science that hope for the complete restoration of her faculties would depend upon time, nature and constitution. Her effort to collect her thoughts was unmistakable. In her sleep, presently, from her lips fell incoherent words and phrases; but through it all she clung to Reuel's hand, seeming to recognize in him a friend.

A little later the doctors filed in noiselessly and stood about the bed gazing down upon the sleeper with awe, listening to her breathing, feeling lightly the fluttering pulse. Then they left the quiet house of suffering, marvelling at the miracle just accomplished in their presence. Livingston lingered with Briggs after the other physicians were gone.

"This is a great day for you, Reuel," he said, as he laid a light caressing hand upon the other's shoulder.

Reuel seized the hand in a quick convulsive clasp. "True and tried friend, do not credit me more than I deserve. No praise is due me. I am an instrument – how I know not – a child of circumstances. Do you not perceive: something strange in this case? Can you not deduce conclusions from your own intimate knowledge of this science?"

"What can you mean, Reuel?"

"I mean – it is a *dual* mesmeric trance! The girl is only partly normal now. Binet speaks at length of this possibility in his treatise. We have stumbled upon an extraordinary case. It will take a year to restore her to perfect health."

"In the meantime we ought to search out her friends."

"Is there any hurry, Aubrey?" pleaded Reuel, anxiously.

"Why not wait until her memory returns; it will not be long, I believe, although she may still be liable to the trances."

"We'll put off the evil day to any date you may name, Briggs; for my part, I would preserve her incognito indefinitely."

Reuel made no reply. Livingston was not sure that he heard him.

Chapter V

THE WORLD scarcely estimates the service rendered by those who have unlocked the gates of sensation by the revelations of science; and yet it is to the clear perception of things which we obtain by the study of nature's laws that we are enabled to appreciate her varied gifts. The scientific journals of the next month contained wonderful and *wondering* (?) accounts of the now celebrated case – reanimation after seeming death. Reuel's lucky star was in the ascendant; fame and fortune awaited him; he had but to grasp them. Classmates who had once ignored him now sought familiar association, or else gazed upon him with awe and reverence. "How did he do it?" was the query in each man's mind, and then came a stampede for all scientific matter bearing upon animal magnetism.

How often do we look in wonder at the course of other men's lives, whose paths have diverged so widely from the beaten track of our own, that, unable to comprehend the one spring upon which, perhaps, the whole secret of the diversity hinged, we have been fain to content ourselves with summing up our judgment in the common phrase. "Well, it's very strange; what odd people there are in the world to be sure!"

Many times this trite sentence was uttered during the next few months, generally terminating every debate among medical students in various colleges.

Unmindful of his growing popularity. Reuel devoted every moment of his spare time to close study of his patient. Although but a youth, the scientist might have passed for any age under fifty, and life for him seemed to have taken on a purely mechanical aspect since he had become first in this great cause. Under pretended indifference to public criticism, throbbed a heart of gold, sensitive to a fault; desiring above all else the wellbeing of all humanity; his faithfulness to those who suffered amounted to complete self-sacrifice. Absolutely free from the vices which beset most young men of his age and profession, his daily life was a white, unsullied page to the friend admitted to unrestricted intercourse, and gave an irresistible impetus to that friendship, for Livingston could not but admire the newly developed depths of nobility which he now saw unfolding day by day in Reuel's character. Nor was Livingston far behind the latter in his interest in all that affected Dianthe. Enthused by its scientific aspect, he vied with Reuel in close attention to the medical side of the case, and being more worldly did not neglect the material side.

He secretly sought out and obtained the address of the manager of the jubilee singers and to his surprise received the information that Miss Lusk had left the troupe to enter the service of a traveling magnetic physician – a woman – for a large salary. They (the troupe) were now in Europe and had heard nothing of Miss Lusk since.

After receiving this information by cable, Livingston sat a long time smoking and thinking: people often disappeared in a great city, and the police would undoubtedly find the magnetic physician if he applied to them. Of course that was the sensible thing to do, but then the publicity, and he hated that for the girl's sake. Finally he decided to compromise the matter by employing a detective. With him to decide that it was expedient to do a certain thing was the same as to act; before night the case was in the hands of an expert detective who received a goodly retainer. Two weeks from that day – it was December twenty-fourth – before he left his boarding place, the detective was announced. He had found the woman in a small town near Chicago. She said that she had no knowledge of Miss Lusk's whereabouts. Dianthe had remained with her three weeks, and at the end of that time had mysteriously disappeared; she had not heard of her since.

Livingston secured the woman's name and address, gave the man a second check together with an admonition to keep silence concerning Miss Lusk. That closed the episode. But of his observations and discoveries, Aubrey said nothing, noting every phase of this strange happening in silence.

Strangely enough, none of the men that had admired the colored artist who had enthralled their senses by her wonderful singing a few weeks before, recognized her in the hospital waif consecrated to the service of science. Her incognito was complete.

The patient was now allowed the freedom of the corridors for exercise, and was about her room during the day. The returns of the trance-state were growing less regular, although she frequently fell into convulsions, thereby enduring much suffering, sometimes lying for hours in a torpid state. Livingston had never happened to be present on these occasions, but he had heard of them from eye-witnesses. One day he entered the room while one was occurring. His entrance was unnoticed as he approached lightly over the uncarpeted floor, and stood transfixed by the scene before him.

Dianthe stood upright, with closed eyes, in the middle of the room. Only the movement of her bosom betrayed breath. The other occupants of the room preserved a solemn silence. She addressed Reuel, whose outstretched arms were extended as if in blessing over her head.

"Oh! Dearest friend! Hasten to cure me of my sufferings. Did you not promise at that last meeting? You said to me, 'You are in trouble and I can help you? And I answered, 'The time is not yet.' Is it not so?"

"Yes," replied Reuel. "Patience a while longer; all will be well with you."

"Give me the benefit of your powerful will," she continued. "I know much but as yet have not the power to express it: I see much clearly, much dimly, of the powers and influences behind the Veil, and yet I cannot name them. Some time the full power will be mine; and mine shall be thine. In seven months the sick will be restored – she will awake to worldly cares once more." Her voice ceased; she sank upon the cot in a recumbent position. Her face was pale; she appeared to sleep. Fifteen minutes passed in death-like stillness, then she extended her arms, stretched, yawned, rubbed her eyes – awoke.

Livingston listened and looked in a trance of delight, his keen artistic sense fully aroused and appreciative, feeling the glamour of her presence and ethereal beauty like a man poring over a poem that he has unexpectedly stumbled upon, losing himself in it, until it becomes, as it were, a part of himself. He felt as he watched her that he was doing a foolish thing in thus exposing himself to temptation while his honor and faith were pledged to another. But then, foolishness is so much better than wisdom, particularly to a man in certain stages of life. And then he fell to questioning if there could be temptation for him through this girl – he laughed at the thought and the next instant dismay covered him with confusion, for like a flash he realized that the mischief was already done.

As we have already hinted, Aubrey was no saint; he knew that fickleness was in his blood; he had never denied himself anything that he wanted very much in his whole life. Would he grow to want this beautiful woman very much? Time would tell.

* * *

It was Christmas-time – a good, sensible seasonable day before Christmas, with frost and ice in abundance, and a clear, bright, wintry sky above. Boston was very full of people – mostly suburban visitors – who were rushing here and there bent on emptying their purses on the least provocation. Good-nature prevailed among the pedestrians; one poor wretch stood shivering, with blue, wan face, on the edge of the sidewalk, his sightless eyes staring straight before him, trying to draw a tune from a consumptive violin – the embodiment of despair. He was, after all, in the minority, to judge by the hundreds of comfortably-clad forms that hurried past him, breathing an atmosphere of peace and prosperity.

Tomorrow the church bells would ring out tidings that another Christmas was born, bidding all rejoice.

This evening, at six o'clock, the two friends went to dine in a hotel in a fashionable quarter. They were due to spend the night and Christmas day at the Vance house. As they walked swiftly along with the elastic tread of youth, they simultaneously halted before the blind musician and pressed into his trembling hand a bountiful gift; then they hurried away to escape his thanks.

At the hotel Livingston called for a private dining room, and after the coffee was served, he said:

"Tell me, Briggs, what is the link between you and your patient. There is a link, I am sure. Her words while in the trance made a great impression upon me.

There was a pause before Reuel replied in a low tone, as he rested his arm on the opposite side of the table and propped his head up on his hand:

"Forgive me, Aubrey!"

"For what?"

"This playing with your confidence. I have not been entirely frank with you."

"Oh, well! You are not bound to tell me everything you know. You surely have the right to silence about your affairs, if you think best."

"Listen, Aubrey. I should like to tell you all about it. I would feel better. What you say is true; there is a link; but I never saw her in the flesh before that night at the Temple. With all our knowledge, Aubrey, we are but barbarians in our ideas of the beginning, interim and end of our creation. Why were we created? for whose benefit? Can anyone answer that satisfactorily?

"'Few things are hidden from the man who devotes himself earnestly and seriously to the solution of a mystery,' Hawthorne tells us," replied Aubrey. "Have not you proved this, Reuel?"

"Well, yes – or, we prove rather, that our solution but deepens the mystery or mysteries. I have surely proved the last. Aubrey, I look natural, don't I? There's nothing about me that seems wrong?"

"Wrong! No."

"Well, if I tell you the truth you will call me a lunatic. You have heard of people being haunted by hallucinations?"

Aubrey nodded. "I am one of those persons. Seven weeks ago I saw Dianthe first, but not in the flesh. Hallow-eve I spoke to her in the garden of the haunted house, but not in the flesh. I thought it strange to be sure, that this face should lurk in my mind so much of the time; but I never dreamed what a crisis it was leading up to. The French and German schools of philosophy have taught us that going to places and familiar passages in books, of which we have had no previous knowledge, is but a proof of Plato's doctrine – the soul's transmigration, and reflections from the invisible world surrounding us.

"Finally a mad desire seized me to find that face a living reality that I might love and worship it. Then I saw her at the Temple – I found her àt the hospital – *in the flesh*! My desire was realized."

"And having found her, what then?" He waited breathlessly for the reply.

"I am mightily pleased and satisfied. I will cure her. She is charming; and if it is insanity to be in love with her, I don't care to be sane."

Livingston did not reply at once. His face was like marble in its impassiveness. The other's soft tremulous tones, fearless yet moist eyes and broken sentences, appeared to awaken no response in his breast. Instead, a far-off gleam came into his blue eyes. At last he broke the silence with the words:

"You name it well; it is insanity indeed, for you to love this woman."

"Why?" asked his friend, constrainedly.

"Because it is not for the best."

"For her or me?"

"Oh, for *her* —!" he finished the sentence with an expressive gesture.

"I understand you, Aubrey. I should not have believed it of you. If it were one of the other fellows; but you are generally so charitable."

"You forget your own words: 'Tramps, stray dogs and Negroes —,'" he quoted significantly. "Then there is your professional career to be considered – you mean honorable, do you not? How can you succeed if it be hinted abroad that you are married to a Negress?"

"I have thought of all that. I am determined. I will marry her in spite of hell itself! Marry her before she awakens to consciousness of her identity. I'm not unselfish; I don't pretend to be. There is no sin in taking her out of the sphere where she was born. God and science helping me, I will give her life and love and wifehood and maternity and perfect health. God, Aubrey! You, with all you have had of life's sweetness, petted idol of a beautiful world, you who will soon feel the heartbeats of your wife against your breast when lovely Molly is eternally bound to you, what do you know of a lonely, darkened life like mine? I have not the manner nor the charm which wins women. Men like me get love from them which is half akin to pity, when they get anything at all. It is but the shadow. This is my opportunity for happiness; I seize it. Fate has linked us together and no man and no man's laws shall part us."

Livingston sipped his wine quietly, intently watching Reuel's face. Now he leaned across the table and stretched out his hand to Briggs; his eyes looked full into his. As their hands met in a close clasp, he whispered a sentence across the board. Reuel started, uttered an exclamation and flushed slowly a dark, dull red.

"How – where – how did you know it?" he stammered.

"I have known it since first we met; but the secret is safe with me."

Chapter VI

THE SCENE which met the gaze when an hour later the young men were ushered into the long drawing-room of the Vance house was one well-calculated to remove all gloomy, pessimistic reasoning. Warmth, gaiety, pretty women, luxury – all sent the blood leaping through the veins in delightful anticipation.

Their entrance was greeted by a shout of welcome.

"Oh, Aubrey! I am so glad you are come," cried Molly from the far end of the room. Fancy tomorrow being Christmas! Shall we be ready for all that company tomorrow night and the ballroom, dining room and hall yet to be trimmed? Is it possible to be ready?"

"Not if we stand dwadling in idle talk." This from 'Adonis', who was stretched full length on the sitting-room sofa, with a cigarette between his lips, his hands under his handsome head, surrounded by a bevy of pretty, chattering girls, prominent among whom was Cora Scott, who aided and abetted Charlie in every piece of mischief.

Molly curled her lip but deigned no reply.

Bert Smith, from a corner of the room where he was about ascending a step-ladder, flung a book heavily at Adonis's lazy figure.

"Don't confuse your verbs," exclaimed Aubrey. "How can you stand when you are lying clown, and were you ever known to do anvthing else but dwadle, Adonis – eh?"

"I give it up," said Charlie, sleepily, kicking the book off the sofa.

"Is this an amateur grocery shop, may I ask, Miss Vance?" continued Aubrey as he and Briggs made their way to their hostess through an avalanche of parcels and baskets strewn on the tables and the floor.

Molly laughed as she greeted them. "No wonder you are surprised. I am superintending the arrangement of my poor people's gifts," she explained. "They must all be sent out tonight. I don't know what I should have done without all these good people to help me. But there are *piles* to be done yet. There is the tree, the charades, etc., etc.," she continued, in a plaintive little voice.

"More particularly cetra, cetra," said Aubrey from Bert's corner where he had gone to help along the good works of placing holly wreaths.

"Oh, you, Aubrey – stop being a magpie." Aubrey and Molly were very matter of fact lovers.

"Molly," again broke in Charlie, "suppose the box from Pierson's has never come, won't you be up a tree?" and the speaker opened his handsome eyes wide, and shook off his cigarette ash.

Molly maintained a dignified silence toward her brother. The firelight danced and dwelt upon her lovingly. She was so pretty, so fair, so slender, so graceful. Now in her gray plush tea-gown, with her hair piled picturesquely on the top of her small head, and fixed there with a big tortoise-shell pin, it would have been difficult to find a more delightful object for the gaze to rest upon.

"We shall have to fall back upon the wardrobes," she said at length. "You are a horrid wet-blanket, Charlie! I am sure I—"

Her remarks were cut short as the door opened, and with laughter and shouting a bevy of young people who had been at work in another part of the house rushed in. "It is come; it's all right; don't worry, Molly!" they sang in chorus.

"Do be quiet all of you; one can hardly hear oneself speak!"

The box from the costumer's had arrived; the great costume party was saved; in short, excitement and bustle were in full swing at Vance Hall as it had been at Christmas-time since the young people could remember.

Adonis lifted himself from the sofa and proposed to open the box of dresses at once, and try them on.

"Charlie, you are a brick! – the very thing!"

"Oh! Yes, yes; let us try them on!"

Molly broke through the eager voices:

"And we have not done the ballroom yet!" she said reproachfully.

"Oh! Bother the ballroom!" declared Adonis, now thoroughly aroused. "We have all night. We can't do better than to don our finery."

Molly sat down with an air of resigned patience. "I promised Mr. Pierson," she observed quietly, "that the box should not be touched until he was here to superintend matters."

"Oh, Pierson be blowed!" elegantly observed her brother. But Reul Briggs suddenly dropped his work, walked over, and sided with Molly.

"You are quite right, Miss Molly; and you Charlie and Aubrey and the rest of you men. if you want to open the box tonight you must first decorate the ballroom, business before pleasure."

"Saved! – Saved! Sec my brave, true knight defends his lady fair." Molly danced, practicing the step she was about to astonish the company with on Christmas-night. "I think I am what the Scotch call 'fey'" she laughed. "I don't know why I feel so awfully jolly tonight. I could positively fly from sheer excitement and delight."

"Don't you know why?" observed Cora. "I will tell you. It is because this is your last Christmas as Molly Vance; next year—"

"Ah, do not!" interrupted Molly, quickly. "Who knows what a year may bring forth. Is it not so, Dr. Briggs?" she turned appealingly to Reuel.

"Grief follows joy as clouds the sunlight. 'Woe! Woe! Each heart must bleed, must break.'" was his secret thought as he bowed gravely. But on his face was a look of startled perplexity, for suddenly as she spoke to him it appeared that a dark veil settled like a pall over the laughing face at his side. He shivered.

"What's the matter, Briggs?" called out Adonis. They had reached the ballroom and were standing over the piles of holly and evergreen, ready for an onslaught on the walls.

"Don't be surprised if Briggs acts strangely," continued Charlie. "It is in order for him to whoop it up in the spirit line."

"Why, Charlie! What do you mean?" questioned Molly with an anxious glance at Reuel.

"Anything interesting, Charlie?" called out a jolly girl across the room.

"Briggs is our 'show' man. Haven't you heard, girls, what a celebrity is with you tonight? Briggs is a philosopher – mesmerism is his specialty. Say, old man, give the company a specimen of your infernal art, can't you? He goes the whole hog, girls; can even raise the dead."

"Let up, Charlie," said Aubrey in a low tone. It's no joking matter."

There were screams and exclamations from the girls. With reckless gaiety Adonis continued,

"What is to be the outcome of the great furore you have created, Briggs?"

"Nothing of moment, I hope," smiled Reuel, good-naturedly. I have been simply an instrument; I leave results to the good angels who direct events. What does Longfellow say about the arrow and the song?

'Long:, long afterwards, in an oak
I found the arrow still unbroke;
And the song, from beginning to end,
I found in the heart of a friend.'

May it be so with my feeble efforts."

"But circumstances alter cases. In this rase, the 'arrow' is a girl and a devilish handsome one, too; and the 'air' is the whole scientific world. Your philosophy and mysticism gave way before Beauty. Argument is a stubborn man's castle, but the heart is still unconvinced."

"'I mixed those children up, and not a creature knew it,'" hummed Pert Smith. "Your ideas are mixed, Don; stick to the ladies, you understand girls and horseflesh; philosophy isn't in your line."

"Oh, sure!" said Adonis unruffled by his friend's words.

"Charlie Vance," said Molly severely, "if we have any more *swearing* from you tonight, you leave the room until you learn to practice good manners. I'm surprised at your language!"

"Just the same, Briggs is a fraud. I shall keep my eye on him. It's a case of beauty and the beast. Oh," he continued in malicious glee, "wouldn't you girls turn green with envy, every man jack of you, if you could see the beauty!"

Thereupon the girls fell to pelting him with holly wreaths and evergreen festoons, much to the enjoyment of Mr. Vance, who had entered unperceived in the general melee.

"What is it all about, Dr. Briggs?" asked Molly in a low voice.

"It is the case of a patient who was in a mesmeric sleep and I was fortunate enough to awaken her. She is a waif; and it will be months before she will be well and strong, poor girl."

"Do you make a study of mesmerism, Doctor?" asked Mr. Vance from his armchair by the glowing fire.

"Yes sir; and a wonderful science it is." Before Mr. Vance could continue, Livingston said: "If you folks will be still for about ten minutes, I'll tell you what happened in my father's house when I was a very small boy; I can just remember it."

"If it's a ghost story, make it strong, Aubrey, so that not a girl will sleep tonight. Won't the dears look pretty blinking and yawning tomorrow night? We'll hear 'em, fellows, in the small hours of the morning, 'Molly, Molly! I'm so frightened. I do believe someone is in my room; may I come in with you, dear?'"

"Charlie, stop your nonsense," laughed his father, and Adonis obediently subsided.

"My father was Dr. Aubrey Livingston too," began Aubrey, "and he owned a large plantation of slaves. My father was deeply interested in the science of medicine, and I believe made some valuable discoveries along the line of mesmeric phenomena, for some two or three of his books are referred to even at this advanced stage of discovery, as marvellous in some of their data.

"Among the slaves was a girl who was my mother's waiting maid, and I have seen my father throw her into a trance state many times when I was so small that I had no conception of what he was doing.

"Many a time I have known him to call her into the parlor to perform tricks of mind-reading for the amusement of visitors, and many wonderful things were done by her as the record given in his books shows.

"One day there was a great dinner party given at our place, and the elite of the county were bidden. It was about two years before the civil war, and our people were not expecting war; thinking that all unpleasantness must end in their favor, they gave little heed to the ominous rumble of public opinion that was arising at the North, but went on their way in all their pride of position and wealth without a care for the future.

"Child as I was I was impressed by the beauty and wit of the women and the chivalric bearing of the men gathered about my father's hospitable board on that memorable day. When the feasting and mirth began to lag, someone called for Mira – the maid – and my father sent for her to come and amuse the guests.

"My father made the necessary passes and from a serious, rather sad Negress, very mild with everyone, Mira changed to a gay, noisy, restless woman, full of irony and sharp jesting. In this case this peculiar metamorphosis always occurred. Nothing could be more curious than to see her and hear her. 'Tell the company what you see, Mira,' commanded my father.

"You will not like it, captain; but if I must, I must. All the women will be widows and the men shall sleep in early graves. They come from the north, from the east, from the west, they sweep to the gulf through a trail of blood. Your houses shall burn, your fields be laid waste, and a down-trodden race shall rule in your land. For you, captain, a prison cell and a pauper's grave."

The dinner-party broke up in a panic, and from that time my father could not abide the girl. He finally sold her just a few months before the secession of the Confederate States, and that was the last we ever knew of her."

"And did the prophecy come true about your father?" asked Mr. Vance.

"Too true, sir; my father died while held as a prisoner of war, in Boston Harbor. And every woman at the table was left a widow. There is only too much truth in science of mesmeric phenomena. The world is a wonderful place."

"Wonderful!" declared his hearers.

"I am thinking of that poor, pretty creature lying ill in that gloomy hospital without a friend. Men are selfish! I tell you what, folks, tomorrow after lunch we'll make a Christmas visit to the patients, and carry them fruit and flowers. As for your beautiful patient, Dr. Briggs, she shall not be friendless any longer, she shall come to us at Vance Hall."

"Molly!" broke simultaneously from Aubrey and Charlie.

"Oh, I mean it. There is plenty of room in this great house, and here she shall remain until she is restored to health."

Expostulation was in vain. The petted heiress was determined, and when Mr. Vance was appealed to he laughed and said, as he patted her hand:

"The queen must have her own."

At length the costumer's box was opened amidst jest, song and laughter. The characters were distributed by the wilful Molly. Thus attired, to the music of Tannhauser's march, played by one of the girls on the piano, the gay crowd marched and counter-marched about the spacious room.

In the early morning hours, Aubrey Livingston slept and dreamed of Dianthe Lusk, and these words haunted his sleep and lingered with him when he woke:

"She had the glory of heaven in her voice, and in her face the fatal beauty of man's terrible sins."

Aubrey Livingston knew that he was as hopelessly lost as was Adam when he sold his heavenly birthright for a woman's smile.

Chapter VII

THROUGH DAYS AND DAYS, and again through days and days, over and over again, Reuel Briggs fought to restore his patient to a normal condition of health. Physically, he succeeded; but mentally his treatment was a failure. Memory remained a blank to the unhappy girl. Her life virtually began with her awakening at the hospital. A look of wonder and a faint smile were the only replies that questions as to the past elicited from her. Old and tried specialists in brain diseases and hypnotic states came from every part of the Union on bootless errands. It was decided that nothing could be done; rest, freedom from every care and time might eventually restore the poor, violated mind to its original strength. Thus it was that Dianthe became the dear adopted daughter of the medical profession. Strange to say, Molly Vance secured her desire, and wearing the name of Felice Adams, Dianthe was domiciled under the roof of palatial Vance hall, and the small annuity provided by the generous contributions of the physicians of the country was placed in the hands of Mr. Vance, Sr., to be expended for their protege.

The astonishing nature of the startling problems he had unearthed, the agitation and indignation aroused in him by the heartless usage to which his patient must have been exposed, haunted Briggs day and night. He believed that he had been drawn into active service for Dianthe by a series of strange coincidences, and the subtle forces of immortality; what future acts this service might require he knew not, he cared not; he registered a solemn promise to perform all tasks allotted him by Infinity, to the fullest extent of his power.

The brilliant winter days merged themselves into spring. After one look into Dianthe's eyes, so deep, clear and true, Molly Vance had surrendered unconditionally to the charm of the beautiful stranger, drawn by an irresistible bond of sympathy. "Who would believe," she observed to Livingston, "that at this stage of the world's progress one's identity could be so easily lost and one still be living. It is like a page from an exciting novel."

With the impulsiveness of youth, a wonderful friendship sprang up between the two; they rode, walked and shopped together; in short, became inseparable companions. The stranger received every attention in the family that could be given an honored guest. Livingston and Briggs watched her with some anxiety; would she be able to sustain the position of intimate friendship to which Molly had elected her? But both breathed more freely when they noted her perfect manners, the ease and good-breeding displayed in all her intercourse with those socially above the level to which they knew this girl was born. She accepted the luxury of her new surroundings as one to the manner born.

"We need not have feared for her; by Jove, she's a thorough-bred!" exclaimed Aubrey one day to Reuel. The latter nodded as he looked up from his book.

"And why not? Probably the best blood of the country flows in the poor girl's veins. Who can tell? Why should she not be a thorough-bred."

"True," replied Aubrey, as a slight frown passed over his face.

"I am haunted by a possibility, Aubrey," continued Reuel. "What if memory suddenly returns? Is it safe to risk the unpleasantness of a public reawakening of her sleeping faculties? I have read of such things."

Aubrey shrugged his handsome shoulders. "We must risk something for the sake of science; where no one is injured by deception there is no harm done."

"Now that question has presented itself to me repeatedly lately: Is deception justifiable for any reason? Somehow it haunts me that trouble may come from this. I wish we had told the exact truth about her identity."

"'If 'twere done when 'tis done, then 'twere well it were done quickly'" murmured Aubrey with a sarcastic smile on his face. "How you balk at nothing, Reuel," he drawled mockingly.

"Oh, call me a fool and done with it, Aubrey, I suppose I am; but one didn't make one's self."

Drives about the snow-clad suburbs of Cambridge with Briggs and Molly, at first helped to brighten the invalid; then came quiet social diversions at which Dianthe was the great attraction.

It was at an afternoon function that Reuel took courage to speak of his love. A dozen men buzzed about 'Miss Adams' in the great bay window where Molly had placed Dianthe, her superb beauty set off by a simple toilet. People came and went constantly. Musical girls, generally with gold eyeglasses on aesthetic noses, played grim classical preparations, which have as cheerful an effect on a gay crowd as the perfect, irreproachable skeleton of a bygone beauty might have; or articulate, with cultivation and no voices to speak of, arias which would sap the life of a true child of song to render as the maestro intended.

The grand, majestic voice that had charmed the hearts from thousands of bosoms, was pinioned in the girl's throat like an imprisoned song-bird. Dianthe's voice was completely gone along with her memory. But music affected her strangely, and Reuel watched her anxiously.

Her face was a study in its delicate, quickly changing tints, its sparkle of smiles running from the sweet, pure tremor of the lovely mouth to the swift laughter of eyes and voice.

Mindful of her infirmity, Reuel led her to the conservatory to escape the music. She lifted her eyes to his with a curious and angelic light in them. She was conscious that he loved her with his whole most loving heart. She winced under the knowledge, for while she believed in him, depended upon him and gathered strength from his love, what she gave in return was but a slight, cold affection compared with his adoration.

He brought her refreshments in the conservatory, and then told his love and asked his fate. She did not answer at once, but looked at his plain face, at the stalwart elegance of his figure, and again gazed into the dark, true, clever eyes, and with the sigh of a tired child crept into his arms, and into his heart for all time and eternity. Thus Aubrey Livingston found them when the company had departed. So it was decided to have the wedding in June. What need for these two children of misfortune to wait?

Briggs, with his new interest in life, felt that it was good just to be alive. The winter passed rapidly, and as he threaded the streets coming and going to his hospital duties, his heart sang. No work was now too arduous; he delighted in the duty most exacting in its nature. As the spring came in it brought with it thoughts of the future. He was almost penniless, and he saw no way of obtaining the money he needed. He had not been improvident, but his lonely life had lived a reckless disregard of the future, and the value of money. He often lived a day on bread and water, at the same time sitting without a fire in the coldest weather because his pockets were empty and he was too proud to ask a loan, or solicit credit from storekeepers. He now found himself in great difficulty. His literary work and the extra cases which his recent triumph had brought him, barely sufficed for his own present needs. Alone in his bachelor existence he would call this luxury, but it was not enough to furnish a suitable establishment for Dianthe. As the weeks rolled by and nothing presented itself, he grew anxious, and finally resolved to consult Livingston.

All things had become new to him, and in the light of his great happiness the very face of old Cambridge was changed. Fate had always been against him, and had played him the shabbiest of tricks, but now he felt that she might do her worst, he held a talisman against misfortune while his love remained to him. Thinking thus he walked along briskly, and the sharp wind brought a faint color into his sallow face. He tried to think and plan, but his ideas were whirled away before they had taken form, and he felt a giant's power to overcome with each inspiring breath of the crisp, cool March air. Aubrey should plan for him, but he would accomplish.

Livingston had apartments on Dana Hill, the most aristocratic portion of Cambridge. There he would remain till the autumn, when he would marry Molly Vance, and remove to Virginia and renew the ancient splendor of his ancestral home. He was just dressing for an evening at the theatre when Briggs entered his rooms. He greeted him with his usual genial warmth.

"What!" he said gaily, "the great scientist here, at this hour?"

Then noticing his visitor's anxious countenance he added:

"What's the matter?"

"I am in difficulties and come to you for help," replied Reuel.

"How so? What is it? I am always anxious to serve you, Briggs."

"I certainly think so or I would not be here now," said Reuel. "But you are just going out, an engagement perhaps with Miss Molly. My business will take some time—"

Aubrey interrupted him, shaking his head negatively. "I was only going out to wile away the time at the theatre. Sit down and free your mind, old man."

Thus admonished, Reuel flung himself among the cushions of the divan, and began to state his reasons for desiring assistance: when he finished, Livingston asked:

"Has nothing presented itself?"

"O yes; two or three really desirable offers which I wrote to accept, but to my surprise, in each case I received polite regrets that circumstances had arisen to prevent the acceptance of my valuable services. That is what puzzles me. What the dickens did it mean?"

Aubrey said nothing but continued a drum solo on the arm of his chair. Finally he asked abruptly: "Briggs, do you think anyone knows or suspects your origin?"

Not a muscle of Reuel's face moved as he replied, calmly: "I have been wondering if such can be the case."

"This infernal prejudice is something horrible. It closes the door of hope and opportunity in many a good man's face. I am a Southerner, but I am ashamed of my section," he added warmly.

Briggs said nothing, but a dark, dull red spread slowly to the very roots of his hair. Presently Aubrey broke the painful silence.

"Briggs, I think I can help you."

"How?"

"There's an expedition just about starting from England for Africa; its final destination is, I believe, the site of ancient Ethiopian cities; its object to unearth buried cities and treasure which the shifting sands of Sahara have buried for centuries. This expedition lacks just such a medical man as you; the salary is large, but you must sign for two years; that is my reason for not mentioning it before. It bids fair to be a wonderful venture and there will be plenty of glory for those who return, beside the good it will do to the Negro race if it proves the success in discovery that scholars predict. I don't advise you to even consider this opportunity, but you asked for my help and this is all I can offer at present."

"But Dianthe!" exclaimed Reuel faintly.

"Yes," smiled Aubrey. "Don't I know how I would feel if it were Molly and I was in your place? You are like all other men, Reuel. Passion does not calculate, and therein lies its strength. As long as common sense lasts we are not in love. Now the answer to the question of ways and means is with you; it is in your hands. You will choose love and poverty I suppose; I should. There are people fools enough to tell a man in love to keep cool. Bah! It is an impossible thing."

"Does true love destroy our reasoning faculties?" Reuel asked himself as he sat there in silence after his friend ceased speaking. He felt then that he could not accept this offer. Finally he got upon his feet, still preserving his silence, and made ready to leave his friend. When he reached the door, he turned and said: "I will see you in the morning."

For a long time after Briggs had gone, Aubrey sat smoking and gazing into the glowing coals that filled the open grate.

All that night Reuel remained seated in his chair or pacing the cheerless room, conning ways and means to extricate himself from his dilemma without having recourse to the last extremity proposed by Aubrey. It was a brilliant opening; there was no doubt of that; a year – six months ago – he would have hailed it with delight, but if he accepted it, it would raise a barrier between his love and him which could not be overcome – the ocean and thousands of miles.

"Oh, no!" he cried, "a thousand times no! Rather give up my ambitions."

Then growing more rational he gazed mournfully around the poor room and asked himself if he could remain and see his wife amid such surroundings? That would be impossible. The question then, resolved itself into two parts: If he remained at home, they could not marry, therefore separation; if he went abroad, marriage and separation. He caught at the last thought eagerly. If then they were doomed to separate, of two evils why not choose the least? The African position would at least bind them irrevocably together. Instantly hope resumed its sway in Reuel's breast so fertile is the human mind in expedients to calm the ruffled spirit; he began to estimate the advantages he would gain by accepting the position: He could marry Dianthe, settle a large portion of his salary upon her thus rendering her independent of charity, leave her in the care of the Vance family, and return in two years a wealthy man no longer fearing poverty. He had never before builded golden castles, but now he speculated upon the possibility of unearthing gems and gold from the mines of ancient Meroe and the pyramids of Ethiopia. In the midst of his fancies he fell asleep. In the morning he felt a wonderful relief as he contemplated his decision. Peace had returned to his mind. He determined to see Aubrey at once and learn all the particulars concerning the expedition. Providentially, Aubrey was just sitting down to breakfast and over a cup of steaming coffee Reuel told his decision, ending with these words: "Now, my dear Aubrey, it may be the last request I may ever ask of you, for who can tell what strange adventures may await me in that dark and unknown country to which Fate has doomed me?"

Livingston tried to remonstrate with him.

"I know what I am saying. The climate is murderous, to begin with, and there are many other dangers. It is better to be prepared. I have no friend but you."

"Between us, Reuel, oaths are useless; you may count upon my loyalty to all your interests," said Aubrey with impressiveness.

"I shall ask you to watch over Dianthe. I intrust her to you as I would intrust her to my brother, had I one. This is all I ask of you when I am in that far country."

With open brow, clear eyes and grave face, Aubrey Livingston replied in solemn tones:

"Reuel, you may sail without a fear. Molly and I will have her with us always like a dear sister."

Hand clasped in hand they stood a moment as if imploring heaven's blessing on the solemn compact. Then they turned the conversation on the business of securing the position at once.

Chapter VIII

REUEL WAS greatly touched during the next three months by the devotion of his friend Livingston, whose unselfishness in his behalf he had before had cause to notice. Nor was this all; he seemed capable of any personal sacrifice that the welfare of Briggs demanded.

Before many days had passed he had placed the young man in direct communication with the English officials in charge of the African expedition. The salary was most generous; in fact, all the arrangements were highly satisfactory. Whatever difficulties really existed melted, as it were, before Aubrey's influence, and Reuel would have approached the time of departure over a bed of roses but for the pain of parting with Dianthe.

At length the bustle of graduation was over. The last article of the traveler's outfit was bought. The morning of the day of departure was to see the ceremony performed that would unite the young people for life. It was a great comfort to Reuel that Charlie Vance had decided to join the party as a tourist for the sake of the advantages of such a trip.

The night before their departure Aubrey Livingston entertained the young men at dinner in his rooms along with a number of college professors and other learned savans. The most complimentary things were said of Reuel in the after-dinner toasts, the best of wishes were uttered together with congratulations on the marriage of the morrow for they all admired the young enthusiast. His superiority was so evident that none disputed it; they envied him, but were not jealous. The object of their felicitations smiled seldom.

"Come, for heaven sake shake off your sadness; he the happy groom upon whom Fortune, fickle jade, has at last consented to smile," cried Adonis. So, amid laughter and jest, the night passed and the morrow came.

After his guests had departed, Aubrey Livingston went to the telegraph office and sent a message:

> To Jim Titus,
> Laurel Hill, Virginia:
> Be on hand at the New York dock, Trans-Atlantic Steamship Co., on the first. I will be there to make things right for you. Ten thousand if you succeed the first six months.
> A.L.

* * *

It was noon the next day and the newly wedded stood with clasped hands uttering their good-byes.

"You must not be unhappy, dear. The time will run by before you know it, and I shall be with you again. Meanwhile there is plenty to occupy you. You have Molly and Aubrey to take you about. But pray remember my advice – don't attempt too much; you're not strong by any means."

"No, I am not strong!" she interrupted with a wild burst of tears. "Reuel, if you knew how weak I am you would not leave me."

Her husband drew the fair head to his bosom, pressing back the thick locks with a lingering lover's touch.

"I wish to God I could take you with me," he said tenderly after a silence. Dear girl, you know this grief of yours would break my heart, only that it shows how well you love me. I am proud of every tear." She looked at him with an expression he could not read; it was full of unutterable emotion – love, anguish, compassion.

"Oh," she said passionately, "nothing remains long with us but sorrow and regret. Every good thing may be gone tomorrow – lost! Do you know, I sometimes dream or have waking visions of a past time in my life? But when I try to grasp the fleeting memories they leave me groping in darkness. Can't you help me, Reuel?"

With a laugh he kissed away her anxieties, although he was dismayed to know that at most any time full memory might return. He must speak to Aubrey. Then he closed her lips with warm lingering kisses.

"Be a good girl and pray for your husband's safety, that God may let us meet again and be happy! Don't get excited. That you *must* guard against."

And Reuel Briggs, though his eyes were clouded with tears, was a happy man at heart that day. Just that once he tasted to the full all that there is of happiness in human life. Happy is he who is blessed with even *one* perfect day in a lifetime of sorrow. His last memory of her was a mute kiss and a low "God bless you," broken by a sob. And so they parted.

In the hall below Molly Vance met him with a sisterly kiss for good-bye; outside in the carriage sat Mr. Vance, Sr., Charlie and Aubrey waiting to drive to depot.

* * *

Reuel Briggs, Charlie Vance and their servant, Jim Titus, sailed from New York for Liverpool, England, on the first day of July.

* * *

The departure of the young men made a perceptible break in the social circle at Vance Hall. Mr. Vance buried himself in the details of business and the two girls wandered disconsolately about the house and grounds attended by Livingston, who was at the Hall constantly and pursued them with delicate attentions.

By common consent it was determined that no summer exodus could be thought of until after the travellers had reached August, all being well, they would seek the limit of civilized intercourse in Africa. While waiting, to raise the spirits of the family, it was decided to invite a house party for the remainder of July, and in the beauties of Bar Harbor. Soon gaiety and laughter filled the grand old rooms; the days went merrily by.

Two men were sitting in the billiard loom lounging over iced punch. Light, perfumed and golden, poured from the rooms below upon the summer night, and the music of a waltz made its way into the darkness.

"What an odd fish Livingston has grown to be," said one, relighting a thin, delicate-looking cigar. "I watched him out of curiosity a while ago and was struck at the change in him."

"Ah!" drawled the other sipping the cooling beverage. "Quite a Priuli on the whole, eh?"

"Y-e-s! Precisely. And I have fancied that the beautiful Mrs. Briggs is his Clarisse. What do you think? She shudders every time he draws near, and sinks to the ground under the steady gaze of his eye. Odd, isn't it?"

"Deucedly odd! About to marry Miss Vance, isn't he?"

"That don't count. Love is not always legitimate. If there's anything in it, it is only a flirtation probably; that's the style."

"What you say is true, Skelton. Let's drink the rest of this stuff and go down again. I know we're missed already."

When they had swallowed the punch and descended, the first person they saw was Livingston leaning against the door of the salon. His face was abstracted and in dead repose, there lurked about the corners of his full lips implacable resolution. The waltz was ended.

Some interminable argument was going on, generally, about the room. Conversation progressed in sharp, brisk sentences, which fell from the lips like the dropping shots of sharpshooters. There was a call for music. Molly mentally calculated her available talent and was about to give up the idea and propose something else, when she was amazed to see Dianthe rise hurriedly from her seat on an ottoman, go to the piano unattended and sit down. Unable to move with astonishment she watched in fascination the slender white fingers flash over the keys. There was a strange rigid appearance about the girl that was unearthly. Never once did she raise her eyes. At the first sharp treble note the buzz in the room was hushed at stillness. Livingston moved forward and rested his arm upon the piano fastening his gaze upon the singer's quivering lips.

Slowly, tremulously at first, pealed forth the notes:

> *"Go down, Moses, way down in Egypt's land,*
> *Tell or Pharaoh, let my people go."*

Scarcely was the verse begun when every person in the room started suddenly and listened with eager interest. As the air proceeded, some grew visibly pale, and not daring to breathe a syllable, looked horrified into each other's faces. "Great heaven!" whispered Mr. Vance to his daughter, "do you not hear another voice beside Mrs. Briggs'?"

It was true, indeed. A weird contralto, veiled as it were, rising and falling upon every wave of the great soprano, and reaching the ear as from some strange distance. The singer sang on, her voice dropping sweet and low, the echo following it, and at the closing word, she fell back in a dead faint. Mr. Vance caught her in his arms.

"Mrs. Briggs has the soul of an artiste. She would make a perfect prima donna for the Grand Opera," remarked one man to Molly.

"We are as surprised as anyone," replied the young girl; "we never knew that Mrs. Briggs was musical until this evening. It is a delightful surprise."

They carried her to the quiet, cool library away from the glaring lights and the excitement, and at her request left her there alone. Her thoughts were painful. Memory had returned in full save as to her name. She knit her brow in painful thought, finally leaning back among her cushions wearily, too puzzled for further thought. Presently a step paused beside her chair. She looked up into Livingston's face.

"Are you feeling better?" he asked, gently taking in his slender wrist and counting the pulse-beats.

Instead of answering his question, she began abruptly: "Mr. Livingston, Reuel told me to trust you implicitly. Can you and will you tell me what has happened to me since last I sang the song I have sung here tonight? I try to recall the past, but all is confusion and mystery. It makes my head ache so to think."

Livingston suddenly drew closer to her.

"Yes, Felice, there is a story in your life! I can save you."

"Save me!" exclaimed the girl.

"Yes, and will! Listen to me." In gentle accents he recounted to her there in the stillness, with the pulsing music of the viols beating and throbbing in her ears like muffled drums, the story of Dianthe Lusk as we have told it here. At the close of the tale the white-faced girl turned to him in despair the more eloquent because of her quietness.

"Did Reuel know that I was a Negress?"

"No; no one recognized you but myself."

She hid her face in her hands.

"Who ever suffered such torture as mine?" she cried, bitterly. "And there is no rest out of the grave!" she continued.

"Yes, there is rest and security in my love! Felice, Dianthe, I have learned to love you!"

She sprang from his touch as if stung.

He continued: "I love you better than all in the world. To possess you I am prepared to prove false to my friend – I am prepared to save you from the fate that must be yours if ever Reuel learns your origin."

"You would have me give up all for you?" she asked with a shudder.

"Ay, from your husband – from the world! We will go where none can ever find us. If you refuse, I cannot aid you."

"Pity me!"

She sank upon her knees at his feet.

"I give you a week to think it over. I can love, but cannot pity."

In vain the girl sought to throw off the numbing influence of the man's presence. In desperation she tried to defy him, but she knew that she had lost her will power and was but a puppet in the hands of this false friend.

Chapter IX

"THE DOCTOR is so good to you about letters; so different from poor Charlie. I can't imagine what he finds to write about."

It was the first of August, and the last guest had left the mansion; tomorrow they started for Bar Harbor. Molly, Dianthe and Livingston sat together in the morning room.

"He tells me the incidents of the journey. This is the last letter for three months," said Dianthe, with a sigh.

"Of course, there is no love-making," said Aubrey, lazily letting fall his newspaper, and pushing his hands through his bright hair. He was a sight for gods and men. His handsome figure outlined against the sky, as he stood by the window in an attitude of listless grace, his finely-cut face, so rich in color and the charm of varying expression, turned indolently toward the two women to whom the morning mail had brought its offering.

"Have you ever read one of Reuel's letters?" Dianthe said, quietly. "You may see this if you like." A tap sounded on the door.

"Miss Molly, if you please, the dressmaker has sent the things."

"Oh, thank you, Jennie, I'll come at once!" and gathering up her letters, Molly ran off with a smile and a nod of apology.

Aubrey stood by the window reading Reuel's letter. His face was deadly white, and his breath came quick and short. He read half the page; then crushed it in his hand and crossed the room to Dianthe. She, too, was pale and there was something akin to fear in the gaze that she lifted to his face.

"How dare you?" he asked breathlessly; "but you are a woman! Not one of you has any delicacy in her heart! Not one!"

He tore the letter across and flung it from him.

"I do not suffer enough," he said in a suffocated voice. "You taunt me with this view of conjugal happiness – with his *right* to love and care for you."

"I did not do it to hurt you," she answered. "Do you have no thought for Molly's sufferings if I succumb to your threats of exposure and weakly allow myself to be frightened into committing the great wrong you contemplate toward two true-hearted people? I thought you could realize if you could know how Reuel loves and trusts me, and how true and noble is his nature."

"Do you think I have room to pity Reuel – Molly – while my own pain is more than I can bear? Without you my ambition is destroyed, my hope for the future – my life is ruined."

He turned from her and going to a distant part of the room, threw himself into a chair and covered his face with his hands. Against her will, better promptings and desires, the unfortunate girl is drawn by invisible influences across the room to the man's side. Presently he holds her in his eager, strong embrace, his face and tears hidden against her shoulder. She does not struggle in his clasp, only looks into the future with the hopeless agony of dumb despair.

At length he broke the silence. "There is nothing you can feel, or say to me that I do not realize – the sin, the shame, the lasting disgrace. I know it all. I told you once I loved you; I tell you now that I cannot *live* without you!"

An hour later Dianthe sat alone in the pleasant room. She did not realize the beauty of the languid mid-summer day. She thought of nothing but the wickedness of betraying her friends. Her perfect features were like marble. The dark eyes had deep, black circles round them and gazed wistfully into the far, far distance, a land where spirit only could compass the wide space. As she sat there in full possession of all her waking faculties, suddenly there rose from out the very floor, as it were, a pale and lovely woman. She neither looked at Dianthe nor did she speak; but walked to the table and opened a book lying upon it and wrote; then coming back, stood for a moment fixed; then sank, just as she rose, and disappeared. Her dress was that of a servant. Her head was bare; her hair fell loosely around her in long black curls. Her complexion was the olive of mulattoes or foreigners. As the woman passed from her view, Dianthe rose and went to the table to examine the book. She did not feel at all frightened, recognizing instantly the hand of mysticism in this strange occurrence. There on the open page, she perceived heavy marks in ink, under-scoring the following quotation from the 12th chapter of Luke: "For there is nothing covered that shall not be revealed." On the margin, at the end of this passage was written in a fine female hand, the single word, "Mira".

* * *

After luncheon Aubrey proposed that they go canoeing on the river. The idea was eagerly embraced and by five o'clock the large and luxurious canoe floated out from the boat house upon the calm bosom of the lovely Charles rocking softly to the little waves that lapped her sides.

The day had been oppressive, but upon the river a refreshing breeze was blowing now that the sun had gone down. For the time all Dianthe's cares left her and her tortured mind was at peace. Molly was full of life and jested and sang and laughed. She had brought her mandolin with her and gave them soft strains of delicious waltzes.

On, on they glided under the impetus of the paddle-strokes in Aubrey's skilful hands, now past the verdure-clad pine hills, now through beds of fragrant waterlilies getting gradually farther and farther from the companionship of other pleasure-seekers. On, into the uninhabited portion where silent woods and long green stretches of pasture-land added a wild loneliness to the scene.

How lovely was the evening sky with its white clouds dotting the azure and the pink tinting of the sunset casting over all its enlivening glow; how deep, and dark was the green of the water beneath the shadowing trees. From the land came the lowing of cows and the sweet scent of freshly spread hay.

Suddenly Aubrey's paddle was caught and held in the meshes of the water-lily stems that floated all about them. He leaned far over to extricate it and in a moment the frail craft was bottom up, its living freight struggling in the river. Once, twice, thrice a thrilling call for help echoed over the darkening land; then all was still.

Chapter X

THE EXPEDITION with which Reuel Briggs found himself connected was made up of artists, savans and several men – capitalists – who represented the business interests of the venture. Before the white cliffs of the English coast were entirely lost to view, Reuel's natural propensities for leadership were being fully recognized by the students about him. There was an immediate demand for his professional services and he was kept busy for many days. And it was the best panacea for a nature like his – deep and silent and self-suppressing. He had abandoned happiness for duty; he had stifled all those ominous voices which rose from the depth of his heart, and said to him: "Will you ever return? And if you return will you find your dear one? And, if you find her, will she not have changed? Will she have preserved your memory as faithfully as you will preserve hers?

A thousand times a day while he performed his duties mechanically, his fate haunted him – the renunciation which called on him to give up happiness, to open to mishap the fatal door absence. All the men of the party were more or less silent and distrait, even Charlie Vance was subdued and thoughtful. But Briggs suffered more than any of them, although he succeeded in affecting a certain air of indifference. As he gradually calmed down and peace returned to his mind, he was surprised to feel the resignation that possessed him. Some unseen presence spoke to his inner being words of consolation and hope. He was shown very clearly his own inability to control events, and that his fate was no longer in his own hands but ordered by a being of infinite pity and love. After hours spent in soul-communion with the spirit of Dianthe, he would sink into refreshing slumber and away in peace. Her letters were bright spots, very entertaining and describing minutely her life and daily occupation since his departure. He lived upon them during the voyage to Tripoli, sustained by the hope of finding one upon arriving at that city.

One fine evening when the sun was setting, they arrived at Tripoli. Their course lay toward the southward, and standing on deck, Reuel watched the scene – a landscape strange in form, which would have delighted him and filled him with transports of joy; now he felt something akin to indifference.

The ripples that flit the burnished surface of the long undulating billows tinkled continually on the sides of the vessel. He was aware of a low-lying spectral-pale band of shore. That portion of Africa whose nudity is only covered by the fallow mantle of the desert gave a most sad impression to the gazer. The Moors call it 'Bled el Ateusch', the Country of Thirst; and, as there is an intimate relation between the character of a country and that of its people, Reuel realized vividly that the race who dwelt here must be different from those of the rest of the world.

"Ah! That is our first glimpse of Africa, is it?" said Adonis's voice, full of delight, beside him.

He turned to see his friend offering him a telescope. "At last we are here. In the morning we shall set our feet on the enchanted ground."

In the distance one could indeed make out upon the deep blue of the sky the profile of Djema el Gomgi, the great mosque on the shores of the Mediterranean. At a few cable lengths away the city smiles at them with all the fascination of a modern Cleopatra, circled with an oasis of palms studded with hundreds of domes and minarets. Against a sky of amethyst the city stands forth with a penetrating charm. It is the eternal enchantment of the cities of the Orient seen at a distance; but, alas! set foot within them, the illusion vanishes and disgust seizes you. Like beautiful bodies they have the appearance of life, but within the worm of decay and death eats ceaselessly.

At twilight in this atmosphere the city outlines itself faintly, then disappears in dusky haze. One by one the stars came into the sky until the heavens were a twinkling blaze; the sea murmured even her soft refrain and slept with the transparency of a mirror, flecked here and there with fugitive traces of phosphorescence.

The two young men stood a long time on the deck gazing toward the shore.

"Great night!" exclaimed Adonis at length with a long-drawn sigh of satisfaction. "It promises to be better than anything Barnum has ever given us even at a dollar extra reserved seat."

Reuel smiled in spite of himself; after all, Charlie was a home-line warranted to ward off homesickness. On board there was the sound of hurrying feet and a murmur of suppressed excitement, but it had subsided shortly; an hour later "sleep and oblivion reigned over all".

In the morning, amid the bustle of departure the mail came on board. There were two letters for Reuel. He seated himself in the seclusion of the cabin safe from prying eyes. Travelling across the space that separated him from America, his thoughts were under the trees in the garden of Vance Hall. In the fresh morning light he thought he could discern the dress of his beloved as she came toward him between the trees.

Again he was interrupted by Charlie's jolly countenance. He held an open letter in his hand. "There, Doc, there's Molly's letter. Read it, read it; don't have any qualms of conscience about it. There's a good bit in it concerning the Madam, see? I thought you'd like to read it." Then he sauntered away to talk with Jim Titus about the supplies for the trip across the desert.

Jim was proving himself a necessary part of the expedition. He was a Negro of the old regime who felt that the AngloSaxon was appointed by God to rule over the African. He showed his thoughts in his obsequious manner, his subservient "massa", and his daily conversation with those about him. Jim superintended the arrangement of the table of the exploring party, haggled over prices with the hucksters, quarreled with the galley cooks and ended by doing all the cooking for his party in addition to keeping his eye on "Massa Briggs". All of this was very pleasant, but sometimes Reuel caught a gleam in Jim's furtive black eye which set him thinking and wondering at the latter's great interest in himself; but he accounted for this because of Livingston's admonitions to Jim to "take care of Dr. Briggs".

Willing or not, the company of travellers were made to take part in the noisy scene on deck when a horde of dirty rascals waylaid them, and after many uses and combination of all sorts over a few cents, they and their luggage were transported to the Custom House. "Ye gods!" exclaimed Charlie in deep disgust, "what a jostling, and what a noise."

All the little world about them was in an uproar, everyone signalling, gesticulating, speaking at once. Such a fray bewilders a civilized man, but those familiar with Southern exuberance regard it tranquilly, well knowing the disorder is more apparent than real. Those of the party who were familiar with the scene, looked on highly amused at the bewilderment of the novices.

Most of them had acquired the necessary art of not hurrying, and under their direction the examination of the baggage proceeded rapidly. Presently, following a robust porter, they had traversed an open place filled with the benches and chairs of a 'café', and soon the travellers were surprised and amused to find themselves objects of general curiosity. Coffee and nargiles were there merely as a pretext, in reality the gathering was in their honor. The names of the members of the expedition were known, together with its object of visiting Meroe of ancient fame, the arrival of such respectable visitors is a great event. Then, too, Tripoli is the natural road by which Africa has been attacked by many illustrious explorers because of the facility of communication with the country of the Blacks. Nowhere in northern Africa does the Great Desert advance so near the sea. The Atlas range rises from the Atlantic coast, extending far eastward. This range loses itself in the gulf of Little Syrta. and the vast, long-pent-up element, knowing no more barrier, spreads its yellow, sandy waves as far as the Nile, enveloping the last half-submerged summits which form a rosary of oases.

Under the Sultan's rule Tripoli has remained the capital of a truly barbaric state, virgin of improvements, with just enough dilapidated abandon, dirt and picturesqueness to make the delight of the artist. Arabs were everywhere; veiled women looked at the Christians with melting eyes above their wrappings. Mohammedanism, already twelve centuries old, has, after a period of inactivity, awakened anew in Africa, and is rapidly spreading. Very unlike the Christians, the faithful of today are the same fervid Faithful of Omar and Mohammed. Incredulity, indifference, so widely spread among other sects are unknown to them.

Supper-time found the entire party seated on the floor around a well-spread tray, set on a small box. They had taken possession of the one living-room of a mud house. It was primitive but clean. A post or two supported the thatched ceiling. There were no windows. The furniture consisted of a few rugs and cushions. But the one idea of the party being sleep, they were soon sunk in a profound and dreamless slumber.

The next day and the next were spent in trying to gain an audience with the Sheik Mohammed Abdallah, and the days lengthened into weeks and a month finally rolled into oblivion. Meantime there were no letters for Dr. Briggs and Charlie Vance. Everyone else in the party had been blessed with many letters, even Jim was not forgotten.

Reuel had learned to be patient in the *dolce far niente* of the East, but not so Charlie. He fumed and fretted continually after the first weeks had passed. But promptly at two, one hot afternoon the Sheik knocked at the door of their hut. He was a handsome man of forty years – tall, straight, with clear brown eyes, good features, a well-shaped moustache and well-trimmed black beard. Authority surrounded him like an atmosphere. He greeted the party in French and Arabic and invited them to his house where a feast was spread for them. Presents were given and received and then they were introduced to Ababdis, an owner of camels who was used to leading parties into the wilderness. After much haggling over prices, it was decided to take fifteen camels and their drivers. Supplies were to consist of biscuit, rice, tea, sugar, coffee, wax candles, charcoal and a copious supply of water bags. It was decided not to start until Monday, after the coming of the mail, which was again due. After leaving Tripoli, it was doubtful when they would receive news from America again. The mail came. Again Jim was the only one who received a letter from the United States. Reuel handed it to him with a feeling of homesickness and a sinking of the heart.

Monday morning found them mounted and ready for the long journey across the desert to the first oasis. From the back of a camel Charlie Vance kept the party in good humor with his quaint remarks. "Say, Doc, it's worth the price. How I wish the pater, your wife and Molly could see us now, Livingston wouldn't do a thing to these chocolate colored gentry of Arabia."

"And Miss Scott? Where does she come in?" questioned Reuel with an assumption of gaiety he was far from feeling.

"Oh," replied Charlie, not at all nonplussed. "Cora isn't in the picture; I'm thinking of a houri."

"Same old thing, Charlie – the ladies?"

"No," said Charlie, solemnly. "It's business this time. Say, Briggs, the sight of a camel always makes me a child again. The long-necked beast is inevitably associated in my mind with Barnum's circus and playing hookey. Pop wants me to put out my sign and go in for business, but the show business suits me better. For instance," he continued with a wave of his hand including the entire caravan, "Arabs, camels, stray lions, panthers, scorpions, serpents, explorers, etc., with a few remarks by yours truly, to the accompaniment of the band – always the band you know, would make an interesting show – a sort of combination of Barnum and Kiralfy. The houris would do Kiralfy's act, you know. There's money in it."

"Were you ever serious in your life, Charlie?"

"What the deuce is the need of playing funeral all the time, tell me that, Briggs, will you?"

The great desert had the sea's monotony. They rode on and on hour after hour. The elements of the view were simple. Narrow valleys and plains bounded by picturesque hills lay all about them. The nearer hills to the right had shoulders and hollows at almost regular intervals, and a skyline of an almost regular curve. Under foot the short grass always seemed sparse, and the low sage-shrubs rather dingy, but as they looked over the plain stretching away in every direction, it had a distinctly green tint. They saw occasionally a red poppy and a purple iris. Not a tree was to be seen, nor a rock. Sometimes the land lay absolutely level and smooth, with hardly a stone larger than a bean. The soft blue sky was cloudless, the caravan seemed to be the only living creature larger than a gazelle in the great solitude. Even Reuel was aroused to enthusiasm by the sight of a herd of these graceful creatures skimming the plain. High in the air the larks soared and sang.

As they went southward the hot sun poured its level rays upon them, and the song of the drivers was a relief to their thoughts. The singing reminded travellers of Venetian gondoliers, possessing as it did the plaintive sweetness of the most exquisite European airs. There was generally a leading voice answered by a full chorus. Reuel thought he had never heard music more fascinating. Ababdis would assume the leading part. "Ah, when shall I see my family again; the rain has fallen and made a canal between me and my home. Oh, shall I never see it more?" Then would follow the chorus of drivers: "Oh, what pleasure, what delight, to see my family again; when 1 see my father, mother, brothers, sisters, I will hoist a flag on the head of my camel for joy!" About the middle of the week they were making their way over the Great Desert where it becomes an elevated plateau crossed by rocky ridges, with intervening sandy plains mostly barren, but with here and there a solitary tree, and sometimes a few clumps of grass. The caravan was skirting the base of one of these ridges, which culminated in a cliff looking, in the distance, like a half-ruined castle, which the Arabs believed to be enchanted. Reuel determined to visit this cliff, and saying nothing to anyone, and accompanied only by Jim and followed by the warnings of the Arabs to beware of lions, they started for the piles of masonry, which they reached in a couple of hours. The moon rose in unclouded splendor, and Moore's lines came to his heart:

> O, such a blessed night as this,
> I often think if friends were near,
> How we should feel, and gaze with bliss
> Upon the moonlight scenery here.

He strolled into the royal ruin, stumbling over broken carvings, and into hollows concealed by luminous plants, beneath whose shades dwelt noisome things that wriggled away in the marvelous white light. Climbing through what was once a door, he stepped out on a ledge of masonry, that hung sheer seven hundred feet over the plain. Reuel got out his pipe and it was soon in full blast, while the smoker set to building castles in the curls of blue smoke, that floated lightly into space. Jim with the guns waited for him at the foot of the hill.

Under the influence of the soothing narcotic and the spell of the silver moon, Reuel dreamed of fame and fortune he would carry home to lay at a little woman's feet. Presently his castle-building was interrupted by a low vail – not exactly the mew of a cat, nor yet the sound of a lute.

.Again the sound. What could it be?

"Ah, I have it!" muttered Reuel; "it's the Arabs singing in the camp."

Little did he imagine that within ten paces of him crouched an enormous leopard.

Little did he imagine that he was creeping, creeping toward him, as a cat squirms at a bird.

He sat on the ruined ledge of the parapet, within two feet of the edge; seven hundred feet below the desert sand glittered like molten silver in the gorgeous moonlight.

He was unarmed, having given Jim his revolver to hold.

Reuel sat there entirely unconscious of danger; presently a vague feeling struck him, not of fear, not of dread, but a feeling that if he turned his head he would see an enemy, and without knowing why, he slowly turned his head.

Great heavens! What did he see? A thrill of horror passed through him as his eyes rested upon those of an enormous brute, glaring like hot coals set in blood-red circles.

Its mouth was wide open, its whiskers moving like the antennae of a lobster. It lay on its belly, its hindquarters raised, its forepaws planted in the tawny sand ready to spring.

The moon played on the spots of its body. The dark spots became silvered, and relapsed into darkness as the animal breathed, while its tail lashed about, occasionally whipping the sand with a peculiar whish.

How was he to withstand its spring?

The weight of its body would send him over the precipice like a shot.

Strange to say a grim satisfaction came to him at the thought that the brute must go down with him. Where could he hold? Could he clutch at anything? he asked himself.

He dared not remove his eyes from those of the leopard. He could not in fact. But in a sort of introverted glance he saw that nothing stood between him and space but a bare, polished wall, that shone white beneath the moonbeams.

"Was there a loose stone – a stone that would crush in the skull of the bloodthirsty animal?" Not so much as a pebble to cast into the depths, for he had already searched for one to fling over, as people do when perched on imminences. He cried for help, "Jim! Jim! O-o-o-h, Jim!"

There came no reply; not the slightest sound broke the stillness as the sound of his cries died away.

Reuel was now cool – cool as a cucumber – so cool that he deliberately placed himself in position to receive the rush of the terrific brute. He felt himself moving gently back his right foot, shuffling it back until his heel came again an unevenness in the rock, which gave him a sort of purchase – something to back it.

He gathered himself together for a supreme effort, every nerve being at the highest condition of tension.

It is extraordinary all the thoughts that pass like lightning in a second of time, through the mind, while face to face with death. Volumes of ideas flashed through his brain as he stood on the stone ledge, with eternity awaiting him, knowing that this would be the end of all his hopes and fears and pleasant plans for future happiness, that he would go down to death in the embrace of the infuriated animal before him, its steel-like claws buried in his flesh, its fetid breath filling his nostrils. He thought of his darling love, and of how the light would go out of her existence with his death. He thought of Livingston, of the fellows who had gathered to bid him God speed, of the paragraphs in the papers. All these things came as harrowing pictures as he stood at bay in the liquid pearl of the silent moon.

The leopard began to move its hindquarters from side to side. A spring was at hand.

Reuel yelled then – yelled till the walls of the ruined castle echoed again – yelled as if he had 10,000 voices in his throat – yelled, as a man only yells when on his being heard depends his chance for dear life.

The beast turned its head sharply, and prepared to spring. For a second Briggs thought that a pantomime trick might give him a chance. What if he were to wait until the animal actually leaped, and then turn aside?

Carried forward by its own weight and momentum it would go over the ledge and be dashed to pieces on the rocks below.

It was worth trying. A drowning man catches at a straw. Instinctively Reuel measured his distance. He could step aside and let the brute pass, but that was all. The ledge was narrow. He was, unhappily, in very good condition. The sea voyage had fattened him, and it was just a chance that he could escape being carried over by the brute.

He accepted the chance.

Then came the fearful moment.

The leopard swayed a little backward!

Then, to his intense delight, he heard a shout of encouragement in Vance's well-known voice, "Coming, Briggs, coming!"

The next moment a hand was laid on his shoulder from a window above; it was Charlie, who trembling with anxiety had crept through the ruin, and, oh, blessed sight! handed Reuel his revolver.

Briggs made short work of the leopard: he let him have three barrels – all in the head.

Vance had become alarmed for the safety of his friend, and had gone to the ruin to meet him. When very nearly there, he had heard the first cry for help, and had urged his camel forward. Arrived at the castle he had found Jim apparently dead with sleep, coiled up on the warm sand. How he could sleep within sound of the piercing cries uttered by Briggs was long a mystery to the two friends.

Chapter XI

THE CARAVAN had halted for the night. Professor Stone, the leader of the expedition, sat in Reuel's tent enjoying a pipe and a talk over the promising features of the enterprise. The nearer they approached the goal of their hopes – the ancient Ethiopian capital Meroe – the greater was the excitement among the leaders of the party. Charlie from his bed of rugs listened with ever-increasing curiosity to the conversation between the two men.

"It is undoubtedly true that from its position as the capital of Ethiopia and the enterpret of trade between the North and South, between the East and West, Meroe must have held vast treasures. African caravans poured ivory, frankincense and gold into the city. My theory is that somewhere under those pyramids we shall find invaluable records and immense treasure."

"Your theories may be true, Professor, but if so, your discoveries will establish the primal existence of the Negro as the most ancient source of all that you value in modern life, even antedating Egypt. How can the Anglo-Saxon world bear the establishment of such a theory?" There was a hidden note of sarcasm in his voice which the others did not notice.

The learned savan settled his glasses and threw back his head.

"You and I, Briggs, know that the theories of prejudice are swept away by the great tide of facts. It is a *fact* that Egypt drew from Ethiopia all the arts, sciences and knowledge of which she was mistress. The very soil of Egypt was pilfered by the Nile from the foundations of Meroe. I have even thought," he continued meditatively, "that black was the original color of man in prehistoric times. You remember that Adam was made from the earth; what more natural than that he should have retained the color of the earth? What puzzles me is not the origin of the Blacks, but of the Whites. Miriam was made a leper outside the tents for punishment; Naaman was a leper until cleansed. It is a question fraught with big possibilities which Cod alone can solve. But of this we are sure – all records of history, sacred and profane, unite in placing the Ethiopian as the primal race."

"Gee whiz!" exclaimed Charlie from his bed on the floor "Count me out!"

"Don't touch upon the origin of the Negro: you will find yourself in a labyrinth, Professor. That question has provoked more discussion than any other concerning the different races of man on the globe. Speculation has exhausted itself, yet the mystery appears to remain unsolved."

"Nevertheless the Biblical facts are very explicit, and so simple as to force the very difficulties upon mankind that Divinity evidently designed to avoid."

"The relationship existing between the Negro and other people of the world is a question of absorbing interest. For my part, I shall be glad to add to my ethnological knowledge by anything we may learn at Meroe." Thus speaking Reuel seemed desirous of dismissing the subject. More conversation followed on indifferent subjects, and presently the Professor bade them good night and retired to his own tent.

Reuel employed himself in making entries in his journal, Charlie continued to smoke, at times evincing by a musical snore that he was in the land of dreams. Jim sat at some distance reading a letter that he held in his hand.

The night was sultry, the curtains of the tent undrawn; from out the silent solitude came the booming call of a lion to his mate.

Suddenly a rush of balmy air seemed to pass over the brow of the scribe, and a dim shadow fell across the tent door. It was the form of the handsome Negress who had appeared to Dianthe, and signed herself "Mira".

There was no fear in Reuel's gaze, no surprise; it was as if a familiar and welcome visitor had called upon him. For a moment an impulse to spring away into the wide, wide realms of air, seemed to possess him; the next, the still, dreamy ecstasy of a past time; and then he saw Jim – who sat directly behind him – placed like a picture on his very table. He saw him knit his brow, contract his lip, and then, with a face all seamed with discontent, draw from his vest a letter, seemingly hidden in a private pocket, reading thus:

> Use your discretion about the final act, but be sure the letters are destroyed. I have advised the letters sent in your care as you will probably be detailed for the mail. But to avoid mishap call for the mail for both parties. Address me at Laurel Hill – Thomas Johnson.
> A.L.

Twice did the visionary scene, passing *behind* the seer, recross his entranced eyes; and twice did the shadowy finger of the shining apparition in the tent door point, letter by letter, to the pictured page of the billet, which Jim was at that very moment perusing with his natural, and Reuel Briggs with his spiritual eyes. When both had concluded the reading, Jim put up his letter. The curtains of the tent slightly waved; a low, long sigh, like the night's wind wail, passed over the cold, damp brow of the seer. A shudder, a blank. He looked out into the desert beyond. All was still. The stars were out for him, but the vision was gone.

Thus was explained to Reuel, by mesmeric forces, the fact that his letters had been withheld.

He had not once suspected Jim of perfidy. What did it mean? he asked himself. The letter was in Livingston's handwriting! His head swam; he could not think. Over and over again he turned the problem and then, wishing that something more definite had been given him, retired, but not to sleep.

Try as he would to throw it off, the most minute act of Jim since entering his service persisted in coming before his inner vision. The night when he was attacked by the leopard and Jim's tardiness in offering help, returned with great significance. What could he do but conclude that he was the victim of a conspiracy.

"There is no doubt about it," was his last thought as he dropped into a light doze. How long he slept he could not tell, but he woke with a wild, shrill cry in his ears: "Reuel, Reuel, save me!"

Three times it was repeated, clear, distinct, and close beside his ear, a pause between the repetitions.

He roused his sleeping friend. "Charlie, Charlie! Wake up and listen!"

Charlie, still half asleep, looked with blinking eyes at the candle with dazzled sight.

"Charlie, for the love of God wake up!"

At this, so full of mortal fear were his words, Adonis shook off his drowsiness and sat up in bed, wide awake and staring at him in wonder.

"What the deuce!" he began, and then stopped, gazing in surprise at the white face and trembling hands of his friend.

"Charlie," he cried, "some terrible event has befallen Dianthe, or like a sword hangs over our heads. Listen, listen!"

Charlie did listen but heard nothing but the lion's boom which now broke the stillness.

"I hear nothing, Reuel."

"O Charlie, are you sure?"

"Nothing but the lion. But that'll be enough if he should take it into his mind to come into camp for his supper."

"I suppose you are right, for you can hear nothing, and I can hear nothing now. But, oh Charlie! It was so terrible, and I heard it so plainly; though I daresay it was only my – Oh God! There it is again! Listen! Listen!"

This time Charlie heard – heard clearly and unmistakably, and hearing, felt the blood in his veins turn to ice.

Shrill and clear above the lion's call rose a prolonged wail, or rather shriek, as of a human voice rising to heaven in passionate appeal for mercy, and dying away in sobbing and shuddering despair. Then came the words:

"Charlie, brother, save me!"

Adonis sprang to his feet, threw back the curtain of the tent and looked out. All was calm and silent, not even a cloud flecked the sky where the moon's light cast a steady radiance.

Long he looked and listened; but nothing could be seen or heard. But the cry still rang in his ears and clamored at his heart; while his mind said it was the effect of imagination.

Reuel's agitation had swallowed up his usual foresight. He had forgotten his ability to resort to that far-seeing faculty which he had often employed for Charlie's and Aubrey's amusement when at home.

Charlie was very calm, however, and soothed his friend's fears, and after several ineffectual attempts to concentrate his powers for the exercise of the clairvoyant sight of the hypnotic trance, was finally able to exercise the power.

In low, murmuring cadence, sitting statuesque and rigid beneath the magnetic spell, Reuel rehearsed the terrible scene which had taken place two months before in the United States in the ears of his deeply-moved friend.

"Ah, there is Molly, poor Molly; and see your father weeps, and the friends are there and they too weep, but where is my own sweet girl, Dianthe, love, wife! No, I cannot see her, I do not find the poor maimed body of my love. And Aubrey! What! Traitor, false friend! I shall return for vengeance.

"Wake me, Charlie," was his concluding sentence.

A few upward passes of his friend's hands, and the released spirit became lord of its casket once more. Consciousness returned, and with it memory. In short whispered sentences Reuel told Vance of his suspicions, of the letter he read while it lay in Jim's hand, of his deliberate intention to leave him to his fate in the leopard's claws.

The friends laid their plans – they would go on to Meroe, and then return instantly to civilization as fast as steam could carry them, if satisfactory letters were not waiting them from America.

Chapter XII

LATE ONE AFTERNOON two weeks later, the caravan halted at the edge of the dirty Arab town which forms the outposts to the island of Meroe.

Charlie Vance stood in the door of his tent and let his eyes wander over the landscape in curiosity. Clouds of dust swept over the sandy plains; when they disappeared the heated air began its dance again, and he was glad to re-enter the tent and stretch himself at full length in his hammock. The mail was not yet in from Cairo, consequently there were no letters; his eyes ached from straining them for a glimpse of the Ethiopian ruins across the glassy waters of the tributaries of the Nile which encircled the island.

It was not a simple thing to come all these thousands of miles to look at a pile of old ruins that promised nothing of interest to him after all. This was what he had come for – the desolation of an African desert, and the companionship of human fossils and savage beasts of prey. The loneliness made him shiver. It was a desolation that doubled desolateness, because his healthy American organization missed the march of progress attested by the sound of hammers on unfinished buildings that told of a busy future and cosy modern homeliness. Here there was no future. No railroads, no churches, no saloons, no schoolhouses to echo the voices of merry children, no promise or the life that produces within the range of his vision. Nothing but the monotony of past centuries dead and forgotten save by a few learned savans.

As he rolled over in his hammock, Charlie told himself that next to seeing the pater and Molly, he'd give ten dollars to be able to thrust his nose into twelve inches of whiskey and soda, and remain there until there was no more. Then a flicker of memory made Charlie smile as he remembered the jollities of the past few months that he had shared with Cora Scott.

"Jolly little beggar," he mentally termed her. "I wonder what sort of a fool she'd call me if she could see me now whistling around the ragged edge of this solid block of loneliness called a desert."

Then he fell asleep and dreamed he was boating on the Charles, and that Molly was a mermaid sporting in a bed of water-lilies.

Ancient writers, among them Strabo, say that the Astabora unites its stream with the Nile, and forms the island of Meroe. The most famous historical city of Ethiopia is commonly called Carthage, but Meroe was the queenly city of this ancient people. Into it poured the traffic of the world in gold, frankincense and ivory. Diodorus states the island to be three hundred and seventy-five miles long and one hundred and twenty-five miles wide. The idea was borne in upon our travellers in crossing the Great Desert that formerly wells must have been established at different stations for the convenience of man and beast. Professor Stone and Reuel had discovered traces of a highway and the remains of cisterns which must have been marvellous in skill and prodigious in formation.

All was bustle and commotion in the camp that night. Permission had been obtained to visit and explore the ruins from the Arab governor of the Province. It had cost money, but Professor Stone counted nothing as lost that would aid in the solution of his pet theories.

The leaders of the enterprise sat together late that night, listening to the marvellous tales told by the Professor of the city's ancient splendor, and examining closely the chart which had remained hidden for years before it fell into his hands. For twenty-five years this apostle of learning had held the key to immense wealth, he believed, in his hands. For years he had tried in vain to interest the wealthy and powerful in his scheme for finding the city described in his chart, wherein he believed lay the gold mines from which had come the streams of precious metal which made the ancient Ethiopians famous.

The paper was in a large envelope sealed with a black seal formed to resemble a lotus flower. It was addressed:

TO THE STUDENT WHO, HAVING COUNTED THE COST, IS RESOLUTE TO ONCE MORE REVEAL TO THE SCEPTICAL, THE ANCIENT GLORY OF HOARY MEROE.

Within the envelope was a faded parchment which the Professor drew forth with trembling hands. The little company drew more closely about the improvised table and its flickering candle which revealed the faded writing to be in Arabic. There was no comment, but each one listened intently to the reader, who translated very fully as he went along.

"Be it known to you, my brother, that the great and surpassing wealth mentioned in this parchment is not to be won without braving many dangers of a deadly nature. You who may read this message, then, I entreat to consider well the perils of your course. Within the mines of Meroe, four days' journey from the city toward Arabia, are to be found gold in bars and gold in flakes, and diamonds, and rubies whose beauty excels all the jewels of the earth. For some of them were hidden by the priests of Osiris that had adorned the crown of the great Semiramis, and the royal line of Queen Candace, even from ancient Babylon's pillage these jewels came, a spectacle glorious beyond compare. There, too, is the black diamond of Senechus's crown (Senechus who suffered the captivity of Israel by the Assyrians), which exceeds all imagination for beauty and color.

"All these jewels with much treasure beside you will gain by following my plain directions.

"Four days' journey from Meroe toward Arabia is a city founded by men from the Upper Nile; the site is near one of its upper sources, which still has one uniform existence. This city is situated on a forked tributary, which takes its rise from a range of high, rocky mountains, almost perpendicular on their face, from which descend two streams like cataracts, about two miles apart, and form a triangle, which holds the inner city. The outer city occupies the opposite banks on either side of the streams, which after joining, form a river of considerable size, and running some five miles, loses itself in the surrounding swamps. The cities are enclosed within two great walls, running parallel with the streams. There are also two bridges with gates, connecting the inner and outer cities; two great gates also are near the mountain ranges, connecting the outer city with the agricultural lands outside the walls. The whole area is surrounded *by extensive swamps, through which a passage, known only to the initiated runs, and forms an impassible barrier to the ingress or egress of strangers.*

"But there is another passage known to the priests and used by them, and this is the passage which the chart outlines beneath the third great pyramid, leading directly into the mines and giving access to the city.

"When Egypt rose in power and sent her hosts against the mother country, then did the priests close with skill and cunning this approach to the hidden city of refuge, where they finally retired, carrying with them the ancient records of Ethiopia's greatness, and closing forever, as they thought, the riches of her marvellous mines, to the world.

"Beneath the Sphinx' head lies the secret of the entrance, and yet not all, for the rest is graven on the sides of the cavern which will be seen when the mouth shall gape. But beware the tank to the right where dwells the sacred crocodile, still living, although centuries have rolled by and men have been gathered to the shades who once tended on his wants. And beware the fifth gallery to the right where abide the sacred serpents with jewelled crowns, for of a truth are they terrible.

"This the writer had from an aged priest whose bones lie embalmed in the third pyramid above the Sphinx."

With this extraordinary document a chart was attached, which, while an enigma to the others, seemed to be perfectly clear to Professor Stone.

The letter ended abruptly, and the chart was a hopeless puzzle to the various eyes that gazed curiously at the straggling outlines.

"What do you make of it, Professor?" asked Reuel, who with all his knowledge, was at sea with the chart. "We have been looking for mystery, and we seem to have found it."

"What do I make of it? Why, that we shall find the treasure and all return home rich," replied the scholar testily.

"Rubbish!" snorted Charlie with fine scorn.

"How about the sacred crocodile and the serpents? My word, gentlemen, if you find the back door key of the Sphinx' head, there's a chance that a warm welcome is awaiting us."

Charlie's words met with approval from the others, but the Professor and Reuel said nothing. There was silence for a time, each man drawing at his pipe in silent meditation.

"Well, I'm only travelling for pleasure, so it matters not to me how the rest of you elect to shuffle off this mortal coil, I intend to get some fun out of this thing," continued Charlie.

There was a shout of laughter from his companions.

"Pleasure!" cried one. "O Lord! You've come to the wrong place. This is business, solid business. If we get out with our skins it will be something to be thankful for."

"Well," said Reuel, rousing himself from a fit of abstraction, "I come out to do business and I have determined to see the matter through if all is well at home. We'll prove whether there's a hidden city or not before we leave Africa."

The Professor grasped his hand in gratitude, and then silence fell upon the group. The curtains of the tent were thrown back. Bright fell the moonlight on the sandy plain, the Nile, the indistinct ruins of Meroe, hiding all imperfections by its magic fingers. It was a wonderful sight to see the full moon looking down on the ruins of centuries. The weird light increased, the shadows lengthened and silence fell on the group, broken only by the low tones of Professor Stone as he told in broken sentences the story of ancient Ethiopia.

"For three thousand years the world has been mainly indebted for its advancement to the Romans, Greeks, Hebrews, Germans and Anglo-Saxons; but it was otherwise in the first years.

Babylon and Egypt – Nimrod and Mizraim – both descendants of Ham – led the way, and acted as the pioneers of mankind in the untrodden fields of knowledge. The Ethiopians, therefore, manifested great superiority over all the nations among whom they dwelt, and their name became illustrious throughout Europe, Asia and Africa.

"The father of this distinguished race was Cush, the grandson of Noah, an Ethiopian."

"Old Chaldea, between the Euphrates and Tigris rivers, was the first home of the Cushites. Nimrod, Ham's grandson, founded Babylon. The Babylonians early developed the energy of mind which made their country the first abode of civilization. Canals covered the land, serving the purposes of traffic, defense and irrigation. Lakes were dug and stored with water, dykes built along the banks of rivers to fertilize the land, and it is not surprising to learn that from the earliest times Babylonia was crowded with populous cities. This grandeur was brought about by Nimrod the Ethiopian."

"Great Scott!" cried Charlie, "you don't mean to tell me that all this was done by *niggers*!"

The Professor smiled. Being English, he could not appreciate Charlie's horror at its full value.

"Undoubtedly your Afro-Americans are a branch of the wonderful and mysterious Ethiopians who had a prehistoric existence of magnificence, the full record of which is lost in obscurity.

"We associate with the name 'Chaldea' the sciences of astronomy and philosophy and chronology. It was to the Wise Men of the East to whom the birth of Christ was revealed; they were Chaldeans – of the Ethiopians. Eighty-eight years before the birth of Abraham, these people, known in history as 'Shepherd Kings', subjugated the whole of Upper Egypt, which they held in bondage more than three hundred years."

"It is said that Egyptian civilization antedates that of Ethiopia," broke in Reuel. "How do you say, Professor?"

"Nothing of the sort, nothing of the sort. I know that in connecting Egypt with Ethiopia, one meets with most bitter denunciation from most modern scholars. Science has done its best to separate the race from Northern Africa, but the evidence is with the Ethiopians. If I mistake not, the ruins of Meroe will prove my words. Traditions with respect to Memnon connect Egypt and Ethiopia with the country at the head of the Nile. Memnon personifies the ethnic identity of the two races. Ancient Greeks believed it. All the traditions of Armenia, where lies Mt. Ararat, are in accordance with this fact. The Armenian geography applies the name of Cush to four great regions – Media, Persia, Susiana, Asia, or the whole territory between the Indus and the Tigris. Moses of Chorene identifies Belus, king of Babylon with Nimrod.

"But the Biblical tradition is paramount to all. In it lies the greatest authority that we have for the affiliation of nations, and it is delivered to us very simply and plainly: 'The sons of Ham were Cush and Mizraim and Phut and Canaan…and Cush begot Nimrod…and the beginning of his kingdom was Babel and Erech and Accad and Calneh, in the land of Shinar.' It is the best interpretation of this passage to understand it as asserting that the four races – Egyptians, Ethiopians, Libyans and Canaanites – were ethnically connected, being all descended from Ham; and that the primitive people of Babylon were a subdivision of one of these races; namely, of the Cushite or Ethiopian.

"These conclusions have lately received important and unexpected confirmation from the results of linguistic research. After the most remarkable of Mesopotamian mounds had yielded their treasures, and supplied the historical student with numerous and copious documents, bearing upon the history of the great Assyrian and Babylonian empires, it was determined to explore Chaldea proper, where mounds of considerable height marked the site of several ancient cities. Among unexpected results was the discovery of a new form of speech, differing greatly from the later Babylonian language. In grammatical structure this ancient tongue resembles dialects of the Turanian family, but its vocabulary has been pronounced to be decidedly Cushite or Ethiopian; and the modern languages to which it approaches nearest are thought to be the Mahen of Southern Arabia and the Galla of Abyssinia. Thus comparative philology appears to confirm old traditions. An Eastern Ethiopia instead of being the invention of bewildered ignorance, is rather a reality which it will require a good deal of scepticism to doubt, and the primitive race that bore sway in Chaldea proper belongs to this ethnic type. Meroe was the queenly city of this great people."

"It is hard to believe your story. From what a height must this people have fallen to reach the abjectness of the American Negro," exclaimed a listener.

"True," replied the Professor. "But from what a depth does history show that the Anglo-Saxon has climbed to the position of the first people of the earth today."

Charlie Vance said nothing. He had suffered so many shocks from the shattering of cherished idols since entering the country of mysteries that the power of expression had left him.

"Twenty-five years ago, when I was still a young man, the camel-driver who accompanied me to Thebes sustained a fatal accident. I helped him in his distress, and to show his gratitude he gave me the paper and chart I have shown you tonight. He was a singular man, black hair and eyes, middle height, dark-skinned, face and figure almost perfect, he was proficient in the dialects of the region, besides being master of the purest and most ancient Greek and Arabic. I believe he was a native of the city he described.

"He believed that Ethiopia antedated Egypt, and helped me materially in fixing certain data which time has proved to be correct. He added a fact which the manuscript withholds – that from lands beyond unknown seas, to which many descendants of Ethiopia had been borne as slaves, should a king of ancient line – an offspring of that Ergamenes who lived in the reign of the second Ptolemy – return and restore the former glory of the race. The preservation of this hidden city is for his reception. This Arab also declared that Cush was his progenitor."

"That's bosh. How would they know their future king after centuries of obscurity passed in strange lands, and amalgamation with other races?" remarked the former speaker.

"I asked him that question; he told me that every descendant of the royal line bore a lotus-lily in the form of a birthmark upon his breast."

It might have been the unstable shadows of the moon that threw a tremulous light upon the group, but Charlie Vance was sure that Reuel Briggs started violently at the Professor's words.

One by one the men retired to rest, each one under the spell of the mysterious forces of a past life that brooded like a mist over the sandy plain, the dark Nile rolling sluggishly along within a short distance of their camp, and the ruined city now a magnificent Necropolis. The long shadows grew longer, painting the scene into beauty and grandeur. The majesty of death surrounded the spot and its desolation spoke in trumpet tones of the splendor which the grave must cover, when even the memory of our times shall be forgotten.

Chapter XIII

NEXT MORNING the camp was early astir before the dawn; and before the sun was up, breakfast was over and the first boatload of the explorers was standing on the site of the ruins watching the unfolding of the apparatus for opening solid masonry and excavating within the pyramids.

The feelings of every man in the party were ardently excited by the approach to the city once the light of the world's civilization. The great French writer, Volney, exclaimed when first his eyes beheld the sight, "How are we astonished when we reflect that to the race of Negroes, the object of our extreme contempt, we owe our arts, sciences and even the use of speech!"

From every point of view rose magnificent groups of pyramids rising above pyramids. About eighty of them remaining in a state of partial preservation. The principal one was situated on a hill two and a half miles from the river, commanding an extensive view of the plain. The explorers found by a hasty examination that most of them could be ascended although their surfaces were worn quite smooth. That the pyramids were places of sepulture they could not doubt. From every point of view the sepulchres were imposing; and they were lost in admiration and wonder with the first superficial view of the imposing scene.

One of the approaches or porticoes was most interesting, the roof being arched in regular masonic style, with what may be called a keystone. Belonging without doubt to the remotest ages, their ruined and defaced condition was attributed by the scientists to their great antiquity. The hieroglyphics which covered the monuments were greatly defaced. A knowledge of these characters in Egypt was confined to the priests, but in Ethiopia they were understood by all showing that even in that remote time and place learning and the arts had reached so high a state as to be diffused among the common people.

For a time the explorers wandered from ruin to ruin, demoralized as to routine work, gazing in open astonishment at the wonders before them. Many had visited Thebes and Memphis and the Egyptian monuments, but none had hoped to find in this neglected corner, so much of wonder and grandeur. Within the pyramids that had been opened to the curious eye, they found the walls covered with the pictures of scenes from what must have been the daily life – death, burial, marriage, birth, triumphal processions, including the spoils of war.

Reuel noticed particularly the figure of a queen attired in long robe, tight at neck and ankles, with closely fitted legs. The Professor called their attention to the fact that the entire figure was dissimilar to those represented in Egyptian sculpture. The figure was strongly marked by corpulency, a mark of beauty in Eastern women. This rotundity is the distinguishing feature of Ethiopian sculpture, more bulky and clumsy than Egypt, but pleasing to the eye.

The queen held in one hand the lash of Osiris, and in the other a lotus flower. She was seated on a lion, wearing sandals resembling those specimens seen in Theban figures. Other figures grouped about poured libations to the queen, or carried the standards graced and ornamented by the figures of the jackal, ibis and hawk. At the extremity of each portico was the representation of a monolithic temple, above which were the traces of a funeral boat filled with figures.

Professor Stone told them that Diodorus mentions that some of the Ethiopians preserved the bodies of their relatives in glass cases (probably alabaster), in order to have them always before their eyes. These porticoes, he thought, might have been used for that purpose. The hair of the women was dressed in curls above the forehead and in ringlets hanging on their shoulders.

One who had visited the chief galleries of Europe holding the treasures accumulated from every land, could not be unmoved at finding himself on the site of the very metropolis where science and art had their origin. If he had admired the architecture of Rome and the magnificent use they had made of the arch in their baths, palaces and temples, he would be, naturally, doubly interested at finding in desolate Meroe the origin of that discovery. The beautiful sepulchres of Meroe would give to him evidence of the correctness of the historical records. And then it was borne in upon him that where the taste for the arts had reached such perfection, one might rest assured that other intellectual pursuits were not neglected nor the sciences unknown. Now, however, her schools are closed forever; not a vestige remaining. Of the houses of her philosophers, not a stone rests upon another; and where civilization and learning once reigned, ignorance and barbarism have reassumed their sway.

This is the people whose posterity has been denied a rank among the human race, and has been degraded into a species of talking baboons!

> *Land of the mighty Dead!*
> *There science once display'd*
> *And art, their charms;*
> *There awful Pharaohs swayed*
>
> *Great nations who obeyed;*
> *There distant monarchs laid*
> *Their vanquished arms.*
> *They hold us in survey—*
>
> *They cheer us on our way—*
> *They loud proclaim,*
> *From pyramidal hall—*
> *Prom Carnac's sculptured wall—*
> *Prom Thebes they loudly call—*
> *"Retake your fame!"*
>
> *"Arise and now prevail*
> *O'er all your foes;*
> *In truth and righteousness—*
> *In all the arts of peace –*
> *Advance and still increase,*
> *Though hosts oppose"*

Under the inspiration of the moment, Charlie, the irrepressible, mounted to the top of the first pyramid, and from its peak proceeded to harangue his companions, lugging in the famous Napoleon's: "From the heights of yonder Pyramids forty centuries are contemplating you," etc. This was admirably done, and the glances and grimaces of the eloquent young American must have outvied in ugliness the once gracious-countenanced Egyptian Sphinx.

We may say here that before the excavations of the explorers were ended, they found in two of the pyramids, concealed treasures – golden plates and tables that must have been used by the priests in their worship. Before one enormous image was a golden table, also of enormous proportions. The seats and steps were also of gold, confirming the ancient Chaldean records which tell of 800 talents of metal used in constructing this statue.

There was also a statue of Candace, seated in a golden chariot. On her knees crouched two enormous silver serpents, each weighing thirty talents. Another queen (Professor Stone said it must be Dido from certain peculiar figures) carried in her right hand a serpent by the head, in her left hand a sceptre garnished with precious stones.

All of this treasure was collected finally, after indemnifying the government, and carefully exported to England, where it rests today in the care of the Society of Geographical Research.

They never forgot that sunset over the ancient capital of Ethiopia at the close of the first day spent on the city's site, in the Desert. The awe-inspiring Pyramids throwing shadows that reminded one of the geometrical problems of his student days; the backsheesh-loving Arabs, in the most picturesque habiliments and attitudes; the patient camels, the tawny sands, and the burnished coppery sunlight! They had brought tents with them, leaving the most of the outfit on the opposite bank under the care of Jim Titus, whom Reuel had desired the professor to detail for that duty. Somehow since his adventure in the ruins with the leopard, and the mysterious letter-reading, he had felt a deep-seated mistrust of the docile servant. He concluded not to keep him any nearer his person than circumstances demanded. In this resolve Charlie Vance concurred; the two friends resolved to keep an eye on Titus, and Ababdis was sent for the mail.

Reuel Briggs had changed much. Harassed by anxieties which arose from his wife's silence, at the end of two months he was fast becoming a misanthrope. Charlie felt anxious as he looked at him walking restlessly up and down in the pale moonlight, with fiery eyes fixed on space. Charlie suppressed his own feelings over the silence of his father and sister to comfort Reuel.

"You ought not, my dear Briggs," he would say. "Come, for heaven's sake shake off that sadness which may make an end of you before you are aware." Then he would add, jestingly, "Decidedly, you regret the leopard's claws!"

On this night the excitement of new scenes had distracted the thoughts of both men from their homes, and they lay smoking in their hammocks before the parted curtains of the tent lazily watching Ababdis advancing with a bundle in his hand. It was the long expected mail!

Chapter XIV

IT WAS SOME THREE WEEKS after this before Briggs was able to assume his duties. The sudden shock of the news of his wife's death over-weighted a brain already strained to the utmost. More than once they despaired of his life – Professor Stone and Vance, who had put aside his own grief to care for his friend. Slowly the strong man had returned to life once more. He did not rave or protest; Fate had no power to move him more; the point of anguish was passed, and in its place succeeded a dumb stupidity more terrible by far, though far more blessed.

His love was dead. He himself was dead for any sensibility of suffering that he possessed. So for many days longer he lay in his hammock seemingly without a thought of responsibility.

They had carried him back to the camp across the river, and there he spent the long days of convalescence. What did he think of all day as he moved like a shadow among the men or swung listlessly in the hammock? Many of the men asked themselves that question as they gazed at Briggs. One thought repeated itself over and over in his brain, "Many waters cannot quench love, neither can the floods drown it." "Many waters" – "many waters" – the words whispered and sung appealingly, invitingly, in his ears all day and all night. "Many waters, many waters."

One day he heard them tell of the removal of the door in the pyramid two and one-half miles on the hill. They had found the Sphinx' head as described in the manuscript, but had been unable to move it with any instrument in their possession. Much to his regret, Professor Stone felt obliged to give the matter up and content himself with the valuable relics he had found. The gold mines, if such there were, were successfully hidden from searchers, and would remain a mystery.

The white orb of the moon was high in the heavens; the echoeless sand gave back no sound; that night Reuel rose, took his revolver and ammunition, and leaving a note for Vance telling him he had gone to the third pyramid and not to worry, he rowed himself over to Meroe. He had no purpose, no sensation. Once he halted and tried to think. His love was dead – that was the one fact that filled his thoughts at first. Then another took its place. Why should he live? Of course not; better rejoin her where parting was no more. He would lose himself in the pyramid. The manuscript had spoken of dangers – he would seek them.

As he went on the moon rose in full splendor behind him. Some beast of the night plunged through a thicket along the path.

The road ascended steadily for a mile or more, crossing what must have once been carriage drives. Under the light of the setting moon the gradually increasing fertility of the ground shone silver-white. Arrived at the top of the hill, he paused to rest and wipe the perspiration from his face. After a few minutes' halt, he plunged on and soon stood before the entrance of the gloomy chamber; as he stumbled along he heard a low, distinct hiss almost beneath his feet. Reuel jumped and stood still. He who had been desirous of death but an hour before obeyed the first law of nature. Who can wonder? It was but the re-awakening of life within him, and that care for what has been entrusted to us by Omnipotence, will remain until death has numbed our senses.

The dawn wind blew all about him. He would do no more until the dawn. Presently the loom of the night lifted and he could see the outlines of the building a few yards away. From his position he commanded the plain at his feet as level as a sea. The shadows grew more distinct, then without warning, the red dawn shot up behind him. The sepulchre before him flushed the color of blood, and the light revealed the horror of its emptiness.

Fragments of marble lay about him. It seemed to the lonely watcher that he could hear the sound of the centuries marching by in the moaning wind and purposeless dust.

The silence and sadness lay on him like a pall and seemed to answer to the desolation of his own life.

For a while he rambled aimlessly from wall to wall examining the gigantic resting place of the dead with scrupulous care. Here were ranged great numbers of the dead in glass cases; up and up they mounted to the vaulted ceiling. His taper flickered in the sombreness, giving but a feeble light. The air grew cold and damp as he went on. Once upon a time there had been steps cut in the granite and leading down to a well-like depression near the center of the great chamber. Down he went holding the candle high above his head as he carefully watched for the Sphinx' head. He reached a ledge which ran about what was evidently once a tank. The ledge ran only on one side. He looked about for the Sphinx; unless it was here he must retrace his steps, for the ledge ran only a little way about one side of the chamber.

He was cold and damp, and turned suddenly to retrace his steps, when just in front of him to the left the candle's light fell full on the devilish countenance of the Ethiopian Sphinx.

He moved quickly toward it; and then began an examination of the figure. As he stepped backward his foot crushed through a skull; he retreated with a shudder. He saw now that he stood in a space of unknown dimensions. He fancied he saw rows of pillars flickering drunkenly in the gloom. The American man is familiar with many things because of the range of his experience, and Reuel Briggs was devoid of fear, but in that moment he tasted the agony of pure, physical terror.

For the first time since he received his letters from home, he was himself again filled with pure, human nature. He turned to retrace his steps; something came out of the darkness like a hand, passed before his face emitting a subtle odor as it moved; he sank upon the ground and consciousness left him.

* * *

From profound unconsciousness, deep, merciful, oblivious to pain and the flight of time, from the gulf of the mysterious shadows wherein earth and heaven are alike forgotten, Reuel awoke at the close of the fourth day after his entrance into the Great Pyramid. That Lethean calm induced by narcotic odors, saved his reason. Great pain, whether physical or mental, cannot last long, and human anguish must find relief or take it.

A soft murmur of voices was in his ears as he languidly unclosed his eyes and gazed into the faces of a number of men grouped about the couch on which he lay, who surveyed him with looks of respectful admiration and curiosity mingled with awe. One of the group appeared to be in authority, for the others listened to him with profound respect as they conversed in low tones, and were careful not to obtrude their opinions.

Gradually his senses returned to him, and Reuel could distinguish his surroundings. He gazed about him in amazement. Gone were all evidences of ruin and decay, and in their place was bewildering beauty that filled him with dazzling awe. He reclined on a couch composed of silken cushions, in a room of vast dimensions, formed of fluted columns of pure white marble upholding a domed ceiling where the light poured in through rose-colored glass in soft prismatic shades which gave a touch of fairyland to the scene.

The men beside him were strangers, and more unreal than the vast chamber. Dark-visaged, he noticed that they ranged in complexion from a creamy tint to purest ebony; the long hair which fell upon their shoulders, varied in texture from soft, waving curls to the crispness of the most pronounced African type. But the faces into which he gazed were perfect in the cut and outline of every feature; the forms hidden by soft white drapery, Grecian in effect, were athletic and beautifully moulded. Sandals covered their feet.

The eyes of the leader followed Reuel's every movement.

"Where am I?" cried Briggs impetuously, after a hurried survey of the situation.

Immediately the leader spoke to his companions in a rich voice, commanding, but with all the benevolence of a father.

"Leave us" he said. "I would be alone with the stranger."

He spoke in ancient Arabic known only to the most profound students of philology. Instantly the room was cleared, each figure vanished behind the silken curtains hanging between the columns at one side of the room.

"How came I here?" cried Reuel again.

"Peace," replied the leader, extending his arms as if in benediction above the young man's head. "You have nothing to fear. You have been brought hither for a certain purpose which will shortly be made clear to you; you shall return to your friends if you desire so to do, after the council has investigated your case. But why, my son, did you wander at night about the dangerous passages of the pyramid? Are you, too, one of those who seek for hidden treasure?"

In years the speaker was still young, not being over forty despite his patriarchal bearing. The white robe was infinitely becoming, emphasizing breadth of shoulder and chest above the silverclasped arm's-eye like nothing he had seen save in the sculptured figures of the ruined cities lately explored. But the most striking thing about the man was his kingly countenance, combining force, sweetness and dignity in every feature. The grace of a perfect life invested him like a royal robe. The musical language flowed from his lips in sonorous' accents that charmed the scholar in his listener, who, to his own great surprise and delight, found that conversation between them could be carried on with ease. Reuel could not repress a smile as he thought of the astonishment of Professor Stone if he could hear them rolling out the ancient Arabic tongue as a common carrier of thought. It seemed sacrilegious.

"But where am I?" he persisted, determined to locate his whereabouts.

"You are in the hidden city Telassar. In my people you will behold the direct descendants of the inhabitants of Meroe. We are but a remnant, and here we wait behind the protection of our mountains and swamps, secure from the intrusion of a world that has forgotten, for the coming of our king who shall restore to the Ethiopian race its ancient glory. I am Ai, his faithful prime minister."

Hopelessly perplexed by the words of the speaker, Reuel tried to convince himself that he was laboring under a wild hallucination; but his senses all gave evidence of the reality of his situation. Somewhere in Milton he had read lines that now came faintly across his memory:

> Eden stretched her lines
> From Auran eastward to the royal tow'rs
> Of great Seleucia, built by Grecian kings,
> Or where the sons of Eden long before
> Dwelt in Telassar.

Something of his perplexity Ai must have read in his eyes, for he smiled as he said, "Not Telassar of Eden, but so like to Eden's beauties did our ancestors find the city that thus did they call it."

"Can it be that you are an Ethiopian of those early days, now lost in obscurity? Is it possible that a remnant of that once magnificent race yet dwells upon old mother Earth? You talk of having lived at Meroe; surely, you cannot mean it. Were it true, what you have just uttered, the modern world would stand aghast."

Ai bowed his head gravely. "It is even so, incredible though it may seem to you, stranger. Destroyed and abased because of her idolatries, Ethiopia's arrogance and pride have been humbled in the dust. Utter destruction has come upon Meroe the glorious, as was predicted. But there was a hope held out to the faithful worshippers of the true God that Ethiopia should stretch forth her hand unto Eternal Goodness, and that then her glory should again dazzle the world. I am of the priestly caste, and the office I hold descends from father to son, and has so done for more than six thousand years before the birth of Christ. But enough of this now; when you are fully rested and recovered from the effect of the narcotics we were forced to give you, I will talk with you, and I will also show you the wonders of our hidden city. Come with me."

Without more speech he lifted one of the curtains at the side of the room, revealing another apartment where running water in marble basins invited one to the refreshing bath. Attendants stood waiting, tall, handsome, dark-visaged, kindly, and into their hands he resigned Reuel.

Used as he was to the improvements and luxuries of life in the modern Athens, he could but acknowledge them as poor beside the combination of Oriental and ancient luxury that he now enjoyed. Was ever man more gorgeously housed than this? Overhead was the tinted glass through which the daylight fell in softened glow. In the air was the perfume and lustre of precious incense, the flash of azure and gold, the mingling of deep and delicate hues, the gorgeousness of waving plants in blossom and tall trees – palms, dates, orange, mingled with the gleaming statues that shone forth in brilliant contrast to the dark green foliage. The floor was paved with varied mosaic and dotted here and there with the skins of wild animals.

After the bath came a repast of fruit, game and wine, served him on curious golden dishes that resembled the specimens taken from ruined Pompeii. By the time he had eaten night had fallen, and he laid himself down on the silken cushions of his couch, with a feeling of delicious languor and a desire for repose. His nerves were in a quiver of excitement and he doubted his ability to sleep, but in a few moments, even while he doubted, he fell into a deep sleep of utter exhaustion.

Chapter XV

WHEN HE AROSE in the morning he found that his own clothing had been replaced by silken garments fashioned as were Ai's with the addition of golden clasps and belts. In place oi his revolver was a jewelled dagger literally encrusted with gems.

After the bath and breakfast, Ai entered the room with his noiseless tread, and when the greetings had been said, invited him to go with him to visit the public buildings and works of Telassar. With a swift, phantomlike movement, Ai escorted his guest to the farther end of the great hall. Throwing aside a curtain of rich topaz silk which draped the large entrance doors he ushered him into another apartment opening out on a terrace with a garden at its foot – a garden where a marvellous profusion of flowers and foliage ran riot amid sparkling fountains and gleaming statuary.

Through a broad alley, lined with majestic palms, they passed to the extreme end of the terrace, and turning faced the building from which they had just issued. A smile quivered for a moment on Ai's face as he noted Reuel's ill-concealed amazement. He stood for a moment stock-still, overcome with astonishment at the size and splendor of the palace that had sheltered him over night. The building was dome-shaped and of white marble, surrounded by fluted columns, end fronted by courts where fountains dashed their spray up to the blue sky, and flowers blushed in myriad colors and birds in gorgeous plumage flitted from bough to bough.

It appeared to Reuel that they were on the highest point of what might be best described as a horse-shoe curve whose rounded end rested on the side of a gigantic mountain. At their feet stretched a city beautiful, built with an outer and inner wall. They were in the outer city. Two streams descended like cataracts to the plain below, at some distance from each other, forming a triangle which held another city. Far in the distance like a silver thread, he could dimly discern where the rivers joined, losing themselves in union. As he gazed he recalled the description of the treasure city that Professor Stone had read to the explorers.

As far as the eye could reach stretched fertile fields; vineyards climbed the mountain side. Again Reuel quoted Milton in his thoughts, for here was the very embodiment of his words:

> *Flowers of all hue, and without thorn the rose,*
> *Another side, umbrageous grots and caves*
> *Of cool recess, o'er which the mantling vine*
> *Lays forth her purple grape, and gently creeps*
> *Luxuriant; meanwhile murmuring waters fall*
> *Down the slope hills, dispersed, or in a lake,*
> *That to the fringed bank with myrtle crown'd*
> *Her crystal mirror holds, unite their streams.*
> *The birds their choir apply; airs, vernal airs,*
> *Breathing the smell of field and grove, attune*
> *The trembling leaves, while universal Pan,*
> *Knit with the Graces and the Hours in dance,*
> *Led on th' eternal spring.*

Far below he could dimly discern moving crowds; great buildings reared their stately heads towards a sky so blue and bewildering beneath the sun's bright rays that the gazer was rendered speechless with amazement. Shadowy images of past scenes and happenings flitted across his brain like transient reflection of a past perfectly familiar to him.

"Do you find the prospect fair?" asked Ai at length, breaking the settled silence.

"Fairer than I can find words to express; and yet I am surprised to find that it all seems familiar to me, as if somewhere in the past I had known just such a city as this."

Ai smiled a smile of singular sweetness and content; Reuel could have sworn that there was a degree of satisfaction in his pleasure.

"Come, we will go down into the city. You who know the wonders of modern life at its zenith, tell me what lesson you learn from the wonders of a civilization which had its zenith six thousand years before Christ's birth."

"Six thousand years before Christ!" murmured Reuel in blank stupidity.

"Aye; here in Telassar are preserved specimens of the highest attainments the world knew in ancient days. They tell me that in many things your modern world is yet in its infancy."

"How!" cried Reuel, "do you then hold communion with the world outside your city?"

"Certain members of our Council are permitted to visit outside the gates. Do you not remember Ababdis?"

"Our camel-driver?"

Ai bowed. "He is the member who brought us news of your arrival, and the intention of the expedition to find our city for the sake of its treasure."

More and more mystified by the words and manner of his guide, Reuel made no reply. Presently they entered a waiting palanquin and were borne swiftly toward the city. The silken curtains were drawn one side, and he could drink in the curious sights. They soon left the country behind them and entered a splendid square, where stately homes were outlined against the dense blue of the sky. A statue of an immense sphinx crouched in the center of the square, its giant head reaching far into the ethereal blue. Fountains played on either side, dashing their silvery spray beyond the extreme height of the head. Under umbrageous trees were resting places, and on the sphinx was engraved the words: "That which hath been, is now; and that which is to be, hath already been; and God requireth that which is past."

Suddenly a crowd of men surged into the square, and a deep-toned bell sounded from a distance. Swiftly sped the bearers, urged forward by the general rush. The booming of the bell continued. They reached the end of the avenue and entered a side street, through a court composed of statues. They paused before a stately pile, towering in magnificence high in the heavens, a pile of marvellously delicate architecture worked in stone. The entrance was of incomparable magnificence. Reuel judged that the four colossal statues before it represented Rameses the Great. They were each sculptured of a single block of Syene granite of mingled red and black. They were seated on cubical stones. The four Colosses sitting there before that glittering pile produced a most imposing effect.

The steps of the temple were strewn with flowers; the doors stood open, and music from stringed instruments vibrated upon the air. The bearers stopped at a side entrance, and at a sign from Ai, Reuel followed him into the edifice.

All was silence, save for the distant hum of voices, and the faint sound of music. They halted before a curtain which parted silently for their entrance. It was a small room, but filled with a light of soft colors; when Reuel could command his gaze, he beheld about twenty men prostrated before him. Presently they arose and each filed past him, reverently touching the hem of his white robe. Among them was Ababdis, so transformed by his gorgeous robes of office as to be almost unrecognizable.

Ai now assumed an azure robe embroidered in silver stars and crescents that formed a sunburst in shape of a Grecian cross. He then advanced towards Reuel bearing on a silken cushion a magnificent crown, where the principal aigrette was shaped as a cross set with gems priceless in value. Astounded at the sight, the young man stood motionless while it was adjusted by golden chains about his head. The gems blazed with the red of the ruby, the green of the emerald, the blue of the sapphire, the yellow of the topaz, the cold white of priceless diamonds. But dulling all the glories of precious stones, peerless in their own class, lay the center ornament – the black diamond of Senechus's crown, spoken of in Professor Stone's record. A white robe of silken stuff was added to his costume, and again his companions filed past him in deepest reverence. Reuel was puzzled to understand why so great homage was paid to him. While he turned the thought in his mind, a bugle sounded somewhere in the distance, sweet and high. Instantly, he felt a gliding motion as if the solid earth were slipping from beneath his feet, the curtains before him parted silently, and he found himself alone on a raised platform in the center of a vast auditorium, crowded with humanity. Lights twinkled everywhere; there was the fragrance of flowers, there were columns of marble draped in amber, azure and green, and glittering lamps encrusted with gems and swung by golden chains from the sides of the building. A blazing arch formed of brilliant lamps raised like a gigantic bow in the heavens and having in its center the words

HAIL! ERGAMENES!

in letters of sparkling fire, met his startled gaze. Then came a ringing shout from the throats of the assembled multitude, "Ergamenes! Ergamenes!" Again and again the throng lifted up the joyous cry. Presently as Reuel stood there undecided what to do – not knowing what was expected of him, as silently as he had come, he felt the motion of the platform where he stood. The crowd faded from sight, the curtains fell; once more he stood within the little room, surrounded by his companions.

"Ababdis, Ai," he demanded, sternly, "What is the meaning of this strange happening, more like a scene from the Arabian Nights? Who is Ergamenes?"

"Thou art Ergamenes – the long-looked-for king of Ethiopia, for whose reception this city was built! But we will return to the palace, now that the people have satisfied somewhat their curiosity. At supper you shall know more."

Once more the bearers carried them swiftly beyond the confines of the city, and soon the palace walls rose before them. Reuel had hardly collected his scattered wits before he found himself seated at table and on either side of the board the Council reclined on silken cushions. His own seat was raised and placed at the head of the table. There was no talking done while what seemed to be a solemn feast was in progress. Servants passed noiselessly to and fro attending to their wants, while from an alcove the music of stringed instruments and sweetest vocal numbers was borne to their ears.

After supper, they still reclined on the couches. Then from the hidden recesses the musicians came forth, and kneeling before Reuel, one began a song in blank verse, telling the story of Ergamenes and his kingdom.

> *"Hail! oh, hail, Ergamenes!*
> *The dimmest sea-cave below thee,*
> *The farthest sky-arch above,*
> *In their innermost stillness know thee,*
> *And heave with the birth of Love.*
> *"All hail!*
> *We are thine, all thine, forevermore;*

Not a leaf on the laughing shore,
Not a wave on the heaving sea,
Nor a single sigh
In the boundless sky,
But is vowed evermore to thee!"

"Son of a fallen dynasty, outcast of a sunken people, upon your breast is a lotus lily, God's mark to prove your race and descent. You, Ergamenes, shall begin the restoration of Ethiopia. Blessed be the name of God for ever and ever, for wisdom and might are His, and He changeth the times and seasons; He removeth kings and countries, and setteth them up again; He giveth wisdom unto the wise, and knowledge to them that know understanding! He revealeth the deep and secret things; He knoweth what is in the darkness, and the light dwelleth with Him!

"Great were the sins of our fathers, and the white stranger was to Ethiopia but a scourge in the hands of an offended God. The beautiful temples of Babylon, filled with vessels of silver and gold, swelled the treasures of the false god Bel. Babylon, where our monarchs dwelt in splendor, once the grandest city to be found in the world. Sixty miles round were its walls, of prodigious height, and so broad that seven chariots could be driven abreast on the summit! One hundred gates of solid brass gave entrance into the city, guarded by lofty towers. Beautiful buildings rose within, richly adorned and surrounded by gardens. One magnificent royal palace was girdled by three walls, the outermost of which was seven miles and a half in compass. In its grounds rose the far-famed hanging gardens, terraces built one above another to the height of three hundred and fifty feet, each terrace covered with thick mould, and planted with flowers and shrubs, so that the skill of man created a verdant hill on a plain. Nearly in the centre rose the lofty temple of Belus, the tower of Babel, whose builders had hoped to make its summit touch the very skies. Millions of dollars in gold were gathered in the chambers of the temple. The wealth, power and glory of the world were centered in the mighty city of Babylon.

"On the throne of this powerful city sat your forefathers, O Ergamenes!"

Part of the story had been given in recitative, one rich voice carrying grandly the monotonous notes to the accompaniment of the cornet, flute, sackbut, dulcimer and harp. Reuel had listened to the finest trained voices attempting the recitative in boasted musical circles, but never in so stately and impressive a manner as was now his privilege to hear. They continued the story.

"And Meroe, the greatest city of them all, pure-blooded Ethiopian. Once the light of the world's civilization, now a magnificent Necropolis.

"Standing at the edge of the Desert, fertile in soil, rich in the luxuries of foreign shores; into her lap caravans poured their treasures gathered from the North, South, East and West. All Africa poured into this queenly city ivory, frankincense and gold. Her colossal monuments were old before Egypt was; her wise men monopolized the learning of the ages, and in the persons of the Chaldeans have figured conspicuously the wisdom of ages since Meroe has fallen.

"Mother of ancient warfare, her horsemen and chariots were the wonder and terror of her age; from the bows of her warriors, the arrows sped like a flight of birds, carrying destruction to her foes – a lamb in peace, a lion in time of war."

Once more the measure changed, and another voice took up the story in verse.

"Who will assume the bays
That the hero wore?
Wreaths on the Tomb of Days
Gone evermore!

Who shall disturb the brave
Or one leaf of their holy grave?
The laurel is vow'd to them,
Leave the bay on its sacred stem!
But hope, the rose, the unfading rose,
Alike for slave and freeman grows!

"On the summit, worn and hoary,
Of Lybia's solemn hills,
The tramp of the brave is still!
And still is the poisoned dart,
In the pulse of the mighty hearts,
Whose very blood was glory!

Who will assume the bays
That the hero wore?
Wreaths on the Tomb of Days
Gone evermore!"

Upon Reuel a strange force seemed working. If what he heard were true, how great a destiny was his! He had carefully hidden his Ethiopian extraction from the knowledge of the world. It was a tradition among those who had known him in childhood that he was descended from a race of African kings. He remembered his mother well. From her he had inherited his mysticism and his occult powers. The nature of the mystic within him was, then, but a dreamlike devotion to the spirit that had swayed his ancestors; it was the shadow of Ethiopia's power. The lotus upon his breast he knew to be a birthmark. Many a night he had been aroused from childhood's slumbers, to find his mother bending above him, candle in hand, muttering broken sentences of prayer to Almighty God as she examined his bosom by the candle's rays. He had wondered much; now he guessed the rest. Once more the clanging strings of the instruments chained his attention. The recitative was resumed.

"The Most High ruleth in the kingdom of men, and giveth it to whomsoever He will. He delivereth and rescueth, and He worketh signs and wonders in heaven and in earth. Pre-eminent in peace, invincible in war – once the masters of mankind, how have we fallen from our high estate!

"Stiff-necked, haughty, no conscience but that of intellect, awed not by God's laws, worshipping Mammon, sensual, unbelieving, God has punished us as he promised in the beginning. Gone are our ancient glories, our humbled pride cries aloud to God in the travail of our soul. Our sphinx, with passionless features, portrays the dumb suffering of our souls.

Their look, with the reach of past ages, was wise,
And the soul of eternity thought in their eyes.

"By divine revelation David beheld the present time, when, after Christ's travail for the sins of humanity, the time of Ethiopia's atonement being past, purged of idolatry, accepting the One Only God through His Son Jesus, suddenly should come a new birth to the descendants of Ham, and Ethiopia should return to her ancient glory! Ergamenes, all hail!

"You come from afar
   From the land of the stranger,
The dreadful in war,
   The daring in danger;
Before him our plain
   Like Eden is lying;
Behind him remain
   But the wasted and dying.

"The weak finds not ruth,
   Nor the patriot glory;
No hope for the youth,
   And no rest for the hoary;
O'er Ethiop's lost plains
   The victor's sword flashes,
Her sons are in chains,
   And her temples in ashes!

"Who will assume the bays
   That the hero wore?
Wreaths on the Tomb of Days
   Gone evermore!"

Upon his companions the song of the past of Ethiopia had a strange effect. Soothing at times, at times exciting, with the last notes from the instruments the company sprang to their feet; with flashing dark eyes, faces reflecting inward passions, they drew their short, sabrelike arms and circled about Reuel's throne with the shout "Ergamenes! Ergamenes!"

Chapter XVI

ONCE MORE Reuel found himself alone with Ai. It was far into the night, but he felt sleepless and restless. At last Ai broke a long silence:

"Tell me of the country from which you come, Ergamenes. Is it true that the Ethiopian there is counted less than other mortals?"

"It is true, Ai," replied Reuel. "There, the dark hue of your skin, your waving hair with its trace of crispness, would degrade you below the estate of any man of fair hue and straight locks, belonging to any race outside the Ethiopian, for it is a deep disgrace to have within the veins even one drop of the blood you seem so proud of possessing."

"That explains your isolation from our race, then?"

Reuel bowed his head in assent, while over his face passed a flush of shame. He felt keenly now the fact that he had played the coward's part in hiding his origin. What though obstacles were many, some way would have been shown him to surmount the difficulties of caste prejudice.

"And yet, from Ethiopia came all the arts and cunning inventions that make your modern glory. At our feet the mightiest nations have worshipped, paying homage to our kings, and all nations have sought the honor of alliance with our royal families because of our strength, grandeur, riches and wisdom. Tell me of all the degradation that has befallen the unfortunate sons of Ham."

Then in the deep, mysterious silence of the night, Reuel gave in minutest detail the story of the Negro, reciting with dramatic effect the history of the wrongs endured by the modern Ethiopian.

To his queries as to the history of these mountain-dwelling Ethiopians, Ai gave the following reply:

"We are a singular people, governed by a female monarch, all having the same name, Candace, and a Council of twenty-five Sages, who are educated for periodical visits to the outer world. Queen Candace is a virgin queen who waits the coming of Ergamenes to inaugurate a dynasty of kings. Our virgins live within the inner city, and from among them Candace chooses her successor at intervals of fifteen years.

"To become a Sage, a man must be married and have at least two children; a knowledge of two out-world languages, and to pass a severe examination by the court as to education, fitness and ability. After an arduous preparation they are initiated into the secrets of this kingdom. They are chosen for life. The inner city is the virgins' court, and it is adorned with beautiful gardens, baths, schools and hospitals. When a woman marries she leaves this city for the outer one.

"We have a great temple, the one you entered, dedicated to the Supreme or Trinity. It is a masterpiece of beauty and art. The population assembles there twice a year for especial service. It seats about 12,000 persons. The Sages have seen nothing equal to it in the outer world.

"Octagonal in shape, with four wings or galleries, on opposite sides; the intervening spaces are filled with great prism columns, twenty-five feet high, made of a substance like glass, malleable, elastic and pure. The effect is gorgeous. The decorations of the hall are prepared natural flowers; that is, floral garlands are subjected to the fumes of the crystal material covering them like a film and preserving their natural appearance. This is a process handed down from the earliest days of Ethiopian greatness. I am told that the modern world has not yet solved this simple process," he said, with a gentle smile of ridicule.

"We preserve the bodies of our most beautiful women in this way. We suspend reflecting plates of the crystal material arranged in circles, pendant from the ceiling of the central hall, and thus the music of the instruments is repeated many times in sweetest harmony.

"We have services at noon every seventh day, chiefly choral, in praise of the attributes of the Supreme. Our religion is a belief in One Supreme Being, the center of action in all nature. He distributed a portion of Himself at an early age to the care of man who has attained the highest development of any of His terrestrial creatures. We call this ever-living faculty or soul Ego.

"After its transition Ego has the power of expressing itself to other bodies, with like gift and form, its innate feeling; and by law of affinity, is ever striving to regain its original position near the great Unity; but the physical attractions of this beautiful world have such a fascination on the organism of man that there is ever a contention against the greater object being attained; and unless the Ego can wean the body from gross desires and raise it to the highest condition of human existence, it cannot be united to its Creator. The Ego preserves its individuality after the dissolution of the body. We believe in re-incarnation by natural laws regulating material on earth. The Ego can never be destroyed. For instance, when the body of a good man or woman dies, and the Ego is not sufficiently fitted for the higher condition of another world, it is re-associated with another body to complete the necessary fitness for heaven."

"What of the Son of man? Do you not know the necessity of belief in the Holy Trinity? Have not your Sages brought you the need of belief in God's Son?" Ai looked somewhat puzzled.

"We have heard of such a God, but have not paid much attention to it. How believe you, Ergamenes?"

"In Jesus Christ, the Son of God," replied Retiel solemnly.

"O Ergamenes, your belief shall be ours; we have no will but yours. Deign to teach your subjects."

When at last Reuel closed his eyes in slumber, it was with a feeling of greater responsibility and humility than he had ever experienced. Who was he that so high a destiny as lay before him should be thrust upon his shoulders?

* * *

After these happenings, which we have just recorded, every day Reuel received callers in state. It seemed to him that the entire populace of that great hidden city turned out to do him homage. The Sages, clad in silver armor, attended him as a bodyguard, while soldiers and officials high in the councils of the State, were ranged on both sides of the immense hall. The throne on which he sat was a massive one of silver, a bronze Sphinx couched on either side. The steps of the throne were banked with blossoms, offerings from the procession of children that filed slowly by, clad in white, wearing garlands of roses, and laying branches of palm, oleander flowers, lilies and olive sprays before their king.

Offerings of gold, silver and gems, silken cloths, priceless articles moulded into unique and exquisite designs, sword of tempered steel, beside which a Damascus blade was coarse and unfinished, filled his artist soul with delight and wonder. Later, Ai escorted him to the underground workshops where brawny smiths plied their trades; and there the secrets of centuries dead and gone were laid bare to his curious gaze.

How was it possible, he asked himself again and again, that a nation so advanced in literature, science and the arts, in the customs of peace and war, could fall as low as had the Ethiopian? Even while he held the thought, the answer came: As Daniel interpreted Nebuchadnezzar's dream, so has it been and is with Ethiopia. "They shall drive thee from men, and thy dwelling shall be with the beasts of the field, and they shall make thee to eat grass as oxen, and they shall wet thee with the dew of heaven, and seven times shall pass over thee, till thou knowest that the Most High ruleth in the kingdom of men, and giveth it to whomsoever He will. Thy kingdom shall be sure unto thee; after that thou shalt have known that the heavens do rule."

But the excitement and changes through which he had passed began to tell upon a constitution already weakened by mental troubles. Ai observed with much concern, the apathy which foretold a serious illness. Hoping to arouse him from painful thoughts which now engrossed his mind, Ai proposed that the visit to the inner city, postponed by the pressure of other duties, be made the next day.

That morning a company, of which the Sages formed a part, started for the inner city. They were to spend the night in travel, resting by day. The progress of the party was very slow, and in a direction Reuel had not yet explored. A deep yellow glow suffused the sky. This soon gave way to the powerful but mellow light of the African moon, casting long shadows over the silvery green of the herbage and foliage. They encountered a perfect network of streams, pursuing their way through virgin forests, brilliant by daylight with beautiful flowers. The woods were inhabited by various kinds of birds of exquisite note and plumage. There were also a goodly number of baboons, who descended from the trees and ranged themselves on the ground to obtain a nearer view of the travellers. They grinned and chattered at the caravan, seeming to regard them as trespassers in their domains.

The character of the country improved as they neared the interior. Reuel noticed that this was at variance with the European idea respecting Central Africa, which brands these regions as howling wildernesses or an uninhabitable country. He found the landscape most beautiful, the imaginary desert "blossomed like the rose", and the "waste sandy valleys" and "thirsty wilds", which had been assigned to this location, became, on close inspection, a gorgeous scene, decorated with Nature's most cheering garniture, teeming with choice specimens of vegetable and animal life, and refreshed by innumerable streams, branches of the rivers, not a few of which were of sufficient magnitude for navigation and commerce. But Reuel remembered the loathsome desert that stood in grim determination guarding the entrance to this paradise against all intrusion, and with an American's practical common sense, bewailed this waste of material.

Proceeding along a mountain gorge, our travellers found the path straitened between the impending mountain on one side and a rapid and sparkling stream on the other. On the opposite side of the ravine the precipices rose abruptly from the very edge of the water. The whole appearance of this mountain pass was singularly grand, romantically wild and picturesquely beautiful. They were often obliged to clamber over huge masses of granite, fallen from the cliffs above; and, on this account, progress was slow and toilsome. On turning an angle of the rock, about the centre of the gorge, the party were suddenly confronted by a huge, tawny lion, which stood directly in the path, with not a wall and scarce a space between. The path was so narrow in this place that it would have been impossible to pass the brute without touching him. Used to the king of the African jungle, the company did not shrink, but faced the animal boldly, although not without some natural physical fear. The lion, too, seemed to be taken by surprise. Thus the opponents stood at a distance of five yards, each staring at the other for several minutes. Had the travellers shown the least signs of fear, or had they attempted to escape, the fate of one, at least, would have been sealed. Now appeared an exhibition of the power of magnetism. Reuel stepped in advance of the foremost bearer, fixed his wonderful and powerful eyes upon the beast, literally transfixing him with a glance, poured the full force of his personal magnetism upon the animal, which almost instantly responded by low growls and an uneasy twisting of the head; finally, the terrible glance remaining inflexible and unwavering, the beast turned himself about and slowly withdrew with a stately and majestic tread, occasionally looking back and uttering a low growl, as if admonishing the travellers to keep their distance.

Murmurs of wonder and admiration broke from Reuel's companions, who were aware of the danger attending the meeting of a hungry lion at close quarters. His admirable intrepidity, and the remarkable powers which were his birthright, had preserved him and his companions.

"Truly, he is the King!" they murmured among themselves. And more than ever Ai watched him with increasing love and the fondness of a father.

Without further adventure they reached the portals of the inner city. Their arrival was evidently anticipated, for they were received by a band of young females under the guardianship of a matron. By this escort they were shown to the palace and into the rooms set apart for their reception. Having rested for an hour, bathed and dined, they were ready for the ceremony of introduction. Another guard of women took them in charge, and the procession started down one passage, crossed a great, aisle-like hall, and came to a corresponding passage on the other side. On through seemingly endless colonnades they passed, till they came to a huge door formed of great winged creatures. Reuel had thought that nothing could surpass the palace in the outer city for beauty and luxury, but words failed him as his eyes drank in the glories of the lofty apartment into which they stepped, as an Amazon in silver mail threw wide the glittering doors, disclosing the splendor of the royal Presence-chamber. It was a lofty saloon lined with gilded columns, the sunlight falling from the open roof upon the mosaic floor beneath. The tapestries which lined the walls bore exquisite paintings of love and warfare.

As the door opened, a voice called. The company halted before a curtained recess, guarded by a group of beautiful girls. Never had Reuel beheld such subtle grace of form and feature, such masses of coal-black hair, such melting eyes of midnight hue. Each girl might have posed for a statue of Venus.

The heavy curtains were lifted now, and discovered the Queen reclining upon a pile of silken cushions – a statue of Venus worked in bronze.

"The Queen is here!" exclaimed a voice. In an instant all present prostrated themselves upon the floor. Reuel alone stood erect, his piercing eyes fixed upon the woman before him.

Grave, tranquil and majestic, surrounded by her virgin guard, she advanced gracefully, bending her haughty head; then, gradually her sinuous body bent and swayed down, down, until she, too, had prostrated herself, and half-knelt, half-lay, upon the marble floor at Reuel's feet.

"O Ergamenes, hast thou indeed returned to thine inheritance?" murmured a voice like unto silver chimes. Reuel started, for it seemed to him that Dianthe's own voice was breathing in his ears.

Knowing now what was expected of him, he raised the Queen with one hand, addressed her courteously in Arabic, led her to her silken couch, seated himself, and would have placed her beside him, but she, with a gesture of dissent, sank upon the cushions at his feet that had served her for footstools.

By this time the Sages had risen and now reclined on the silken couches with which the apartment was well supplied. Ai advanced and addressed the Queen; during this exchange of courtesies, Reuel gazed upon her curiously. She reminded him strongly of his beautiful Dianthe; in fact, the resemblance was so striking that it was painful, and tears, which were no disgrace to his manhood, struggled to his eyes. She was the same height as Dianthe, had the same well-developed shoulders and the same admirable bust. What suppleness in all her movements! What grace, and, at the same time, what strength! Yes; she was a Venus, a superb statue of bronze, moulded by a great sculptor; but an animated statue, in which one saw the blood circulate, and from which life flowed. And what an expressive face, full of character! Long, jet-black hair and totally free, covered her shoulders like a silken mantle; a broad, square forehead, a warm bronze complexion; thick black eyebrows, great black eyes, now soft and languishing – eyes which could weep in sorrow or shoot forth lightning in their anger; a delicate nose with quivering nostrils, teeth of dazzling whiteness behind lips as red as a rose; in her smile of grace and sweetness lurked a sense of power. He was astonished and lost in admiration in spite of himself. Her loveliness was absolutely and ideally perfect. Her attitude of unstudied grace accorded well with the seriousness of her face; she seemed the embodiment of all chastity.

The maidens of her household waited near her – some of them with baskets of flowers upheld in perfect arms. Some brought fruit in glittering dishes and wine in golden goblets of fairy-like fretwork, which were served from stands of ivory and gold. One maiden knelt at her lyre, prepared to strike its chords at pauses in the conversation.

The attendants now retired modestly into the background, while Ai and the other Sages conversed with the Queen. She listened with downcast eyes, occasionally casting a curious, though deferential glance at the muscular figure beside her.

"And dost thou agree, and art thou willing to accept the destiny planned by the Almighty Trinity for thee and me from the beginning of all things, my lord?" she questioned at length in her flute-like voice.

"Queen Candace, thy beauty and graciousness dazzle me. I feel that I can love thee with all my heart; I will fulfill my destiny gladly, and I will cleave to thee until the end."

"Now," answered the Queen with sweet humility, "now, when thou, my lord, doth speak so royally, it doth not become me to lag in generosity. She paused.

Reuel, gazing into her beautiful face, was deeply moved by strong emotions. Again she spoke:

"Behold! In token of submission I bow to my lord, King Ergamenes." She bent herself slowly to the ground, and pressed her knees for one instant upon the mosaic floor. "Behold," and she touched his forehead lightly with her lips, "in earnest of connubial bliss, I kiss thee, King Ergamenes. Behold," and she placed her hand upon his heart, "I swear to thee eternal fealty by the Spirit – the never-changing Trinity." This ceremony ended she seated herself once more beside him. Reuel felt himself yielding readily to her infinite attractiveness. In the azure light and regal splendor of the fragrant apartment, there was rest and satisfaction. All the dreams of wealth and ambition that had haunted the feverish existence by the winding Charles, that had haunted his days of obscure poverty in the halls of Harvard, were about to be realized. Only once had he known joy in his checkered life, and that was when he basked in the society of Dianthe, whom he now designated his spirit-bride. The delirium of that joy had ended in lamentation. Doubts and misgivings had assailed him in the silence of the night when Ai had left him and his influence was withdrawn. Then he had but a faint-hearted belief in the wonderful tale told to him, but here, under Queen Candace's magic influence, all doubts disappeared, and it seemed the most natural thing in the world to be sitting here among these descendants of the ancient Ethiopians, acknowledged as their King, planning a union with a lovely woman, that should give to the world a dynasty of dark-skinned rulers, whose destiny should be to restore the prestige of an ancient people.

Verily, if the wonders he had already seen and heard could be possible in the nineteenth century of progress and enlightenment, nothing was impossible. Dianthe was gone. The world outside held nothing dear to one who had always lived much within himself. The Queen was loving, beautiful – why not accept this pleasant destiny which held its alluring arms so seductively towards him? A sudden moisture filled his eyes; a curious vague softness and tenderness stole over him. Turning abruptly toward his hostess, he held out his own swimming goblet:

"Drink we a loving cup together, oh Queen Candace!" he said in a voice that trembled with earnestness. "I pledge my faith in return for thine!"

The Queen returned his ardent gaze with one of bright surprise and joyous happiness, and bending her head, drank a deep draught of the proffered wine.

"Almost thou lovest me, Ergamenes. May the Eternal Trinity hold fast our bonds!" With a graceful salute she returned the goblet. Reuel drank off in haste what remained within it.

"Behold! I have prepared against this happy hour," continued the Queen, and going to an inlaid cabinet at one side of the room, she took from it a curious ring of dull gold, bearing one priceless gem cut in the form of a lotus lily. "Hold forth thy hand," she said, and on his finger placed the ring.

"Thus do I claim thee for all eternity."

The Sages had watched the actors in this life-drama with jealous eyes that noted every detail with open satisfaction. At Queen Candace's last words, Ai extended his arms with the solemn words:

"And now it is done and never can be undone or altered. Let us hence, that the union may be speedily accomplished."

Chapter XVII

IN A MONTH the marriage was to be celebrated with great pomp and rejoicing. Preparations began as soon as the interview between the Queen and the prospective King was over.

After his return from this betrothal, the power of second sight which seemed to have left Reuel for a time, returned in full force. Restlessness was upon him; Dianthe's voice seemed ever calling to him through space. Finally, when his feelings became insupportable, he broached the subject to Ai.

The latter regarded his questioner gravely. "Of a truth thou art a legitimate son of Ethiopia. Thou growest the fruits of wisdom. Descendant of the wise Chaldeans, still powerful to a degree undreamed of by the pigmies of this puny age, you look incredulous, but what I tell you is the solemn truth."

"The Chaldeans disappeared from this world centuries ago," declared Reuel.

"Not all – in me you behold their present head; within this city and the outer world, we still number thousands."

Reuel uttered an exclamation of incredulous amazement. "Not possible!"

Silently Ai went to his cabinet and took down a small, square volume which he placed in Reuel's hand. "It is a record of the wisdom and science of your ancestors."

Reuel turned it over carefully – the ivory pages were covered with characters sharply defined and finely engraved.

"What language is this? It is not Hebrew, Greek nor Sanskrit, nor any form of hieroglyphic writing."

"It is the language once commonly spoken by your ancestors long before Babylon was builded. It is known to us now as the language of prophecy."

Reuel glanced at the speaker's regal form with admiration and reverence.

"Teach me what thou knowest, Ai," he said humbly, "for, indeed, thou art a wonderful man."

"Gladly," replied Ai, placing his hand in loving tenderness upon the bowed head of the younger man. "Our destiny was foreordained from the beginning to work together for the upbuilding of humanity and the restoration of the race of our fathers. This little book shall teach your soul all that you long to know, and now grasp but vaguely. You believe in the Soul?"

"Most assuredly!"

"As a Personality that continues to live after the body perishes?"

"Certainly."

"And that Personality begins to exert its power over our lives as soon as we begin its cultivation. Death is not necessary to its manifestation upon our lives. There are always angels near! To us who are so blessed and singled out by the Trinity there is a sense of the supernatural always near us – others whom we cannot see, but whose influence is strong upon us in all the affairs of life. Man only proves his ignorance if he denies this fact. Some in the country from which you come contend that the foundations of Christianity are absurd and preposterous, but all the prophecies of the Trinity shall in time be fulfilled. They are working out today by the forces of air, light, wind – the common things of daily life that pass unnoticed. Ethiopia, too, is stretching forth her hand unto God, and He will fulfill her destiny. The tide of immigration shall set in the early days of the twentieth century, toward Africa's shores, so long bound in the chains of barbarism and idolatry."

Reuel listened entranced, scarce breathing.

"I was warned of your coming long before the knowledge was yours. The day you left your home for New York. I sat within my secret chamber, and all was revealed to me."

"Ay, Ai," Reuel answered, feebly. "But how?"

"You believe that we can hold communion with the living though seas divide and distance is infinite, and our friends who have passed to the future life of light are allowed to comfort us here?"

"I believe."

"Tis so," continued Ai. "Half by chance and half by learning, I long ago solved one of the great secrets of Nature. Life is wonderful, but eternity is more wonderful." He paused, regarding affectionately Reuel's troubled face.

"I will answer thy question presently. But can I do aught for thee? Dost memories of that world from which thou hast recently come disturb thee, Ergamenes? I have some feeble powers; if thou wilt, command them." Ai fell into the use of 'thee' and 'thou' always when greatly moved, and Reuel had become very dear to him.

"I would know some happenings in the world I have left; could my desire be granted, I might, perchance, lose this restlessness which now oppresses me."

Ai regarded him intently. "How far hast thou progressed in knowledge of Infinity?" he asked at length.

"You shall be the judge," replied Reuel. And then ensued a technical conversation on the abstract science of occultism and the future state.

"I see thou are well versed," said Ai finally, evidently well pleased with the young man's versatility. "Come with me. Truly we have not mistaken thee, Ergamenes. Wonderfully hast thou been preserved and fitted for the work before thee."

Reuel had the freedom of the palace, but he knew that there were rooms from which he was excluded. One room especially seemed to be the sanctum sanctorium of the Sages. It was to this room that Ai now conducted him.

Reuel was nearly overpowered with the anticipation of being initiated into the mysteries of this apartment. He found nothing terrifying, however, in the plain, underground room into which he was ushered. A rough table and wooden stools constituted the furniture. The only objects of mystery were a carved table at one end of the apartment, with a silken cloth thrown over its top, and a vessel like a baptismal font, cut in stone, full of water. Air and light came from an outside source, for there were no windows in the room. After closing the door securely, Ai advanced and removed the cloth from the table. "Sit," he commanded. "You ask me how I knew of your coming to my land. Lo, I have followed your career from babyhood. Behold, Ergamenes! What would you see upon the mirror's face? Friend or foe?"

Reuel advanced and looked upon the surface of a disk of which the top of the table was composed. The material of which the polished surface was composed was unknown to Reuel; it was not glass, though quite transparent; it was not metal, though bright as polished steel.

Reuel made no wish, but thought of the spot where the accident had occurred upon the River Charles weeks before. He was startled to observe a familiar scene where he had often rowed for pleasure on pleasant summer evenings. Every minute particular of the scenery was distinctly visible. Presently the water seemed to darken, and he saw distinctly the canoe containing Aubrey, Molly and Dianthe gliding over the water. He started back aghast, crying out, "It is magical!"

"No, no, Ergamenes, this is a secret of Nature. In this disk I can show thee what thou wilt of the past. In the water of the font we see the future. Think of a face, a scene – I will reflect it for thee on this disk. This is an old secret, known to Ethiopia, Egypt and Arabia centuries ago. I can reflect the past and the faces of those passed away, but the living and the future are cast by the water."

Reuel was awed into silence. He could say nothing, and listened to Ai's learned remarks with a reverence that approached almost to worship before this proof of his supernatural powers. What would the professors of Harvard have said to this, he asked himself. In the heart of Africa was a knowledge of science that all the wealth and learning of modern times could not emulate. For some time the images came and went upon the mirror, in obedience to his desires. He saw the scenes of his boyhood, the friends of his youth, and experienced anew the delights of life's morning. Then he idly desired to see the face of his loved Dianthe, as she last appeared on earth. The surface of the disk reflected nothing!

"You have not reached perfection then, in this reflector?"

"Why think you so?" asked Ai gravely.

"I have asked to see the face of a friend who is dead. The mirror did not reflect it."

"The disk cannot err," said Ai. "Let us try the water in the font."

"But that reflects the living, you say; she is dead."

"The disk cannot err," persisted Ai. He turned to the font, gazed in its surface, and then beckoned Reuel to approach. From the glassy surface Dianthe's face gazed back at him, worn and lined with grief.

"'Tis she!" he cried, "her very self."

'Then your friend still lives," said Ai, calmly.

"Impossible!"

"Why do you doubt my word, Ergamenes?"

Then with great suppressed excitement and much agitation, Reuel repeated the story of Dianthe's death as brought to him by the last mail he had received from America.

"You say that 'Molly' as you call her, was also drowned?"

"Yes."

"Let us try the disk."

They returned to the mirror and instantly the face of Molly Vance gazed at them from the river's bed, surrounded by seaweed and grasses.

"Can a man believe in his own sanity!" exclaimed Reuel in an agony of perplexity.

Ai made no reply, but returned to the font. "I think it best to call up the face of your enemy. I am sure you have one." Immediately the water reflected the debonair face of Aubrey Livingston, which was almost instantly blotted out by the face of Jim Titus.

"Two!" murmured Ai. "I thought so."

"If she then lives, as your science seems to insist, show me her present situation," cried Reuel, beside himself with fears.

"I must have a special preparation for the present," said Ai, calmly. He set about preparing a liquid mixture. When this was accomplished he washed the face of the disk with a small sponge dipped in the mixture. A film of sediment instantly formed upon it.

"When this has dried, I will scrape it off and polish the mirror, then we shall be ready for the demonstration. One picture only will come – this will remain for a number of days, after that the disk will return to its normal condition. But, see! The sediment is caked. Now to remove it and finish our test." At last it was done, and the disk repolished. Then standing before it, Ai cried, in an earnest voice:

"Let the present appear upon the disk, if it be for the benefit of Thy human subjects!"

Ai appeared perfectly calm, but his hands shook. Reuel remained a short remove from him, awaiting his summons.

"Come, Ergamenes."

For a few moments Reuel gazed upon the plate, his eyes brilliant with expectation, his cheeks aglow with excitement. Then he involuntarily shuddered, a half-suppressed groan escaped him, and he grew ashy pale. In a trice he became entirely unnerved, and staggered back and forth like a drunken man. Greatly alarmed, and seeing he was about to fall, Ai sprang to his side and caught him. Too late. He fell to the floor in a swoon. The picture reflected by the disk was that of the ancestral home of the Livingstons. It showed the parlor of a fine old mansion; two figures stood at an open window, their faces turned to the interior. About the woman's waist the man's arm was twined in a loving embrace. The faces were those of Aubrey and Dianthe.

Late that night Reuel tossed upon his silken couch in distress of mind. If the disk were true, then Dianthe and Aubrey both lived and were together. He was torn by doubts, haunted by dreadful fears of he knew not what. If the story of the disk were true, never was man so deceived and duped as he had been. Then in the midst of his anger and despair came an irresistible impulse to rise from his bed. He did so, and distinctly felt the pressure of a soft hand upon his brow, and a yielding body at his side. The next instant he could have sworn that he heard the well-known tones of Dianthe in his ears, saying:

"Reuel, it is I."

Unable to answer, but entirely conscious of a presence near him, he had presence of mind enough to reiterate a mental question. His voiceless question was fully understood, for again the familiar voice spoke:

"I am not dead, my husband; but I am lost to you. Not of my own seeking has this treachery been to thee, O beloved. The friend into whose care you gave me has acquired the power over me that you alone possessed, that power sacred to our first meeting and our happy love. Why did you leave me in the power of a fiend in human shape, to search for gold? There are worse things in life than poverty."

Calming the frenzy of his thoughts by a strong effort, Reuel continued his mental questions until the whole pitiful story was his. He knew not how long he continued in this communion. Over and over he turned the story he had learned in the past few hours. Ungovernable rage against his false friend possessed him. "Blind, fool, dupe, dotard!" he called himself, not to have seen the treachery beneath the mask of friendship. And then to leave her helpless in the hands of this monster, who had not even spared his own betrothed to compass his love for another.

But at least revenge was left him. He would return to America and confront Aubrey Livingston with his guilt. But how to get away from the hidden city. He knew that virtually he was a prisoner.

Still turning over ways and means, he fell into an uneasy slumber, from which he was aroused by a dreadful shriek.

Chapter XVIII

IT WAS NOW two months since Reuel's strange disappearance from the camp of the explorers. Day after day they had searched every inch of the ground within and about the pyramids, with no success. Charlie Vance was inconsolable, and declared his intention of making his home at Meroe until Reuel was found. He scouted the idea of his death by falling a prey to wild beasts, and hung about the vicinity of the Great Pyramid with stubborn persistence. He was no longer the spoiled darling of wealth and fashion, but a serious-minded man of a taciturn disposition.

He spent money like water in his endeavor to find the secret passage, believing that it existed, and that in it Reul was lost.

One morning he and Jim Titus laid bare a beautifully worked marble wall, built of fine masonry, with even blocks, each a meter and a half long, and below the exquisitely worked moulding two further layers of well-worked calcareous stone. The whole formed a foundation for a structure which had fallen into ruins about two and a half meters high. But this wall continued for thirteen meters only, and then returned at right angles at each end. On the inner side this marble structure was backed by large blocks of calcareous stone, and in the inner angles, they had with much labor to break up and remove two layers of blocks superimposed at right angles, one upon another. The entire party was much puzzled to learn what this structure could have been.

Sculptures and paintings lined the walls. As usual, there was a queen, attired in a long robe. The queen had in one hand the lash of Osiris and in the other a lotus flower.

At the extremity of each portico was the representation of a monolithic temple, above which were the traces of a funeral boat filled with figures.

After two days' work, the skilled diggers assured the explorers that they could do nothing with the debris but to leave it, as it was impossible to open the structure. Rut in the night, Charlie was kept awake by the thought that this curious structure might hold the expedition's secret; and remembering that perseverance was never beaten, set to work there the next morning, digging into the interior and breaking up the huge blocks which impeded his progress. The next day another impediment was reached, and it was decided to give it up. Again Charlie was awake all night, puzzling over the difficulties encountered, and again he made up his mind not to give it up. Charlie was learning many needed lessons in bitterness of spirit out in these African wilds. Sorrow had come to him here in the loss of his sister, and the disappearance of his friend. As Reuel had done in the night weeks before, so he did now, rising and dressing and securing his weapons, but taking the precaution to awaken Jim, and ask him to accompany him for a last visit to the Pyramid.

Jim Titus seemed strangely subdued and quiet since Reuel's disappearance. Charlie decided that their suspicions were wrong, and that Jim was a good fellow, after all.

As they trudged along over the sandy paths in the light of the great African moon, Charlie was glad of Jim's lively conversation. Anecdotes of Southern life flowed glibly from his tongue, illustrated by songs descriptive of life there. It really seemed to Vance that a portion of the United States had been transported to Africa.

They entered the great Pyramid, as Reuel had done before them, lit their torches, and began slowly and carefully to go over the work of excavation already done.

They passed down a side passage opening out of the outer passage, down a number of steps and along an underground shaft made by the workmen. Suddenly the passage ended. They halted, held up the lamps and saw such a scene as they were not likely to see again. They stood on the edge of an enormous pit, hedged in by a wall of rock. There was an opening in the wall, made by a hinged block of stone. This solid door had opened noiselessly, dlark figures had stolen forth, and had surrounded the two men. As they discovered their strange companions, weapons of burnished steel flashed and seemed to fill the vault. Not a sound was heard but the deep breathing of men in grim determination and on serious business bent. Instantly the two travellers were bound and gagged.

* * *

Instantly, after the seizure, the eyes of the prisoners were blindfolded; then they were half led, half dragged along by their captors. As he felt the grip of steel which impelled a forward movement, Charlie bitterly cursed his own folly in undertaking so mad a venture. "Poor Reuel," he lamented, "was this the explanation of his disappearance?" Reuel had been the life of the party; next to Professor Stone, he was looked up to as leader and guide, and with his loss, all interest seemed to have dropped from the members of the expedition.

For half an hour they were hurried along what must have been deep underground passages. Charlie could feel the path drop beneath his feet on solid rock which seemed to curve over like the edges of a waterfall. He stumbled, and would have fallen if strong arms had not upheld him.

He could feel the rock worn into deep gutters smoother than ice. For the first time he heard the sound of his captors' voices. One in command gave an order in an unknown tongue. Charlie wished then that he had spent more time in study and less in sport.

"Oh," he groaned in spirit, "what a predicament for a free-born American citizen, and one who has had on the gloves with many a famous ring champion!" He wondered how Jim was faring, for since the first frightened yell from his lips, all had been silence.

There came another brief command in the unknown tongue, and the party halted. Then Charlie felt himself lifted into what he finally determined was a litter. He settled himself comfortably, and the bearers started. Charlie was of a philosophical nature; if he had been born poor and forced to work for a living, he might have become a learned philosopher. So he lay and reflected, and wondered where this experience would end, until, lulled by the yielding motion and the gentle swaying, he fell asleep.

He must have slept many hours, for when he awoke he felt a strong sensation of hunger. They were still journeying at a leisurely pace. Charlie could feel the sweet, fresh air in his face, could hear the song of birds, and smell the scented air, heavy with the fragrance of flowers and fruits. Mentally thanking God that he still lived, he anxiously awaited the end of this strange journey. Presently he felt that they entered a building, for the current of air ceased, and the soft footsteps of the bearers gave forth a metallic sound. There came another command in the unknown tongue, and the bearers stopped; he was told to descend, in unmistakable English, by a familiar voice. He obeyed the voice, and instantly he was relieved of his bandage; before his sight became accustomed to the semi-darkness of the room, he heard the retreating steps of a number of men. As his sight returned in full, he saw before him Ai and Abdallah and Jim.

Abdallah regarded him with a gaze that was stolid and unrecognizing. The room in which he stood was large and circular. Floors and walls were of the whitest marble, and from the roof light and air were supplied. There were two couches in the room, and a divan ran about one of its sides. There was no door or entrance visible – nothing but the unvarying white walls and flooring.

"Stranger," said Ai, in his mellow voice, speaking English in fluent tones, "Why hast thou dared to uncover the mysteries of centuries? Art thou weary of life that thou hast dared to trifle with Nature's secrets? Scarce an alien foot has traversed this land since six thousand years have passed. Art weary of living?" As he asked the last question, Charlie felt a chill of apprehension. This man, with his strange garb, his dark complexion, his deep eyes and mystic smile, was to be feared and reverenced. Summoning up all his *sang froid* and determination not to give in to his fears, he replied:

"We came to find old things, that we may impart our knowledge to the people of our land, who are eager to know the beginning of all things. I come of a race bold and venturesome, who know not fear if we can get a few more dollars and fresh information."

"I have heard of your people," replied Ai, with a mysterious sparkle in his eyes. "They are the people who count it a disgrace to bear my color; is it not so?"

"Great Scott!" thought Charlie, turning mental somersaults to find an answer that would placate the dignitary before him. "Is it possible that the ubiquitous race question has got ahead of the expedition! By mighty, it's time something was done to stop this business. Talk of Banquo's ghost! Banquo ain't in it if this is the race question I'm up against." Aloud he said, "My venerable and esteemed friend, you could get there all right with your complexion in my country. We would simply label you 'Arab, Turk, Malay or Filipino' and in that costume you'd slide along all right; not the slightest trouble when you showed your ticket at the door. Savee?" He finished with a profound bow.

Ai eyed him sadly for a moment, and then said:

"O, flippant-tongued offspring of an ungenerous people, how is it with my brother?" and he took Jim's unresisting hand and led him up to Charlie. "Crisp of hair," and he passed his hand softly over Jim's curly pate. "Black of skin! How do you treat such as this one in your country?"

Charlie felt embarrassed in spite of his assurance. "Well, of course, it has been the custom to count Africans as our servants, and they have fared as servants."

"And yet, ye are all of one blood; descended from one common father. Is there ever a flock or herd without its black member? What more beautiful than the satin gloss of the raven's wing, the soft glitter of eyes of blackest tint or the rich black fur of your own native animals? Fair-haired worshippers of Mammon, do you not know that you have been weighed in the balance and found wanting? That your course is done? That Ethiopia's bondage is about over, her travail passed?"

Charlie smiled in inward mirth at what he called the "fossilized piece of antiquity". "Touched in the forehead; crank," was his mental comment. "I'd better put on the brakes, and not aggravate this lunatic. He's probably some kind of a king, and might make it hot for me." Aloud he said, "Pardon, Mr. King, but what has this to do with making me a prisoner? Why have I been brought here?"

"You will know soon enough," replied Ai, as he clapped his hands. Abdallah moved to the side of the room, and instantly a marble block slid from its position, through which Ai and he departed, leaving the prisoners alone.

For a while the two men sat and looked at each other in helpless silence. Then Jim broke the silence with lamentations.

"Oh, Lord! Mr. Vance, there's a hoodoo on this business, and I'm the hoodoo!"

"Nonsense!" exclaimed Vance. "Be a man, Jim, and help me find a way out of this infernal business."

But Jim sat on the divan, lamenting and refusing to be comforted. Presently food was brought to them, and then after many and useless conjectures, they lay down and tried to sleep.

The night passed very comfortably on the whole, although the profound silence was suggestive of being buried alive. Another day and night passed without incident. Food was supplied them at regular intervals. Charlie's thoughts were varied. He – fastidious and refined – who had known no hardship and no sorrow – why had he left his country to wander among untutored savages? None were there to comfort him of all his friends. These walls would open but to admit the savage executioner. He ground his teeth. He thought of Cora Scott; doubtless she thought him dead. Dead! No; nor would he die. He'd find a way out of this or perish; he'd go home and marry Cora. Now this was a most surprising conclusion, for Charlie had been heard to say many times that "he'd be drawn and quartered before he'd tie up to a girl of the period," which Cora undoubtedly was. As if aroused from a dream, he jumped up and going over to Jim, shook him. The Negro turned uneasily in his sleep and groaned. Again he shook him.

"Get up, Jim. Come, I'm going to try to get out of this."

"I'm afraid, Mr. Vance; it's no use."

"Come on, Jim; be a man."

"I'm ready for anything, only show me the way," replied Jim in desperation. Their pistols had been taken from them, but their knives remained. They stored what food remained about their persons and began a thorough examination of the room.

"They certainly find an exit here somewhere, Jim, and we must find it too."

"Easier said than done, I fear, sir."

An hour – two hours, passed in fruitless search; the marble walls showed not a sign of exit or entrance. They rested then, sitting on the sides of the divans and gazing at each other in utter helplessness. The full moonlight showered the apartment with a soft radiance from the domed roof. Suddenly, Jim sprang forward and inserted his knife in a crevice in the floor. Instantly Charlie was beside him, working like mad on the other side. The slab began to waver to and fro, as though shaken by a strong force – the crack widened – they saw a round, flat metal button – Jim seized it with one hand and pried with the knife in the other – a strong breeze of subterranean air struck through the narrow opening – and with a dull reverberation half the flooring slid back, revealing what seemed to be a vast hole.

The men recoiled, and lay panting from their labors on the edges of the subway. Charlie blessed his lucky stars that hidden in his clothes was a bundle of tapers used by the explorers for just such emergencies. By great good fortune, his captors had not discovered them.

"What's to be done now, Jim?"

"Git down there and explore, but hanged if I want the job, Mr. Vance."

"We'll go together, Jim. Let's see," he mused, "What did Prof. Stone's parchment say? 'Beware the tank to the right where dwells the sacred crocodile, still living, although centuries have rolled by, and men have been gathered to the shades who once tended on his wants. And beware the fifth gallery to the right where abide the sacred serpents with jewelled crowns, for of a truth are they terrible,'" quoted Charlie, dreamily.

"You don't suppose this is the place you were hunting for, do you?" queried Jim, with eyes big with excitement.

"Jim, my boy, that's a question no man can answer at this distance from the object of our search. But if it is, as I suspect, the way to the treasure will lead us to liberty, for the other end must be within the pyramid. I'm for searching this passage. Come on if you are with me."

He lighted his taper and swung it into the abyss, disclosing steps of granite leading off in the darkness. As his head disappeared from view, Jim, with a shudder, followed. The steps led to a passage or passages, for the whole of the underground room was formed of vaulted passages, sliding off in every direction. The stairs ended in another passage; the men went down it; it was situated, as nearly as they could judge, directly beneath the room where they had been confined. Silently the two figures crept on, literally feeling their way. Shortly they came to another passage running at right angles; slowly they crept along the tunnel, for it was nothing more, narrowing until it suddenly ended in a sort of cave, running at right angles; they crossed this, halting at the further side to rest and think. Charlie looked anxiously about him for signs, but saw nothing alarming in the smooth sandy floor, and irregular contorted sides. The floor was strewn with bowlders like the bed of a torrent. As they went on, the cavern widened into an amphitheatre with huge supporting columns. To the right and left of the cave there were immense bare spaces stretching away into immense galleries. Here they paused to rest, eating sparingly of the food they had brought. "Let us rest here," said Charlie, "I am dead beat."

"Is it not safer to go on? We cannot be very far from the room where we were confined."

"I'll sit here a few moments, anyhow," replied Charlie. Jim wandered aimlessly about the great vault, turning over stones and peering into crevices.

"What do you expect to find, Jim, the buried treasure?" laughed Charlie, as he noted the earnestness of the other's search.

Jim was bending over something – wrenching off a great iron cover. Suddenly he cried out, "Mr. Vance, here it is!"

Charlie reached his side with a bound. There sat Jim, and in front of him lay, imbedded in the sand of the cavern's floor, a huge box, long and wide and deep, whose rusted hinges could not withstand the stalwart Negro's frantic efforts.

With a shuddering sigh the lid was thrust back, falling to one side with a great groan of almost mortal anguish as it gave up the trust committed to its care ages before. They both gazed, and as they gazed were well-nigh blinded. For this is what they saw:

At first, a blaze of darting rays that sparkled and shot out myriad scintillations of color – red, violet, orange, green, and deepest crimson. Then by degrees, they saw that these hues came from a jumbled heap of gems – some large, some small, but together in value beyond all dreams of wealth.

Diamonds, rubies, sapphires, amethysts, opals, emeralds, turquoises – lay roughly heaped together, some polished, some uncut, some as necklaces and chains, others gleaming in rings and bracelets – wealth beyond the dreams of princes.

Near to the first box lay another, and in it lay gold in bars and gold in flakes, hidden by the priests of Osiris, that had adorned the crowns of queens Candace and Semiramis – a spectacle glorious beyond compare.

"The Professor's parchment told the truth," cried Charlie, after a few moments, when he had regained his breath. "But what shall we do with it, now we have it?" asked Jim in disconsolate tones. "We can't carry it with us."

"True for you, Jim," replied Vance, sadly. "This wealth is a mockery now we have it. Jim, we're left, badly left. Here we've been romping around for almost six months after this very treasure, and now we've got it we can't hold it. This whole expedition has been like monkeying with a saw mill, Jim, my boy, and I for one, give in beaten. Left, I should say so; badly left, when I counted Africa a played-out hole in the ground. And, Jim, when we get home, if ever we do, the drinks are on me. Now, old man, stow some of these glittering baubles in your clothing, as I am going to do, and then we'll renew our travels." He spoke in jest, but the tears were in his eyes, and as he clasped Jim's toil-hardened black hand, he told himself that Ai's words were true. Where was the color line now? Jim was a brother; the nearness of their desolation in this uncanny land, left nothing but a feeling of brotherhood. He felt then the truth of the words, "Of one blood have I made all races of men."

As they stooped to replace the cover, Jim's foot knocked against an iron ring set in the sandy flooring. "I believe it's another box, Mr. Vance," he called out, and dropping his work, he pulled with all his might.

"Careful, Jim," called Charlie's warning voice. Too late! The ring disappeared at the second tug, revealing a black pit from which came the odor of musk. From out the darkness came the sweeping sound of a great body moving in wavelets over a vast space. Fascinated into perfect stillness, Vance became aware of pale emerald eyes watching him, and the sound of deep breathing other than their own. There was a wild rattle and rush in the darkness, as Jim, moving forward, flung down his taper and turned to flee.

"The serpents! The serpents! Fly for your life, Jim!" shouted Charlie, as he dashed away from the opening. Too late! There came a terrible cry, repeated again and again. Charlie Vance sunk upon the ground, overcome with horror.

Chapter XIX

IT MUST HAVE BEEN about one o'clock in the morning when Reuel started out of a fitful slumber by the sound of that terrible scream. He sprang to his feet and listened. He heard not a sound; all was silence within the palace. But his experience was so vivid that reason could not control his feelings; he threw wide the dividing curtains, and fled out upon the balcony. All was silence. The moonlight flooded the landscape with the strength of daylight. As he stood trying to calm himself, a shadow fell across his path, and raising his eyes, he beheld the form of Mira; she beckoned him on, and he, turning, followed the shadowy figure, full of confidence that she would show him the way to that fearful scream.

On they glided like two shadows, until the phantom paused before what seemed a solid wall, and with warning gaze and uplifted finger, bade him enter. It was a portion of the palace unfamiliar to him; the walls presented no hope of entrance. What could it mean? Mira faded from his gaze, and as he stood there puzzling over this happening, suddenly the solid wall began to glide away, leaving a yawning space, in which appeared Ai's startled and disturbed face.

"Back!" he cried, as he beheld his King. "Back, Ergamenes! How come you here?"

"What was the cry I heard, Ai? I cannot rest. I have been led hither," he continued, significantly. Then, noticing the other's disturbed vision, he continued, "Tell me. I command you."

With a murmured protest, Ai stepped aside, saying, "Perhaps it is best."

Reuel advanced into the room. The hole in the floor was securely closed, and on the divans lay Charlie Vance, white and unconscious, and Jim Titus, crushed almost to a jelly but still alive. Abdallah and a group of natives were working over Vance, trying to restore consciousness. Reuel gave one startled, terrified glance at the two figures, and staggered backward to the wall.

Upon hearing that cry, Jim Titus stirred uneasily, and muttered, "It's him!"

"He wishes to speak with you," said Ai, gravely.

"How came they here, and thus?" demanded Reuel in threatening anger.

"They were searching for you, and we found them, too, in the pyramid. We confined them here, debating what was best to do, fearing you would become dissatisfied. They tried to escape and found the treasure and the snakes. The black man will die."

"Are you there, Mr. Reuel?" came in a muffled voice from the dying man.

Reuel stood beside him and took his hand – "Yes, Jim, it is I; how came you thus?"

"The way of the transgressor is hard," groaned the man. "I would not have been here had I not consented to take your life. I am sure you must have suspected me; I was but a bungler, and often my heart failed me."

"Unhappy man! How could you plot to hurt one who has never harmed you?" exclaimed Reuel.

"Aubrey Livingston was my foster brother, and I could deny him nothing."

"Aubrey Livingston! Was he the instigator?"

"Yes," sighed the dying man. "Return home as soon as possible and rescue your wife – your wife, and yet not your wife – for a man may not marry his sister."

"What!" almost shrieked Reuel. "What!"

"I have said it. Dianthe Lusk is your own sister, the half-sister of Aubrey Livingston, who is your half-brother."

Reuel stood for a moment, apparently struggling for words to answer the dying man's assertion, then fell on his knees in a passion of sobs agonizing to witness. "You know then, Jim, that I am Mira's son?" he said at length.

"I do. Aubrey planned to have Miss Dianthe from the first night he saw her; he got you this chance with the expedition; he kept you from getting anything else to force you to a separation from the girl. He bribed me to accidentally put you out of the way. He killed Miss Molly to have a free road to Dianthe. Go home, Reuel Briggs, and at least rescue the girl from misery. Watch, watch, or he will outwit you yet." Reuel started in a frenzy of rage to seize the man, but Ai's hand was on his arm.

"Peace, Ergamenes; he belongs to the ages now."

One more convulsive gasp, and Jim Titus had gone to atone for the deeds done in the flesh.

With pallid lips and trembling frame, Reuel turned from the dead to the living. As he sat beside his friend, his mind was far away in America looking with brooding eyes into the past and gazing hopelessly into the future. Truly hath the poet said:

The evil that men do lives after them.

And Reuel cursed with a mighty curse the bond that bound him to the white race of his native land.

* * *

One month after the events narrated in the previous chapter, a strange party stood on the deck of the out-going steamer at Alexandria, Egypt – Reuel and Charlie Vance, accompanied by Ai and Abdallah in the guise of servants. Ai had with great difficulty obtained permission of the Council to allow King Ergamenes to return to America. This was finally accomplished by Ai's being surety for Reuel's safe return, and so the journey was begun which was to end in the apprehension and punishment of Aubrey Livingston.

Through the long journey homeward two men thought only of vengeance, but with very different degrees of feeling. Charlie Vance held to the old Bible punishment for the pure crime of manslaughter, but in Reuel's wrongs lay something beyond the reach of punishment by the law's arm; in it was the accumulation of years of foulest wrongs heaped upon the innocent and defenceless women of a race, added to this last great outrage. At night he said, as he paced the narrow confines of the deck, "Thank God, it is night;" and when the faint streaks of dawn glowed in the distance, gradually creeping across the expanse of waters, "Thank God, it is morning." Another hour, and he would say, "Would God it were night!" By day or night some phantom in his ears holloes in ocean's roar or booms in thunder, howls in the winds or murmurs in the breeze, chants in the voice of the sea-fowl – "Too late, too late. 'Tis done, and worse than murder."

Westward the vessel sped – westward while the sun showed only as a crimson bull in its Arabian setting, or gleamed through a veil of smoke off the English coast, ending in the grey, angry, white-capped waves of the Atlantic in winter.

Chapter XX

IT WAS BELIEVED by the general public and Mr. Vance that Molly and Dianthe had perished beneath the waters of the Charles River, although only Molly's body was recovered. Aubrey was picked up on the bank of the river in an unconscious state, where he was supposed to have made his way after vainly striving to rescue the two girls.

When he had somewhat recovered from the shock of the accident, it was rumored that he had gone to Canada with a hunting party, and so he disappeared from public view.

But Dianthe had not perished. As the three struggled in the water, Molly, with all the confidence of requited love, threw her arms about her lover. With a muttered oath, Aubrey tried to shake her off, but her clinging arms refused to release him. From the encircling arms he saw a sight that maddened him – Dianthe's head was disappearing beneath the waters where the lily-stems floated in their fatal beauty, holding in their tenacious grasp the girl he loved. An appalling sound had broken through the air as she went down – a heart-stirring cry of agony – the tone of a voice pleading with God for life! The precious boon of life! That cry drove away the man, and the brute instinct so rife within us all, ready always to leap to the front in times of excitement or danger, took full possession of the body. He forgot honor, humanity, God.

With a savage kick he freed himself and swam swiftly toward the spot where Dianthe's golden head had last appeared. He was just in time. Grasping the flowing locks with one hand and holding her head above the treacherous water, he swam with her to the bank.

Pretty, innocent, tender-hearted Molly sank never to rise again. Without a word, but with a look of anguished horror, her despairing face was covered by the glistening, greedy waters that lapped so hungrily about the water-lily beds.

As Aubrey bore Dianthe up the bank his fascinated gaze went backward to the spot where he had seen Molly sink. To his surprise and horror, as he gazed the body rose to the surface and floated as did poor Elaine:

> In her right hand the lily,
> —All her bright hair streaming down—
> —And she herself in white,
> All but her face, and that clear-featured face
> Was lovely, for she did not seem as dead,
> But fast asleep, and lay as tho' she smiled.

Staggering like a drunken man, he made his way to a small cottage up the bank, where a woman, evidently expecting him, opened the door without waiting for his knock.

"Quick! Here she is. Not a word. I will return tonight." With these words Livingston sped back to the riverbank, where he was found by the rescuing party, in a seemingly exhausted condition.

For weeks after these happenings Dianthe lived in another world, unconscious of her own identity. It was early fall before her full faculties were once more with her. The influence which Livingston had acquired rendered her quiescent in his hands, and not too curious as to circumstances of time and place. One day he brought her a letter, stating that Reuel was dead.

Sick at heart, bending beneath the blight that thus unexpectedly fell upon her, the girl gave herself up to grief, and weary of the buffets of Fate, yielded to Aubrey's persuasions and became his wife. On the night which witnessed Jim Titus's awful death, they had just returned to Livingston's ancestral home in Maryland.

It would be desecration to call the passion which Aubrey entertained for Dianthe, love. Yet passion it was – the greatest he had ever known – with its shadow, jealousy. Indifference on the part of his idol could not touch him; she was his other self, and he hated all things that stood between him and his love.

It was a blustering night in the first part of November. It was twilight. Within the house profound stillness reigned. The heavens were shut out of sight by masses of sullen, inky clouds, and a piercing north wind was howling. Within the room where Dianthe lay, a glorious fire burnt in a wide, low grate. A table, a couch and some chairs were drawn near to it for warmth. Dianthe lay alone. Presently there came a knock at the door. "Enter," said the pale woman on the couch, never once removing her gaze from the whirling flakes and sombre sky.

Aubrey entered and stood for some moments gazing in silence at the beautiful picture presented to his view. She was gowned in spotless white, her bright hair flowed about her unconstrained by comb or pin. Her features were like marble, the deep grey eyes gazed wistfully into the far distance. The man looked at her with hungry, devouring eyes.

Something, he knew not what, had come between them. His coveted happiness, sin-bought and crime-stained, had turned to ashes – Dead-Sea fruit indeed. The cold gaze she turned on him half froze him, and changed his feelings into a corresponding channel with her own.

"You are ill, Dianthe. What seems to be your trouble? I am told that you see spirits. May I ask if they wear the dress of African explorers?"

It had come to this unhappy state between them.

"Aubrey," replied the girl in a calm, dispassionate tone, "Aubrey, at this very hour in this room, as I lay here, not sleeping, nor disposed to sleep, there where you stand, stood a lovely woman; I have seen her thus once before. She neither looked at me nor spoke, but walked to the table, opened the Bible, stooped over it a while, seeming to write, then seemed to sink, just as she rose, and disappeared. Examine the book, and tell me, is that fancy?"

Crossing the room, Aubrey gazed steadfastly at the open book. It was the old family Bible, and the heavy clasps had grown stiff and rusty. It was familiar to him, and intimately associated with his life-history. There on the open page were ink lines underscoring the twelfth chapter of Luke: "For there is nothing covered that shall not be revealed, neither hid that shall not be known." At the end of this passage was written the one word "Nina".

Without a comment, but with anxious brows, Aubrey returned to his wife's couch, stooped and impressed several kisses on her impassive face. Then he left the room.

Dianthe lay in long and silent meditation. Servants came and went noiselessly. She would have no candles. The storm ceased; the moon came forth and flooding the landscape, shone through the windows upon the lonely watcher. Dianthe's restlessness was soothed, and she began tracing the shadows on the carpet and weaving them into fantastic images of imagination. What breaks her reverie? The moonlight gleams on something white and square; it is a letter. She left the couch and picked it up. Just then a maid entered with a light, and she glanced at the envelope. It bore the African postmark! She paused. Then as the girl left the room, she slipped the letter from the envelope and read:

> *Master Aubrey – I write to inform you that I have not been able to comply with your wishes. Twice I have trapped Dr. Briggs, but he has escaped miraculously from my hands. I shall not fail the third time. The expedition will leave for Meroe next week, and then something will surely happen. I have suppressed all letters, according to your orders, and both men are feeling exceedingly blue. Kindly put that first payment on the five thousand dollars to my sister's credit in a Baltimore bank, and let her have the bank book. Next mail you may expect something definite.*
> *Yours faithfully,*
> *Jim Titus.*

Aubrey Livingston had gone to an adjoining city on business, and would be absent three or four days.

That night Dianthe spent in his library behind locked doors, and all about her lay open letters – letters addressed to her, and full of love and tenderness, detailing Reuel's travels and minutely describing every part of his work.

Still daylight found her at her work. Then she quitted it, closed up the desk, tied up the letters, replaced them, left the room, and returned to her boudoir to think. Her brain was in a giddy whirl, and but one thought stood out clearly in her burning brain. Her thoughts took shape in the one word 'Reuel', and by her side stood again the form of the pale, lovely mulattress, her long black curls enveloping her like a veil. One moment – the next the room was vacant save for herself.

Reuel was living, and she a bigamist – another's wife! Made so by fraud and deceit. The poor overwrought brain was working like a machine now – throbbing, throbbing, throbbing. To see him, hear his voice – this would be enough. Then came the thought – lost to her, or rather she to him – and how? By the plans of his would-be murderer. O, horrible, inhuman wretch! He had stolen her by false tales, and then had polluted her existence by the breath of murder. Murder! What was murder? She paused and gasped for breath; then come the trembling thought, "Would he were dead!"

He would return and discover the opening of the letters. "O, that he were dead!"

She wandered about the grounds in the cold sunshine, burning with fever, and wild with a brain distraught. She wished the trees were living creatures and would fall and crush him. The winds in their fury, would they but kill him! O, would not something aid her? At last she sat down, out of breath with her wanderings and wearied by the tumult within her breast. So it went all day; the very heavens beckoned her to commit a deed of horror. She slept and dreamed of shapeless, nameless things that lurked and skulked in hidden chambers, waiting the signal to come forth. She woke and slept no more. She turned and turned the remainder of the night; her poor warped faculties recalled the stories she had read of Cenci, the Borgias, and even the Hebrew Judith. And then she thought of Reuel, and the things he had told her on many an idle day, of the properties of medicine, and how in curiosity she had fingered his retorts used in experiments. And he had told her she was apt, and he would teach her many things of his mysterious profession. And as she thought and speculated, suddenly something whispered, as it were, a name – heard but once – in her ear. It was the name of a poison so subtle in its action as to defy detection save by one versed in its use. With a shudder she threw the thought from her, and rose from her couch.

We know we're tempted. The world is full of precedents, the air with impulses, society with men and spirit tempters. But what invites sin? Is it not a something within ourselves? Are we not placed here with a sinful nature which the plan of salvation commands us to overcome? If we offer the excuse that we were tempted, where is the merit of victory if we do not resist the tempter? God does not abandon us to evil prompters without a white-robed angel, stretching out a warning hand and pointing out the better way as strongly as the other. When we conquer sin, we say we are virtuous, triumphant, and when we fall, we excuse our sins by saying, "It is fate."

The days sped on. To the on-looker life jogged along as monotonously at Livingston Hall as in any other quiet home. The couple dined and rode, and received friends in the conventional way. Many festivities were planned in honor of the beautiful bride. But, alas! These days but goaded her to madness. The uncertainty of Reuel's fate, her own wrongs as a wife yet not a wife, her husband's agency in all this woe, the frailness of her health, weighed more and more upon a mind weakened by hypnotic experiments. Her better angel whispered still, and she listened until one day there was a happening that turned the scale, and she pronounced her own dreadful doom – "For me there's no retreat."

Chapter XXI

IT WAS PAST MIDDAY about two weeks later that Dianthe wandered about the silent woods, flitting through the mazes of unfamiliar forest paths. Buried in sad thoughts she was at length conscious that her surroundings were strange, and that she had lost her way. Every now and then the air was thick and misty with powdery flakes of snow which fell, or swept down, rather, upon the brown leaf-beds and withered grass. The buffeting winds which kissed her glowing hair into waving tendrils brought no color to her white cheeks and no light to her eyes. For days she had been like this, thinking only of getting away from the busy house with its trained servants and its loathsome luxury which stifled her. How to escape the chains which bound her to this man was now her only thought. If Reuel lived, each day that found her still beneath the roof of this man whose wife she was in the eyes of the world, was a crime. Away, away, looking forward to she knew not what, only to get away from the sight of his hated face.

Presently she paused and looked about her. Where was she? The spot was wild and unfamiliar. There was no sight or sound of human being to question as to the right direction to take, not that it mattered much, she told herself in bitterness of spirit. She walked on more slowly now, scanning the woods for signs of a human habitation. An opening in the trees gave a glimpse of cultivated ground in a small clearing, and a few steps farther revealed a typical Southern Negro cabin, from which a woman stepped out and faced her as if expecting her coming. She was very aged, but still erect and noble in form. The patched figure was neat to scrupulousness, the eye still keen and searching.

As the woman advanced slowly toward her, Dianthe was conscious of a thrill of fear, which quickly passed as she dimly remembered having heard the servants jesting over old Aunt Hannah, the most noted 'voodoo' doctor or witch in the country.

"Come in, honey, and res'," were her first words after her keen eyes had traveled over the woman before her. Dianthe obeyed without a murmur; in truth, she seemed again to have lost her own will in another's.

The one-roomed cabin was faultlessly neat, and the tired girl was grateful for the warmth of the glowing brands upon the wide hearth. Very soon a cup of stimulating coffee warmed her tired frame and brought more animation to her tired face.

"What may your name be, Auntie?" she asked at length, uneasy at the furtive glances cast by the eyes of the silent figure seated in the distant shadow of the chimney-corner. The eyes never wavered, but no answer was vouchsafed her by the woman in the corner. Somewhere she had read a description of an African princess which fitted the woman before her.

> I knew a princess; she was old,
> Crisp-haired, flat-featured, with a look
> Such as no dainty pen of gold
> Would write of in a fairy book.
>
> …
>
> Her face was like a Sphinx's face, to me,
> Touched with vast patience, desert grace,
> And lonesome, brooding mystery.

Suddenly a low sound, growing gradually louder, fell upon Dianthe's ear; it was the voice of the old woman crooning a mournful minor cadence, but for an instant it sent a chill about the girl's heart. It was a funeral chant commonly sung by the Negroes over the dead. It chimed in with her gloomy, despairing mood and startled her. She arose hastily to her feet to leave the place.

"How can I reach the road to Livingston Place?" she asked with a shudder of apprehension as she glanced at her entertainer.

"Don't be 'feared, child; Aunt Hannah won't hurt a ha'r of that purty head. Hain't it these arms done nussed ev'ry Livingston? I knowed your mother, child; for all you're married to Marse Aubrey, you isn't a white 'ooman."

"I do not deny what you say, Auntie; I have no desire so to do," replied Dianthe gently.

With a cry of anguish the floodgates of feeling were unloosed, and the old Negress flung her arms about the delicate form. "Gawd-a-mercy! My Mira's gal! My Mira's gal!" Then followed a harrowing scene.

Dianthe listened to the old story of sowing the wind and reaping the whirlwind. A horrible, paralyzing dread was upon her. Was she never to cease from suffering and be at rest? Rocking herself to and fro, and moaning as though in physical pain, the old woman told her story.

"I was born on de Livingston place, an' bein' a purty likely gal, was taken to de big house when I was a tot. I was trained by ol' Miss'. As soon as I was growed up, my mistress changed in her treatment of me, for she soon knowed of my relations with massa, an' she was hurt to de heart, po' 'ooman. Mira was de onlies' child of ten that my massa lef' me for my comfort; all de res' were sold away to raise de mor'gage off de prop'rty.

"Ol' marse had only one chil', a son; he was eddicated for a doctor, and of all the limb o' de devil, he was de worst. After ol' marse an' ol' miss' was dead he took a shine to Mira, and for years he stuck to her in great shape. Her fust child was Reuel—"

"What!" shrieked Dianthe. "Tell me – quick, for God's sake! Is he alive, and by what name is he known?" She was deathly white, and spread out her hands as if seeking support.

"Yes, he's living, or was a year ago. He's called Dr. Reuel Briggs, an' many a dollar he has sent his ol' granny, may the good Marster bless him!"

"Tell me all – tell me the rest," came from the lips of the trembling girl.

"Her second child was a girl – a beautiful, delicate child, an' de Doctor fairly worshipped her. Dat leetle gal was yourself, an' I'm your granny."

"Then Reuel Briggs is my brother!"

"Certain; but let me tell you de res', honey. Dese things jes' got to happen in slavery, but I isn't gwine to wink at de debbil's wurk wif both eyes open. An' I doesn't want you to keep on livin' with Marse Aubrey Livingston. It's too wicked; it's flyin' in de face ob Almighty God. I'se wanted to tell you eber sense I knowed who he'd married. After a while de Doctor got to thinkin' 'bout keepin' up de family name, an' de fus' thing we knows he up an' marries a white lady down to Charleston, an' brings her home. Well! When she found out all de family secrets she made de house too hot to hol' Mira, and it was ordered that she mus' be sold away. I got on my knees to Marse an' I prayed to him not to do it, but fi give Mira a house on de place where she could be alone an' bring up de childrun, an' he would a done it but for his wife."

The old woman paused to moan and rock and weep over the sad memories of the past. Dianthe sat like a stone woman.

"Den I believe de debbil took possession of me body and soul. A week before my po' gal was to be sol', Misses' child was born, and died in about an hour; at about de same time Mira gave birth to a son, too. In de 'citemen' de idea come to me to change de babies, fer no one would know it, I being alone when de chil' died, an' de house wil' fer fear misses would die. So I changed de babies, an' tol' Marse Livingston dat Mira's boy was de dead one. So, honey, Aubrey is your own blood brother an' you got to quit dat house mejuntly."

"My brother!"

Dianthe stood over the old woman and shook her by the arm, with a look of utter horror that froze her blood. "My brothers! Both those men!"

The old woman mumbled and groaned, then started up.

Aunt Hannah breathed hard once or twice. Minute after minute passed. From time to time she glanced at Dianthe, her hard, toil-worn hands strained at the arms of her chair as if to break them. Her mind seemed wavering as she crooned:

"My Mira's children; by de lotus-lily on each leetle breast I claim them for de great Osiris, mighty god. Honey, hain't you a flower on your breast?"

Dianthe bowed her head in assent, for speech had deserted her. Then old Aunt Hannah undid her snowy kerchief and her dress, and displayed to the terrified girl the perfect semblance of a lily cut, as it were, in shining ebony.

"Did each of Mira's children have this mark?"

"Yes, honey; all of one blood!"

Dianthe staggered as though buffeted in the face. Blindly, as if in some hideous trance, reeling and stumbling, she fell. Cold and white as marble, she lay in the old woman's arms, who thought her dead. "Better so," she cried, and then laughed aloud, then kissed the poor, drawn face. But she was not dead.

Time passed; the girl could not speak. The sacrilege of what had been done was too horrible. Such havoc is wrought by evil deeds. The first downward step of an individual or a nation, who can tell where it will end, through what dark and doleful shades of hell the soul must pass in travail?

> The laws of changeless justice bind
> Oppressor and oppressed;
> And close as sin and suffering joined,
> We march to Fate abreast.

The slogan of the hour is "Keep the Negro down!" but who is clear enough in vision to decide who hath black blood and who hath it not? Can anyone tell? No, not one; for in His own mysterious way He has united the white race and the black race in this new continent. By the transgression of the law He proves His own infallibility: "Of one blood have I made all nations of men to dwell upon the whole face of the earth," is as true today as when given to the inspired writers to be recorded. No man can draw the dividing line between the two races, for they are both of one blood!

Bending a little, as though very weak, and leaning heavily upon her old grandmother's arm, Dianthe at length set out for the Hall. Her face was lined and old with suffering. All hope was gone; despair was heavy on her young shoulders whose life was blasted in its bloom by the passions of others.

As she looked upward at the grey, leaden sky, tears slowly trickled down her cheeks. "God have mercy!" she whispered.

Chapter XXII

FOR TWO DAYS Mrs. Livingston brooded in her chamber. Fifty times a day Aubrey asked for her. The maid told him she was ill, but not alarmingly so; no physician was called. She was simply indisposed, could not be seen.

Gazing in Dianthe's face, the maid whispered, "She sleeps. I will not disturb her."

Alone, she springs from her couch with all the energy of life and health. She paced the room. For two long hours she never ceased her dreary walk. Memories crowded around her, wreathing themselves in shapes which floated mistily through her brain. Her humble school days at Fisk;

her little heart leaping at the well-won prize; the merry play with her joyous mates; in later years, the first triumphant throb when wondering critics praised the melting voice, and world-admiring crowds applauded. And, O, the glorious days of travel in Rome and Florence! The classic scenes of study; intimate companionship with Beethoven, Mozart and Hayden; the floods of inspiration poured in strains of self-made melody upon her soul. Then had followed the reaction, the fall into unscrupulous hands, and the ruin that had come upon her innocent head.

The third day Mrs. Livingston arose, dressed, and declaring herself quite well, went to walk. She returned late in the afternoon, dined with her husband, conversed and even laughed. After dinner they walked a while upon the broad piazzas, beneath the silent stars and gracious moon, inhaling the cold, bracing air. Then Aubrey begged her for a song. Once again she sang 'Go down, Moses', and all the house was hushed to drink in the melody of that exquisite voice.

To mortal eyes, this young pair and their surroundings marked them as darlings of the gods enjoying the world's heaped-up felicity. Could these same eyes have looked deeper into their hearts, not the loathsome cell of the wretch condemned to death could have shown a sight more hideous. 'Twas late. Pausing at her chamber door, Aubrey raised her hand to his lips with courtly grace, and bade her good night.

* * *

It was the first hours of the morning. From the deepest and most dreamless slumber that had ever sealed his eyes, Aubrey awoke just as the clock was striking two. 'Twas quite dark, and at first he felt that the striking clock had awakened him; yet sleep on the instant was as effectually banished from his eyes as if it were broad daylight. He could not distinguish the actual contact of any substance, and yet he could not rid himself of the feeling that a strong arm was holding him forcibly down, and a heavy hand was on his lips. He saw nothing, though the moon's rays shone full into the room. He felt nothing sensuously, but everything sensationally; and thus it was that with eyes half-closed, and seemingly fixed as by an iron vice, he beheld the door of his dressing-room – the private means of communication with Dianthe's rooms – very cautiously opened, and Dianthe herself, in a loose robe, crept into the room, and stealthily as a spirit glide to the side of his bed.

Arrested by the same trance-like yet conscious power that bound his form but left perception free, Aubrey neither spoke nor moved. And yet he felt, and partially beheld her stoop over him, listen to his breathing, pass her hand before his eyes to try if they would open; then he, with sidelong glance, beheld her, rapidly as thought, take up the night glass standing on his table, and for the glass containing clear cold water, which it was his custom to swallow every morning upon first awakening, substitute one which, he had seen from the first, she carried in her hand. This done, the stealthy figure moved away, gently drew back the door, and would have passed; but no – the spell was broken. A hand was on her shoulder – a hand of iron. Back it dragged her – into the room just left, shut the door and locked it, held her in its sinewy strength till other doors were locked, then bore her to the bed, placed her upon it, and then released her. And there she sat, white and silent as the grave, whilst before her stood Aubrey, pale as herself, but no longer silent.

Taking the glass which she had substituted, he held it to her lips, and pronounced the one word – "Drink!" But one word; but O, what a world of destiny, despair, and agony hung on that word; again and again repeated. Her wild and haggard eyes, her white, speechless lips, all, alas! bore testimony to her guilt – to a mind unbalanced, but only added determination to Aubrey's deep, unflinching purpose.

"Drink! Deeper yet! Pledge me to the last drop; drink deep; drink all!"

"Aubrey, Aubrey! Mercy, as you look for it! Let me explain—" The shrinking woman was on her knees, the half-drained glass in her hand.

"Drink!" shouted Aubrey. "Drain the glass to Reuel!"

"To Reuel!" gasped Dianthe, and set the glass down empty. Once more Aubrey led his bride of three months back to the door of her room. Once more before her chamber door he paused; and once again, but now in mockery, he stooped and kissed her hand.

"Farewell, my love," he said. "When we meet, 'twill be—"

"In judgment, Aubrey; and may God have mercy on our guilty souls!"

Chapter XXIII

'**TWAS A COLD GRAY MORNING**; the dawn of such a day as seems to wrap itself within the shroud of night, hiding the warm sun in its stony bosom, and to creep through time arrayed in mourning garments for the departed stars. Aubrey was up by the earliest glimpse of dawn. Uncertain what to do or where to go, he made a pretence of eating, sitting in solemn state in the lonely breakfast room, where the servants glided about in ghostly silence, which was too suggestive for the overwrought nerves of the master of all that magnificence. Fifty times he asked the maid for Mrs. Livingston. The woman told him she was ill – not alarmingly so; no physician's services were needed, neither his own nor another's. He did not ask to see her, yet with a strange and morbid curiosity, he kept on questioning how she was, and why she kept her chamber, until the knowing laugh and sly joke about the anxiety of bridegrooms over the welfare of brides made the servants' quarters ring with hilarity. At length, tired of his aimless wandering, he said he'd go. His valet asked him where. He could not tell. "Pack up some things."

"For how long a time, sir?"

"I cannot tell, James."

"Shall I order the carriage?"

"Anything, something! A horse; yes. I'll have the swiftest one in the stable. A valise – no more; no, you need not come. I must be alone."

In Dianthe's room the attendants tread noiselessly, and finally leave her to enjoy her feigned slumber. She waits for the closing of the door, to spring from her couch with all the seeming energy of life and health. First she went to the window and flung wide the hangings, letting in a flood of light upon the pale, worn face reflected in the mirror. What a wondrous change was there! The long white drapery of her morning robe fell about her like a shroud, yet, white as it was, contrasted painfully with the livid ash-hue of her skin. Her arms were thin and blue, her hands transparent; her sunny hair hung in long dishevelled, waving masses, the picture of neglect; the sunken, wan brow, and livid lips, the heavy eyes with deep, black halos round them – all these made up a ruined temple.

"When he comes he will not know me," she murmured to herself; then sighing deeply, turned and paced the room. What she thought of, none could say. She spoke not; never raised her eyes from off the ground, nor ceased her dreary walk for two long hours. She sometimes sobbed, but never shed a tear.

Here we drop the veil. Let no human eye behold the writhings of that suffering face, the torture of that soul unmoored, and cast upon the sea of wildest passion, without the pilot, principle, or captain of all salvation, God, to trust in – passion, adoration of a human idol, hereditary traits entirely unbalanced, generous, but fervid impulses, her only guides. She knew that her spiritual person must survive the grave, but what that world was where her spirit was fast tending, only the dread tales of fear and superstition shadowed truth; and now, when her footsteps were pressing to it, horror and dread dogged every footprint.

Hour after hour elapsed alone. O, 'twas agony to be alone! She could not bear it. She would call her maid; but no, her cold, unimpassioned face would bring no comfort to her aching heart, aching for pity, for some cheering bosom, where she might sob her ebbing life away. The door opens – and O joy! Old Aunt Hannah's arms enfold her. For hours the two sat in solemn conference, while the servants wondered and speculated over the presence of the old witch.

At last night fell. "Mother," murmured the dying girl, raising her head from off her damp pillow. "A very golden cloud is printed with the fleecy words of glory. 'I will return.'" She pointed to the golden clouds banking the western sky. "O, will our spirits come, like setting suns, on each tomorrow of eternity?"

For answer, the old woman raised her hand in warning gesture. There sounded distinct and clear – three loud, yet muffled knocks on the panel directly above the couch where Dianthe lay.

"'Tis nothing, mother; I'm used to it now," said the girl with indifference.

"You say 'tis nuffin, honey; but yer limbs are quiverin' wif pain, and the drops ob agony is on yer po' white face. You can't 'ceive me, chile; yer granny knows de whole circumstance. I seed it all las' night in my dreams. Vengeance is mine; I will repay. One comes who is de instrumen' ob de Lord." And the old woman muttered and rocked and whispered.

Whatever was the cause of Mrs. Livingston's illness, its character was unusual and alarming. The maid, who was really attached to the beautiful bride, pleaded to be allowed to send for medical aid in vain. The causes for her suffering, as stated by Dianthe, were plausible; but her resolve to have no aid, inflexible. As evening advanced, her restlessness, and the hideous action of spasmodic pains across her livid face, became distressing. To all the urgent appeals of her servants, she simply replied she was waiting for someone. He was coming soon – very soon and then she would be quite well.

And yet he came not. From couch to door, from door to window, with eager, listening ear and wistful eyes the poor watcher traversed her chamber in unavailing expectancy. At length a sudden calm seemed to steal over her; the incessant restlessness of her wearied frame yielded to a tranquil, passive air. She lay upon cushions piled high upon the couch commanding a view of the broad hallways leading to her apartments. The beams of the newly risen moon bathed every object in the dim halls. Clear as the vesper bell, sounding across a far distant lake, strains of delicious music, rising and falling in alternate cadence of strong martial measure, came floating in waves of sound down the corridor.

Dianthe and Aunt Hannah and the maid heard the glorious echoes; whilst in the town the villagers heard the music as of a mighty host. Louder it grew, first in low and wailing notes, then swelling, pealing through arch and corridor in mighty diapason, until the very notes of different instruments rang out as from a vast orchestra. There was the thunder of the organ, the wild harp's peal, the aeolian's sigh, the trumpet's peal, and the mournful horn. A thousand soft melodious flutes, like trickling streams upheld a bird-like treble; whilst ever and anon the muffled drum with awful beat precise, the rolling kettle and the crashing cymbals, kept time to sounds like tramping of a vast but viewless army. Nearer they came. The dull, deep beat of falling feet – in the hall – up the stairs. Louder it came and louder. Louder and yet more loud the music swelled to thunder! The unseen mass must have been the disembodied souls of every age since Time began, so vast the rush and strong the footfalls. And then the chant of thousands of voices swelling in rich, majestic choral tones, joined in the thundering crash. It was the welcome of ancient Ethiopia to her dying daughter of the royal line.

Upspringing from her couch, as through the air the mighty hallelujah sounded, Dianthe with frantic gestures and wild distended eyes, cried: "I see them now! The glorious band! Welcome, great masters of the world's first birth! All hail, my royal ancestors – Candace, Semiramis, Dido, Solomon, David and the great kings of early days, and the great masters of the world of song. O, what long array of souls divine, lit with immortal fire from heaven itself! O, let me kneel to thee! And to thee, too, Beethoven, Mozart, thou sons of song! Divine ones, art thou come to take me home? Me, thy poor worshipper on earth? O, let me be thy child in paradise!"

The pageant passed, or seemed to pass, from her whose eyes alone of all the awe-struck listeners, with mortal gaze beheld them. When, at length, the last vibrating echoes of the music seemed to die away in utter vacant silence to the terrified attendants, Dianthe still seemed to listen. Either her ear still drank in the music, or another sound had caught her attention.

"Hark, hark! 'Tis carriage wheels. Do you not hear them? Now they pass the railroad at the crossing. Hasten, O hasten! Still they have a long mile to traverse. O, hasten! They call me home."

For many minutes she sat rigid and cold as marble. The trembling maid wept in silent terror and grief, for the gentle bride was a kind mistress. Old Aunt Hannah, with a fortitude born of despair, ministered in every possible way to the dying girl. To the great relief of all, at last, there came to their ears the very distant rumbling of wheels. Nearer it came – it sounded in the avenue – it paused at the great entrance, someone alighted – a stir – the sound of voices – then footsteps – the ascent of footsteps on the stairs. Nearer, nearer yet; hastily they come, like messengers of speed. They're upon the threshold – enter. Then, and not till then, the rigid lady moved. With one wild scream of joy she rushed forward, and Reuel Briggs clasped her in his arms.

For a few brief moments, the wretched girl lived an age in heaven. The presence of that one beloved – this drop of joy sweetened all the bitter draught and made for her an eternity of compensation. With fond wild tenderness she gazed upon him, gazed in his anxious eyes until her own looked in his very soul, and stamped there all the story of her guilt and remorse. Then winding her cold arms around his neck, she laid her weary head upon his shoulder and silently as the night passed through the portals of the land of souls.

Chapter XXIV

'TWAS MIDNIGHT. The landscape was still as death. Hills, rocks, rivers, even the babbling brooks, seemed locked in sleep. The moonbeams dreamt upon the hillside; stars slept in the glittering sky; the silent vales were full of dreaming flowers whose parti-colored cups closed in sleep. In all that solemn hush of silence one watcher broke the charmed spell. 'Twas Aubrey Livingston. Now he moves swiftly over the plain as if some sudden purpose drove him on; then he turns back in the self-same track and with the same impulsive speed. What is he doing in the lonely night? All day, hour after hour, mile on mile, the scorching midday sun had blazed upon his head, and still he wandered on. The tranquil sunset purpled round his way and still the wanderer hastened on. In his haggard eyes one question seems to linger – "I wonder if she lives!"

Many, many dreary times he said this question over! He has a secret and 'tis a mighty one; he fears if human eye but look upon him, it must be revealed. Hark! Suddenly there falls upon his ear the sound of voices, surely someone called! Again! His straining ear caught a familiar sound.

"Aubrey! Aubrey Livingston!"

"By heaven, it is her voice!" he told himself. And as if to assure him still more of who addressed him, close before his very eyes moved two figures. Hand in hand they passed from out a clump of sheltering trees, and slowly crossed his path. One face was turned toward him, the other from him. The moon revealed the same white robe in which he had last beheld her, the long, streaming hair, her slippered feet – all were there. Upon his wondering eyes her own were fixed in mute appeal and deepest anguish; then both figures passed away, he knew not where.

"'Twas she, and in full life. God of heaven, she lives!"

Pausing not to think he was deceived, enough for him, she lived. He turned his steps toward his home, with flying feet he neared the hall. Just as he reached the great entrance gates, he saw the two figures slightly in advance of him. This time Dianthe's face was turned away, but the silver moonbeams threw into bold relief the accusing face of Molly Vance!

With a sudden chill foreboding, he entered the hall and passed up the stairs to his wife's apartments. He opened wide the door and stood within the chamber of the dead.

There lay the peaceful form – spread with a drapery of soft, white gauze around her, and only the sad and livid, poisoned face was visible above it; and kneeling by the side of her, his first love and his last – was Reuel Briggs.

Rising from the shadows as Aubrey entered, Charlie Vance, flanked on either side by Ai and Ababdis, moved to meet him, the stern brow and sterner words of an outraged brother and friend greeted him:

"Welcome, murderer!"

* * *

Dianthe was dead, poisoned; that was clear. Molly Vance was unduly done to death by the foul treachery of the same hand. All this was now clear to the thinking public, for so secluded had Aubrey Livingston lived since his return to the United States, that many of his intimate associates still believed that he had perished in the accident on the Charles. It was quite evident to these friends that his infatuation for the beautiful Dianthe had led to the commission of a crime. But the old adage that, 'the dead tell no tales', was not to be set aside for visionary ravings unsupported by lawful testimony.

Livingston's wealth purchased shrewd and active lawyers to defend him against the charges brought by the Vances – father and son – and Reuel Briggs.

One interview which was never revealed to public comment, took place between Ai, Ababdis, Aunt Hannah, Reuel Briggs and Aubrey Livingston.

Aubrey sat alone in his sumptuous study. An open book was on his knees, but his eyes were fixed on vacancy. He was changed and his auburn locks were prematurely grey. His eyes revealed an impenetrable mystery within into whose secret depths no mortal eye might look. Thus he sat when the group we have named above silently surrounded him. "Peace, O son of Osiris, to thy parting hour!"

Thus Ai greeted him. There was no mistaking these words, and gazing into the stern faces of the silent group Aubrey knew that something of import was about to happen.

Aubrey did not change countenance, although he glanced at Reuel as if seeking mercy. The latter did not change countenance; only his eyes, those strange deep eyes before whose fixed gaze none could stand unflinching, took on a more sombre glow. Again Ai spoke:

"God has willed it! Great is the God of Ergamenes, we are but worms beneath His feet. His will be done." Then began a strange, weird scene. Round and round the chair where Aubrey was seated walked the kingly Ai chanting in a low monotone in his native tongue, finally advancing with measured steps to a position directly opposite and facing Livingston, and stood there erect and immovable, with arms raised as if in invocation. His eyes glittered with strange, fascinating lights in the shaded room. To the man seated there it seemed that an eternity was passing.

Why did not these two men he had injured take human vengeance in meting out punishment to him? And why, oh! why did those eyes, piercing his own like poniards, hold him so subtly in their spell?

Gradually he yielded to the mysterious beatitude that insensibly enwrapped his being. Detached from terrestrial bonds, his spirit soared in regions of pure ethereal blue. A delicious torpor held him in its embrace. His head sank upon his breast. His eyes closed in a trancelike slumber.

Ai quitted his position, and approaching Aubrey, lifted one of the shut eyelids. "He sleeps!" he exclaimed.

Then standing by the side of the unconscious man he poured into his ear – speaking loudly and distinctly – a few terse sentences. Not a muscle moved in the faces of those standing about the sleeper. Then Ai passed his hands lightly over his face, made a few upward passes, and turning to his companions, beckoned them to follow him from the room. Silently as they had come the group left the house and grounds, gained a waiting carriage and were driven rapidly away. In the shelter of the vehicle Charlie Vance spoke, "Is justice done?" he sternly queried.

"Justice will be done," replied Ai's soothing tones.

"Then I am satisfied."

But Reuel spoke not one word.

* * *

One day not very long after this happening, the body of Aubrey Livingston was found floating in the Charles river at the very point where poor Molly Vance had floated in the tangled lily-bed. The mysterious command of Ai, "death by thine own hand", whispered in his ear while under hypnotic influence, had been followed to the last letter.

Thus Aubrey had become his own executioner according to the ancient laws of the inhabitants of Telassar. Members of the royal family in direct line to the throne became their own executioners when guilty of the crime of murder.

* * *

Reuel Briggs returned to the Hidden City with his faithful subjects, and old Aunt Hannah. There he spends his days in teaching his people all that he has learned in years of contact with modern culture. United to Candace, his days glide peacefully by in good works; but the shadows of great sins darken his life, and the memory of past joys is ever with him. He views, too, with serious apprehension, the advance of mighty nations penetrating the dark, mysterious forests of his native land.

"Where will it stop?" he sadly questions. "What will the end be?"

But none save Omnipotence can solve the problem.

To our human intelligence these truths depicted in this feeble work may seem terrible – even horrible. But who shall judge the handiwork of God, the Great Craftsman! Caste prejudice, race pride, boundless wealth, scintillating intellects refined by all the arts of the intellectual world, are but puppets in His hand, for His promises stand, and He will prove His words, "Of one blood have I made all races of men."

Space Traitors

Walidah Imarisha

In conversation with Derrick Bell's short story 'Space Traders'.

THE TRILLING of the phone was almost equal to the pounding in Jamar's head. He reached out his hand without bothering to open his eyes, groping blindly for the phone. Dirty sock, dirty underwear, dirty dish, not even sure what that is…he finally found the phone and lifted it to his ear.

"Someone better be dead," he rasped menacingly into the phone.

"Yeah, it's about to be you, if you keep up that tone with me," his sister Malika snapped back.

Jamar grabbed his head and groaned at the sound of her voice. Malika was a beautiful woman, no doubt about that – after all, she was his sister so she got her share of the good genes – but she had a demeanor that would make a drill sergeant envious, and a voice to match. If she started that militant revolutionary shit right now, he hoped he couldn't be held responsible in a court of law for his response.

"Malika, can you call me back at a reasonable time. Say, 2 p.m. next Tuesday?" His voice, already crackled, was further muffled by the pillow he had pushed over his face to block out the sunlight.

"What? I can't understand a damn thing you're saying," Malika spit into the phone. "It's not my fault you keep your ass out all night long drinking with those loser friends of yours at that dive bar! I know Black folks everywhere are celebrating Obama's election and all – which you know is really just a neoliberal plot to diffuse the power of the oppressed masses, by giving us a figurehead when our people are suffering in the street every day! But shit, get up, 'cause the world as we know it is about to change!" Her voice sparkled with fervor. "You're going to miss everything! Your lazy ass will thank me for this later."

Jamar licked his lips, so dry they were painful, like a dress two sizes too small. She was right about one thing at least – shoulda drank more water and less whiskey last night. But then that wasn't a new story for him, the only difference was, for once, he had all the Black folks in Harlem, most of the Puerto Ricans and half the liberal white folks with him. Jamar didn't really care about politics. In fact, he had been too ashamed to say he hadn't voted for Obama. Shit, he hadn't voted for anybody since junior high school president… and then he'd voted for himself. But seeing Old Man Joe, a permanent fixture at Remy's Bar, crying like a baby as he talked about his father who had been lynched dreaming that such a day would come, Jamar was proud to raise up a toast. Or six.

But, of course, that meant he was in a very familiar position, along with eighty-five percent of the nation's Black population – hungover, pissed off and losing any shreds of patience he had left. "What am I gonna miss? A good day's rest? Too late, I already missed it."

"What?" Her voice hit an octave designed to make his head crack open like a walnut shell. "You mean you really have been in bed all this time? You haven't even got up to do anything at all? Brush your teeth? Nothing? Jamar, just cause you ain't got a job, again, doesn't mean you need to be the saddest person on this planet. I'm not telling you to go work for some capitalist white supremacist oppressor, but there are so many community programs and centers that could use a brotha like you. Don't buy into this post racial madness sweeping the nation – you know Obama in the White House ain't fitting to change the material conditions of the brothas and sistas on the streets! You should be involved in our community! You could be helping young cats stay out of the gang.

"At the very least you could get up and wash ya ass once in a while, damn!" Malika sighed a heavy sigh, laden with the burden of being born the younger sister to such a shiftless counter revolutionary fool.

Jamar rubbed the short dreadlocks springing out from his head in all directions and rolled his eyes. He really did not need this shit, not so early in the afternoon… okay then, not so early in the evening. Sure, he had lost his job a week ago. And sure, it had been the ninth job this year. Yes, he had drunk up the last of his money last night and slept so long today he hadn't had a chance to get out to look for work, like he had planned. Like he had planned every day this week. But damn, that's why he needed to drink – 'cause he was broke and jobless.

And her old power to the people routine was just too tired. Their parents had been part of the Philly chapter of the Black Panthers. They had both done time, gotten their asses beat by cops, to make a better world for their kids. Had given both Jamar and Malika African names, celebrated Kwanzaa and all that super Black shit. But this wasn't 1968 anymore. America had just proved that last night, hadn't it? This was a new day, one where Black people could truly do anything, even become president.

Power to the people, my ass. The only power Jamar was worried about right now was his electricity, since he hadn't paid the bill in about two months.

Satisfied that Jamar was properly chastised, Malika continued, "Well, if you *had* been awake at a decent hour you would have heard about the most incredible shit I ever imagined. This is a dawning of a new day for oppressed peoples around the world, big brother! And I ain't talking 'bout that Black puppet in the White House! Who would have thought when the revolution happened, it would come not from the third world but from another world!" She giggled uncontrollably, and for a minute, Jamar remembered the ashy-kneed little girl in braids who used to squeal when he pushed her on the rusty swing set in the school yard, demanding to be pushed higher and higher.

But of course, she had to ruin that moment. "Look, are you ready for this stuff? You sitting down? Well, knowing you, you're probably still laying down. I at least hope you have some drawers on, 'cause you know I hate talking to you when you naked…"

"Will you just tell me what the fuck is going on or leave me the hell alone?!" Jamar's frustrated yell felt like a hammer to his head, but he just couldn't take it anymore.

"Muthafucking aliens, muthafucka! Okay?!" She threw the words out like daggers. "There are muthafucking aliens, they just arrived this morning, and in exactly two minutes, they are fitting to address us."

Jamar was silent for a minute. Then he said, rage leaking out of his tone at all sides, "You woke me up when I have a pounding headache to play some stupid ass game with me. So help me, Malika…"

"It's true," Malika yelled back. "These aliens from outer space are here and they want to talk! And just wait to you hear whose voice they talking with!"

The silence was deafening.

"Damnit, turn on the TV – it's all they're talking about and watch it for your damn self. That is," she retorted, "if that busted ass set of yours can even pick up a decent picture. Don't know why I even bother with you. I swear... Malcolm X, give me strength," was her parting goodbye as she hung up the phone.

"She thinks she's so funny," he muttered to himself as he tossed the phone back into the dead sea that was his bedroom floor, from where it came.

I'm not turning on the TV, he said to himself firmly, I'm not playing along with whatever game she's up to.

Jamar closed his eyes and rolled over.

And over.

And over.

"Ah what the hell," he said, throwing off the blanket, "I'm up, I might as well see what's on."

He threw some sweatpants over the boxers Malika would be so glad to know he was wearing, padded into the living room, and dropped down onto the couch. He dug the remote out of the crevice of the couch, along with a pizza crust, a peppermint candy still in its wrapper, and a lint ball the size of a baby's head.

He clicked the worn power button.

His pout quickly changed to a look of disbelief and amazement. His jaw dropped.

A giant chrome spaceship hovering over the capitol filled the screen on every station he flipped to. It was fairly flat and had a number of prongs that stretched out from the base. Jamar realized ruefully that it sort of looked like a space age afro pick. No wonder Malika was so excited.

The audio running with the image was of the aliens, who had used the voice pattern of revolutionary poet Gil Scott Heron. Everything they said sounded like it should have been set to the beat of a congo drum, performed in front of audiences that would snap at the completion and then go burn down some white-owned stores.

"We reach out in solidarity to the scarred peoples of the planet Earth. We do not come in peace, but in justice.

"We have traveled many light years to engage your populations in a revolutionary exchange. We have technology that can cure many diseases, that can create sustainable food growth, for soil purification, for renewable sources of energy. We have resources and knowledge, to bring power to your scarred communities and enable you to establish autonomous spaces that you administer and defend. The power to determine the destinies of your own communities."

Autonomous spaces? Damn, Jamar said, they must have been reading those big ass, dull books Malika was always trying to push on him.

"We want to be clear. We cannot just give these to you. It is not that we do not wish it. But our technology is not like yours. We do not build something independent of ourselves. To create something new, we, all of us, must grow it together, each putting in pieces of ourselves. By giving, we are all enriched."

Jamar snorted. Sounds like a pyramid scam. If they threw in a trip to Hawaii, they'd get more suckers to bite.

"But we can commit to staying here and working with you until these technologies are fully birthed. Please understand, though, this is not charity, but an act of solidarity."

If this was a Gil Scott poem, this is where everyone would have snapped.

"Because we must devote individuals, equipment and resources, we can only focus on a part of your planet at a time. So right now, our offer is only open to those scarred peoples in the country called the United States of America."

Scarred peoples? Jamar thought. Is that what this cat keeps saying? Did he mean scared and it was just a glitch in the translation?

"In exchange for this, we ask that the scarred people of the United States of America commit to joining us in liberating other scarred peoples in the galaxy for the next eight of your earth years and help us create autonomous communities open to all scarred people everywhere. This is how we are able to bring this to your planet, and we believe it only right to continue to pass on the aid we receive.

"Scarred people of the United States, we picked you because we monitored your recent history. We saw all scarred communities coming together to protest unjust wars, challenge abuses of power, and work to create a new world. We saw your young take to the streets in rage and hope. We heard the voices of your greatest philosophers, like the one whose voice I now use to speak to you, and it resonated deeply in us as we too know that the revolution will not be televised, the revolution will be no rerun brothas (and sistas) the revolution will be live."

Jamar started. They were talking about the 1960s – but that was so long ago. Either they got their wires crossed and messed up on the time, or time passes real different for them than for us humans, us scarred people, whatever that is. Malika must be shitting herself with joy.

"Scarred people of the United States, you have a week to decide. Dig it."

The end of the transmission created a typhoon of commentary on television and radio stations: What did an autonomous community mean? What would they be liberating? And what the hell were scarred people?"

Gil Scott's rich voice cut back in, silencing the cacophony. "We understand. Scarred peoples is the term we have created to represent all of us who have experienced the exploitation of our labor, our culture, our histories and our bodies by populations promulgated upon a fraudulent hierarchical genetic supposition based on visual demarcations of difference."

The silence was deafening.

"Look," Gil said starting to sound a little irked, "we come from many planets, many races and species. We have joined together because we have been oppressed on our home worlds. I am of those who the first scarred peoples to rise up. We freed ourselves, with the solidarity of scarred peoples from a nearby star. We made the commitment to do the same for others, and to grow our ranks of scarred liberators. We are here, speaking to the scarred peoples of the Unites States of America. Those who have suffered from this brutality so familiar to our own, what you call white supremacy, racism, colonization.

"We are speaking only to those who have decided to call yourselves 'people of color.' Can you dig it now?"

Gil must not have been as confident in our power of collective comprehension because he added, "So those of y'all who ain't white. We await your reply."

The airwaves exploded. Phone lines jammed as people across the country called into talk radio. On Fox News, commentators foamed at the mouth, each screaming over each other, "This is reverse discrimination!" "We should take this as a direct attack against our way of life!" "These aliens are jealous of normal Americans' freedoms!" "The U.S. military knows more about bringing freedom to places than anywhere else on the globe: just look at Iraq and Afghanistan – just ask Vietnam! Maybe we should show these aliens a little of how we bring liberation, American style!"

The calls for military action were, however, somewhat muted after the display of power by the alien spaceship which, with one burst of its lasers, disabled every weapon in all of the Washington D.C. area, down to every warhead, missile, bomb and hand gun.

What about Obama? People, especially white people, implored. *We just elected the first Black president in the history of the country yesterday. Doesn't that count for anything?*

"Not really," Gil was definitely more than a little peeved at the unexpected slowness. Guess he was planned on landing in the middle of a Black Panther rally, Jamar thought. "On our planet we had some of our kind who were in positions of power. That in no way changed the conditions of the masses of scarred people who were enslaved and exploited. We know, from centuries of experience working in intergalactic solidarity, that this will not change your situation for the better, and perhaps it will make it much worse. We have seen that after a token advancement such as this, the backlash against the scarred peoples is indescribable, often setting back the cause for liberation decades. But, as it should be, as it ever was, the choice is yours, scarred peoples of USA."

Jamar leaned back on his ratty couch, absentmindedly unwrapped the peppermint candy and popped it in his mouth, which was still hanging open. "Well, the shit's bout to hit the fan now, isn't it?" Jamar asked the empty room in wonder.

The Line of Demarcation

Patty Nicole Johnson

DOELLE STARED at the faded sunset poster. She'd only been in the cramped part-conference, part storage room once before, during orientation. Back then, empty of the many boxes now stacked three high, the lights had seemed brighter somehow.

Now a series of shadows cast a stain on the already muted countryside landscape. The phrase, *Work hard now for a brighter tomorrow* was printed in an overused italic font.

She wanted to understand. But the rapid words from her four supervisors faded into murmurs no matter how hard she tried. But one thing was clear. She would have to decide soon.

* * *

Doelle had committed most of the Neolimb website to memory.

You may feel a slight itching sensation at the site of the incision, but for most it goes away within the first few weeks.

The terms and conditions section was her bed mate most evenings. Before the procedure, she had looked up the definitions of the most indecipherable legalese, ultimately becoming semi-fluent in Latin. Yet even among the redundancy, there had been no hint at the agony she'd been facing for nearly five months.

Today, as she prepared for work, a familiar fire erupted in her throat. She tamped it down with a strong cough. She had to remain calm, her last bout of rage interfered with the sensory receptors of the prosthetic arms. So she sat still, slouched over in her twin bed, twitching at irregular intervals.

"Doelle, wake up! You'll be late for your shift." Deidra called from the kitchen.

"I'm up, sis," Doelle said, shaking her head.

Deidra's convulsions, dizziness, and anxiety attacks hadn't abetted until 4 a.m. despite weeks of increased insulin. Years of deficiency had taken its toll and doctors said it would take time for her body to rebuild its stores.

Yet even being sleep deprived and enduring chronic pain, Deidra still was up by dawn. Sweeping, folding laundry and completing other housework she assigned herself. Doelle shook her head in frustration. Why didn't she take it easier on her body when it obviously needed the rest?

Doelle walked to the row of sleeveless Forage blue shirts that hung in the closet, waiting to brand her day. Tossing on the closest one over the pants she'd slept in, she was ready for her 10 a.m. to 10 p.m. shift.

Every time she donned the Forage uniform, her face tightened. *There's no need for sleeves when you have Neolimbs. Show the honor proudly.*

The Neolimb site promised a perfect skin tone match. But its lies were abound. The left arm was a faded honey hue while the other was a high-gloss caramel. Neither was close to her true russet skin tone.

Yet each limb did mirror each other in weight. Both the left and right arm sported the same considerable heft. Each time she'd raise a limb over her head or operate both at the same time, she'd take a deep inhale to ward off the dizzy spell.

Behavior adjustments, like this, were perceived as acceptable modifications of the Neolimb system. *They will adapt to you and you must adapt to them,* the FAQ page read under the question: *How will my life change after a Neolimb transplant?*

The FAQs were thousands of words long, breaking at sections to delineate different types of concerns. The skin-to-metal line of demarcation had been of most interest to Doelle before undergoing the procedure. What would the transition look like? Would it be seamless like when kitchen tiles kissed the drywall or abrupt like a worm getting caught under a screen door?

It was more of the latter, of course. Yet Doelle's vanity could wearily survive the perforation of skin butted against unnaturally cool titanium, if the pain wasn't so assaulting.

The saddest part? She'd grown accustomed to it. The fiery stabs were a loyal reminder of the path she'd chosen.

A short jolt of haptic feedback prickled Doelle's fingers. At least that feature worked as advertised. In ten minutes, a self-driving Forage Pool vehicle would arrive at her front door to drop her off with exactly enough time to arrive fifteen minutes early.

As Doelle entered the kitchen, Deidra was at the stove piling a mound of scrambled eggs onto a slice of toast. She topped it with another piece of bread and wrapped it in a paper towel. "Here. You can scarf this down in the car."

"Thanks," Doelle said in almost a whisper. Even though she'd done so much for her, she found it difficult to accept any reciprocated kindness when it was her duty to support her. And until recently, she wasn't doing a very good job.

She glanced at the stove's clock. "Come on, it's time."

Deidra looked over and nodded in silence and walked over to the fridge. As she reached the door, Doelle extended her right arm and opened it wide. Smiling, Deidra removed the day's insulin dosage and sat at the table.

The first post-Neolimb injection Doelle had given her sister had been an awkwardly hilarious occasion. The finely crafted digits of the Neolimb were used by doctors to complete delicate surgeries. But, back then, Doelle couldn't even work the thumbs. She had concentrated so much as the ribbed digit teetered over the spring-loaded injector that sweat was building at her temples. When a drop had finally succumbed to gravity the two couldn't hold in their giggles.

The next time hadn't been so funny, though. The pain medicine Doelle took was becoming less effective. And she refused to take a larger dose, as she knew the end to that story all too well.

She'd held her breath, hiding the pain, long enough that she'd passed out right on the table. When Doelle awoke, there was a fear in Deirda's eyes that she never wanted to see again.

This morning was uneventful, though. The two were old pros at their new arrangement.

As Doelle slid into the drone-operated vehicle and nodded to her normal route mates, she tinkered with her right limb.

Any vandalization, modification, unauthorized repairs, or adjustments will forfeit the warranty and result in immediate suspension from Forage.

She remembered the phrase embedded within the fine print. Doelle thought it fitting to threaten everything but termination. Forage was the highest sought-after distribution center job.

Multiple write-ups got you transferred to one of Forage's less desirable subsidiaries. With sixteen-hour shifts at one of those faraway distribution centers most people didn't return home most evenings. If Doelle didn't give Deidra her injections or protect her head during a seizure, who would? Doelle took her fingers off the tiny bolt and pressed her hand into her lap.

Fulfillment associates, called Foragers, had the privilege of qualifying for the Neolimb program only after exceeding performance metrics six months in a row and living the Forage brand value of extreme customer dedication. Doelle had accomplished both by mistake.

Her previous job at MartAll demanded twice the rate of loading boxes into the delivery drone. The muscle memory of taking the odd pack of AAA batteries and shoving it into a box with baby formula came naturally to her.

The purposefully vague secondary requirement occurred as one of her supervisors either spied or overheard her speaking to a newb.

Doelle had seen countless of them cry in their first week at Forage. She didn't even stop to look anymore. Yet she found herself pulling a sobbing girl into a corner at the tail end of a weekend shift.

"You need to start considering yourself lucky," she said in a sharp whisper, as she held the girl's slight shoulders firmly. "This is your first ever job, right?"

The wobbly, curly-haired teenager looked down and nodded. Her bent head revealed a streak of faded red, skipping halfway down her kinky tendrils.

"Your allotment is one-fourth of everyone's here. This is as easy as it's going to get."

"But I'm only twelve," the girl said as a renegade tear formed a new path down her cheek. "I just want to go back to seventh grade."

Doelle's breath caught. She heard rumblings about parent's signing waivers to let their children work. But she hadn't encountered any at her own distribution center before.

She pressed her lips together. "Learn the shortcuts. It's faster through Block D if you go through the gaps in the aisles instead of taking the lanes. Just look around, everyone's doing it. Stop feeling bad for yourself and think about ways to get it done."

That was all it took. Doelle had been fast tracked into the program. Supervisors Meredith, Lindsay, Colin and Tyler gyrated in sequence in Conference Room 567 as they invited her to the Forage Neolimb Reward Program. They immediately dove into a timetable of pre-op and post-op requirements as if she'd already signed the contract.

Nearly reaching their stark, dead eyes were taut smiles and wild gestures as they modeled their Neolimbs as visuals aids.

"This gift's impact will reverberate throughout your entire life," said Meredith.

"Today people pass you on the street, never paying a second mind," Tyler added. "In your new tomorrow, you'll be part of a supreme class that represents what's to come for the human race."

Each promised platitude of a double Neolimb life flew past Doelle. She didn't care that the esteemed elite had undergone cybernetics surgery for decades. She wanted the bottom line.

It came soon enough.

"In your first three months as you become acclimated to your new titanium limbs your pay will double," Tyler said.

Doelle grasped her seat. After she finished her training and physical therapy, her salary could soar into the six figures. Each promise had its own line-item on the contract.

She figured the math in her head. Immediately her sister's daily half-dose of insulin could rise to a full injection. And in six months, she could afford the prescribed two daily injections if inflation hadn't risen again by then.

They had her. With the Supreme Court's overturn of HIPAA, they knew every detail of her family's medical history. The Forage HR department had positioned the salary increases perfectly so she could afford the insulin, in time.

As the vehicle drove over bumpy roads and passed vacant lots positioned between three-flats and large apartment buildings, it wasn't uncommon to see Neolimbs. Most people worked in distribution centers, after all. A guy leaning against a gate raised a metal hand to wave at Doelle as she waited at an intersection. She returned the gesture as the sun hit one of his titanium bolts and glimmered its own greeting.

Minutes later, the Forage Pool neared the middle-class area of town where single-family houses lined the streets. No Neolimbs in sight. Only the very wealthy or the desperate poor ever underwent the procedure.

Fully autonomous androids had been outlawed years ago. When they had first awoken, their sentience had been welcomed. The robot race was considered a kind and helpful counterpart to humans. But the humanoid machines hadn't seen their existence that way.

The anti-servitude protests had lasted years. They wrote their demands on their angular bodies and held a general strike. Yet their chants about the value of a machine's life ultimately fell on deaf ears.

Like a barking dog begging to be let out, her AI counterparts grew tired of asking for their autonomy. After steel bodies of sanitation workers, mail deliverers, hospice aids and more littered the streets, the United Nations enacted a sweeping measure for the abolition of synthetic beings.

Back then, a young Doelle listened as her aunts and uncles cheered for the working class. They believed their jobs and dignity would be restored. But Forage and their kin couldn't be stopped. Cybernetic divisions at the top seven tech firms were born, each with their own employee incentive program.

As soon as the drone reached the east wing of Forage's Midwest campus, the doors flung open. The other Foragers scattered, filing in empty-handed to their stations – personal items were discouraged as no break rooms were provided.

Doelle shoved the crumpled paper towel into her pocket. She had 15 minutes to go the mile and a half through the endless single-story building to reach her station in housewares.

She kept a brisk pace, passing suicide hotline signs in English, Spanish and Arabic. She noted bays with various amalgamations of her coworkers. Some were upfitted with rolling wheels instead of legs. Many had arms like hers as that was thought to be the least invasive entry point. Once in a while, you would see an Ether. They were changed beyond recognition. More limbs than four. A high-powered respirator replaced the lungs. Some even had magnified eyes that protruded from their skulls, making them resemble oversized insects.

As Doelle made it to her bay, beads of sweat were dripping down her lower back. With this job, she'd never need to diet. No matter how much rice and beans she ate.

Her limbs vibrated as the countdown began. Four, three, two, one...

A handheld vacuum directly in front of her yet five shelving levels high, lit up. Her lens reader noted it was due in Albuquerque Heights in 30 minutes. Its order companion, a paperback copy of *The Jungle* by Upton Sinclair, was due then too but it was in a warehouse on the far southside of the city. They would have to meet enroute.

Doelle raised her head and concentrated on the box yards above. With a desired object inside the target area they'd extend, forgoing the need of a ladder. She couldn't prove it, but she suspected they acted milliseconds before her command was issued.

With a deep breath her hands rose in unison, taking seconds to ratchet up to their full length. The burning intensified, causing her to sweat more.

Swaying on outstretched legs, she'd have to master this stance if she'd ever wanted to reach six figures. When the vacuum was secure within her locked grasp, she began walking the quarter mile to the packaging area, making note of the extension cord in her queue that was due for packaging in the next three minutes.

It always took an hour or so for Doelle to warm up to her average pace. In her head, she calculated a speed of 180 steps a minute to reach her next milestone. Naturally, the beginning and end portions were when she received the most speed dings. She tracked her pace with the wrist scanner and noticed she was progressing well. At this rate, she'd hit her stride earlier than normal. It was best not to make eye contact with anyone. You'd be surprised how many seconds that could steal from your shift.

She sped up, almost skipping. Her arms beeped showing she was within the 90th percentile of her native leg counterparts. Without stopping she outstretched her left hand, grasping the item while only slowing two percentage points.

A pale Neolimb stretched in unison and snatched the cord out of Doelle's hand. As her arm went limp, she made out Meredith, Tyler, Colin, and Lindsay grinning in her periphery.

* * *

Still in unison, their dance was different this time. Their titanium limbs weren't so expressive. They rose and fell like a sly wave.

A contract slid in front of her. The words 'legs' and 'Neolimb' jumped off the page. As Doelle sat, her left knee bounced with nervous energy. The page was now a blur. She looked ahead and saw the sunset poster. And even in its propagandized form, she wanted to leap inside and escape past the horizon.

After blinking a bit to reset her eyes, she looked for familiar characters like dollar signs and commas.

The supervisor quartet now sung to accompany their dance. "You deserve this. Don't let this opportunity go amiss."

Did their song mention salary and she glossed over it? Doelle grimaced. Fire swam throughout each finger. She tried deep breathing, waiting for the burning to subside. A few coughs. Nothing.

A brash pounding on the desk startled Doelle as much as it did the others. Yet it was her own arms that pushed off the table, lifting her core from the seat. Her feet dangled inches from the floor.

Cold hands patted her back and head. They brought the contract closer. Doelle saw it written plain as day. Enough zeros to pay for insulin generation surgery. This meant she'd never again find her sister on the bathroom floor seizing from low blood sugar. No more donating blood to afford a doctor's appointment. Deidra wouldn't die. Not from this treatable disease.

Her arms released the table and her feet once again touched the floor.

At 10:30 p.m. Doelle sat on her bed with her legs stretched out. She noticed a few stray thick hairs near her ankle that she always failed to see when shaving. Hints of a scar traced the bottom of her right knee. She'd earned it while learning how to ride a bike on Humboldt Boulevard.

Grasping her phone, she went to the Neolimb website – the leg section. She studied the interactive diagram that showed how the hip joint would be replaced with a titanium-cast sphere and lengthened, retractable legs.

Neolimb leg replacement offers a range of benefits, such as the elimination of breaks and sprains due to biological overuse.

The surgery was scheduled for next week. As with all Neolimb contracts, they promised she had until the time of surgery to back out. But she wouldn't. No Forager ever would. The Neolimb website, her employer and the entire system excelled at transparently obfuscating reality. Their line of demarcation was a fallacy.

Yet, hers was too.

The familiar gargling and thrashing sounds of a seizure came in from the next room. Doelle rose and for one of the last times rushed over to her sister on her own two feet.

Light Ahead for the Negro

Edward Johnson

Chapter I
The Lost Airship – Unconsciousness

FROM MY youth up I had been impressed with the idea of working among the Negroes of the Southern states. My father was an abolitionist before the war and afterward an ardent supporter of missionary efforts in the South, and his children naturally imbibed his spirit of readiness and willingness at all times to assist the cause of the freedmen.

I concluded in the early years of my young manhood that I could render the Negroes no greater service than by spending my life in their midst, helping to fit them for the new citizenship that had developed as a result of the war. My mind was made up throughout my college course at Yale; and, while I did not disclose my purpose, I resolved to go South as soon as I was through college and commence my chosen life-work. In keeping with this design, I kept posted on every phase of the so-called "Negro problem"; I made it my constant study. When I had finished college I made application to the Union Missionary Association for a position as teacher in one of their Negro schools in a town in Georgia, and after the usual preliminaries I received my certificate of appointment.

It was June, 1906, the year that dirigible airships first came into actual use, after the innumerable efforts of scores of inventors to solve final problems, which for a long time seemed insurmountable. Up to this time the automobile – now relegated to commercial uses, or, like the bicycle, to the poorer classes – had been the favored toy of the rich, and it was thought that the now common one hundred and one hundred and fifty horse-power machines were something wonderful and that their speed – a snail's pace, compared with the airship – was terrific. It will be remembered that inside of a few months after the first really successful airships appeared a wealthy man in society could hardly have hoped to retain his standing in the community without owning one, or at least proving that he had placed an order for one with a fashionable foreign manufacturer, so great was the craze for them, and so widespread was the industry – thanks to the misfortune of the poor devil who solved the problem and neglected to protect his rights thoroughly. Through this fatal blunder on his part, their manufacture and their use became world-wide, almost at once, in spite of countless legal attempts to limit the production, in order to keep up the cost.

A wealthy friend of mine had a ship of the finest Parisian make, the American machines still being unfashionable, in which we had often made trips together and which he ran himself. As I was ready to go to my field of labor, he invited me to go with him to spend from Saturday to Sunday in the City of Mexico, which I had never seen, and I accepted.

We started, as usual, from the new aërial pier at the foot of West Fifty-ninth Street, New York City, then one of the wonders of the world, about one o'clock, in the midst of a cloud of machines bound for country places in different parts of the United States and we were peacefully seated after dinner, enjoying the always exhilarating sensation of being suspended in space without support – for my friend had drawn the covering from the floor of clear glass in the car, which was coming into use in some of the new machines – when there was a terrific report. The motor had exploded!

We looked at each other in horror. This indeed was what made air-travelling far-and-away the most exciting of sports. Human beings had not yet come to regard with indifference accidents which occurred in mid-air.

My friend picked his way through a tangled mass of machinery to the instruments. We were rising rapidly and the apparatus for opening the valve of the balloon was broken. Without saying a word, he started to climb up the tangle of wire ropes to the valve itself; a very dangerous proceeding, because many of the ropes were loosened from their fastenings. We suddenly encountered a current of air that changed our course directly east. (We had been steering south and had gone about six hundred miles.) It drew us up higher and higher. I glanced through the floor but the earth was almost indistinguishable, and was disappearing rapidly. There was absolutely nothing that I could do. I looked up again at my friend, who was clambering up rather clumsily, I remember thinking at the moment. The tangle of ropes and wires looked like a great grape vine. Just then the big ship gave a lurch. He slipped and pitched forward, holding on by one hand. Involuntarily, I closed my eyes for a moment. When I opened them again, *he was gone*!

My feelings were indescribable. I commenced to lose consciousness, owing to the altitude and the ship was ascending more rapidly every moment.

Finally I became as one dead.

Chapter II
To Earth Again – One Hundred Years Later

ONE DAY an archaic-looking flying machine, a curiosity, settled from aërial heights on to the lawn of one Dr. Newell, of Phœnix, Georgia.

When found I was unconscious and even after I had revived I could tell nothing of my whereabouts, as to whither I was going, or whence I had come; I was simply there, "a stranger in a strange land," without being able to account for anything.

I noticed however that the people were not those I had formerly left or that I expected to see. I was bewildered – my brain was in a whirl – I lapsed again into a trance-like state.

When I regained my full consciousness I found myself comfortably ensconced in a bed in an airy room apparently in the home of some well-to-do person. The furniture and decorations in the room were of a fashion I had never seen before, and the odd-looking books in the bookcase near the bed were written by authors whose names I did not know. I seemed to have awakened from a dream, a dream that had gone from me, but that had changed my life.

Looking around in the room, I found that I was the only occupant. I resolved to get up and test the matter. I might still be dreaming. I arose, dressed myself – my suit case lay on a table, just as I had packed it – and hurriedly went downstairs, wondering if I were a somnambulist and thinking I had better be careful lest I fall and injure myself. I heard voices and attempted to speak and found my voice unlike any of those I heard in the house. I was just passing out of the front door, intending to walk around on the large veranda that extended on both sides of the house, when I came face to face with a very attractive young lady who I subsequently learned was the niece of my host and an expert trained nurse. She had taken charge of me ever since my unexpected arrival on her uncle's lawn.

She explained that she had been nursing me and seemed very much mortified that I should have come to consciousness at a moment when she was not present, and have gotten out of the room and downstairs before she knew it. I could see chagrin in her countenance and to reassure her I said, "You needn't worry about your bird's leaving the cage, he shall not fly away, for in the first place he is quite unable to, and in the second place why should he flee from congenial company?"

"I am glad you are growing better," she said, "and I am sure we are all very much interested in your speedy recovery, Mr. – What shall I call you?" she said hesitatingly.

I attempted to tell her my name, but I could get no further than, "My name is—" I did not know my own name!

She saw my embarrassment and said, "O, never mind the name, I'll let you be my anonymous friend. Tell me where you got that very old flying machine?"

Of course I knew, but I could not tell her. My memory on this point had failed me also. She then remarked further that papers found in my pocket indicated that a Mr. Gilbert Twitchell had been appointed to a position as teacher in a Missionary School in the town of Ebenezer, Georgia, in the year 1906, and inquired if these "old papers" would help me in locating my friends. She left me for a moment and returned with several papers, a diary and a large envelope containing a certificate of appointment to said school.

She stated that inquiry had already been made and that "old records" showed that a person by the name of Twitchell had been appointed in 1906, according to the reading of the certificate, and that while *en route* to his prospective field of labor in an air-ship he was supposed to have come to an untimely death, as nothing had been seen or heard of him since. Further than that the official records did not go.

"Now, we should be very glad to have you tell us how you came by that certificate," she suggested.

I was aghast. I was afraid to talk to her or to look about me. And the more fully I came to myself the more I felt that I did not dare to ask a question. The shock of one answer might kill me.

I summoned all my strength, and spoke hurriedly, more to prevent her speaking again than to say anything.

"Perhaps I can tell you something later on," I said hoarsely. "I find my memory quite cloudy, in fact, I seem to be dreaming."

She saw my misery and suggested that I go into "the room used to cure nervousness" and that I remain as long as possible. I passed stupidly through the door she held open for me and had hardly sat down before I felt soothed. The only color visible was violet, – walls, ceiling, furniture, carpet, all violet of different shades. An artificial light of the same color filled the room. And the air! – What was there in it?

A desk was at the other end of the large apartment. As my eyes roved about the strange looking place I saw on it an ordinary calendar pad, the only thing in the room that closely resembled objects I had seen before. The moment that I realized what it was I felt as though I was about to have a nervous chill. I dared not look at it, even from that distance. But the delicious air, the strength-giving light revived me in spite of myself. For full five minutes I sat there, staring, before starting over to look at it; for though I knew not who I was, and though I had passed through only two rooms of the house, and had met only one person, I had divined the truth a thousand times.

As I slowly neared it I saw the day of the month, the twenty-fourth. Nearer and nearer I came, finally closing my eyes as the date of the year in the corner became *almost* legible – just as I had done in the car of the air-ship, that awful moment. I moved a little nearer. I could read it now! I opened my eyes and glanced, then wildly tore the pads apart, to see if they were all alike – and fell to the floor once more.

It was the year *two thousand and six*, just one hundred years from the date of my appointment to the position of a teacher in the South!

In a short time I regained complete consciousness, and under the influence of that wonderful room became almost myself again. I learned that I had not really been left alone but had been observed, through a device for that purpose, by both the doctor and his niece, and on her return I related my whole story to her as far as I could then remember it.

The strangest and most unaccountable part was that though I had been away from the earth about one hundred years, yet, here I was back again still a young man, showing no traces of age and I had lived a hundred years. This was afterward accounted for by the theory that at certain aerial heights the atmosphere is of such a character that no physical changes take place in bodies permitted to enter it.

The physical wants of my body seemed to have been suspended, and animation arrested until the zone of atmosphere immediately surrounding the earth was reached again, when gradually life and consciousness returned.

I have no recollection of anything that transpired after I lost consciousness and the most I can say of it all is that the experience was that of one going to sleep at one end of his journey and waking up at his destination.

Chapter III
At the Public Library with Irene

THE NEXT TIME I met my nurse was by chance. I saw her at the public library near Dr. Newell's house, where I often went to sit and think the first few days after my rebirth into the world. She had left the Newell residence on the night of the day she had put me in the violet room, being called to some special duty elsewhere. I approached her with a kindly salutation which she reciprocated in a manner indicating that she was pleased to meet me. In the meantime I had found out her name – Irene Davis – and had also found out that an elective course in a training school for scientific nursing was according to the custom of the times, which regarded such a course as indispensable to the education of a liberally trained young woman.

Our conversation drifted along as to my personal comforts until I told her that I had heard that I was to be called upon to deliver a written account of my recollections of the past, especially in reference to the Negro question.

"I suppose Dr. Newell is at the bottom of that," she remarked, "he is so intensely interested in the Negro question that he would be the first one to make the suggestion. I really believe that he refused to allow you to be taken to the City Hospital when you were found on his lawn because he almost divined that you might have a message from another age for him on that subject. The city authorities yielded to his wishes and assigned me to assist in caring for you at his residence, instead of at the hospital.

"I found very little to do, however, but would like to recall to you the beneficial effects of the violet room, which I see had the desired results. It always does, and many people who can afford it, especially physicians, are now installing these rooms in their houses for the benefit of neurotic patients, on whom the violet rays of electricity, coupled with neurium, a newly discovered chemical preparation, similar to radium, has a most remarkable effect."

I remarked that I had taken no medicine and really felt better than ever in either of my lives.

"Well," said she, laughing, "I trust you may be able to recall all about the past and give a most excellent account of it in your paper for the Bureau of Public Utility – and don't fail to send me a copy!"

"Are you at all interested in the question," I asked.

"All Southerners are interested in that question. I am a teacher in a Sunday School for Negro children and a member of a Young Ladies' Guild which was organized expressly for reaching Negro children that may need help. We visit the families and talk with the parents, impress on them ideas of economy, direct them in caring for the sick, and instruct them in the most scientific methods of sanitation. I am really fond of these people and the happiest moments of my life are spent with them – they are of a different temperament from us, so mild and good natured, – so complacent and happy in their religious worship and their music is simply enchanting! – Don't you like to hear them sing, Mr. Twitchell?"

I remarked that I was very fond of their singing, and that I had been delighted with a visit I had recently made to the Dvorak Conservatory, where the Negro's musical talent seemed to have been miraculously developed.

I further remarked, to myself, "How congenial in tastes and sympathy we seem to be, and how beautiful you are!" She moved me strangely as she stood there with her black hair, rosy cheeks, large good-natured black eyes, her Venus-like poise of neck and shoulders, and a mouth neither large nor small but full of expression, and showing a wealth of pearls when she laughed – and all this coupled with such noble aspirations, and such deep womanly sympathy.

I said to her, "Miss Davis, I am certainly glad to learn that our sentiments on the Negro question coincide so thoroughly and if any encouragement were needed, I should certainly feel like offering it, as a stimulus in your efforts."

"All humanity needs encouragement," she replied, "and I am human; and so are these people around us who are of a different race. They need encouragement and in my humble way I hope to be of some service to them. Their chances have not been as favorable as ours, but they have been faithful and true with the talents they have."

"So I understand you are assisting in this work more from a sense of duty than as a diversion?" I observed.

"Yes, that is true," she said, "but nevertheless I really get considerable recreation in it. I find these people worthy of assistance and competent to fill many places that they otherwise could not but for the help of our Guild."

"So you have found that success does not always come to the worthy," I suggested, "if those who are worthy have no outside influence? I can remember people who worked hard all their lives for promotion and who not only did not get it, but often witnessed others less skilled and deserving than themselves pushed forward ahead of them. This was especially true of the Negro race in my time. The Negroes were told that Negro ability would sell for as much in the market as white, but while this was encouraging in some respects and true in many cases, it could by no means be laid down as a rule."

"I agree with you," she said, "in part; for the feeling no doubt prevails among some people that the lines of cleavage should move us naturally to do more for our own than for a different race, and that spirit occasionally crops out, but the spirit of helpfulness to Negroes has now become so popular that it permeates all classes and there is practically no opposition to them."

"You are a long way removed from the South of the past," said I, "where to have done such work as you are engaged in would have disgraced you, and have branded you for social ostracism."

She replied that there was no criticism at all for engaging in such work but only for doing more for one race than another.

"You Georgians had degenerated in my day," I remarked. "The Southern colonies under such men as Oglethorpe seemed to have higher ideals than had their descendants of later times. Oglethorpe was opposed to slavery and refused to allow it in the Colony of Georgia while he was governor; he was also a friend to the Indians and to Whitfield in his benevolent schemes, but the Georgian of my day was a different character altogether from the Oglethorpe type. He justified slavery and burned Negroes at the stake, and the 'Cracker class' were a long ways removed from the Oglethorpe type of citizenship, both in appearance and intelligence. I notice, too, Miss Davis, that you never use the words 'colored people' but say 'Negro,' instead."

"That is because these people themselves prefer to be called Negroes. They are proud of the term Negro and feel that you are compromising if you refer to them as 'colored people.'"

"That is quite a change, too," said I, "from the past; for in my time the race did not like the term Negro so well because it sounded so much like 'nigger,' which was a term of derision. I notice that this term also has become obsolete with you – another sign of progress. In fact, I fear that the ideas I had in 1906, when I started on my trip to work as a missionary among the Negroes, would be laughed at now, so far have you progressed beyond me. Indeed, I am quite confused at times in trying to conform to my new conditions."

At this juncture she suggested that she had almost broken an engagement by chatting with me so long, and would have to hurry off to meet it. In taking her departure she remarked that perhaps it was worth while to break an engagement to talk with one who had had so unusual an experience. "I may be quite an unusual character," said I, "but probably too ancient to be of interest to so modern a person as yourself."

She did not reply to this, but left with a smile and a roguish twinkle in her eye.

I found on inquiry at the library that Negroes in the South were now allowed the use of the books, and that they were encouraged to read by various prizes, offered especially for those who could give the best written analyses of certain books which were suggested by the library committee.

Chapter IV
Now and Then

I HAD SCARCELY recovered my equilibrium and become able to give an account of myself before I was formally called on by the "Chief of the Bureau of Public Utility" of the country to make a statement about the Negro problem in my time, Dr. Newell having informed him that I was interested in that subject.

Here follows the substance of what I wrote as I read it over to Dr. Newell before sending it:

"Many changes considered well nigh impossible one hundred years ago have taken place in almost all phases of the so-called Negro problem. One of the most noticeable instances to me is the absence of slurs at individual Negroes and at the race as a whole in your newspapers. Such headlines as 'Another Coon Caught,' 'The Burly Black Brute Foiled,' 'A Ham Colored Nigger in the Hen House' and 'This Coon Wants to be Called Mister,' are, to me, conspicuous by their absence. In the old days, in referring to a Negro who had made a speech of some merit he was called 'Professor,' but in making a reference to him as being connected with politics the same person was dubbed 'Jim' or 'Tom.' Fights between three white men and two Negroes were published, under glaring headlines, as 'Race Riots.' The usual custom of dealing out the vices of the Negro race as a morning sensation in the daily papers evidently fell into 'innocuous desuetude,' and the daily papers having dropped the custom, the weeklies, which were merely echoes of the dailies, also left off the habit, so that now neither the city people nor farmers have their prejudices daily and weekly inflamed by exaggerated portrayals of the Negroes' shortcomings.

"The character of no individual and in fact of no race can long endure in America when under the persistent fire of its newspapers. Newspapers mould public opinion. Your organization for the dissemination of news has it in its power to either kill or make alive in this respect. Our organization, called the News Distributing Bureau, was formerly in the hands of people whose policy designedly necessitated the portrayal of the Negro in his worst light before the people, in order that certain schemes against the race might be fostered, and seemed to take special delight in publishing every mean act of every bad Negro, and leaving unrecorded the thousands of credible acts of the good ones.

"Like Lincoln's emancipation proclamation, this wholesale assassination of Negro character in the newspapers was strictly a political 'war measure,' intended for political use only. Its design was to prejudice the race in the eyes of the world and thus enable the white supremacy advocates, North and South, to perfect the political annihilation of the Negro. The Negro farmer knew little about what was going on; he was making corn and cotton, and to tell him in public assemblies would be considered 'incendiary,' and 'stirring up strife between the races,' and the individual who might be thus charged would certainly have to leave 'between two suns,' as the phrase was. However, the general desire among leading Negroes was for peace at any sacrifice, and they studiously labored to that end. The South ought to have thanked the Negro preachers and the Negro school teachers for the reign of peace in that section, because it was due almost wholly to their efforts.

"Then, too, the public schools, which were at that period the boast of the South, in support of her contention of friendliness to the Negro, served the purpose of quieting many a Negro who might otherwise have been disposed to 'talk too much.' [1] Be it remembered that at this time it was considered virtually a social crime to employ a Negro as a clerk in a store or elsewhere. This feeling extended from Delaware to Texas, and the thousands of Negroes who were coming out of the various public schools, and the institutions for higher training established by Northern philanthropists, had practically no calling open to them, as educated men and women, save that of teaching. The door of hope was shut in their face and they were censured for not doing better under such impossible handicaps. It was like closing the stable door and whipping the horse for not going in! A few entered the professions of law, pharmacy and medicine, some engaged in business, but no great number for the following reasons:

"First – In the professions the white professional man was by habit and custom very generally employed by the colored people, while the colored professional man, by the conventional laws of society, was rarely or never employed by white people.

"Second – The natural disposition of the colored people to patronize white merchants and professional men in preference to their own was a factor to be reckoned with in looking for the *causas rerum* – a kind of one-sided arrangement whereby the whites got the Negroes' money but the Negroes could not get theirs – in the professions. In many of the small lines of business, however, the Negro was patronized by the whites.

"So that – with the News Bureau making capital every morning of the corruption in the race; with the efforts of Southern ministers who had taken charge of Northern pulpits, to strew seeds of poison by proclaiming, on the commission of every offense by a Negro, 'We told you that the Negro was not worth the freedom you gave him,' 'We told you he wasn't fit for citizenship and that the money you have spent for his education is worse than wasted;' with the constant assertions that his only place is 'behind a mule,' that education made him a greater criminal, that 'the Southern people are his best friends' because 'we overlook his follies' and 'treat him kindly if he will stay in his place;' with the money interests clamoring for the South 'to be let alone' with the Negro question, for fear of unsettling business and causing a slump in Southern securities; with the claims that, to keep the railroads earning dividends, to keep the cotton market active, the Negro must be handled according to the serfdom or shotgun plan, and that the best task master so far found was the Southern white man, who had proven himself wonderfully adept in getting good crops from Negro labor – with these and many other excuses, the question of raising the Negro in the scale of civilization was left to posterity.

"'What is he worth to us now?' That is the only question with which we are concerned, was the ruling thought, if not the open confession.

"Let it be understood that statistics (which the Negro did not compile) showed that the race at that time was, as a mass, the most illiterate, the least thrifty, and the most shiftless and criminal of any class of American citizens – dividing the population into natives – Irish emigrants, German emigrants, Italians, Jews, and Poles. This was a fact that hurt, regardless of who was responsible for it.

"Then the question of color cut no small figure in this problem. The Negro's color classified him; it rang the signal bell for drawing 'the color line' as soon as he was seen, and it designated and pointed him out as a marked man, belonging to that horrible criminal class whose revolting deeds were revealed every day in the newspapers. No wonder he was shunned, no wonder the children and women were afraid of him! The great mass of the people took the newspaper reports as true. They never read between the lines and seldom read the corrections of errors[2] that had been made. In some cases the first report had been that a Negro had committed a crime, and later it was discovered that a white man with his face blacked had been the perpetrator. Some one has said, 'Let me write the songs of a people and I will control their religious sentiments.' In a country like America where the newspapers are so plentiful and where people rely on them so implicitly, those who control the newspapers may be said to control the views of the people on almost any public question. With 30 per cent of the Negro population illiterate, with a criminal record double that of any of the emigrant classes above outlined, with the News Distributing Bureau against it, with no political or social standing – pariahs in the land – with Northern capital endorsing serfdom, with their inability to lose their race identity, on account of their color – we realize how heavy the odds were against the Negro race at that time.

"As a Negro orator once put it, 'De Southern white man's on top'er de nigger and de Yankee white man's on top er de Southern white man and de bad nigger's on top er dem bofe!'

"I now come to some of the proposed solutions of the problem. Various meetings were held all over the country to discuss the Negro problem, and many a mediocre white man who thirsted for a little newspaper notoriety, or political preferment, in both the North and the South, had his appetite in this direction satisfied by writing or saying something on the Negro question. One Thomas Dixon tried to out Herod Herod in taking up the exceptional cases of Negro criminality and using them in an attempt to convince his readers of the Negro's unfitness for citizenship. A public speaker named John Temple Graves[3] made lecture tours advocating deportation as the only solution of the problem, rejecting as unsound the theories of Booker Washington, who was advocating industrial education as the main factor in solving the problem, because of the consequent clash that would arise between white and colored mechanics – rejecting also as unsound the theory of higher education; because that would develop in the Negro a longing for equality which the white man would not give and was never known to give an inferior race, a statement which all honest white people must regard as a base slander upon their Christianity.

"Bishop Turner, senior bishop of the African Methodist-Episcopal Church, one of the leading organizations of the Negro race, also advocated emigration to Africa as the only solution of the problem, on the grounds that the white people would never treat the Negro justly and that history furnished no instance where a slave race had ever become absolutely free in the land of its former owners, instancing that to be free the Jews had to leave Egypt; that William the Conqueror and his followers slaughtered the native Britons, rather than attempt to carry out what seemed to them an impossible task, that of teaching two races, a conquered race and a conquering one, to live side by side in peace.

"One Professor Bassett made enemies of the Southern newspapers and politicians by proposing *justice* and *equality* as a solution of the problem. The 'most unkindest cut of all' of Professor Bassett's saying was that Booker Washington was 'the greatest man, save Robert E. Lee, that the South had produced in a hundred years.' The politicians and their sympathizers seized upon this statement as being a good opportunity to keep up the discussion of the Negro issue, which many better disposed people were hoping would be dropped, according to promise, as soon as the Negroes had been deprived of the ballot by the amendments then being added to the constitutions of the Southern States. They rolled it over as a sweet morsel under their tongues. 'Othello's occupation,' they realized, would be gone without the 'nigger in the wood pile.' The politicians disfranchised the Negro to get rid of his vote, which was in their way, and they kept the Negro scarecrow bolstered up for fear that the whites might divide and that the Negro might then come back into possession of the ballot.

"The politicians proposed no measures of relief for the great mass of ignorance and poverty in their midst. The modicum of school appropriations was wrung from them, in some instances, by the threats of the better element of the people. They were obstructionists rather than constructionists. One Benjamin Tillman boasted on the floor of the United States Senate that in his state he kept the Negroes 'in their place' by the use of the shot-gun, in defiance of law and the constitution, and that he expected to keep it up. If left alone, the feeling against Negroes would have subsided to some extent and mutual helpfulness prevailed, but the politicians had to have an issue, even at the sacrifice of peace between the races and at the expense of a loss of labor in many sections where it was once plentiful – as many Negroes left for more liberal states, where they not only received better wages but also better treatment. The Southern farmer and business man was paying a dear price for office holders when he stood by the politicians and allowed them to run off Negro labor, by disfranchisement and political oppression. It was paying too much for a whistle of that quality.

"Many Negroes thought, with Bishop Turner and John Temple Graves, that emigration was the solution of the problem; not necessarily emigration from the United States, but emigration individually to states where public sentiment had not been wrought up against them. But the Negro, owing to his ignorance, and also to his affection for the land of his birth, and on account of a peculiar provincialism that narrowed his scope of vision of the world and its opportunities, could not bring himself to leave the South, so far as the great mass was concerned. Then, too, he had been told that the Yankees would not treat him like the Southerner, and Southern newspapers took especial pains to publish full details of all the lynchings that occurred in the North and make suggestive comments on them, in which they endeavored to show that the whole country was down on the Negro, and that while in the South the whites lynched only the one Negro against whom they had become enraged, in the North they mobbed and sought to drive out *all* the Negroes in the community where the crime had been committed. (The two clippings below occurred in the same issue of a Southern paper and showed how, while the North was mobbing a Negro, the South was honoring one.) [4]

"Instances of white mechanics North who were refusing to work with Negroes, and instances of Northern hotels refusing them shelter were also made the most of and served the purpose of deterring Negro emigration from the Southern States. Frequently some Negro was brought home dead, or one who had contracted disease in the North came home and died. These occurrences were also used as object lessons and had their effect.

"In fact, the Southern white people did not want the Negroes to leave. They wanted them as domestics, on the farm, and as mechanics. They knew their value as such. 'Be as intelligent, as capable as you may but acknowledge my superiority,' was the unspoken command.

"Many individual Negroes acted on this suggestion and by shrewd foresight managed to accumulate considerable property, and so long as they 'minded their own business,' and 'stayed out of politics' they did well, and had strong personal friends among the white people. Their property rights were recognized to a very large extent, in fact the right of Negroes to hold property was very generally conceded. This was true even to the extent, in several instances, of causing reimbursement for those who were run away from their homes by mobs. In some states laws were passed giving damages to the widows of those who were lynched by mobs, said damages to be paid by the county in which the lynching occurred. In fact the South had long since discovered the Negro's usefulness and the feeling against him partook more of political persecution than race hatred. The paradoxical scheme of retaining six million Negroes in the population with all the rights and duties of citizenship, less social and political standing, was the onus of the problem in the South. Such a scheme as this was bound to breed more or less persecution and lawlessness, as did the slave system. It was a makeshift at best, and though in the main, honestly undertaken, it was impossible of performance.

"The Southern people seemed to have no objection to personal contact with Negroes in a servile capacity. Many Negro women made their living as 'wet nurses,' and the Southern 'black mammy' had become stereotyped. Then, too, the large number of mulatto children everywhere was some evidence of personal contact, on the part of the men. Negro servants swarmed around the well-to-do Southern home, cooked the food and often slept with the children; the Southerner shook hands with his servants on his return home from a visit and was glad to see them; but if any of these servants managed by industry and tact to rise to higher walks of life, it became necessary, according to the unwritten law, to break off close relations. Yet, in the great majority of cases, the interest and good feeling remained, if the Negro did not become too active politically – in which case he could expect 'no quarter.'

"The subject of lynching became very serious. This evil custom, for a while, seemed to threaten the whole nation. While Negroes were the most common victims, yet the fever spread like a contagion to the lynching of white criminals as well.

"At first it was confined to criminals who committed assaults on women, and to brutal murderers, but it soon became customary to lynch for the slightest offense, so that no man's life was safe if he was unfortunate enough to have had a difficulty with some individual, who had friends enough to raise a mob at night who would go with him to the house of his victim, call him out, and either shoot, or unmercifully beat him. The refusal of the officers of the law to crush out this spirit in its embryonic stage resulted in its growing to such enormous proportions that they found, too late, that they could neither manage nor control it. The officers themselves were afraid of the lynchers.

"The method of lynching Negroes was usually by hanging or by burning at the stake, sometimes in the presence of thousands of people, who came in on excursion trains to see the sight, and, possibly, carry off a trophy consisting of a finger joint, a tooth or a portion of the victim's heart. If the lynching was for a crime committed against a woman, and she could be secured, she was consigned to the task of starting the flames with her own hands. This was supposed to add to the novelty of the occasion. [5]

"'Why did not the Negro offer some resistance to these outrages?' you may ask.

"That question, no doubt, is often propounded by those who read of the horrors of this particular period. Different theories are advanced. One is that the Negro was overawed by numbers and resources – that he saw the uselessness of any such attempt. Another theory is that during the whole history of Negro slavery in this country there occurred only one or two rebellions worthy of the name. One was the 'Nat Turner Insurrection' in Southampton County, Virginia, in 1831. This was soon put down and the ringleader hung, together with several of his misguided followers. So it must be concluded, since the Negro bore two hundred and fifty years of slavery so patiently, and made only a few feeble attempts to liberate himself, that he is not naturally of a rebellious nature – that he easily fits into any place you put him, and with the fatalistic tendency of all barbaric races, except the Indian, makes the best of circumstances. It is possibly true that the Negro would be a slave among us to-day if some one else had not freed him. The sentiment, 'He who would be free must first himself strike the blow,' did not appeal to him.

"Another reason cited for the Negro's submission so long to oppression both before and since the American Civil War of 1860 to 1865 was his inability to organize. The white man learned this art by thousands of years of experience and of necessary resistance for the protection of those rights which he holds most dear. The Negroes were never able to make any concerted movement in their own behalf. They clashed too easily with one another and any individual would swamp the ship, as it were, to further his own scheme. The 'rule or ruin' policy prevailed and the necessity of the subordination of individuality for the good of the whole was lost in a storm of personal aggrandizement whenever an attempt was made at anything bordering on Negro national organization. This was one of the fruits of slavery, which encouraged jealousy and bickering. Several religious organizations had a successful existence for some time and quite a number of business and benevolent enterprises, but in politics all was chaos. The Negroes cast their ballots one way all of the time; it was known just as well ten years before an election how they would vote, as it was after the ballots were counted. No people of political calibre like that could measure arms with the white man politically; his rebelling in such a condition would have been preposterous. The Negro took his cue in matters of race policy from his white friends – he did not fight until the signal was given by them. No Negro gained any national reputation without first having been recognized by the white race, instead of his own. The Negroes recognized their leaders after the whites picked them out – not before.

"The Negro nature at this time was still a pliable one, after many years of drill training, but it was much more plastic in the days of slavery, and for the first forty years after reconstruction. The master labored to subordinate the will of the slave to his own, to make him like clay in the hands of the potter. In this he had an eye to business. The nearer the slave approached the horse, in following his master's guidance, the nearer perfect he was, and this lesson of putting himself absolutely at the mercy of his master was thoroughly learned, and it was learned easily because there seemed to exist a natural instinctive awe on the part of the Negro for the white man. He had that peculiar fondness for him that the mule has for the horse. You can mount one horse and lead a thousand mules, without bit or bridle, to the ends of the earth.

"The Negro sought to please his master in all things. He had a smile for his frowns and a grin for his kicks. No task was too menial, if done for a white master – he would dance if he was called upon and make sport of the other Negroes, and even pray, if need be, so he could laugh at him. He was trustworthy to the letter, and while occasionally he might help himself to his master's property on the theory of a common ownership, yet woe be unto the other Negro that he caught tampering with his master's goods! He was a 'tattler' to perfection, a born dissembler

– a diplomat and a philosopher combined. He was past grand master in the art of carrying his point when he wanted a 'quarter' or fifty cents. He knew the route to his master's heart and pocketbook and traveled it often. He simply made himself so obliging that he could not be refused! It was this characteristic that won him favor in the country from college president down to the lowest scullion. Had he been resentful and vindictive, like the Indian, he would have been deported or exterminated long since.

"The Negro's usefulness had also bound him to the South. The affection that the master and mistress had for the slave was transmitted in the blood of their children.

> *"As unto the bow the cord is,*
> *So unto the man is woman,*
> *Though she bends him, she obeys him,*
> *Though she draws him, yet she follows;*
> *Useless each without the other,"*

applied to the relations between the Negro and his white master. In the Civil War between the states, many a slave followed his master to the front. Here he was often the only messenger to return home. He bore the treasured watch, or ring, or sword, of the fallen soldier, and broke the sad news to the family; and there were black tears as well as white ones spilled on such occasions.

"The white males went to the war leaving the family and farm in charge of the blacks thereon. They managed everything, plowed, sowed, reaped, and sold, and turned over all returns to the mistress. They shared her sorrows and were her protection.

When Union soldiers came near, the trusted blacks were diligent in hiding property from the thieves and bummers of the army. They carried the horses to the woods and hid them in the densest swamps, they buried the jewelry and silver and gold plate; they secreted their young mistresses and the members of the family where they could not be found, and not one instance was there ever heard of improper conduct, out of a population of nearly four million slaves; in spite of the fact that the war was being maintained by their masters for the perpetuation of the shackles of slavery on themselves! The Negro was too fond of his master's family to mistreat them, he felt almost a kinship to them. The brutes of later days came from that class of Negroes who had been isolated from the whites, on the quarters of large plantations.

"Was there ever a more glorious record? Did ever a race deserve more fully the affection of another race than these southern Negroes, and did not we owe it to their descendants to save them from both deportation and serfdom?

"You ask, 'Why was it that after the war there was so much race prejudice, in the face of all these facts?'

"The answer to that question is fraught with much weight and bears strongly on the final solution of the Negro problem. The friends of the Negro had this question to battle with from the beginning, for the enemies of the race used every weapon at hand in the long and terrible fight against Negro citizenship.

"To begin with, I will state that after the war the Negro became a free citizen and a voter – he was under no restraint. His new condition gave him privileges that he had never had before; it was not unnatural that he should desire to exercise them. His attempts to do so were resisted by the native whites, but his vote was needed by the white men who had recently come into the South to make it their home – and to get office – and also for his own protection. It was necessary that he should vote to save himself from many of the harsh laws that were being proposed at the time. Some of them were that a Negro should not own land, that a Negro's testimony was incompetent in the courts, that a Negro should not keep firearms for his defense, that he should not engage in business without paying a high and almost prohibitive tax, that he must hire himself out on a farm in January or be sold to the highest bidder for a year, the former owner to have the preference in bidding.

"These laws were unwisely urged by those whites who did not desire to accept the consequences of the war. To make the laws effective, it was thought necessary by their advocates to suppress the Negro voters; for, if they were allowed to vote, there were so many of them, and so many of the whites had been disfranchised because of participation in the war, that defeat was certain. Here is where the bitterness, which for a long time seemed to curse our country, had its origin. The Negroes and their friends were lined up on one side and their opponents on the other.

"The 'Ku Klux Klan' was a secret organization whose purpose was to frighten and intimidate Negroes and thus prevent their voting. It had branch organizations in the different Southern states during the reconstruction period. When the members went out on raids, they wore disguises; some had false heads with horns and long beards, some represented his satanic majesty, some wore long gowns, others wrapped themselves in sheets of different colors, and all sorts of hideous shapes and forms, with masks representing the heads of different animals, such as goats, cows and mules. They proceeded on the principle of using mild means first, but when that failed, they did not hesitate to resort to harsher methods. The object seemed to be only to so frighten Negroes that they would not attempt to vote. But in carrying out this scheme they often met resistance, whereupon many outrages were perpetrated upon people who made a stand for their rights under the law of the land. In obstinate cases and toward the end of their careers "klans" would visit Negro cabins at night and terrify the inmates by whipping them, hanging them up by their thumbs, and sometimes killing them. Many Negroes who assumed to lead among their people were run from one county into another. Some were run out of their states, and even white men who led the Negroes in thickly settled Negro counties were driven out.

"The story was told of one case where a white man named Stephens, the recognized political leader of the Negroes as well as a few whites, in one of the states, was invited into one of the lower rooms of the courthouse of his county while a political meeting by his opponents was in progress above, and there told he must agree to leave the county and quit politics or be killed then and there.

He refused to do either, whereupon two physicians, with others who were present, tied him, laid him on a table and opened his jugular veins and bled him to death in buckets provided for the occasion. Meanwhile the stamping of feet and the yelling above, where the speaking was going on, was tremendous, being prearranged to deaden any outcry that he might make. It is said that Stephens's last words before he was put on the table were a request that he might go to the window and take a final look at his home, which was only a few rods away. This was granted, and as he looked his wife passed out of the house and his children were playing in the yard. Stephens's dead body was found by a Negro man who suspected something wrong and climbed to the window of the room in search for him.

"Such acts as these spread terror among the Negro population, as well as bad feeling, and dug a wide political pit between the Negro and the Democratic party which organized these methods of intimidation.[6] The 'Ku Klux Klan' was finally annihilated by the strong hand of President Grant, who filled the South with sufficient militia to suppress it. A favorite means of evading the arrests made by the militia was to have the prisoners released on *habeas corpus* by the native judges. To stop this the writ of *habeas corpus* was suspended by some of the provisional governors. One governor who did this was impeached by the Democratic party when it returned to power and he died broken hearted, without the removal of his disabilities. You can easily see from these facts how the political differences between the Negro and the Democratic party arose."

Here my paper ended. When I had read it over to Dr. Newell, he rose and went over to his desk, saying,

"While looking over some old papers belonging to my grandfather, I found the following article inside of an old book. On it is a statement that it was written in the year 1902 and republished in 1950. I have often desired to get at the true status of this question, and when I found this my interest was doubly aroused. The so-called Negro problem was truly a most crucial test of the foundation principles of our government a century ago, and I feel proud of my citizenship in so great a country when I reflect that we have come through it all with honor and that finally truth has won out and we are able at last to treat the Negro with justice and humanity, according to the principles of Christianity! This problem tested our faith as with fire."

He handed me the article, and gave his attention to other matters until I had read it:

"Reconstruction and Negro Government

"In the ten years culminating with the decade ending in 1902, the American Negroes have witnessed well nigh their every civil right invaded. They commenced the struggle as freemen in 1865; at the close of the civil war both races in the South began life anew, under changed conditions – neither one the slave of the other, except in so far as he who toils, as Carlyle says, is slave to him who thinks. Under the slave system the white man had been the thinker and the Negro the toiler. The idea that governed both master and slave was that the slave should have no will but that of his master.

"The fruits of this system began to ripen in the first years of freedom, when the Negro was forced to think for himself. For two hundred and forty years his education and training had been directed towards the suppression of his will. He was fast becoming an automaton. He was taught religion to some extent, but a thoughtless religion is little better than mockery and this it must have been when even to read the Bible in some states was a crime. It is, therefore, not surprising that freedom's new suit fitted the recently emancipated slave uncomfortably close; he hardly knew which way to turn for fear he would rend a seam. Consultation with his former owners was his natural recourse in adjusting himself to new conditions.

"In North Carolina a meeting was called at the capital of the state by the leading colored men, and their former masters, and the leading white men were invited to come forward, to take the lead and to tell them what was best for them to do. It is a lamentable fact that the thinking white men did not embrace this opportunity to save their state hundreds of lives that were afterwards sacrificed during reconstruction. Many other evils of the period, might have been thus averted. It was a fatal blunder that cost much in money and blood, and, so far as North Carolina is concerned, if the Negroes in reconstruction were misled it was the fault of those who were invited and refused this opportunity to take hold and direct them properly.

"The Negro, turned from the Southern white man's refusal, followed such leaders as he could find. In some instances these proved to be corrupt camp followers, in others ambitious and unscrupulous Southern men who made the Negroes stepping stones to power or pelf. The Negroes of the state received very little of the honor or harvest of

reconstruction, but very much of dishonor, and they are now charged with the sins both of omission and commission of that period. A pliant tool he may have been in the hands of demagogues, yet in the beginning he sought the leadership of wise men. In this he showed a noble purpose which at least relieves him – whatever was charged to his account afterwards – of the charge of malicious intent.

"Here is a list of prominent white leaders in North Carolina who controlled the ship of state for the first ten years after the war, from 1869 to 1876:

"Wm. E. Rodman (Southern white), Judge Dick (Southern white), W. W. Holden, Governor (Southern white), Byron Baffin (Southern white), Henry Martindale (Ohio white), Gen'l Ames (Northern), G. Z. French, legislator (Maine), Dr. Eugene Grissom, Superintendent Insane Asylum Raleigh, North Carolina (Southern white), Tyre York, legislator and party leader (Southern white), Governor Graham (Southern white), Judge Brooks (Southern white), S. J. Carrow (Southern white).

"This list shows that those who had the reins of government in hand were not Negroes. The truth is, that if the team went wrong the fault was that of the white drivers and not that of the Negro passengers who, to say the most, had only a back seat in the wagon of state.

"But the enemies of Negro suffrage and advocates of the mistakes of reconstruction avow that the sway of reconstruction demagoguery could never have prevailed but for Negro suffrage; that had the Negro not been a voter he could never have been made the tool of demagogues. This is obvious but the argument is sufficiently met by the fact that the Negroes offered the brain and culture of the South the opportunity of taking charge of affairs. Instead of doing so they stiffened their necks against Negro suffrage, the Howard Amendment, and the other propositions of the government at Washington, looking towards the reconstruction of the lately seceded states. If there had been less resistance there would have been less friction, but the South had its own ideas of how the thing should be done and resisted any others to the point of a revolution which had to be put down by government troops. The government's plans were carried finally at the point of the bayonet, when they might have gone through smoothly, had the Negro's call for Southern leadership been heeded. Had this been done, the 'Ku-Klux' would never have developed. The South came back into the Union, 'overpowered,' it said, 'but not conquered.' So far as the Negro question is concerned that is true but in other matters the South is essentially loyal. Although it came back pledged never to deprive any citizen of his rights and privileges 'on account of color or previous condition of servitude,' it is now engaged in a bold and boasting attempt to do this very thing. Louisiana, Mississippi, Alabama, South Carolina, North Carolina and Virginia have all adopted amendments to their constitutions which practically nullify the Fourteenth and Fifteenth Amendments to the United States Constitution, which the honor of these states was pledged not to do when they were re-admitted into the Union at the close of the war of secession! In Virginia the amendment was established without submitting the question to the popular vote. To secure these amendments in other states, fraud and intimidation is alleged to have been used, and the Southern states that have not amended their constitutions have effected the same results by a system of political jugglery with the Negro's ballots.

"The Southern states seem to live in mortal dread of the Negro with a ballot. They imagine a Pandora's box of evils will open upon them if the Negro is allowed to vote. This feeling arises more from the fact that the whites want the offices than from any other cause. Past experience shows that Negroes have never attempted to *claim all of the offices, even where they did ninety-nine per cent. of the voting. It is a notable fact that in North Carolina during the reconstruction times, when few white men voted and Negroes had a monopoly of the ballot, that white men were put forward for official positions. The same condition existed in the period from 1894 to 1898, during the 'Fusion Movement,' when out of ninety-six counties, each of which had three commissioners elected by the people, only four counties out of the ninety-six had a Negro commissioner; and the commissioners in two-thirds of the counties were elected principally by Negro votes – in many of the eastern counties, almost wholly by them. Out of ninety-six counties the Negroes never demanded a single sheriff or a mayor of a city, town or village. There were a few Negro magistrates in the eastern counties, but always more white ones near by and under a provision of a North Carolina statute any defendant who thinks he cannot get justice before the magistrate in whose court he is summoned for trial, can have his case moved to some other justice.*

"The evils of reconstruction were due to the general demoralization which followed the Civil War, rather than to the Negro. War is 'hell' and so is its aftermath.

"Another pet assertion of the opponents of Negro suffrage is that Negro government is expensive. Those who despair of reaching the American conscience in any other way hope to do so through the pocket argument, commercialism if you please. This argument, like the others, has no facts for a basis. It is a phantom, a delusion and is intended to affect the business element of the North, which people sometimes mistakenly think has more respect for prices than principles.

It will not do, however, to listen to the siren of commercialism whose songs are composed by advocates of Negro disfranchisement. There is method in the spell she would bring upon you, and her story is literally nothing but a song.

"The truth is that during the whole period of the 'Fusion Movement' North Carolina never had a more economical government – taxes then were 93c. on a hundred dollar valuation; taxes now are $1.23. North Carolina six per cent. bonds then sold for $1.10; they now sell for $1.09. The Fusion government made the state penitentiary self-supporting; the white supremacy government has run it into debt to the amount of $50,000. Under the Fusion government, most of the counties paid off their debts and had a surplus in their treasuries for the first time since the war. Under the Fusion government more miles of railroad were built than in any period of the same length before or since, more cotton factories were established; one of them being owned and operated by Negroes. A silk mill operated entirely by Negro labor, from foremen down, was also established. The fees of public officers were cut down about one-third. These are some of the phases of the Fusion government – a government based almost entirely on Negro votes – that the enemies of Negro suffrage do not discuss.

"It is useless to refer to the period of reconstruction to disprove the theory that Negro suffrage would entail an expensive government on the South, when we have the recent experiment in North Carolina before us. For the sake of argument, we might admit that the Negro was unfit for suffrage forty years ago, but that by no means proves that he is unfit now. Forty years of experience under American institutions have taught him many lessons. He is no longer the 'child-man,' as the white supremacy advocates call him. These people are as false in their theories as were the pro-slavery advocates who maintained the absurd proposition that if the Negro was emancipated he would soon perish, for want of sufficient ability to feed and clothe himself. Forty years after emancipation – about as long as Moses was in the wilderness – in spite of these false prophecies, we can now find some of the sons of the prophets fearing and foretelling, not that the Negroes will perish, but that they will outstrip them in the race of life! So the white man in the new constitution is to be allowed to vote on his 'grand-daddy's'[7] merits and the Negro must vote on his own.

"These politicians were afraid to base the right to vote on merit, as they feared the Negro would win.[8] Among these people a Negro has to be twice as smart as a white man to merit the same favors, yet in a recent Civil Service examination in Atlanta 19 Negroes out of 40 passed, while only 26 whites out of 115 succeeded. In an examination of law students by the Supreme Court of North Carolina only 40 per cent. of the whites passed, while 100 per cent. of the colored got licenses. A hundred other illustrations might be made showing the speciousness of the arguments put forth as to Negro incompetency. The fact is that there is no use in arguing such a proposition.

The effort made to suppress the Negro has no just basis. There has simply been a determination to do it, right or wrong. The advocates of white supremacy who watch the current of events, have seen that the decitizenization of the Negro can be accomplished with the shot-gun, without trouble to themselves, and they have accomplished the task. They have asked to be let alone with the Negro problem; they have been let alone since 1876, when the Republican party dropped the Negro question as an issue. Since that time they have been politically tying the Negroes' hands. Realizing his industrial usefulness, the aim has been to eliminate him from politics and at the same time use him as a tax-payer and a producer. The paradoxical task of defining his citizenship as that of one with all the burdens and duties, less the rights and privileges thereof, has been quite successfully performed.

"The white supremacy advocates seem to have selected a propitious period for this work – a time when the Negro's friends in the Republican party are occupied with similar problems in Cuba and the Philippines. 'If the Republicans deny self-government to the Philippines, Porto Rico and Cuba,' inquire the Southerners, 'why haven't we the right to do the same to Negroes? Why allow Negroes in the South to rule and deny the same to Negroes in Hawaii?' are questions they are asking with some force. Whatever else the advocates of white supremacy may lack they are not lacking in shrewdness. Their disfranchising schemes have flaunted themselves under the very nose of the government, and bid it defiance in the National Senate with unmistakable boldness, since the Spanish-American War and the policy growing out of it. However there seems to be a man in the White House who wants to set no example that white supremacy can follow; so far as his indicated policy in dealing with Cuba was concerned, President Roosevelt determined that the black people of Cuba should be free.

"But the subordination of the Negro cannot last, there will always be white people in this country who will believe in his equality before the law. These principles are too firmly entrenched in the hearts of Americans to be utterly subverted. They are the bed rock on which the government was founded – on which the Civil War was maintained. Too much of blood and treasure has been spent now to go backwards. These principles have been established at too great a cost to abandon them so soon. It is true that the white supremacy advocates seem now in control of the situation, but that also seemed true of the advocates of slavery before the war. While the enemies of liberty have always been cunning, yet like all other advocates of false doctrines who get power, they usually abuse it; the South might have held her slaves for many years longer, had she not overstepped *the mark by trying to force the institution on the North. She attempted to extend slavery into new territories, she even attempted to capture her slaves in the streets of anti-slavery cities like Boston, by the Fugitive Slave Law – under the very noses of the abolitionists! Had the pro-slavery people been satisfied with restricted slavery, the abolitionists might have had harder work in dethroning the institution.*

"If the question of lynching had been confined to Negroes guilty of assaults on females some justification might exist, but it has been extended to all crimes; and not satisfied with hanging, burning by slow fire has been substituted, accompanied by stabbing, the cutting off of finger joints, the digging out of eyes, and other torture.

"On the question of civil equality, the 'Jim-crow' system has not sufficed; like the horse leech, they continually call for more. If practiced only in the South it might stand, but an attempt has been made to cover the country, and the President himself must not treat a colored gentleman otherwise than as a scullion – according to the advocates of white supremacy. In their doctrine all Negroes are to be humiliated. This tendency to dictate to others and go to extremes is characteristic, and it means that we may always depend on this class of individuals to go too far, and by over-stepping the mark to turn the country against them.

"If a fool has rope enough the end is easy to see."

After reading the article, I turned to the Doctor, and said, "These statements are essentially correct, according to my recollection of those times, and I will say further that there were grave doubts one hundred years ago as to the permanency of our institutions under the strain of the Negro problem; and no less prominent was the labor agitation or the war between capital and labor. It is a happy realization for me to return to my country and find these questions peaceably adjusted and that the South, which was for a long time considered obdurate on this subject, has led in bringing about this happy solution, in spite of the prophecies of many writers like this one. But the problem I have been laboring with ever since my second advent, as it were, is, how was it all done?

"Well, we Southern people changed our leaders. We took men of noble character; men who appealed to reason and humanity, rather than pandered to the lowest passions of the people," he said.

"Tell me, Dr. Newell, how the labor question was settled and how the labor unions learned to leave off discriminating against Negroes. According to my best recollections the American labor organizations, almost without exception, excluded Negro members."

"Yes," replied Dr. Newell, "that is correct, as I have gleaned from the history of your times, but – as all injustice must – this particular instance followed the fixed rule and finally gave way to truth. Such discriminations were incompatible with the spirit and trend of our government. The labor leaders, however, yielded in the end more from a sense of necessity than of justice to the Negro. As Lincoln said, the nation could not exist half slave and half free, and as Blaine said, in his famous Augusta speech, no imaginary line could continue to divide free labor from serf labor. The labor leaders found, after serious second thought, that it would be better to emancipate Negro labor than to lend their efforts towards keeping it in serfdom. For a long time the labor organizations desired the Negroes deported, as a solution of the problem for themselves alone. They found various influences, especially capital, opposed to this; as one writer put it, 'the Dollar was no respecter of persons and would as soon hop into the hands of a black man, in consideration of the performance of a service, as in those of a white one.' Capital wanted the work done and the man who could do it the cheapest and best was the man that got the Dollar every time. This phase of the question was a constant menace to organized labor, and finally caused a revolution in its tactics. White labor began to see that it would be better to lift the Negro up to the same scale with itself, by admitting him into their organization, than to seek his debasement. If Negroes were in a condition to work for fifty cents per day and would do so, and capital would employ them, then white men must accept the same terms or get no work! This, followed to its last analysis, meant that white laborers must provide for their families and educate their children on fifty cents per day, if the Negroes could do it."

"Did not the South object to the organization of Negro labor?" I asked.

"The Southern people, at first, strongly objected.

"The laboring white people of the South have made serious blunders in their position on the Negro problem, having acted all along on the presumption that the proper solution was to 'keep the Negro down.' Towards this end, they bent their best energies, under the mistaken idea of conserving their own interests, not realizing the all-important fact that as long as there was a large number of Negroes in their midst who would work for only fifty cents per day as above stated, and capital was disposed to employ them, just so long would every laboring white man have to accept the same wages as the Negro.

"The intelligent solution of the problem was found by making the Negro see what his interests were, by taking him into the labor unions, where he could be educated up to an intelligent appreciation of the value of his labor; instead of seeking further to degrade him by oppression, with the consequent result of lowering the white man's scale of wages. Further it has been found that oppression does not oppress when aimed at the Negro – he rather thrives under it. In those communities where he was most oppressed and the hand of every laboring white man seemed to be against him, the Negro thrived and prospered to a marked degree. Oppression simply drives negroes together, they concentrate their trade in their own stores and spend their wages among themselves to a greater extent than otherwise – and thus it more often than otherwise happened, that Negro laborers as a mass, in such communities, lived in better homes, and educated their children better than the white laborers. The eyes of the Southern white laboring men began to see this point and a change of base took place, and now they are and have been for a long time, seeking to elevate the Negro laborer to their own standard to keep him from pulling them down – a most intelligent view of the matter!

"The South had congratulated itself on being free from the strikes and lock-outs caused by organized labor in the North. Their contention was that the Negroes could not act intelligently in any organization, and that serious consequences would certainly follow. But all such predictions failed to materialize after the Negroes were organized. The work of organizing did not stop with their admission into labor unions but courses of instruction were mapped out and competent people were employed to drill the members in the principles of the order; and, so far as possible, in the advanced methods of handling tools. The result was the creation of a much better class of workmen, better wages and better living for all.

"The unions also opened their doors to women in separate meetings. Schools of Domestic Science were established and those who employed servants soon found that they could leave the household and kitchen work to a master-hand. The wives and mothers of employers were emancipated from constantly 'overseeing.' There was a vast difference between the professional domestic servant, who needed only orders, which would be carried out faithfully, and the 'blunderbuss,' who was continually at sea in the absence of the directing hand and mind of her mistress. The Southern people began to recognize the difference, and soon became the firm champions of the new system, and welcomed the new efforts of the labor unions as a blessing rather than a curse."

"But, Doctor, am I to understand that there are no labor problems at all in the country at present?"

"No, not exactly that; organized labor still has its problems, but you must remember that they are not of the same character as those of a hundred years ago. The essentials of life, such as coal, iron, oil and other natural products are now handled by the National Government, and the government is pledged to see to it that labor in the production of these commodities is paid a fair share of the surplus accruing from sales. No attempt at profit is allowed; the management is similar to that of the Post Office Department, which has been conducted from the beginning for the convenience of the people, and not for revenue to the Government. The workmen are paid well and the cost to the consumer is lessened by discarding the profits that formerly went into private purses. We have no more strikes and lock-outs; the chief concern of the labor unions now is to raise their less skillful members to a higher standard (for a long time this effort was especially directed toward the Negro members), and to assist those who, because of infirmity and disease, find themselves incapacitated for further service. It may be well said that the problem of 'wherewithal shall we be clothed' is solved in this country, so far as organized labor is concerned, and more time is now left for the perfection of skill and individual improvement."

"A delightful situation, as compared with the past as I recollect it to be," I remarked – "when labor was paid barely enough to live on, while enormous wealth was being accumulated in the hands of a few fortunate people who happened to be born into opportunities – or, better still, born rich.

"As I remember the past, the laboring people in coal and iron mines earned barely enough for subsistence and their hours of toil were so long that anything like self-improvement was impossible. They were in a continual row with their employers, who revelled in luxury and rebelled against a 10 per cent. increase in wages, and who in many instances, rather than pay it, would close down the mines until their workmen were starved into submission. I never could reconcile myself to the logic of the principle that it was lawful for capital to thus oppress labor. I think the legal maxim of *sic utere tuo ut alienum non laedas* (so use your own as not to injure another) applies with force in this instance. The application of it is usually made in suits for damages, where one person has injured another by negligence. But the force of the maxim is applicable to capital as well, and he who would use money (though in fact it be *legally* his own) to oppress others has violated both the letter and spirit of the maxim. In saying this I would not be understood as indulging in that sickly sentimentality which despises all rich people simply because they are rich, but rather to condemn the illegitimate use of riches. A rich man can be a blessing as well as a curse to his community, and I am indeed happy to learn and see for myself that this is now the rule, rather than the exception, as formerly.

"There is another phase of the question that you have not yet referred to. What is the condition of the farm laborers of the Southern States?" I asked. "When I left they were working from sunrise to sunset, the men earning fifty cents and the women thirty-five cents per day, and they lived in huts with mud chimneys – often a family of six or eight in one room. They had a three months' school during the winter season, when there were no crops, and these were not too often taught by skilled teachers. Has their condition improved so that it is in keeping with the times?"

At this juncture the Doctor was called out of the room before he could reply.

While waiting for him to return, I had a surprise. His private secretary came in and seated himself at a phonographic typewriter which took down the words in shorthand, typewrote them on a sheet for preservation in the office, and at the same time sent the letter by telephone to its destination. But my surprise was awakened by the fact that this private secretary was a Negro; not full black, but mixed blood – in color, between an Indian and a Chinaman. I ascertained from this young man that it was now "quite common" for Southern white men of large affairs to employ Negroes for higher positions in their offices, counting rooms, and stores. (They had a precedent for this in the custom of the Romans, who used their educated Greek slaves in this way.) He also told me that the matter of social equality was not mentioned. He naturally associated with his own people. He simply wanted to do his work faithfully, and neither expected nor asked to sit by his employer's fireside. In a word, he showed that to give the Negro an education need not necessarily "turn his head." [9]

The young man said, "Our theory has kept the two races pure and has developed both the Saxon and the Negro types and preserved the best traits of each."

I noticed that the subdued look of the old time Negro was absent and that, without any attempt at display, this man possessed "*le grande air*" which is a coveted attribute in the highest walks of life. I had already observed that an advance in civilization produced more individuality and more personal freedom in choosing one's associates. It was not expected that a man was the social equal of another because he worked at the same bench with him, or rode in the same car on the railroad. That was now considered the postulate of an ignoramus.

Individuality is a marked development of advanced civilization – of this I have always been aware, the more so since witnessing the changes wrought during my absence. Individuality gives room for thought, out of which is born invention and progress. When the individual is not allowed to separate from the crowd in thought and action, the aggregate will, the aggregate thought, is his master and he "dare not venture for fear of a fall." Progress is measured only by the degree of swiftness made by the mass. Some individuals may be able to make better speed, but the mass holds them back. Four horses are pulling a load; two may be able to go faster than the others, but the speed of the team is measured by the speed of the slowest horse.

This does not always appear apropos of the progress of communities, for a community may be led by a few progressive spirits who seem to reflect upon it their own standard and tone, but the less progressive members of such a community have merely subordinated their wills for the time being and may on any occasion see fit to exercise them; and at this point the illustration becomes true again.

"Now," said Doctor Newell, on his return, "I am sorry our conversation was interrupted, but let us proceed. I believe you desired to ask me some questions about the Negro farm laborers, did you not?"

I replied that I did, and recalled my statement as to their condition when I last knew of them.

"Oh, it is very different from that now, Mr. Twitchell. Many changes; many, many, have occurred! You will recall that, about the time you left, the different Southern states were re-reconstructing themselves, as it were, by making amendments to their constitutions which virtually disfranchised a large proportion of the Negro voters – enough to put the offices of the states absolutely into the hands of white men, as outlined in the magazine article you have just read, and as you stated in your brochure for the Bureau of Public Utility. Some passages from a book I have on the subject may remind you of the discussion of this question that was going on then."

Signifying to his secretary what he wanted, he read to me the following excerpts from the history of those times:

"Negro Disfranchisement

"What Dr. F.A. Noble Thinks
"In civil as in business affairs there is nothing so foolish as injustice and oppression; there is nothing so wise as righteousness. By the letter of the amended Constitution, by the spirit and aim of the amendments, and by all the principles of our American democracy, the Negro is in possession of the elective franchise. Men differ in their views as to whether it was good policy to confer this right upon him at the time and in the way, and especially to the extent to which it was done; but the right was conferred, and it is now his. To deprive him of this right, for no other reason than that he is a Negro, is to nullify the fundamental law of the land, discredit one of the most sacred results of Emancipation, and flaunt contempt in the face of the idea of a government of the people and by the people and for the people. To discourage the Negro from attempting to exercise the right of the ballot is to belittle him in his own estimation, put him at a serious disadvantage in the estimation of others, and by so much remand him back to the old condition of servitude from which he was rescued at such cost to the nation. Wrong done to the colored race involves the white race in the catastrophe which must follow. To withhold justice is worse than to suffer injustice. A people deprived of their rights by the state will not long be faithful to their duties to the state.

"What Hon. Carl Schurz Thinks
"That the suppression of the Negro franchise by direct or indirect means is in contravention of the spirit and intent of the Fifteenth Amendment to the Constitution of the United States hardly admits of doubt. The evident intent of the Constitution is that the colored people shall have the right of suffrage on an equal footing with the white people. The intent of the provisions of the State Constitutions in question, as avowed by many Southern men, is that the colored people shall not vote. However plausible it may be demonstrated by ingenious argument that the provisions in the State Constitutions are not in conflict with the National Constitution, or that if they were their purpose could not be effectively thwarted by judicial decisions, yet it remains true that by many, if not by all, of their authors they were expressly designed to defeat the universally known and recognized intent of a provision of the national Constitution.

"The only plausible reason given for that curtailment of their rights is that it is not in the interest of the Southern whites to permit the blacks to vote. I will not discuss here the moral aspect of the question whether A may deprive B of his rights if A thinks it in his own interest to do so, and the further question, whether the general admission of such a principle would not banish justice from the earth and eventually carry human society back into barbarism. I will rather discuss the question whether under existing circumstances it would really be the true interest of the Southern whites generally to disfranchise the colored people.

"Negro suffrage is plausibly objected to on the ground that the great bulk of the colored population of the South are very ignorant. This is true. But the same is true of a large portion of the white population. If the suffrage is dangerous in the hands of certain voters on account of their ignorance, it is as dangerous in the hands of ignorant whites as in the hands of ignorant blacks. To remedy this two things might be done: To establish

an educational test for admission to the suffrage, excluding illiterates; and, secondly, to provide for systems of public instruction so as to gradually do away with illiteracy – subjecting whites and blacks alike to the same restrictions and opening to them the same opportunities.

"But most significant and of evil augury is the fact that with many of the Southern whites a well-educated colored voter is as objectionable as an ignorant one, or even more objectionable, simply on account of his color. It is, therefore, not mere dread of ignorance in the voting body that arouses the Southern whites against the colored voters. It is race antagonism, and that race antagonism presents a problem more complicated and perplexing than most others, because it is apt to be unreasoning. It creates violent impulses which refuse to be argued with.

"The race antipathy now heating the Southern mind threatens again to curtail the freedom of inquiry and discussion there – perhaps not to the same extent, but sufficiently to produce infinite mischief by preventing an open-minded consideration of one of the most important interests. And here is the crucial point: There will be a movement either in the direction of reducing the Negroes to a permanent condition of serfdom – the condition of the mere plantation hand, 'alongside of the mule,' practically without any rights of citizenship – or a movement in the direction of recognizing him as a citizen in the true sense of the term. One or the other will prevail.

"That there are in the South strenuous advocates of the establishment of some sort of semi-slavery cannot be denied. Governor Vardaman, of Mississippi, is their representative and most logical statesman. His extreme utterances are greeted by many as the bugle-blasts of a great leader. We constantly read articles in Southern newspapers and reports of public speeches made by Southern men which bear a striking resemblance to the pro-slavery arguments I remember to have heard before the Civil War, and they are brought forth with the same passionate heat and dogmatic assurance to which we were then accustomed – the same assertion of the Negro's predestination for serfdom; the same certainty that he will not work without 'physical compulsion'; the same contemptuous rejection of Negro education as a thing that will only unfit him for work; the same prediction that the elevation of the Negro will be the degradation of the whites; the same angry demand that any advocacy of the Negro's rights should be put down in the South as an attack upon the safety of Southern society and as treason to the Southern cause.

"Thus may it be said, without exaggeration, that by striving to keep up in the Southern States a condition of things which cannot fail to bring forth constant irritation and unrest; which threatens to burden the South with another 'peculiar institution,' by making the bulk of its laboring force again a clog to progressive development, and to put the South once more in a position provokingly offensive to the moral sense and the enlightened spirit of the world outside, the reactionists are the worst enemies the Southern people have to fear.

"A body of high-minded and enlightened Southerners may gradually succeed in convincing even many of the most prejudiced of their people that white ignorance and lawlessness are just as bad and dangerous as black ignorance and lawlessness; that black patriotism, integrity, ability, industry, usefulness, good citizenship and public spirit are just as good and as much entitled to respect and reward as capabilities and virtues of the same name among whites; that the rights of the white man under the Constitution are no more sacred than those of the black man; that neither white nor *black can override the rights of the other without eventually endangering his own; and that the Negro question can finally be settled so as to stay settled only on the basis of the fundamental law of the land as it stands, by fair observance of that law and not by any tricky circumvention of it. Such a campaign for truth and justice, carried on by the high-minded and enlightened Southerners without any party spirit – rather favoring the view that whites as well as blacks should divide their votes according to their inclinations between different political parties – will promise the desired result in the same measure as it is carried on with gentle, patient and persuasive dignity, but also with that unflinching courage which is, above all things, needed to assert that most important freedom – the freedom of inquiry and discussion against traditional and deep-rooted prejudice – a courage which can be daunted neither by the hootings of the mob nor by the supercilious jeers of fashionable society, but goes steadily on doing its work with indomitable tenacity of purpose.*

"What The New York Evening Post Thinks

"This analysis of existing conditions and tendencies in the South is one to which the South itself and the entire nation should give heed. Mr. Schurz clearly perceives a dangerous drift. Slavery ideas are again asserting themselves. The movement to extinguish the Negro's political rights is unconcealed. By craftily devised and inequitable laws the suffrage is taken from him. With all this go naturally the desire and purpose to keep him forever 'alongside the mule.' Negro education is looked upon with increasing hostility.

Every door of hope opening into the professions is slammed in the face of black men merely because they are black. The South works itself up into hysterics over the President's spontaneous recognition of manhood under a black skin. While philanthropists and teachers are laboring to raise the Negro to the full level of citizenship, an open and determined effort is making at the South to thrust him back into serfdom. As Mr. Schurz says, the issue is upon the country, for one tendency or the other must prevail.

"It is his view of the great urgency of the juncture which leads him to address a moving appeal to the South's best. He implores its leading men to bestir themselves to prevent the lamentable injustice which is threatened, and partly executed. By withstanding the mob; by upholding the law; by ridding themselves of the silly dread of 'social equality'; by contending for Negro education of the broadest sort; by hailing every step upward which the black man may take; by insisting upon the equality of all men before the law, they can, Mr. Schurz argues forcibly, do much to save the South and the country from the disgrace and calamity of a new slavery. To this plea every humane patriot will add his voice.

Mr. Schurz's paper is also a challenge to the mind and conscience of the North. Unless they, too, respond to the cause of the Negro – which to-day is the cause of simple justice – it will languish and die.

"What The Outlook Thinks

"It must not be forgotten that the so-called race question is the only capital which a small group of Southern politicians of the old school still possess. They have no other questions or issues; they depend upon the race question for a livelihood, and they use every occasion to say the most extreme things and to set the match to

all the inflammable material in the South. To these politicians several occurrences which have happened lately have been a great boon, and they are making the most of them. But there is a large, influential and growing group of Southern men, loyal to their section, equally loyal to the nation, open-minded and high-minded, who are eager to give the South a new policy, to rid it of sectionalism, to organize its spiritual, moral and intellectual forces, to develop education, and to treat great questions from a national rather than from a sectional point of view; men like Governor Aycock, of North Carolina, and Governor Montague, of Virginia. There is a whole group of educational leaders who represent the best of the Old South and the best of the New. It is the duty of wise, patriotic men in the North to cooperate with these new leaders; to strengthen their hands; to recognize and aid the best sentiment in the South, and to stimulate its activity. The Negro question can be settled by cooperation of the North with the South, by sympathy, by understanding; it can never be settled in any other way.

"What Gov. Aycock, of North Carolina, Thinks

"I am proud of my state because we have solved the Negro problem, which recently seems to have given you some trouble. We have taken him out of politics, and have thereby secured good government under any party, and laid foundations for the future development of both races. We have secured peace and rendered prosperity a certainty. I am inclined to give you our solution of this problem. It is, first, as far as possible, under the Fifteenth Amendment, to disfranchise him; after that, let him alone; quit writing about him; quit talking about him; quit making him 'the white man's burden'; let him 'tote his own skillet'; quit coddling him; let him learn that no man, no race, ever got anything worth the having that he did not himself earn; that character is the outcome of sacrifice, and worth is the result of toil; that, whatever his future may be, the present has in it for him nothing that is not the product of industry, thrift, obedience to law and uprightness; that he cannot, by resolution of council or league, accomplish anything; that he can do much by work; that violence may gratify his passions, but it cannot accomplish his ambition; that he may rarely eat of the cooking equality, but he will always find when he does that there is death in the pot. Let the white man determine that no man shall by act or thought or speech cross this line, and the race problem will be at an end."

After reading these the Doctor explained that, about the time I left, the Negro population of the South began to drift towards the Northern states, where better wages were offered, on account of the improvements going on there.

"The farms were the first to be affected by this turn in affairs," said the Doctor. "In fact, the Negroes who had no land very generally left the farms and this so crippled the cotton industry that within ten years after the disfranchising acts were passed, there wasn't a 'ten horse' farm (to quote the expression used in the records) to be found in some of the Southern states for miles and miles. Every Negro laborer who went North found times so much better that he wrote back for his friends. The disfranchising acts seemed to give the disorderly element in Southern society a free hand. The result was that Negroes were mobbed with impunity for the slightest offences. In one instance I read of a Negro who accidentally stepped on a white man's foot. He was promptly knocked down. As it occurred in a public place where a small crowd had gathered to look at base-ball bulletins, seven or eight of the white by-standers in the crowd took a kick and a knock at him. A policeman appeared on the scene, who arrested the Negro and put him under lock and key – because he got knocked down! – as my father used to say in relating the story. Then, too, the newspapers continued to hold the Negro up to ridicule and whereas he formerly had some of his race on juries, they were now excluded.[10]

"You can imagine that it was getting very uncomfortable for the Negroes in the South about that time. Many of them left for the North and West. Quite a number went to Africa – and Bishop Smith of the African Methodist Church induced many to go to Hayti. Vast tracts of land in the Southwestern part of the United States were opened up to the cultivation of cotton by a national system of irrigation, and the Government employed Negroes on these improvements and also in the cultivation of the plant itself, after the irrigation system was perfected."

"What happened to the Southern white farmers?" I inquired.

"They moved to the cities in large numbers and engaged in manufacturing. As you will see when you begin to travel with me the South is now a great manufacturing country. This, they found later, was a mistake, as they lost race vitality and became virtually the slaves of the manufacturers, on whom they had to depend for bread from week to week. The National Government, however, came to the relief of the South in quite a substantial way (at the same time that it assumed control of all coal and iron mines, and oil wells) by buying up the cotton lands and parcelling them out to young Negroes at a small price, accompanied with means and assistance for the production of the crop. This was an act of the highest statesmanship and a great help in the solution of the Negro problem. It should have come immediately after reconstruction, but the intervening interests of political parties and ambitious men prevented it. A matter of serious moment for a long time was how to eliminate party and personal interests from the equation of politics. Too often good measures were opposed by the different political parties with an eye singly to these interests. The great work of General O. O. Howard in connection with what was known as the Freedmen's Bureau was greatly hampered and met an untimely end because of the selfishness and partisanship of that period. In fact, this one feature has stood in the way of progress in this Government from its earliest existence. Example after example might be cited where party policy and personal interest has blocked the wheels of useful legislation.

"Oxenstiern said, 'See my son, with how little wisdom nations are governed.'

"It is wonderful how tolerant the people of the world have been in respect to bad government. No group of business men would have allowed its directors to spend the company's earnings in the way the rulers of the world have done from time immemorial. America has overlooked many of these points because of the unlimited opportunities here for money making – let the high tide of prosperity once ebb and then these defects become apparent! There were usually in a government office twice as many employed to do small tasks as any business organization would have thought of hiring, and they were paid excellent salaries. In other words, the more places a boss could fill with his constituents or friends, the more public money he could cause to be spent in his district, the more sinecures he could get for his constituents, the more popular he became. In addition to all this, he wasted the people's money with long speeches which were often printed and distributed at the Government's expense. The National Congress formerly was a most expensive institution. Its methods of business were highly extravagant and very often the time consumed resulted in accomplishing nothing more than a mere pittance, perhaps, of the work to be done; and that was carried through because of party advantage or personal interest."

Chapter V
A Visit to Public Buildings

THE TIME had now arrived for our promised visit to some of the public buildings of the city and we seated ourselves in an electric motor car which the Doctor had summoned by touching a button. To my surprise, it made the trip alone, by traversing a course made for this purpose, somewhat on the order of the cash delivery systems formerly used in our large stores, being elevated some twenty feet above the surface. The coaches were arranged to come at a call from any number on certain streets.

The Doctor suggested that we should first visit the "Administration Building." I was expecting to find Congress or some such body in session, but to my surprise I was told by the Doctor that Congress had been abolished, and that the country was run on what I had formerly understood as the corporation plan; except that the salaries were not so large. The business of the Government was entrusted to bureaus or departments, and the officers in them were chosen for their fitness by an improved system of civil service.

"Who is president now," I inquired.

"President!" replied the Doctor, in surprise, "why we have none. I never saw a president. We need none. We have an Executive Department which fills his place."

"What as to proposing new measures?" I asked. "Who writes the annual messages suggesting them?"

"All this is left to a bureau chosen for that purpose, whose duties are to keep the nation informed as to its needs, and to formulate new plans, which are carried out along the idea of the *initiative* and *referendum* system with which you are doubtless somewhat acquainted, as I notice that it was discussed as early as 1890."

I replied that I had a recollection of seeing the terms but I could not give an intelligent definition of them. Whereupon the Doctor explained the system.

"You see," he said, "that the time wasted in Congressional debate is saved and the chance to block needed legislation is reduced to a minimum.

There are no political offices to parcel out to henchmen, and the ambitions of demagogues are not fostered at the expense of the people. England, you will recollect, has had a king only in name for four hundred years. The American people have found out there is no necessity for either king, president, parliament or congress, and in that respect we may be able sooner or later to teach the mother country a lesson."

"To say I am surprised at all this, Dr. Newell, is to express my feelings but mildly," said I, "but I can now see how the changes in reference to the Negro have been brought about. Under our political system, such as I knew it to be, these results could not have been reached in a thousand years!"

"Yes, Mr. Twitchell," replied the Doctor, "our new system, as it may be called, has been a great help in settling, not only the Negro problem, but many others; for instance the labor question, about which we have already conversed, – and the end is not yet, the hey-day of our glory is not reached and will not be until the principles of the Golden Rule have become an actuality in this land."

I here remarked that I always felt a misgiving as to our old system, which left the Government and management of the people's affairs in the hands of politicians who had more personal interest than statesmanship; but I could not conceive of any method of ridding the country of this influence and power, and had about resolved to accept the situation as a part of my common lot with humanity.

Doctor Newell stated that there was much opposition to the parcelling out of land to Negro farmers. It was jeered at as "paternalism," and "socialistic," and "creating a bad precedent."

"But," said he, "our Bureau of Public Utility carried out the idea with the final endorsement of the people, who now appreciate the wisdom of the experiment. The government could as well afford to spend public money for the purpose of mitigating the results of race feeling as it could to improve rivers and harbors. In both instances the public good was served. If bad harbors were a curse so was public prejudice on the race question. It was cheaper in the long run to remove the cause than to patch up with palliatives. If the Negro was becoming vicious to a large extent, and the cause of it was the intensity of race prejudice in the land, which confined him to menial callings, and only a limited number of those; and race prejudice could not be well prevented owing to the misconception of things by those who fostered it; and if an attempt at suppression would mean more bitterness toward the Negro and danger to the country, then surely, looking at the question from the distance at which we are to-day, the best solution was the one adopted by our bureaus at the time. At least, we know the plan was successful, and 'nothing succeeds like success!'

"I am inclined to the opinion that the politicians, judging by the magazine article I gave you," said he, "were quite anxious to keep the Negro question alive for the party advantage it brought. In the North it served the purpose of solidifying the Negro vote for the Republicans, and in the South the Democrats used it to their advantage; neither party, therefore, was willing to remove the Negro issue by any real substantial legislation. Enough legislation was generally proposed *pro* and *con* to excite the voters desired to be reached, and there the efforts ended."

I could not but reflect that the triumph of reason over partisanship and demagoguery had at last been reached, and that the American people had resolved no longer to temporize with measures or men, but were determined to have the government run according to the original design of its founders, upon the principle of the greatest good to the greatest number.

No President since Grant was ever more abused by a certain class of newspapers and politicians than President Roosevelt, who adopted the policy of appointing worthy men to office, regardless of color. He said that fitness should be his rule and not color. In his efforts to carry out this policy he met with the most stubborn resistance from those politicians who hoped to make political capital out of the Negro question. To his credit let it be said that he refused to bow the knee to Baal but stood by his convictions to the end.

I found from the published reports of the Bureau of Statistics that the Negro's progress in one hundred years had been all that his friends could have hoped for. I give below a comparative table showing the difference:

	A.D. 1900	A.D. 2004
Aggregate Negro Wealth	$890,000,000	$2,670,000,000
Aggregate Negro population	8,840,789	21,907,079
Per cent. of illiteracy	45 per cent.	2 per cent.
Per cent. of crime	20 per cent.	1 per cent.
Ratio of home owners	1 in 100	1 in 30
Ratio of insane	1 in 1000	1 in 500
Death rate	20 per M.	5 per M.
Number of lawyers	250	5,282

Number of doctors	800	11,823
Number of pharmacists	150	2,111
Number of teachers	30,000	200,603
Number of preachers	75,000	250,804
Number of mechanics	80,000	240,922

I noticed that Negroes had gained standing in the country as citizens and were no longer objects for such protection as the whites thought a Negro deserved. They stood on the same footing legally as other people. It was a pet phrase in my time for certain communities to say to the Negro that they "would protect him in his rights," but what the Negro wanted was that he should not have to be protected at all! He wanted public sentiment to protect him just as it did a white man. This proffered help was all very good, since it was the best the times afforded, but it made the Negro's rights depend upon what his white neighbors said of him, – if these neighbors did not like him his rights were *nil*. His was an ephemeral existence dependent on the whims and caprices of friends or foes. True citizenship must be deeper than that and be measured by the law of the land – not by the opinion of one's neighbors.

But the voice of the politician who wished to contort civil into social equality was now hushed. He no more disgraced the land, and a Negro could have a business talk with a white man on the street of a Southern city without either party becoming subjects of criticism for practicing "social equality."

Chapter VI
A Ride with Irene

SOON AFTER this talk Miss Davis and I visited prominent places in the city of Phoenix. I had anxiously waited for this opportunity. An uncontrollable desire to fulfill this engagement had grown on me, from the day she informed me that she had planned the outing. We visited McPherson's monument, and standing with head uncovered in its shadow, I said that I was glad to see that the cause he fought for was recognized as a blessing to the South as well as to the North. She replied that some of her relatives perished in defense of the South, but she had been often told by her father that her ancestors considered slavery a great wrong and liberated their slaves by will.

"In fact," she remarked with womanly intuition, "I can see no reason for their having had slaves at the outset. Why couldn't the Negroes have served us, from the first, as *freemen*, just as they did after their emancipation? What was the necessity for adopting a system that gave a chance for the brutal passions of bad men to vent themselves? The whole country has suffered in its moral tone because of slavery, and we are not as pure minded a nation to-day as we should have been without it."

I replied that it was commercialism that fixed slavery in the nation and rooted and grounded it so deep that scarcely could it be eradicated without destroying the nation itself. I noticed that she had none of the Southern woman's prejudice against "Yankees," so prevalent in my day, and that she was far enough removed from the events of the Civil War to look at them dispassionately.

What a difference doth time make in people and nations. What is wisdom to-day may be the grossest folly to-morrow, and the popular theme of to-day maybe ridiculed later on. Ye "men of the hour" beware! The much despised Yankee has taught the South many lessons in industry, in the arts, sciences and literature, but none more valuable to her than to forsake her prejudice against the evolution of the Negro.

We rode out to Chattahoochee farm, noted for its picturesqueness and "up-to-dateness," a paying institution entirely under the management of Negroes. The superintendent was a graduate from the State Agricultural College for Negroes, near Savannah.

"Are there any other farms of this kind in the state under Negro management," I asked.

She replied that there were many, that a majority of the landowners of the state had found it profitable to turn vast tracts of land over to these young Negro graduates, who were proving themselves adepts in the art of scientific farming, making excellent salaries, and returning good dividends on the investments.

I remarked that I used to wonder why this could not be done with the young Negroes coming out from such schools – since their ante-bellum fathers were so successful in this line – and I further said that this movement might have been inaugurated in my day, but for the opposition of the politicians, who approached the Negro question generally with no sincere desire to get effective results, but to make political capital for themselves.

She at once suggested, "And so you believe it was a good idea then to dispense with the politicians?"

"Indeed," said I, "they were horrible stumps in the road of progress."

We ended our ride after a visit to the park, which was a beautiful spot. It served not only as a place of recreation, but Musical, Zoölogical, Botanical and Aquarian departments were open to the public, and free lectures were given on the latest inventions and improvements, thus coupling information with recreation, and elevating the thoughts and ideas of the people. I noticed the absence of the old time signs which I had heard once decorated the gates of this park, "Negroes and dogs not allowed." Of course Irene had never seen or heard of such a thing and I therefore did not mention my thoughts to her. She was a creature of the new era and knew the past only from books and tradition. I had the misfortune, or pleasure, as the case may be, of having lived in two ages and incidents of the past would continually rise before me in comparison with the present.

On reaching my room that evening I felt that my trip with Miss Davis had been very agreeable and very instructive, but still there was an aching void – for what I did not know. Was it that we did not converse on some desired subject?

Chapter VII
Dr. Newell and Work of the Young Ladies' Guilds

"THESE GUILDS," said Dr. Newell, taking my arm as we left the dinner table one afternoon, "are most excellent institutions. Nothing has done more to facilitate a happy solution of the so-called Negro problem of the past than they, and their history is a most fascinating story, as it pictures their origin by a a a young Southern heroine of wealth and standing with philanthropic motives, who while on her way to church one Sunday morning was moved by the sight of a couple of barefooted Negro children playing in the street. Her heart went out to them. She thought of the efforts being made for the heathen abroad, when the needy at our very doors were neglected. Moved towards the work as if by inspiration, she gave her whole time and attention and considerable of her vast wealth to organizing these guilds all over the country. She met with much opposition and was ridiculed as the 'nigger angel,' but this did not deter her and she lived to see the work she organized planted and growing in all the Southland. Cecelia was her name and the incorporated name of these organizations is the Cecilian Guild."

"I should be glad to read the history of this movement," said I, "for all I have learned about it through Miss Davis and yourself is exceedingly interesting."

LIGHT AHEAD FOR THE NEGRO

"One of the problems met with in the outset was that of the fallen woman," said the Doctor, "although the Negroes were never so immoral as was alleged of them. You will recall that after the Civil War many of the slave marriages were declared illegal and remarriage became necessary. Twenty-five cents was the license fee. Thousands showed their faithfulness to each other by complying with this law – a most emphatic argument of the Negro's faithfulness to the marriage vows. Day after day long files of these sons of Africa stood in line waiting with their 'quarters' in hand to renew their vows to the wife of their youth. Many were old and infirm – a number were young and vigorous, there was no compulsion and the former relations might have been severed and other selections made; but not so, they were renewing the old vows and making legal in freedom that which was illegal now because of slavery. Would the 500,000 white divorcees in America in your time have done this?" the doctor asked.

"Let me relate to you a story connected with the work of one of the Cecilian Guilds," said the doctor. "A bright faced octoroon girl living in one of our best Southern homes became peculiarly attractive to a brother of her mistress, a young woman of much character, who loved her maid and loved her brother. The situation grew acute; heroic treatment became necessary as the octoroon related to her mistress in great distress every approach and insinuation made by the young Lothario, his avowals of love, his promises to die for her, his readiness to renounce all conventionalities and flee with her to another state. To all this the octoroon was like ice. Her mother had been trained in the same household and was honored and beloved. Her father was an octoroon – and the girl was a chip of both old blocks. The mistress remonstrated, threatened and begged her brother to no avail, and finally decided to send the girl North, as a last resort, a decision which pleased the maid, who desired to be rid of her tormentor.

"But the trip North only made matters worse. Two years after Eva had made her home with a family in Connecticut, John Guilford turns up. He had been married to his cousin, whom he didn't love, and while practising medicine in one of the leading cities had become distinguished in his profession. He met Eva during a professional visit to her new home in Connecticut. The old flame was rekindled. He concealed the fact of his marriage and offered her his hand, stating that he must take her to another town and keep her incognito, to avoid ruining his practice by the gossip which his marriage to a servant girl would naturally create. Fair promises – which generally do 'butter parsnips,' in love affairs, at least – overcame the fair Eva; she consented to marry the young physician. She lived in another town, she bore him children, he loved her. Finally the real wife, who had borne him no offspring, ascertained the truth. Her husband pleaded hard with her, told her of his love for the girl and how, under the spell of his fondness for children, and following the example of the great Zola, he had yielded to the tempter. 'But,' he begged, 'forgive me because of your love – save my name and our fortune.' This she finally did. Poor Eva, when her second child was four years old, died, never knowing but that she was the true wife of her deceiver. Her children were adopted by the Guilfords as their own, grew up and entered society under the Guilford name and no one to-day will charge them with their father's sin."

Chapter VIII
With Irene Again

I FREQUENTLY saw Irene during the few weeks of my sojourn at the Newell residence, but hers was a busy life and there was not much time for *tête-à-tête*. One evening, however, she seated herself by my side on the veranda and amid the fragrance of the flowers and the songs of the birds we had an hour alone which passed so swiftly that it seemed but a moment. Time hangs heavy only on the hands of those who are not enjoying it. I had noticed her anxiety for a letter and her evident disappointment in the morning when the pneumatic tube in the Newell residence did not deliver it.

Not purposely, but unavoidably, I saw a few days later an envelope postmarked, "Philippines." I ventured to say, with an attempt at teasing, that I trusted she was in good humor to-day since her letter had come, and surmised that it bore "a message of friendship or love" for her. She adroitly avoided the subject, which was all the evidence I wanted to assure me of the truth of my theory as to its contents. The clue was given which I intended to establish in asking the question. Love may be blind but it has ways for trailing its game.

Finding no encouragement for pursuing this subject further, I turned to the discussion of books and finally asked if she had read an old book which in my day used to be referred to as, "Tom Dixon's Leopard's Spots." She said she had not, but had seen it instanced as a good example of that class of writers who misrepresented the best Southern sentiment and opinion. She stated that her information was that there was not a godly character in the book, that it represented the Southern people as justifying prejudice, and ill treatment of a weaker race, whose faults were admittedly forgivable by reason of circumstances. She also stated that "the culture of the present time places such writers in the same class with that English Lord who once predicted that a steamer could never cross the Atlantic for the reason that she could never carry enough fuel to make the voyage."

"And probably in such cases the wish was father to the thought," I added.

She also had heard of those false prophets whom history had not forgotten, but who lived only in ridicule and as examples of error. She seemed to be ashamed of the ideas once advocated by these men, and charitably dismissed them with the remark that, "It would have been better for the cause of true Christianity had they never been listened to by so large a number of our people, as they represented brute force rather than the Golden Rule."

I heard with rapt attention. Although I had already seen much to convince me of the evolution of sentiment in the South, these words sank deeper than all else. Here was a woman of aristocratic Southern blood, cradled under the hills of secession and yet vehement in denunciation of those whom I had learned to recognize as the beacon lights of Southern thought and purpose! And when I reflected that her views were then the views of the whole South, I indeed began to realize the wonderful transformation I was being permitted to see. I silently prayed, "God bless the New South!" My heart was full, I felt that I had met a soul that was a counterpart of my own, – "Each heart shall seek its kindred heart, and cling to it, as close as ever."

The pent-up feelings of my breast must find some expression of admiration for her lofty ideals of joy, for the triumph I had been permitted to see of truth over error in the subjugation of America's greatest curse, *prejudice*, and finally of the meeting with a congenial spirit in flesh and blood, and of the opposite sex; which alone creates for man a halo peculiarly its own.

I was hardly myself, and I burst forth with, "Irene, are you engaged to the man in the 'Philippines'?"

I was rather presumptuous, but the gentle reply was, "I will tell you some other time" – and we parted.

Chapter IX
The Prize Essay

IN LOOKING for the cause of so many improvements I found that the Bureau of Public Utility had been of great service to the country in bringing about such a happy solution of the Negro problem. Among other novel methods adopted I found they had established public boarding schools. I was astonished to learn that they were based on some suggestions made by a Negro of my own times, in an essay which had won a prize of $100 offered by a Northern philanthropist. The writer was a Southern Negro from the state of North Carolina. His ideas were carried out in a general scheme of education for the Negro.

The good results of this course have proved their wisdom; in fact the results were of such importance as to warrant my reproducing part of what he wrote:

The Kind of Education the Negro Needs

"I have noticed a growing tendency in the writings of those whites who discuss the racial question, in the newspapers, towards helpfulness and kindness to the Negro race. Some articles are very bitter, abusive, and unfair, the writers seeming to be either playing to the galleries of a maudlin sentiment or venting personal spleen – but in the main this is not so. The Negroes, who withal had rather love than hate white people, are generally thankful for all expressions favorable to themselves. They realize as a mass that there has grown up within the last thirty years an idle, vicious class of Negroes whose acts and habits are of such a nature as to make them objectionable to their own race, as well as to the whites. What to do with this class is a problem that perplexes the better element of Negroes, more, possibly, than it does the whites; since their shortcomings are generally credited to the whole Negro race, which is wrong as a fact and unjust in theory.

"This vicious element in the race is a constant subject of discussion in Negro churches and in private conversation. It is a mistake to say that crime is not condemned by the better class of Negroes.

There may be a class that attend the courts when their 'pals' are in jeopardy and who rejoice to see them exonerated, but the real substantial Negro man is seldom seen 'warming the benches' of court rooms. Unlike the white spectators, who are men of leisure and spend their time there out of interest in what is going on, and often to earn a per diem as jurors, – the leisure class in the Negro race is generally composed of those who have 'served time' in prison or of their associates.

"The Negro problem, as now considered, seems, so far as the discussion of it is concerned, to be entirely in the hands of white people for solution, and the Negro himself is supposed to have no part in it, other than to 'wait and tend' on the bidding of those engaged at the job. He is 'a looker on in Venice.' I therefore offer my suggestion as to method or plan with fear of being asked to stand aside. Yet, in my zeal for the work and in my anxiety to have it accomplished as speedily and correctly as possible, I venture a few suggestions, the result of twenty years' observation and experience in teaching, which appear to my mind as the best way to go at this Herculean task.

"In the first place I suggest that the boarding school is the only one fitted for the final needs of the young of the race – a school where culture and civility would be taught hand in hand with labor and letters. The main object in education is training for usefulness. 'Leading out' is the meaning of the term education, and what the young of the race needs is to be lead out, and kept out of vice, until the danger period is passed. The public schools turn out the child just at that period when temptations are most alluring. From the age of puberty to twenty-one is the danger time, and the time of forming character. The kind of character then formed remains. If the child can be steered over this period, under right influences and associations, the problem of his future is comparatively settled for good, otherwise for bad. Too much is expected of the public schools as now constituted, if it is presumed that they can mould both the mind and the heart of the child; when they usually drop him just at the period that he begins to learn he has a heart and a mind! He is mostly an animal during the period allotted to him in the public schools. Many are fortunate enough to have parents who have the leisure and ability to train them properly. Some follow up the course in the public schools with a season in a boarding school – these are fortunate, but where is the great mass? They became boot-blacks, runaways, 'dudes,' or temporary domestics, in which calling they earn money more to satisfy their youthful propensities than for any settled purpose for the future of their lives.

"Out of six hundred pupils who had left one public school in Virginia I found only 85 who had settled down with any seemingly fixed purpose. I counted 196 who had become domestics, and, either married or single, are making orderly citizens. The rest have become mere bilge water and are unknown. Among the girls fourteen are of the demirep order. The public schools are doing some work it is true – a great work, all things considered – but their 'reach' is not far enough. What the young of the Negro race needs, beyond all things, is training – not only of the head, but of the heart and hand as well. The boarding school would meet the requirements, if properly conducted. The girl and boy should remain at useful employment under refined influences until the habit of doing things right and acting right is formed. How can the public schools mould character in a child whom they have for five hours, while the street gamins have him for the rest of the day? And further, as before stated, when the child leaves the public schools at the time when most of all he is likely to get into bad habits?

"Good home training is the salvation of any people. Many Negro children are necessarily lacking in this respect, for the reason that their parents are called off to their places of labor during the day and the children are left to shift for themselves. Too often when the parents are at home the influence is not of the most wholesome, thus there is a double necessity for the inauguration of a system of training that will eliminate this evil. The majority of working people do not earn sufficient wages to hire governesses for their children, – if they should quit work and attempt the task for themselves the children would suffer for bread, and soon the state would be called upon to support them as paupers. The state is unable in the present condition of public sentiment to pass upon the sufficiency of wages from employer to employee, but it can dictate the policy of the school system. All selfish or partisan scruples should be eliminated and the subject should be approached with wisdom and foresight, looking solely to accomplishing the best results possible.

"My idea is to supplement the term of the public schools, which might be reduced to four years, by a three years' term in a public boarding school in which the pupil could do all the work and produce enough in vacation to make the school self-sustaining; except the item of the salaries of the teachers, who would be employed by the state. Make three years in these schools compulsory on all who are not able to or do not, select a school of their own choice. Three years' military service is demanded of the adults in most of the European states, which is time almost thrown away so far as the individual is concerned, but a three years' service in schools of this kind would be of the greatest advantage of the child and state as well.

"How it can be done

"There is idle land enough to be used for the establishment of such schools in every township in the South, and with the proper training in them, the pupils from such institutions would come out and build up hundreds of places that are now going to waste for lack of attention. The solution of the race problem cannot be effected by talk alone, nor by a reckless expenditure of public funds, but if the state is to undertake the education of its children with good citizenship in view – thus becoming as it were the parens patriæ, then let the job be undertaken as a parent would be likely to go at it for his own children. In well regulated communities wayward children are placed in homes which the wisdom of experience has found to be the best place for them, and they come out useful citizens. If the youth of the colored race is incorrigible because of instinct or environment, or both, the place for them is in some kind of home where they can be protected against themselves and society, and trained and developed. Let them have four years of training in the public schools and emerge from these into 'a boarding and working school.' This would be far better than furnishing a chain gang system for them to go into after bad character has been formed.

"'An ounce of prevention is worth a pound of cure' right here, and is a cheaper and a more substantial investment. Experience shows that the vicious become more vicious by confinement in the chain gangs, and it not infrequently happens that individuals, after having been degraded by a first sentence, become outcasts and spend from a half to two-thirds of their lives thereafter in prison. The chain gang system can hardly be urged in any sense as a reformatory, and from the frequent returns thereto of the criminal class can be hardly styled as a first-class preventive of crime. It is simply an institution in which criminals can be kept out of their usual occupations. While they are so confined crime is that much decreased, but it opens up again on their exit.

"The value of the boarding school idea as a supplement to the public school system is borne out by the statistics of the boarding schools already established for colored people by private funds. The pupils turned out by these schools are a credit to the race and the state. They are good citizens, they accumulate property, they are industrious and upright. There is not one case in a thousand where you find them on the court records. They are the genuine 'salt of the earth,' so far as the product of the schools for the freedmen is concerned. The public schools have been the feeders in a large measure of these private schools, but only a small percentage of those who leave the public schools ever reach private schools. Under the plan above suggested all pupils will spend three years in a private school, or a school of that nature which will accomplish the same end.

"If the Negro has a greater native tendency to crime than the other races, as is urged by some, then it is necessary to take more care in protecting him against it. If his disease is of a more malignant type than ordinary when it attacks him, then the more heroic should be the remedy. It is as illogical to apply a system of education to a child who is not prepared for it as it would be to treat a patient for appendicitis when he has the eczema. Results are what the state wants, and if the schools now established are not giving them, the system should be changed to one that for thirty years has been a success. The money sent South by Northern charity has not been wasted. Some people think it has destroyed some farm hands – this may be true, but it has created larger producers in other lines fully as beneficial to the state as farming.

"The state is suffering because of its criminal class both white and black, and it will continue to do so until this cloud is removed, and in undertaking the education of its citizens, the state is not working for the farmers especially (as some seem to imply by their arguments on this subject) but for a higher type of citizenship along *all lines. 'More intelligence in farming, mining, manufacturing, and business' is the motto, a general uplift in which all shall be benefited. Neither the farmer, the miner nor the manufacturer can hope to build up a serf class for his special benefit. The state has not established the school system for that purpose, and should the theory once obtain that it was so established, the handwriting would at once appear on the wall. The ideal school system is that in which each citizen claims his part with all the rest. No line should be drawn in the division of the funds to the schools, and as a fit corollary to this, they should not be established to foster the financial interests of any one class of citizens as against another. Pro bono publico is their motto and may it ever remain so!"*

I might add that as a substantial proof of the great success of the new system of Negro education the Southern states have joined in preparing a great Negro Exposition, open to Negroes all over the world, in which, it is expected, a fine showing will be made by members of the race in almost every field of human endeavor.

Chapter X
Sad News for Irene

TWO YEARS have passed since Irene promised, on the veranda of the Newell residence, to tell Gilbert Twitchell if her hand was pledged to the man in the Philippines from whom she had received a letter. Other and sadder news had come since that time. The young officer (Kennesaw Malvern) was dead. He was accidentally shot during a target practice on a U.S. vessel cruising in the Philippines, where by the way peace and independence have long prevailed. Irene was now in black for him. She saw Gilbert Twitchell not quite so often as before, but her mourning robes made it unnecessary that she should answer the question he propounded to her on the veranda.

At the first opportunity, however, Gilbert told her that he loved her, but that he would not ask her hand in marriage till such a time as she thought proper. Her reply was that her whole soul was a complete wreck. She felt as if the world had no further charm, and that death would be welcome if she knew she would be with him.

But time works many changes, even in such a constant and abiding force as a true woman's love. God made them sincere, it may be said, but few there are that stand the test of time, and the assaults of a persistent man's devotion. Many would freeze their hearts if they could, but the manly temperature is too high in most cases and they melt sooner or later under its radiations. Sometimes in her despair, in her dilemma, in her war between the heart force and the will, she resolves to marry her beseecher "to be rid of him," too considerate of his feelings to say "no," and too true to former pledges to say "yes." What tunes indeed may "mere man" play on such heart-strings!

All this was not the case with Irene exactly, but it was true in some particulars, for Irene was a woman, and the only important truth to Gilbert was that the year 2007 saw them husband and wife and that the love that once went to the Philippines was bestowed on the man she helped rescue from his trip in an air ship.

Footnotes for *Light Ahead for the Negro*

1. The white supremacy people accomplished this by employing them as teachers. If they continued to talk too much, they lost their jobs.

2. "Errors" like the following, for instance: "A special dispatch from Charleston, S. C., to the Atlanta Journal, reads: 'While dying in Colleton county, former Section Foreman Jones, of the Atlantic Coast Line Road, has confessed being the murderer of his wife at Ravenel, S. C., fourteen miles from Charleston, in May, 1902, for which crime three Negroes were lynched. The crime which was charged to the Negroes was one of the most brutal ever committed in this State, and after the capture of the Negroes quick work was made of them by the mob.'

"Comment is certainly superfluous. What must be the feelings of those who participated in the lynching." (*Raleigh, N. C., Morning Post.*)

3. The following were the views of Mr. Noah W. Cooper, a Nashville lawyer, on one of Mr. Graves' addresses:

"John Temple Graves' address in Chicago contains more errors and inconsistencies about the so-called Negro problem than any recent utterance on the subject.

"He says that God has established the 'metes and bounds' of the Negro's habitation, but he never pointed out a single mete nor a single bound. He says, 'Let us put the Negro kindly and humanely out of the way;' but his vision again faded and he never told us where to put the darkey.

"If Mr. Graves' inspiration had not been as short as a clam's ear and he had gone on and given us the particular spot on the globe to which we should 'kindly and humanely' kick the darkey 'out of the way,' then we might have asked, who will take the darkey's place in the South? Who will plow and hoe and pick out 12,000,000 bales of cotton? Who will sing in the rice fields? Who will raise the sugar cane? Who will make our 'lasses and syrup? Who will box and dip our turpentine? Who will cut and saw the logs, and on his body bear away the planks from our thousands of sawmills? Who will get down into the mud and swamps and build railroads for rich contractors? Who will work out their lives in our phosphate mines and factories, and in iron and coal mines? Who will be roustabouts on our rivers and on our wharves to be conscripted when too hot for whites to work? Who will fill the darkey's place in the Southern home?

"Oh, I suppose Mr. Graves would say, we will get Dutch and Poles, and Hungarians, Swedes or other foreigners; or we will ourselves do all the work of the Negro. To me this is neither possible nor desirable.

"The South don't want to kick the Negro out, as I understand it. The separation of the Negro from us now – his exile, *nolens volens* – would be a greater calamity to us than his emancipation or his enfranchisement ever has been. We need him and he needs us.

"Mr. Graves says that God never did intend that 'opposite and antagonistic races should live together.'

"That seems to me to be as wild as to say that God intended all dogs to stay on one island; all sheep on another; all lions on another; or to say that all corn should grow in America and all wheat in Russia.

"Mr. Graves cites no 'thus saith the Lord' to back up his new revelation that antagonistic races must live separated.

"What God is it whose mind Mr. Graves is thus revealing? Surely it can't be the God of the Bible – for He allowed the Jews to live 400 years among the Egyptians; then over 500 years in and out of captivity among the Canaanites; then in captivity nearly 100 years in

Babylon; then under the Romans; then sold by the Romans; and from then to now the Jews – the most separate and exclusive of peoples – God's chosen people of the Old Covenant – they have lived anywhere, among all people. Surely Mr. Graves is not revealing the mind of the God to whom the original thirteen colonies bowed down in prayer; the God of the Declaration of Independence and the God of George Washington and Thomas Jefferson. For how many different races were planted in this new world? English, Dutch, Swedes, Quakers, Puritans, Catholics, French Huguenots, the poor, the rich – more antagonism than you can find between 'Buckra' and the 'nigger.' Yet all these antagonisms, such as they were, did not prevent our forefathers from uniting in one country, under one flag, in the common desire for political freedom, moral intelligence and individual nobility of character.

"Under Mr. Graves' God every colony would have become a petty nation, with a Chinese wall around it. Mr. Graves' inconsistencies reached a climax when he said in one breath, 'I appeal for the imperial destiny of our mighty race,' and then in the next breath says, 'let us put the Negro out.' Is it any more imperial to boss the Filipino abroad than it is to boss the Negro at home?

"The God of the Bible commands peace among races and nations, not war; friendship, not antagonism and hatred. Did not Paul, a Jew, become a messenger to the Gentiles? Did he not write the greater part of the New Testament of Christianity while living in Gentile and pagan Rome? Did not Christ set example to the world when He, a Jew, at Jacob's well, preached His most beautiful sermon to a poor Samaritan woman? Winding up that great sermon by telling the woman and the world that not the place of his abode and worship, but the good character of man – 'in spirit and in truth' – was the only true worship. And that is the only exclusive place whose metes and bounds God has set for any man to live, 'in spirit and in truth.'

"How idle to talk of shutting off each race, as it were, into pens like pigs to fatten them. This penning process will neither fatten their bodies, enlighten their minds nor ennoble their souls. Can Mr. Graves tell us how much good the great Chinese wall has done for man? If he can, he can tell us how much good will come to us by putting the darkey out, and locking the door. Mr. Graves' idea would reverse all the maxims of Christianity. It would be much better for Mr. Graves' idea of the separation of antagonisms to be applied to different classes of occupations, of persons that are antagonistic. For instance, the dram-seller is antagonistic to all homes and boys and girls; therefore, put all dram-sellers and dram-shops on one island, and all the homes and boys and girls on another island, far, far away! Now there is your idea, Mr. Graves! Then, again, all horse thieves, bank breakers, train robbers, forgers, counterfeiters are antagonistic to honest men; so here, we will put them all in the District of Columbia and all the honest men in Ohio, and build a high wall between. All the bad boys we would put in a pen; and all us good boys, we will go to the park and have a picnic and laugh at the nincompoop bad boys whose destiny we have penned up! Ah, Mr. Graves could no more teach us this error than could he reverse the decree of Christ to let the wheat and tares grow together until harvest. The seclusion or isolation of an individual or a race is not the road that God has blazed out for the highest attainments. The Levite of the great parable drew his robes close about him and 'passed by on the other side' – like Mr. Graves would have us do the Negro, except that instead of passing him by we would 'put him behind us' – a mere difference of words. But the good Samaritan got down and nursed the dirty, wounded bleeding Jew; sacrificed his time and money to heal his wounds. Now that Levite must be Mr. Graves' ideal Southerner! He says the Negro is an unwilling, blameless, unwholesome, unwelcome element. So was the robbed and bleeding Jew to the Levite; but did that excuse the Levite's wrong? Ought the Levite to have put the groaning man 'out of the way' of his 'imperial destiny' by kicking him out of the road?

"Nay, verily. By the time that Mr. Graves gets all of the antagonistic races and all the antagonistic occupations and people of the world cornered off and fenced up in their God-prescribed 'metes and bounds,' and fences them each up, with stakes and riders to hold them in – by that time I am sure he will envy the job of Sysiphus. But there is a grain of sober truth in one thing Mr. Graves says – that the Negro is blameless."

4.

Negro Torn from Jail by an Ohio Mob

SHOT DEAD ON THE GROUND, THEN HANGED FROM TELEGRAPH POLE – YELLS OF LAUGHTER – FOR HALF AN HOUR THE SWINGING CORPSE SERVES AS A TARGET FOR THE MOB WHICH POURS LEAD INTO IT, SHRIEKING WITH DELIGHT.

(By the Associated Press.)

Springfield, Ohio, March 7, 1904. – Richard Dixon, a Negro, was shot to death here to-night by a mob for the killing of Policeman Charles Collis, who died to-day from wounds received at the hands of Dixon on Sunday.

Collis had gone to Dixon's room on the Negro's request. Dixon said his mistress had his clothes in her possession. Collis accompanied Dixon to the room, and in a short time the man and woman engaged in a quarrel, which resulted in Dixon shooting the woman, who is variously known as Anna or Mamie Corbin, in the left breast just over the heart. She fell unconscious at the first shot and Collis jumped towards the Negro to prevent his escape from the room. Dixon then fired four balls into Collis, the last of which penetrated his abdomen. Dixon went immediately to police headquarters and gave himself up. He was taken to jail.

As soon as Collis' death became known talk of lynching the Negro was heard and to-night a crowd began to gather about the jail.

The mob forced an entrance to the jail by breaking in the east doors with a railroad iron.

At 10:30 the mob melted rapidly and it was the general opinion that no more attempts would be made to force an entrance. Small groups of men, however, could be seen in the shadows of the court house, two adjacent livery stables and several dwelling houses. At 10:45 o'clock the police were satisfied that there was nothing more to fear and they with other officials and newspaper men passed freely in and out of the jail.

Shortly before 11 o'clock a diversion was made by a small crowd moving from the east doors around to the south entrance. The police followed and a bluff was made at jostling them off the steps leading up to the south entrance.

The crowd at this point kept growing, while yells of "hold the police," "smash the doors," "lynch the nigger" were made, interspersed with revolver shots.

All this time the party with the heavy railroad iron was beating at the east door, which shortly yielded to the battering ram, as did the inner lattice iron doors. The mob then surged through the east door, overpowered the sheriff, turnkey and handful of deputies and began the assault on the iron turnstile leading to the cells. The police from the south door were called inside to keep the mob from the cells and in five minutes the south door had shared the fate of the east one.

In an incredibly short time the jail was filled with a mob of 250 men with all the entrances and yard gates blocked by fully 2,500 men, thus making it impossible for the militia to have prevented access to the Negro, had it been on the scene.

The heavy iron partition leading to the cells resisted the mob effectually until cold chisels and sledge hammers arrived, which were only two or three minutes late in arriving. The padlock to the turnstile was broken and the mob soon filled the corridors leading to the cells.

Seeing that further resistance was useless and to avoid the killing of innocent prisoners the authorities consented to the demand of the mob for the right man. He was dragged from his cell to the jail door and thence down the stone steps to a court in the jail yard.

Fearing an attempt on the part of the police to rescue him, the leaders formed a hollow square. Some one knocked the Negro to the ground and those near to him fell back four or five feet. Nine shots were fired into his prostrate body, and satisfied that he was dead, a dozen men grabbed the lifeless body, and with a triumphant cheer the mob surged into Columbia street and marched to Fountain Avenue, one of the principal streets of the town. From here they marched south to the intersection of Main street, and a rope was tied around Dixon's neck. Two men climbed the pole and threw the rope over the topmost crosstie and drew the body about eighteen feet above the street. They then descended and their work was greeted with a cheer.

The fusillade then began and for thirty minutes the body was kept swaying back and forth, from the force of the rain of bullets which was poured into it. Frequently the arms would fly up convulsively when a muscle was struck, and the mob went fairly wild with delight. Throughout it all perfect order was maintained and everyone seemed in the best of humor, joking with his nearest neighbor while re-loading his revolver.

A Negro Honored
COLUMBUS, GEORGIA, ERECTS A MONUMENT TO A HEROIC LABORER.
(By the Associated Press.)
Macon, Ga., March 9, 1902. – A Columbus, Ga., dispatch to the Telegraph says a marble monument has been erected by the city to the memory of Bragg Smith, the Negro laborer who lost his life last September in a heroic but fruitless effort to rescue City Engineer Robert L. Johnson from a street excavation. On one side is an inscription setting forth the fact, while on the other side is chiseled,
"Honor and shame from no condition rise;
Act well thy part, there all the honor lies."

5.

Burning of Negroes
Birmingham, Ala., Special. – The Age-Herald recently published the following letter from Booker T. Washington:
"Within the last fortnight three members of my race have been burned at the stake; of these one was a woman. Not one of the three was charged with any crime even remotely connected with the abuse of a white woman. In every case murder was the sole accusation. All of these burnings took place in broad daylight, and two of them occurred on Sunday afternoon in sight of a Christian church.

"In the midst of the nation's prosperous life, few, I fear, take time to consider whither these brutal and inhuman practices are leading us. The custom of burning

human beings has become so common as scarcely to attract interest or unusual attention. I have always been among those who condemned in the strongest terms crimes of whatever character committed by members of my race, and I condemn them now with equal severity, but I maintain that the only protection to our civilization is a fair and calm trial of all people charged with crime, and in their legal punishment, if proved guilty. There is no excuse to depart from legal methods. The laws are, as a rule, made by the white people, and their execution is by the hands of the white people so that there is little probability of any guilty colored man escaping. These burnings without trial are in the deepest sense unjust to my race, but it is not this injustice alone which stirs my heart. These barbarous scenes, followed as they are by the publication of the shocking details, are more disgraceful and degrading to the people who influence the punishment than to those who receive it.

"If the law is disregarded when a negro is concerned, will it not soon also be disregarded in the case of the white man? And besides the rule of the mob destroys the friendly relations which should exist between the races and injures and interferes with the material prosperity of the communities concerned.

"Worst of all, these outrages take place in communities where there are Christian churches; in the midst of people who have their Sunday schools, their Christian Endeavor Societies and Young Men's Christian Associations; collections are taken up to send missionaries to Africa and China and the rest of the so-called heathen world.

"Is it not possible for pulpit and press to speak out against these burnings in a manner that will arouse a sentiment that shall compel the mob to cease insulting our courts, our governors and our legal authority, to cease bringing shame and ridicule upon our Christian civilization.

"BOOKER T. WASHINGTON.

"Tuskegee, Ala."

6. Tourgée relates this incident in "A Fool's Errand."

7. The grandfather clause in the North Carolina constitution, as recently amended, gives illiterate whites the right to vote if their grandfathers voted *prior to* 1867. The negroes were enfranchised in 1867 and their grandfathers therefore could not have voted prior to that time. So, while all negroes must be able to read and write the constitution, in order to vote, the illiterate white man may do so because his "grand-daddy" voted prior to 1867.

8. As Mr. A. V. Dockery, who is a competent authority, so tersely said in the New York Age, June 23, 1904, the Negro has been practically the only natural Republican in the South. That a considerable number of soldiers were furnished by the South to the Union army during the Civil War is not contested, and proves little as to political conditions then and for several decades later. It is well known that the mountain section of North Carolina, Tennessee, Kentucky and Virginia sent many soldiers to the Northern army; it may not be so well known that Madison county, North Carolina, the home of Judge Pritchard, contributed more soldiers to the Union cause, in proportion to population, than any other county in the whole United States.

It was not asserted that all those soldiers were then, or afterwards became, Republicans. Before the emancipation, there were some Republicans in this sparsely settled section, it is true, but aggressive Republicanism in the South *got its impetus and had its birth* in the actual emancipation, not necessarily the enfranchisement, of the Negro.

Yet when this remnant of white Republicans could no longer protect the Negro in his right to vote, and successive Congresses supinely consented to his disfranchisement, the South's contribution to Congress consisted of less than half a dozen Republican congressmen, and these only from the aforesaid mountain district.

The Negro, being held up as a terrible hobgoblin to political white folks, it was necessary to destroy his citizenship; which was accomplished by wily and cruel means. About one and a half million citizens were disfranchised and yet we have a paradox. This vast mass of manhood is represented in Congress – in what way? By arbitrarily nullifying the constitution of the Nation. It was the boast in 1861 that one Southern man could whip ten Yankees. May not this same class of Southern politicians now proudly and truly boast that one Southern vote is equal to ten Yankee votes?

Have the ten million American Negroes any more direct representation in Congress than the ten million Filipinos?

In 1896 there was only one party in the South and its primaries elected the congressmen. Seven congressional districts in South Carolina cast a total of less than 40,000 votes for the seven congressmen elected to the Fifty-seventh Congress.

For the same Congress, Minnesota cast a total of 276,000 votes for seven congressmen, an average of 39,428 votes each; whereas the average in South Carolina was less than 6,000 votes per congressman. In other words, one South Carolina congressman is equal to seven of the Minnesota article.

If every "lily white" Democrat in the old fighting South during the last decade of the twentieth century (the "lily white" age) had received an office, no benefit for the so-called Negro party would have been attained, and the South would have remained as solid as ever. The men there who amassed fortunes as a result of the Republican policy of protection, remained Democrats, notwithstanding the elimination of the Negro as a political factor. The "lily white" party had no other principle except greed for office. It was a delicious sham and the people knew it, white and blacks alike. It was distinctly proven that as long, and no longer, as there was any Federal office in the South to be filled there was a Democrat or a "lily white" handy and anxious to fill it and willing to keep his mouth shut only during the occupation.

It is not surprising, therefore, that President Roosevelt early in his administration gave the "lily-white" party to understand that it was *persona non grata* at the White House. As a true patriot and an honest man he could not have done less.

9. A. A. Gunby, Esq., a member of the Louisiana bar, in a recently published address on Negro education, read before the Southern Educational Association, which met in Atlanta, 1892, took diametrically opposite ground to those who oppose higher education because it will lead to the amalgamation of the races. Mr. Gunby said: "The idea that white supremacy will be endangered by Negro education does not deserve an answer. The claim that their enlightenment will lead to social equality and amalgamation is equally untenable. The more intelligent the Negro becomes the better he understands the true relations and divergences of the races, the less he is inclined to social intermingling with the whites. Education will really emphasize and widen the social gulf between the whites and blacks to the great advantage of the State, for it is a heterogeneous, and not a homogeneous, people that make a republic strong and progressive."

10.

> *Does the Negro get Justice in Our Courts?*
> *(Charlotte, N. C., News.)*
>
> *The Charlotte Observer makes the sweeping statement regarding the Negro: "He is not ill-treated nor improperly discriminated against except in the courts, and for the injustice done him there, there seems to be no remedy."*

A Close Contest
(Charlotte, N. C., Observer.)

We always feel sorry for a North Carolina jury which gets hold of a case in which a black man is the plaintiff and the Southern Railway Company the defendant. A jury in Rowan superior court last week had such a case and must have been greatly perplexed about which party to the suit to decide against. After due deliberation, however, it decided – how do you suppose – Why, against the railroad. But the problem was one which called for fasting and prayer.

e-race

Russell Nichols

[STARTING TOMORROW, racism in America will be history!]

When the urgent notification popped up in his eye-mail, the very old man swatted it away.

How was he still getting these damn things? He unsubscribed twenty times at least from this mailing list he never even signed up for. Tried to block them. What part of no means no didn't these parasites understand? Last week he was so fed up with the spamming, he called the U.S. Department of Reparations toll-free number to strongly suggest they go straight to hell, but nobody answered.

[Today marks the deadline for compliance. After midnight, all non-members of the new e-race will face severe penalties, including...]

He slapped at the air again, deleting the message mid-scroll. Then groaned, rolling over in bed. The nubs where his legs used to be itched. The sign of a storm coming. Then: Boom! Boom! Boom! On the door of his senior living pod. He pulled the cover over his head, but knew he couldn't hide.

"Police!" came the voice from the other side. "Open up, Mr. Ellison!"

* * *

Fifteen minutes later, the security guard dragged Ellison into a crowded microsurgery clinic.

"Get your hands off me!" Ellison hollered, fighting but failing to break free. "I'm exempt!"

The guard took Ellison to reception. "Got another 406 for ya."

"Wunderbar!" said the receptionist. She aimed an ID scanner, clicked, and a blue light flashed. The data loaded onto her computer. "Waldo Ellison. Been playing a little hooky, have we?"

"No, no, seriously, I—I'm handicapped, look—" Ellison showed off his robotic prosthetics. "I'm supposed to get a pass."

The guard bent down like talking to a toddler. "Can you say man-da-tory?"

"Please," Ellison pleaded. "I'm not supposed to be here."

"Righteo, you're supposed to be over there." The receptionist pointed to the long line of people waiting to go through pre-op body scanners. Then she pressed an intercom and muttered, "Need a fix on a 406," as the guard escorted Ellison away.

"Hold up, I can't do this. I don't do hospital beds, I break out real bad—"

"If you try to break out of here, it won't be good. Trust me."

The guard patted Ellison's shoulder and left him in the back of the line. The line was a snarl-up, going nowhere, like a scene from the DMV back in the day, before autonomous cars. A shame that cars learned to be autonomous before people. Look at them. More like drones in skin wrapping paper. With zero perspective beyond their eye-mail. Look at them, staring all blank, scrolling through retinal feeds, the contents of which Ellison could only guess – e-race fashion dos and don'ts: Do wear bright colors and you'll be fab! Don't wear gray or you'll look drab!

Didn't they see what was happening?

[The Indivisible Nation Act will level the playing field by eliminating the perception of skin color from the visual cortex...]

Ellison whacked the notification away with a grunt.

Then: a voice behind him. "What's the matter, legacy?"

[Legacy [leg-uh-see] noun, offensive: An old or obsolete person with machine parts]

Ellison dismissed the pop-up definition, turned around. "Whatchu call me?!"

Standing in line behind him was a boy, maybe fifteen, wearing an LED shirt that kept flashing *Now You See Me* then *Now You Don't.*

"No trigger, no trigger," he said with his hands up. "Just launching dialogue with you. Looking like we'll be frozen here a minute."

Ellison almost asked the boy where his parents were, but then remembered he didn't give a shred of damn. He turned back around, hoping a non-response would shut him up.

But the boy asked: "Why you all sad-faced?"

Ellison turned around. "Lookie here, you—"

"Call me Disher."

"I'm tired and it's about to rain and I'm just tryna get out of here. And I got a hunch that if you zip those lips of yours, that'll happen a helluva lot faster, you got me?"

Ellison turned back around.

"I think I got you," Disher said.

Ellison turned around. "No, no, you clearly don't, see, 'cause that was a rhetorical question. That means you're not supposed to answer."

"I know what rhetorical means."

"Then why are you still talking to me?"

Disher frowned. "Is that rhetorical?"

Ellison shook his head, turned back around.

"Why the downvotes, legs? I mean, judging by your body-mods, that last-gen suit and your buggy social skills, I'm getting a strong centenarian signal. I fig, what, a buck oh-five? Buck ten? Point being, this should be an achievement day for you."

Ellison scoffed. "Achievement day."

"No more color lines. Equality all around. That's God particle!"

Ellison glared at Disher. Was he born remedial? Or was that LED shirt offing brain cells?

"It's Trojan horse-shit," Ellison said.

"Edit: Okay, maybe not God particle, but at least it's a step in—"

"—Trojan horse-shit."

"Whatchu infected with? Verify, I'm not as ancient as you. Still I've d-loaded enough history to know it was all glitched up back in your era. But now, thanks to this program, I can be somebody."

Ellison palmed his face. "A monochrome somebody."

"Legs, you can't act like complexion don't matter. You know how long it took me to find a job? How many opps declined me because my skin tone? How about all the undocs looking for sanctuary?" Disher motioned to the people in line. "Like or dislike, this new law levels the playing—"

"Spare me the sound bites, alright? It's the same field, different game." Then, without thinking, Ellison shouted: "You fools really think not seeing color will make racism disappear?!"

"Who's a fool?" came a voice from the crowd.

Ellison felt all eyes on him. But he got an idea: If he could get enough of these drones riled up, the guard would have to step in, and Ellison could step right the hell out.

"Who's a fool?" he asked. "Everybody in this line, that's who."

"Who this legacy think he trolling?" somebody asked, rhetorically.

"I speak the truth!" he said. "You're all getting herded up like cattle. In the name of equality. Am I the only one seeing this?"

"Amigo, you're going to be seeing a whole lot less if you keep at it," somebody said.

Ellison kept at it. "Discrimination never dies. If not the color of your skin, it'll be your accent." Pointing to various people around him. "Or your eyes. Or your nose. Your height. Or your weight." Ellison pointed to Disher. "That hair." To himself. "These legs." A man in a color-changing hijab. "That Christmas ornament on your head."

His partner pushed Ellison's hand away. "You crossed the line."

"See, exactly, that's my point! There will *always* be a line."

The security guard waved a finger at Ellison. A warning to stop.

Ellison didn't stop. "Do any of you know what it feels like to get hit in the face by a high-pressure fire hose? I'm talking enough water pressure to tear bark off a tree or brick off a wall. Of course you don't, but I do. See, I was out there, Kelly Ingram Park, singing 'Ain't Gonna Let Nobody Turn Me Around' while getting sprayed to the ground by pigs."

The security guard didn't budge.

"Bet you never even heard that song, huh? Listen, don't be mad at me, I'm only speaking truth! I grew up in the segregated South. Marches, boycotts, sit-ins. Out there fighting for my rights. My life. But see, that's what's wrong with you kids today. You don't know nothing about sacrifice!"

The security guard wasn't intervening.

"And now look at you, staring all blank, scrolling through retinal feeds, for what? e-race fashion dos and don'ts? Do wear bright colors and you'll be fab! Don't wear gray or you'll look drab! Ha! You're standing in line for a mandatory surgery to be colorblind and that's supposed to be quote-unquote great for America? I didn't vote for this. Did you vote for this?"

Why wasn't the security guard intervening?!

"But wasn't this the end game?" Disher said. "A future where we don't see color? That means all the protests paid off, right? Isn't this the world Dr. Martin Luther King Jr. dreamed of?"

The question wasn't exactly rhetorical. But Ellison didn't answer fast enough, and the tension evaporated with murmurs of "That's true," "Good point," "Preach!"

Ellison hollered: "I know where I stand!"

Somebody hollered back: "Yeah, in line just like the rest of us!"

The crack drew laughs. Moment gone, just like that. Everybody went back to their business. Scrolling through retinal feeds. The security guard raised his fist in the air like "power to the people."

Ellison, rage boiling over, stepped out of line. Power walking. Straight for the guard.

[Starting tomorrow, racism in America will be history!]

Ellison punched the notification.

The guard held his ground, grabbed his nightstick.

Ellison closing in.

Tunnel vision.

[Starting tomorrow, racism in America will be history! Today marks the deadline...]

Ellison batted the air. He'd show them a deadline.

The guard stepped forward, winding up.

"Don't take another step!" he said.

Ellison didn't stop. But a default safety feature made his legs slow down.

The guard lit up, convinced of his godlike power.

Ellison pushed himself forward, but Disher's hand grabbed his arm, holding him back.

"No ban, mods," Disher told the guard. "I'll take care of him."

"Get off of me!" Ellison said.

But Disher used the energy to pivot and escort Ellison to the vacant restroom.

Inside: there was a window up in the wall, getting pummeled by pellets of rain. Disher locked the door and went to a urinal. Ellison leaned over the sink, adrenaline coming back to Earth.

"What were you thinking?" he said, staring at his reflection.

"You're welcome," Disher said. "And don't start spamming me about colored-only restrooms."

Ellison splashed his face with water. "I don't know nothing about colored-only restrooms."

"Riiight."

"That's the truth. I never stepped foot in one in my life."

"But you said—"

"I never marched. Never boycotted. The only sit-in I ever did was at home, alone on my couch, when I didn't feel like being bothered with people. Which was all the damn time."

Disher washed his hands, keeping his mouth shut.

"Back then I felt like, if I could work hard, make something of myself, anybody could. And everybody blaming racism was just using that as an excuse. I really thought that."

"Where's the error?" Disher said. "Race is a social construct. If you don't believe in ghosts, they can't attack you."

"I used to say, 'I don't believe in race.' But see, to say that, I was denying the struggle of the oppressed. Hell, my own struggle! I was in denial of myself." Ellison turned to Disher. "Look, I know you think this Indivisible Nation Act is the end-all, be-all, but I'm here to tell you, it's not even close. Racism is grafted into the skin of America. You can't remove it without spilling a whole lot of blood."

Disher seemed to consider this, staring up at the window.

"Look at me: I'm 125 years old. Lost my legs in a car crash. Before autonomous cars took over. Didn't fight for any kind of rights. But here I am, a survivor, and I can't live with the guilt of doing nothing. I have to resist. I want to make a difference and ... I will not let our history get wiped away."

"History lives on," Disher said. "Right here."

Disher pointed to his chest. Ellison figured he was talking about his heart, but all he could see was the shirt flashing *Now You See Me* then *Now You Don't.*

The room was silent, except for the patter of heavy rain.

Disher looked at the window again. "Ready to ex outta here?"

"You and me?" Ellison felt a surge of pride, but he knew the weather would force his prosthetics into safe mode. Probably wouldn't get two blocks. "I don't know—"

Disher tapped Ellison's arm. "That was a rhetorical question."

Ellison chuckled. Took a deep breath. And positioned himself under the window.

Then: Boom! Boom! Boom! On the restroom door.

Ellison's legs held steady under the weight as Disher stood on his shoulders.

Disher opened the window, looked down at Ellison. "You following?"

Ellison heard keys at the door. "You go on. I'll see you on the other side."

"No you won't."

"Go on! I'll find you – you just go and keep going. And don't look back, you got me?"

Disher gave him a sad smile. "I got you, legacy."

The boy pulled himself up, crawled out of the window and into the storm.

When the security guard burst in, the very old man fell to his mechanical joints.

[Starting tomorrow, racism in America will be history!]

* * *

Moments later, Ellison came out of the restroom on a stretcher. Eyes heavy. The world fading as a sedative took hold. Body going numb, but he could still feel the weight on his shoulders, where the boy had been standing. An orderly pushed him through the pre-op area. Past the line of drones he gave no damns about. He sacrificed himself to make a difference and nobody could take that away.

"You can't make me do this!" a woman hollered at reception. A kindred spirit.

As the orderly pushed him through a door and down a white hall, toward the operating rooms, Ellison heard the receptionist over the intercom: "Need a fix on a 406."

And that was when he saw it. At first he thought it was side effects from the sedative or his old eyes playing tricks on him. But no! There, through the window of a waiting room, he saw a group of kids sitting completely still, their heads plugged into the walls. And one of them, a girl, maybe fifteen, unplugged herself and walked out toward the pre-op area, in the same LED shirt they all wore flashing *Now You See Me* then *Now You Don't*.

Giant Steps

Russell Nichols

Hear those engines roar / rumbling
Feel those fires burn
Blasting off / blasting off / blasting off / blasting off
Step back.
Hear those engines roar / rumbling
Feel those fires burn
Bear the cross / bear the cross / bear the cross / bear the cross

* * *

THE BLUE MARBLE is shrinking; as *Orion II* lifts off, ripping from the grasping tentacles of Earth's gravity, the world gets smaller, smaller, a blot on the cosmic sheet of infinite blackness, which closes in like a camera iris in a classic film's final shot.

Picture the planet's surface, where the wonders of the old world buckle at the top of the hour under the weight of new wars; where down below all those little people fall to their knees, desperate voices crying, crying out to their deity-du-jour for deliverance. There is no answer. Prayers unheard, wishes ungranted, for they've made their bed and now liars must lie.

But not Dr. Jenkins.

Strapped in this single-person spacecraft, plugged into tubes for food, water and waste, the thirty-three-year-old astrophysicist from South Carolina and soon-to-be first ever human to step foot on Titan never felt freer in her life. As the Richard Strauss tone poem, 'Also sprach Zarathustra,' rises in her ears, like the sun in her eyes, Dr. Charlene Jenkins turns away from her homeworld, never minding who she left behind. A long ride ahead – five years, two months, give or take – with gravity assists from Venus and Jupiter flinging *Orion II* like a slingshot to the destination. She hates that word, destination. Too close to destiny. Too far from reality.

"You cain't defy you and I, baby, this some destiny-level shit here," Dave used to say before he got clean, before Trane was born, before Gramma passed. Was that destiny too? Or did Gramma *refuse* to take her 'med'sin'?

It's choice, not chance, that defines who we are, where we end up.

Or down.

Or 1.2 billion kilometers away on Saturn's largest moon, which may or may not be inhabited by giants, depending on who you ask.

"I don't believe in giants," Dr. Jenkins was quoted by the *Honolulu Star-Advertiser*.

Not giants. Not the Nephilim. Definitely not the banduns Gramma used to tell stories about back in the day. No, she didn't believe in that nonsense. Not anymore.

The same can't be said for the world at large; a lonely world of blind believers, who see what they want to see. Take, for instance, the leaked images from NASA's Jet Propulsion Laboratory in Pasadena, California, which captured the public imagination – and common sense. Were these the lost 350 photographs from the Cassini-Huygens mission? The European Space Agency, on the record, said not a chance. But denial only added fuel to the viral wildfire as the mysterious pictures spread to all corners of the globe:

What looked to be 'giant footprints' on Titan, on the northwest shoreline of Ligeia Mare, a hydrocarbon lake larger than Lake Superior. Twenty-four prints total, in a single-file pattern; each one sixty centimeters long, twenty wide, three deep, according to various imaging teams. These 'footprints' could've been impact craters, land erosion, shadows from methane clouds. But cold, hard facts don't solidify in the minds of the masses, *Homo ignoramuses*, sheep in people's clothing who'd rather believe in Goliath than science.

"People lie to themselves," she told the reporter.

But not Dr. Jenkins.

She quit playing those mind games long ago, smart enough to know the human brain looks for patterns, seeks them out religiously, to deny the claustrophobia of utter insignificance. But who wants to hear that?

Definitely not the thousands of so-called 'printers' who saw her quote online and flooded public eye-feeds with their own from Genesis 6:4 – 'There were giants in the earth in those days; and also after that, when the sons of God came in unto the daughters of men, and they bare children to them, the same became mighty men which were of old, men of renown' – who shared links to news stories about massive footprints discovered in China, Bolivia and South Africa; who signed off messages with the sincerest of valedictions:

- Still don't believe in giants? Suck my giant dick.

- Stick to picking cotton, tar baby bitch!!

- DIE SPACE MONKEY

She's heard worse, seen worse, reflected in the green eyes of strangers and coworkers, men and women, those who resent her for making rapid strides against all odds.

"Initiating hypersleep," says Rigel, *Orion II's* sentient computer.

Silent shaming rings the loudest. A look here, a look there, a look away. Ironed-on, Made-in-America smiles that say, *You're not supposed to be here.*

"Don't you go believing all that she she talk," she hears Gramma's words echoing now, like rolling thunder, as she drifts into hypersleep. "The Lawd got you here for a reason."

She sees Gramma now, coming into focus, reclining on the porch of her saddlebag house in Fairfield County, humming "Way Beyawn' duh Moon" with a pop-up choir of crickets. Gramma was what southerners called 'a force of nature,' mythic in style and stature with the head of a queen and heart of a bull, spilling stories for days. Dr. Charlene Jenkins – back when she was just Leenie – was raised on these stories; homegrown hand-me-downs from her great-grandmother and *her* great-grandmother, coming from the Lowcountry, namely St. Helena Island – a near-casualty of climate change that became one of the first UNESCO Bubble Cities.

"Leenie, come'yuh, lemme get them knockers out your head," Gramma would call out from her porch on those muggy summer days. Between Gramma's knees, Leenie fidgeted, feeling those rough hands pulling her pigtails and stretching her kinky hair like she always did to train it against shrinkage.

"Gramma, could you tell me about the banduns again?"

"If you keep still," Gramma said, bouncing her right leg, which used to be for dancing, but now had a strange habit of losing feeling. She was tired all the time, too. But she could talk from sunup to sundown about her kin: the Gullah-Geechee people, descendants of enslaved Africans who survived and thrived for centuries on the Sea Islands of South Carolina and Georgia. How back in the day, after the praise meeting, they would gather round to take part in the legendary ring shout.

A songster kicked things off, call-and-response style; a stickman played the beat, slow at first, then faster, faster; as the joyful congregation moved in a circle, hand-clapping, feet-tapping, shouting and shuffling, dancing on the devil till he begged for sweet mercy, Gramma would say.

"But every now and again," she said, looking around, then leaning forward to make sure no one else could hear, "some sanctified body would step in that ring there, wailing, flailing all furious-like. And lo and behold, that man, filled with the spirit, would up and start growing."

"Growing like a beanstalk?" Leenie asked every time.

"Child, bigguh than a beanstalk. Bigguh than anything in this whole world. Hold this." She handed Leenie her blue knockers. "Just kept growing and growing till they was big enough to reach for the clouds, then climb up to the sky and gone'way."

"Gone where?"

Gramma lifted a hand to the heavens. "Off into the big black yonder."

Sitting there on the porch, Leenie cupped the knockers in her palm. Staring into the little blue orb, she pictured a far-away world. A land of banduns. A place where she might, for once in her life, feel free and feel big and feel like she belongs. Or find her mother.

"Put them knockers in the box 'fore you lose them," Gramma said.

She did as she was told and tucked her small world in a container with the other worlds. And it was these stories of free Black giants that inspired Leenie to learn all she could about the 'big black yonder.' In the process, she learned a bigger truth: Gramma, too, was a liar.

At the heart of every belief is a lie. A stretched truth. Facts distorted like the space inside a wormhole. Vows made to be broken. Like when somebody promises to return and never does. This, she learned, was the real world, so she did what disillusioned optimists do: Leenie grew up.

Never again would she fall victim to faith, be betrayed by hope, or led astray by love. Which is why, outside the Mount Wilson Observatory, when Dave popped the question …

… she popped him on the head. "What are you thinking?!"

"I'm thinking it's high time you and I settle down for real for real, do the family thing."

"Dave … I can't do that. I told you I don't want to be a wife, I don't want kids."

"What kinda woman don't want kids?"

"My kind," she said, closing the ring box and the conversation.

It wasn't him. Not all him. Somewhat him, but not all. He was a good man. Not educated in the conventional sense, not extremely ambitious, but a laid-back, lighthearted type of man. The type who knew just how to touch her and where and asked when, if he wasn't sure.

There he goes now, up on stage in the spotlight, wailing, while she's down in the shadows, clapping. But this is no ring shout. This was the night they met in New York at some underground jazz club with Dave on the sax. She watched his cheeks puff up, a man possessed. And, being a scientist-in-training, she wanted to test out a hypothesis: that a player who could maneuver his fingers and fix his lips to make that instrument scream could do the same to hers. No strings, just a release. She initiated, he obliged. For seven years he obliged, tuning her body between the sheets. But as she moved up in status, he fell back on old habits.

An old habit, like history, repeats itself. What goes around comes around like a satellite. A record. Needles dropping. Heroin and insulin. Dave and Gramma, injecting and rejecting shots, respectively. Two peas in the wrong pods. Putting faith in false gods.

"Baby, that's all in the past," Dave told her the first week of his twelve-step program. And by the sixth week, he figured he could replace his defunct jazz band with a wedding band.

But what is marriage if not another drug? A lifelong dependence on a manmade substance that ultimately leads to abuse?

She'd heard that song time and time again. Lamentations of belittled women. Givers of life beaten down, swallowed whole by the vacuum of the fragile male ego. Born-to-be brides. Born again wives. Ever-shrinking women with self-deflating voices who were raised to submit (from the Latin submittere: 'to yield, lower, let down, put under, reduce'), to keep silent and to take up as little space as possible.

But not Dr. Jenkins.

She is not the one. She wouldn't follow in the fading footsteps of those who walk down the aisle and wind up getting walked over. Didn't matter how magical his fingers felt on the nape of her neck, how musical his lips felt massaging the length of her labia. She refused to sacrifice her identity on the altar of intimacy. She rejected a ring on her finger to see the rings of Saturn because life is too short to live in the land of make-believe.

"Wake up, Dr. Jenkins," Rigel says.

And roused from hypersleep, she sees before her The Ringed Planet, grander and more glorious than she ever imagined, a swirling pastel ball with bands of clouds running around it. But how is this possible? Reading her confused expression, Rigel declares: "We are now approaching Saturn. Destination: Titan."

She unstraps herself.

"It is advised that you remain strapped in, Dr. Jenkins."

No. Something's not right here. Why does the computer show a flight time of only four years, one month and seventeen days? How could she be a full year ahead of schedule?

"Rigel," she says, her voice like gravel, "how long has it been since the launch?"

"This is the forty-seventh day of the fourth year. We made good time."

Before she can ask how this happened so fast, an alarm goes off as the spacecraft's autopilot tries to maneuver through tiny particles running from or being sucked into the delicate, narrow outer band of Saturn's F ring, herded by the shepherd-moon Prometheus. Stray pieces batter the composite shell of *Orion II* like sleet.

"A change of course is advised," Rigel says.

"No, no, stay on current trajectory."

"Dr. Jenkins, at this rate, you won't be able to sustain—"

"Stay on course, I said!"

Keeping her eyes dead ahead, the AR interface labels the various satellites in view and right there, like a ripe Carolina peach bobbing in a deep, dark sea, the big, bright moon draws her nearer, as the warning alarm keeps ringing in her ears.

"'Giant Steps!'" Dave shouted the day he saw the viral Titan photos.

This was last Fall in the living room of their downsized apartment in Berkeley. Dave was bouncing baby Trane on his right leg, a twelve-month-old girl with curious wide brown eyes, as Dr. Jenkins stood over them, projecting a hologram of images from her palmtab.

"No, Dave, these … these aren't footprints." She sighed. "I mean, they could be anything: impact craters, land erosion, shadows from methane clouds—"

"Nah," he said. "You're not hearing me. See this right here? Look at this. See that pattern? Yeah I'd recognize those opening chords anywhere. That's Trane." He tickled the baby girl. "That's you, huh? Huh, little star?"

Dr. Jenkins knew legendary jazz saxophonist John Coltrane was his idol, his influence, the namesake of their newborn. But he was taking this too far. Was he using again?

"Charlene." He set the girl down on the self-cleaning carpet. "Don't look at me like that."

"I'm not looking at you like anything."

He walked out, leaving Dr. Jenkins alone with the baby. She'd only held her a few times since giving birth. Now she watched the little girl lift herself to stand and start sort of walking. But she kept falling back, then smirking up like she'd get in trouble for trying to defy gravity.

Gramma wasn't walking either by then. She was on bed rest, post-amputation.

"The Lawd ain't through with little ol' me," she proclaimed on more than one occasion. "I'll be back on my feet in no time, you watch."

Which Dr. Jenkins determined was a lie for three reasons:

1) 'The Lawd' isn't real.

2) Gramma didn't have feet, plural. Diabetes hijacked her right foot. She had one left.

3) By the time she did leave that bed, she had to be carried out, never to tell a story again.

"Check this out here," Dave said, coming back into the living room with sheets of paper. "You'll appreciate this. I'm finna blow your mind right here. You know what this is?"

Before she could answer, he explained: It was a diagram of Coltrane's Tone Circle, a variation of the classic 'Circle of Fifths' with a pentagram and vanishing point in the middle. "Been listening to these jazz and physics audiobooks, right?" he said. "And this Coltrane circle, it's drawing on the same geometric principles your boy Einstein was working with. Quantum theory, mathematics, relativity – all that heavy-duty scientific shit you went to school for."

"Dave, what does this have to do with anything?"

"I'm saying, it's all connected, everything's connected." He set the palmtab next to the diagram on the legless LeviTable and ran over to stop the little girl from climbing up the stairs. "Trane was out of this world, we know that. Straight-up transcendent. But I always thought to myself: What if that cat was, you know, channeling? Like possessed?"

She stifled a laugh to spare his feelings. "You can't be serious."

"Why not though? The way he improvised? Go listen to *Ascension* and *Interstellar Space*. Listen to *Om* and tell me I'm lying." He lifted the little girl's arms to help her walk. "What if, tucked under those 'sheets of sound,' Trane was tryna tell us the truth?"

"And what truth would that be, my dear? Aliens?"

"Could be. Or a warning. Instructions on how to be free, hell, I don't know," he said. "You the big, bad scientist."

Never copulate with a conspiracy theorist. An obscure scientific law she learned too late. She never told Dave about the banduns. The man believed everything he heard, never bothering to fact-check. In this day and age, you can't afford not to fact-check. Dr. Jenkins volunteered to fly 1.2 billion kilometers just to fact-check.

"Brace for impact," Rigel says.

A massive chunk of ice comes out of nowhere, slamming into *Orion II* like a fist. Knocking the craft off its trajectory. Dr. Jenkins, her heart pounding, looks around to find Titan, but the AR interface has shut off.

"Return to course," she commands.

"Shields down to seventy-five percent," Rigel says. "Life support systems damaged."

"Return to course, return to course, go to Titan!"

"Navigation offline."

"You ain't told him?" Gramma asked from her hospital bed and soon-to-be deathbed. "That man's the father of your child, for crying out loud!"

"He didn't tell me he was planning to get hooked on smack. How come he gets to do what he wants when he wants, and I can't?"

"That's a cross you gotsta bear."

"But that's not … look, it was his idea. *He* wanted to have a baby. Now I need to do what I need to do for me. I don't wanna be one of those kind of women—"

"What woman is that, huh?"

"Never mind."

"Oh no, no, don't get all hush-mouthed now. What kind of woman? You don't wanna be like me is what you saying. Tell the truth, shame the devil."

"Gramma … I have big dreams."

"And what? You think I didn't?"

"You've lived in that same house since before I was born, weaving sweetgrass baskets, whipping up some Frogmore Stew, humming your *spurrituals*. You always said you wanted to get out of Carolina and dance on a big stage, and you could have. You really could have, but you never did. And now you're refusing to get a bionic foot."

"First off, don't worry 'bout my foot. And second, best believe I *chose* to be here. Everybody and they mama got to migrating, up and over to the big cities, fooling theyselves thinking they could outrun racism. But I wasn't fixing to leave my people like that. No ma'am, not me. I stayed my Black behind right here so I could raise you and this the thanks I get?"

"Gramma, this isn't about you. This is about me. I want to explore."

"'Clare to Gawd. So what, you think you Neil Armstrong? Hopscotching round the heavens like ain't nothing better to do? 'You wanna explore.' Shuh. How 'bout you go explore being a mother? That's some uncharted territory for that ass."

"I'm not supposed to be here."

"Oh. I'm sorry. Are you the Creator of the Universe? Didn't think so. So who is you to say where you s'posed to be, huh?" Gramma sighs, then scoots over in bed and pats the mattress. "Leenie, come'yuh. Come sit."

Dr. Jenkins shakes her head, staring at her single foot wiggling under the white sheets.

"Child, I know you scared. Seeing me all shriveled up like this, with one foot literally in the grave. Thinking 'bout Dave and his crookety self. You worried you'll be left to raise that child by your lonesome, I understand that—"

"The only thing I'm scared of is looking back on my life and realizing I was too scared to live. You raised me, Gramma. By yourself. You're the one who taught me to think bigger."

"Bigguh don't mean running from your motherly duties."

"I'm not running, I'm trying to grow!"

And as she said this, it dawned on her: Of the countless times Gramma sat on that porch, telling the story of the banduns, she never ever described these free Black giants as women. Leenie never pictured them as women. Never even thought to ask if any of them were women. The same way most people assume Dr. Jenkins is a man.

"I want to grow, Gramma. Like the banduns."

Gramma shook her head, chuckling to herself. "You so smart, huh? 'Like the banduns.' You even know why they was called banduns?"

Silence. Dr. Jenkins never thought to ask that question either.

"Means abandon," Gramma said. "As in: Your mother *abandoned* you to quote-unquote find herself and what happened? She fell off a cliff in them Himalayas."

More silence.

The space between them filled by the ever-expanding agony of unforgotten grief.

Dr. Jenkins wanted to say something. Something like 'I'm not her' or 'She only went out there to escape from that monster she married.' These words wouldn't matter to Gramma.

"Know what your problem is, Leenie? Got your head all swell-up with facts and figures, only believing what you can see and prove, but child," she tapped her ear, "you not listening."

"Listening to what?"

Gramma gestured as if to say, "My point exactly." And passed away three months later. Two months after that Dr. Jenkins was boarding *Orion II*. Not depressed or guilty or ambivalent like one might expect. She was ready.

"Go to Titan now!" she commands again.

"Shields down to fifty percent," Rigel says. "Navigation still offline."

She plugs the coordinates to the target site into the computer manually: 78° N, 249° W. "Initiate emergency landing procedures!"

"Initiating emergency landing procedures."

She *was* ready.

But right now, as the single-person spacecraft plummets toward Titan, she wonders if she made the biggest mistake of her life. Did she come on this mission to discover something? Or prove something? Maybe both. But why? Why this constant need to prove herself? Why couldn't she escape the long shadow of feeling less-than? Inferior? The feeling that no matter how high she climbs in her career, she'll always be looked down on, a speck of a speck of a speck in spacetime and the eyes of society. And that the slightest misstep will cause irreparable damage, not just to her life, but the lives of others like her.

Who can live in those conditions? Under that kind of pressure?

The nitrogen-rich tholin haze wouldn't break her fall. The dense methane shroud of clouds wouldn't break her fall. Nothing would break her fall, save the moon's freezing surface. She pictures herself outside herself, like a methane droplet in a chemical downpour, falling, in a tragically slow descent toward the north polar region.

Falling …

"I want to make an impact," she said. "Why can't you understand that?"

"What I understand is, you going through a lot right now," Dave said. This was the night after Gramma's funeral, at Gramma's house, as they were packing up Gramma's belongings. "C'mon now, let's be serious."

Falling …

"I'm dead serious."

"How you talking 'bout going to space and your grandma's body not even cold yet?"

"This is my chance to do something that matters."

Falling …

"Oh so this don't matter?" He moved his right hand in circles, like tracing an orbit, referring to him, her and sleeping baby Trane. "We don't matter?"

She was about to say, 'That's not what I meant,' but right then, her eyes caught something in one of Gramma's sweetgrass baskets. It was the box. She snuck outside to peek at her childhood in private. On the porch, in the warm solitude of the starry night as male crickets called out for mates, she opened the box and inside, all those colorful knockers, all those small worlds were still clustered together, though much smaller than she remembered. With her thumb and index finger, she held the orange one up to the clear new moon sky.

Falling …

The screen door creaked open behind her. Dave stepped out, Trane resting on his chest. He kept silent for a moment, observing; and when he did speak, his voice trembled, his words drifting out on the wavering wings of a half-whisper.

"Listen, baby, I understand you wanna go exploring, see what else is out there … I know you hate being boxed in. You been saying that since day one." He took a step forward, gazing up at the sky with her. "Now you tell me you wanna go to outer space to see if some moon can sustain human life. But here's a human life right here," he said, his long fingers on Trane's spine, like how he used to hold his sax. "Ain't she worth sustaining?"

The question echoes as if it came straight from the mouth of Ligeia Mare, which lies below her now, wide open and ready to devour Titan's first human trespasser. In the seconds before splashdown, she watches Trane, growing up so fast, bigger and bigger by the day, walking, talking, asking questions, learning to read, about to turn five, losing her baby teeth, printing her first bot buddy, wanting her own space.

Her own space.

A little girl on the porch looking up at the stars.

"Where are you, Mommy?" she calls out into the big black yonder.

But this little girl isn't Trane; it's her, Dr. Jenkins, in stretched pigtails and bright knockers, a little girl who actually believed prayer could bring her battered mother back home.

"Ain't she worth sustaining?"

Jolted by the splashdown, she opens her eyes as *Orion II* converts into a hovercraft.

Floating.

"We've arrived on Titan, Dr. Jenkins," Rigel says. "Connect to the bioport for me to check for any injuries you may have sustained."

"Give me a second." She breathes deeply, to slow her heart rate. Five-second inhale. Five-second exhale. "Do you hear something? Like a hum?"

"Systems currently in standby mode for damage assessment and repair protocols—"

"No, not … not in here," she says. "I'm going out."

"Dr. Jenkins, for your safety, it is advised that you first connect to the bioport for me to check for any injuries—"

"I'll be right back."

And moments later, she is outside the spacecraft, looking over the vast landscape that stretches out past the lake's edge, where the subdued terrain then takes over, saturated in a hazy sepia tint, something out of a dream. A deathly cold dream. Negative 180 degrees Celsius cold. Her only shield against the elements, the smart skinsuit compressed to her body; a banged-up body with bruised muscles and potentially internal bleeding that would deter anybody else.

But not Dr. Jenkins.

Below her, Ligeia Mare is still once again, like a mysteriously murky sheet of glass. What unknown creatures could be lurking in the deep? How many invisible hands might reach out to touch her, grab her, pull her under?

She replaces those thoughts with thoughts of her mother. And jumps.

She knew the viscosity of liquid methane was about a tenth that of liquid water, but the airy feeling catches her aching body off guard. She struggles to make her way, less swimming than gliding, to the shallows of the northwest shore. Crawling out of the lake and onto the land.

The surface feels somewhat solid, not all the way stable, like slush. She looks around to get her bearings and when she does, she sees it – right there, right in front of her: the footprints. She drags her wounded self forward and puts her gloved hand in the first indentation, deeper than originally estimated. When she touches it, she hears that hum once again, a familiar voice, like rolling thunder, humming 'Way Beyawn' duh Moon,' the looping soundtrack to those muggy Carolina summers, the song that helped Gramma survive and thrive, like other songs did for so many before her, and led Dr. Jenkins to being inevitably here, now.

She clutches her belly, buckles over in utter agony, her helmet hitting the frosty ground. Thinking about Gramma and her stories. And Dave and his sax. How truth, like spacetime, is relative and the beliefs we hold onto, the beliefs that keep us alive cannot, consequently, be lies.

That thought gives her the strength to lift herself to stand and start sort of walking. But she falls down, not used to the gravity being fourteen percent what it is on Earth. She stands again and the atmospheric pressure pushes against her, which feels like walking in a swimming pool, but she staggers on. Following the marked path. One excruciating leap at a time. As she goes on she discovers a different tune, a fact she can't prove, but a truth that can't be denied: Dr. Charlene Jenkins does believe in giants. She was raised by one.

And as she comes to the end of the single-file footprints, she collapses on her knees and lifts her head, and the sight, suddenly, steals from her any semblance of speech, as if the same force beckoning the billions of rocks and ice and dust to bear witness to Saturn has seized the bulk of her words as well; and the sacred few she managed to salvage can be neither spoken nor swallowed, for they remain stuck in her throat, forming a lump as her eyes grow wider, wider, filling up with all the wonder in the world.

* * *

Hear those engines roar / rumbling
Feel those fires burn
Blasting off / blasting off / blasting off / blasting off
Step back.
Hear those engines roar / rumbling
Feel those fires burn
At a loss / at a loss / at a loss / at a loss

Almost Too Good to Be True

Temi Oh

WERE YOU the first person to notice it? That winter you turned eighteen and fell out with all of your friends and London began to feel like a party you'd arrived at too late — laughter long-faded, shattered mulch of broken piñata shells crumbled under careless feet.

You'd white-knuckled it through exams and kept your eyes peeled for spring. Which arrived three months too early on the green outside the corner store at the end of your road. Little eruptions of popcorn white on the boughs of a large tree. And then, a week later, an explosion of cherry blossoms. What kind of tree was it? City-born, you can identify almost no species of plant or bird by sight alone. This one was marooned on an island of traffic. Overdressed, flaunting its cotton-candy canopy like a ballgown amongst the skeletal birches.

What kind of tree was it? The kind that sprays tiny petals like confetti down the cracked concrete before Valentine's day when the ground is still iron-hard and dusted every morning with frost.

How could anyone fail to notice it? The type of tree with leaves that turn Merlot-red right in the middle of the summer and flay off when everyone is still sunbathing. The kind that's naked all autumn long. A time-traveling tree.

Whenever you walked past it, you would nod your head and say — to your mother in her winter coat, or your grandma with her shopping trolley, or your brother whose face was lit blue by the screen of his blackberry — "that's the time-traveling tree." And they would always nod distractedly as if they had always known. As if they had discovered it.

You are time-traveling too, in the only direction. Through university and then your twenties. You turn thirty on Ash Wednesday one year. You're not catholic, but you go for the nostalgia. Lining up with the other congregants that chilly evening reminds you of being fifteen, in the school's gymnasium, waiting with your friends for the priest to apply the ashes and say, "Remember that you are dust and to dust you shall return."

During the sermon, you write down everything that you want on the leather binding in the back of your planner. You write: buy a house, finish a book, have a baby, and then you cross off two.

You've been wondering 'what if I got pregnant?' at the end of every month for the past 17 years. Wondering with a roil of dread that has curdled from nervous excitement to anticipation, and, now, to hope.

This year, the winter was particularly unhappy. No money saved, nothing but rejection letters and disappointments, a couple of snowfalls, and the overground canceled. A bad flu from which you never properly recovered. Six months of cold feet, cold fingers, and cheeks.

If you make it to spring again, you promise yourself, you'll almost forget that the cold ever happened. You always do. After the first t-shirt weather afternoon you'll sun out on the common and tell yourself that you've left those bad old days behind you, maybe forever. Maybe, for a life of late nights and warm gloaming, sitting on the rooftop of your friend's flat-share drinking dandelion and burdock, summer forever, laughing at the whole of the future.

You want a baby. You want it like a joke that's not funny anymore.

A couple of months ago, when your husband asked, "Should I pull out?", on some wild caprice you said, "Don't!" It was then that the notion crystallized in your mind. You went from not wanting it to wanting nothing but. Spent the next two weeks wondering, 'did we?' 'did we? Did we make a person?' You actually liked the thought of it; ten months of company. Their bones knit from your bones. It sounded like a love story.

Why do you want to be a mother?

On your wedding day, you watched a friend of yours dance with her mother. There is a softly lit picture of it on Instagram, the two of them are the same height, with the same haircut, the same round upper-arms, time-displaced reflections of each other. It's one of your favourite pictures of the night. The two of them laughing on the dance floor, hands softly laced into each others. Eyes closed in blind devotion. "Did we make a baby?" You asked, your sweat cooling on the rug. Are you a fool for wanting the answer to be 'yes'?

You've heard it all: about money, about global warming about a pram in the hall and how expensive childcare is, about never sleeping again. Your father in law said, "It's impossible to prepare for it."

"Okay," you said, "so I won't prepare for it."

"It's ninety percent drudgery, ten percent transcendence." Your mother has said.

Why do it? Why ever do it? If your body can make a human, though, how can you *not* do it?

Fourteen days later, you wake up as soon as the bleeding starts, at 2 am. A lonely claustrophobic hour. The moment it starts always feels like the moment before an earthquake begins, sub-frequency seismic waves. You wad tissue between your thighs, clutched by a sudden despair. You'd spend half a month hoping you were not alone, hyper-aware of your body, imagining a magic trick unfolding inside you. And now it's 2.12 am. Lightning bolts of pain in your iliac crest, your back on fire, quiet tears of disappointment. You were vain for hoping. Your husband rolls over and says, "We'll get it next time." The type of thing people say when they toss a basketball at a net and it bounces off the hoop. "It will never be this one, though," you say. "This one will never be."

* * *

You've read that women are born with all of their eggs. A fact that you've been turning over in your head for some time. It means that when your grandmother was pregnant with your mother she was also carrying some part of you. A thought that makes your head spin as you imagine a long line of mothers and their mothers and their mother's mothers, back and back to the fall of Rome, the dawn of civilization, Russian dolls of mothers inside mothers.

"Once, you carried me," you tell your grandmother who is picking bay leaves from the tree in her back garden. When you were a child, she used to tie you to her back with long swathes of cloth. You'd fall asleep with your head on the nape of her neck as she boiled pots of stew. "I've always carried you," she says.

* * *

By the next spring, you've been trying for almost a year. Trying and failing, you tell your doctor who, unhelpfully, draws a picture of your ovaries on a yellow post-it. Strange orchid. "Every month," he starts like a teacher, "you release an egg…"

He answers not one of your questions.

The only thing anyone ever tells you is not to worry. But you've seen the stats, and you know they're no longer in your favour.

* * *

Your husband goes away for two weeks. The longest time you've been apart since you were married. Last month, flush with a little cash after payday, you spent all your savings on seeds. You don't have a garden but you have a windowsill, the light-filled ledge where maybe you can grow herbs.

"We'll have all the thyme in the world," you kept joking to each other. You remember the thrill of washing dishes one evening, leaning over to find their green little blades in amongst the black soil. Your husband was delighted by them.

The week he leaves there is a lunar eclipse. You promised yourself you'll stay awake for it but drift like a wave in and out of sleep. All the lights on in the room, diagonal in the bed, feeling totally alone.

When you wake up the next morning all the plants have given up growing. "I'm a bad plant mother," you say when he comes back. "You are," he laughs but then smiles as if it could have happened to either of you … but it happened to you.

* * *

Another month, this time, you're a day late. You go to work and your mind floats happily back to the seed pearl inside you. Probably inside you. Then sob over the porcelain sink at lunch when you discover the seat of your pants wet like toffee. The hope put you to shame. Now stagger through the week, your gut wringing itself out like a dishcloth. You thought you had company.

The most exhausting thought is doing it again. The fact that your body can't help but do it again. The days after the bleeding like coming up for air. This time you'll sow seeds and this time they'll grow. This time you'll sow seeds and this time they'll grow.

* * *

You cry, now, every month. You dream about not getting out of bed. You spent everything you had on a round of treatment that failed and in the days after you imagine everyone you've ever known — your primary school best friend, your first-ever boyfriend, the handsome receptionist at your dentist's office — coming like the magi with gifts to comfort you. Champagne, pink gin and elderflower tonic, nail varnish and baklava, a Venetian mask, thing after thing and not one of them the one you want.

Everyone has their story about what finally worked and you will come round to believing all of them; acupuncture, ubiquinol, yoga, prayers to Saint Gerard Majella. When you rub the holy water your great aunt brought from Lourdes on your pelvic arch, you feel like a villager caught doing a rain dance. There is nothing you won't believe. 'Imagine your baby', the YouTube meditation tells you. You do so often that you miss her.

So maybe that's why you decide to believe in the tree.

* * *

Were you ever in a forest and thought that you heard the ground under your feet whispering? A friend of yours tells you that trees are social creatures. That they can talk to each other through a network of roots and fungi. 'The wood wide web' tells you that a mother tree may push nutrients to her saplings, or a plant under attack from pests may warn its neighbors.

Walking past that tree on the corner, you can't help but wonder what it can tell you about the future.

Another early January, and it's a riot of blossoms. You make a detour towards it on your way into the office. It's still dark, and the grass glitters with specks of ice. With a gloved hand, you touch the bark and when you turn to leave you notice that under the canopy of the tree the street looks different. The sky is flushed pink with sunrise and there is a display of easter eggs in the window of a local corner store.

Strange, you think. Though, stranger still, when you step out from underneath its canopy, the road is dark again, the sky iron-clad, a heavy mist lingering by your ankles.

Some odd trick of the light? You rub your head in confusion.

When you step back under the leaves of the tree, the street has transformed again. It's springtime. The sky is cloud-mottled and cerulean.

"Could it be true?" That peering under the dark canopy of your time-displaced tree, you can see the street a season in the future?

* * *

Now you go every day. Sometimes, twice a day. On your way to work and back. Throughout January, you watch the street from under the tree. You watch spring turn to summer. You watch as construction sites become buildings. You glimpse shop displays and magazine covers three months in advance.

Across the road the old public library — the one that smelled of mildew — begins its transformation into a ballet school. The nettle-choked playground — where teens on undersized bikes gather to smoke weed — is paved over and a couple of new shops open. An artisan coffee store in a pristine arcade. An organic food market, a bike shop.

Really, you go every day in hopes that you will catch a glimpse of yourself. How do you look in the future? Your birthday is coming up and you wonder how you look at thirty-two. You've been trying and failing so long that it has become the central sadness in both of your lives. You can see it in each other's faces a certain hopefulness extinguished. A naive faith in life. Some people try all their lives and never manage to have a baby. You consult the tree as one might a tarot-card reader or a psychic. You want some sign that you will not be one of them.

* * *

"Hope deferred makes the heart sick," says the priest at another Ash Wednesday service when you tell him that you only come once a year. He tells you about Sarah and Elizabeth and Hannah who told Jacob, "Give me children, or else I die" and then invites you back for Easter. You make no promises.

But you want something to believe in. So every day of Lent that year, you go twice. Daily pilgrimage, trudging across the unkempt grass and watching the road from under its leaves.

You see the corner store turn into a Waitrose. Somebody gets arrested, police tape tied between lampposts, oil-slick of blood on the sidewalk. You try, three months later, to stop it, but arrive a minute too late, just at the moment of collision; motorbike, jogger, bollard.

* * *

That Thursday you promise your grandmother you will accompany her to 'stations of the cross' but you go to the tree instead. To the same spot, you've worn away with your heels.

This time, when you look back at the road, you sense that you are seeing it almost two decades in the future. Everything is different. There are high-rises where there used to be squat red-bricks, glass-clad apartments like shark's teeth. People you've never seen before live there. Throngs are gathered in the square outside the dance school. Students smoking between lessons. Anxious parents, juniors with impeccable hair bun and gym bags, practicing in the sun or perched on the marble lip of a fountain you've never seen.

A girl strides across the green where you stand. She has skin dark as coffee beans, long neck, long arms, blue summer dress that shows off the curve of her thighs. Your arms, your thighs, that unmistakable arrow of your own chin. She has wireless earbuds in, a gym-bag slung lazily over one shoulder. She pulls one of her earbuds out and turns suddenly as if something surprising has caught her eye. You.

She regards you with a gasp and you see in her granite eyes that this girl knows you. Knows you've wished her into being. Her name is almost at the tip of your tongue. You want to shout it, but instead, you ask, hoping it's true, "is this the whole of the future?". Springtime eventually. Nothing but laughter from then on.

She opens her mouth to say the word but the bus comes up the road and catches her eye. She hesitates for a moment and then runs for it. Gets on. She might be looking at you through the window, her palm pressed against the glass but the sun lights the pane silver, and then she's gone.

* * *

The next day, the tree is gone. A crater in the ground like a rotten tooth. "No!" You shout when you spot it at the end of the road. Panic lances through you as you rush to the torn-up patch of ground and bury your face in the acid dirt.

They are going to build flats on top of it. Construction starts after the bank holiday.

"What's the matter?" Your husband asks, crossing the road after you.

"It's gone," you tell him.

"What?"

"The tree. The time-traveling tree."

"What are you talking about?" The fact that he doesn't know confirms that he never really believed you. What's the use in explaining now?

"I just want to know that everything turns out alright," you say with tears in your eyes, "then I could bear all of this."

* * *

On Easter Sunday, you wake up with that same old pain in your gut. There's going to be another royal baby, everyone is talking about it on the news. Every baby is someone else's baby.

It's such a good Sunday. The first real spring day, with temperatures suddenly shot up to the mid-twenties, people out on the streets in glasses and sun-hats, the sky immaculate cobalt. You wear your favourite yellow-cotton sundress, with no tights and no cardigan for the first time that year, and feel the warm air on your back as you walk to church.

On your way there, nearly 270 people are killed in a suicide bombing in churches and hotels in Sri Lanka. When you hear the news it makes you sick. All while everyone is singing hymns, your vision is blurred with tears and you think 'Why is it so hard to be born and so easy to die?'

"Easter joy is for the melancholy," says a woman from the pulpit. Her voice is high and tremulous as if also balanced on the edge of tears. She asks, "Are you tired of death too? Aren't you tired of disappointment?" She promises that you live in a world where impossible things occasionally happen. Where water sometimes turns to wine and some dead things come back to life. "There will be some joy. Complete satisfaction," she says, clutching the lectern so tightly her fingers are white. She speaks with the certainty of someone who has glimpsed the future too. Someone who has returned only to tell you. "It's impossible to believe," she says, "it's almost too good to be true. But it will be true."

You May Run On

Megan Pindling

THE DAY BEFORE the River flooded Hard Bloom and destroyed Mister Hampton's cotton crop, Mollie knelt down by the River and whispered, "I'm gonna get me free." Later that night, she whispered in her mother's ear, lips pressed against the outer shell, "I'm gonna get me free" and her mother whispered back, "Yes."

Mollie and Rosana went down into the River and stood as close to the center as they could. Mollie had with her a knife lifted from Mister Hampton's kitchen and the clothes on her back. Brackish water wet and cooled their skin. Rosana looked up at the sky and saw that the moon had hidden herself away.

"Very well," Rosana said pressing dry kisses to her daughter's forehead and eyelids. "I don't expect to see you again soon. And I am not sorry."

The River undulated and pushed Mollie towards the shore, willing to give up her River child for her to get some free.

Mollie ran because Mollie had two legs and legs are meant for running.

* * *

The first time Rosana ran from Hard Bloom to get her some free, Mister Hampton's men caught her after two days of tromping through the woods and returned with Rosana bound between their shoulder blades, splinters in their fingers. The men's breath labored under Rosana's weight, though she was not by any stretch, a large woman. One man could have held her. One man did – the first time they caught her.

When they caught her, she was sleeping beside a fallen tree trunk. The men stared at their quarry for a fraction of a heartbeat before one man snatched a fistful of her hair and pulled her out of the bramble.

"Look what I've found boys," he said smiling with all of his teeth even as Rosana snapped hers at them.

He held on to her hair as they made their way back to Hard Bloom. With one hand. He should have tied her, some part of her, down. He should have held on with both hands, but he wanted his other hand free to touch the parts of her that weren't her hair. He held on to her with one hand. And when she twisted in his one hand, it surprised him, and he let her hair go. She ran a distance of three tree trunks when they brought her down.

The slaves of Hard Bloom stilled in the fields and in the kitchens to watch Rosana's procession. Each man had a hand or two on some part of her. Mister Hampton looked to see that it was her and went back to his house and shut the door. He didn't have the stomach for demonstrative violence. He preferred the fleeting violence of a pinched bottom or a tweaked nose. When a slave had to be beaten, he went into his house and closed the curtains, but he listened at the cracks to be sure that it was done.

The night after Rosana's first beating, Mollie's father counted the scars that stretched like persistent tree branches across Rosana's back.

"I count eleven."

Eleven kisses on her back.

Twenty-nine kisses on his back.

Mister Hampton sold Mollie's father before either he or Rosana knew that Mollie had begun to begin. Rosana would look down into Mollie's face and see the face of a man who would never know what he had helped to create.

* * *

Mollie was born once upon a time in a rush of water.

The waters came fast.

Rosana went down to the River when her back bowed and Mollie began to fight her way out of Rosana's body. She laid down her clothing on the Riverbank and walked to the edge, until water brushed the underside of her toes. It was cold. The sky above her, hard and wide, holding its breath. She walked until hard, cold rock became soft and gave way to her footsteps. The River was ravenous. It could, and it would, consume her. It nipped at her ankles with razor sharp teeth and then her calves and then her thighs and all of spaces in between her thighs. Hungry. At her hips, the water gentled and caressed. It warmed. She cupped her hand to collect a little water and brought it to her lips for she had become suddenly and unaccountably thirsty.

The child moved. She tore and she bit her way through gristle, desperate to breathe. Mollie punched through, fist first and swam the rest of the way out. She swam so far and so quick, Rosana had to reach out her arms to catch her River child. With her fingertips Rosana grasped Mollie's heel when the baby would have floated down the length of the River.

The waves tried to swallow Mollie into its open mouth, but Rosana would not relinquish her child to the River. Rosana stretched her hand and circled Mollie's ankle between her thumb and forefinger. The River opened her mouth wider. They tugged on Mollie's tiny body, mother and River goddess fighting for what they saw as theirs. Rosana's body clenched, ready to dispel the afterbirth, and she made the River a promise. "You can have the rest. The rest, I will give you freely." The greedy River devoured the offering, taking no time to savor in the consuming frenzy.

On the Riverbank, Rosana brought Mollie to her breast but the baby latched on to a spot just above Rosana's nipple and sucked at the drops of water there. She brought Mollie to her nipple, but the baby wouldn't drink the milk that had begun to flow. Milk slipped down Rosana's torso and into the ground.

The River watched Rosana walk back towards the slave cabins and whispered, "For now" to Rosana's back. By the flex of her spine, the River knew that she had heard her. Rosana promised to love Mollie, "though not, perhaps, as well as the River would have loved you." She wove a basket out of sweet grass and placed Mollie in the heart of it and imagined that it could carry her precious baby down the River, far from Hard Bloom.

* * *

Hard Bloom produced annually 8,000 pounds of cotton, 7,000 pounds of rice and 3,000 pounds of sugar. Mister Hampton crowed his success to anyone who would hear, owing it to the richness of the land, not to the people who worked the land.

"Good earth will prove itself." If someone asked him how he managed to find gold in Georgia, he would pull out a handful of dirt from his pockets and show them his gold. He never left Hard Bloom without bringing a piece of his land with him. At church on Sundays when the reverend instructed his parishioners to give thanks, Mister Hampton slipped his hand into his suit pocket where the dirt browned the insides. There was always dirt under his fingernails.

He wore Hard Bloom cotton and would not allow it to be dyed. He wanted to wear it as white as it came out of the ground. He loved nothing more than wading through the ocean of cotton. Smelling the cotton, smelling himself.

Rosana produced annually, 600 pounds of cotton, 300 pounds of rice and 100 pounds of sugar. With her hands she made Mister Hampton rich. She picked so quickly her hands bled from the cotton burrs that resisted the loss of their meat. She fought the resistance and left cotton painted red.

Like her mother, Mollie bled all over Hard Bloom, picked cotton faster and faster anticipating the blood that would well from her fingertips and palms and meant that she was alive. At the end of each day, Mollie washed her bloodied hands in the River and watched as blood like puffs of breath danced around and around. She used two hands to cup and bring water to her lips, but when the water wouldn't come fast enough, she lay on her belly until her lips kissed the surface. She drank. Great inhalations of water. Until her entire head disappeared beneath the surface and all you could see were the pearls bisecting her back.

Rosana grabbed fistfuls of her daughter's clothes and pulled her back from the water's edge. "You can't have her yet," Rosana told the River and reminded herself that she didn't have Mollie at all. She didn't waste time being jealous that Mollie loved the River as much as she loved her. She didn't mind sharing so long as Mollie laid her head on Rosana's breast at night. The older women warned Rosana not to let her love overflow.

"It wouldn't do, when the Master can take and sell your body and whatever comes out of it." Dee, who at sixty produced the same number of bushels of cotton that she did at twenty, did not say this out of unkindness, but out of a truth tattooed on her womb where her own children had been.

* * *

When Mollie was sixteen and Hard Bloom produced annually for the first time 4,000 pounds of sugar, Rosana attempted free for the fourth and final time. Mollie grew and Rosana added to the growth on her back, several more branches that bent when she bent and stretched when she stretched. After the third time, Mollie had given her mother one hundred and one kisses. It took her half the night.

The night before Rosana ran for the fourth time, she told Mollie, "Free is the whole world. The whole sky and the ground beneath your feet. I drank free from the dew caught in the leaves. I ate free in heavy peaches. I let free get sticky around my mouth. I left free everywhere. In my footprints. Every time I touched a tree trunk. Mister Hampton doesn't know that kind of free."

Mollie leaned in close to her mother to catch a whiff of free that clung to her skin.

"What kind of free, mama?"

"Free lost and found."

Rosana whispered free into her daughter's hair as they lay on the pallet. She kneaded it into her daughter's back after harvest. She breathed it into her with a kiss on the mouth. When she ran and then was caught, she made sure to bring back enough to share with her daughter. Mollie ingested free more readily than she had her mother's milk. Mollie and Rosana whispered free to each other until Mollie's body pressed against her mother's and was a match in length and width. Mollie grew with free whispered in her hair.

* * *

Mister Hampton watched from the portico as his men brought Rosana back a fourth time. He watched his men remove Rosana's arms from her dress one at a time the way they would undress a small child. They tied her arms to a thick tree branch above her head and her body bent like a wave. The first lash didn't land until the door to the great house latched.

The buzz of insects couched the sound of the whip slicing through the air. Hampton's man took up a natural rhythm. He beat Rosana with percussive intent. Mollie covered her ears, but kept her eyes opened. Rosana's blood rolled down the hill.

After, the women gathered to clean Rosana's open back. They used needle points to prick the swollen skin until the pus burst out, the white meat bloomed in the jagged incisions that latticed from the top of her buttocks to curve of her neck. Putrefaction was a living thing on Rosana's back. The women re-opened old scars for better access. Turpentine and red pepper were pressed into Rosana's wounds. Mollie kissed her mother's nose and forehead, and then her mouth that was swollen from screaming. Two women at Rosana's back pressed down, getting blood under their fingertips.

Mollie ran down to the River and gathered water in her cupped palms and brought it to her mother's broken back. Before the women could stop her, she poured the water into the wounds.

Dee slapped Mollie across the face. "Stupid girl! The dirty River water will cause illness." She slapped her again because she could not slap Rosana.

"Your mama don't know what's good for her and her mama ain't around to tell her, so I have to."

"Is mama going to die?" she asked Dee, but Dee didn't answer.

"Is mama going to die?" she asked the River. And the River said, "Not yet."

"Are you going to die," she asked her mother. And her mother said, "Take me to the River."

Mollie led Rosana to the River by a hand, and mother, daughter and River were reunited. Rosana dipped herself into the River seven times.

* * *

The night before the River flooded Hard Bloom, Mollie walked through rows of cotton with hands outspread until blood dripped from her fingertips. She ran from Hard Bloom. She ran from her mothers. Away.

Just beyond Mister Hampton's house stood a great wood, thick and green and brown. She fled to it and the forest swallowed Mollie, eager to receive her. In her bare feet, she clung to the earth with each step. Grateful for its dryness. She ran through earth, covered in earth and learned what it meant to be free. She ate fruit from the trees that hung heavy in the canopy during the day and mingled blood and earth to cover herself at night.

The morning after Mollie ran from Hard Bloom, Mister Hampton stood on the porch and looked at his land and his people and felt like a king of his own making. When one of his men walked up to the porch, hat in hand, to tell him that one of his slaves had run, Mister Hampton took a sip from the hot coffee in his hands.

"Break her this time. She won't be bend." It was approaching the heat of the day, and still Mister Hampton took a draught of the hot liquid that dulled his teeth and tickled his eyelashes.

"It isn't Rosana this time sir." He said the words slowly, the combination and order foreign. "Her daughter."

Mister Hampton sent out five men on horseback after Rosana's daughter. He watched the men and their horses disappear after Mollie before turning back to his cotton.

* * *

Rosana stepped into the River before the first of Mister Hampton's men entered the wood, gone after Mollie. Rosana could see her reflection in the water's surface. She looked like a mother, she thought. The water brushed her collar bone and she walked on. The water flowed between her lips and she walked on. The water washed the sweat from her scalp and the water finally had what she wanted. The water was warmer than it ought to be at that time of year, salivating it was, for her.

"Eat," she told the River. "Eat." She slipped beneath the surface.

* * *

The River flooded her banks. She dismantled the irrigation channels. She spoiled the crop out of spite. Her waters consumed cotton and licked at the heels of the slaves as they fled the fields. The overseers did not look behind them as they ran from the waters and Hard Bloom. They covered their noses as they ran.

Mister Hampton had his slaves build a mud dam to stave off the River's most vigorous aggression. But she made the mud part of herself. All was mud, and the rest, the residue of mud. Her waters raced ashore and overcame any man-made barrier.

"Use stones!" he said feeling less like a king.

He snatched the whip out of a fleeing overseer's hand and beat any man, white or black, in the circumference of its arc. Even his malignant benevolence evaporated in the face of his concern for economy. "The cotton cannot stand all of this water," he said to himself as his voice could not be heard over the marauding waters.

The River passed over the slave quarters and raced for Mister Hampton's House. She licked the lip of the portico and threatened to overtake the white-washed steps. The house trembled, a child holding back tears and losing the fight.

The River nipping at his ankles, Mister Hampton fled into his house and shut the door – some water followed him inside. Cotton growers surrounded Mister Hampton's house with roughhewn stones. They walled their master in his house. Up high, the stones reached the height of their heads.

The slaves tried to fight back the waters, but they could not compete with the rage of her rush. The River cried out, filling every available crevice. Hampton's head rang with the force of it. It echoed inside his head, rattled his bones.

* * *

Hampton's men found Mollie easily before the sun had set on the third day. It was her first run for free and her feet were too heavy on the ground.

"See if you can catch her," their leader said to his men and their dogs. Her feet were heavy and they were on horseback. They corralled her in a clearing, smirks painted across their mouths not knowing that Hard Bloom was under water.

"Come girl," their leader said, "It's obvious you're tired and you've been caught." His men laughed in a fractured chorus.

"I'm disappointed," he said with mock paternal regret. "Your mother would have gotten farther than this."

Like they would with her mother, the men tightened their circle. Mollie stilled. One eager young man slid from the stirrups and approached her, hand outstretched. Mollie took the knife from her pocket. Thinking she meant to strike at him, the young man jumped back. Boots shook the ground as the rest of the men dismounted. Mollie placed the knife along her throat.

Water trickled from the corner of her eyes. She stuck out her tongue and when she tasted salt, she ran the blade along the delicate skin at her neck. Water spilled from the wound with enough force to make her stumble. When she righted herself, she took the blade, stuck it between her breasts and twisted the knife. Water shot out and hit the shirtfront of the man directly before her. The men jumped back and the dogs ran, their staccato barks echoing in the trees and off of the waters growing from the hole in Mollie's chest. She cut down the middle, from just under her breasts to her belly and sighed at the overwhelming relief of having emptied the weight she'd carried inside of her. Rivers are heavy, she reminded herself.

Hampton's man tried to take hold of her, but she slipped through his fingers. The men fled, following the dogs who knew better, but Mollie chased after them. Her waters cut deep grooves in the ground. She reached down and found more water, hidden beneath bedrock. They joined her and they charted a path for Hard Bloom.

Mollie as River. Hard Bloom under her. Mollie happy to return to her mothers.

Suffering Inside, But Still I Soar

Sylvie Soul

March 11, 2019

ARRGH!!! Claire can be such a two-faced jerk sometimes. She KNOWS how I feel about Devin, and yet she still flirts with him during third period Biology. I swear, if she does it again, I'm going to slap her.

March 13, 2019

Claire and I had a huge argument at her place tonight. She told me she hoped Devin would ask her out to the Spring Dance and I let her have it. She was still screaming at me from the front porch when I left. So immature. Why was I cursed with such garbage friends???

March 15, 2019

Wow, I almost died today.

I was walking home after soccer practice (ALONE – thanks a lot, Claire) when something fell out of the sky and slammed into the ground really close to me! Thankfully, I was okay. I went to investigate and found the culprit: a small glowing rock sticking out of a crater. As soon as I touched it, I felt this immense wave of energy pass over me, then the glowing stopped.

I'm not a dork. I mean, I don't collect rocks or anything. But it was really pretty, so I took it.

Then this little brown animal showed up out of nowhere and started rubbing against me like a cat. At least I thought it was a cat at first. Actually, it looked more like a squirrel – it had a tail and stood on its hind legs. But its ears were HUGE. It looked straight at me and started chattering at me cutely.

So against my better judgment, I brought the squirrel-thing home. I figured it was hungry, so I snuck it some lettuce from my kitchen (I have no idea what squirrels eat LOL).

After eating, the squirrel-thing seemed content, and decided to snuggle with me. It was nice, like having a living stuffed animal.

Ha – I am the world's worst daughter. I'm smuggling a live animal in my bedroom.

Mom and Dad are cool…MOST of the time. But they most definitely aren't big on pets. Even if they were, I doubt they'd let me keep the thing. Their first question would be what it is, and their second would be if it has rabies. Since I can't answer either question, I'll decide to keep it a secret. For now.

March 17, 2019

I've made the rock I found into a cute little necklace. Hope Devin notices.

March 18, 2019

OMG – Devin talked to me today! Claire was so jealous. This necklace is my lucky charm, I'm never taking it off.

March 19, 2019

OMG!

I can fly!!!

I am actually writing this while sitting on somebody's roof! This is so wild!!!

I woke up in the middle of the night and found that I was hovering a few inches off the ground in my sleep! Of course I panicked – who wouldn't? – and fell right back down into my bed. At first, I was convinced that I was actually dreaming and ignored it. But a few seconds later, it happened again! This time, I didn't freak out, I just sort of floated around my room while on my back.

I hovered over to my window and flew outside. I was slow at first, opting to hover around my rooftop.

Then I flew around the neighborhood and came back for my diary so I could record this for posterity and prove that I'm not dreaming. I still can't believe I'm writing this. I CAN FLY!!!!!!!!

March 22, 2019

I decided to give the squirrel-thing a name. I call it Chance, because I feel like it was pure chance that I would stumble upon a new pet and these crazy powers just a few days apart. Somehow I feel like they're both connected.

I really love flying. Not because I'm the only one who can do it – although that IS a pretty good reason – but because of how it feels to me. It's hard to describe. It's like when you have a dream, and in that dream you have something special, or are really good at something and it just feels natural. Like you've always had that ability. That's what flying is like for me. It feels like I always had this power.

Not just power, but freedom. Ultimate freedom. If I was walking down the street and looked up, I could wish to be there, and then I can fulfill that wish. I could feel the freeing sensation of my feet leaving the ground. I can feel my will, like imaginary wings, taking me where I want to go, with no rules, no restrictions, no fear.

Yesterday, I flew during the morning for the first time. I know St. John's isn't super busy like Toronto or New York City, but I still took a huge risk that someone would see me fly up to Signal Hill. I can't help it. Now that I can fly, it seems like the most obvious place to go.

From Cabot Tower, I can see all of St. John's. That's all of my life right there, encapsulated in a snapshot of The Rock. It seemed so big from the ground – it was huge to me the first time I came up here on foot for a Grade 3 field trip.

But when I'm up there on Signal Hill, I feel like I've seen all I need to see of St. John's. That I've conquered it. My whole life is here – my friends and my family. I couldn't ask for anything else.

I love my town. I love it more now that it's all within my reach.

March 23, 2019

Chance was acting really crazy today. I took him (I'm still not sure if Chance is a boy or girl, but I've been calling him a boy) out for a walk to see if he would calm down. He led me close to the water, near the docks, to this deserted part of town. The crystal around my neck glowed when we arrived.

When I got there, this shadow figure emerged in front of me. Like, it literally materialized before my eyes, clawing out of the ground like a demon and snarling.

I was so scared. I'm pretty sure I screamed at the top of my lungs and ran all the way back home.

March 25, 2019

Some really gruesome news going around town. Dad says several dogs have gone missing from homes of their owners. Some were located, dead. Their bodies were ripped to shreds, like some sort of larger animal mauled it to ribbons. Cops think it was wolves, or a wild bear, but I can't shake the feeling those claw marks belong to that thing I stumbled upon the other day.

Is it my fault those dogs are dead?

March 26, 2019

I decided to stop being a coward. I let Chance lead me back to the shadow creature.

This time, he led me to a vacant lot not far from Jellybean Row. When Chance stopped and started to bristle, I knew he'd found it. Right on cue, the shadow appeared.

Suddenly I felt that warm energy from before permeating in the pit of my stomach. I realized that I was glowing, and an aura of fire-like energy covered my entire body.

I felt bold, like I could take on the world. I ran up to the shadow and punched it, and it exploded into a million pieces that dissipated like smoke. That was cool.

The part that was NOT cool was when I calmed down from my energy high and I realized those flames had eaten away my clothes. I was TOTALLY NAKED!! Thank GOD I had some dirty gym clothes in my backpack, otherwise I'd have no idea how I would've gotten home!

I must've been given these powers, and Chance, for a reason. I guess he wants me to fight these shadow things and protect my city.

I don't really want to do this. But I also don't want to be responsible for a bunch of murdered pets around St. John's. Or worse. What if next time, it's not just a pet?

What choice do I have?

April 10, 2019

Wow, so busy. I'm getting the hang of incorporating 'fighting evil' into my daily routine. I've developed a system for combatting monsters while still juggling schoolwork and maintaining an active social life. We just had our Spring Dance, and Claire and I both got to slow dance with Devin (I know she's my best friend and all, but she really needs to find someone else to crush on, because Devin is MINE). I had to drop out of soccer, though. That was simply too much on my plate.

Every Saturday, after Mom and Dad are in bed, I sneak out with Chance and patrol the streets of St. John's. I use the rock from my necklace as a beacon to find the shadow creatures. Once I find them, I power-up and punch them so they disappear. Easy-peasy.

I've also mastered the whole 'clothes melting off' issue. Turns out I have to be calm when I use my powers. That means if I'm stressed or scared or tired or even hungry, then my powers 'flame on' and eat away at whatever I'm wearing. But I've planned ahead by bringing my backpack with a spare change of clothes, just in case. So when I'm finished handling the shadow monsters, I can change quickly and without any hassle.

Chance accompanies me on all of the hunts, so I never feel alone. Though I do miss spending time with Claire, even if she gets on my nerves.

May 12, 2019

DEVIN IS OFFICIALLY ANCIENT HISTORY.

I heard from someone in English class that he asked Claire out.

That's alright, because I found someone even better.

His name is Jeff. I met him after one of my nightly rounds led me to George Street, the party district in St. John's.

I had a rough go with one of the shadows. My clothes weren't completely melted off, but I went from wearing a turtleneck sweater and jeans to a crop top and distressed jean shorts. That apparently got Jeff's attention.

We spent the night talking, walking up and down that single strip of George Street (I'm still not old enough to drink). I learned that Jeff didn't go to school, and that he worked in the area, at a nearby manufacturing plant.

The only place we could get into was a karaoke bar at the end of George Street. I should've went home right after my fight, but instead Jeff and I sang the night away with cheesy 90s one-hit wonders. Claire can stick to her little boys. I got myself a GROWN MAN.

June 27, 2019

Thank GOD it's summer. I've had enough of this school year.

My grades have tanked in the last few weeks. Guess I wasn't juggling my responsibilities as well as I thought. Heh. Mom and Dad aren't too happy about that.

Oh yeah – and they finally found out about Chance. Either that, or they were tired of pretending like they didn't hear all those squeals and foot patters coming from my room. Naturally, they wanted him out. Chance seems self-sufficient, but I still worry about him. I sneak him snacks whenever I can.

There was an uptick in dead animal cases. Mainly strays, but a few pets again. The monsters have been appearing more frequently, which means I have to go on my walks every night. And they've been getting stronger, and more aggressive.

I was fighting a few days ago, and this particularly fast shadow managed to sneak behind me and slice my shoulders with its claws. That frickin' hurt.

I came home with blood seeping down my clothes, which were already in dwindling short supply. Not really a sight I could explain to my parents, who stayed up late to wait for me. FML.

Question: how do you tell your Mom and Dad that you're essentially protecting them from the creatures that go bump in the night? Answer: you don't. You lie, you deflect, and in the process they begin to trust you less and less.

I've become distant from my friends as well. Especially Claire. Claire and I are no longer on speaking terms. Honestly, I don't think we have anything in common anymore. And after the whole Devin/Spring Dance debacle, our on-again, off-again friendship might permanently be in the off position.

Oh well. At least I still have Jeff. We've been hanging out a lot more throughout the week.

There have been times when I had to leave class in the middle of the day to deal with the monsters. I would use that as an opportunity to take a quick detour and see Jeff at the park or at a coffee shop. Sometimes people give us strange looks, but I couldn't care less. I've got what they can't have so they're probably jealous.

July 8, 2019

I think I've found the shadows nest. (Do shadows have nests? If they do, are they even CALLED nests? Whatever. That's what I'm calling it.)

There was a massive electrical storm last night that cut out all the power in St. John's. The thunder woke me up; the first thing I saw was the crystal around my neck, and it was glowing so brightly it lit up the entire room. Then I saw Chance tapping at my window frantically.

I snuck out of the house under cloak of rain and darkness and followed Chance until I found an army of shadows assembling in the downtown core. I knew what I had to do. I powered up and prepared to fight.

A mass of gnashing teeth and claws came at me in a flurry of rage. It was unpleasant. Actually, scratch that – it SUCKED. I had to go into it with my full power.

When I was finally done, I stood alone in the middle of the street, the eviscerated carcasses of the beasts smoldering despite the heavy downpour of rain. As usual, my clothes had melted off, but this time I forgot to bring my backpack. I grabbed a nearby black tarp and wrapped it around my body like a toga.

Suddenly, I heard this loud creaking noise. I couldn't see the source from my vantage point, so I flew straight up in the air to investigate.

St John's is quite a sight in the rain. I mean, it's breathtaking when it's blue sky on a clear day, but in less ideal weather, it takes on a whole different persona. On foggy days, it's like a ghost town; on snowy days it feels like a cozy little picturesque village you'd see as the December spread of a landscape calendar.

But in a rainstorm, St. John's was bipolar. All the charm and character that people talk about when they mention our town? Gone out the window. Especially during hurricane season, St. John's a veritable hellscape, lacking all the things that make it so endearing.

And it felt like hell floating in the air, in the middle of a thunderstorm. The waves whipped about like crazy, like God himself was ticked off about something and needed to let off some steam.

I've had nightmares like this. Wind and rain would whip around madly in a dark, deserted city without any light or comfort. Flying afforded me a lot of unique views, but this was one I could definitely do without.

In the distance, I spotted a freighter being tossed around like a toy boat in the bathtub of an overly enthusiastic toddler. As I watched the scene unfold, a giant wave overtook the freighter and it capsized.

I grappled for some time with the idea of letting others know about my powers. I couldn't abandon people in peril, so I flew to the freighter.

Everything was sideways when I had arrived. I found a door and kicked it in, then descended into the depths of the freighter looking for survivors. I found a man, holding on for dear life to bars attached to the walls. I saw another man, but he wasn't moving; it looked like his neck was snapped. It was the first time I had ever seen a dead body.

The survivor looked at me with bugged out eyes, like I was the Grim Reaper, coming to collect his soul. I guess that made sense – I was wearing the oversized black tarp that sort of resembled the cloak of death.

The man pointed out I was bleeding. Apparently, my arm was slashed from a wound I didn't even realize I had sustained.

I safely lowered the man to where the body was and instructed him to carry it (well I wasn't going to do it). I found out the man's name was Carl, and his unlucky friend was John. So I scooped Carl into my arms and flew into the air (the perks of having super strength). As I flew away from the wreckage, an explosion erupted from the freighter; it quickly disappeared under the water.

I lowered Carl and his cargo onto solid ground, then I flew back to Cabot Tower. I landed on the roof of the tower and collapsed on my back, the rain pelting my face and beaten body. Mood: exhausted but exhilarated.

That night was a turning point for me. I actually saved someone! Not just someone's dumb dog! I actually made a difference in someone's life. Maybe these powers are good for something after all.

September 1, 2019

Wow. SO MUCH has changed since I last wrote in this diary.

Mom and Dad caught wind of me skipping school through people around town. Apparently, the owner of one of the coffee shops Jeff and I frequented was friends with my homeroom teacher, and she was the one who spilled the beans to my folks. We had a massive blowout in August. I didn't need the aggravation, so I packed my bag and moved out. I'm currently living with Jeff on the other side of town.

The shadow creatures stopped appearing in St. John's after the night of the electrical storm. I haven't seen my necklace glow since.

Thank God Jeff is cool with pets; Chance has been living with me again.

Chance has been quiet lately. He's seemed to have aged six years in the six months that I've owned him. His energy has really taken a nosedive, and most of the time he just lulls around my room, sleeping. He's been eating a lot less, too – I hope there's nothing wrong with him.

Oh yeah. I've dropped out of school. Jeff says I don't need it, and he's right. Who needs school when you've got superpowers?

I decided to give being a local superhero a try. I wear a mask and I've made myself a costume by dyeing an old cheerleading outfit I found at a thrift shop pink and purple. I even thought up a cool name – Valiant.

So far I've done some basic stuff: broken up bar fights on George Street, pulled a baby from a burning car after a collision, rescued a cat from a tree (cliché, I know).

I've told Jeff that I could fly early on in our relationship; he scoffed and asked if I was high, so I dropped it. But he's technically the only other person who knows about what I can do.

I'm hoping to eventually do something truly heroic, like when I saved Carl in the freighter. Maybe then I can smooth things out with my parents and they'll see that I'm not a screw-up and that they were wrong to doubt me.

October 3, 2019

Chance is dead.

When I woke up this morning, I found his limp body lying on a pile of clothes in the corner of the room. He seemed so small. Like a stuffed animal. Like the first night when he snuggled with me.

I was devastated. I didn't know what to do…so I didn't do anything. I left the apartment and went for a walk. I knew I could fly, but in that moment, flying didn't seem appropriate. So, I walked for a few hours. Nowhere in particular. When I returned, the pile of clothes was gone and so was Chance.

I asked Jeff about it. He told me he bundled it all up and threw it in a nearby dumpster. Then he asked when I was going to get a job and contribute to the rent.

October 21, 2019

My heart is reeling.

I knew things weren't great between me Jeff – it started getting bad as soon as I moved in. But things went south real fast. He was always criticizing me, calling me lazy and stupid and useless for not having a job. Either he forgot what I told him about my powers or he didn't believe me. I never felt like reminding him.

But what he did last night was absolutely unforgiveable.

Jeff invited one of his friends over. I didn't think anything of it – Jeff had his work buddies over all the time.

But this guy was different. I remember getting a really weird vibe as soon as he entered the living room.

I was watching TV on the couch when suddenly Jeff had grabbed my arms and pinned me down.

"If you're gonna stay, you're gonna earn your keep," he growled in my ear. His breath reeked of booze.

The other guy loomed over me and attempted to grab my legs.

I fought back; I kicked the guy in the face. I'm sure he lost a few teeth.

I escaped Jeff's grip and scrambled to my feet and ran to the room I slept in, locking the door immediately.

Jeff started pounding on the door and calling me all sorts of horrible names. At that point, I knew there was no way I was leaving the apartment the way I came in.

I filled my backpack with everything I could carry and escaped out the window.

I could've flown to my favorite spot – Cabot Tower – but I couldn't bear to sully that place with these disgusting memories so I slept behind a coffee shop. The same coffee shop where I confessed to Jeff that I loved him.

I've never felt so low in my life.

October 23, 2019

My necklace glowed today. It hadn't done that for months. To get my mind off my current situation, I flew around until I pinpointed the source: a white commercial van that I hadn't seen around town before.

I followed the van to an abandoned building in the industrial part of town. Instead of a shadow creature, a shady-looking guy emerged from the van. He was overweight, with a lumberjack's beard and a shaved head; he wore grey sweatpants and a dark grey hoodie that barely fit over his belly. He went inside the building while holding a bag of fast food. I snuck inside after him. He stopped beside a door leading into a small dark room and tossed the bag into the shadows, then he walked down the hall and disappeared behind a door at the opposite end.

When he was out of sight, I crept into the first room and turned on the light. My heart sank.

A girl was lying on the ground on her side. I didn't recognize her, but she looked to be about my age, maybe a little younger. It's very likely she could have gone to my school. She was alive, because I could see her chest rise and fall, but she looked very weak. Her brown hair clung limply to her face. She had an arm outstretched; she was trying to reach for the contents of the fast-food bag but she was chained to the wall.

I backed away from the room. I walked down the hall to where the man had exited and opened the door. By the time I entered the room, the glow of my necklace was blindingly bright.

The man was sitting on a chair watching a show on a laptop. He looked up at me and swore.

The rest was a blur.

When I fought the shadows, it didn't really register to me that I was destroying an actual life. It felt more like extinguishing the flame of a candle. There was a presence with tangible energy, and then there wasn't.

With a human body, every bit of contact has feedback. Every connection lingers: the snap of bone, the echo of screams against the wall, the slippery sensation of blood and other bodily fluids.

Unlike a shadow, a human being is messy.

I returned to the room with the girl. I ripped the chains clear out of the wall and took her into my arms. When I rescued Carl, my super strength kept him from being a burden. But this girl felt so small, she didn't even feel real. I held her tightly to my chest; she was like a doll in my old room, at my parents' house. But she was warm. She felt like Chance. Her shallow breathing snapped me out of it and reminded me that she wasn't a thing. I was upset that some people in the world needed to be reminded that she wasn't a commodity.

I flew until I found a group of older guys outside playing basketball. The teens had forgotten all about their game when I dropped from the sky. I handed the girl to one of the teens; his eyes were wide with questions.

I answered none of them. I couldn't. I turned around and flew away. Then I cried. I haven't stopped crying.

October 29, 2019

I can't do this anymore.

I'm so tired.

The flying, the powers – they're honestly the worst things to ever happen to me. When I found out I could fly, I was so happy. I thought it would be fun, that it would open doors to endless possibilities. Instead, those doors have been closed shut to me. I have nothing now, except this diary and this rock around my neck: a constant reminder of my lost innocence. I'm no longer the naïve girl who once thought she could change the world.

I have no future; I became a dropout just to chase this insane dream of becoming a superhero. I thought I could make a difference. I was wrong.

I can never go back to Mom and Dad. It's only a matter of time before the cops track me down as the person who murdered that kidnapper.

I know I did the right thing, so why do I feel like the monster?

I need to leave St John's.

This will be my last entry. To whoever visits Signal Hill and finds this diary, please give it to my parents. Let them know that I'm sorry.

Let them know they encouraged me to spread my wings and fly. To soar above the limits of my surroundings.

I'm doing it now. Though my feet no longer touch the ground, my head is no longer in the clouds. Goodbye.

Val

The Pox Party

Lyle Stiles

UGH. I CAN'T BELIEVE I'M HERE. This dump smells horrible. The nasty ass smell of rotten eggs and copper from this hill of trash is unbearable. But I can't leave now. I know I saw it here. I dig through piles of broken toys, old box-computers, and used diapers before I spot it again.

The top of the dingy silver board stands out from rest of the junk. I grip the tip of the board, as Juan shouts from the bottom of the trash heap.

"Yo Keisha, you done yet?!"

"I *said* give me a minute." I shout. Grunting, I yank the board out with all my strength and fall backwards, tumbling down the hill of trash. I hit the dirt floor hard – but I've still got the board in my hands.

"Swayze!" I smirk and pull a stray wire from the poof in the back of my pulled hair.

"You got me standing out in this heat for that?" Juan wipes his face, shifting the black hair stuck to his light-skinned forehead. He stares at the board in my hand and shakes his head. "I could've gotten you a better one."

"Nah, I'm good." I say. "I don't want your stolen stuff."

I throw the board down the dirt road between the garbage mounds. It hits the ground and slides.

"Figured it would be busted." I whisper, walking over to it. With the pants legs of my dingy blue overalls rolled up, I sit on the ground. The exposed brown skin on my legs itch from the dirt. It sucks but I gotta start now. The guilt will kill me if I don't.

"At least my stolen stuff works…" Juan mutters, like a gnat behind my ear. "Why do you even need that thing anyway? Tell me you're not still going through with your plan."

"Since when have I backed down from anything round here?" I say without looking up. I flip the elongated oval board around trying to find the right spot.

"It's not around *here*. That's the problem." Juan counters.

I tap the gold band on my wrist. A light-projected vid appears over it, and a clip of a woman fixing a silver board plays.

"*Yes*, I'm still going through with it." I respond, trying to hear the low sounds from the vid. "Now *hush*."

Juan sucks his teeth then pulls a vid-game out of his pocket.

I tap the band, raising the vid's volume. The woman in the holo talks about the board's ion-drive and shows schematics.

"This is the thing that's prolly broke…" I pull the ion drive out of the board's bottom panel. Squinting and staring at the square piece, I'm sure it's the same part in the vid. I snatch a few tools out of my overalls. I snip out the old qubit and solder a new one in its place. The one I brought looks a little too big, but it's gonna have to do.

"Done." I say, sliding the repaired ion drive back into the board. It glows green. I toss the board a few feet away. It rights itself and hovers above the ground.

"Schway!" I thought this part would take weeks. "Aight. The hard part is done. Now all I gotta do is find that lady."

Juan stops his game and looks at the floating board. "Hmm. Not bad for a *ten*."

"Would you stop with that?" I snap. "If I'm a *ten*, you're damn sure a *ten*."

I hate it when he uses that word. Only highlanders call us that, and Juan only says it cause he swears he's moving there. I'm tired of those rich *bicks* in their high-rises calling us 'tens' and 'untennables' just because we live in tenements. If they ever said that to my face, I'd tell 'em my name for *them* – human trash.

We don't even live in actual tenements anymore. Since the global warming part of 'the Pox' got worse, the rains and flooding did too. Most lowland buildings have structural damage, and no one's got *greenz* to fix them. They haven't been safe since I was in diapers. We mostly just live in tents now – easier to pick up when it floods, and you don't worry about them collapsing on you. They probably don't help much with the name though.

"Being a ten is temporary." Juan responds. "I won't be here for long."

I roll my eyes. "Yeah, ok. Good luck with that." I walk to the hovering board and step on it. It sways, and I wobble around until it finally steadies. I lean forward but the board ain't moving.

"What's wrong?" I mutter.

"Maybe it's not really fixed."

"Oh, shut up."

I kneel and reach beneath the board, pushing in the underside panel because it might be loose. Suddenly, it flashes red and shoots me up into the air. My stomach hits the board. I wrap my arms around it, trying not to look down, but I can see the whole dump site and our 'tenement' of tents nearby. Eventually, the board stops, hovering high in the air. I pant.

Somehow, I'm still alive. I hug the board tighter, and accidentally hit the bottom panel again.

"Thank goooo—" The board drops. It plummets all the way back down, stopping right before it hits the ground and hovers.

"Oh god." I say, huffing.

Juan gasps. "See?! That's a sign. You shouldn't go through with this. It's just a *muk* watch."

I roll off the board, as it turns green again. Still huffing, I stare at my gold wristband. "I don't care. I stole this iRiST, so I'm gonna return it."

Trust me, I'm not proud of it. I swiped it from a woman at an abandoned transport stop. This *bick* had to be a highlander. She stared at everyone like it was a zoo. The woman was so busy ogling everyone and notetaking, she stopped paying attention to her second iRiST next to her. My old ass box-computer was dying, so I snatched it. So what? Everyone takes stuff. It doesn't matter how much say it. I know what mom would think, so the guilt is killing me.

"Look, I..." Juan stops himself. "It's only been two weeks, maybe you should wait and see how you feel..."

"I know how I feel!" I snap. "I want to give this thing back." I expect a smart-*muk* comeback, but he pauses. Him trying to avoid the subject makes it worse. If he can't talk about the bigger issue, there's no way I can.

"But..." He scratches the buzzed-cut side of his head. "I mean...you never really listened to your mom before. Why start now?"

Already, I feel like I have to hold back tears.

"Because she would've wanted me to..." The words hang in the air for way too long.

My mind's in another world now. I tap the iRiST, as my eyes get misty. A light panel of vids appears – all thirty-one show mom. When she was sick, she recorded life-lesson vids for me. I ported them from my dying box-computer to this iRiST.

The vids loop. This is my mom, so of course the first one is about stealing.

I hesitate but select it anyway. Her frail face visualizes. I drag my finger across the holo, skipping through much of it. I'm too scared to hear her confirm I'm not living 'God's way.' My finger cramps, and the vid plays. "Just cause it's the apocalypse, it don't mean you should carry on…" I pause it and exhale.

Juan opens his mouth but closes it again.

I smile a bit, remembering how she'd say the whole word, 'apocalypse'. Everyone else just calls these times the 'pox', but she was old school. She taught me about stuff before the pox – things most teenagers don't get to hear. Before it was *us* versus the mega rich, or *us* versus the floods, or *us* versus everything else, society was stable. She was my age then, so she taught me old life lessons, thinking those days would return.

"I shouldn't've mentioned it. I'm sorry…" Juan tosses his board over the ground. It hovers and flashes a rainbow of colors. It's one of the newest models – that he stole from people in the highlands.

"Don't be. You didn't kill her." I say, steeling myself and stepping on my board.

"I'm coming too." Juan hops on his hoverboard and steadies himself easily because of its updated features.

"No one invited you." I cut him a side-eye. "Besides, you just wanna come cause there's a party."

"I have to go." He whines. "Who schedules parties like that? She must be mega rich."

For some reason, this *bick* has *many* parties scheduled in her iRiST calendar. One for today is listed as 'T. Party' and the address is in the description.

"It doesn't mean you can go." I glance at the gold band. "And it sure as hell doesn't mean you can go to steal stuff."

"Doesn't matter what *I* want to do. Question is 'how else you gonna get there?'"

Secretly, I'm happy he's intruding. If this address is real, she parties deep in the highlands. A place only Juan has been.

"Don't think this has anything to do with you." He says. "I've got *business* over there."

"I know. That's the problem." I respond. "Since when did stealing things and selling them to other people become 'business?'"

"Since always." He chuckles.

"Fine! Let's go." I try to hide my smile. I lean forward, making my board glide ahead. "Anything's better than being here. This place smells horrible."

* * *

After heading back to the tents for body sanitizer, we head towards the highlands.

I bump wrists with some people from our tenement and wave to friends in the distance, as we hover by.

Juan just stares at the sight on the horizon – the highlands. Small townhouses are aligned in rows, overshadowed by the tall high-rises. They don't have to worry about the flooding – or anything as much as we do. From my side-eye, I see Juan's eyes widen and his mouth curl upward.

His goal's always been to leave and live in the highlands. He figures he'll make enough *greenz* by stealing their stuff and selling it back to them – but he has no clue what he'll do once lives there. He'll probably be lonely, but that doesn't stop him from looking forward with a huge smile.

"It's not that great, you know." I scoff. "Most of them are schooling or working all day. And you're still a teenager. Even if you make enough money, they're gonna make you do vid-school."

He turns with an arched eyebrow. "Nah. I'm not doing that." He replies. "Up there I'd have *so* much *greenz*, I'd just buy my way out. When you get enough, it's like having a magic wand. *Poof* school. Be gone." We chuckle.

"Yeah, but it's still not worth it." I say, recovering. "You would just be there by yourself. If you can't bring the rest of the tenement with you, what's the point?"

His board slows and trails behind me. I turn around and meet his stone-faced gaze. "To not have to live in a tent." His voice lowers. "To not have to worry bout food all the time. To not have people look down on you. To live a good life."

My head whips forward. I may have pushed him too far. I think about changing the subject, but luckily I don't have to because we start nearing the *rough* blocks.

We pass guys with no tenement hanging out on the sidewalks and make *zero* eye contact. A young kid stumbles at the intersection ahead – naked and filthy. I look away from his tear-dried face and blank stare. Maybe he's high on *Luzid* or maybe someone just took advantage of him. Stuff like that happens more than I like to admit. Most women are smart enough not to chill outside their tenements for long. Usually it's the dudes who risk hanging out, so some people are *really* interested in them – especially the younger ones who can't put up as much of a fight.

Once we pass those blocks things get less sketchy, we near the huge 'temporary' bridge. "Finally!" Juan shouts.

The bridge has no lanes for pedestrians or boarders – cars only. It's the only way to the highlands now since the floods wrecked the other routes. Most of us are too broke for cars though. Mom said it's how they keep us out. If they wanna make it hard for 'tens' to get to the highlands, it's *muk* for them – cause we're gonna do it anyway.

We scan for the Peace Officers who usually guard the bridge. None in sight. They're probably patrolling.

Our boards glide over the rough asphalt then over the bridge's smooth concrete. Juan and I stay close to the shoulder. The wide lane is a little scary, knowing speeding cars could hit us. I keep looking back to check.

"Hey. Look-it!" Juan points up ahead. The yellow arrows look like huge stickers stuck on a white road. They're real ugly, but they're not for looks. They speed up ion-drive cars. Juan moves his board from the shoulder to the middle of the lane.

"You know those are for cars, right?" I yell, constantly looking back to see if one is coming.

"No *muk*. But they work on boards too!"

"I..I…" I stutter, wondering what happened to all my *steelz*.

"Come on." He says. "It'll take us an hour to cross this bridge if we don't use it. Then we'll be stuck out here at night. We gotta do it."

"Ok…" I say, looking forward. "Let's try it."

Juan slows down, and my board catches up to his. We near the sticker. As soon as we glide over the yellow arrow, our boards shoot forward.

"Woah!" I shout, zipping down the lane with air whipping in my eyes. I turn to the side, and the bridge's pillars flicker by. As soon as our boards slow, we race over more stickers, speeding down the lane.

I do a one-eighty on the board and smile, accidentally facing Juan. He flashes his 'I-told-you-so' look. I roll my eyes. Okay, I was wrong. This is *schway* fun.

We get to the other side of the bridge. Our boards slow, gliding over even more finely paved roads. One of the first things I spot are the nice manicured lawns. Both sides of the street are filled with the greenest grass, but the neighborhood is empty. Not a soul out here.

We hover to the sidewalk and pass several two-story houses. Whenever I peep inside, I see silhouettes. Most of them are on VR-machines moving files around – mindlessly working like bots. A woman in her kitchen looks out her plasma window and shoots us a disapproving glare. I stop looking in their windows.

* * *

After an hour, Juan points out a high-rise up ahead. "That's the place."

I check my iRiST again. It does seem like the one in this woman's pictures, but they all look the same to me. The block granite design looks as *muk* as the other high-rises nearby.

"I hope so, cuz we've been out in this heat too long." I say, wiping the sweat on my forehead. "This woulda only taken us twenty minutes if we had a car."

We glide towards the building. Stairs lead to it, surrounded by stepped-grassy lawns on both sides. We hop off our boards, sticking them under our arms, and start walking.

"I thought this place looked familiar." Juan says, walking over another step. "I did business here last week. This'll be easy. I'll slip past the front desk bot and let you in the side door."

He jerks his neck and points to the left side of the building. "Go wait over there."

"You sure this is a good idea?"

"Why are you so worried about everything, now?"

"Cause this place is *real* different from the lowlands, and it's starting to get at me."

"I tried to warn you earlier." Juan says. "But it's too late. We're here. You need to find that *steelz* you have back home – and bring it here."

Juan rushes up the steps, swinging his board, then walks past the plasma front doors. All I know is this boy better not get us caught. I came to return a watch, not get thrown in a holding cell.

I walk off the stepped stone path onto the grass, taking high steps over each ascending grassy field. Eventually, I make it to the building's side and stand next to the door. Rainbow lights flash from a floor above, and I hear thumps of music.

Sounds schway... I nod to the familiar beat, trying to think about anything other than getting caught.

I gotta calm down. I tap my wristband and watch the previews of my mom's last vids.

My eyes start to get misty again, but I stop as soon as I hear Juan yelling and cursing near the front of the building. He suddenly turns the corner and faces me with a torn shirt, a bruised cheek, and a broken board.

"What happened?!" I ask.

He ignores me, spitting on the ground. A clear glob of spit lies on the grass.

"No blood huh? That *bick* is lucky." He looks up and finally responds to me. "It wasn't a bot this time. A real person was at the front desk. He said residents complained about someone who looked like me selling stuff. Two tenants argued last week because one had the other's recently stolen stuff. The *bick* said I'm ruining their community and some other *muk*. Then he jumped at me."

"Told you they were trash..."

"They're the ones who bought it!" Juan says, exasperated. "The guy who lives there knew exactly where I got it from. He even made a joke about it."

I flash him my 'I-told-you-so' face.

"Sorry I couldn't get you in." Juan says. "Guess we'll head back now."

"Nah." I say, staring up at the window with the flashing lights and the tiny balcony. "We're still going."

His eyebrow arches. "Look-it. We're one board down, my face feels like *muk*, and we don't have a way in."

I view the party details listed in the calendar. Third floor. It must be the same place. "Yeah, we do. We can get up there with this." I say, tossing my board.

"Oh, you mean the thing that you 'fixed' that almost killed you?"

"It's been fine the whole ride. And look who's scared now." I say. "Look-it. I can't keep staring at my mom's face in these vids knowing I didn't do everything I could."

"You're crazy." Juan says. "But, whatever, let's do it. I won't say 'no' to getting new merch."

Looking up, I spot the multi-colored flashes over the small ass terrace on the third floor.

The board hovers unsteadily. Luckily, I know what mistake I made last time – so I'll just make it again, carefully. I lay down on the board.

"Aight. Get on."

Juan lays down on my back. I tap the underside of the board.

"Are you—" Juan is interrupted, as the board rockets upwards. The force presses my face against the board and Juan's face to my back. We rocket past the second floor. When I spot the third, I tap the board's underside again.

We hop off onto the terrace and peer inside. Looking through the plasma door, the place is like nothing I've ever seen.

On the inside of the really nice apartment, a short flight of stairs leads to a huge living room. People are standing around in ratty clothes, but they look weirdly neat. The rips on their shirts and jeans look too even, like they made the tears with a laser blade.

"I know those guys." Juan says, pointing out a few people. "I'm going in."

Juan forces the plasma door aside.

"I'll be in there for a bit to see what I can grab." He says, sticking his head inside. "You coming?" Juan rushes inside without even waiting for a response.

"Yeah..." My voice fades, as he sprints down the stairs. "Be there in a sec."

I recognize the *bick* I took the iRiST from standing in the living room. She's rocking a gold and silver iRiST on each arm.

My legs freeze. All the *steelz* I had just melted away. We don't belong here.

As if trying to prove me wrong, Juan makes it downstairs and walks around the living room. I watch him integrate into the party. People actually seem to know him. He bumps wrists with a few before he moves out of view to another room.

Before I step inside, a naked man covered in makeup splotches that look like dirt spots limps into the room. His exaggerated motions shake the silver platter on his hand. The woman grabs a thin green strip from the platter, placing it on her tongue. Other guests in their tattered clothes do the same. Their eyes widen as the music blasts.

They must be getting high on Luzid. I think, shaking my head. *Does it matter though? She's right there. I can return the iRiST now...*

If I do what mom wants, it means no more vids of mom. I'll have nothing else to play them on. I grab the wristband still frozen, waiting.

I could at least delete the vids. I tap the wristband. All her vids play on short, silent loops in the preview display. My finger nears the 'Delete All' panel.

Below, the naked guy disappears and reappears with an object shaped like a thick penis, snatching my attention. The woman and the other guests take turns chucking iRiSTs at it. I can't hear what's happening well, but I think she starts arguing about game rules or something.

She gets mad and throws one of her iRiSTs to the ground. It breaks into pieces. A man she was arguing with puts another green strip on her tongue. They start talking about something else.

What kind of twisted party is this? These bicks are crazy.

I stare at the broken iRiST on the floor.

I stare at mom's vids. Would she still tell me to give it back? I don't know. All I know is this watch means more to me than it does to this highlander. If mom was here, she might say giving it back is the 'right thing to do' – but she's not here. And one of the few things that keeps me from forgetting her is this wristband.

I move my finger through the 'Cancel' button instead. The display disappears.

Below, the naked guy collects the broken iRiST pieces. He then offers people a platter of something brown – that doesn't look like food. They take handfuls and start smearing what I hope isn't feces on each other's faces.

I close the door, turning away from the scene inside. I'm done with this place.

Eventually, Juan comes back and pulls the terrace door open. I get hit by the nasty ass smell inside.

"You give the watch back?" Juan holds some multi-colored iRiSTs and a large pillowcase with the rest of the stuff he couldn't carry.

"Nah. I didn't."

Before he can respond, I raise my palm, silencing him.

"It's not cause I'm trying to get *greenz* or anything like that..." I say, as a smirk stains his face. "You know what? I'm not even gonna bother."

I turn and glance back at the plasma door. "Should I even ask what's going on in there?"

"Oh yeah." Juan says. "Found out it's a *Ten* party, where they pretend to be people from—"

"Nope!" I raise my palm again and shake my head. "I don't wanna know any more."

I toss the board between us.

"Let's go." I say, stepping step on it. "There's nothing left for us here."

The Regression Test

Wole Talabi

THE CONFERENCE ROOM is white, spacious, and ugly.

Not ugly in any particular sort of way: it doesn't have garish furniture or out-of-place art or vomit-colored walls or anything like that. It's actually quite plain. It's just that everything in it looks furfuraceous, like the skin of some diseased albino animal, as if everything is made of barely attached bleached Bran Flakes. I know that's how all modern furnishing looks now – SlatTex, they call it – especially in these high-tech offices where the walls, doors, windows, and even some pieces of furniture are designed to integrate physically, but I still find it off-putting. I want to get this over with and leave the room as soon as possible. Return to my nice two-hundred-year-old brick bungalow in Ajah where the walls still look like real walls, not futuristic leper-skin.

"So, you understand why you're here and what you need to do, Madam?" Dr. Dimeji asks me.

I force myself to smile and say, "Of course – I'm here as a human control for the regression test."

Dr. Dimeji does not smile back. The man reminds me of an agama lizard. His face is elongated, reptilian, and there is something that resembles like a bony ridge running through the middle of his skull from front to back. His eyes are sunken but always darting about, looking at multiple things, never really focused on me. The electric-blue circle ringing one iris confirms that he has a sensory-augmentation implant.

"*Sorites* regression test," he corrects, as though the precise specification is important or I don't know what it is called. Which I certainly do – I pored over the yeye data-pack they gave me until all the meaningless technobabble in it eventually made some sense.

I roll my eyes. "Yes, I'm here as a human control for the sorites regression test."

"Good," he says, pointing at a black bead with a red eye that is probably a recording device set in the middle of the conference room table. "When you are ready, I need you to state your name, age, index, and the reason why you are here today while looking directly at that. Can you do that for me, Madam?"

He might be a professor of memrionics or whatever they're calling this version of their A.I. nonsense these days, but he is much younger than me, by at least seven decades, probably more. Someone should have taught him to say please and to lose that condescending tone of voice when addressing his elders. His sour attitude matches his sour face, just like my grandson Tunji, who is now executive director of the research division of LegbaTech. He's always scowling, too, even at family functions, perpetually obsessed with some work thing or other. These children of today take themselves too seriously. Tunji's even become religious now. Goes to church every Sunday, I hear. I don't know how my daughter and her husband managed to raise such a child.

"I'll be just outside observing if you need anything," Dr. Dimeji says as he opens the door. I nod so I don't accidentally say something caustic to him about his home training or lack thereof. He shuts the door behind him and I hear a lock click into place. That strikes me as odd but I ignore it. I want to get this over with quickly.

"My name is Titilope Ajimobi," I say, remembering my briefing instructions advising me to give as much detail as possible. "I am one hundred and sixteen years old. Sentient Entity Index Number HM033-2021-HK76776. Today I am in the Eko Atlantic office of LegbaTech Industries as the human control for a sorites regression test."

"Thank you, Mrs. Ajimobi," a female voice says to me from everywhere in the room, the characteristic nonlocation of an ever-present A.I. "Regression test initiated."

I lean back in my chair. The air conditioning makes me lick my lips. For all their sophistication, hospitality A.I.s never find the ideal room temperature for human comfort. They can't understand that it's not the calculated optimum. With human desires, it rarely is. It's always just a little bit off. My mother used to say that a lot.

Across the conference room, lines of light flicker to life and begin to dance in sharp, apparently random motions. The lights halt, disappear, and then around the table, where chairs like mine might have been placed, eight smooth, black, rectangular monoliths begin to rise, slowly, as if being extruded from the floor itself. I don't bother moving my own chair to see where they are coming from; it doesn't matter. The slabs grow about seven feet tall or so then stop.

The one directly across from me projects onto the table a red-light matrix of symbols and characters so intricate and dense it looks like abstract art. The matrix is three-dimensional, mathematically speaking, and within its elements patterns emerge, complex and beautiful, mesmerizing in their way. The patterns are changing so quickly that they give the illusion of stability, which adds to the beauty of the projection. This slab is putting on a display. I assume it must be the casing for the memrionic copy being regression tested.

A sorites regression test is designed to determine whether an artificial intelligence created by extrapolating and context-optimizing recorded versions of a particular human's thought patterns has deviated too far from the way the original person would think. Essentially, several previous versions of the record – backups with less learning experience – interrogate the most recent update in order to ascertain whether they agree on a wide range of mathematical, phenomenological, and philosophical questions, not just in answer, but also in cognitive approach to deriving and presenting a response. At the end of the experiment, the previous versions judge whether the new version's answers are close enough to those they would give for the update to still be considered 'them', or could only have been produced by a completely different entity. The test usually concludes with a person who knew the original human subject – me, in this case – asking the A.I. questions to determine the same thing. Or, as Tunji summarized once, the test verifies that the A.I., at its core, remains recognizable to itself and others, even as it continuously improves.

The seven other slabs each focus a single stream of yellow light into the heart of the red matrix. I guess they are trying to read it. The matrix expands as the beams of light crawl through it, ballooning in the center and fragmenting suddenly, exploding to four times its original size then folding around itself into something I vaguely recognize as a hypercube from when I still used to enjoy mathematics enough to try to understand this sort of thing. The slabs' fascinating light display now occupies more than half of the table's surface and I am no longer sure what I am looking at. I am still completely ensorcelled by it when the A. I. reminds me why I am here.

"Mrs. Ajimobi, please ask your mother a question."

I snap to attention, startled at the sentence before I remember the detailed instructions from my briefing. Despite them, I am skeptical about the value of the part I am to play in all this.

"Who are you?" I ask, even though I am not supposed to.

The light matrix reconstructs itself, its elements flowing rapidly and then stilling, like hot water poured onto ice. Then a voice I can only describe as a glassy, brittle version of my mother's replies.

"I am Olusola Ajimobi."

I gasp. For all its artifice, the sound strikes at my most tender and delicate memories and I almost shed a tear. That voice is too familiar. That voice used to read me stories about the tortoise while she braided my hair, each word echoing throughout our house. That voice used to call to me from downstairs, telling me to hurry up so I wouldn't be late for school. That voice screamed at me when I told her I was dropping out of my PhD program to take a job in Cape Town. That voice answered Global Network News interview questions intelligently and measuredly, if a bit impatiently. That voice whispered, "She's beautiful," into my ear at the hospital when my darling Simioluwa was born and I held her in my arms for the first time. That voice told me to leave her alone when I suggested she retire after her first heart attack. It's funny how one stimulus can trigger so much memory and emotion.

I sit up in my chair, drawing my knees together, and try to see this for what it is: a technical evaluation of software performance. My mother, Olusola Ajimobi – 'Africa's answer to Einstein,' as the magazines liked to call her – has been dead thirty-eight years and her memrionic copies have been providing research advice and guidance to LegbaTech for forty. This A.I., created after her third heart attack, is not her. It is nothing but a template of her memory and thought patterns which has had many years to diverge from her original scan. That potential diversion is what has brought me here today.

When Tunji first contacted me, he told me that his team at LegbaTech has discovered a promising new research direction – one they cannot tell me anything about, of course – for which are trying to secure funding. The review board thinks this research direction is based on flawed thinking and has recommended it not be pursued. My mother's memrionic copy insists that it should. It will cost billions of Naira just to test its basic assumptions. They need my help to decide if this memrionic is still representative of my mother, or whether has diverged so much that it is making decisions and judgement calls of which she would never have approved. My briefing instructions told me to begin by revisiting philosophical discussions or debates we had in the past to see if her positions or attitudes toward key ideas have changed or not. I choose the origins of the universe, something she used to enjoy speculating about.

"How was the universe created?" I ask.

"Current scientific consensus is—"

"No," I interrupt quickly, surprised that her first response is to regurgitate standard answers. I'm not sure if A.I.s can believe anything and I'm not supposed to ask her questions about such things, but that's what the human control is for, right? To ask questions that the other A.I.s would never think to ask, to force this electronic extrapolation of my mother into untested territory and see if the simulated thought matrix holds up or breaks down. "Don't tell me what you think. Tell me what you *believe*."

There is a brief pause. If this were really my mother she'd be smiling by now, relishing the discussion. And then that voice speaks again: "I believe that, given current scientific understanding and available data, we cannot know how the universe was created. In fact, I believe we will never be able to know. For every source we find, there will be a question regarding its own source. If we discover a god, we must then ask how this god came to be.

If we trace the expanding universe back to a single superparticle, we must then ask how this particle came to be. And so on. Therefore, I believe it is unknowable and will be so indefinitely."

I find it impressive how familiarly the argument is presented without exact parroting. I am also reminded of how uncomfortable my mother always was around Creationists. She actively hated religion, the result of being raised by an Evangelical Christian family who demanded faith from her when she sought verifiable facts.

"So you believe god could exist?"

"It is within the realm of possibility, though highly unlikely." Another familiar answer with a paraphrastic twist.

"Do you believe in magic?"

It is a trick question. My mother loved watching magicians and magic tricks but certainly never believed in real magic.

"No magical event has ever been recorded. Cameras are ubiquitous in the modern world and yet not a single verifiable piece of footage of genuine, repeatable magic has ever been produced. Therefore, it is reasonable to conclude, given the improbability of this, that there is no true magic."

Close enough but lacking the playful tone with which my mother would have delivered her thoughts on such matters.

I decide that pop philosophy is too closely linked to actual brain patterns for me to detect any major differences by asking those questions. If there is a deviation, it is more likely to be emotional. That is the most unstable solution space of the human equation.

"Do you like your great-grandson, Tunji?"

Blunt, but provoking. Tunji never met his great-grandmother when she was alive and so there is no memory for the A.I. to base its response on. Its answer will have to be derived from whatever limited interaction he and the memrionic have engaged in and her strong natural tendency to dislike over-serious people. A tendency we shared. Tunji is my daughter's son and I love him as much as our blood demands, but he is an insufferable chore most of the time. I would expect my mother to agree.

"Tunji is a perfectly capable executive director."

I'm both disappointed and somehow impressed to hear an A.I. playing deflection games with vocabulary.

"I have no doubt that he is," I say, watching the bright patterns in the light matrix shift and flow. "What I want to know is how you feel about him. Do you like him? Give me a simple yes or no."

"Yes."

That's unexpected. I sink into my chair. I was sure she would say no. Perhaps Tunji has spent more time interacting with this memrionic and building rapport with it than I thought. After all, everything this memrionic has experienced over the last forty years will have changed, however minutely, the system that alleges to represent my mother. A small variation in the elements of the thought matrix is assumed not to alter who she is fundamentally, her core way of thinking. But, like a heap of rice from which grains are removed one by one, over and over again, eventually all the rice will be gone and the heap will then obviously be a heap no more. As the process proceeds, is it even possible to know when the heap stops being, essentially, a heap? When it becomes something else? Does it ever? Who decides how many grains of rice define a heap? Is it still a heap even when only a few grains of rice are all that remain of it? No? Then when exactly did it change from a heap of rice to a new thing that is not a heap of rice? When did this recording-of-my-mother change to not-a-recording-of-my-mother?

I shake my head. I am falling into the philosophical paradox for which this test was named and designed to serve as a sort of solution. But the test depends on me making judgements based on forty-year-old memories of a very complicated woman. Am I still the same person I was when I knew her? I'm not even made of the exact same molecules as I was forty years ago. Nothing is constant. We are all in flux. Has my own personality drifted so much that I no longer have the ability to know what she would think? Or is something else going on here?

"That's good to hear," I lie. "Tell me, what is the temperature in this room?"

"It is twenty-one-point-two degrees Celsius." The glassy iteration of my mother's voice appears to have lost its emotional power over me.

"Given my age and physical condition, is this the ideal temperature for my comfort?"

"Yes, this is the optimum."

I force a deep breath in place of the snort that almost escapes me. "Olusola." I try once more, with feeling, giving my suspicions one more chance to commit hara-kiri. "If you were standing here now, beside me, with a control dock in your hand, what temperature would you set the room to?"

"The current optimum – twenty-one-point-two degrees Celsius."

There it is.

"Thank you. I'm done with the regression test now."

The electric-red hypercube matrix and yellow lines of light begin to shrink, as though being compressed back to their pretest positions, and then, mid-retraction, they disappear abruptly, as if they have simply been turned off. The beautiful kaleidoscope of numbers and symbols, flowing, flickering and flaring in fanciful fits, is gone, like a dream. Do old women dream of their electric mothers?

I sigh.

The slabs begin to sink back into the ground, and this time I shift my chair to see that they are descending into hatches, not being extruded from the floor as they would if they were made of SlatTex. They fall away from my sight leaving an eerie silence in their wake, and just like that, the regression test is over.

I hear a click and the door opens about halfway. Dr. Dimeji enters, tablet in hand. "I think that went well," he says as he slides in. His motions are snake-like and creepy. Or maybe I'm just projecting. I wonder who else is observing me and what exactly they think just happened. I remember my data-pack explaining that regression tests are typically devised and conducted by teams of three but I haven't seen anyone except Dr. Dimeji since I entered the facility. Come to think of it, there was no one at reception, either. Odd.

"Your questions were few, but good, as expected. A few philosophical ones, a few personal. I'm not sure where you were going with that last question about the temperature, but no matter. So tell me, in your opinion, Madam, on a scale of one to ten, how confident are you that the tested thought analogue thinks like your mother?"

"Zero." I say, looking straight into his eyes.

"Of course." Dr. Dimeji nods calmly and starts tapping at his tablet to make a note before he fully registers what I just said, and then his head jerks up, his expression confounded. "I'm sorry, what?"

"That contrivance is not my mother. It thinks things that she would but in ways she would never think them."

A grimace twists the corners of Dr. Dimeji's mouth and furrows his forehead, enhancing his reptilian appearance from strange to sinister. "Are you sure?" He stares right at me, eyes narrowed and somehow dangerous. The fact that we are alone presses down on my chest, heavy like a sack of rice. Morbidly, it occurs to me that I don't even know if anyone will come if he does something to me and I scream for help. I don't want to die in this ugly room at the hands of this lizard-faced man.

"I just told you, didn't I?" I bark, defensive. "The basic thoughts are consistent, but something is fundamentally different. It's almost like you've mixed parts of her mind with someone else's to make a new mind."

"I see." Dr. Dimeji's frown melts into a smile. Finally, some human expression. I allow myself to relax a little.

I don't even notice the humming near my ear until I feel the sting in the base of my skull where it meets my neck and see the edge of his smile curl unpleasantly. I try to cry out in pain but a constriction in my throat prevents me. My body isn't working like it's supposed to. My arms spasm and flail then go rigid and stiff, like firewood. My breathing is even despite my internal panic. My body is not under my control anymore. Someone or something else has taken over. Everything is numb.

A man enters the room through the still half-open door and my heart skips a beat.

Ah! Tunji.

He is wearing a tailored gray suit of the same severe cut he always favors. Ignoring me, he walks up to Dr. Dimeji and studies the man's tablet. His skin is darker than the last time I saw him and he is whip-lean. He stands there for almost thirty seconds before saying, "You didn't do it right."

"But it passed the regression test. It passed," Dr. Dimeji protests.

Tunji glowers at him until he looks away and down, gazing at nothing between his feet. I strain every muscle in my body to say something, to call out to Tunji, to scream – *Tunji, what the hell is going on here?* – but I barely manage a facial twitch.

"If she could tell there was a difference," Tunji is telling Dimeji, "then it didn't pass the regression test, did it? The human control is here for a reason and the board insists on having her for a reason: she knows things about her mother no one else does. So don't fucking tell me it passed the regression test just because you fooled the other pieces of code. I need you to review her test questions and tell me exactly which parts of my thought patterns she detected in there and how. Understand? We can't take any chances."

Dr. Dimeji nods, his lizard-like appearance making it look almost natural for him to do so.

Understanding crystallizes in my mind like salt. Tunji must have been seeding the memrionic A.I. of my mother with his own thought patterns, trying to get her to agree with his decisions on research direction in order to add legitimacy to his own ideas. Apparently, he's created something so ridiculous or radical or both that the board has insisted on a regression test. So now he's trying to rig the test. By manipulating me.

"And do it quickly. We can't wipe more than an hour of her short-term memory before we try again."

Tunji stands still for a while and then turns calmly from Dimeji to me, his face stiff and unkind. "Sorry, Grandma," he says through his perfectly polished teeth. "This is the only way."

Omo ale jati jati! I curse and I swear and I rage until my blood boils with impotent anger. I have never wanted to kill anyone so much in my life but I know I can't. Still, I can't let them get away with this. I focus my mind on the one thing I hope they will never be able to understand, the one thing my mother used to say in her clear, ringing voice, about fulfilling a human desire. An oft-repeated half-joke that is now my anchor to memory.

It's never the optimum. It's always just a little bit off.

Dr. Dimeji wearily approaches me as Tunji steps aside, his eyes emotionless. Useless boy. My own flesh and blood. How far the apple has fallen from the tree. I repeat the words in my mind, trying to forge a neural pathway connecting this moment all the way back to my oldest memories of my mother.

It's never the optimum. It's always just a little bit off.

Dr. Dimeji leans forward, pulls something grey and bloody out of my neck, and fiddles. I don't feel anything except a profound discomfort, not even when he finishes his fiddling and rudely jams it back in.

It's never the optimum. It's always just a little bit off.

I repeat the words in my mind, over and over and over again, hoping even as darkness falls and I lose consciousness that no matter what they do to me, my memory, or the thing that is a memory of my mother, I will always remember to ask her the question and never forget to be surprised by the answer.

Biographies & Sources

James Beamon
An Empty, Hollow Interview
(First Publication)
James Beamon has been all over the world but most times it was to places no one else wants to go. The author of over forty short stories in publications such as *Lightspeed*, *Intergalactic Medicine Show* and the *Magazine of Fantasy & Science Fiction*, he's currently serving as a Director-at-Large for SFWA. He can't remember if he lost his hair before self-publishing his *Pendulum Heroes* series or because of it. These days he lives in Virginia with his wife, son and cat.

W.E.B. Du Bois
The Comet
(Originally Published in *Darkwater: Voices From Within the Veil*, 1920)
William Edward Burghardt Du Bois (1868–1963) was an American civil rights activist, socialist and historian as well as a writer and editor. He was a strong leader in opposing racism in its many forms, particularly in education and employment settings. He was a prolific author and is perhaps best known for popularizing the term 'colour line' in *The Souls of Black Folk* (1903), as well as his most highly regarded work, *Black Reconstruction in America*. 'The Comet' was published in Du Bois' *Darkwater: Voices From Within the Veil*, a collection of autobiographical writings, essays and poems.

K. Tempest Bradford
Élan Vital
(Originally Published in *Sybil's Garage* No. 6, 2009)
K. Tempest Bradford is a science-fiction and fantasy writer, writing instructor, media critic, reviewer, and podcaster. Her short fiction has appeared in multiple anthologies and magazines including Strange Horizons, PodCastle, *Sunspot Jungle, In the Shadow of the Towers*, and many more. She's the host of *ORIGINality*, a podcast about the roots of creative genius, and contributes to several more. Her media criticism and reviews can be found on NPR, io9, and in books about Time Lords. When not writing, she teaches classes on writing inclusive fiction through LitReactor and Writing the Other.com. Visit her website at ktempestbradford.com.

Tara Campbell
The Orb
(First Publication)
Tara Campbell (www.taracampbell.com) is a writer, teacher, Kimbilio Fellow, and fiction editor at Barrelhouse. She received her MFA from American University in 2019. Previous publication credits include *SmokeLong Quarterly, Masters Review, Jellyfish Review, Booth, Strange Horizons*, and *Escape Pod/Artemis Rising*. She's the author of a novel, *TreeVolution*, and three collections: *Circe's Bicycle, Midnight at the Organporium*, and *Political AF: A Rage Collection*. Originally from Anchorage, Alaska, she has also lived in Oregon, Ohio, New York, Germany and Austria. She currently lives in Washington, D.C.

Martin R. Delany

Blake, or The Huts of America

(Originally Published in the *Anglo-African Magazine*, 1859 [part one] and the *Weekly Anglo-African Magazine*, 1861–62 [part two])

Martin Robertson Delany (1812–85) was an abolitionist, writer, soldier and physician. He was one of the first three men to be accepted into Harvard Medical School; however, he was sadly removed after widespread protests. In 1839, he became competent in dental care and worked as a physician's assistant, in the South and Southwest of America. He would eventually become a leading Pittsburgh Physician. His writings include essays and novels, and Delany founded a weekly newspaper called the *Mystery*. In 1856 Delany moved to Canada as a response to the oppressive conditions in the United States, only returning at the beginning of the Civil War to help recruit troops for the 54th Massachusetts Volunteers, for which he was recruited as a surgeon.

Michelle F. Goddard

The Floating City of Pengimbang

(Originally Published in *Water*, 2017)

Michelle F. Goddard is an AWADJ: artist with a day job. She is a vocalist and musician who has performed around the world, and a composer with credits to her name for works in musicals and films. Her short fiction has been published in B Cubed Press's *Alternative Apocalypse* anthology, Ulthar Press's *Machinations and Mesmerism* anthology, and *Hybrid Fiction* magazine, among others. She is presently working on several short stories and a science fiction novel. You can find her at michellefgoddard.wordpress.com

Dr. Sandra M. Grayson

Introduction

Dr. Sandra M. Grayson is a tenured Full Professor in the English Department at University of Wisconsin-Milwaukee. Her numerous publications include the books *Visions of the Third Millennium: Black Science Fiction Novelists Write the Future*; *Symbolizing the Past: Reading Sankofa, Daughters of the Dust, and Eve's Bayou as Histories*; *A Literary Revolution: In the Spirit of the Harlem Renaissance*; and *Sparks of Resistance, Flames of Change: Black Communities and Activism*.

Harambee K. Grey-Sun

The New Colossuses

(First Publication)

Harambee K. Grey-Sun lives in Northern Virginia and is the author of several works of fiction and poetry, including *Hero Zero*, *Colder Than Ice*, and *Trinity & Its Twin*. Although he writes in a variety of genres, his stories often fall somewhere on the spectrum of horror, ranging from the supernatural to the psychological. His work has most recently appeared in *The Arcanist*. The curious can find more information about him and his ongoing projects at harambeegreysun.com.

Sutton E. Griggs

Imperium in Imperio

(Originally Published in 1899)

Writer, minister, and community leader Sutton Elbert Griggs (1872–1933) was born in

Chatfield, Texas. He graduated from the Richmond Theological Seminary in 1893, following in the footsteps of his father, a Baptist minister who had founded the first black high school and newspaper in the state of Texas. An avid writer, he authored numerous books and pamphlets, including the utopian novel *Imperium in Imperio*, and established his own publishing company in the process. Griggs' work explored themes of social and racial justice, issues for which he passionately advocated in his lifetime.

Emmalia Harrington
Seven Thieves
(Originally Published in *Rococoa*, 2015)
Emmalia (she/her) is a disabled QWOC with a deep love of speculative fiction and history. A trip to Colonial Williamsburg influenced the setting for 'Seven Thieves'. She serves as Acquiring Editor at *FIYAH*, Associate Editor at Podcastle, and a member of *Broad Universe* and *Codex*. Somehow she still finds the time for writing, sewing, cooking, and managing cats. Her work can be found at *FIYAH*, *Glittership*, *Anathema*, and other venues. She can be found on Twitter at @Emmalia_Writes.

Pauline Hopkins
Of One Blood
(Originally Published in *The Colored American Magazine*, 1902–03)
Raised in Boston, Massachusetts, acclaimed African-American novelist and intellectual Pauline Elizabeth Hopkins (1859–1930) first rose to prominence as a playwright and performer before later turning to journalism and literature. Her use of the romantic novel as a medium by which to explore race and social issues, through works such as *Contending Forces: A Romance Illustrative of Negro Life North and South,* made her a pioneer of her time. As an editor and director of *Colored American Magazine*, she wielded significant literary and cultural influence, and went on to write stories and articles for a number of other magazines.

Walidah Imarisha
Space Traitors
(Originally Published in *Buckman Journal 003*, 2019)
Walidah Imarisha is an educator and a writer. She is the co-editor of two anthologies including *Octavia's Brood: Science Fiction Stories from Social Justice Movements*. Imarisha also authored a poetry collection *Scars/Stars*, as well as the nonfiction book *Angels with Dirty Faces: Three Stories of Crime, Prison and Redemption*, which won a 2017 Oregon Book Award. In 2015, she received a Tiptree Fellowship for her science fiction writing. Imarisha currently teaches in Portland State University's Black Studies Department.

Patty Nicole Johnson
The Line of Demarcation
(First Publication)
Patty Nicole Johnson is a Black and Puerto Rican science-fiction writer. In her Chicago bungalow, she weaponises time travel, holograms, multiverses and more to envision a more equitable society. Her work has been published or is forthcoming in *New American Legends*, *On the Seawall*, *Midnight & Indigo*, and *Constelación*. She primarily writes flash fiction and short stories, yet she's revising her debut novel, *The*

Rhythm of Reveries. She was also a moderator and panellist for the FIYAHCON 2020 Virtual Conference for BIPOC+ In Speculative Fiction. Read her work at pattynjohnson. com, or find her on Twitter & Instagram at @pattynjohnson.

Edward Johnson
Light Ahead for the Negro
(Originally Published in 1904)
Edward Austin Johnson (1860–1944) lived a remarkable life. Born into enslavement in North Carolina, he was initially educated by a free black woman. After emancipation, Johnson was able to continue his education formally, going on to earn a law degree from Shaw University – while working as a school principle. A successful lawyer, he became increasingly active in the Republican party, and was eventually elected to the New York State Legislature in 1917. Over the course of his lifetime he wrote a number of books, including two textbooks intended to teach children about the achievements of black Americans, and his best-known work, the utopian novel *Light Ahead for the Negro*.

Russell Nichols
e-race
(Originally Published in *Terraform*, 2019)
Giant Steps
(Originally Published in *Lightspeed Magazine*, 2020)
Russell Nichols is a speculative fiction writer and endangered journalist. Raised in Richmond, California, he got rid of all his stuff in 2011 to live out of a backpack with his wife, vagabonding around the world ever since. Usually set in the near future, his stories revolve around concepts of race, mental health, technology, and the absurdity of existence. Find his work in *FIYAH*, *Apex Magazine*, *Lightspeed Magazine*, *Terraform*, *Strange Horizons*, and others. Look for him at russellnichols.com.

Temi Oh
Almost Too Good to Be True
Foreword
Temi Oh graduated with a BSci in Neuroscience. Her degree provided great opportunities to write and learn about topics ranging from 'Philosophy of the Mind' to 'Space Physiology'. While at KCL, Temi founded a book club called 'Neuroscience-fiction', where she led discussions about science fiction books which focus on the brain. In 2016, she received an MA in Creative Writing from the University of Edinburgh. Her first novel, *Do You Dream of Terra-Two?*, was published by Simon & Schuster in 2019 and won the American Library Association's Alex Award. She has loved and gifted Flame Tree's beautiful books for many years and is thrilled to be part of this project.

Megan Pindling
You May Run On
(First Publication)
Megan Pindling is a speculative fiction writer and archivist. She teaches writing and literature at Queens College where she attempts to convince her students that they really do like poetry, they've just been reading the wrong poems. Megan writes poems that aren't very poetic, literary criticism that is a little too poetic, and short stories that are novels in

disguise. She is suspicious of words like 'literary' and 'genre' and is probably, more than likely, daydreaming at this very moment.

Tia Ross
Associate Editor
Tia Ross is the Founder of Black Writers Collective (BlackWriters.org), Founder/Managing Editor for Black Editors & Proofreaders (BlackEditorsProofreaders.com), Editor for ColorOfChange.org and Senior Editor for WordWiserInk.com. She is a polymath entrepreneur who is passionate about great writing, as well as forging successful businesses as an information architect and event organiser.

Sylvie Soul
Suffering Inside, But Still I Soar
(First Publication)
Sylvie Soul is a dual American/Canadian citizen living in Toronto, Canada. Since she was a little girl, Sylvie has been enamoured by stories of fantasy of magic. To this day, as a devoted fan of *Sailor Moon* and retro video games, she is still a big kid at heart. Sylvie hopes to inspire the next generation of little girls to use their imaginations and create something beautiful the world can enjoy. Sylvie has written for numerous publications, including *Screen Rant, The Spool* and *Midnight & Indigo*. She is currently writing her first YA novel; follow her writing journey at sylviesoul.com.

Lyle Stiles
The Pox Party
(First Publication)
Lyle Stiles is a recovering researcher nursing a growing love for poetry and science fiction. As an African American raised in Brooklyn, New York, who trained in the discipline of neuroscience, he brings his unique blend of personal experiences and scientific background into his fiction. He works with a talented group of published writers, the Saturday Speculative Fiction Group, who critique and celebrate members' developing works. This ultimately led to having some of his writings being selected for publication including his poem 'Tourists' and his short story 'The Xenobot Paradox'. You can follow him and his ramblings on Twitter: @thewritestiles.

Wole Talabi
The Regression Test
(*The Magazine of Fantasy and Science Fiction*, 2017)
Wole Talabi is a full-time engineer, part-time writer and some-time editor from Nigeria. His stories have appeared in *F&SF, Lightspeed, Omenana, Terraform*, and several other places. He has edited three anthologies and co-written a play. His fiction has been nominated for several awards including the Caine Prize for African Writing and the Nommo Award which he won in 2018 and 2020. His debut collection of stories, *Incomplete Solutions*, is published by Luna Press. He likes scuba diving, elegant equations and oddly shaped things. He currently lives and works in Malaysia. Find him online at wtalabi.wordpress.com and @wtalabi on Twitter.

FLAME TREE PUBLISHING
Epic, Dark, Thrilling & Gothic
New & Classic Writing

Flame Tree's Gothic Fantasy books offer a carefully curated series of new titles, each with combinations of original and classic writing:

Chilling Horror • Chilling Ghost • Science Fiction • Murder Mayhem
Crime & Mystery • Swords & Steam • Dystopia Utopia • Supernatural Horror
Lost Worlds Time Travel • Heroic Fantasy • Pirates & Ghosts • Agents & Spies
Endless Apocalypse • Alien Invasion • Robots & AI • Lost Souls • Haunted House
Cosy Crime • American Gothic • Urban Crime • Epic Fantasy Detective
Mysteries • Detective Thrillers • A Dying Planet • Footsteps in the Dark
Bodies in the Library • Strange Lands • Lovecraft Mythos • Terrifying Ghosts

**Also, new companion titles offer rich collections of
classic fiction, myths and tales in the gothic fantasy tradition:**

George Orwell: Visions of Dystopia • H.G. Wells • Lovecraft
Sherlock Holmes • Edgar Allan Poe • Bram Stoker • Mary Shelley
African Myths & Tales • Celtic Myths & Tales • Greek Myths & Tales
Norse Myths & Tales Chinese Myths & Tales • Japanese Myths & Tales
Irish Fairy Tales • Native American Myths & Tales • Heroes & Heroines Myths & Tales
Witches, Wizards, Seers & Healers Myths & Tales • Gods & Monsters Myths & Tales
Alice's Adventures in Wonderland • King Arthur & The Knights of the Round Table
The Divine Comedy • Hans Christian Andersen Fairy Tales • Brothers Grimm
The Wonderful Wizard of Oz • The Age of Queen Victoria

Available from all good bookstores, worldwide, and online at
flametreepublishing.com

See our new fiction imprint
FLAME TREE PRESS | FICTION WITHOUT FRONTIERS
New and original writing in Horror, Crime, SF and Fantasy

And join our monthly newsletter with offers and more stories:
FLAME TREE FICTION NEWSLETTER
flametreepress.com

GOTHIC FANTASY